THE
DRAGON
BOOK

THE
DRAGON
BOOK

EDITED BY
Jack Dann and Gardner Dozois

ANDERSEN PRESS

20 Vauxhall Bridge Road London SW1V 2SA
www.andersenpress.co.uk

First published in UK in 2009 by Andersen Press Limited
First published in USA in 2009 by The Berkley Publishing Group
part of Penguin Group (USA) Inc
This edition published by Andersen Press Limited in 2011
1 3 5 7 9 10 8 6 4 2

British Library Cataloguing in Publication Data available.

ISBN 978 184 939 100 9

Printed and bound in Great Britain by CPI Mackays, Chatham, ME5 8TD

CONTENTS

Contents

Preface

Dragons are by far the most potent and widespread of all mythological beasts, and dragons or dragonlike creatures appear in just about every mythology in the world. So omnipresent is the image of the dragon, and so powerful the emotions that it evokes, that Carl Sagan, among others, has suggested that dragons are actually a racial memory of dinosaurs, left over from the days when our remote ancestors were tiny, tree-dwelling insectivores who cowered in shivering terror whenever one of the immense flesh eaters like *Tyrannosaurus rex* came crashing through the forest.

Whatever the truth of that, it's certainly true that dragons are one of the few mythological creatures that it's almost pointless to bother describing. As Avram Davidson once put it, "Although the wombat is real and the dragon is not, nobody knows what a wombat looks like and everyone knows what a dragon looks like."

There are variations, of course—sometimes the dragon is wingless and rather like a gigantic worm, sometimes like a huge snake, most often like an immense, winged lizard. Sometimes it breathes fire, sometimes not. But, for the most part, the rule holds. With very few exceptions, almost everyone does know what a dragon looks like, which is why it is one of the master-symbols of fantasy. (Or perhaps it's the other way around.)

Although the Eastern Dragon (and particularly the Chinese Dragon) is usually depicted as a wise and benevolent creature, a divine being associated with the bringing of the life-giving rains, what we have been describing here primarily fits the Western Dragon . . . and, not surprisingly, it is the Western Dragon, the terrible fire-breathing dragon of folklore and fairy tales, that has been the dominant image of the dragon in Western literature and art, and which is the kind of dragon we'll encounter most frequently in the stories that follow (although there are a number of benign dragons included as well, just for spice, some in the role of teacher or protector, some who are morally neutral or ambiguous, some who are just friendly).

In addition to its well-known fondness for snacking on princesses, the Western Dragon is a covetous beast and can often be found guarding the immense treasures of gold and jewels that it has pillaged from human realms. Although sometimes portrayed as merely a huge, mindless beast, the dragon is just as often depicted as having the gift of speech: in this guise, it is frequently a sorcerer, an active magic-user itself as well as being a magical creature. In fact, some say that Dragon Magic is the strongest and most ancient magic of all . . .

The strength of that magic, and the sheer power to enchant and fascinate that the dragon still possesses, even in our busy modern world, is amply demonstrated in the pages of the stories that follow.

We asked some of the very best modern fantasists—Cecelia Holland, Naomi Novik, Jonathan Stroud, Kage Baker, Jane Yolen, Adam Stemple, Liz Williams, Peter S. Beagle, Diana Gabaldon, Samuel Sykes, Garth Nix, Sean Williams, Tad Williams, Harry Turtledove, Diana Wynne Jones, Gregory Maguire, Bruce Coville, Tanith Lee, Tamora Pierce, Mary Rosenblum, and Andy Duncan—to write stories about this potent fantasy archetype, the dragon. The book you hold in your hands is the result. Here you'll find dragons both ancient and newly hatched; dragons evil and rapacious and wise and benign; dragons hunted to the death by humans and dragons who count humans as their closest friends; ensorcelled dragons and dragons with vast magical powers of their own; dragons who coexist with our own modern world, prowling its busy streets and alleys, and dragons who pace the landscapes of ancient Rome, tsarist Russia, medieval Europe, darkest Africa, and a few fantasy worlds that exist only in the imagination. You'll even find a few stories told from the *dragon's* point of view, giving their own unique perspective on things.

We hope you enjoy them.

THE
DRAGON
BOOK

Dragon's Deep

CECELIA HOLLAND

Cecelia Holland is one of the world's most highly acclaimed and respected historical novel-ists, ranked by many alongside other giants in that field such as Mary Renault and Larry McMurtry. Over the span of her forty-year career, she's written almost thirty historical novels, including The Firedrake, Rakóssy, Two Ravens, Ghost on the Steppe, The Death of Attila, Hammer for Princes, The King's Road, Pillar of the Sky, The Lords of Vaumartin, Pacific Street, The Sea Beggars, The Earl, The Kings in Winter, The Belt of Gold, *and more than a dozen others. She also wrote the well-known science fiction novel* Floating Worlds, *which was nominated for a Locus Award in 1975, and of late has been working on a series of fantasy novels, including* The Soul Thief, The Witches' Kitchen, *and* The Serpent Dreamer. *Her most recent novel is* The High City, *and upcoming is* The Kings of the North, *the last of the Soul Thief books.*

Here she tells the poignant story of a woman ripped from her proper place who must learn to survive under difficult conditions, yearning all the while for home—only to rediscover the old wisdom that says that you can't go home again. Or that maybe you're better off if you don't.

ॐ

ONCE, in the fishing village of Saint Mary Under The Hill, in the duchy of Asturias, there lived a girl named Perla. One summer day, she sat outside with her sister, packing dried fish into casks, to feed them through the winter, and her sister began giving her advice.

"You're a fool not to marry Ercule, Perla. Heed me. We're not rich, you aren't that pretty, and you're too clever. Take Ercule. Who else wants you?"

Perla set her teeth together, her face rough with embarrassment, and watched her hands shoving dried fish into the salt. Her sister had married the biggest lout in the village and already had two babies; Perla thought she wanted company, and some hot words to that effect sizzled in her throat. She glanced up, ready to snap back, and saw her sister looking past her toward the road, her mouth falling open in astonishment.

"Sweet Heaven!" Her sister sprang up and ran through the little circle of huts toward the beach, waving her arms to the men along the shore. Left behind, Perla straightened slowly to her feet, her eyes on the glittering parade of horsemen prancing down the road toward her.

One galloped forward, waving a stick. "Down! Down, you little fool, for the Duke!"

She went to her knees, gaping up at them. There were half a hundred mounted men, but the first few were the ones she stared at. They wore mail, with long coats over them figured in gold and silver thread, spurs on their steel-covered feet, their horses sleek and fine. The one in the middle wore a gold circlet over his helmet. The one with the stick hit her across the shoulders.

"Down!"

"I *am* down," she cried, and doubled up, her arms over her head.

"*All* of you, down," the crier shouted, and she heard voices behind her and knew that the rest of the village had gathered, and she was glad not to be alone. Another of the knights began to shout, talking the way the priest did when he recited something he had by memory.

"You people of the fish and the sea! People of the village you call for the Holy Mother of God! This is to inform you that His Highness the Duke has discovered that you are the best fishermen in his country. This village has taken in more fish in the past years than any other."

There went up an uncertain cheer. The bull-throated voice went on. "Therefore, the Duke has decided that henceforth you will give him double the amount of taxes. And we are here now to take what you owe."

The cheer fell into a stunned silence. Perla, still curled up on the ground, looked backward past her feet toward the rest of her people behind her. Most of them had gone to their knees. Now the rest did also, their faces tilted up, pleading.

All except her brother, Marco. He stepped forward, past Perla, going out there all alone before the Duke, and said, "Sir, we cannot. Already we give most of our catch to you. We have to live."

Cautiously, Perla lifted her head out of her arms and saw the Duke there before her, his horse's feet pattering at the ground. His stirrups were covered with chased silver. Fringe hung from his saddlecloth, his reins.

Behind him were too many horsemen for her to count. She began to plan how she would run when they charged.

"Then catch more fish," said the Duke, between his teeth, and waved his arm. His knights jogged forward. For a moment, Perla's brother stood, his feet widespread, his hat in one hand, and the other hand still out, beseeching, and then he hurried backward and went to his knees. The knights scattered through the village, and the pillaging began. Perla sprinted toward the nearby woods, staying low to the ground.

When they had gone, when they had taken everything, and the girls and women who had been able to escape had crept back to their trampled huts, the villagers gathered as they were accustomed to in the evening, building a fire in the shelter of the cliff and cooking what little remained to eat.

Perla sat with her arms wrapped tight around her sister, who had not gotten away. The Duke's men had caught her with her babies, and in exchange for their lives, she had let them rape her. She had saved her children, she kept on saying this, while the two little ones sobbed into her skirts, and her husband would not look at her.

Ercule, whom her sister wanted her to marry, sat there with the other men, behind Perla's brother, Marco. Ercule had done nothing, not even a useless plea like Marco's. She lowered her eyes, clutching her sister against her.

The night came, and the light of the fire shone on them all. Usually when they gathered, they drank, they talked and joked, sang the old songs, and retold the old stories; but this time they huddled somberly together and considered what had happened to them.

"We can't stay here," said one, and a few here and there grunted, agreeing.

"Where else should we go? There's always somebody like the Duke."

Perla hugged her sister, angry. It was unseemly for a woman to speak up, at least until all the men had spoken, but now they were all calling out stupid ideas, like hiding, or running, or changing who they were. Someone—old Juneo—even said, "We can be pirates."

Now Marco stood. He was short, square-shouldered, strong as an ox from casting nets and rowing; Perla's heart leapt for him, brave and sensible. He would have an answer. Everybody quieted, seeing him. Everybody respected Marco.

He said, "We need to make one more great catch, before the winter. The Duke won't come back this year. He thinks he has it all. If we can pull in one great catch, we can all live through this."

"The fish are going," said an old man. "This is the bad time of the year for fish along this coast."

"Here," her brother said, his voice steady. "And south of here, where everybody fishes. But in the north, where the coast turns eastward, there are always great schools."

A general grumble. A sharp voice called out, "That's too risky."

"It's not for nothing called Dragon's Deep," someone else said—a woman's voice; Perla looked around, started, and saw one of the fishwives standing up, her hands in her skirt.

Now Ercule stood. "Most of the other fleets avoid those waters. But I've always heard they're prime fishing waters, just that there are a lot of reefs."

He gave a look at Perla, to see that she saw him doing this; he puffed out his chest a little.

Perla's sister's husband called out in a hoarse voice. "Bad storms hit that cape. I've heard there's an eddy under the cliff. Bad currents. Nobody goes there."

"There's a reason there isn't a village for miles off that headland."

Marco stood, his hands at his sides, waiting for the clamor to die down. In the first lull, he said, "Or we could get all our scaling knives and gaffs together and attack the Duke and his men, and take our fish back from him." He was smiling; he gave a little shrug.

Nobody said anything. In the firelight, Perla saw them look from side to side and down, one man after another, and the wives also, one to the next, and there was a long silence.

Marco said, "Then we fish Dragon's Deep."

Perla's sister's husband flung his hands out and stepped back, away from the rest. "Not me. I have a wife and children. I'll take them into the forest first."

Marco wheeled, casting his gaze like a net over the other men. "Who else is a coward? Who else is afraid of rumors and gossip?"

No one spoke for a moment; the men were looking at one another, and a few shook their heads, then Perla jumped to her feet.

"I will go, Marco! I will go with you, if nobody else dares!"

Marco gave her a broad smile and held out his hand. His voice swelled. "Who else is as brave as a girl? All you men. Will you let a girl go first?"

Ercule cried, "I am going."

Then, in a rush, others called out. "Yes, me, I will go, I will go," in a jumble of voices, until all but a few had agreed. But then they stood nervously, looking around, their faces fretted.

Marco stood smiling around him, his hands on his hips. "Good. We'll start tomorrow. It will take us a couple of days to get up there."

၄ၖ

"BEAUTIFUL," she murmured, and shivered.

The bay stretched out before them, dark blue to the north, paler as the water shallowed toward the beach, and the beach itself an arc of pale brown sand. The wind was driving from the west, but the headland behind them blocked most of it, and the little combers that ran into the sand were tame and mild. In the shallower, green-blue water, she could see the dark reefs. There was a reef directly below their boat now, the lumpy stone waving green with seaweed and alive with fish.

Yet the broad bay was empty, desolate. No village showed, no smoke, not even a single hut. From the edge of the beach, the sheer headland stood up like a tower, flanked by steep green slopes, and, beyond them, the snow-caps of the mountains.

All along the clean, pale beach, in the high line of driftwood, were the ribs and planks of boats, old wrecks, sun-bleached. Some looked burnt. And down on the bottom in the clear blue depths, she saw a boxy stern and part of a thwart poking out of the sand. Nowhere was there a sign of a living man, except those newly come.

A gull wheeled above them, screeching. She thought, for an instant, that she caught a note of warning in its voice.

Marco was giving crisp orders. "Perla, you go ashore and make us a camp. We should have brought some other women with us to help you, but we'll pitch in when we get ashore this afternoon. Ercule, Juneo, shake out the nets." He put his hands around his mouth, to shout to the other two boats, and Perla grabbed his arm.

"I'm not going ashore! I didn't come this far to *watch* you, Marco."

Around them on the boat, the other men laughed and nudged each other. Juneo said, "Marco, I hope you're handling the lines better than you handle her!"

A general hooting followed that. Perla lowered her eyes, ashamed, thinking she had made a fool of herself, and of Marco. But her brother took her by the chin and turned her face up.

He was smiling. He said, "Yes, you should fish with us." He glanced over his shoulder at the rest of the crew. The other two boats had drawn closer. He said, "I remember when you were the only brave one in the village."

That sobered the other men. Ercule and Juneo turned to the barrels that held the fishing nets, and Lucco and the skinny boy, Grep, sat on the two front rowing benches and ran the oars out. Perla lingered there, in the middle, wondering what to do, and Marco put his hand in hers and drew her back beside him at the tiller.

The other boats rowed in a widespread line across the bay from west to east, the headland behind them looming up above the unbroken stretch of beach. Marco called out for the oarsmen to raise their oars. The warm sun glistened on the bay; looking over the side, Perla watched fish as long as her arm, in schools that seemed endless, weaving slowly through the open water. The men had trailed the net out behind them, and Marco let the boat drift slowly along, down the sun from the fish.

The yell from Juneo jerked them all upright. The netsman was hauling on his net, and beside him Ercule bellowed also: "Help! Help!"

With a roar, the two rowers bounded to grip the nets, to try to haul in the catch. Marco gave a whoop. He pushed the tiller into Perla's hands and leapt back there to join them. She gripped the tiller with both hands and looked back, amazed, as they dumped a huge slithering silver avalanche of fish into the back hold of the boat.

Marco came hurrying back, his face ready, his smile abeam. "I knew this would work." He slid onto the bench beside her and grabbed the tiller away. "Row!" He lifted his voice to shout orders. "Row!"

Perla laid her hand on the gunwale; down the bay, she saw the other two boats also hauling in their catches, and the tiny figures waved their hands over their heads, and she could hear their thin cheering voices. Marco laid the tiller over.

"Down there! Under the headland, where the water's sheltered—Row!"

The boat felt different now, even Perla could sense it, heavier with the load of fish. The men pulled strongly; Lucco squirmed deftly out of his shirt between strokes. The sun blazed on the water, but as they drew nearer, the high stone crag blocked it and cast a shadow out over the deep.

Marco called, and the men shipped their oars and ran to the nets. The other boats were rowing fast after them. Perla stood up; this time she meant to join them bringing the nets in.

She felt the boat under her quiver slightly.

Marco called, "Juneo, cast the net!"

"I—I—" Juneo was balanced on the stern of the boat, the rolled net gripped in his hands; he turned his white face toward Marco, and then the boat began to slide sideways.

Marco yelled. Perla grabbed hold of the gunwale with both hands. The boat was spinning along at the edge of a whirling circle of water; at the center, the water sank down, and down, all spinning and widening, so that their boat now lurched and swayed, tipped halfway into the vortex. Perla shouted, "Marco, what should I do?"

Then up through the center of the eddy came the dragon.

Its great horned head reared up into the air, its long neck arched, its shoulders thrusting through the whirl of the water. For an instant, the men on Perla's boat stood frozen where they were, their faces lifted, and then Marco bounded toward the mast and the gaff tied to it.

"Get back, Perla!"

She took a step back, but the red, horned head towering over her was turning toward her, toward the boat, and the long jaws parted and a gust of green flame erupted from its throat. The ball of fire hit the boat by the forward thwart, and it exploded into flames. Perla leapt overboard.

She swam away from the boat, but the whirlpool caught her; in spite of her thrashing arms, she went skidding down the side of the eddy. The beast loomed over her, enormous, its red scales streaming water. She saw its head dart past her again and rear up, a man clutched in its jaws. She screamed; that was Lucco, from her boat, his arms waving. The dragon flipped him up into the air, so that he fell headfirst, and swallowed him on the way down. The huge head swung around again. Away from her. She struggled in the furious current, trying to swim across the tow, get out of the whirlpool, but it was carrying her swiftly downward, always closer to the dragon. A scream reached her ears, and she saw the wedge-shaped red head rise again, another man in its teeth.

Then the wave of the whirlpool brought her directly against the dragon's side. Her fingers scraped over the slick red scales, trying to grab hold. Above her, the beast's spines rose like giant barbs, and she lunged up and caught one and held on.

The beast was still rising. Clutching the spine, she was borne higher up into the air. All around her, below her, the water tossed, full of men, some screaming and waving their arms and some trying to swim, and the dragon caught another, and another, its head darting here and there at the end of its long neck. She tied her belt to the spine, to stay on. She saw Marco down there, on the lip of the eddy, and tried to yell, but he disappeared in a gust of steam. The dragon breathed out again, and the last of the boats burst into flame.

She clung to the spine, thick as a tree bough, polished smooth and sleek as gold; she was sick to her stomach, numb with fear, sure that Marco was dead, that they were all dead. The beast whirled and her head struck the spine hard enough to daze her. The sky whirled by her, then, abruptly, the dragon was plunging down.

She flung her head back, startled alert again, and fought to untie her belt. The wet knot was solid. She fought to pull the belt loose off the spine, while the dragon dove down into the dark green water, but the belt held her, and just as the sea closed over her head, she gasped in a deep lungful of air.

The sea rushed past her. They were going down into the darkness. She looked up, saw a body floating limp in the shrinking patch of pale water. Then the dragon was swimming sideways, into an underwater cave or a tunnel.

The light vanished. In the pitch darkness, surging along on the dragon's back, she could not imagine an end. She had to breathe. Her lungs hurt. The dark water rippled on her skin. Her fists were clenched around the spine, her body flying along above the strong-swimming beast. She had to breathe! She kept still a moment longer, counting. When she got to ten, she counted again. Her lungs ached. She could see nothing. Strange lights burst in her eyes, in the dark, and were gone. Nausea rose in her throat. Then the dragon was swimming upward, toward the pale surface.

She counted again, on the ragged edge of giving up and breathing in water, and at eight, she burst into the light and the air.

She gasped, clinging to the spine, looking around her. Her whole body shuddered. They were inside the headland; some underwater passage connected it to the sea. Sheltered inside the sheer rock walls lay a lagoon with a little brown beach. The dragon was swimming toward the beach. She gripped her belt. With a leap of relief, she saw that it had frayed almost apart in the wild ride, and, with her fingers, she ripped it off just as the dragon reached the shallow water. She plunged down the red-scaled side and ran up onto the sand.

The brown cliff there rose impossibly high and steep. But the face was runneled and cleft with caves and seams. She ducked into the nearest of hollows and went back as far as it went, only a few feet of a narrow twisting gorge that pinched together into nothing.

Far enough, she thought. It can't reach me here. She crept cautiously up nearer the beach, to see out.

The dragon had lain down right in front of her, only about ten feet of sand between her cave and its head. So it knew she was there. But it stretched out, relaxed, well fed, half-asleep. She leaned against the rock wall behind her and looked it over.

The red, horned head lay half-turned toward her, the eyes closed, rimmed in gold, the wide curled nostrils also gold-trimmed, oddly delicate. The long red neck led back into ridged shoulders with scales as big as a house. At ease, the beast sprawled between its forepaws, their curved claws outstretched. The massive bulk of its body curled away, its tail half in the water still, a net wrapped around one spine.

She watched it until the daylight was gone. Once, in its sleep, its jaws parted and gave a soft greenish burp, and a little round stone rolled out. As the beast still slept, its long red tongue licked over its lips, and it settled deeper on the sand.

The sun went down. In the night, she thought, she could escape, and she edged closer to the beach. Just as she reached the mouth of the crevice, the dragon's near eye opened, shining in the dark, fixed on her. Perla scuttled back into the deep of the crevices, all her hair on end. She thought she heard a low growl behind her.

She wept; she wept for Marco and Lucco and the other men, and for herself, because she knew she was lost. At last, she slept a little. When she woke, it was morning, and she was so hungry and thirsty she went back to the mouth of the crevice.

The dragon was still there. It stood looking away from her, the sun blazing on its magnificence, the red scales, darker at the edges, and the shining spines along its backbone. Then the narrow-jawed head swung toward her, high above her on the long, arched neck. On the broad space between its eyes was a disk of gold. Its eyes were big as washtubs, brilliant red, flecked and edged with gold.

It said, in a voice so deep and huge that she imagined she heard it through the bones of her head, not her ears, "Why don't you come out so I can eat you?"

"Please don't eat me," she said.

"Why shouldn't I? You'll just die in there anyway." It gave a cold chuckle. "And by then you'd be too thin to bother digging for. Tell me what you'll give me if I don't eat you. Will someone ransom you?"

She stood at the mouth of the crevice, her hands clammy and her throat thick with fear. No one from her village had anything to ransom her with, if the village even still survived, with all its men gone. She thought desperately of what she herself could do: weave, sew, cook, haul water.

"Can you dance? Sing?"

"I—"

The dragon said, "Tell me a story."

A cold tingle went down her spine. "A story," she said.

"If it's good enough, I won't eat you." The dragon settled himself down, his forepaws curled under him like a cat's, waiting.

She gulped. The village's stories were old and worn, which was why the villagers told them, and retold them, like the imperishable favorite about how old Pandan had his eye put out while looking through a knothole in the bathhouse at the women bathing. She knew at once such stories would not satisfy the dragon, much less save her life.

He was waiting, patient, his jeweled eyes on her. She realized that since he had begun speaking to her, she had thought of him as "he."

That gave her a wisp of an idea. She sat down in the mouth of the cave, her heart thundering, and began, "Once there was a King. An evil King." Like the Duke. Her mind sorted through the possibilities. "He stole everything from his people, and he killed many. But he did have one thing he loved, his beautiful daughter."

She spent some time describing the beautiful daughter, so that she could plan the next part. The dragon was utterly silent, his eyes steadily watching her, his long lips slightly smiling.

"He was so jealous of her that he put her in a tower by the sea." The story was growing stronger in her mind, and she let her voice stride out confidently, telling of the tower, and the wild storms, the sunlight, and the birds that came to sing to her in her window. "There she lived lonely, singing to the birds, and grew even more beautiful, but no man saw her except her father.

"But one day a Prince came by." She made the prince like Marco, solid and honest and brave. Dead now, probably, dead in this dragon's belly. Her voice trembled, but she fought herself back under control. She gave the Prince a red charger and red hair, which she saw amused the dragon. "The Prince heard her singing and climbed up the tower wall to her window. They fell in love at once, because she was beautiful and good, and he was handsome and brave and good. But before he could carry her off, the King burst in on them."

The dragon twitched, and she leaned toward him a little, intent, knowing now she had him. "The King had his sword, and although the Prince tried to fight back, he had no weapon. So the King got him down quickly."

The dragon growled. She kept her voice steady, speaking over the rumble. "But he did not kill him. Instead, he told the Prince that, since he was such a lizard that he could scale a castle wall, he would become the greatest lizard. And he turned him into a dragon and cast him into the sea."

The dragon lifted its head and roared, not at her, but to the sky, then quickly sank down again, his eyes blazing.

"But the Princess. What happened to her?"

Perla was ready to run for the end of the crevice if this did not suit. She fixed the dragon eye to eye. "Her heart was broken. She fled from her father—"

"Good."

"And now she wanders through the world looking for her Prince. Only her love can change him back from the dragon. But every day she grows older, and every day, the dragon grows more like a dragon, and less like the Prince."

She was poised to run. But the dragon's eyes were shining. His long lips drew back from his dagger-teeth, and he nodded once. Turning, he plunged into the lagoon.

She went cautiously out onto the open sand. On the beach, water spilled down the cliff in a long fall, and she went there and quenched her thirst, all the while looking for some other way out of the lagoon. The cliff ran all around it like a wall.

In the lagoon, too soon, the whirling appeared, and the eddy deepened, and the dragon's head rose through it and he swam to the beach and dragged himself out onto the sand. In his jaws, he held a long, flopping sea bass, which he flung down on the sand.

"Wait." The voice was like speaking bronze. He reared his head back and shot forth a bolt of flame, which blasted around the fish for several seconds.

She went warily up to it, knelt, and touched the carcass. It was nicely cooked. She peeled back the skin and ate the hot, flaky white meat. It was delicious, but it tasted a little sharp.

The dragon was crouched there, head and shoulders settled above its sprawled forepaws, his long neck curved, watching her. When she was done, and sitting there licking her fingers, he lay down around her, his head stretched along his paws, half embrace, half prison. The great red eye blinked once in a flash of gold. "Tell me another story."

AFTER that, the dragon let her roam as she pleased around the lagoon, as long as she told him stories whenever he asked. She made up stories about dragons, about princesses, about evil Kings, good and handsome Princes, about the brothers of Princesses, crisscrossing them, sometimes using the same people in one story after another. She tried to make every one different, but to her they seemed to all be the same, about wanting to go home, to be with whom she loved, and where she belonged.

She was sitting in the sun one afternoon, longing for home, and tears began to roll down her cheeks. The dragon said, "What's the matter?"

"You ate my brother," she said bitterly. "You ate all my people. I hate you."

He gave one of his throaty chuckles, unperturbed. "You eat the fish. You don't care about *their* brothers."

She cast off the thought of fish, which she had always eaten. "Do you have no family? No tribe? Where did you come from?"

He looked surprised. His huge eyes blazed red as the heart of a fire. "I was always here." But his stare shifted, and as much of a look of perplexity as she had ever seen came over his long, snakelike face. "There were more of us, once. But not many more." He turned, and flopped away into the lagoon and disappeared.

During the day, he often slept in the sun, or went down into the lagoon and was gone for a long while. She guessed that he went out the tunnel to the open sea. She wandered the beach, drinking from the waterfall that tumbled down from the top of the cliff and spread its shining skirts across the sand, eating berries growing down the stone wall, and seaweed, crabs, and clams, or anything else she could find. She worked out stories as she walked, saving bits and pieces when she could not make them whole, and remembering it all in a big overstory she would never tell him, about a girl taken captive by a dragon, who was rescued in the end by a Prince.

When he came back, he always had a fish for her and cooked it with the fire of his breath; no matter what the fish, bass, bonito, or shark, the meat always had a faintly sharp, spicy taste. If he had fed well, he burped up lots of stones, some as big as her fist, most toe-sized, clear lumps of colored crystal, red and blue and green. If he had eaten nothing or little, he complained and glowered at her and licked his lips at her, and talked of eating her instead, his red eyes wicked and his tongue flickering.

"I don't have to listen to you," she said, holding herself very straight. She turned back to the crevice, where she could get away from him.

Behind her, the deep rumbling voice said, "If you try to escape, I will definitely eat you."

She spun toward him. "But I want to go home. You should let me go home."

At that, he gave off a burst of furious heat and exhaled a stream of green fire. She dodged him and ran toward the crevice.

One huge forepaw came down directly in front of her. When she wheeled, his other paw came down, fencing her in.

"You can't leave!"

She put her hands over her ears, the roar shaking her whole body. The ground trembled under her. He was lying down, curled around her. She lowered her hands. He was calm again, but his great scaled bulk surrounded her. Only a few feet away, the enormous eye shut and opened again. "Tell me a story."

So she had to escape. During the day, she followed the seams and gullies worn into the cliff, hoping to find another way out, but they all pinched out or ended in falls of broken rock. Once, in the shadows at the back of a defile, she found a skeleton, still wearing tattered clothes—a cloak with fur trim, and pretty, rotten shoes, even rings on the fingerbones.

The bones were undisturbed. Whoever this was, however he had gotten here, he had never even left the cave.

She had left the cave. She found herself a little proud of that.

One evening, after she told him a story about some adventures of the Prince as dragon, she turned to go back into the crevice, where she usually slept. Before she could reach the cliff, he caught her lightly with his forepaw—the long curved claws like tusks inches from her face—and tossed her backward. She stumbled off across the beach, wondering what she had done wrong. The other paw met her and sent her reeling back. She whirled, frightened, her hands out, and he batted her around again. His head suspended over her watched her with a cold amusement. He was *playing*, she realized, in a haze of terror, not really hurting her. She caught hold of his scaly paw and held tight, and he stopped.

But he did not let her go. He reached down and took her between his long jaws, gently as a mother with an egg. She lay, rigid, her breath stopped, between two sets of gigantic teeth, the long tongue curled around her. He lay down, stretched out, and carefully set her on the sand between his forepaws. He put his head down on his paws, so that she lay in the hollow under his throat, and went to sleep.

She lay stiff as a sword under him. Something new had happened, and she had no notion what he might mean by this. What he might do next. Yet the cavern under his throat was warm, and she fell asleep after a while.

The next day, he dove into the lagoon and was gone, and she began to search from one end of the cliff to the other for a way out. She went back through every crevice, tried to chimney up the sides, and crawled along the top of huge mounds of rubble. Always, the space came to an end, the cliff pressed down on her, dark and cold.

She crept back out to the sunlit lagoon again. The beauty of it struck her, as it always did, the water clear and blue and dark at the center, and paler in toward the shore, the tiny ripples of the waves, the cream-colored sand. The sky was cloudless. The cliff vaulted up hundreds of feet high, sheer as glass.

As she stood there, wondering what to do, the blue water began to whirl, eddying around, and the dragon's great head thrust up through the center of it, a white fish between his long jaws.

He saw her, and came to her, cast down the fish, and breathed on it with the harsh fire of his breath, and then, as usual, stood there watching her eat it. She was hungry and ate all the pale, flaky meat. Being close to him made her edgy. She had thought of a good story to tell him, with a long chase through a forest, and the dragon's escape at the end. She could not look at him, afraid of what she might see brimming in the great red eyes.

He sat quietly throughout the story, as he always did. She had learned to feel the quality of his attention, and she knew he was deep into this story. She brought it to an end and stood.

His head moved, fast as a serpent, and he caught her between his jaws. He laid her down on her back between his forepaws. She lay so stiff her fists were clenched, looking up at the wedge-shaped head above her, and then he began to lick her all over.

His tongue was long and supple, silky smooth, longer than she was tall, so that sometimes he was licking her whole body all at once. She was afraid to move. He licked at her dress until it was bunched up under her armpits. His touch was soft, gentle, even tender; stroking over her breasts, he paused an instant, his warm tongue over her, and against her will, she gasped.

He said, in his deep, harsh voice, "It's only me, the Prince," and chuckled. He slid his tongue down her side and curled it over her legs.

She clutched her thighs together, but the tip of his tongue flicked between them, into the cleft of her body. She shut her eyes. She held her whole body tight, as if she could make an armor of her skin. Her strength was useless against him.

But nothing more happened. He slept, eventually, his head over her. She dozed fitfully, starting up from nightmares.

In the morning, he went off as usual, and she searched desperately along the cliff face. At the waterfall, she stood in the tumbling water, thinking of his tongue on her, wondering what else he would do.

Behind the streaming water, she noticed a narrow crevice.

She stepped into it, behind the water, and saw that the slit in the rock angled back into the dark. She pressed herself into it. Water ran three inches deep along the bottom of the crevice. As she worked her way back, and the dark shut down around her, her hands along the walls on either side passed through sheets of water coming down.

She came to a place where the gorge divided in two, one side running to her left, one to her right. It was totally dark. She stood still a while, her mind blocked with fear, and then she realized that there was water trickling over the toes of her right foot, and the other was dry. She followed the water.

The crevice walls came so close together that her nose scraped in front and the back of her head scraped behind her. The tunnel twisted, turned. In the dark, she fumbled along, her heart thundering. She should have brought water. Food. She should have planned this. Thought ahead. Was it night, now, was it dark out, as it was so dark in here? Blindly, she crept forward through the crevice in the rock. She could not go back now. He was back there by now; he knew that she was gone.

The tunnel narrowed and kinked. In the kink, for an instant, she could not move, buried there in the belly of the cliff, caught in the wedge of the stone, and she almost screamed. Instead, she made herself relax. There was water running over her ankles. She had only to follow the water. She pushed slowly, gently forward, most of her body stuck fast; but her foot moving, then her thigh, her hip, until she worked her way around the bump in the rock.

The tunnel widened. It began to climb upward, twisting and turning, but always up in the dark, until she was helping herself along with her outstretched hands. Then the climb came to an end in a blank rock wall, with water spilling down its surface.

She felt her way along the rock wall, found a place where she could climb, and went up. Her hands groped ahead of her for holds, and her feet pressed against the rock. If she fell from here, she might die. Break her leg. Die slowly. Then, reaching up, she realized that she could see her hand.

She followed that grip into brighter light. She could see where to put her hands now, and the stone was warm. Above, beyond the edge of rock, was pink sky: the sun just going down. She pulled herself the last few feet up to the grass beside the pool of water, and lay down, exhausted, and closed her eyes, and slept.

꒰ꕥ꒱

SHE had nothing to eat, but the spring had come; the meadow was full of mushrooms, and the trees of birds' nests and eggs. She walked a whole day and much of the night, through a brilliant full moon, before she came at last to the high road where it came down from the mountain passes and veered toward the sea. It was deserted. Even from its crests, she could not see the coast. Off toward the ocean, a plume of thick black smoke clotted the air; she wondered if the farmers were burning off their fields for the spring planting.

She walked on, eating whatever she could find—roots, nuts, even flowers and grubs. On the third day, she came on some travelers, who gave her some bread.

They were surprised to find her walking alone; they said, "Be careful, there are robbers on the highway. The Duke has gone south to a war, and there is no law."

"And raiders on the sea," said another. "Be careful."

So she watched out for strangers, walking along, but she thought that she was near her own village and looked for the path down to it. She wondered what she would find there—if anything were left there. She wept once, thinking of Marco. But she was still walking along the high road, her feet sore, and every muscle aching, when someone shouted, and a skinny boy bounded down out of the rocks toward her.

"Perla! Perla!"

It was Grep, who had rowed third oar on Marco's boat at Dragon's Deep. She laughed, astonished, her hopes surging.

Grep bounded around her, laughing. "You're alive! You're alive! Come, hurry—Marco will—"

"Marco," she cried, running down the steep path beside him. "Marco is alive?"

"Marco, Ercule, Juneo, me," he said. They slowed to a crawl under a fallen tree. "Everybody else went down in the storm."

"The storm," she said, startled.

He put his finger to her lips. "But you're alive!" He laughed again, joyous, as if nothing else mattered. "Come on—" He ran out ahead up a short, steep slope and onto the flat top of the sea cliff, shouting.

"Look here, everybody! Look here!"

She stood there, looking around her. She knew this cliff, which had stood behind her village. Now on its narrow height stood a cluster of huts inside a ditch—half as many huts as the old village, and now from each one, faces peered out.

And she laughed, delighted, and stretched out her arms, and they were running toward her, her sister, all tears, and her friends.

"Perla! Perla! You came back!" She flung herself into their arms, and for a while nothing mattered.

"Where are the men?" she asked, in her sister's hut. Her sister set a piece of fish before her, a slab of bread, and she reached greedily as a child for them.

"They're out," her sister said vaguely. She said, "The few there are. Marco has been the saving of us."

Perla looked around the hut, smaller than before, stoutly made with stone footings, a withy wall domed overhead, and covered with straw. There was only one bed, and that small. Her eyes went to the doorway, where half a dozen children hung in the opening, watching her wide-eyed.

She turned to her sister. "Are your children—"

"I lost my little girl in the winter. It was hard."

"Oh, no. Your husband?"

"He's dead," her sister said. She picked up the knife again, to cut the bread. "Do you want more? We have plenty of food."

"But—he didn't go with us to Dragon's Deep," Perla said.

"He died when Marco took the men up to the highway," her sister said. She laid the loaf down on the board and hacked off another slab. "That's how we have lived, Perla, we rob the highway. And, at last, we have enough."

Perla gave a shudder, horrified. "Until the Duke comes," she said, but she remembered that she had heard that he had gone away.

"Why should we not?" her sister said. "Have we not been everybody else's prey?" Her eyes glittered. "When the Duke comes, Marco will have a plan. Marco always has a plan." She thrust out the piece of bread. "He brought me this bread. The men all follow him, and he makes sure all of us widows are fed. Just obey Marco. Everything will come well."

Perla took the bread. "I hope you are right."

Later, when the men came back, they gathered together in the evening.

The men saw her and cheered, and Marco came and hugged her, and she endured also the sweaty hugs of Ercule, and they all shouted her name. "How did you get home? Where have you been?"

She sat down in the circle to tell them her story. They had built a bright fire, and all their faces shone in the light. She began, "You remember how we set off to the north, to Dragon's Deep, to fish there. Because the Duke had come and stolen all our food."

They murmured, agreeing, and looked at one another. Marco, beside her, leaned forward, a little frown on his face. She fought off the feeling that he was not liking this.

"And we got there, you remember, and the fish were thick as grass on the meadow, and we hauled in one great catch—"

"And then the storm came," Marco said.

The listeners gave a louder rumble of agreement, and Ercule called out, "One boat after another foundered."

Juneo said, "The sky was dark as night, and the lightning flashed—"

"No," Perla said, astonished.

"I made it to the shore," Grep said. "I don't know how, and then I saw Marco trying to carry Ercule in, and Juneo hanging to both of them, and went to help them."

"No," Perla said.

"We don't want to talk about it anymore," Marco said, and the other men loudly agreed with him again, and the women gestured and nodded and agreed, and Perla sat there dumb and amazed.

They sang some songs, which she had known from her babyhood, and she came near tears to hear them. Then someone told the old story about how Pandun had gotten his eye put out, looking through the hole in the bathhouse wall at the women.

After, she saw Marco to one side, and went to him. He wrapped his muscular arms around her again. "I'm glad you're back. I was sure you were dead." He kissed her hair.

"Marco," she said, "what is this about a storm?"

"We were wrecked in a sudden storm," he said, smiling. "I don't know how you got through it. I really don't know how I did."

"Marco, there was a dragon."

He laughed. "You don't say. Aren't you a little addled, maybe, from all that time alone? That must be it." He pressed his lips to her forehead. "There. See? Ercule is watching you. Go to him, he's missed you too."

"I hate Ercule," she burst out.

"Well, you're going to marry him," said Marco. He was still smiling. Nothing seemed to bother him. She supposed if he had already swallowed the storm story, then he was ready for anything.

She said, "What about the Duke?"

"Hah," he said.

"My sister told me what you're doing."

His eyebrows jacked up and down. That at least ruffled him; his face tightened. "I had four men left and a dozen families with children," he said. "And it was *my* fault, Perla. I took them there. You were gone. Lucco. All the boats but one. Lost in a storm." He took a deep breath, drawing back into the shell he had made for himself, the one that smiled all the time. He smiled. "So I did what I had to do. And so will you. Ercule is very useful to me. I want you to marry him." He leaned over and laid his cheek against hers and walked away.

More like a dragon than a Prince, she thought, nearly in tears again. She had not come home after all. She crept back to her sister, to find a place to sleep.

During the following days, she drowned herself in work, making her own house, bringing up stones and withies from the deserted village on the beach. The trail up the cliff was steep and hard, but well-worn, and the other women helped her. During the day, the men went off. She was afraid to ask what they did, but they did not take out the only boat left, which lay always on the beach in the lee of the rock, its nets rotting on the sand. They brought back stories from the highway, gossip, news. At night, when they returned, Ercule came on her.

She held him off for several nights, pushing, shoving, angry, making him shy, but she saw Marco talking to him. After that, he was bolder, he forced her to kiss him, and the next night, while he kissed her, he grabbed her breast in his hand. She wrenched away from him and went inside. It was just past the full moon, and the light shone through the holes in her dome-shaped roof, which had not yet been thatched over. She saw him come in, saw his toothy grin, and could not stop him.

The next day, he went off with Marco somewhere, and she sat inside the hut and cried. Her sister came and sat by her and patted her shoulder. But when next the men came back, they had bread and meat and blankets and a cask of wine, and it was Ercule who sat beside her, and she could not keep him off.

She was afraid to tell stories, and without the constant telling, the stories stopped coming to her.

One late afternoon, Grep rushed in from the path, leading a stumbling, exhausted stranger. "He was on the sea trail," he said to Marco. "I thought you should hear him."

The villagers had all come out to see what was happening, and the stranger staggered into their midst. He was in rags, his face hollow with thirst and grief. One of the women went quickly to him, brought him water, made him sit, and comforted him. The others gathered around him.

He said, "I never saw them—I was asleep—I woke up to find the place burning. Everybody's gone. Everybody's gone."

Marco said, "Where?"

The stranger said the name of the next village up the coast. He was devouring bread and cheese and milk. The widow beside him had already claimed him, whether he knew it or not. His mouth full, he went on, "I hid in the cesspit. The whole village burnt to the ground. When I got out in the morning, everybody was gone, or dead."

Perla thought, Not him, then. Not him. He hunts in the daylight. But her heart leapt.

"You didn't see them?"

"That's how I lived. If I'd seen them, they would have seen *me*."

Ercule said, "It's that same bunch who took San Male."

"Maybe," Marco said. "When did this happen?"

"Two days ago," the stranger said. "The night of the full moon."

Marco gave a short grunt. He turned to Ercule. "I think there was a full moon the night they took San Male. Go up on the high road, ask around."

"I will," Ercule said.

Perla thought, He hunts in the daylight. But on his home hunting ground. Off his range, he would be more cautious. Her palms were clammy. *If you try to escape, I will definitely eat you.*

Marco said, "And find out where the Duke is. I heard he was coming back north."

Ercule said, "I will, Marco."

Perla swallowed, her hands pressed together at her breast, and looked down at the sea beach below the cliff, where once the village had been—where still a lot of the village remained. A story began to form in her mind, but she had no one to tell it to. If she kept it silent, it would go away. She looked out at the broad, rippled sea, burnished in the setting sun.

Ercule said, "What's got you so pinch-faced? I'll be back in a couple of days." He showed his teeth in his ugly grin. "Then we'll have a good time."

"I'd rather be eaten," she said.

Ercule came back with a buzz of news. To her relief, Perla's courses had begun, and for once she slept untroubled and alone. A few days later, the Duke himself rode down toward the village on the beach.

His charger was black, with reins worked with silver, and silver stirrups. Marco met him at the foot of the trail up the cliff; the villagers all watched from the height.

The Duke's voice was clear and loud. "I know who you are. Word came to me even in the south, where I was fighting Saracens. Help me defeat these northern sea-raiders, and I'll make you Count of this place. You can go on robbing, unh, taking your tolls on the highway. Just give me half."

Perla, horrified, saw her brother bow down, agreeing to this. The Duke wheeled his horse and rode away, and Marco came back up the trail to the village.

Perla went to him as soon as she saw him without Ercule. She said, "He is lying! He is *lying*. Can't you see that?"

Marco smiled at her. "It's all right, my darling." He kissed her. "I was lying too." More a dragon every day.

Marco said, "They come on the full moon. The Duke agrees with me, says there have been three attacks this year, all north of here, but moving down the coast. They come in the night of the full moon, burn the village, seize all the people, go before daylight comes. Slavers, obviously. We can figure they'll come here, if not the next full moon, then the one after. Especially if we all move back to the village on the beach."

Perla clamped her lips shut. They would be safe on the cliff.

If they stayed on the cliff, the dragon would be safe from them.

Now Marco was telling the plan. "We'll dig a ditch just above the high-tide line. The Duke will bring archers, who will hide in the ditch, and knights, who will wait in the village. When the raiders come in, we'll get them between, and we'll have them."

Perla bit her knuckle. Ercule swung around toward her. "Well, what do you think of that?" He picked her up and swung her around. "When I am a lord, you'll be a lady. Hah! Then you'll like me better." She clenched her teeth, angry, and thought of getting a knife somewhere and sticking it up between his ribs.

But for the next few weeks, all the men worked hard digging the ditch, and Ercule mostly left her alone. The moon was waxing. The women went back to living on the beach, in the shells of the old huts; with the summer coming on, these were pleasant in the evening breezes, and close by the water for the children. They talked of taking out the boat to fish, until someone noticed the holes in the nets.

A few days before the next full moon, the Duke rode in and galloped his black horse on the beach at low tide, all the while staring out to sea. Perla watched him morosely. Talk was, his war in the south had not gone well. He needed to defeat someone. Her gaze went to Marco, working hard in the heat to shore up the side of the ditch. Surely he was making a fool out of Marco, who was doing all the work, while the Duke would get all the glory.

The Duke's handsome young son raced after him. He practiced with his sword, pretending to do battle with hundreds.

Just one, she thought, her heart hammering, and looked out over the sea. Or maybe she had dreamt it. Just a story, after all. Maybe there was nothing but the likes of Ercule, the Duke, and Marco.

Her sister came to her, and said, "The moon will be full tonight. We are going into the woods again. Will you come?"

Perla said, "I want to stay."

"It's been said—" Her sister's mouth kinked. "If the Duke can't have his sea-raiders, he'll take Marco."

She said, "I will stay."

"Ah, you've always been a fool, Perla! Now I think you're a little crazy."

She knew that Marco had spread that word about her, that she was crazy.

She was beginning to wonder, what difference did it make, if everybody else believed something else? Surely they were right?

The sun set, and the round moon rose. She alone of all the women stayed in the beach village, where the Duke's knights spread out to eat their supper among the huts. Wary of them, she walked down toward the water. She circled the end of the ditch, full of men with bows. Out before everybody else was Marco, with the other villagers.

She climbed up onto the rock at the end of the beach. The moonlight made everything silver and black, glistening sand, the inky pit of the ditch. The sea ran soft and quiet in the windless night, just curling over along the beach. She thought, The knights are ready, either for the attack from the sea, or to attack Marco. Marco had only five men, and the Duke one hundred.

She sat on the rock in the moonlight, dozing, and she dreamt of the great red eye, gold-rimmed, and the deep voice saying, "Tell me a story."

She opened her eyes. The moon was sinking into the west. Her hair tingled up. Out there, an eddy was forming on the rippled water.

She stiffened, her breath frozen in her lungs. Behind her, a man called out sleepily, "What's that?"

Marco shouted, "Perla! What are you doing there? Run!"

She twisted to see him running away from the water, dashing for the cliff. The other villagers followed him. So that was his plan! He remembered the dragon after all. Without waiting for her, Ercule and the others at his heels, he raced toward the trail up the cliff, leaving the Duke's men behind to fight.

The Duke's men ignored him. To them, nothing was happening. A few of the archers in the ditch lifted their bows. One called out, "What are we shooting at?"

The sentry shouted, "Something's out there."

Standing in his stirrups to see, the Duke rode to the edge of the ditch, his son behind him, his face stretched in a lopsided yawn. Out on the sea, the eddy whirled larger and deeper, sleek and dark in the moonlit water around it. The edge broke hard on the beach. Then the horned head shot up, and the dragon lunged into the air.

Perla leapt down from the rock. "No! Go back—it's a trap! Go back—" Something struck her hard in the back, and she fell headlong, almost in the water.

A tremendous brazen roar drowned everything. She felt the waves lapping at her hands, and crawled up toward the dry sand, out of the way. Her back hurt, and blood ran down her side; she twisted her arm around carefully to feel behind her, but touched only her sodden dress. Whatever had hit her had glanced off. She sank down, gasping with pain. Then the dragon hurtled up out of the sea past her.

As he went, he shot out a green bolt of flame that scorched the ditch from end to end. When the few men who could raised their bows, he swept them up in his jaws. Some he ate, and some he cast aside to go after more. He crossed the smoldering ditch with a bound. Perla, crouched by the rock, heard the ping of the arrows striking his scales.

A horn blew. In a long single line, the knights charged down the beach. The Duke led them, his sword drawn. They swept in around the dragon like a surging wave, their swords hacking, the horses whirling and struggling against spurs and bits.

Then another green flame sizzled out and knocked the dark wave back, and, with a shriek, the dragon reared up, his head high, the Duke between his jaws. Even from the side, Perla could hear the armor crunch. A wail went up from the Duke's men, and they scurried back, away.

The Duke's son galloped forward. "Rally! Rally—"

The dragon hurled the Duke's body down and went straight for the son, and the boy wheeled his horse and ran. The great jaws snapped shut at the horse's tail. The knights followed in a stream. The dragon grabbed another as they fled, and ate him, spitting out the coat of mail and the helmet.

Perla rose, stiff with pain, and limped toward him. He was bleeding from a dozen places, a slash on his neck, a deep gash in his breast, arrows sticking into his scales. She held out her arms to him.

"Are you all right?"

The dragon turned to her, and she saw the first dawnlight glisten on the golden disk between his eyes. His voice was harsh. He said, "I am sore wounded, my heart's blood flows on these sands. If not for your warning, they would have had me. I swore I would devour you, if I found you. But you saved me, and suffered for it." He turned, swaying back toward the sea. "And I remember the stories."

She said, "I want to go with you."

He stopped, his neck arched, his head hanging down. His wounds dropped thick globs of blood that burnt a moment on the sand and then went out in a wisp of smoke. "I remember the stories. I do not know where these wounds and the sea will carry me."

"Yet I will go with you, whatever happens."

His head swung toward her. The great red eyes glimmered, brimming. The long tongue flicked out tenderly over her bare feet. She climbed up over his shoulder and onto his back, sitting astride, holding with both hands to the great spine before her. She had only enough time to draw a deep breath before he plunged back into the sea.

Vici

NAOMI NOVIK

Here's a demonstration that "Seize the day!" is often good advice, even if taking it gets you entangled with a dragon—in ways that you never could have anticipated!

Born in New York City, where she still lives with her mystery-editor husband and six computers, bestselling author Naomi Novik is a first-generation American who was raised on Polish fairy tales, Baba Yaga, and Tolkien. After doing graduate work in computer science at Columbia University, she participated in the development of the computer game Neverwinter Nights: Shadows of Undrentide *and then decided to try her hand at novels. A good decision! The resultant Temeraire series—consisting of* His Majesty's Dragon, Throne of Jade, Black Powder War, *and* Empire of Ivory— *describing an alternate version of the Napoleonic Wars where dragons are used as living weapons, has been phenomenally popular and successful. Her most recent book is a new Temeraire novel,* Victory of Eagles.

❧

"WELL, Antonius," the magistrate said, "you are without question a licentious and disreputable young man. You have disgraced a noble patrician name and sullied your character in the lowest of pursuits, and we have received testimony that you are not only a drunkard and a gambler—but an outright murderer as well."

With an opening like that, the old vulture was sending him to the block for sure. Antony shrugged philosophically; he'd known it was unlikely his family could have scraped together enough of a bribe to get him let go. Claudius's family was a damn sight richer than his; and, in any case, he could hardly imagine his stepfather going to the trouble.

"Have you anything to say for yourself?" the magistrate said.

"He was a tedious bastard?" Antony offered cheerfully.

The magistrate scowled at him. "Your debts stand at nearly 250 talents—"

"Really?" Antony interrupted. "Are you sure? Gods, I had no idea. Where *does* the money go?"

Tapping his fingers, the magistrate said, "Do you know, I would dearly love to send you to the arena. It is certainly no less than you deserve."

"The son of a senator of Rome?" Antony said, in mock appall. "They'd have you on the block, next."

"I imagine these circumstances might be considered mitigating," the magistrate said. "However, your family has petitioned for mercy most persuasively, so you have an alternative."

Well, that was promising. "And that is?" he said.

The magistrate told him.

"Are you out of your mind?" Antony said. "How is that mercy? It's twelve men to kill a dragon, even if it's small."

"They did not petition for your life," the magistrate said patiently. "*That* would have been considerably more expensive. Dragon-slaying is an honorable death, and generally quick, from my understanding; and it will legally clear your debts. Unless you would prefer to commit suicide?" he inquired.

Dragons could be killed, guards might be bribed to let you slip away, but a sword in your own belly was final. "No, thanks anyway," Antony said. "So where's the beast? Am I off to Germanica to meet my doom, or is it Gaul?"

"You're not even leaving Italy," the magistrate said, already back to scribbling in his books, the heartless bugger. "The creature came down from the north a week ago with all its hoard and set itself up just over the upper reaches of the Tiber, not far from Placentia."

Antony frowned. "Did you say its *hoard*?"

"Oh yes. Quite remarkable, from all reports. If you do kill it, you may be able to pay off even your debts, extraordinary as they are."

As if he'd waste perfectly good gold in the hand on anything that stupid. "Just how old a beast are we talking about, exactly?"

The magistrate snorted. "We sent a man to count its teeth, but he seems to be doing it from inside the creature's belly. A good four to six elephantweight from local reports, if that helps you."

"Discord gnaw your entrails," Antony said. "You can't possibly expect me to kill the thing alone!"

"No," the magistrate agreed, "but the dragon-hunter division of the ninth is two weeks' march away, and the populace is getting restless in the meantime. It will be as well to make a gesture." He looked up again. "You will be escorted there by a personal guard provided by Fulvius Claudius Sullius's family. Do you care to reconsider?"

"Discord gnaw *my* entrails," Antony said bitterly.

ALL right, now this was getting damned unreasonable. "It breathes *fire*?" Antony said. The nearest valley was a blackened ruin, orchard trees and houses charred into lumps. A trail of debris led away into the hills, where a thin line of smoke rose steadily into the air.

"Looks like," Addo, the head of the guards, said more enthusiastically than was decent. Anyone would've thought he'd won all the man's drinking money last night, instead of just half. There hadn't even been a chance to use it to buy a whore for a last romp.

The guards marched Antony down to the mouth of the ravine—the only way in or out, because the gods had forsaken him—and took off the chains. "Change your mind?" Addo said, smirking, while the other two held out the shield and spear. "It's not too late to run onto it, instead."

"Kiss my arse." Antony took the arms and threw the man his purse. "Spill a little blood on the altar of Mars for me, and have a drink in my memory," he said, "and I'll see you all in Hell."

They grinned and saluted him. Antony stopped around the first curve of the ravine and waited a while, then glanced back: but the unnaturally dedicated *pedicatores* were sitting there, dicing without a care in the world.

All right: nothing for it. He went on into the ravine.

It got hotter the farther in he went. His spear grip was soaked with sweat by the last curve, and then he was at the end, waves of heat like a bath furnace shimmering out to meet him. The dragon was sleeping in the ravine, and *merda sancta*, the thing was the size of a granary! It was a muddy sort of green with a scattering of paler green stripes and spots and spines, not like what he'd expected; there was even one big piebald patch of pale green, splotchy on its muzzle. More importantly, its back rose up nearly to the height of the ravine walls, and its head looked bigger than a wagon cart.

The dragon snuffled a little in its nose and grumbled, shifting. Pebbles rained down from the sides of the ravine walls and pattered against its hide of scales lapped upon scales, with the enameled look of turtle shell. There was a stack of bones heaped neatly in a corner, stripped clean—and behind that a ragged cave in the cliff wall, silver winking where some of the coin had spilled out of the mouth, much good would it do him.

"Sweet Venus, you've left me high and dry *this* time," Antony said, almost with a laugh. He didn't see how even a proper company would manage this beast. Its neck alone looked ten cubits long, more than any spear could reach. And breathing fire—

No sense in dragging the thing out. He tossed aside his useless shield—a piece of wood against this monster, a joke—and took a step toward the dragon, but the shield clattering against the ravine wall startled the creature. It jerked its head up and hissed, squinty-eyed, and Antony froze. Noble resignation be damned; he plastered himself back against the rock face as the dragon heaved itself to its feet.

It took two steps past him, stretching out its head with spikes bristling to sniff suspiciously at the shield. The thing filled nearly all the ravine. Its side was scarcely an arm's length from him, scales rising and falling with each breath, and sweat was already breaking out upon his face from the fantastic heat: like walking down the road in midsummer with a heavy load and no water.

The shoulder joint where the foreleg met the body was directly before his face. Antony stared at it. Right in the armpit, like some sort of hideous goiter, there was a great swollen bulge where the scales had been spread out and stretched thin. It was vaguely translucent, and the flesh around it had gone puffy.

The dragon was still busy with the shield, nosing at it and rattling it against the rock. Antony shrugged fatalistically and, taking hold of the butt of his spear with both hands, took a lunge at the vulnerable spot, aiming as best he could for the center of the body.

The softened flesh yielded so easily that the spear sank in until both his hands were up against the flesh. Pus and blood spurted over him, stinking to high heaven, and the dragon reared up, howling, lifting him his height again off the ground before the spear ripped back out of its side, and he came down heavily. Antony hit the ground and crawled toward the wall, choking and spitting, while rocks and dust came down on him. "Holy Juno!" he yelled, cowering, as one boulder the size of a horse smashed into the ground not a handspan from his head.

He rolled and tucked himself up against the wall and wiped his face, staring up in awe while the beast went on bellowing and thrashing from side to side above, gouts of flame spilling from its jaws. Blood was jetting from the ragged tear in its side like a fountain, buckets of it, running in a thick black stream through the ravine dust. Even as he watched, the dragon's head started to sag in jerks: down and pulled back up, down again, and down, then its hindquarters gave out under it. It crashed slowly to the ground with a last long hiss of air squeezing out of its lungs, and the head fell to the ground with a thump and lolled away.

Antony lay there staring at it a while. Then he shoved away most of the rocks on him and dragged himself up to his feet, swaying, and limped to stand over the gaping, cloudy-eyed head. A little smoke still trailed from its jaws, a quenched fire.

"Sweet, most-gracious, blessed, gentle Venus," he said, looking up, "I'll never doubt your love again."

He picked up his spear and staggered down the ravine in his blood-soaked clothing, and found the guards all standing and frozen, clutching their swords. They stared at him as if he were a demon. "No need to worry," Antony said, cheerfully. "None of it's mine. Any of you have a drink? My mouth is unspeakably foul."

℘ↄ

"WHAT in stinking Hades is that?" Secundus said, as the third of the guards came out of the cave, staggering under an enormous load: a smooth-sided oval boulder.

"It's an egg, you bleeding *capupeditum*," Addo said. "Bash it into a bloody rock."

"Stop there, you damned fools; it stands to reason it's worth something," Antony said. "Put it in the cart."

They'd salvaged the cart from the wreckage of the village and lined it with torn sacking and, to prove the gods loved him, even found a couple of sealed wine jars in a cellar. "Fellows," Antony said, spilling a libation to Venus while the guards loaded up the last of the treasure, "pull some cups out of that. Tomorrow we're going to buy every whore in Rome. But tonight, we're going to drink ourselves blind."

They cheered him, grinning, and didn't look too long at the heap of coin and jewels in the cart. He wasn't fooled; they'd have cut his throat and been halfway to Gaul by now if they hadn't been worried about the spear he'd kept securely in his hand, the one stained black with dragon blood.

That was all right. He could drink any eight men under the table in unwatered wine.

He left the three of them snoring in the dirt and whistled as the mules plodded down the road, quickly: they were all too happy to be leaving the dragon corpse behind. Or most of it, anyway: he'd spent the afternoon hacking off the dragon's head. It sat on top of the mound of treasure now, teeth overlapping the lower jaw as it gradually sagged in on itself. It stank, but it made an excellent moral impression when he drove into the next town over.

❧

THE really astonishing thing was that now, when he had more gold than water, he didn't need to pay for anything. Men quarreled for the right to buy him a drink, and whores let him have it for free. He couldn't even lose it gambling: every time he sat down at the tables, his dice always came up winners.

He bought a house in the best part of the city, right next to that pompous windbag Cato on one side and Claudius's uncle on the other, and threw parties that ran dusk until dawn. For the daylight hours, he filled the courtyard with a menagerie of wild animals: a lion and a giraffe that growled and snorted at each other from the opposite ends where they were chained up, and even a hippopotamus that some Nubian dealer brought him.

He had the dragon skull mounted in the center of the yard and set the egg in front of it. No one would buy the damn thing, so that was all he could do with it. "Fifty sesterces to take it off your hands," the arena manager said, after one look at the egg and the skull together.

"What?" Antony said. "I'm not going to pay *you*. I could just smash the thing."

The manager shrugged. "You don't know how far along it is. Could be it's old enough to live a while. They come out ready to fight," he added. "Last time we did a hatching, it killed six men."

"And how many damned tickets did it sell?" Antony said, but the bastard was unmoved.

It made a good centerpiece, anyway, and it was always entertaining to mention the arena manager's story to one of his guests when they were leaning against the egg and patting the shell, and watching how quickly they scuttled away. Personally, Antony thought it was just as likely the thing was dead; it had been sitting there nearly six months, and not a sign of cracking.

He, on the other hand, was starting to feel a little—well. Nonsensical to miss the days after he'd walked out of his stepfather's house for good, when some unlucky nights he'd had to wrestle three men in a street game for the coin to eat—since no one would give him so much as the end of a loaf of bread on credit—or even the handful of times he'd let some fat, rich lecher paw at him just to get a bed for the night.

But there just wasn't any juice in it anymore. A stolen jar of wine, after running through the streets ahead of the city cohorts for an hour, had tasted ten times as sweet as any he drank now, and all his old friends had turned into toadying dogs who flattered him clumsily. The lion got loose and ate the giraffe, and then he had to get rid of the hippo after it started spraying shit everywhere, which began to feel like an omen. He'd actually picked up a book the other day: sure sign of desperation.

He tried even more dissipation: an orgy of two days and nights where no one was allowed to sleep, but it turned out that even he had limits, and sometime in the second night, he had found them. He spent the next three days lying in a dark room with his head pounding fit to burst. It was August, and the house felt like a baking oven. His sheets were soaked through with sweat, and he still couldn't bear to move.

He finally crawled out of his bed and let his slaves scrub and scrape him and put him into a robe—of Persian silk embroidered with gold, because he didn't own anything less gaudy anymore—and then he went out into the courtyard and collapsed on a divan underneath some orange trees. "No, Jupiter smite you all, get away from me and be quiet," he snarled at the slaves.

The lion lifted its head and snarled at him, in turn. Antony threw the wine jug at the animal and let himself collapse back against the divan, throwing an arm up over his eyes.

He slept again a while, and woke to someone nudging his leg. "I told you mange-ridden dogs to leave me the hell alone," he muttered.

The nudging withdrew for a moment. Then it came back again. "Sons of Dis, I'm going to have you flogged until you—" Antony began, rearing up, and stopped.

"Is there anything more to eat?" the dragon asked.

He stared at it. Its head was about level with his, and it blinked at him with enormous green eyes, slit-pupiled. It was mostly green, like the last one, except with blue spines. He looked past it into the courtyard. Bits and chunks of shell were littering the courtyard all over, and the lion—"Where the hell is the lion?" Antony said.

"I was hungry," the dragon said unapologetically.

"You ate the lion?" Antony said, still half-dazed, and he stared at the dragon again. "You ate the *lion*," he repeated, in dawning wonder.

"Yes, and I would like some more food now," the dragon said.

"Hecate's teats, you can have anything you want," Antony said, already imagining the glorious spectacle of his next party. "Maracles!" he yelled. "Damn you, you lazy, sodding bastard of a slave, fetch me some goats here! How the hell can you talk?" he demanded of the dragon.

"*You* can," the dragon pointed out, as if that explained anything.

Antony thought about it and shrugged. Maybe it did. He reached out tentatively to pat the dragon's neck. It felt sleek and soft as leather. "What a magnificent creature you are," he said. "We'll call you—Vincitatus."

⸙

IT turned out that Vincitatus was a female, according to the very nervous master of Antony's stables, when the man could be dragged in to look at her. She obstinately refused to have her name changed, however, so Vincitatus it was, and Vici for short. She also demanded three goats a day, a side helping of something sweet, and jewelry, which didn't make her all that different from most of the other women of Antony's acquaintance. Everyone was terrified of her. Half of Antony's slaves ran away. Tradesmen wouldn't come to the house after he had them in to the courtyard, and neither would most of his friends.

It was magnificent.

Vici regarded the latest fleeing tradesman disapprovingly. "I didn't like that necklace anyway," she said. "Antony, I want to go flying."

"I've told you, my most darling one, some idiot guard with a bow will shoot you," he said, peeling an orange; he had to do it for himself, since the house slaves had been bolting in packs until he promised they didn't have to come to her. "Don't worry, I'll have more room for you soon."

He'd already had most of the statuary cleared out of the courtyard, but it wasn't going to do for long; she had already tripled in size, after two weeks. Fortunately, he'd already worked out a splendid solution.

"Dominus," Maracles called nervously, from the house. "Cato is here."

"Splendid!" Antony called back. "Show him in. Cato, my good neighbor," he said, rising from the divan as the old man stopped short at the edge of the courtyard. "I thank you so deeply for coming. I would have come myself, but you see, the servants get so anxious when I leave her alone."

"I did not entirely credit the rumors, but I see you really have debauched yourself out of your mind at last," Cato said. "No, thank you, I will not come out; the beast can eat you, first, and then it will be so sozzled I can confidently expect to make my escape."

"I am not going to eat Antony," Vici said indignantly, and Cato stared at her.

"Maracles, bring Cato a chair, there," Antony said, sprawling back on the divan, and he stroked Vici's neck.

"I didn't know they could speak," Cato said.

"You should hear her recite the *Priapeia*, there's a real ring to it," Antony said. "Now, why I asked you—"

"Those poems are not very good," Vici said, interrupting. "I liked that one you were reading at your house better, about all the fighting."

"What?" Cato said.

"What?" Antony said.

"I heard it over the wall, yesterday," Vici said. "It was much more exciting, and," she added, "the language is more interesting. The other one is all just about fornicating, over and over, and I cannot tell any of the people in it apart."

Antony stared at her, feeling vaguely betrayed.

Cato snorted. "Well, Antony, if you are mad enough to keep a dragon, at least you have found one that has better taste than you do."

"Yes, she is most remarkable," Antony said, with gritted teeth. "But as you can see, we are getting a little cramped, so I'm afraid—"

"Do you know any others like that?" Vici asked Cato.

"What, I suppose you want me to recite Ennius's *Annals* for you here and now?" Cato said.

"Yes, please," she said, and settled herself comfortably.

"Er," Antony said. "Dearest heart—"

"Shh, I want to hear the poem," she said.

Cato looked rather taken aback, but then he looked at Antony—and smiled. And then the bastard started in on the whole damned thing.

Antony fell asleep somewhere after the first half hour and woke up again to find them discussing the meter or the symbolism or whatnot. Cato had even somehow talked the house servants into bringing him out a table and wine and bread and oil, which was more than they'd had the guts to bring out for *him* the last two weeks.

Antony stood up. "If we might resume our business," he said pointedly, with a glare in her direction.

Vincitatus did not take the hint. "Cato could stay to dinner."

"No, he could *not*," Antony said.

"So what was this proposition of yours, Antony?" Cato said.

"I want to buy your house," Antony said flatly. He'd meant to come at it roundabout, and enjoy himself leading Cato into a full understanding of the situation, but at this point he was too irritated to be subtle.

"That house was built by my great-grandfather," Cato said. "I am certainly not going to sell it to you to be used for orgies."

Antony strolled over to the table and picked up a piece of bread to sop into the oil. Well, he could enjoy this, at least. "You might have difficulty finding any other buyer. Or any guests, for that matter, once word gets out."

Cato snorted. "On the contrary," he said. "I imagine the value will shortly be rising, as soon as you have gone."

"I'm afraid I don't have plans to go anywhere," Antony said.

"Oh, never fear," Cato said. "I think the Senate will make plans *for* you."

"Cato says there is a war going on in Gaul," Vincitatus put in. "Like in the poem. Wouldn't it be exciting to go see a war?"

"What?" Antony said.

ୡୡ

"WELL, Antonius," the magistrate said, "I must congratulate you."

"For surviving the last sentence?" Antony said.

"No," the magistrate said. "For originality. I don't believe I have ever faced this particular offense before."

"There's no damned law against keeping a dragon!"

"There is *now*," the magistrate said. He looked down at his papers. "There is plainly no question of guilt in this case; it only remains what is to be done with the creature. The priests of the temple of Jupiter suggest that the beast would be most highly regarded as a sacrifice, if you can arrange the mechanics—"

"I'll set her loose in the Forum first!" Antony snarled. "—No. No, wait, I didn't mean that." He took a deep breath and summoned up a smile and leaned across the table. "I'm sure we can come to some arrangement."

"You don't have enough money for that even now," the magistrate said.

"Look," Antony said, "I'll take her to my villa at Stabiae—" Seeing the eyebrow rising, he amended, "—or I'll buy an estate near Arminium. Plenty of room, she won't be a bother to anyone—"

"Until you run out or money or drink yourself to death," the magistrate said. "You do realize that the creatures live a hundred years?"

"They do?" Antony said blankly.

"The evidence also informs me," the magistrate added, "that she is already longer than the dragon of Brundisium, which killed nearly half the company of the fourteenth legion."

"She's as quiet as a lamb?" Antony tried.

The magistrate just looked at him.

"Gaul?" Antony said.

"Gaul," the magistrate said.

♆

"I hope you're happy," he said bitterly to Vincitatus as his servants, except for the few very unhappy ones he was taking along, joyfully packed his things.

"Yes," she said, eating another goat.

He'd been ordered to leave at night, under guard, but when the escort showed up, wary soldiers in full armor and holding their spears, they discovered a new difficulty: she couldn't fit into the street anymore.

"All right, all right, no need to make a fuss," Antony said, waving her back into the courtyard. The house on the other side had only leaned over a little. "So she'll fly out to the Porta Aurelia and meet us on the other side."

"We're not letting the beast go spreading itself over the city," the centurion said. "It'll grab some lady off the street, or an honorable merchant."

He was for killing her right there and then, instead. Antony was for knocking him down, and did so. The soldiers pulled him off and shoved him up against the wall of the house, swords out.

Then Vincitatus put her head out, over the wall, and said, "I think I have worked out how to breathe fire, Antony. Would you like to see?"

The soldiers all let go and backed away hastily in horror.

"I thought you said you couldn't," Antony hissed, looking up at her; it had been a source of much disappointment to him.

"I can't," she said. "But I thought it would make them let you go." She reached down and scooped him up off the street in one curled forehand, reached with the other and picked up one of the squealing, baggage-loaded pack mules. And then she leaped into the air.

"Oh, Jupiter eat your liver, you mad beast," Antony said, and clutched at her talons as the ground fell away, whirling.

"See, is this not much nicer than trudging around on the ground?" she asked.

"Look out!" he yelled, as the Temple of Saturn loomed up unexpectedly.

"Oh!" She said, and dodged. There was a faint crunch of breaking masonry behind them.

"I'm sure that was a little loose anyway," she said, flapping hurriedly higher.

He had to admit it made for quicker traveling, and at least she'd taken the mule loaded with the gold. She hated to let him spend any of it, though, and in any case, he had to land her half a mile off and walk if he wanted there to be anyone left to buy things from. Finally, he lost patience and started setting her down with as much noise as she could manage right outside the nicest villa or farmhouse in sight, when they felt like a rest. Then he let her eat the cattle and made himself at home in the completely abandoned house for the night.

That first night, sitting outside with a bowl of wine and a loaf of bread, he considered whether he should even bother going on to Gaul. He hadn't quite realized how damned *fast* it would be, traveling by air. "I suppose we could just keep on like this," he said to her idly. "They could chase us with one company after another for the rest of our days and never catch us."

"That doesn't sound right to me at all," she said. "One could never have eggs, always flying around madly from one place to another. And I want to see the war."

Antony shrugged cheerfully and drank the rest of the wine. He was half looking forward to it himself. He thought he'd enjoy seeing the look on the general's face when he set down with a dragon in the yard and sent all the soldiers running like mice. Anyway, it would be a damned sight harder to get laid if he were an outlaw with a dragon.

Two weeks later, they cleared the last alpine foothills and came into Gaul at last. And that was when Antony realized that he didn't know the first damn thing about where the army even was.

He didn't expect some Gallic wife to tell him, either, so they flew around the countryside aimlessly for two weeks, raiding more farmhouses—inedible food, no decent wine, and once some crazy old woman hadn't left her home and nearly gutted him with a cooking knife. Antony fled hastily back out to Vincitatus, ducking hurled pots and imprecations, and they went back aloft in a rush.

"This is not a very nice country," Vincitatus said, critically examining the scrawny pig she had snatched. She ate it anyway and added, crunching, "And that is a strange cloud over there."

It was smoke, nine or ten pillars of it, and Antony had never expected to be glad to see a battlefield in all his life. His stepfather had threatened to send him to the borders often enough, and he'd run away from home as much to avoid that fate as anything else, nearly. He didn't mind a good fight, or bleeding a little in a good cause, but as far as he was concerned, that limited the occasions to whenever it might benefit him.

The fighting was still going on, and the unmusical clanging reached them soon. Vincitatus picked up speed as she flew on toward it, then picked up still more, until Antony was squinting his eyes to slits against the tearing wind, and he only belatedly realized that she wasn't going toward the camp or the rear of the lines; she was headed straight for the enemy.

"Wait, what are you—" he started, too late, as her sudden stooping dive ripped the breath out of his lungs. He clung to the rope he'd tied around her neck, which now felt completely inadequate, and tried to plaster himself to her hide.

She roared furiously, and Antony had a small moment of satisfaction as he saw the shocked and horrified faces turning up toward them from the ground, on either side of the battle, and then she was ripping into the Gauls, claws tearing up furrows through the tightly packed horde of them.

She came to ground at the end of a run and whipped around, which sent him flying around to the underside of her neck, still clinging to the rope for a moment as he swung suspended. Then his numb fingers gave way and dumped him down to the ground, as she took off for another go. He staggered up, wobbling from one leg to the other, dizzy, and when he managed to get his feet under him, he stopped and stared: the entire Gaulish army was staring right back.

"Hades *me fellat*," Antony said. There were ten dead men lying down around him, where Vincitatus had shaken them off her claws. He grabbed a sword and a shield that was only a little cracked, and yelled after her, "Come back and get me out of here, you damned daughter of Etna!"

Vincitatus was rampaging through the army again and didn't give any sign she'd heard, or even that she'd noticed she'd lost him. Antony looked over his shoulder and put his back to a thick old tree and braced himself.

The Gauls weren't really what you'd call an army, more like a street gang taken to the woods, but their swords were damned sharp, and five of the barbarians came at him in a rush, howling at the top of their lungs. Antony kicked a broken helmet at one of them, another bit of flotsam from the dead, and as the others drew in, he dropped into a crouch and stabbed his sword at their legs, keeping his own shield drawn up over his head.

Axes, of course they'd have bloody axes, he thought bitterly, as they thumped into the shield, but he managed to get one of them in the thigh and another in the gut, and then he heaved himself up off the ground and pushed the three survivors back for a moment with a couple of wide swings, and grinned at them as he caught his breath. "Just like playing at soldiers on the Campus Martius, eh, fellows?" They just scowled at him, humorless *colei*, and they came on again.

He lost track of the time a little: his eyes were stinging with sweat, and his arm and his leg where they were bleeding. Then one of the men staggered and fell forward, an arrow sprouting out of his back. The other two looked around; Antony lunged forward and put his sword into the neck of one of them, and another arrow took down the last. Then another one thumped into Antony's shield.

"Watch your blasted aim!" Antony yelled, and ducked behind the shelter of his tree as the Gauls went pounding away to either side of him, chased with arrows and dragon-roaring.

"Antony!" Vincitatus landed beside him and batted away another couple of Gauls who were running by too closely. "There you are!"

He stood a moment, panting, then he let his sword and shield drop and collapsed against her side.

"Why did you climb down without telling me?" she said reproachfully, peering down at him. "You might have been hurt!"

He was too out of breath to do more than feebly wave his fist at her.

❧

"I don't care if Jupiter himself wants to see me," Antony said. "First I'm going to eat half a cow—yes, sweetness, you shall have the other half—and then I'm going to have a bath, and *then* I'll consider receiving visitors. If any of them are willing to come to me." He smiled pleasantly and leaned back against Vincitatus's foreleg and patted one of her talons. The legionary looked uncertain, and backed even farther away.

One thing to say for a battlefield, the slaves were cheap and a sight more cowed, and even if they were untrained and mostly useless, it didn't take that much skill to carry and fill a bath. Antony scrubbed under deluges of cold water and sank with relief into the deep trough they'd found somewhere. "I could sleep for a week," he said, letting his eyes close.

"Mm," Vincitatus said drowsily, and belched behind him, a sound like a thundercloud. She'd gorged on two cavalry horses.

"You there, more wine," Antony said, vaguely snapping his fingers into the air.

"Allow me," a cool patrician voice said, and Antony opened his eyes and sat up when he saw the general's cloak.

"No, no." The man pushed him back down gently with a hand on his shoulder. "You look entirely too comfortable to be disturbed." The general was sitting on a chair his slaves had brought him, by the side of the tub; he poured wine for both of them and waved the slaves off. "Now, then. I admired your very dramatic entrance, but it lacked something in the way of introduction."

Antony took the wine cup and raised it. "Marcus Antonius, at your command."

"Mm," the general said. He was not very well-favored: a narrow face, skinny neck, hairline in full retreat and headed for a rout. At least he had a good voice. "Grandson of the consul?"

"You have me," Antony said.

"Caius Julius, called Caesar," the general said, and tilted his head. Then he added, thoughtfully, "So we are cousins of a sort, on your mother's side."

"Oh, yes, warm family relations all around," Antony said, raising his eyebrows, aside from how Caesar's uncle had put that consul grandfather to death in the last round of civil war but one.

But Caesar met his dismissive look with an amused curl of his own mouth that said plainly he knew how absurd it was. "Why not?"

Antony gave a bark of laughter. "Why not, indeed," he said. "I had a letter for you, I believe, but unfortunately I left it in Rome. They've shipped us out to"—he waved a hand—"be of some use to you."

"Oh, you will be," Caesar said softly. "Tell me, have you ever thought of putting archers on her back?"

Bob Choi's Last Job

JONATHAN STROUD

Jonathan Stroud is one of the most popular and acclaimed authors in young adult fantasy today. He's best known for his Bartimaeus Trilogy, depicting the adventures and misadventures of a genie, and including The Amulet of Samarkand, The Golem's Eye, and Ptolemy's Gate, but his stand-alone novels include Heroes of the Valley, The Last Siege, The Leap, and Buried Fire. He's also written several illustrated puzzle books for young readers, including The Viking Saga of Harri Bristlebeard and The Lost Treasure of Captain Blood, and one nonfiction title: Ancient Rome, in the Sightseers series. He lives in Great Britain.

In the powerful story that follows, he takes us along with a grimly determined dragon hunter out on a dangerous job—one that may turn out to be more dangerous than he had ever imagined it could be.

OF the victim's body, only scorched bones remained, and these had been neatly stacked in the refuse bag for disposal in the trash. The pelvis lay at the bottom, with the leg and arm bones set diagonally across to form a platform for the skull. The ribs, vertebrae, and smaller fragments had been piled around the skull in snug, intersecting layers, but the arrangement had collapsed when Bob Choi opened the bag.

Bob made a sad, dispirited sound behind his teeth. He removed a glove, and, with the tips of his fingers, touched the dome of the skull. Just the faintest trace of heat. So—one hour since the feeding, maybe two. The creature would be soporific in its room.

Bob bent low, so that his long coat sighed and whispered in the alley dirt. The smell upon the bag was fresh and strong: pitchstone, copper sulphate, a subtle mix of other mineral residues. Not a hatchling, then. An old one, subtle and experienced . . . Bob Choi clicked his tongue against his teeth.

Straightening, he looked up at the apartment block that rose above him in the rain, a slight, stoop-shouldered man with dark, receding hair. Small drips of water beaded his forehead and ran across his face. He did not move to brush them away but held himself still and watchful. His face was doughy, soft and unspectacular, his eyes weary and a little lined.

From a window on the fourth floor of the apartment building, an orange-yellow radiance gleamed. It might be a simple light or lantern; then again, it might not. Bob Choi shook his head, blowing out his cheeks. Why couldn't they stick with legal meat? They didn't *have* to kill, and no one would be any the wiser if they just stayed quiet—their cloaks worked all too well. But no, they were beasts, of course; their hunger was ungovernable. They had to screw up every time. Some of them took years to show themselves, but it always ended the same way. With his gloved hand, he patted the pockets of his coat to check the location of the weapons. Always the same way.

He grasped the bag, and, heedless of the rattles and cracking of the shifting bones, dragged it down the alley to a recessed doorway out of the rain. Slinging the bag into the corner, he climbed the step and took up position, watching the apartment block. A few minutes passed. Drizzle dropped from an iron sky. A hundred yards away, the crowd noises on Bryce Street rose and fell. In the silence of the alley, Bob Choi allowed his hand to slip beneath the coat and draw out the silver flask. It was not a good time for it, but the cold and fear needed pushing back a little. No one would know. He set the flask to his lips.

"Mr. Choi."

Bob Choi coughed, swore, jerked round, right hand darting to his coat. A young man stood beside him, close enough to touch. He looked the same as he had that morning and the night before: trim, blue-eyed, with blond hair slicked back behind his rimless glasses, his suit crisp, uncreased, his face bleached clean of expression. As on the previous occasions, he held a paper packet in his hand.

Bob shoved the flask from view. "How do you *do* that? I should have heard you."

"That's not your talent, is it?" the young man said. His brow corrugated above his little nose. "You know you've got to keep your gloves *on*, Choi. Regulations. You're breaking the fifth protocol. Putting me at risk."

Bob put his glove on. He said, "What have you got for me, Parsons?"

"Szechuan noodles. Beef and ginger. Coffee." The young man opened the paper packet and took out a polystyrene tray, covered with film.

"Good. I've been the only one round here *not* eating." Bob indicated the bag.

The young man inspected the contents, frowning with distaste. "The estate agent?"

"I should think so. Noodles, please. I'm starved."

Despite the hand being safely encased in its black leather glove, the young man passed over the tray with ostentatious care, keeping his fingers out of reach and darting them back quickly. Bob said nothing. He bent a little forward to shield the noodles from the rain, picked up the little plastic fork, and began to eat. The young man stood silent, watching how the steam rising from the food veered sharply aside before it reached Bob's face, how it rounded the contours of his head at speed and continued rising. There was a layer of cold, clear air around Bob's skin that the steam could not penetrate.

Bob's mouth was full. He coughed and swallowed: "Coffee too, you said?"

"Yes."

Bob nodded, twisting noodles savagely, forking them into his mouth. "Okay."

The young man said: "I'll come again at nine. Will you be here or back in the street?"

A shake of the head; the last of the food was shoveled in, soy juice drunk, the tray tossed aside. "I'm not waiting any longer," Bob Choi said. "I know which one it is."

The young man had bent fastidiously and was picking up the tray. He looked up sharply. "You do? Who?"

"The old man in 4A. He'll be up there now, fat as a snake from the feast."

The pale brow furrowed. "Mr. Yang? Did you see him leave the bones here?"

"No. I was round the front. I missed the drop. Give me the coffee, please."

The young man stared at his feet, moved a slim black shoe. "We don't want another mistake, Choi."

"There won't *be* another mistake. It's Yang. I watched him on Bryce this morning, shuffling along in his little slippers, all white-haired and frail. Ahh! This is hot." Bob wiped coffee from his mouth. "It's in the way he *walks*, Parsons."

"*I've* seen him walk," the young man said. "I didn't notice anything."

"It's in the way he walks," Bob Choi said again. "It's in the jerky way the shoulders swing, the way the skinny neck cranes out as the head moves side to side. You've seen crocodiles at the zoo, Parsons? Seen tortoises? Watch how they move. You can get glimpses even through the cloak, if you look hard enough. If you know what you're looking for."

Parsons said: "I don't like this. There are others it might be just as easily. Zhou on the fifth floor fits the pattern: he's a loner too—solitary occupation, background hard to trace. All fits. And the woman, Lau, on the fourth floor opposite to Yang. Records say she was in Shanghai during the last hunt there. Lived in the same suburb as the victims. Now she's here. No record of her travelling with the airlines."

Bob Choi shrugged; he stared at his cup. "Maybe she took a boat. Or walked."

"Or," Parsons said, "she flew." He folded the paper packet neatly with pale fingers, placed it in the empty tray. "If you wait till tomorrow, Burns can be here. They're bringing him in from Hanoi."

"I'm not waiting for Burns. This is a fresh feed. Yang'll be slow and torpid now."

"He'll still be torpid when Burns gets here," the young man said. "*If* it's him."

"I've seen him walk," Bob said, stubbornly. "There won't be two of them."

The young man's glasses flashed as he glanced toward the apartment block. His voice was bored. "Well, I won't try to dissuade you, Choi. If it's Yang, go kill him. But don't run to me for help if you mess it up."

Bob had his head back, draining the last of the coffee. He held the cup out. "Here. Seeing as how you hate a mess."

He looked across. The alley was empty. The young man and the bag of bones were gone.

IN the broad, lit canyon of Bryce Street, umbrellas were up against the rain. A hundred gold and scarlet disks spun and bobbed above the pavement and across the thoroughfare, reflected to infinity in the mirrored glass of the cafes and pleasure-bars. There was a swish of skirts and a pattering of canes. Laughter tumbled over Bob Choi as he slowly climbed the seven steps to the entrance of the apartment block, a hunched figure in a long black coat, hatless, with weary pouches beneath his eyes.

A gloved hand pushed gently at the door. No luck: locked fast, opened electronically by switches in each apartment. On the wall hung a rank of buzzers, each with its room and name tag, some typed neatly, others scrawled. The lettering for *4A: Yang*, was written in blue ink—an ornately cursive script, sinuous and flexible. Bob stared at it briefly, then dropped his gaze to the lowest label. *1C: Murray, Caretaker.*

The noise of the buzzer was ugly and indelicate. While he waited, Bob Choi stared up at the rain and the wall of the building: big brownstone blocks, rough-hewn, easy enough to climb if necessary. A voice sounded in the intercom. "Yes?"

Bob bent close. "Parcel delivery, sir."

"Who for?"

"You, sir."

"I haven't ordered anything." The voice was curt. "Oh, hell—wait there."

Bob Choi waited on the step. From an inside pocket, he took a pen and a small slip of yellow paper. Then he removed the glove from his right hand.

The door opened. A man in a crumpled brown suit stood there. He had fair hair, red cheeks, and bloodshot, raddled eyes. He regarded Bob Choi with blank hostility.

"Where's the parcel?"

"In the van, sir. If you could just sign this." Bob Choi proffered the pen and paper. Behind the man's curtain of alcohol, he smelt faint traces of bitumen and sulphur—the usual chemical tang—drifting down through the darkness of the hall. He glimpsed the stairwell at the far end.

"Where's the van? I don't see a van." But the man took the paper, then the pen, his hand brushing against Bob Choi's fingertips as he did so. He frowned, first at the blankness of the paper, then at the onrushing chill coursing through his blood, the numb cold enveloping his brain. Bob Choi was already stepping through the doorway as the man fell; he caught him, swung the door shut, lowered the body to the floor, all in one fluid movement, and stood motionless in the hallway, listening to the noises of the house.

Water gurgled in pipes, floorboards shifted, rats moved behind plaster; men and women breathed, moved, talked to each other in soft whispers and with voices raised in anger. Alone in the squalor of the hall, Bob Choi listened.

High in the building he heard the slow, slow rasp of shifting scales as the creature settled itself for slumber.

He stood still a moment, remembering the reptile walk of the old man in the street. He remembered the fight at Fukuoka, when the one cloaked like a little girl had risen from the pile of bones and speared Sam Johnson through the chest.

He remembered the flask in his breast pocket.

Bob Choi made a soft, sad sound. Patting the weapons beneath his coat, he stepped past the body on the floor and proceeded up the stairs.

The stairwell was empty, worn and desolate, with aged linoleum underfoot, yellowed wallpaper, light fittings made of oval glass at intervals on the walls. Each landing had a short lobby, four closed doors, a window at the end. Bob went slowly, carefully, listening to noises from the rooms, smelling the air. With each step, the rustling grew more obvious, the mineral taint hung heavier on his palate.

As he approached the third landing, he took a small black canister from his coat and sprayed its contents back and forth on the stairs, the floor, and the walls about him. A thin mist settled and vanished. Bob Choi continued climbing, past the landing and up the next flight, spraying the mist every few paces.

Rounding the final half-landing, Bob Choi went more slowly than ever, but the stairs were clear right to the fourth floor. Ahead was the lobby, its window showing a bright, wet light and falling rain. To the left was the door to Apartment 4A. Somewhere close came a dry rasping, like something heavy sliding among dead leaves. Bob Choi halted, scratching the back of his neck with gloved fingers. He opened his coat and unclipped a fastening within. With his left hand, he pulled out a long-barrelled gun, fitted with a vicious barb-headed dart.

He took a long breath and glanced around.

Opposite 4A was the door to 4C, closed and quiet. He heard nothing from there, or the other two rooms further along the lobby. From 4A, the apartment of old Mr. Yang, the rustling sound had quieted. The thing was still now, continuing its digestion.

Bob Choi sighed, stepped quickly across the lobby, drew back the fist of his right hand, and struck the door just beside the handle, where the locks were. The wood split, the frame cracked; with another blow, Bob drove the door wide open.

Before stepping through, he used the canister again. Now the mist revealed secret characters written on the threshold of the door. When Bob bent close, the inscription glowed an angry emerald green. When he stood up, it faded. Taking care not to touch the curse rune, he jumped over it, landing in the apartment safely.

The hall was short and narrow, hung with pictures, floored with dark wood. To the left was a bureau supporting a Chinese lantern, three letters, a telephone and address book, a ring of keys. Fixed to the opposite wall was a metal rail, the kind used by the elderly and infirm.

Bob Choi put away the canister, and, thrusting his right hand under his coat, drew out an ebony stick, shiny, bone-handled, long as his fore-arm. He moved quickly down the hall toward an open door.

The room he entered occupied the corner of the apartment block, and had a window overlooking the alley. It was cluttered with shabby furniture and belongings: a radio, a television set resting on a table, a magazine rack, a frayed rug on a linoleum floor, a wheeled walking frame. The air smelled strongly of carbolic cleaning fluid.

In an armchair in the centre of the rug, facing towards the door, sat an old man, arms bent, hands folded contentedly across the belly of his shirt. His legs, stick-thin beneath the nylon trousers, were crossed at the ankles. He wore white socks and canvas slippers. His eyes were closed; a faint smile played upon his lips. White wisps of grandfatherly hair lay upon his placid forehead and on the antimacassar of the armchair.

An old man sleeping: there was nothing to suggest otherwise.

Bob Choi looked at him. This moment was always the hardest: the cloak was just so good. Even when you'd seen the curse rune, even when you knew—

The old man's eyes flicked open; his face sagged with bewilderment. "Who—who are you? What are you doing?" The voice was feeble, quaver-ing. "You want my money? I have none! I am a poor man."

Bob Choi licked his lips. The cloak was just so good. But he smelt cop-per sulphate and pitchstone even beneath the odour of the cleaning fluid—and he could smell blood also. He noticed that the floor of the room was newly scrubbed—here and there, it shone damp from washing.

A bucket of water sat beside an arch to the kitchen. The water was a dirty brown.

Bob Choi raised his gun.

The old man began to sit up, his mouth slack, his rheumy eyes blinking. "Sir, take my television, take my radio, but please, sir, do not hurt me!"

His stomach was grotesquely swollen beneath the tightness of his shirt.

"Please, sir—"

Bob Choi shot the old man through the chest.

The barbed dart embedded itself in the wood of the chair back, jerking the old man back so that his arms and legs leapt like a puppet's limbs. For an instant, bright scaled coils writhed in the armchair, claws flexed in agony, teeth like steak knives snapped together—then the old man was back, floundering and clawing at the flanged iron stub protruding from the centre of his shirt, straining himself forward, seeking to break free.

Bob Choi tucked the dart-gun back inside his coat. He pressed a button on the ebony stick so that a long metal blade snicked from the end. It was made of three fused strips of steel, strong enough to shear through neck scales. He stepped towards the chair.

No blood showed in the centre of the old man's shirt. His face was impassive. He pulled steadily at the dart that transfixed him, watching as Bob Choi approached. Suddenly, his mouth opened. The voice that emerged was similar to the tremulous voice of the old man but was now altogether stronger and more urgent. "Wait!" it said. "Listen! I will give you treasure!"

Bob Choi said nothing. He rounded the table.

"I can show you piled hoards undreamt of, caves in Persia filled with gemstones—diamonds, turquoise, lapis, and cornelian! I can give you sapphires big as human fists! You want these? Fine! Just remove the iron!"

Bob Choi walked close, stood before the old man. He adjusted the sword-stick so that he held it with both hands.

The old man rocked back and forth, plucking at the dart. "I can clothe you in silk! I will slay your enemies! You will be a prince among men!"

Before making the stroke, Bob Choi pushed the television further away across the table so that it would not obstruct his swing. He raised the sword-stick.

From the old man's mouth spurted a six-foot jet of flame. Bob Choi's head and upper body were enveloped; he was knocked back on his heels by the force of the blast. The plasterboard ceiling beyond him blackened and popped; his coat began to burn. But the heat-repellent layer on his skin held firm. From the midst of the inferno, he looked at the old man and steadily shook his head.

The old man threw his hands in the air in a gesture of disgust. His head fell forwards. With a gasping breath, he sucked the jet of fire back into him.

Bob Choi said, "Sit quiet now. Let us finish this."

As he adopted the stance necessary for the decisive stroke, he heard a rustling of scales behind him. A soft voice said: "Sir, why do you hurt my grandfather?"

Bob Choi stood with his blade at the old man's neck, his coat still smouldering, and looked back at the young woman standing at the entrance of the room. She was small, slender, neatly dressed in the European style, with a wide-boned face and big, dark eyes. Such was their vanity when they hid as females. He had never seen a plain one yet.

He thought wearily of Parsons's warnings in the alley; of Burns on the plane from Hanoi. He thought of the difficulties of facing two of them alone.

"Miss Lau?"

"That is my present name."

"Mr. Yang is your grandfather?"

The mouth smiled; she had pretty little teeth. "Not precisely in your terms. But we share a lineage, and bonds of honour too subtle for you to comprehend. In short, I do not want him dead."

"He *is* dead already, by virtue of his recent crimes," Bob Choi said. "I just confirm the sentence. You know the way it goes."

"Crimes?" Again the smile. "What crimes are these?"

Bob Choi noticed that the old man, by a process of discreet wriggling, was succeeding in pulling himself forwards. The barbed dart was almost out of the armchair. Raising a boot, he pressed it firmly down on the distended stomach, pushing him back into the chair. Even through the leather sole, he felt the heat from the firestones lodged in the centre of the belly. The old man made a snarling noise and spoke words in a language Bob Choi did not understand.

Bob said mildly: "Three murders, perhaps four: a man, two women, and a child. Those are the crimes that bring me here. I suppose I need to kill you as well."

She laughed—a high, delightful sound. "Murder? By what definition? You eat pork-meat, I suppose. You eat beef."

Bob Choi rolled his eyes. "Oh, please."

"Do you stand trial for the death of those animals?" Miss Lau said. She raised her delicate hands, small shoulders shrugging. "Should we be condemned for *our* feeding? I see not a scrap of difference. And there are *so*, so many of you. What is one human more or less in this world?"

"We are not pigs or cattle," Bob Choi said. "We protect ourselves, as is our right."

Slim eyebrows arched. " 'We'? 'Ourselves'? You count yourself among them?"

"I am human enough."

"*Are* you? You, who sniffs us out in the midst of this teeming city? Who breaks with bare fists through the door? Who withstands the blast of our breath and lives? Whose skin carries poison so that he cannot touch another man—or woman—without protection? With such enhancements, *are* you truly human still? I hardly think so," the girl said, smiling. "Not any more. Like us, you merely *look* like one."

Bob Choi's mouth was screwed down at the corners now, clamped tight shut. His face was a little pale. He adjusted his grip upon the sword-stick. "I suggest you leave," he said thickly. "While you still can. You won't get another chance."

From the depths of the armchair, his hands plucking furiously at the iron stub in the centre of his chest, the old man nodded. "He's right, Grand-daughter. Go, before you too get into trouble. I can deal with this."

"You are not the *only* one who can sniff things out," the girl said, ignoring the old man. "Let me tell you what *you* smell of, sir—aside from alcohol, of course. Solitude. You stink of it. It rolls off you like vapour from a mountaintop. You are alone always, are you not, as you go about your hunting?" She sighed. "Truly, that is a sad fate. *I* have my grandfather and he has me, and there are others of our kind in many places, concealed from you, so that even amid the swarm of men, we are not alone. But *you* . . ."

The old man spoke testily. "Please, Granddaughter, is this any way to talk with him? Pointing out his abject misery will only make him angrier." He whispered to Bob Choi sidelong. "So you lack friends, family, or lovers? The solution is simple. Take the bolt from my chest and put away that stick. With the riches I give you, you will be able to *buy* whatever company you need."

Bob Choi cleared his throat, which had become constricted. "Be still, both of you."

The girl laughed. "Now you stink of rage."

"Be *still.*"

The old man said, "He is uncertain of his strength, else he would have surely killed me by now. His gun is empty, Granddaughter. Listen—I give you my blessing. When he strikes me dead, seize him in your coils and crush him before he can rearm."

"He will not strike," the girl said. Then, to Bob Choi, quietly: "At least, I do not think so. None of the other hunters would have hesitated as you have. Despite what your masters have made you, I think you're different—more aware of what you are and what you do. Is that not so?"

Bob Choi did not respond. He looked at the blade he held against the old man's neck.

"Perhaps you *are* still human," the girl went on. "In your fashion. Perhaps I was wrong before. Who knows, perhaps despite all your many . . . *alterations*, you might one day cast off this lonely life of yours and walk freely among the crowds out there."

She gestured towards the window. Bob Choi, instinctively following her gaze, remembered too late that the window looked on the empty alley, not the crowded aisles of Bryce Street. He swivelled back, arm muscles flexing, to find the girl had sprung across the room; she was right beside him. Her slim, pale arm swiped at his face. He felt claws strike him, felt his doctored bones creak with the impact of the blow, found himself thrown back across the room and through the dividing wall, to land in a shower of wood and plaster against the fridge unit in the kitchen.

Bob Choi could feel blood running down the side of his face, knew the heat-resistant layer was punctured. Rising stiffly, hands working automatically to fix a new bolt into the barrel of his gun, he saw through the ruin of the wall the girl pulling the iron bolt clear of her grandfather. The old man got to his feet, a jagged hole right through him: the magnitude of the wound was such that he could not maintain his cloak successfully. His form flickered: for an eye's blink—once, twice, and then again—his human shape was replaced by an undulating flex of bloodied coils. Now his granddaughter's arm was around him; the cloak stabilised. Limping, staggering on his canvas slippers, he passed with the girl into the hall and out of view.

Bob Choi swore quietly to himself, smashed through the remaining fragments of wall, picked up his sword-stick from where it lay upon the rug, and strode off in pursuit, long coat billowing behind him.

Out into the lobby, where the door opposite stood open. He saw them straight ahead, going arm in arm down the little hallway of the girl's apartment. The old man stumbled, tottered; his companion ushered him on, whispering, cajoling.

Beyond them rose a rectangle of light: balcony doors open to the sky.

This was bad, but he had them still. Without breaking stride, Bob Choi lifted the gun and aimed it directly at the back of the girl's neck. As he did so, he crossed into the apartment, stepping onto a curse rune inscribed upon its threshold. There was an explosion of green fire: Bob Choi was blown against the ceiling, tumbling to the floor again in a cascade of plaster, glass, and sparking electrical flex.

He raised himself and limped on fast as he was able, just in time to see the girl and her grandfather crouching on the balcony balustrade, barefooted now, gripping the metal rail like birds. The girl looked back at him. Then they launched themselves off, moving straight up above the whistling bolt that Bob Choi fired, above the glistening gold and scarlet of the crowded street, above the grey buildings and dark, wet roofs, into the sky where the clouds were breaking. Arriving on the balcony with dragging, painful steps, Bob Choi watched them for as long as he was able, saw their cloaks relax at last, saw their shapes change, saw the gold scales glittering beneath the long, slow wing-beats as they wheeled into the sun. Then they were lost to him, and he was left on the balcony alone, with the crowds passing along the boulevards far below.

Bob Choi put the gun and sword-stick back in the pockets of his coat and stood watching the patterns of the crowd. Time passed. His gaze became unfocused. Turning away at last, he noticed that his right hand was still gloveless. Bob Choi did not instantly locate the spare gloves carried in his coat as regulations demanded, and his hand was still bare when he at last went back inside.

Are You Afflicted with *Dragons?*

KAGE BAKER

Well, are you? If so, Kage Baker would like you to know that there's something you can do about it. Although the cure may be worse than the disease.

One of the most prolific new writers to appear in the late nineties, Kage Baker made her first sale in 1997, to Asimov's Science Fiction, and has since become one of that magazine's most frequent and popular contributors with her sly and compelling stories of the adventures and misadventures of the time-traveling agents of the Company; of late, she's started two other linked sequences of stories there as well, one of them set in as lush and eccentric a high-fantasy milieu as any we've ever seen. Her stories have also appeared in Realms of Fantasy, Sci Fiction, Amazing Stories, and elsewhere. Her first Company novel, In the Garden of Iden, was also published in 1997 and immediately became one of the most acclaimed and widely reviewed first novels of the year. More Company novels quickly followed, including Sky Coyote, Mendoza in Hollywood, The Graveyard Game, The Life of the World to Come, The Machine's Child, and The Sons of Heaven, as well as a chapbook novella, The Empress of Mars, and her first fantasy novel, The Anvil of the World. Her many stories have been collected in Black Projects, White Knights; Mother Aegypt and Other Stories; The Children of the Company; and Dark Mondays. Among her most recent books are Or Else My Lady Keeps the Key, about some of the real pirates of the Caribbean, and the fantasy novel The House of the Stag. Her latest book is the novel The Empress of Mars. In addition to her writing, Baker has been an artist, actor, and director at the Living History Center, and has taught Elizabethan English as a second language. She lives in Pismo Beach, California.

THERE must have been a dozen of the damned things up there.

Smith walked backward across the hotel's garden, glaring up at the roofline. The little community on the roof went right on with its busy social life, preening, squabbling over fish heads, defecating, spreading stubby wings in the morning sunlight, entirely unaware of Smith's hostile scrutiny.

As he continued backward, Smith walked into the low fence around the vegetable patch. He staggered, tottered, and lurched backward, landing with a crash among the demon-melon frames. Instantly, a dozen tiny reptilian heads turned; a dozen tiny reptilian necks craned over the roof's edge. The dragons regarded Smith with bright, fascinated eyes. Smith growled at them helplessly as he flailed there, and they went into tiny reptilian gales of piping laughter.

Disgusted, Smith got to his feet and dusted himself off. Mrs. Smith, who had been having a quiet smoke by the back door, peered at him.

"Did you hurt yourself, Smith?"

"We have to do something about *those*," said Smith, jerking a thumb at the dragons. "They're getting to be a nuisance."

"And possibly a liability," said Mrs. Smith. "Lady What's-her-name, the one with that pink palace above Cable Steps, had dinner on the terrace last night with a party of friends. I'd just sent Mr. Crucible out with the Pike Terrine when one of these little devils on the roof flies down, bold as you please, and lights on the lady's plate. She screamed, and for a moment, everyone was amused, you know, and one or two of them even said the horrible little creature was cute. Then it jumped up on her shoulder and started worrying at her earring.

"Fortunately, Crucible had the presence of mind to come after it with the gravel rake, and it flew away before it could do Milady any harm, but she wasn't pleased at all. I had to give them free pudding all around and two complimentary bottles of Black Gabekrian."

Smith winced. "That's expensive."

"Not as expensive as Milady's bullies coming down here and burning the hotel over our heads. What if the little beast had managed to pull out her earring and flown off with it, Smith?"

"That'd finish us, all right." Smith rubbed his chin. "I'd better go see if I can buy some poison at Leadbeater's."

"Why don't we simply call in an exterminator?" Mrs. Smith puffed smoke.

"No! They charge a duke's ransom. Leadbeater's got something; he swears it does the job or your money back."

Mrs. Smith looked doubtful. "But there was this fellow in the marketplace only the other day, had a splendid pitch. 'Are you afflicted with DRAGONS?' he shouted. Stood up on the steps of Rakut's monument, you know, and gave this speech about his secret guaranteed methods. Produced a list of testimonials as long as your arm, all from grateful customers whose premises he'd ridded of wyrmin."

Smith grunted. "And he'd charge a duke's ransom and turn out to be a charlatan."

Mrs. Smith shrugged. "Have it your way, then. Just don't put it off any longer, or we'll be facing a lawsuit at the very least."

જ્જ

LEADBEATER'S & Son's was an old and respected firm, three dusty floors' worth of ironmongery with a bar in the cellar. Great numbers of the city's population of males of a certain age disappeared through its doors for long hours at a time; some of them practically lived there. Smith was by no means immune to its enchantment.

Regardless of what he needed, Smith generally began with climbing up to the third floor to stare at Bluesteel's Patented Improved Spring-driven Harvester, a gleaming mystery of wheels, gears, blades, leather straps, and upholstery, wherein a man might ride at his leisure while simultaneously cutting down five acres of wheat. Mr. Bluesteel had assembled it there for the first Mr. Leadbeater, long years since, and there it sat still, because it was so big no one had been able to get it down the stairs, and the only other option was taking off the roof and hoisting it out with a crane.

Smith had a long, satisfying gawk at it, then continued on his usual progress: down to the second floor to browse among the Small Iron Goods, to see whether there were any hinges, bolts, screws, or nails he needed, or whether there might be anything new and stylish in the way of drawer pulls or doorknobs. Down, then, to the ground floor, where he idled wistfully among the tools in luxuriant profusion, from the bins full of cheap hammers to the really expensive patent wonders locked behind glass. At last, sadly (for he could not admit to himself that he really needed a clockwork reciprocating saw that could cut through iron bars with its special diamond-dust attachment), Smith wandered back through the barrels of paint and varnish to the Compounds area, where young Mr. Leadbeater sat behind the counter doing sums on a wax tablet.

"Leadbeater's son," said Smith by way of greeting.

"Smith-from-the-hotel," replied young Leadbeater, for there were a lot of Smiths in Salesh-by-the-Sea. He stuck his stylus behind his ear and stood. "How may I serve? Roofing pitch? Pipe sealant? Drain cleaner?"

"What have you got for dragons?"

"Ah! We have an excellent remedy." Young Leadbeater gestured for Smith to follow him and went sidling back between the rows of bins. "Tinplate's Celebrated Gettemol! Very cleverly conceived. Here we are." He raised the lid on a bin. It was full of tiny pellets in a riot of brilliant colors.

"It looks delicious," said Smith.

"That's what your wyrmin will think," said young Leadbeater. "They'll see this and they'll leave off hunting fish, see? They'll fill their craws with it and, tchac! It'll kill them dead. How bad is your infestation?"

"There's a whole damned colony of them on the roof," said Smith.

"*Well*. You'll want a week's worth—I can sell you a couple of buckets to carry it in—and for that kind of volume, we throw in a statue of Cliba and the Cliba Prayer; put a shrine where the dragons can see it and keeps 'em from coming back, very efficacious—and then of course you'll need new roofing and gutters once you've cleaned your dragon colony out—"

"What for?"

"Because if you've got that many of them on your roof, ten to one they've been prying up the leading to hide things under it, and once their droppings get underneath on your roof beams, they eat right through, and you don't want that, trust me. Highly corrosive droppings, dragons. Just about impossible to get the stink out of plaster, too. Had them long?"

"There'd always been a couple," said Smith. "We're at the damned seaside, right? You expect them. But in the last month or two we've got some kind of wyrmin rookery up there."

"Yes. I daresay it's the weather. Lot of people coming in with the same trouble. Well, let me fetch you a pair of good big buckets . . ."

"Yes, but no roofing stuff just yet, all right?" Smith followed him over to the Containers section. "I'll wait until I get up there and see how bad it is. And what do I do with it? Just scatter it around? We've got a baby at our place, and I wouldn't want him picking it up and eating it."

"Not at all. You've got a big tree on your grounds, haven't you? Just hang the buckets in the tree branches. Neat and tidy. They're naturally curious, see? They'll fly down to eat it, and then all you'll need to do is call the umbrella-makers," said young Leadbeater, with a grin.

"What for?" Smith was mystified until he remembered the commercial uses for dragon wings. "Oh! Right. Will they come and collect the dead ones for us?"

"Usually. You can get a good price for them, too." Young Leadbeater winked.

ço

SMITH trudged home with two gallon buckets of Tinplate's Celebrated Gettemol, and the little statue of Cliba—a minor god of banishments— with its prayer on a slip of paper, in his pocket. He set a ladder against the trunk of the big canopy-pine and, climbing the ladder, went up himself to hang the buckets where they would be clearly visible. While up there, he peered across at his roof but saw no gaping holes evident. Whistling, he climbed back down and spent the rest of the afternoon in the work shed making a shrine for Cliba out of an old wine jar.

ço

NEXT morning, Smith was carrying a case of pickles up from the hotel's cellar when he heard Mrs. Smith calling him, with thunder in her voice. He emerged to find her clutching her grandchild.

"What?"

"Perhaps you'd better go and see what Baby found when I took him outdoors for his sunbath," she said grimly. Smith, expecting a dead dragon, sighed and trudged off to the garden, followed closely by Mrs. Smith. When he stepped through the back door, he beheld the garden and back terrace scattered with thousands of rainbow-colored pellets.

"And guess what Baby went straight for, when I set him down? *'Yum yum, look at all this candy!'*" said Mrs. Smith.

"Gods below!" Smith looked up into the tree and saw the two empty pails swinging on one end of gnawed-through cord. Five or six dragons perched along the branch above it, watching Smith with what looked like malicious glee in their little slit-pupiled eyes. As Smith stared, they defecated in unison and flew back to the hotel's roof.

"I trust you'll have Mr. Crucible sweep it up immediately," said Mrs. Smith with icy hauteur.

"Damned right I will," said Smith. "And then I'm taking it back to Leadbeater's and demanding a refund."

"And what'll you do then?"

Smith rubbed the back of his neck, scowling. "Go ask a priest for intercession?"

"A fat lot of good that'll do! What self-respecting god gets rid of house-hold pests, Smith? No, go and do what we ought to have done in the first place and hire a professional. There's that fellow in the marketplace. 'Are you afflicted with DRAGONS?' and all that. A big fellow in oilskins. One-eyed."

ళ్ల

AFTER a brief unpleasant interview with the Leadbeaters father and son, Smith walked out of their emporium counting his money. He put his wallet away, and, sighing, looked around. He spotted the column of Duke Rakut's monument, two streets away.

"May as well," Smith muttered to himself. Picking his way between fishnets spread out for mending, he made his way over to the marketplace in Rakut Square.

Approaching the monument, Smith saw only a skinny youth seated on its steps, next to a handcart loaded with empty cages. The youth, who had a rather bruised and melancholy look to him, was feeding shrimps to a fat little dragon perched on his shoulder. The dragon ate greedily. The youth watched it with a mother's tender regard.

"Is there a man hereabouts says he can get rid of those?" Smith inquired, staring at the dragon. He had never seen a tame one before.

"That'd b-be my m-m-master," said the youth, not meeting Smith's eyes.

"Well, where is he?"

By way of answer, the youth pointed at the wineshop across the way.

"Back soon?"

The youth nodded. Smith sat down on the steps to wait. The dragon climbed batlike down to the youth's knee and squeaked at Smith. It ducked its head and shook its wings, which resembled fine red leather, at him.

"What's it doing?"

"Sh-she's begging you for t-t-treats," said the youth.

"Huh." Smith scratched his head. "Smart dragon." The youth nodded. The dragon waited expectantly for treats, and, when none were forthcoming from Smith, it squealed angrily at him and clambered back up the front of the youth's tunic, where it settled down to groom itself, now and then casting an indignant glance at Smith.

A man emerged from the wineshop. Smith, watching him as he walked across the square, saw that he was big, wore a curious long coat made of oilskin, and had one eye. A leather patch hid where the other had been.

The man was red-faced and genial-looking, even more so than might be accounted for by having just emerged from a wineshop.

"C-c-customer, Master," said the youth. The man rubbed his hands together, grinning at Smith.

"Are you, sir? Are you afflicted with—"

"Dragons, yes, I am. What're your rates like?"

"I will completely eradicate your dragons for absolutely free!" the man told him. His voice was a hoarse bawl. He grabbed Smith's hand in his gauntleted own and shook it heartily.

"Free! What's the catch?"

"No catch, my friend. Etterin Crankhandle, at your service. And let me tell you what those services include! No appointment necessary. I will personally come to your premises and arrange for on-site removal of any and all dragons infesting your property. All wyrmin are humanely trapped—no dangerous poisons or other chemical preparations used. I will then conduct a complete and thorough examination of your roof, shed, or outbuildings, and remove any nests or caches and repair any damage I find such as loose leading, tiles, or slates. I, of course, reserve the right to any contents of said nests or caches. Your roof, shed, or outbuildings will then be sprayed with my Miracle Wyrm Repellent, guaranteed to prevent any reinfestation for a full year. All absolutely free. Interested?"

��

"I wish I'd run into you before I spent a fortune on that Gettemol crap," said Smith, panting as he helped Crankhandle and his assistant push their cart up the street. Crankhandle laughed and shook his head.

"Ah, sir, if I had a gold crown for every time I'd heard someone say that, I'd be a wealthy man!"

"You ought to charge something, then," said Smith, leaning away from the dragon on the youth's shoulder, as it stuck its neck out and nipped at him.

"Oh, no," said Crankhandle. "The dragons themselves are payment enough. And in any case, you wouldn't have found me there before last month. I'm new here."

"A traveler, then?"

"I am, sir. Have to be. When I clear wyrmin out of a town, they don't come back. Pretty soon business dries up, doesn't it?"

"I suppose it would. Here we are," said Smith, opening the garden gate. They wheeled the cart in over the lawn and parked it under the canopy-pine. As Crankhandle's assistant scrambled to slide chocks under the wheels, Crankhandle turned and peered up at the roof. The dragons looked down at him. Crankhandle grinned wide. Smith saw that his teeth had been capped with gold.

"There you are! Uncle's come with treats, my little darlings. Oh, yes he has."

ૐ

SMITH went indoors, got a beer, and came back out to watch as the youth unloaded all the cages from the cart. He set them up in a row and opened each one. His master, meanwhile, opened a panel in the floor of the cart, and, from a recess, brought out an iron strongbox. When he opened it, Smith glimpsed a dense greenish stuff, looking like damp compressed sawdust. Crankhandle broke off a cake of it and went to each of the cages, baiting each cage with bits of the cake. The dragon on his assistant's shoulder turned its head and watched jealously. It began to squeak, doing the same head-bobbing and wing-fluttering routine it had gone through at Smith.

"Here you are, little sweeting," said Crankhandle, holding out a morsel of the stuff. The little dragon snapped at it avidly and gobbled it down. "That's the way. Now! Arvin, send her up there."

The youth, Arvin, took the dragon in both his hands. He kissed the top of her head—she tried to bite him—and tossed her up in the air toward the roof. She unfolded her wings and flew to the roofline, landing among the other dragons there. They hissed at her, but only for a moment; presumably, they had caught the scent of the cake on her jaws, for they suddenly mobbed her, biting her in their excitement, snapping at crumbs. She squawked and fled, jumping off the edge and flapping back down to Arvin's waiting hands. He clutched her to himself and dodged behind the open cages, holding her against his chest protectively as the other dragons came winging after her.

But the whole flock—and Smith saw now there were a lot more than a dozen, more like twenty—pulled up and wheeled in midair as they noticed the bait. For a moment there was a confusion of beating wings, loud as spattering rain on rock, then each dragon had zipped into one of the cages and was ravenously eating the green cake. Crankhandle stepped forward and slammed the cages shut, one after another. Arvin stepped around to help him, as his dragon scrambled back on his shoulder.

"And it's done," said Crankhandle, beating his gauntlets together.

Arvin's dragon peeped and begged. "And here's your reward, good girl!" Crankhandle added, going to the strongbox and taking out a last bit of cake. He handed it to Arvin to feed to her and put the strongbox back in its compartment, shutting the panel.

"Damn," said Smith. Crankhandle swung round to him, grinning, and held up an index finger.

"But wait! I have not completed my comprehensive removal! Arvin, get the ladder."

"Yes, Master," said Arvin, as the dragon screamed in temper and bit him because the last of the cake was gone. He dabbed absentmindedly at the blood streaming from his ear and went to pull an extendable ladder from the side of the cart.

Crankhandle loaded a basket with tools and, slinging it on his back, climbed the ladder one-handed, while Smith steadied the ladder for him and Arvin loaded the cages back on the cart. Arvin sustained a number of other bites doing this, amid a tremendous racket, because the dragon flock was in a group rage and hurling themselves against the bars; but Arvin kept working and only paused to tie a couple of bandages on his wounds before throwing netting over the cart's top to fasten everything down.

"I've got it figured out," said Smith, who had wandered over to watch the dragons once Crankhandle was safely on the roof. "He sells the little bastards to the umbrella-makers, doesn't he?"

Arvin shot him a pained look. "N-n-n-n-n-no!" he said reproachfully. "He l-lets them g-go. G-goes inland a l-long way and r-releases them. G-gone for w-weeks sometimes."

"Aha," said Smith. "Yes, of course."

⚗

CRANKHANDLE was up on the roof a long while, scraping and clunking and hammering. Mrs. Smith came out to see what was going on, and, on learning, was very pleased indeed with Smith, so much so that she went back indoors to prepare his favorite fried eel for dinner.

Having repaired the leads, removed the nests, and dug dragon shit out of all the rain gutters, Crankhandle came back down the ladder at last, looking smug.

"Very nice haul," he said, slinging the basket down and pulling a tank with a spraying rig from under the cart. Smith got up and looked in the basket. He glimpsed something bright glinting among the ruin of nests and flat, sun-dried dragon corpses.

"There's something gold in here—" Smith reached for it, but Crank-handle whirled around with the tank in his hands.

"Ah-ah-ah! That's my perquisite, sir. 'Contents of said nests or caches,' I said, didn't I? Anything I found up there's *mine*, see? Or I can just let the little dears loose again, and I shouldn't think you'd want that, not with the spiteful mood they're in."

"All right, all right," said Smith, but he brushed aside the rubbish for a better look anyway. His jaw dropped. In the bottom of the basket was a clutch of gold crown-pieces, a gold anklet, a silver bracelet set with moon-stones, a length of gold chain, three gold signet rings, the brass mouthpiece from a trumpet, assorted earrings . . .

"Wait a minute." Smith grabbed out a gold stickpin, a skull with ruby eyes. "This is mine! Went missing from my washstand!"

"Mine now, mate," said Crankhandle, shaking his head. "Those were my terms. Wyrmin steal bright metal; everybody knows that. Anyplace they nest, there's going to be a hoard. Now you know how I can afford to do this free of charge."

"Well yes, but . . ." Smith turned the stickpin in his fingers. "Come on. This was a gift. A gift from a demon-lord, if you want to know, and I wouldn't want to offend him by losing it. Can't I keep just this pin? Trade you for it."

"Such as what?" Crankhandle was busy fastening the tank's harness on his back.

"Lady of the house is a gourmet cook. Seriously, the Grandview's res-taurant rated five cups in the city guide. Exclusive, understand? All the lords and ladies are regulars here, so you can imagine the wine cellar's stocked with nothing but the best. We'll give you the finest table and serve you the finest meal you'll ever eat in your life, eh? And whatever you like to drink, as much as you can hold!"

"Really?" Crankhandle's eye gleamed. "Right, then; you get the table ready. I'm just going up to finish the job. I warn you, I've got a good appetite."

❦

HE wasn't joking. Crankhandle set his elbows on the table and worked his way through a whole moor-fowl stuffed with rice and groundpeas, a crown roast of venison with a blackberry red wine reduction sauce, golden-fried saffron crab cakes, two glasses of apricot liqueur, and a quart and a half of porter. Smith played the companionable host and took his dinner of fried eel at the table with his guest, watching in awe as the man ate and drank.

He took it on himself to have some fried eel sent out to Arvin as well, marooned in the garden keeping watch over the cages.

Refilling Crankhandle's glass, Smith inquired: "How did you get into this line of business, if you don't mind my asking?"

"Ha-ha!" Crankhandle belched, grinned, and placed a slightly unsteady finger beside his nose. "That's the story, isn't it? What's for pudding? Got any fruitcake?"

Smith waved down one of the waiters and told him to bring out a fruitcake.

"How'd I get into my line of business. Well. Always interested in dragons, from the time I was a kid. I grew up back in the grainlands, see, way inland. Way upriver. And the dragons, you know, they're bigger there—twice the size of these little buggers. I remember standing on the tail of my father's cart and watching 'em cruise across the sky, just gliding, you know, on these scarlet wings. Most beautiful thing I'd ever seen in my life. Ah!"

The waiter brought the fruitcake to the table. It was dark, solid, drenched in liquor, heavy as a couple of bricks and covered in molten sugar, and the mere sight of it was enough to give Smith indigestion. The waiter deftly set out a plate and took up his cake knife, poised to serve. "How big a slice would Sir like?"

"Leave the whole thing," said Crankhandle, a bit testily. The waiter looked sidelong at Smith, who nodded. The waiter set the fruitcake on the table and left. Crankhandle seized the knife and, a little unsteadily, sawed out a slice. Gloating, he held it up to the candle, so the light shone through the red and amber and green fruit. "Look at that! Looks like jewels. Looks like a dragon's trove. Nothing about them isn't beautiful, dragons." He stuffed the slice of cake in his mouth and cut himself another.

"So anyway—I wanted to know everything about 'em, growing up. Asked everybody in my village what they knew about dragons. Nobody knew much. Used to watch the dragons dive in the river for fish. Found out the sorts of things they like to eat when they can't get fish, found out what they physic themselves with when they're ill, that sort of thing.

"And then, one time, I followed one back to the cliffs where it nested and climbed up there to have a look, and that was when I found its hoard. All this gold! Nobody in my village had any, you can be sure. I reached in and grabbed this goblet with rubies on it—got my arm bitten pretty badly too—and carried it home.

"The schoolmaster had a look at it and said it was *old*. Come out of some old king's tomb somewhere, he said. The mayor said it likely had a curse on it and he confiscated it, to keep the curse off me, he said, but he was a greedy bastard and I knew he wanted it for himself. Pour me some more of that apricot stuff, eh?"

Smith obliged him. Crankhandle grinned craftily, took a mouthful of liqueur, and leaned quickly toward the candle. He swallowed, belched. The candle flame shot out sideways for a second, a jet of fire.

"Is that how dragons do it?" said Smith.

"No. See, that's a popular misconception about dragons, that they breathe fire. I'm here to tell you they don't, and I'd know. Been studying 'em my whole life. I know more about dragons than anybody else in the world, now." Crankhandle cut himself a huge slab of cake, took half of it in one bite, and chewed thoughtfully.

"Such as?"

"Such as, they're smart. They can learn things. I learned to train 'em. Mind you, it isn't easy"—Crankhandle pointed at the patch covering his eye socket—"because they're willful, and temperamental, and quick. You have to want them more than an eye, or a fingertip, or an earlobe. The boy's learning that. The other thing is, you can only really train wyrmin to do better what they already want to do anyway." He reached for the knife to cut the last quarter of fruitcake into eighths, changed his mind, and simply picked up the whole wedge and bit into it.

"Well. So I learned all there was to know about dragons, see? Discovered a secret, and I didn't learn it from any priests or mages either, I worked it out for myself. There's something dragons need in their diets—and I'm not telling you what it is, but it's either animal, vegetable, or mineral, ha-ha—and if they don't get it, they don't grow. That's why they're so puny, here by the sea. Lots of fish, but no Mystery Ingredient. So I worked out a special food formula for dragons, right? A little of this, a little of that, a lot of the Mystery Ingredient, and that's my bait.

"Not even the boy knows the recipe. I make it up myself, in a locked room. And the little bastards love it! Can't get enough of it. Have to be careful doling it out to them, because they do get bigger when they eat it, and you can spend a fortune on cages. But oh, how they come to the bait!"

"So . . . you travel around with this stuff, cleaning out wyrmin colonies, and collecting all the gold they've stolen and hoarded," said Smith. "You must have earned a fortune by now! But if it's that dangerous, why don't you retire?"

"Haven't made enough yet," said Crankhandle, pouring himself some more liqueur. "I'm saving it up. You might say I've got a hoard of my own. Besides, this isn't where the real money is!"

"Oh no?"

"No indeed. Rings and pins and bracelets . . . ha. That's the petty stuff the little ones bring in. They're not strong enough to lift anything bigger. You don't get a real payoff until you've got the big ones troving for you."

"Troving?"

"Going out looking for gold. It's instinctive. The big dragons where I grew up, they could tell where there was old gold. Tombs, mounds, other dragons' hoards. You should see *their* nests! I told you how I got this, didn't I?" He rolled up his oilskin sleeve to reveal a brawny arm, tattooed with swirling patterns, and a distinct U-shape of white, scarred tooth marks.

"You did. Stealing a cup."

"Right, well, I learned that what you do is, you get 'em when they're little enough to be easily managed, and you *train* 'em, see? You get 'em used to you. You get 'em so they believe they'd better do what you want 'em to do, to get those lovely wyrmin treats. And then you feed 'em so they get of a bigness to raid tombs and such, and you take 'em back into the inlands where the old places are and you let 'em go.

"Then it's just a matter of making a chart of where they build their nests and going around every now and then to see what they've collected for you. They remember *me,* old Uncle Treats, and I dump out a great sack of special formula for 'em, and while they're busy gobbling it down, I can take what I like out of the hoard. Works every time!"

"You ought to be stinking rich pretty soon, all the same," said Smith in awe. "Going to retire and pass your secret on to the boy?"

Crankhandle made a face. He drained his glass and shook his head. "No. He's a bit of a fool, really. Good enough for pulling the cart, but he's too soft for the work. He *loves* dragons, like they were people. And, you know, you really can't love, in this business." He reached for the emptied bottle and tilted it, sticking his tongue up the neck to get the last drops.

"You're a lot like a dragon, yourself," said Smith.

Crankhandle belched and grinned, and his gold teeth glinted in the candlelight. "Why, thank you," he said.

ᚷᚻ

THAT night, Smith put his stickpin away in a drawer. It had occurred to him that there was another thing Crankhandle might have trained his wyrmin to do, and that was to fly through open windows and rob houses.

The more he thought about it, the more he wondered whether the sudden infestation at the Grandview had happened entirely by chance.

But the dragons did not return, at least. When next Milady from the pink palace stopped in as one of a party ordering lunch on the terrace, she asked, with an unpleasant smile, whether she was likely to be attacked by an animal again. Smith assured her that all the dragons had been extermi-nated, which seemed to please her.

ℰℬ

SIX months later, Smith had business down in Rakut Square. He glanced at the base of the monument as he walked by, and saw no cart. He thought to himself that Crankhandle must have moved on to another city.

He was a little surprised, therefore, as he walked back toward the Grandview, to find the boy Arvin mending a fishing net. The little dragon was still perched on his shoulder, sleepily basking in the sunlight. She opened one slit-pupiled eye to regard Smith, and then closed it, dismissing him as not worth her attention.

"Hello!" said Smith. "Where's your master these days?"

Arvin looked up at him. He shook his head sadly. "Dead," he replied.

"Dead! How?"

"He t-told you about the b-bait we used, how it m-makes dragons bigger?"

"Right, he did."

"It makes them s-smarter, too."

The Tsar's Dragons

JANE YOLEN AND ADAM STEMPLE

One of the most distinguished of modern fantasists, Jane Yolen has been compared to writers such as Oscar Wilde and Charles Perrault, and has been called "the Hans Christian Andersen of America." Primarily known for her work for children and young adults, Yolen has produced more than three hundred books, including novels, collections of short stories, poetry collections, picture books, biographies, twelve songbooks, two cookbooks, and a book of essays on folklore and fairy tales. She has received the World Fantasy Award, the Golden Kite Award, the Caldecott Medal, and three Mythopoeic Awards, and has been a finalist for the National Book Award, as well as winning two Nebula Awards, for her stories "Lost Girls" and "Sister Emily's Lightship." Her more adult-oriented fantasy has appeared in collections such as Sister Emily's Lightship and Other Stories, Once Upon a Time (She Said), Storyteller, and Merlin's Booke. Her novels include Cards of Grief, Sister Light/Sister Dark, White Jenna, The One-Armed Queen, Dragon's Blood, Heart's Blood, A Sending of Dragons, Dragon's Heart, Briar Rose, The Devil's Arithmetic, and Sword of the Rightful King. She edited The Year's Best Science Fiction & Fantasy for Teens with Patrick Nielsen Hayden. She lives part of the year in Massachusetts and part in Scotland.

A relatively new author—with four published novels (one of which won a Locus Award), a dozen music books for young readers, plus about a dozen published short stories (several of which have been on Year's Best lists)—Adam Stemple has been a professional musician for more than twenty years as lead guitarist for such Minneapolis bands as Cats Laughing, Boiled in Lead, and the Irish band The Tim Malloys. He is best known for his fantasy novels Singer of Souls and Steward of Song for Tor. With Jane Yolen, he has written the novels Pay the Piper and Troll Bridge and an upcoming novel about a boy, a bar mitzvah, and a golem.

In the story that follows, they join forces to show us some desperate people caught between a rock and a hard place—or between a Tsar and a dragon.

꙰

THE dragons were harrowing the provinces again. They did that whenever the Tsar was upset with the Jews. He would go down to their barns himself with a big golden key and unlock the stalls. Made a big show of it.

"Go!" he would cry out pompously, flinging his arm upward, outward, though, having no sense of direction, he usually pointed towards Moscow. That would have been a disaster if the dragons were equally dense. But of course they are not.

So they took off, the sky darkening as their vee formation covered a great swath of the heavens. And as they went, everyone below recited the old rhyme, "Bane of Dragons":

Fire above, fire below,
Pray to hit my neighbor.

Well, it rhymes in the dialect.

Of course, the Jews were all safe, having seeded their shtetls with a new kind of drachometer—an early-warning device that only they could have invented. The Tsar should have listened to me when I told him to gather the Jewish scientists in one place and force them to work for him. Away from their families, their friends. Use them to rid ourselves of the rest. But no, once again I was not heeded.

So deep inside their burrows, the Jews—safe as houses—were drinking schnapps and tea in glasses with glass handles . . . which always seems an odd combination to me, but then, I am not Jewish, not even seven times down the line, which one must prove in order to work for the Tsar.

Balked of their natural prey, the dragons took once more to raking the provinces with fire. This time, it cost us a really fine opera house, built in the last century and fully gilded, plus a splendid spa with indoor plumbing, and two lanes of Caterina the Great houses, plus the servants therein. Thank the good Lord it was summer—all the hoi plus all the polloi were at their summer dachas and missed the fun. The smoke, though, hung over the towns for days, like a bad odor.

I pointed all this out this to His Royal Graciousness High Buttinsky, but carefully, of course. I know that I'm not irreplaceable. No one is. Even Tsars, as we all found out much later. And I wanted my head to remain on my shoulders. At least until my new wife wore me out.

Bowing low, I said, "Do you remember, gracious one, what I said concerning the Jewish scientists?"

The Tsar stroked his beard, shook his head, mumbled a few words to the mad magician who danced attendance on the Tsaritsa, and left abruptly to plan his next pogrom. It would have as little effect as the last. But he was always trying.

Very trying.

Have I mentioned how much Tsar Nicholas is constantly upset with the Jews?

Now the mad magician and I had this in common: we did not think highly of the Tsar's wits. Or his wishes and wants. This did not, of course, stop us from cashing his chits and living at court and finding new young wives at every opportunity, our own and other men's. But where we differed was that Old Raspy thought that he knew a thing or three about dragons. And in that—as it turned out—he was terribly, horribly wrong.

ॐ

SOME twelve feet below the frozen Russian surface, two men sat smoking their cigarettes and drinking peach schnapps next to a blue-and-white-tiled stove. The tiles had once been the best to be had from a store—now long gone—in the Crimea, but in the half-lit burrow, the men did not care about the chips and chinks and runnels on them. Nor would they have cared if the stove were still residing upstairs in the house's summer kitchen. They were more concerned with other things now, like dragons, like peach schnapps, like the state of the country.

One man was tall, gangly, and humped over because of frequent stays in the burrow, not just to escape the dragons either. He had a long beard, gray as a shovelhead. With the amount of talking he tended to do, he looked as if he were digging up an entire nation. Which, of course, he was.

The other was short, compact, even compressed, with a carefully cultivated beard and sad eyes.

The taller of the two threw another piece of wood into the stove's maw. The heat from the blue tiles immediately cranked up, but there was no smoke, due to the venting system, which piped the smoke straight up through ten feet of hard-packed dirt, then, two feet before the surface, through a triple-branching system that neatly divided the smoke so that when it came into contact with the cold air, it was no more than a wisp. Warm enough for wolves to seek the three streams out, but as they scattered when there were dragons or Cossacks attacking the villages, the smoke never actually gave away the positions of the burrows.

"You ever notice," the taller man, Bronstein, began, "that every time we ask the Tsar to stop a war—"

"He kills us," the other, Borutsch, finished for him, his beard jumping. "Lots of us." Bronstein nodded in agreement and seemed ready to go on, but Borutsch didn't even pause for breath. "When he went after Japan, we told him, 'It's a tiny island with nothing worth having. Let the little delusional, we're-descended-from-the-sun-god-and-you-aren't bastards *keep* it. Russia is big enough. Why add eighteen square miles of nothing but volcanoes and rice?"

Bronstein took off the oval eyeglasses that matched his pinched face so well and idly smeared dust from one side of the lenses to the other. "Well, what I mean to say is—"

"And this latest! His high mucky-muck Franz falls over dead drunk in Sarajevo and never wakes up again, and all of a sudden Germany is a rabid dog biting everyone within reach." Borutsch gnashed his teeth at several imaginary targets, setting his long beard flopping so wildly that he was in danger of sticking it in his own eye. "But why should we care? Let Germany have France. They let that midget monster loose on us a century ago; they can get a taste of their own borscht now."

"Yes, well—" But Borutsch was not to be stopped.

"How big a country does one man need? What is he going to do with it? His dragons have torched more than half of it, and his 'Fists' have stripped the other half clean of anything of value."

"Wood and grain," Bronstein managed to interject. *The only things worth more than the dragons themselves,* he thought. *Wood in the winter and grain in the spring—the only two seasons Russia gets. The nine aggregate days that made up summer and fall didn't really count.*

"Yes. So he sends us to fight and die for a country we don't own and that's worth nothing anyway, and if we happen to survive, he sends us off to Siberia to freeze our dumplings off! And if we *complain*?" Borutsch pointed his finger at Bronstein, thumb straight. "Ka-pow!"

Bronstein waited to see if the older man was going to go on, but he was frowning into his schnapps now, as if it had disagreed with something he'd just said.

"Yes, well, that's what I wanted to talk to you about, Pinches."

Borutsch looked up, his eyes sorrowful and just slightly bleary from drink.

"I've got an idea," Bronstein said.

Borutsch's lips curled upward in a quiet smile, but his eyes remained sad. "You always do, Lev. You always do."

ℰℬ

THE mad monk was not so mad as people thought. Calculating, yes. Manipulative, yes. Seductive, definitely.

He stared speculatively at himself in a gilded mirror in the queen's apartments. His eyes were almost gold.

Like a dragon's, he thought.

He was wrong. The dragons' eyes were coal black. Shroud black. Except for the dragon queen. *Hers* were green. Ocean green, black underwater green, with a lighter, almost foamy green color in the center. But then the mad monk had never actually been down to see the dragons in their stalls, or talked to their stall boys. He didn't dare.

If there was one thing that frightened Rasputin, it was dragons. There had been a prophecy about it. And as calculating a man as he was, he was also a man of powerful beliefs. Peasant beliefs.

He who fools with dragons
Will himself be withered in their flames.

It is even stronger in the original Siberian.

Not that you can find anyone who speaks Siberian here in the center of the Empire, the monk thought. *Which is where I belong. In the center.* He'd long known that he was made for greater things than scraping a thin living from the Siberian tundra, like his parents.

Or dying in the cold waters of the Tura, like my siblings.

Shaking off these black thoughts, he made a quick kiss at his image in the mirror.

"Now *there's* an enchanting man!" he said aloud.

His own face always did much to cheer him—as well as cheer the ladies of the court.

"Father Grigori," said a light, breathy child's voice in the vicinity of his hip. "Pick me up."

The mad monk was not so mad as to refuse the order of the Tsar's only son. The boy might be ill, sometimes desperately so. But one day soon, he would be Tsar. The stars foretold it. And the Lord God—who spoke to Father Grigori in his dreams of fire and ice—had foretold it as well.

"As you wish and for my pleasure," he said, bending down and picking up the child in his arms. He bore him carefully, knowing that if he pressed too hard, bruises the size and color of fresh beets would form and not fade for weeks.

The boy looked up at him fondly, and said, "Let's go see Mama," and Father Grigori's mouth broke into a wolfish grin.

"Yes, let's," he said. "As you wish and for *my* pleasure." He practically danced down the long hall with the child.

❧

SO having been balked once again of my chance to persuade the Tsar of the foolishness of his plans, I thought to go back to my apartment and visit with my young wife. We had met not a year earlier at the *Bal Blanc*, she in virginal white, her perfect shoulders bare, diamonds circling that perfect neck like a barrier. I was so thoroughly enchanted, I married again, less than a year after my last wife's death. It was only much later that I discovered the diamonds were her sister's. It was only much, much later that she discovered how little money *I* actually have.

Now, early afternoon, she might be napping. Or she might be entertaining. I hoped she would be available and not with some of her admirers. The problem with taking someone so young to wife is getting one's turn with her. Nights, of course, she is always mine, but who knows what she is doing during the day.

Suddenly realizing that I didn't *want* to know, I turned abruptly on my heel, my new boots on the tiled floor making a squealing noise that was not unlike the sound a sow makes in labor. I have watched many of them at my summer farm.

I'd made a decision, and I made it quickly. It's one of the things the Tsar likes about me since he has so many ditherers around him. Old men, old aristos, who cannot come down on one side or another of any question. Much like the Tsar. I think it's in the bloodlines, along with the many diseases. Inbreeding, you know.

This was my decision: I would go down to the stalls and visit the dragons. See if I could figure them out. There is a strange, dark intelligence there. Or maybe not exactly intelligence as we humans understand it, more like cunning. If only we could harness that as well as we have harnessed their loyalty—from centuries of captivity and a long leash. Much like the Cossacks actually. With a bit of luck, I might figure out this harrowing business. The Tsar might finally make me a Count. New blood might appeal to him. He'd listen to my plans. Then my young wife, Ninotchka, would be available in the afternoons, too. I strode down the hallway smiling. Making decisions always lifts my spirit. I breathed more deeply; my blood began to race. I felt fifty years old again.

It was then that I saw the mad monk, halfway down the hall and coming toward me, carrying the young prince. He's the only one who dares do that without soft lambs'-wool blankets. That child's skin is like old china. It can be smashed by the slightest touch.

"Father Grigori," I said, my hand to my brow in salute. He may be just a *muzhik* by birth, he may be as mad as they say he is, but I would be madder still to neglect the obeisance he demands. He has the ear of the young Tsar. And the young Tsar's mother, Alexandra. Maybe more than just her *ear*, if you believed the rumors.

He glanced at me, my name ashes in his mouth. He never uses my title. Then he smiled, that soft, sensual smile that drives the women wild, though to me it looks like a serpent's smile. "Commend me to your young wife."

It was then that I knew what I had only feared before. My own Ninotchka had fallen under his spell. I would have to kill him. Alone or with others. For Ninotchka's sake, as well as my own.

But how?

The answer, I felt, was down in the stalls with the dragons. So, down I went.

YOU always smell the dragons long before you see them. It is a ripe musk, fills the nostrils, tastes like old boots. But it's not without its seductions. It is the smell of power, a smell I could get used to.

The door squalled when I opened it, and the dragons set up a yowling to match, expecting to be fed. Dragons are always hungry. It has to do with the hot breath, and needing fuel, or so I'd been told.

I grabbed a handful of cow brains out of a nearby bucket and flung it into the closest stall.

There was a quick rustling of their giant bat wings—three or four dragons share a stall because it calms them down. I wiped my hands on the towel hung on the peg for just that purpose. I would need to wash before going back to my apartment, or Ninotchka would never let me touch her tonight.

The Tsar's dragons were slimmer and more snakelike than the Great Khan's dragons from whom they'd been bred. They were black, like eels.

Their long faces, framed with ropy hair, always looked as if they were about to speak in some Nubian's tongue. One expected Araby to issue forth instead of curls of smoke.

I gazed into the eyes of the largest one, careful not to look down or away, nor to show fear. Fear only excites them. *Prey* show fear. His eyes were dark, like the Crimea in winter, and I felt as if I swam in them. Then I sensed that I was starting to drown. Down and down I went, my eyes wide open, my mouth filled with the ashy water—when suddenly I saw the future breaststroking towards me: hot fires, buildings in flames. The Russias were burning. St. Petersburg and Moscow buried in ash. The gold leaf of the turrets on Anichkov Palace and Ouspensky Cathedral peeling away in the heat.

"Enough!" I said, hauling myself away, finding the surface, breaking the spell. "I will not be guiled by your animal magic."

The dragon turned away and nuzzled the last of the cow brains at his feet.

I'd been wrong. There'd be no help from these creatures. And I'd be no help for them.

THE dragons finally gone, the drachometer signaled the all clear, a sound like cicadas sighing. Bronstein and Borutsch crawled out of the burrows and into a morning still thick with dragon smoke. The two squinted and coughed and nodded to the other folks who were emerging besmirched and bleary from their own warrens.

No one exchanged smiles; they were alive and unharmed, but houses had been burned, businesses ruined, fields scorched through the snow. A stand of fine old white birch trees, after which the town was named, were now charred and blackened stumps. And perhaps the next time, the drachometers would fail and there would be no warning. It was always a possibility. *Drek happens*, as the rabbis liked to say.

The *babuschkas* were not so full of bile, but they were realists, too, as they told of the old times before the drachometers, when Tsars with names like "Great" and "Terrible" savaged the lands with their dragons and their armies. The Jews had been nearly wiped out then, and only the invention of the first drachometer—a primitive device by today's standards—had saved them. Borutsch's old grandmother often said, "We live in the better times."

"Better than *what*?" he would tease.

Hearing the old women's stories, the children shuddered at the wanton destruction while the young men scoffed and made chest-puffed proclamations of what they would or wouldn't have done had they been faced with sudden, fiery death from above.

But not Bronstein. He'd always listened intently to the stories and tried to imagine what it was like in the far-off days when you had no time to get safely underground and you had to face the dragons in the open: flame, tooth, and claw against man's feeble flesh. Because he realized something that the other young men seemed not to: technologies fail, or other technologies supplant them, and the contraption you count on one day can be useless the next. *In this, the rabbis are right,* he thought. *Drek really does happen.* There was only one thing you could really count on, and it certainly wasn't a sheep-sized gadget that ran on magnetism and magic and honked like a bull elk in rut when a dragon came within ten miles.

It was power.

Those who have it stand on the backs of those who don't, and no amount of invention or intelligence could raise a person from one to the other. No, to get power you had to grab it by force. And to hold it, you had to use even more force.

We Jews, Bronstein thought, as he led Borutsch out of town, *are unaccustomed to force.* Then, frowning, *Except when it's used against us.*

As they climbed the hills outside the shtetl, both men began to breathe heavily, their breath frosting like dragon smoke in the chill December air. Borutsch shed his outer coat. Bronstein loosened his collar. They walked on. Entering the forest at midday, they moved easily through the massive cedars and spruce, grown so tall as to choke out the undergrowth and even keep the snow from falling beneath them.

Bronstein led confidently, despite seeming to follow no trail. Each time he came here, he took a different route. But it didn't matter. He was as attuned to what he sought as a drachometer to the wings of dragons.

If someone with the Tsar's ear discovers my machinations before I am ready . . .

The results were too dire to consider.

Signaling a halt in a small clearing, he pointed to a fallen log. "Sit," he said, then pulled a loaf of bread from beneath his coat and handed it to Borutsch. "Eat," he said to the older man. "I go to see we aren't followed."

"If I'd known the journey was goin' to be so long, I would have brought more schnapps."

Bronstein smiled and reached into his other coat pocket, revealing a flask. "I'll take it with me to ensure you'll wait."

"Be safe, then," Borutsch mumbled through a mouthful of bread.

Bronstein was not only safe, but quick as well, merely trotting back to the forest's edge and peering down the slope. He could see the shtetl, still swathed in smoke, and, beyond it, the thin strips of burning grain fields. There was no one working the fields at this time of year, though it was little enough they got from the harvest even when they did. The Tsar's *kruks*—the "Fists" that Borutsch had mentioned—took the lion's share and the lamb's as well, leaving them with barely enough to starve on. It was the same with the peasants, only the Tsar did not set his dragons on them.

Seeing nobody climbing the slope after them, Bronstein turned back to the forest.

From field to forest, he thought. *Grain to wood.*

"Up," he said as he reentered the clearing and tossed the flask to Borutsch. "We are almost there."

Bronstein moved quickly now, and Borutsch struggled a bit to keep up. But as Bronstein had said, they were almost there.

They came upon a brook running swift and shallow through snowy banks. Bronstein turned downstream and paralleled it, stopping finally at an old pine tree that had been split by lightning long ago. He paced off thirty steps south, away from the stream, then turned sharply and took another thirty. Flinging himself to the ground, he began pawing through a pile of old leaves and pine needles.

"Grain and wood, Borutsch," Bronstein said. "Two of the three things that give power in this land." He'd cleared away the leaves and needles now and was digging through the cold dirt. The ground should have been frozen and resisting, but it broke easily beneath his fingers. "However, to get either one, you need the third." Stopping his digging, he beckoned Borutsch over.

Borutsch shambled over and stared into the shallow hole Bronstein had dug. "Oh, Lev," he said, his voice somewhere between awe and terror.

Inside the shallow depression, red-shelled and glowing softly with internal heat, lay a dozen giant eggs. Dragon's eggs.

"There's more," Bronstein said.

Borutsch tore his gaze from the eggs and looked around. Clumps of leaves and needles that had appeared part of the landscape before, now looked suspiciously handmade. Borutsch didn't bother to count them, but there were many.

"Oh, Lev," he said again. "You're going to burn the whole world."

ဢ

THE monk carried the child into his mother's apartments. The guards
knew better than to block his way. They whispered to one another when
he could not hear him, calling him "Devil's Spawn," and "Antichrist" and
other names. But always in a whisper, and always in dialect, and always
when he was long gone.

Rasputin went through the door, carrying the sleeping child.

The five ladies-in-waiting scattered before him like does before a wolf-
hound. Their high, giggly voices made him smile. Made him remember the
Khlysts, with their orgiastic whippings. What he would give for a small
cat-o'-nine-tails right now! He gazed at the back of the youngest lady,
hardly more than a girl, her long neck bent over, swanlike, white, inviting.
"Tell your mistress I have brought her son, and he is well, if sleeping."

They danced to his bidding, as they always did, disappearing one at a
time through the door into the Tsaritsa's inner rooms, the door snicking
quietly shut on the last of them.

After a moment, Alexandra came through the same door by herself,
her plain face softened by the sight of the child in the monk's arms.

"You see," he told her, "the child only needs sleep and to be left alone,
not be poked by so many doctors. Empress, you must *not* let them at him
so." He felt deep in his heart that he alone could heal the child. He knew
that the Tsaritsa felt the same.

He handed her the boy, and she took the child from him, the way a
peasant woman would take up her child, with great affection and no fear.
Too many upper-class women left the raising of their children to other
people. The monk admired the Tsaritsa, even loved her, but desired her
not at all, no matter what others might say. He knew that she was totally
devoted to the Tsar, that handsome, stupid, lucky man. Smiling down at
her, he said, "Call on me again, Matushka, Mother of the Russian People.
I am always at your service." He bowed deeply, his black robe puddling at
his feet, and gave her the dragon smile.

She did not notice but tucked the boy away in the bed, not letting a
single one of her ladies help her.

As Rasputin backed away, he instinctively admired the Tsaritsa's form.
She was not overly slim like her daughters, nor plump—*zaftik*, as the Jews
would say. Her hair was piled atop her head like a dragon's nest, revealing
a strong neck and the briefest glimpse of a surprisingly broad back.

Some peasant stock in her lineage somewhere? he thought, then quickly brushed the ungracious thought aside. *Not all of us have to raise ourselves from the dirt to God's grace. Some are given it at birth.*

The rest of her form was disguised by draping linens and silks, as the current fashion demanded, but the monk knew that her waist was capable of being cinched quite tight in the fashions of other times. Her eyes, the monk also knew, were ever so slightly drooping, disguising her stern nature and stubborn resolve—especially when caring for her only son.

She turned those eyes on him now. "Yes, Father Grigori? Do you require something of me?"

The monk blinked twice rapidly, realizing he'd been staring and that perhaps "desiring her not at all" was overstating things a touch.

"Only to implore you once more to keep the bloodsuckers away," he managed to say, covering his brief awkwardness with a bow. The Tsaritsa nodded, and the monk shuffled quickly out of the chamber.

Where is the girl with the swan's neck? he thought. *I should like to take these unworthy feelings out on her.* He rubbed his hands together, marveling at how smooth his palms had become during his time at court. *Perhaps it is not too late to find a whip.*

ॐ

"WHERE did you get them? Where did they come from? What do you plan for them?" Borutsch's voice trembled slightly on the last phrase.

Bronstein felt a sudden urge to slap Borutsch. He'd had no idea his friend was so woman-nervous.

"Quiet yourself. We approach the shtetl."

Borutsch didn't answer, but took another quick sip of the schnapps.

"And if you say anything about . . . about what I have just showed you . . . anything at all . . ."

Bronstein's voice trailed off, but there was a hard edge to it, like nothing Borutsch had ever heard from him before. He took another sip of the schnapps, almost emptying the flask.

"I'll not speak of it, Lev," he said quietly. He tried for the schnapps again, but sloshed it over his shirtfront as Bronstein grabbed him roughly by the shoulders.

"You won't!" Bronstein almost hissed. His eyes seemed to gleam. "I swear to you, Borutsch. If you do . . ."

Borutsch bristled and shook himself free. "Who would I tell? And who would believe an old Jew like me? An old Jew with fewer friends in this world every day." He peered up at Bronstein and saw the manic light slowly dim in his eyes. But suddenly Borutsch realized that he feared his friend more than he feared any dragon. It was a sobering thought.

"I . . . I am sorry, Pinches." Bronstein took off his glasses. Forest dirt was smeared on the lenses. He wiped them slowly on his shirt. "I don't know what came over me."

"They say that caring for dragons can make you *think* like one. Make you think that choosing anything but flame and ruin is a weakness."

Shaking his head, Bronstein said, "No, it's not that. This world is untenable. We cannot wait upon change. Change must be brought about. And change does not happen easily." He frowned. "Or peacefully."

Borutsch took a deep breath before speaking. What he had to say seemed to sigh out of him. "The passage of time is not peaceful? And yet nothing can stand before it. Not men, not mountains. Not the hardest rock, if a river is allowed to flow across it for long enough."

"You make a good, if overeloquent point." Bronstein sighed. "But *he* would disagree."

Borutsch frowned as if the schnapps had turned sour in his mouth. "*He* is not here."

"But he will return. When the dragons hatch . . ."

Borutsch looked stunned. "You have shown him the eggs, too?"

Shaking his head, Bronstein said, "Of course, I have shown him the eggs."

"*If* they hatch, Lev. Do you know what this means?"

"Don't be an idiot. Of course I know what this means. And they *will* hatch. And I will train them."

Neither one of them had spoken above a whisper, as all the Jews of the area had long been schooled in keeping their voices down. But these were sharp, harsh whispers that might just as well have been shouts.

"What do you know about training dragons?"

"What does the Tsar know?"

"You are so rash, my old friend." It was as if Borutsch had never had a drop of the schnapps, for he certainly seemed cold sober now. "The Tsar has never trained a dragon, but his money has. And where will *you*, Lev Bronstein, find that kind of money?"

Bronstein laid a finger to the side of his nose and laughed. It was not a humorous sound at all. "Where Jews always find money," he said. "In other people's pockets."

Bronstein turned and looked at the morning sun. Soon it would be full day. Not that there was that much difference between day and night, this far north in the Russias in the winter. All was a kind of deep gray.

"And when I turn my dragons loose to destroy the Tsar's armies, *he* will return."

"If *he* returns," Borutsch shouted, throwing the flask to the ground, "it will be at the head of a German column!"

"*He* has fought thirty years for the revolution!"

"Not here, he hasn't. By now, Ulyanov knows less about this land than the Tsar's German wife does."

"He is Russian, not German. And he is even a quarter Jew." Bronstein sounded petulant. "And why do you not call him by the name he prefers?"

"Very well," Borutsch said. "Lenin will burn this land to the ground before saving it, just to show that his reading of Marx is more *oisgezeihent* than mine."

Bronstein raised his hand as if to slap Borutsch, who was proud of the fact that he didn't flinch. Then, without touching his friend at all, Bronstein walked away down the hill at a sharp clip. He did not turn to see if Borutsch followed or not, did not even acknowledge his friend was there at all.

"You don't need to destroy the army," Borutsch called after him. "They'd come over to us eventually." Bending over, he picked up the flask. Gave it a shake. Smiled at the reassuring slosh it still made. "Given the passage of time," he said more quietly. Bronstein was already out of earshot.

Borutsch wondered if he'd ever see Bronstein again. Wondered if he'd recognize him if he did. What did it matter? He was not going back to the shtetl; not going to cower in that burrow ever again; not going to drink any more cheap schnapps. "If there's going to be a war with all those dragons," he said to himself, "I will leave me out of it." He'd already started the negotiations to sell his companies. He'd take his family into Europe, maybe even into Berlin. It would certainly be safer than here when the dragon smoke began to cover all of the land. When the Tsar and his family would be as much at risk as the Jews.

⸹

I took the stairs two at a time. Coming around the corner on the floor where my apartments were situated, I told myself that it no longer mattered who was there with Ninotchka. Out they would go. I would send her to her room. Though I rarely gave orders, she knew when she had to listen to me. It's in the voice, of course. After I locked her in, I would send out invitations to those I knew were already against the monk. I counted them on my fingers as I strode down the hall. The Archbishop, of course, because Rasputin had called rather too often for the peasants to forgo the clergy and find God in their own hearts. The head of the army, because of the monk's antiwar passions. To his credit, the Tsar did not think highly of the madman's stance, and when Rasputin had expressed a desire to bless the troops at the front, Nicholas had roared out, "Put a foot on that sacred ground, and I will have you hanged at once!" I had never heard him be so decisive and magnificent before or—alas—since.

Perhaps, I thought, *I should also ask Prince Yusupov and Grand Duke Pavlovich, who have their own reasons for hating him. And one or two others.* But another thought occurred to me. *Too many in a conspiracy will make it fail. We need not a net but a hammer, for as the old* babuschkas *like to say, "A hammer shatters glass but forges steel."*

I already knew that I would have my old friend Vladimir on my side. He had called out Rasputin in the Duma, saying in a passionate speech that the monk had taken the Tsar's ministers firmly in hand. How did he put it? Oh yes, that the ministers "have been turned into marionettes." That was a good figure of speech. I hardly knew he had it in him. A good man with a pistol, though.

But we would have to be careful. Rasputin was thought by the peasants to be unkillable. Especially after that slattern tried to gut him, calling him the Antichrist. She had missed her opportunity. Yes, her knife slid through his soft belly, and he stood before her with his entrails spilled out. But some local doctor pushed the tangled mess back in the empty cavity and sewed him up again.

Oh yes, he might be the very devil to kill.

And realizing that I'd made a joke—rare enough for me—I entered the apartments, giggling.

Ninotchka was alone, working on her sewing. She looked up, the blond hair framing that perfect heart-shaped face. "A joke, my darling?" she asked.

"A joke," I said, "but not one a man can share with his adorable wife." I cupped her chin with my right hand.

She wrinkled her nose. "You stink, my love. What *is* that smell?"

I had forgotten to wash the stench of dragon off my hands.

"It is nothing. I was talking to the horses that pull our carriage, reminding them of what sweet cargo they will have aboard tonight."

"Tonight?" The look in her eyes forgave me the stench. It was not yet the start of the Season, and she was growing feverish for some fun. I would take her to the Maryinski Theater and to dinner afterwards. And she would reward me later.

"I have planned a special treat out for us. It was to have been a surprise." It was amazing how easily the lie came out. "And now I have business," I added. "I beg you to go to your rooms. You and your women."

"Government business?" she asked, so sweetly that I knew that she was trying to find out some bit of gossip she could sell to the highest bidder. After all, I alone could not keep her in jewels. Later in bed, I would sleepily let out a minor secret. Not this one, of course. I am a patriot, after all. I serve the Tsar. Even though the Tsar has not lately served me at all.

I smiled back. "Very definitely government business."

After she went in, I locked the door from the outside. Then I sat at my desk and wrote my letters. Satisfied with the way I had suggested but never actually said what the reason for the meeting was, I called my man in to deliver them and to make a reservation at the Maryinski and *Chez Galouise*, the finest French restaurant in the city, for their last sitting. I knew I could trust Alexie completely. He, at least, would never shop me to my enemies. After all, I had saved his life upon three separate occasions. That kind of loyalty is what distinguishes a man from a woman.

༇

SPRING would break in Russia like the smiles of women Bronstein had known: cautious, cold, and a long time coming. But now they were in the deepest part of the winter. Snow lay indifferently on the ground, as if it knew that it still had months of discomfort to visit on the people, rich and poor alike. *But,* Bronstein told himself, *on the poor even more.* The peasants, at the bottom of the heap, might even have to tear the thatch from their roofs to feed the livestock if things got much worse.

He'd visited the eggs a dozen more times, going each visit by a different route and always brushing away his back trail carefully. He spent hours with the eggs, squatting in the cold, snowy field and talking out his plans as if the dragons could hear him. He had no one else to tell. Borutsch had fled to Berlin, and Bronstein feared that the old man had spilled his secret before leaving. But he spotted no one following him, and the eggs had never been disturbed.

But not this time.

Bronstein could see something was wrong as soon as he spotted the lightning-split pine. The ground beneath it was torn up, the leaves scattered. Running up to the tree, he gaped in horror at a hole in the ground that was completely devoid of eggs.

Mein Gott und Marx, he swore in silent German. *The Tsar's men have found them!*

There was no time to tear his hair or weep uncontrollably; he knew that he had to flee.

Perhaps I can join Borutsch in Berlin. If he'll have me.

Bronstein turned to run but was stopped cold by a rustling sound in the brush behind him.

Soldiers! he thought desperately. Reaching into his pocket and pulling out the small pistol he'd taken to carrying, he waved it at his unseen enemies before realizing how useless it would be against what sounded like an entire company of soldiers.

Swiveling his head from side to side as more rustling came from all around him, he came to a grim decision.

So this is how it ends.

The gun shook as he raised it to his temple.

"Long live the revolution!" he shouted, then winced. *Oh, to have not died with a cliché on my lips!*

His finger tightened on the trigger, then stopped just short of firing as a dragon the size of a newborn lamb—and just as unsteady on its feet—pushed through the bushes and into view.

"Gevalt!"

The dragon emitted a sound somewhere between a mew and a hiss and wobbled directly up to Bronstein, who took an involuntary step back. Even as a hatchling, the creature was fearsome to look at, all leathery hide and oversized bat wings, and came up to his knees. Its eyes were the gold of a full-grown beast, though still cloudy from the albumin that coated its skin and made it glisten in the thin forest light. He wondered if they would stay that color, or change, as babies' eyes do. He'd heard the Tsar's dragons had eyes like shrouds. Of course, the man who told him that could have been exaggerating for effect. And though the pronounced teeth that gave the adult dragons their truly sinister appearance had yet to grow in, the egg tooth at the tip of the little dragonling's beak looked sharp enough to kill if called upon. And the claws that scritch-scratched through the sticks and leaves looked even now as though they could easily gut a cow.

But Bronstein quickly remembered Lenin's advice.

Dragons respect only power. And fresh-hatched, you must be the only power they know.

So he pocketed the pistol that he still held stupidly to his head and stepped forward, putting both hands on the dragon's moist skin.

"Down, beast," he said firmly, pressing down. The beast collapsed on its side, mewling piteously. Grabbing a handful of dead leaves from the trees, Bronstein began scraping and scrubbing, cleaning the egg slime from the dragon's skin, talking the whole time. "Down, beast," and, "Stay still, monster!"

More dragons wandered out of the brush, attracted, no doubt, by the sound of his voice.

Perhaps, Bronstein thought, *they could hear me through their shells these last months.* Whether that was true or not, he was glad that he'd spoken to them all that while.

"Down!" he bade the new dragons, and they, too, obeyed.

As he scraped and scrubbed, Bronstein could see the dragons' color emerging. They were red, not black.

Red, like fire. Red, like blood.

Somehow that was comforting.

༄

THE mad monk had heard talk of dragons. Of course he'd often heard talk of dragons. But this time there was something different in the tenor of the conversations, and he was always alert to changes in gossip.

It had something to do with a red terror, which was odd, since the Tsar's dragons were black. But when his sources were pressed further—a kitchen maid, a bootboy, the man-boy who exercised the Tsar's dogs and slept with them as well—they couldn't say more than that.

Red terror! He tried to imagine what they meant, his hands wrangling together. It could mean nothing or everything. It could have nothing to do with dragons at all and everything to do with assassination attempts. A palace was the perfect place for such plots. Like a dish of stew left on the stove too many days, there was a stink about it.

But if there was a plot, he would know about it. He would master it. He would use it for his own good.

"Find me more about this red terror," he whispered to the kitchen maid, a skinny little thing with a crooked nose. "And we will talk of marriage." That he was already married mattered not a bit. He would find her a mate, and she knew it.

"Find me more about this red terror," he told the bootboy, "and I shall make sure you rise to footman." It was his little joke, that. The boy was not smart enough for the job he already had. But there were always ways to make the boy think he'd tried.

He said nothing more to the dog's keeper. As his old mother used to tell him: A *spoken word is not a sparrow. Once it flies out, you can't catch it.* He knew that the dog boy spoke in his sleep, his hands and feet scrabbling on the rushes the way his hounds did when they dreamed. Everybody listened in.

The truth that peasants speak is not the same as the truth that the powerful know. Having been one and become the other, the mad monk knew this better than most. He wrung his hands once more. "Find me more about this red terror," he muttered to no one in particular.

But even as he asked, he drew in upon himself, becoming moody, cautious, worried. Walking alone by the frozen River Neva, he tried to puzzle through all he'd heard. It was as if the world was sending him messages in code. He asked his secretary, Simanovich, for paper, and wrote a letter to the Tsar telling him of the signs and warning him, too. But he did not send it. It was too soon. Once he found out all about this red terror, he would personally hand the letter to the Tsar.

ℛ

THE red dragons were restless, snapping at their keepers and tugging at their leads. Bronstein tried to keep them in line—he was the only one they really listened to—but even he was having trouble with them tonight.

"Why do they act this way?"

"And why do you not stop them?"

The speakers were Koba and Kamo, two middlemen sent by Lenin to oversee the training of the beasts. Or the "Red Terror," as Lenin had dubbed them. That was so like Lenin, trusting no one. Not even his own handpicked men. He'd told them nothing beside the fact that they would be underground. They'd assumed they were to be spies. And so they were, of a sort.

Bronstein couldn't tell Koba and Kamo apart. And he didn't like their manner: arrogance compounded by . . . by . . . He couldn't quite put his finger on it.

"The dragons are bred to the sky," he said archly, "and this stay underground irks them." He fixed one of them—the one with the slightly thicker moustache, *Koba, maybe*—with a glare. "And you may try to stop them if you wish."

Maybe-Koba looked at the dragons for a moment as if considering it. He didn't look hopeful. But he didn't look frightened either.

Bronstein snapped his fingers. That was it! Arrogance compounded by blind stupidity. They didn't know enough to be afraid of the dragons. Or of Lenin. *Or*—he thought carefully—*of me.*

"My apologies, Comrade Bronstein."

He didn't sound sorry. *The man is an entire library of negatives,* Bronstein thought.

Maybe-Koba went on. "We shall let you return to your work. Comrade Lenin will be here within days. Then we shall release the Red Terror to cleanse this land. Lenin has said it, and now I understand what he means. Come, Kamo."

Koba it is, then, Bronstein thought, adding aloud, "Cleanse it of what? Of Russians?"

Bronstein knew that Koba—or maybe Kamo. Did it matter?—had been a Georgian Social Democrat and nationalist, and, some whispered, a separatist before joining Lenin to free the entire working class. Some said that Koba—or maybe Kamo—still was. The fractures in the revolution made Bronstein's head hurt. Without realizing it, he rubbed his cigarette-stained fingers against his temples.

Koba stared at Bronstein with no trace of emotion on his face. "Of the Tsar. And his followers. Are you feeling ill?" As if a headache dropped Bronstein even further in his estimation.

There was something hard about Koba, Bronstein decided, like his innards were made of stone or steel rather then flesh and blood. But the men followed him. Followed him without question. Not that the men who followed Koba asked a lot of questions. They might fight for the workers, but they looked like idlers and ne'er-do-wells to Bronstein. Actually, they looked like thieves and murderers, and most likely anti-Semites, but sometimes those were the kind of men you needed.

Revolution was a dirty business.

He grunted. So was tyranny.

"I will provide the dragons, Koba, and you provide the men. And together we will *free* this land."

"Comrade Lenin will be here soon. He will say if there will be freedom or not. Make sure his dragons are ready."

With that, Koba turned and left, Kamo right behind.

Lenin's dragons? Bronstein's hand twitched. *Who stayed up nights with the beasts? Who imprinted them? Who fed them by hand?* How he would have loved to wring the necks of these interlopers. But that was not his way. Besides, one of the dragons chose that moment to bite the finger of a young man who was grooming him, and Bronstein had to run and help wrench the digit out of the dragon's mouth before it was swallowed.

Lenin will be here soon, he thought, smacking the dragon on the top of its stone-hard head until it opened its mouth. The finger was still on the creature's tongue, and Bronstein snatched it out before the jaws snapped shut. He tossed it to its bleeding and howling former owner before wiping his hands on his shirt. Perhaps the doctor could sew it back on. Perhaps not.

Fingers, dragons, revolutionaries, his thoughts cascaded. *There's no way we'll be ready in time.*

I had to admit, it was a masterful plan. Especially since my presence was necessary at its execution. I giggled at my play on words, and Ninotchka glanced at me coldly. Her face was as powdered as her hair, which made her look surprisingly old. And haggard.

"Did I say something to amuse you, my husband?"

She'd grown distant over the last weeks, probably due to my spending long hours pulling the threads of my plot together into a web that Father Grigori could not hope to escape. He could neither refuse the invitation nor survive the meal I had planned for him.

And I *would* be there. Nothing on earth could keep me from seeing the look on his arrogant face as he realized who the architect of his destruction was. Did he think he could cuckold me without a response? I had destroyed better men than he in the service of the Tsar. Occasionally I had even killed them on the Tsar's orders. Not with my own hands, of course. But with a word in the right ear, with a bit of money passed carefully. Knowing the right men for such tasks *is* my job. And it seems that I am very good at what I do. If the monk's mad eyes seemed to look through me whenever we met in the palace halls—well, I would soon see them close forever.

"No," I said to Ninotchka. Having planned to dispose of Rasputin on her behalf, I now grew tired of her sniping. A man does what he must to protect his spouse, and if she is especially unappreciative of his efforts, he may very well find himself a new wife who is. "No, you say *nothing* that amuses me these days."

Taking pleasure in the wide-eyed look of surprise she gave me, I spun smartly on my heel and quick-marched from the sitting room, my boots tip-tapping a message to her with every step.

After all, I had a group of high-level men to shore up. Just in case . . . just in case the borscht-cum-poison didn't kill Rasputin on the first go-round.

ꝗᔒ

A week later, in his apartment, Rasputin looked in the great mirror. He grimaced at his reflection, his teeth so white compared to the smiles of the peasants he had known. Brushing his fingers through his beard, he loosened a few scattered bits of bread stuck in the hairs. *Always go to a dinner full,* his mother had warned. *The hungry man looks like a greedy man.* He had no desire to look greedy to these men. Hard, yes. Powerful, definitely. But not greedy. A greedy man is considered prey.

"Prince Yusupov's house in Petrograd at 9," the invitation had read. He knew that Yusupov's palace was a magnificent building on the Nevska, though he'd never before been invited to dine there. He and the prince had parted company some time ago. He'd heard it had a great hall with six equal sides, each guarded by a large wooden door. This morning, after receiving the invitation, he'd played the cards and saw that six would be a number of change for him. He was ready. But then, he was *always* ready. Didn't he always carry a charm around his neck against death by a man's hand? He never took it off, not in the bathhouse, not in bed. A man with so many enemies had to be prepared.

And really, Yusupov is but a boy in man's clothing, Rasputin thought. *He got his place at court through marriage. He needs me more than I need him.* Still, going to the palace would give him the opportunity to meet the prince's wife, the Tsar's lovely niece, Irina of the piercing eyes. He had heard many things about her and all of them wonderful. Rasputin had not yet had the pleasure. *Well, it would be her pleasure, too.*

That dog, Vladimir Purishkevich, was picking him up in a state automobile. He supposed that he could abide the man for the time it took to drive to the prince's palace. Then he would turn his back and mesmerize the princess right there, in front of her husband and his friends. They'd make a game of it. But it would not be a game. Not entirely.

Really, he felt, *no one can stop me.* He began to laugh. It began softly but soon rose to almost maniacal heights.

A knock on the door recalled him to himself.

"Father Grigori," his man asked. "Are you choking?"

"I am laughing, imbecile," he answered, but gently, because the man had been with him since the days of the flagellants, and a man of such fervid loyalty could not be found elsewhere.

The door opened and Father Grigori's man shuffled in, hunched and slow. "My . . . apologies, Father," he stuttered. "But I have news." He hauled one of the dragon boys in with him. The boy had a nose clotted with snot, and he sniveled.

Rasputin waited, but the man said nothing more. *He really is an imbecile,* the mad monk thought. The boy said nothing, either. Waiting, Rasputin assumed, for a sign from his elders. And betters.

Raising an eyebrow, Rasputin finally cued the man. "And this news is . . . ?"

It was the boy who spoke, trembling, the clot loosened, snot running down towards his mouth. "Your Holiness, I . . . I have found the red terror."

Rasputin stood and waved them fully inside his chambers. "Quickly, quickly," he said. "Come in where we will not be overheard. And tell me everything."

"It is about dragons, Father, and there is a man called Lenin who will free them, but he will not be here until the month's end. Three days from now. When the moon is full. Only when he comes . . ."

"Dragons . . ." Rasputin's voice was calm, but underneath his heart seemed to skip a beat. Soon he would be able to tell the Tsar.

ॐ

SHORING up my coconspirators had been tougher work than I'd imagined it would be. *Really, they have no stomach for this stuff. Aristocrats are ever prepared to pronounce sentence but rarely willing to carry that same sentence out themselves.* Not that I liked to get my hands dirty, either—but if you really want something done, occasionally you have to be the one to do it. And these men wanted Father Grigori dead almost as much as I did. And now, a week later, they had knives in their boots and revolvers in their waistbands so they that could finish the job properly if needed. But I could not presume that they would actually *use* their weapons. Better to be prepared myself.

In just a few hours, the mad monk will be dead, I thought.

I practically skipped down the halls of the palace thinking about it. Though first I had a few administrative duties to deal with, afterwards I'd be there to watch Rasputin die.

Except instead of sitting down to drink a beet stew full of poison, that son of a Siberian peasant was marching quickly down the same hall as me, dressed in his best embroidered blouse, black velvet trousers, and shiny new boots.

"Good evening, Father Grigori," I said as calmly as I could. *What is he doing here? He dare not insult the men I set him up with openly. Is he that arrogant? Or is he really that powerful?* My hands began to tremble, and I willed them to stop, to freeze.

Subtly, I put myself into his path, so that he would have to either pull up or plow me down. For a moment, I thought he was going to march right over me, but, at the last second, he stopped, looming above me, uncomfortably close. He smelled of cheap soap. I barely kept myself from wrinkling my nose.

"Out of my way, lackey," he said, eyes as cold as his mother's breast milk must have been. "I have important news for the Tsar."

I was close to panic. What news could he have to cause him to miss his dinner and insult me openly but that of my plans for him? I reached inside my jacket surreptitiously. Got my fingers on the hilt of a dagger I kept hidden there.

I may have to cut him down here in the hall, I thought. I wasn't sure I could. He was far bigger than I and certainly stronger, and if I missed with my first stroke, he could probably snap me in two with his huge peasant's hands.

"Why not give it to me to pass along then, Father," I said, hoping my voice didn't sound as querulous and weak to him as it did to me. "I assume by your outfit that you have somewhere else you must be?"

I was really just trying to buy some time. I needed to be just a few steps back, so that I would have room to draw steel, but not so far away as to be unable to close and strike. I had no idea what I might tell His Majesty to explain my murder of his wife's closest advisor in the halls outside his chambers. But tales could be fabricated, evidence planted. I was not terribly good with a knife, but I had skills in that other department.

But the knife will have to come out first.

With that in mind, I took a small step back and prepared to pull my blade.

But, surprisingly, the mad monk stood just a single moment in thought, then turned and spoke to me.

"You are right, my son. I have somewhere to be. Somewhere important. The Tsar, bless him, is probably already closeted with his beautiful wife. No man should be disturbed at such a time. I will speak to him in the morning, after our prayers." He managed to pack information and insult in five short sentences before turning on his heel and marching away from me.

I stood and watched him disappear around a corner, sweat from my knife hand drip-dripping into my jacket.

MY car followed Rasputin's, but not that closely. I did not want to frighten him off. As we were both going to Prince Yusupov's palace, and I knew where it was—well, didn't everybody?—I could take a slightly longer route.

I'd never actually been to the palace before. The prince was sole heir to the largest fortune in Russia, and I was certainly not in his set. But if I could help pull off this coup, perhaps he would reward me greatly. After all, he had tired of his old friend in carousal, Rasputin, who had gone with him to all the dubious nightclubs long before his marriage.

The prince had said quite plainly a year ago, "Will no one kill this *starets* for me?"

I hadn't known it then, but when I spoke of my own plan to Pavlovich, he brought me in on this one. Because of Pavlovich's extensive social calendar, the first time he was free was this evening, December 31. We didn't want him canceling any of his other engagements and thus arousing suspicion.

I felt marvelous to have been able to move the monk along and could not wait to hear their applause. It warmed me on such a cold night. I leaned forward and told my driver, "Faster! Faster now."

It was pitch-black outside, lit only by the car's lights illuminating the swirling snow. The driver had a heavy foot, and soon we approached the palace.

I went in the back way, as if a servant, as planned. One of the stewards took me down to the cellar room where the dinner was to be. I peeked out from behind the curtain. No one was there yet.

The cellar room was of gray stone with a granite floor. It had a low, vaulted ceiling. *Ah,* I thought, *it already feels like a mausoleum.* Only the carved wooden chairs, the small tables covered with embroidered cloths, and the cabinet of inlaid ebony indicated that it was a place of habitation by the living. A white bearskin rug and a brilliant fire in the hearth further softened the room's cemeterial aspect.

In the center of the room, a table was laid for six: the prince, the monk, Pavolovich, two other conspirators, and the prince's wife, who had been the bait to lure Rasputin to the place. Though he was not to know it, Princess Irina was off in the Crimea with her parents, not here.

I smiled. What a plot we have hatched! What a coil!

A samovar in the middle of the table was already smoking away, surrounded by plates of cakes and dainties. On the sideboard were the drinks, filled with poison, and the glasses, their rims soaked in poison as well. Dr. Lazovert had told me himself that each cake was filled with enough cyanide potassium to kill several men in an instant.

Several! We only wanted to dispatch *one*.

My smile grew larger. All was at the ready. As soon as Rasputin dropped, it would be my job to get the body out of there. But just in case he was slow to die, I had a pistol as well. And my knife.

From upstairs came the sound of music. I think it was "Yankee Doodle Dandy," that damned American song. The music was supposed to be part of a party that Princess Irina was throwing for some women friends before joining the men. I would have to hide again. They would soon be bringing Rasputin down.

I feared being found behind a curtain and situated myself on the other side of the wooden serving door. It had a small window. I could see but not be seen. Perfect.

And then the door opened, and in walked the mad monk himself, followed by a nervous-looking Prince Yusupov. I wanted to shout at him, "Stop sweating! You will give the game away." But we were already well into it. It would play as it would play. I shrank back for a moment, away from the window in the door, took a deep breath, and waited.

જ⊙

RASPUTIN sauntered into the room, smiling. He could feel his body tingling, starting at his feet. That always meant something huge would happen soon. Perhaps Princess Irina would declare her love openly. Perhaps the prince would simply offer her to him.

But no—he preferred the chase, the slow seduction, the whimpering of the whipped dog that would be the prince. He must not jump the fence before it was close enough. His mother always said that. The old folk wisdom was true.

He touched the charm around his neck. The prince would hate him but could not harm him.

"Have some cakes," Prince Yusupov said, gesturing with a hand toward the table. There were beads of sweat on his forehead.

Rasputin wondered at that. It was, indeed, too warm down in the cellar, but he himself was not sweating.

"The cakes were made especially. Especially for you," Yusupov said.

And indeed, they were the very kind of he loved best. Honey cakes topped with crushed almonds, *skorospelki* covered with branches of fresh dill, caviar blinis, and so much more. But Rasputin did not want to appear greedy.

"Please," Yusupov said. "Irina had them made especially. We would not want her to be disappointed."

"No, we would not," Rasputin said, managing to make the four words sound both engaging and insulting at the same time. He picked up a honey cake and a blini and ate them, savoring the taste. Surprisingly, they were too sweet and dry. "Some Madeira, if you please," he told the prince.

Yusupov himself went to the sideboard and poured the wine with exquisite care into a glass.

The first glass went down quickly but barely moved the dry taste out of Rasputin's mouth. Forgetting that he didn't want to appear greedy, he held out the glass for refill.

Eagerly, the prince filled it for him.

"And the princess?" Rasputin said, after downing the second glass.

"Here shortly. She had to see off her own guests and change costume," Yusupov said.

"Ah, women," said the monk. "God bless them. My mother used to say, 'A wife is not a pot, she will not break so easily.' Ha-ha. But I would rather say, 'Every seed knows its time.'"

Yusupov started. "What do you mean by that? What do you mean?" He was sweating again.

Rasputin put his hand out and clapped Yusupov on the shoulder. "Just that women, God bless them, are like little seeds and know their own time, even though we poor fellows do not." He slashed a hand across his forehead. "Is it very hot in here?"

"Yes, very," said Yusupov using a handkerchief to wipe his own forehead.

"Well, sing to me then, to pass the time till your wife gets here," the monk said. He pointed to the guitar that rested against the wall. "I heard you singing often in those far-off days when we went into the dark sides of the city. I would hear you again. For old times' sake. And for your lovely wife Irina's."

Yusupov nodded, gulped, nodded again. Then he went over and picked up the guitar. Strumming, he began to sing.

ℛ♪

I could not believe my ears. Downstairs, someone was singing, slightly off-key. I moved back and peeked carefully through the window. Rasputin was still on his feet. There seemed to be cakes missing from the table. An empty glass stood on the table as well. And Yusupov, that damned upper-class clown, was strumming his guitar and singing. Had he gone faint with worry? Had he decided not to kill his old friend after all? I turned away from the sight, raced up the servants' stairs, and found Dr. L., Purishkev-ich, and Grand Duke Dmitri at the top of the stairs that led down to the cellar.

"For the Lord's sake, what is going on?" I asked, my voice barely more than a whisper. "To my certain knowledge, the man ate several cakes. And had a glass of wine."

"Two at least," said Dr. L. "We heard him ask for a refill. He is . . ." he whispered as well, "not a man at all, but the very devil. There was enough poison to fell an entire unit of Cossacks. I know; I put the stuff in it my-self." He looked wretched and—as we watched—he sank into a stupor.

I took his hands and finally had to slap his face to revive him.

All the while we whispered together, Yusupov's thready voice, singing tune after tune, made its way up the stairs.

"Should we go down?" I asked.

"No, no, no," Purishkevich whispered vehemently, "that will give the game away."

"But surely he is already suspicious."

"He is a peasant," said the Grand Duke, which explained nothing.

I was a-tremble. After all we had planned, for it to come to this? *This, I thought, is the worst possible thing.* Oh, had I but known!

Suddenly the door to the cellar opened, and we all backed up, I the fastest. But it was just poor Yusupov, saying over his shoulder, "Have an-other cake, Father. I will see what is keeping my wife."

And Rasputin's voice, somewhat hoarsened, called up to him, "Love and eggs are best when they are fresh!"

"A peasant," the Grand Duke repeated, as Yusupov came up to find us.

If I was trembling, Yusupov was a leaf on a tree, all aflutter and sweat-ing. "What should I do? What can I do?"

"He cannot be allowed to leave half-dead," Purishkevich said laconically.

The Grand Duke handed Yusupov a pistol. "Be a man." And Yusupov went back down the stairs, holding the pistol behind him.

We heard Rasputin call out, "For the Lord's sake, give me more wine." And then he added, "With God in thought, but mankind in the flesh."

A moment later we heard a shot. And a scream.

"Come," said the Grand Duke, "that will have done it."

I was not so sure, but in this company it was not my place to say.

We ran down the stairs one right after another, the Grand Duke first, Dr. L. second. Purishkevich stayed behind.

The monk had fallen backward onto the white bearskin rug, his eyes closed.

Dr. L. knelt by his side, felt for his pulse. "He is dead."

But of course, that was premature, for not a moment later, Rasputin's left eye, then his right, opened, and he stared straight at Yusupov with those green eyes that reminded me of dragon eyes. They were filled suddenly with hatred. Yusupov screamed.

I could not move, nor could poor Yusupov. The Grand Duke was cursing under his breath. And I thought we were about to lose Dr. L. again.

"Long whiskers cannot take the place of brains," said Rasputin to the ceiling, and as he spoke, he began to foam at the mouth. A moment later, he leaped up, grabbed poor Yusupov by the throat, tore an epaulet from Yusupov's jacket.

Yusupov was sweating so badly that the monk's hand slipped from his throat, and Yusupov broke away from him, which threw Rasputin down on his knees.

That gave Yusupov time to escape, and he turned and raced up the stairs. He was screaming out to Purishkevich to fire his gun, shouting, "He's alive! Alive!" His voice was inhuman, a terrified scream the likes of which I'd never heard before or since.

The three of us watched as Rasputin, foaming and fulminating, and on all fours, climbed after him.

Prince Yusupov made it to his parents' apartments and locked the door after him, but the mad monk, maddened further by all that had happened to him, went straight out the front door. The rest of us followed him to see what he would do, Dr. L. muttering all the while that he was a devil and would probably sprout red wings and fly away.

But he was not flying; he was running across the snow-covered courtyard towards the iron gate that led to the street, shouting all the while, "Felix, Felix, I will tell everything to the Empress."

At last, Purishkevich raised his gun and fired.

The night seemed one long, dark echo. But he had missed.

"Fire again!" I cried. If Rasputin got away, we were all dead men.

He fired again and, unbelievably, missed once more.

"Fool!" the Grand Duke said as Purishkevich bit his own left hand to force himself to concentrate.

When he fired a third time, the bullet struck Rasputin between the shoulders, and he stopped running though he did not fall.

"A devil, I tell you!" cried the doctor.

"I am surrounded by fools," the Grand Duke said, and I was inclined to agree with him.

But Purishkevich shot one last time, and this one hit Rasputin in the head, and he fell to his knees. Purishkevich ran over to him and kicked him hard, a boot to the temple. At that, the monk finally fell down prostrate in the snow.

Suddenly Yusupov appeared with a rubber club and began hitting Rasputin hysterically over and over and over again.

The Grand Duke took hold of Yusupov's shoulders and led him away.

Only then did I take out my knife and plunge it deep into Rasputin's heart. I wanted to say something, anything, but there was nothing more to say.

A servant came out a little later with a rope, and we pulled the body to the frozen Neva and left it there.

"Should we find a hole and push him in?" I asked.

"Let the world see him," the Grand Duke said. "Dead is dead."

I looked at the mad monk splayed out on the ice and wondered at that. By my count, he should have died five times tonight before my knife decided the thing. But, "Dead is dead," I agreed with the Grand Duke, and left him lying there.

I went home but could not scrub away the feel of my hand touching his back, the knife going deep into his body.

"It is ended," I told my image in the mirror. But it had only begun.

༄

THE mad monk lay on the ice. His back hurt abominably where the knife had plunged in. He couldn't move.

"I curse you," he muttered, or tried to. His lips were frozen shut, and anyway, he wasn't sure whom he should be cursing, not knowing who had set the blade deep in his back. Instead, he cursed his old drinking companion, his betrayer.

Felix, may you lose all that is dear to you.

His shoulder and the back of his head hurt, too, though not as badly. Oddly enough his stomach and throat were burning as well. He wondered if the cakes—how many had he eaten?—had disagreed with him. *Trust the* prvidvorny, *the courtiers, to make stale and rotten cakes.* His own mother could have done better.

He was cold, but he had been colder. The Lord knew how cold a *muzhik* from Siberia could get without succumbing. He was wearing his charm, so men couldn't kill him. Nor women, it turned out. The whore who had slit him from stem to sternum had learned that. He would survive this.

But he could not move.

How long till the full moon? he thought. *How long till that fool Lenin arrives and lets the dragons out of their hole?*

Dragons, when caught in their lairs, can be drowned, starved out, slaughtered by massed rifle fire—in fact, killed in any number of ways. It was why the Tsar's dragons' stables were better guarded than his own home. In the skies, they were unstoppable: swift fire from the night skies and death to all who stood against them, like Jews and revolutionaries. But not now.

The fools haven't killed me. But if I don't recover before the moon is full, they will have killed Russia.

He tried to twitch a finger, blink an eyelid. Nothing.

I must rest. I will try again in the morning.

The moon rose over the frozen Neva, a near-perfect circle.

I have perhaps two days, he thought, his mind perfectly clear. *Maybe three.*

꿒

THE red dragons were no longer restless, because, for the first time, they'd been led up into the night air. Long noses sniffed at the sky; wings unfurled and caught the slight breeze. But they were not loosed to fly. Not yet. Not till Lenin gave the word.

The man in question, who had arrived just the night before, stood watching the dragons critically. Bronstein knew that the Bolshevik leader had never seen dragons before tonight, but he was showing neither awe nor fear in their presence. On the contrary, he was eyeing them critically, one hand stroking his beard.

"You are sure they will function, Leon?"

Lenin meant him, Bronstein. He insisted on calling Bronstein by his revolutionary name. Bronstein realized just now that he didn't much care for it. It was an ugly name, *Leon. And Trotsky sounds like a town in Poland.* He wondered how soon he could go back to the name he'd been born with. And he thought at the same time that taking revolutionary names was like a boys' game. *Such silliness!*

"Leon!" Lenin snapped. "Will they function?"

"I . . . I do not know for sure," Bronstein said, too quickly, knowing that he should have lied and said that he was certain. "But they are the same stock as the Tsar's dragons," he added. "And those function well enough."

Bronstein was certain of that at least. He'd traced the rumor of a second brood bred from the Great Khan's dragons with the thoroughness of a Talmudic scholar. Traced the rumor through ancient documents detailing complex treaties and byzantine trades to a kingdom in North Africa. Traced it by rail and camel and foot to a city that drought had turned to desert when the pharaohs were still young. Traced it with maps and bribes and a little bit of luck to a patch of sand that hadn't seen a drop of rain in centuries.

Then he'd dug.

And dug.

And dug some more.

He dug till he'd worn through three shovels and done what he was sure was irreparable damage to his arms and shoulders. Dug till the sun scorched the Russian pall from his face and turned it to dragon-leather. Dug till the desert night froze him colder than any Russian would ever care to admit.

Dug till he found the first new dragon eggs in over 120 years. The Tsar's dragon queen hadn't dropped a hatch of eggs in a century, nor was she likely to anytime soon. And even if she did, it would be years before the eggs would hatch.

Dragon eggs weren't like other eggs. They didn't need warmth and heat to bring forth their hatchlings. They were already creatures of fire; they needed a cool, damp place to develop.

Nothing colder and wetter than a Russian spring, Bronstein knew. So he'd brought them home in giant wooden boxes and planted them on the hillside overlooking his town, doing all the work himself.

Another thing that set dragon eggs apart: they could sit for years, even centuries, until the conditions were right to be born.

"And some would say," Bronstein said to Lenin, "they should be more powerful, having lain in their eggs for so much longer."

Lenin stared at him blankly for a moment, then turned to Koba. "Are your men ready?"

Koba grinned, and his straight teeth reflected orange from the fire of a snorting dragon. The handler calmed the beast as Koba spoke.

"Ready to kill at my command, Comrade."

Lenin turned a stern gaze at the moon as if he could command it to rise faster. Koba glanced at Bronstein and grinned wider.

A dragon coughed a gout of flame, and Koba's eyes reflected the fire. Bronstein looked into those eyes of flame and knew that if he let Koba loose his men before Bronstein launched his dragons, then he had lost. There would be no place for him in the new Russia. The land would be ruled by Georgian murderers and cutthroat thieves; new *kruks* to replace the old, and the proletariat worse off than before. Not the Eden he'd dreamed of. And the Jews? Well, they, of course, would be blamed.

"Lenin," Bronstein said, as firmly as he could. "The dragons are ready."

"Truly?" Lenin asked, not looking back.

"Yes, Comrade."

Lenin waited just a beat, nothing more, then said, "Then let them fly."

Bronstein nodded to Lenin's back and practically leaped toward the dragons. "Fly!" he shouted. "Let them fly!"

The command was repeated down the line. Talon boys dashed bravely beneath broad, scaly chests to cut the webbings that held the dragons' claws together.

"Fly!" Bronstein shouted, and the handlers let slip the rings that held the pronged collars tight to the dragons' necks before scurrying back, as the beasts were now free to gnash and nip with teeth the size of scythe blades.

"Fly!" the lashers shouted as they cracked their long whips over the dragons' heads. But the dragons needed no encouragement. They were made for this. For the night sky, the cool air, the fire from above.

"Fly," Bronstein said softly, as giant wings enveloped the moon, and the Red Terror took to the skies.

Fifty yards away, Lenin turned to Koba. "Release your men to do their duty, as well." And Koba laughed in answer, waving his hand.

Bronstein saw Koba's men scurry away and knew for certain that Russia was lost. Releasing the dragons was a mistake; releasing Koba's men a disaster. Borutsch had been right all along.

It will be years before we struggle free from these twin terrors from land and sky. What I wanted was a clean start. But this is not it.

He shivered in the cold.

I need warmth, he thought suddenly. By that he did not mean a stove in a tunnel, a cup of tea, schnapps. *I want palm trees. Soft music. Women with smiling faces. I want to live a long and merry life, with a* zaftik *wife.* He thought of Greece, southern Italy, Mexico. The dragon wings were but a murmur by then. And the shouts of men.

૯ఠ

IN the blackness before dawn, the mad monk's left index finger moved. It scraped across the ice and the slight *scritching* sound it made echoed loud and triumphant in his ears.

He'd lain unmoving for three days.

A peasant child had thrown rocks at him on the second day, trying to ascertain whether the drunk on the ice was alive or dead. The mad monk was surprised when the child didn't come out on the ice and loot his body. But then he realized why.

The ice was melting.

The days had grown warmer, and the ice was melting. Soon, the mighty Neva would break winter's grip and flow freely to the Baltic Sea once more. Icy water was already pooling in his best boots and soaking his black velvet trousers. It splashed in his left ear, the one that lay against the ice, and he thought that he could feel it seeping through his skin to freeze his very bones.

Terror crept in with the cold as he realized that his attempted murderers would not need to kill him. The river would do their work for them. Drown him, as his sister had drowned, or cause him to waste away in fever, like his brother. He would have shivered with fear or cold, but he could not move.

Night fell, and, for the first time, Father Grigori felt the terror of the mortals he'd ministered to. Through the night, he felt like Jesus on the cross, his iron faith wavering. *Why hast thou forsaken me?*

The night brought no answer, just more cold water in his boots.

But then, before dawn, the finger moved.

If one finger can move, the rest can move as well.

And putting thought to deed, he moved the index finger on his other hand. Moved it as if he'd never been hurt, tapping it on the ice, once, twice, a third time. His spirits soared as the sun broke the horizon, and, with a great effort, he bent up at the waist, levering himself to a sitting position. He was sore. He was cold. Every bit of his body ached. But he was alive. And moving!

However, he was also very tired, and he decided not to try to stand quite yet. Facing the rising sun, he waited for the heat to reach him.

"When I am warmed straight through," he said, his voice calm despite the creaking and popping of his stiff limbs, "I shall go ashore and deal with Felix and the others."

Watching the sun rise and turn from red to gold, he saw a flock of birds pass before it. A big flock of birds, not just in size, but in number, hundreds of them, casting long shadows across the ice.

What are those? he thought. *Egrets leaving their roost?* But it was winter. There were no egrets here.

And the birds were too big. Even from far away, he could tell that they were huge. Suddenly, he knew that he was too late. He'd lain on the ice too long, and Lenin had come to loose the Red Terror on the land.

Now staring in horror, he watched the flock move closer, revealing red scales and leathery wings, smoke curling from their nostrils. He made a small cry, like a rabbit in extremis, and struggled to stand. But the movement that had come so easily just moments ago was a trial now. His limbs cried in protest and refused to budge. Despite straining and sweating, he'd only achieved an ungainly half crouch when the dragons were upon him.

The lead dragon swooped in low and swatted him aside with its forefoot. He went skittering across the ice, feeling his ribs shatter. Crawling for the shore, he dragged himself along far too slowly, and his fingernails broke on the ice. Finally—*finally*—he was able to shiver. But this was in fear. He no longer felt cold. Terror rushed hot in his blood.

A shadow enveloped him, and he looked up into the black eyes of a hovering dragon. Before he could react, the dragon's talons shot toward him, and one long claw pierced him through the chest, pinning him to the ice. It looked as if it were laughing at him, its teeth filling its horrible great mouth. He tried to scream, but suddenly he had no breath. Lungs pierced, he could only stare stupidly as the dragon's wing beats slowed and it landed on the ice beside him, as gently as any songbird.

But the dragon was no songbird, and the ice shattered under its weight. Water splashed the beast's belly, and it roared its displeasure, flapping madly, trying to get aloft. Then it belched out a lash of fire, which further melted the ice around itself and the ice below Rasputin. When the dragon managed to lift out of the water, it slowly shook itself free of water and prey at the same time. The wind from the dragon's wings was so strong that it pushed Father Grigori Rasputin over the melting edge of ice and down into the dark water.

We have put a rope through the nose of Leviathan, he thought as the waves closed over his head. He could still see the dragons, distorted by the water, hovering over the hole in the ice like terns. *But he is king over all the sons of pride.*

And then, like his sister, Maria, so many years before, Father Grigori drowned.

ॐ

I did not wake Ninotchka. All was falling apart. She would need her sleep.

Prying open the old desk where I keep my treasures—the key was long lost—I filled my pockets with gold coinage, my real certificate of birth, my other papers, several strands of rare pearls, my mother's diamonds, my father's gold watch and fob. I would leave my wife with what paltry jewels she had. She would need them. Alas, the Tsar would not look kindly on me and mine once the story of the mad monk's death came out. And come out it would. Servants can be forced to tell what their masters will not. Better that I leave Ninotchka to what fate her beauty could buy her.

As for me, I would cross the line, find the men who held the new reins of terror. Who knows if the Tsar will even last through this time? The wheel turns and turns again. Revolution is a messy business. Yet, there is always a need for a good functionary, a secretary, a man of purpose. I'd always known I was the first two, and now I know I can be hard, too. I can kill. My hand can wield a knife. Yes, I am someone who has much to offer, to *muzhik* or Tsar. And I will let it be known—I work equally well with men and with dragons.

The Dragon of Direfell

LIZ WILLIAMS

Vanquishing a dragon is a big job but may turn out to be not as straightforward a job as it appears—and the dragon may turn out to be the least *of your problems.*

British writer Liz Williams has had work appear in Interzone, Asimov's Science Fiction, Visionary Tongue, Subterranean, Terra Incognita, The Mammoth Book of New Jules Verne Adventures, Strange Horizons, Realms of Fantasy, and elsewhere, and her stories have been collected in The Banquet of the Lords of Night & Other Stories. *Her books include the critically acclaimed novels* The Ghost Sister, Empire of Bones, The Poison Master, Nine Layers of Sky, Snake Agent, The Demon and the City, *and* Darkland. *Her most recent novels are* The Shadow Pavilion *and* Winterstrike. *She lives in Brighton, England.*

ॐ

IT was not fire-breathing, nor did it boast claws. It lay coiled neatly around the hill, its long head resting near the summit. For something so large, it was curiously difficult to see in the twilight: a thin, whiplike body, tapering to a tail like that of some fluke. We were, I was relieved to note, closer to the tail than to the head. Above, near the summit of the hill, there was the sudden glittering glint of a green eye, an emerald star.

I nudged Parch. "I'm assuming that's the dragon you were talking about?"

"Please keep your voice down, Lord Cygne! These devils have the ears of a hunting dog."

Parch, I observed with a modicum of scorn, was prone to nerves. I'd already taken the precaution of casting a concealment spell, a small guise only and too basic to attract the attention of a magic-using creature. We would not be overheard, but Parch was too anxious to listen to me. His plump face was agitated; a faint sweat had broken out across his brow. One must make allowances, I told myself. It had been immediately evident back at the mansion that John Parch, steward to the ninth Duke of Direfell, was not a man of action.

The worm was shifting position, perhaps spotting some unwary prey down in the vale. From the movements of its serpentine head, I knew that the prey was not ourselves; we were perfectly safe beneath our guise in the bushes. But Parch looked so frightened that I thought he might be about to do something stupid. Correspondingly, I suggested that we make a strategic withdrawal, and, with alacrity, he agreed.

��

I had come to Direfell in late summer, under a cloud-riding moon. The mansion, and its dependent villages, lay to the south of my own home of Burnblack, some handful of days distant. As I approached the mansion, riding up over a low roll of hills, I caught sight of corn-lecks whisking out of sight behind the stacked stooks of hay, golden-skinned in the light of the moon, with their wild hair streaming behind them. The hedges were starred with roses, and beech woods billowed across the hills. Direfell did not live up to its name, I thought as I approached the house.

I had never met the ninth duke, Richard Porthlois, though I knew that his ancestor had been granted the holding by Queen Lune, herself the ancestor of our own monarch, Aoife. Faeries being long-lived, there had only been one queen in between, so it may well be that Aoife herself remembered the first duke: rumour said that he'd often ventured beneath the hollow hills of Albion, a risky undertaking for any except the most advanced or foolhardy magician. I considered this as I rode, weighing up political likelihoods: the duke had hired me, for a purpose hinted at but not fully explained, and I had heard nothing from Aoife for over three months. Indeed, I had not set foot in London for nearly a year. This in itself was not unusual. The Queen had a tendency to leave me alone at Burnblack for long periods of time, then snap her green-tinged fingers and expect me to come running. It was a pattern to which the majority of the court (to which, as minor nobility and a major magician, I was only lightly attached) had long since become accustomed. I could hear Aoife's voice now, cold as a wind-chimed icicle: "You think too much, my lord Cygne!"—followed by her chilly, merry laughter.

Perhaps so. But I'd survived, when many of those around me had not. If that was where thought led, I'd go on thinking.

The mansion of Direfell itself squatted in a dip in the hills, a sprawling construction that had clearly been accumulating over the last five hundred years. As I drew closer, I saw that the main house was built of mellowed brick, half-covered in a suffocating blanket of roses. Nothing too dire about that—but in faery-ruled Albion, you learn early to see what lies beneath the glamour, or do not learn at all. No one was waiting for me, and there was no sign of any guards, magical or otherwise—a far cry from my own home of Burnblack, where conjure-shucks prowl the grounds and rend trespassers to ribbons. Frowning, I tethered my horse to a column on which reposed a stone pineapple, and went up the steps to knock upon the door.

It took some while to open, and, when it did, the Duke of Direfell was not the one who stood there. Instead, I saw a young girl, perhaps fifteen, with a pale face like the crescent moon and a long fall of golden hair.

"Lord Cygne?" she said, in a whispering little voice, and gave a curtsey.

"None other."

"My father will be pleased to welcome you," she murmured, and drifted within. It crossed my mind that the duke might have a marriage proposal in mind—it had happened before. If so, this young lady would be safe from the ravages of matrimony, at least as far as I was concerned: I'm not a one for *delicate* and *frail*. But magicians, especially aristocratic ones, like forming dynasties. Wondering, I followed her into the parlour, where, despite the warmth of the evening, the ninth duke was stretching his legs in front of a roaring blaze.

"Lord Porthlois?" I asked, repressing the urge to reach for a kerchief to mop my suddenly dripping brow.

"The same. Lord Cygne?" Porthlois, the ninth Duke of Direfell, rose languidly from the fire and took my hand in a limp grip. Had I seen him at the Queen's court in London, I would have him down for a fop, all powders and primping, but this did not quite sit with the country seat or the presence of the girl, since he added, "My eldest daughter, Rose. There are three of them—you'll find her sisters around somewhere."

"And Lady Porthlois?"

"My first wife is no longer with us," the ninth duke explained with a sigh. "You will meet the girls' stepmother in due course. We've put you in the Blue Chamber. I trust you'll find it to your liking. Perhaps you'd care for a small glass of wine after your journey?"

I stifled the inclination to reply, *No, a large one,* and assured him that this would be delightful. Rose slipped away and returned with a bottle. The wine, when it was poured, turned out to be thick and dark and redolent of hedgerows, rather than the Italian vintages preferred by the court.

"Our own," Porthlois informed me, with a negligent wave of the hand. "Elderberry, mainly."

"Most—unusual." It didn't taste quite like elderberry to me, and with the warmth of the parlour, I decided to pretend to sip. Capturing rival magicians wasn't an unknown phenomenon, either. But thus far, I had no sense that Porthlois was a mage.

"So," I said, taking a seat as far from the fire as possible, "you wrote to me, Lord Porthlois."

"Indeed, indeed." Porthlois appeared to go off into a reverie. I waited, with increasing impatience. At last, he said, "We have a small local difficulty."

"Oh?"

"We have a dragon."

"Oh dear."

"Hasn't been a problem for the last couple of hundred years, but recently, we seem to have acquired one. Been taking sheep, frightening villagers."

"The usual things that dragons do, eh? What kind is it?"

"A laidly one."

"Ah. A worm."

"Did you see the hills on your journey?"

"I did." I'd noted the coiled mazes that striped some of the hillsides, had speculated as to their origins.

"We had a worm plague some three hundred years ago. My ancestor called in a foreign knight—man with a beard, there's a portrait of him on the stairs. He did a good enough job of getting rid of them."

"Dragon slaying's rather gone out of fashion," I mused.

"Due to the lack of dragons. But things change."

"Any notion as to why they've returned?"

"None. They come from stagnant pools, growing from stones laid in the mud, everyone knows that. As to why this particular time—I do not know."

The duke evidently subscribed to one of the popular superstitions regarding the origin of dragons, but I decided to keep my more extensive knowledge to myself for the moment.

"Well," I assured him. "I shall see what can be done."

NEXT morning, I woke early and drew the curtains to see a sylvan land-scape unfolding before me. It did not, on the face of it, look like the kind of terrain favoured by dragons—but then, that was the point. Such worms are attracted to fat pickings: the cattle and sheep mentioned by my host, the flesh of human farmers, and something more—the spirit of abundance that pervades such a place, off which the worms may leech.

But Porthlois had been wrong. Laidly worms don't come from ponds; they are not frogs. They are conjured from the Eldritch Realm, from moondark and shadow, their spirits summoned forth to infest a par-worm or lizard, which then grows to monstrous lengths, bloated by borrowed power.

To conquer a worm, you must first find its master, or failing that, its spirit. Porthlois was the obvious candidate, given that no other magi lived in the vicinity of Direfell—at least, as far as I was concerned, and I'd long ago made it my business to keep up with the mage registers of Albion. But I did not think that the duke was a mage, and besides, Porthlois was un-likely to have summoned a worm to ravage his own lands unless there was some subtlety here of which I was unaware. That left an unknown mage at work, and that was worrying. I also couldn't understand why Porthlois had left his mansion unwarded, when there was a worm slithering about the landscape. It was rare for such beasts to attack the homes of men, but it did happen, and I'd have thought that the duke would be unwilling to take any chances.

Taking the opportunity that early morning afforded me, I dressed, then slipped from the chamber and began to explore the house. It proved to be a typically ancient family seat, with a great deal of oak panelling and stone flags, a general air of slight neglect. I might have said it lacked a woman's touch—but then, there were the three daughters, and the step-mother, to whom I had still not been introduced.

As I came out onto the terrace, I saw to my chagrin that I was no longer alone: I would have liked to have explored the immediate grounds unhindered. The three girls were coming up across the lawns, threading their way through a motley collection of topiaried yew. They sang and laughed as they came—clearly, thoughts of marauding worms had failed to trouble them.

"We have been collecting the morning dew!" Rose informed me as she came up the steps. "These are my younger sisters—Lily and May."

Evidently, one of their parents had enjoyed a floral bent. All the girls looked the same, with the long, gilded locks and pale faces. Not unlike flowers, I supposed; it was a pretty enough conceit. I surmised that they took after their mother, since, beneath the powdered wig, Porthlois's hair was dark. As Rose held out the pail of dew for me to admire, I saw that her fingernails, too, had a slight golden tinge. Odd, though not unattractive.

"You're not worried about the dragon?" I asked.

"Oh, it keeps to its hill," Rose explained, though she cast a somewhat nervous glance over her shoulder as she spoke. "Our father has had a protection put on the grounds."

"Indeed? I noticed no such."

"Father is a man of great subtlety," Lily explained, and an expression that almost amounted to worship crossed the features of all three girls. I smiled in as benign a manner as I could manage.

"Wonderful! I have not yet met Lady Porthlois . . ."

At once, the worship soured. "Oh, *her*," May remarked.

No love lost, then. Hardly an uncommon occurrence.

"Girls!" The duke ambled down the steps with a clap of the hands. "Kindly leave the poor man alone. Don't you have things to do?"

The three golden-haired girls trooped meekly into the house, and Porthlois and I sat over ale and bread for the next hour and made plans. It was not immediately obvious to me how to approach the laidly worm. I'd never dealt with dragons, but I wasn't going to tell Porthlois that. As a magus, one must guard one's areas of inexperience with care.

"The first thing must be the study of the beast," I told the duke.

"Quite so. As you know, they tend to go to ground during the day, appearing as soon as the dusk falls over the land."

This was so: dragons, for all their fiery reputation, are not solar creatures, preferring the shadows from which their spirits emanate. I had some thoughts of locating the thing's nest and burning it out at noon, but first I needed to see exactly what I was dealing with.

"I shall send you out with my steward, Parch," the duke said.

"In the meanwhile, I should like to see a little more of the estate, the terrain . . ."

"I will arrange it."

As he was doing so, I took the chance to explore Direfell Hall itself, wandering down panelled corridors patterned by uncertain shafts of sun, into a book-lined room that bore an astrolabe upon a small table, its captive planets set to spinning by the touch of my hand.

Up a narrow flight of stairs, onto a landing that smelled of beeswax and age. I was about to turn on my heel and return to the parlour, when a voice said, "Who's there?"

It had come from behind a closed door, across the landing. I went to it, and answered, "My name is Lord Cygne."

"Ah, the magician?"

A gratifying enough response.

"Just so."

"Come in, Lord Cygne."

Entering, I found myself in a long chamber, and blinked. A shaft of sunlight had blinded me. I ducked my head, avoiding the light, and eventually my vision cleared to reveal a room hung with mirrors, turning gently in the draught. One of these had directed the blinding sunlight towards me. At the end of the chamber was a bed. A monstrously corpulent woman reposed within it. "I am Lady Porthlois," the woman announced. Her voice was well modulated, even hypnotic. She held out a hand, and I drew closer. "I've heard of you."

"Positively, I hope."

Lady Porthlois grinned, displaying white teeth within the expanse of her face. Yet despite her size, I could see that she had once been a handsome woman: there were the vestiges of angularity beneath the flesh, and her eyes were large and hazel in colour. I wondered about the mirrors. "More or less. You're a favourite of Her Majesty, aren't you?"

"Favourite" didn't quite cover it. "Queen Aoife has been kind enough to grant me a few small boons, yes."

"And Richard has called you in on account of our dragon?"

She might be fat, confined to her bed, and wearing a mob-cap, but there was something about her that captured my interest. "What do you know about dragons?" I asked.

"The usual manner of things. They snatch cattle, occasionally require maidens."

"Have they required maidens?"

"Not yet. My stepdaughters are not fond of me, Lord Cygne. You may have observed this. But it may surprise you to learn that I am fond of them. Their only sin in my eyes, if sin it can be called, is that of missing their mother. And the callowness of youth."

"A commendably forgiving attitude," I said, recalling the sourness of May's expression as she mentioned her dead parent.

"The first lady Porthlois was a beauty," the current incumbent said, "but as poisonous as a serpent. Richard was lucky to lose her as early as he did. But the girls were quite young at the time—no more than children—and her beauty blinded them. All they saw was the sweetness. When Richard married me, three years ago, I was not as you see me now." She gave a grim laugh. "Sometimes I think I have absorbed all the bitterness in this unhappy household, and it has bloated me like a toad."

"Such things have been known," I agreed. "It sounds as though you knew Lady Porthlois."

"Why, so I did. I am her cousin. I knew her from a child, and she was always the same—the first to suggest a trick, then, when the adults found out, the first with tears and a trembling lip and a ready tongue to blame."

"You said you were fond of them. Do any of the girls take after her?"

She hesitated for a fraction of a second. "No, they have all the sweetness and none of the bile, I am thankful to say. Just like *her* own sisters. Well, Lord Cygne, as you can see, I am not well, and I grow weary." She reached out and patted my hand with a beringed finger. "I should like to talk with you again, though. Perhaps when you have experienced our dragon."

It was as effective a dismissal as any I have known. I touched my lips to her hand, a gesture which I could see pleased her. "Until then, Lady Porthlois."

And then I took my leave, wondering as I did so what the exact nature of Lady Porthlois's ailment might be, and why a woman confined to her mirror-ringed bed in a bucolic part of the shires should be wearing on her finger a ring of the Grand College of Magi, an organisation notably opposed to the admission of women.

∾∾

LATER that evening, the steward, Parch, and I found ourselves crouching in a bush and observing a dragon. As we hastily departed, I reflected that the beast I had seen did indeed possess all the characteristics of a laidly worm: it was legless, fireless, and watery in humour, most probably grown from a newt or sluggard-worm. The size, however, appalled me.

"Are they always that big?" I wondered aloud.

"I do not know." Parch shuddered. "The others, all those years ago, were reputedly not so large; but one, at least, appears to have been venomous."

"How deadly did it prove?"

"It dispatched one of the Queen's own knights."

By this, I knew, Parch meant one of the human knights attached to the Royal household, not one of Aoife's fairy kindred. Aoife liked to be surrounded by young gentlemen.

"The Queen sent a knight?" Porthlois had said nothing about this.

"No, no, he did not come from Her Majesty. He was the son of a local family, distant relatives of the duke, and visiting them. Naturally, he felt obliged to do something about the dragon."

"Yes. Young knights usually do."

"The consequences were hideous. It burned him with an acid slime."

"Nasty. I wonder if this is of the same kind?"

In the moonlight, Parch's round face bore an expression that suggested that he was not particularly interested in my biological speculations.

"No doubt. Lord Cygne, I think we should go back to the mansion now." Parch cast a nervous glance at the beast on the hill. There was little more to be gained from lingering, it was true. I could glean no sense that the dragon was particularly magically imbued, at least, not more so than usual. I'd come across cases in which they were predominantly supernatural, more than their souls conjured through the portals between this world and its dark twin, but this was just a large worm. A large, *hungry* worm, I reminded myself as a cow bellowed beyond the hill and fell abruptly silent.

On the way back, swiftly leaving the worm behind us, Parch cursed as a shadow ran through the cornfields to our left.

"What's the matter?"

"Damnable lecks," the steward grumbled. "Running riot in my corn."

"Do they do much damage?" There weren't many cornfields around Burnblack: it wasn't the land for it.

"Most certainly. They riffle the ripening grain, leach it of its vital substance, until it yields not flour but dust."

What with dragons preying on his flocks and corn-lecks poisoning the fields, the steward of Direfell had his work cut out. Parch's face grew yet more sour as I said, "What measures do you take against them?"

"The fields are warded, but somehow they always manage to evade them, no matter what I do."

"I will give the issue some consideration," I promised the disconsolate steward, as the Hall came into view. "There may be something that can be done, for lecks as well as for dragons."

MY reassurances to Parch had been simply that. I had been hired to deal with dragons, not unruly corn spirits, and so the main thrust of my deliberations over the next day was to prepare an antiworming spell.

Conjuring dragons is tough, but it's simple. If you cannot find their master, then dispatching them to their point of origin is also tough, also simple. Whereas a worm's soul, if one might call it such a thing, is brought through from the dark, to remove a worm from one's vicinity, one reverses the process. Once the animating force, the vital essence, is gone, the dragon itself will shrink back to its natural par-worm or newtlike state.

It was this that I proposed to do. To prepare for any magical procedure of this nature is exhaustive—and exhausting—work, and I thus made my requirements very clear to Porthlois.

"A room, set apart from any other. You need not worry about equipment, beyond a brazier—I have brought my own implements. But I shall need a measure of charcoal, if you have it, and also a black cockerel." This last was a relatively modern piece of magic, popular in France. I am not a man to turn to fads and fancies in the matter of necromantic practice, but occasionally even the French come up with something worthwhile, and experiments based upon a recently acquired Continental grimoire had convinced me that this could be useful.

Porthlois grew a little paler when I mentioned the cockerel.

"You plan to make a sacrifice?" he faltered. It never ceases to astound me how men accustomed to the butchery of their own cattle—and not infrequently, of one another in the course of battle—become as squeamish as maidens when confronted with what they imagine to be the bloodier side of the esoteric. I sighed.

"Not at all. Indeed, I trust it will not be necessary and that the bird will be strutting about your barnyard on the morrow as confidently as before. The cockerel is there as a safeguard, to direct eldritch forces from me should anything go awry. Unless, of course, you would prefer to dispense with the risk to the bird and have any dire entities fall upon a member of the household? No? I thought as much."

The black cockerel was waiting for me when I entered the chamber: a small attic annexe. I had not yet quite got my bearings in this maze of a mansion, but I estimated that this room lay not far from the mirrored gloom of Lady Porthlois's own chamber.

Interesting. Lord Porthlois had not taken the trouble to introduce me to his wife, and so, correspondingly, I had not seen fit to mention that we'd already met. An invisible presence, and yet, as unspoken influences often do, that intelligent bulk somehow seemed to dominate the proceedings in a way that I did not thus far comprehend.

Once within the chamber, I locked the door and sealed it magically behind me. No one could get in, and, perhaps more importantly, nothing could get out, either. The cockerel clucked nervously within its iron cage. I took a look out of the small window before warding that, as well.

The long summer evening had not yet drawn to a close, and a smoky dusk lay across the landscape. Just before the rise of the hills, I could see the cornfields, a paler expanse against the dark mass of beech wood. Sparks flitted amongst the stooks: lecks, perhaps, or something even more arcane. A thin moon hung above them upon its back, a sickle smile. It was not far off Lammas, and I could sense the thick tides of the land running sluggishly beneath the surface of my mind. Peasant magic is not for me— my path is the ceremonial one of necromancy—and yet it is irritatingly impossible in this faery-ruled realm to avoid the wheel of the seasons, their inevitable turn, and the nature of the days that they bring. I turned from the window and brought my attention back to the chamber.

A chalice, of black glass and old gold. A wand, with an amber tip. A small bottle of blood: my own, used in the conjuration of shucks. A knife, obsidian-handled.

I took the knife and, murmuring a familiar invocation, cut a circle in the air around me. Now, I stood in the centre of a circle, gleaming black-red.

I began the familiar conjuration of a shuck, dropping blood onto a glass, imbuing it with a snatched fragment of my own essence, concentrating hard upon the invocation. Within the hour, a shuck stood before me in the circle, congealing like fog. Crimson eyes glared from the baleful wedge of its head, and it shook itself once, as if rearranging itself into being.

"Go forth," I told it. "Go forth, and bring me a scale from the worm that coils around the hill." For a moment, I thought that the shuck might disobey me—far from the magical solidity of my own mansion, it had an unfamiliar aspect—but eventually, it gave another shake, and its dark dog shape bounded through the window and out upon the air.

I did not know whether it would be successful. I was forced to wait, watching through the eyes of the shuck as it ran through the cornfields, scattering the smaller spirits, heading for the hill. Once, passing by a hedge, a corn-leck sprang out at it: I glimpsed the sharp teeth, the little yellow eyes. But the leck thought better of it and fell back into the ripening corn.

When the shuck reached the worm, it paused, and I could feel it assessing its various opportunities. It came close to the tail, hunched close to the ground. But the worm sensed that something was amiss. It stirred uneasily, and its great head shifted above that of the shuck. I felt the shuck's sides heave in and out in a mimicry of breath. It sidled forward, towards the worm. Above, I once more saw that emerald glint of eye against the swimming summer stars. The shuck leaped, knowing caution but not fear: it was not, after all, a living thing, and its dissolution meant no more to its consciousness than the passing of a shadow. It snatched at the tail, and its jaws connected with a sudden, jarring sensation on gristle and bone. I started back, within the confines of the circle, and my elbow knocked against a candle. Cursing myself for my clumsiness, I righted the light. The circle had not been broken, but the shuck was in flight: leaping and bounding through the narrow lanes between the beech trees, already far from the hill.

Even all the way in Direfell, I heard the worm's hiss, like a star sizzling out. A moment later, snapped back by the thread of magic, the shuck stood in front of me. A single scale, blue-green as captured water, clung to its gaping jaw.

The conjuration of shucks is a lesser effort, a small part of magical acts. That this episode had drained me made me nervous, more so than I cared to admit. A wiser man might have rested before making the greater part of the spell; but wise men do not become magicians, and I was running out of time. On the stroke of midnight, I lit a candle of black fat, made sure the cockerel was safely in his cage within the circle, and placed the scale upon my tongue.

How to depict the Eldritch Realm, the world beyond the world, where the essences of dragons roam freely? It is far from the world of Earth, and far, too, from the Otherlands from which our rulers come: the faery realms of the Hollow Hills are still a part of our own world, after all. But the Eldritch Realm is otherwhere, a vast darkness shot with crimson light and the giant clouds which birth suns. I spun through a world of stars, not knowing whether I saw a constellation or the eye of some god. Presences too immense for me to comprehend swam past, as if within some infinite sea.

There are colours there for which we have no words, and a sense that one's spirit is stretched to the point of snapping. I have never dared to travel too far within the Eldritch Realm, and yet I had to find the point of origin of the worm: the residual element of its soul, which tied it to its home and so lent it its power. The scale took me, obliging, spiralling down into billows of aquamarine and jade, past sparkling jewelled cliffs and waterfalls of living crystal. There, at the bottom of a crag, was a tiny point of light with a thread snaking from it.

I knew how this was done. Find the start and pull back the thread, reeling it in like the capture of some monstrous fish. Unable to resist a tug from the Eldritch Realm, the worm's soul would recede, coiling back inwards, and ready to be tethered.

It was supposed to be relatively straightforward, or so I'd heard. But magicians are like fishermen: they lie about such things as ease and length. I would just have to give it a go. So, with the scale still resting in my spectral mouth like some unnatural tongue, I put my shimmering hand to the point of origin of the worm's soul and spoke the words to bring it back again.

You may not be entirely surprised to learn that I was not successful. Instead of reeling inwards, the spark that was the worm's soul clung to my hand and pulled. I found myself shooting back through the Eldritch Realm, with the heavy airs of Earth a palpable presence up ahead. I tried every incantation I could think of to break free, but without avail. As the wall that indicated the magical boundaries of Albion shot towards me, I had a sudden, unwelcome vision of what the immediate future was about to bring: myself, hurtling out of a summery sky and dropping beneath a worm's jaws. Attached to the line of its soul, I could not break free.

I crashed through the boundary and cried out, an infant reborn, as the air of my own world tore into my lungs. But it was not the dragon-infested hillside on which I found myself. Instead, it was the interior of Lady Porthlois's mirrored chamber.

This would not, I am sad to say, be the first time in which I'd proved to be an uninvited guest in some lady's boudoir. Sometimes it turned out rather better than anticipated, sometimes not. But my intentions in entering the room of Lady Porthlois were, on this occasion, entirely inadvertent, and I experienced a moment of wholly social panic.

I need not have worried. Her ladyship neither simpered, screamed, nor demanded an explanation. As I stumbled to my feet and fell back against the wall, I saw Lady Porthlois sitting up in bed. Her mouth and her eyes were wide open, and a blue-black light streamed from them, reverberating from the mirrors and illuminating the room like the interior of a thundercloud. Her fists were balled at her sides, and the chamber echoed with magic.

I see no shame in admitting that I tried to run. My efforts were, however, doomed. My movements resembled those of someone caught in a spider's web, a net of treacle in which magic ran so thick and closely packed that there was barely sufficient air to breathe. I fell to my knees, choking, and the magic picked me up and carried me to a nearby chest, made of oak banded with iron. I was deposited within it, the lid slammed shut, and there I lay, gasping for breath, while the spells of another mage boomed and crashed above my uncomprehending head.

EVENTUALLY, it ended. I felt the coming of dawn rather than witnessing it, for no light penetrated the depths of my box. But a true magician always knows what time of the day or night it might be: the presence of the decans of each hour change with their own curious precision as the wheel of the sun turns towards night and back again. Three o'clock, and all was not well. I was expecting my captor to open the lid and gloat over her prize; but she let me be, and that was more galling than anything. I was beginning to suspect that rather than being some special captive, I had simply gotten in her way.

During my time in the box, I had been able to get some measure of her magic, and this was unusual. I had met female magicians before, and some were powerful, some merely cunning. All illicit, borrowed power, of course, for the College will not train those of the female sex: the result of years of jealous rule by faery women, who know what sometimes mortal men do not—that the talent of the fair human sex outstrips that of the male. Small wonder that Aoife and her predecessors have not been able to face the competition. But as it is, the College guards its secrets with close attention: Lady Porthlois wore a mage's ring, but where had she obtained it? From a father, or from her husband? It could not be hers by right, and yet her magic was, I sensed, intimately bound together with the ring, just as mine was bound to the old silver band bearing the black dog's seal, which I wore upon my third finger. And there was something else besides, an immensity of power reaching far beyond the normal skills of mortal humanity. A stout, sick woman in a mob-cap, confined to her bed? Lady Porthlois was far more than this. One never likes to think that one might have met one's match; but lying there in the dark oak box, surrounded by the odours of magic and cedar, I was beginning to feel that this hour, for me, may finally have come.

I lay there for another four hours, listening intently to the sounds from the chamber beyond: a heavy creaking, as if of great steps upon ancient floorboards. I'd already run through all the incantations I could think of, and it would have been just as efficacious if I'd babbled nursery rhymes: it wasn't just that nothing had worked, as that my efforts simply held no power at all. Nothing I'd ever encountered, not even the Faery Queen herself, had so comprehensively stripped me of my abilities.

So I remained, alternatively seething and plotting, until a faint tapping on the lid of the box attracted my attention. I wasn't able to speak—she had taken that, too—but I uttered a grunt, and it seemed that was enough. The lid opened, letting in a shaft of blinding sunlight. It made me blink, but I knew her all the same: Porthlois's eldest daughter, Rose.

As soon as she saw me, she gave a gasp of horror.

"Lord Cygne!"

"Indeed." As if the sunlight had brought back my powers, I could speak again. Experimentally, I flexed small magical muscles. All seemed once more intact.

"Whatever are you doing in that chest?"

I hauled myself out of the box with what I felt to be a lamentable lack of dignity. "Where are we?"

The chest was no longer in Lady Porthlois's mirrored chamber. Instead, I looked out onto a cobwebbed cellar, near a rack on which reposed many bottles of wine. Rose was clutching one of them, like a club.

"In the wine cellar. My father sent me to fetch a bottle of porter, for luncheon. We were wondering where you were."

"How did you know someone was in the box?"

"I–" Rose seemed somewhat at a loss. "The chest should not be here. It belongs upstairs; my stepmother asked Parch to have it moved this morning. I confess, I did not think anyone might be inside it: I was merely curious. What on earth were you doing within it?"

"I think," I said grimly, "that it is time I spoke to your father."

The Duke of Direfell seemed utterly at a loss when I recounted recent events.

"But what does this all mean? You sought a dragon, and found my wife?"

"I will tell you what I believe to be the case," I said. I poured us both another glass of the porter: I needed it after my ordeal, and Richard's own was just beginning. "I went in search of the origin point of the dragon's soul, to bring it fully back into what we call the Eldritch Realm, there to secure it. Once this is done, the body inhabited by the draconian spirit will simply dwindle, becoming perhaps no more than a newt, or a worm in truth. This is normally," I remarked with some grandeur, "a simple enough procedure, both in its concept and its execution. As I instructed your steward, had anything attempted to return with me, it would have passed into the body of the black cockerel and slain it, rather than latching on to I myself. However, on this occasion, something went badly awry. Rather than dispatching the worm's soul to its original home, I found my spirit returning out of the sanctuary of a protective circle and being hauled into the presence of your wife."

"My wife has been very ill," Richard said, frowning. "She has a case of malignant dropsy, which the doctors seems unable to cure. She cannot even stir from her bed. We have tried everything. But she is a woman of the best heart and soul, despite her ailments. I cannot believe that she is some kind of—well, *what*?"

"She wears a mage's ring," I told him.

"That signet ring? That is a legacy of her poor father, who died in a pilgrimage to the Outer Isles."

It was my turn to frown. "Her father was a devotee of the island gods?"

"Quite so. His ancestors came from the furthest north of Albion; sea priests of a cult of Manannan mac Lir."

"Odd, that a son of such a family should end up here in these midlands. We must be further from the coast than any other point of Albion."

"This is what my wife has told me, and I see no need to doubt her word." The duke paused and looked mournful. "You see, she is the cousin of my first spouse."

"Indeed so?" I tried to look encouraging, and he continued. "My beautiful Sara . . . Alas, she died in a plague of the yellow flux, several years ago, leaving me with three small daughters. They needed a mother, and Ilyris—the current Lady Porthlois—was the nearest female relative."

"So you married her. A pragmatic solution."

"It was not simply for the sake of the girls," the duke protested. "At that time, Ilyris may not have been the beauty that her cousin was, but she was a handsome woman all the same—of mature years, it is true, but nonetheless widely admired. It is only since the dropsy came upon her that she has become as she is now."

"And her character?"

"Firm, unyielding on matters of principle, intelligent. We spoke little of the supernatural—I have an aversion to such matters—but I believe her understanding to be considerable, as a consequence of her ancestry."

"An ancestry which was shared by the first lady Porthlois?" I remarked.

A series of possibilities was beginning to creep through my mind, which was busy sorting, sifting, sieving hypotheses . . .

"No—the sea priest was Ilyris's father, whereas Sara was on the maternal side. A very old family. They have been in this area for generations—far longer than even my own family. Cygne, what must we do?" He sounded quite pathetic. I could not entirely blame him. "My wife is a monster, my daughters are in danger—what can be done?"

I stood up and drained the glass of porter. "We must act," I said. "I have a dragon to slay."

Returning the dragon to its point of origin had proved such a significant failure that I decided to resort to cruder measures. I informed the duke of my plans, and he paled.

"But—that would be using her as bait!"

"Quite so. But you must understand that these are desperate times. Your wife has absorbed into herself a draconian spirit. Despite any protestations she might have made to the contrary when in possession of her right senses, the brunt of her anger will shortly fall upon her stepchildren. Dragons," I said glibly, "are territorial creatures, and greatly jealous. Your wife's reasoning is that of a beast—a cunning beast, it is true, but a beast nonetheless. To her mind, once the children are removed, she can begin to breed."

"A hideous prospect!"

"Quite so. However, we cannot at present tackle her in her own chamber. Your comment that she has not left her bed since the illness convinces me that this is the seat of her power. She is too entrenched there—and so we must lure her out. A combination of your eldest daughter and myself might prove sufficient, if I can convince Ilyris that I have changed sides, as it were, and have her own best interests at heart."

"You intend to tell her that you will aid her? Will she believe that?"

"Magicians are renowned for their desire for power. I shall put it to her that with you and your heirs out of the way, she and I can assume the authority of Direfell Hall. Once she has crept forth from her chamber—her seat of power—she will be vulnerable to attack."

The duke gave a reluctant nod. "It is risky—but as you say, this is a desperate situation. However, you will understand that I need to be nearby, in order to protect Rose."

"I should expect nothing less."

ROSE eagerly agreed, and her indignation was considerable. "I always *knew* it," she told me. "Her jealousy of my beloved mother knew no bounds. No doubt she inserted herself into this household in order to usurp my mother's position." She lowered her voice, even more bitterly. "I should not be surprised if she had contributed to my mother's death by the use of her filthy powers."

"Nothing would surprise me at this juncture."

Due to my own incarceration, it was now close to three in the afternoon, and even granted the long summer evenings, there was no time to be lost. With care, I bound Rose's hands and led her upstairs, followed by her father, and, at a safe distance, the quavering Parch. Then I knocked on the door of Lady Porthlois's chamber.

There was no reply. "Madam? Are you within?" I asked sharply. "I know you to be there, in whatever form you have assumed. I have a proposition for you!"

Still no answer, so I continued with my proposal. At its end, I stole a glance at Rose. Her eyes were closed, and she was whispering. A prayer, no doubt. There was a moment of silence from within the chamber, then a sudden flurry of rustling motion behind the door. A minute later the door was flung open, and Lady Porthlois came across the threshold in a rush. Despite her bulk, which I could now see included a bulbous, scaly tail, she moved with appalling speed. Beneath the incongruous mob-cap, the indigo light of the Eldritch Realm still streamed from her eyes like lamps, and she was hissing.

"Now!" I cried, and leaped forward to thrust Rose into her stepmother's path. The duke shouted out a protest, and I spun, knocking his sword aside. Parch, demonstrating a lamentable lack of loyalty to his employer, bolted down the stairs as I stuck out a foot and tripped Richard so that he sprawled at my feet.

Rose screamed, a thin, whistling sound. Ilyris turned, opened her mouth, and emanated a beam of blue light. As a trained mage, I could hear the incantation behind it, but I doubt that Richard did. It struck Rose in the middle of her breast and clung like watery fire. I watched as it spread across the shrieking girl, encompassing her limbs and, at last, her head. Ilyris shut her mouth with an audible snap. As the light faded, so Rose withered, the golden girl shrivelling into a gaunt thing, all bones and claws, with a cluster of sharp teeth. Only the mass of hair remained. Richard made an inarticulate sound. Ripping aside its bonds, the corn-leck sprang at me, snarling. It bowled me over and we both fell down the stairs, struggling. When we reached the bottom, I hit the landing with a force that jarred my spine and left me momentarily stunned. I had a sudden glimpse of the gaping jaws and tiny yellow eyes, and then it was gone in a gush of green blood as the Duke of Direfell struck off his eldest daughter's head.

ೞ

"HOW long have you known?" I asked Ilyris, much later. The body of the corn-leck had been removed to the stables. I had taken a much-needed bath. Richard's remaining children had been placed under close confinement, and the duke himself had retired to his chamber, to consider and to mourn.

Without the bulk of her borrowed spirit, Ilyris proved to be a large but firm-bodied woman, with assured movements. She now sat, twisting her father's ring between her long fingers. Her face was pinched with exhaustion. "Ever since I was a girl. My father married into the family, you understand, and his clan were sea people. He knew little of the earth spirits, the corn-lecks and harvest wights. His own wife, my mother, had none of the family secret—she was human through and through. But her *sister*—Sara's mother—was even more of a leck than the thing you have just seen. We rarely saw her, except for glimpses. She lived in the fields. Sara herself was lovely, but, as I told you, she had a wearisome personality. She died of natural causes, in case you're wondering." Ilyris passed a hand across her broad brow. "I wasn't lying when I told you that I was fond of the children. They are my family, after all. I was happy to marry Richard, to look after them, and they were sweet little girls. But when Rose turned thirteen, her heritage began to make itself felt. She started spending more and more time outside. I caught her coming in at dawn; she wore wildness like a cloak. The crops began to fail, because there was no one to teach Rose how to regulate her powers, and she took too much from the land. Then one of the calves was found dead, with bite marks in its throat. I tried talking to her, but she would have none of it—she spat that I had stolen her father and would pay. When I attempted to raise the subject with Richard, he simply would not listen. It was too late, and I knew that I had to act. But Rose had her mother's magic—the warding powers that lecks use to keep the territory of their fields. She shut me in this chamber, and I could not get out—you understand that I have some magic, but not enough. I am human, after all, and *she* was not. I tried to reflect Rose's magic back to her with the use of the mirrors, but it did not work. Yet my father was a priest, and I still possessed his grimoire. So I called upon a dragonspell that allowed me to bring through a spirit: I held part of its soul within myself, while the dragon grew from a worm on the hill. I governed its movements, made sure that it preyed upon the lecks, and the occasional sheep. Never humans. But I was aiming it at Rose—when the dragon should be fully grown, I planned to bring it here."

"A bold but dangerous plan!"

Ilyris gave a weary nod. "And so it proved. My body was not strong enough to contain the dragon's spirit, even in part. I told Richard that I had dropsy. If you had not acted when you did, I would probably have become a monster. I am sorry, by the way, that I trapped you in the box. I thought you were acting against me."

"I was. But there were too many anomalies. Eventually, I configured the truth."

"And I am grateful. You have probably saved my life and that of my husband."

"What will happen to the remaining girls?"

"Richard has said that he will contact the Court, and they will send a mage to bring the children into captivity. It is too soon to tell if they will take the same path as their sister, but we cannot risk simply releasing them into the fields."

"I wish you well," I said, and meant it.

ฅ৯

RIDING home, the summer sun lay upon the fields in sheaves of gold, as heavy as corn. I did not see anything dodging behind the stooks, nor hiding in the green hedges, but I had no doubt that they were there. I had gained both friends and enemies, not unusual for a mage. At the crest of a hill, I reined in my mare and looked back. Direfell sat in a pool of sun, its harsh edges softened by light. Across the vale, the dragon's hill was still slightly ridged. Somewhere upon it was a tiny, bewildered worm, dreaming of greater things. A metaphor for the human condition? Perhaps, but such philosophical speculations rarely lead to a positive outcome. I turned the mare's head around and rode for home, under the sun.

Oakland Dragon Blues

Peter S. Beagle

A policeman is sworn to protect and serve. But that "protect" part can get a little compli-cated when mythological creatures are involved . . .

Peter S. Beagle was born in New York City in 1939. Although not prolific by genre standards, he has published a number of well-received fantasy novels, at least two of which, A Fine and Private Place and The Last Unicorn, are now considered to be classics of the genre. In fact, Beagle may be the most successful writer of lyrical and evocative mod-ern fantasy since Bradbury. He has won the Locus Award and two Mythopoeic Fantasy Awards, as well as having often been a finalist for the World Fantasy Award. Beagle's other books include the novels The Folk of the Air; The Innkeeper's Song; Tamsin; and a popular autobiographical travel book, I See by My Outfit. His short fiction has ap-peared in places as varied as the Magazine of Fantasy & Science Fiction, the Atlantic Monthly, and Seventeen, and has been collected in Giant Bones, The Rhinoceros Who Quoted Nietzsche and Other Odd Acquaintances, The Line Between, Strange Roads, We Never Talk About My Brother, and Mirror Kingdoms. He won the Hugo Award in 2006 and the Nebula Award in 2007 for his story "Two Hearts." His produced screenplays include the animated versions of The Lord of the Rings and The Last Unicorn, and he has two new novels—Summerlong and I'm Afraid You've Got Dragons—plus several new story collections and nonfiction books scheduled for re-lease in 2009 and 2010.

"I am happy to report," Officer Levinsky said to Officer Guerra, point-ing to the dragon sprawled across the Telegraph and 51st Street in-tersection, "that this one is all yours. I've been off shift for exactly seven minutes, waiting for your ass to get here. Have a nice day."

Guerra stared, paling visibly under his brown skin. Traffic was backed up in all four directions: horns were honking as madly as car alarms, drivers were screaming hysterically—though none, he noticed, were getting out of their cars—and a five-man road crew, their drills, hoses, sawhorses and warning signs scattered by a single swing of the dragon's tail, were adding their bellows to the din. The dragon paid no attention to any of it, but regarded the two policemen out of half-closed eyes, resting its head on its long-clawed front feet, and every now and then burping feeble, dingy flames. It didn't look well.

"How long's it been here?" Guerra asked weakly.

Levinsky consulted his watch again. "Thirty-one minutes. Just plopped out of the sky—damn miracle it didn't crush somebody's car, flatten a pedestrian. Been lying there ever since, just like that."

"Well, you called it in, right?" Guerra wondered what the police code for a dragon in the intersection would be.

Levinsky looked at him as though he had suggested a fast game of one-on-one with an open manhole. "You *are* out of your mind—I always thought so. No, I didn't call it in, and if you have the sense of a chinch bug, you won't either. Just get rid of it, I'm out of here. Enjoy, Guerra."

Levinsky's patrol car was parked on the far side of the intersection. He skirted the dragon's tail cautiously, got in the car, slapped on his siren—for pure emotional relief, Guerra thought—and was gone, leaving Guerra scratching his buzz-cut head, facing both a growing traffic jam and a creature out of fairy tales, whose red eyes, streaked with pale yellow, like the eyes of very old men, were watching him almost sleepily, totally uninterested in whatever he chose to do. But watching, all the same.

The furious chaos of the horns being harder on Guerra's normally placid nerves than the existence of dragons, he walked over to the beast, and said, from a respectful distance, "Sir, you're blocking traffic, and I'm going to have to ask you to move along. Otherwise you're looking at a major citation here."

When the dragon did not respond, he said it again in Spanish; then drew a deep breath and started over in Russian, having taken a course that winter in order to cope with a new influx of immigrants. The dragon interrupted him with a brief hiccup of oily, sulphurous flame halfway through. In a rusty, raspy voice with a faint accent that was none of the ones Guerra knew, it said, "Don't start."

Guerra rested his hand lightly on the butt of the pistol that he was immensely proud of never having fired during his eight years on the Oakland

police force, except for his regular practice sessions and annual recertifi-
cations at the Davis Street Range. He said, "Sir, I am not trying to start
anything with you—I'm having enough trouble just believing in you. But
I've got to get you out of this intersection before somebody gets hurt. I
mean, look at all those people, listen to those damn *horns*." The racket
was already giving him a headache behind his eyes. "You think you could
maybe step over here to the curb, we'll talk about it? That'd work out much
better for both of us, don't you think?"

The dragon raised its head and favored him with a long, considering
stare. "I don't know. I like this place about as well as I like anyplace in
this world, which is not at all. Why should I make things easier for you?
Nobody ever cares about making anything easier for *me*, let me tell you."

Guerra's greatest ambition in law enforcement was to become a hostage negotiator. He had been studying the technique on and off for most
of his tenure on the force, both on-site and through attending lectures
and reading everything he could find on the subject. The lecturers and the
books had a good deal to say concerning hostage-takers' tendency to self-
pity. He said patiently to the dragon, "Well, I'm really trying to do exactly
that. Let's get acquainted, huh? I'm Officer Guerra—Michael Guerra, but
people mostly call me Mike-O, I don't know why. What's your name?"
*Always get on a first-name basis, as early as possible. It makes you two
human beings together—you'll be amazed at the difference it makes.* Now
if only one of those books had ever covered the fine points of negotiating
with a burping mythological predator.

"You couldn't pronounce it," the dragon replied. "And if you tried,
you'd hurt yourself." But it rose to its feet with what seemed to Guerra an
intense and even painful effort, and with some trepidation he led it away
from the intersection to the side street where he had parked his blue-and-
white patrol car. The traffic started up again before they were all the way
across, and if people went on honking and cursing, still there were many
who leaned out of their windows to applaud him. One driver shouted jovi-
ally, "Put the cuffs on him!" while another yelled, "Illegal parking—get
the boot!" The dragon half lumbered, half slithered beside Guerra as se-
dately as though it were on a leash; but every so often it cocked a red eye
sideways at him, like a wicked bird, and Guerra shivered with what felt
like ancestral memory. *These guys used to hunt us like rabbits. I know
they did.*

The phone at his waist made an irritable sound and rattled against
his belt buckle. He nodded to the dragon, grunted "My boss, I better take

this," and heard Lieutenant Kunkel's nasal drone demanding, "Guerra, you there? Guerra, what the hell is going on up in Little Ethiopia?" Lieutenant Kunkel fully expected Eritrean rebels to stage shoot-outs in Oakland sometime within the week.

"Big, nasty traffic jam, Lieutenant," Guerra answered, consciously keeping his voice light and level, even with a dragon sniffing disdainfully at his patrol car. "All under control now, no problem."

"Yeah, well, we've been getting a bunch of calls about I don't know what, some sort of crazy dragon, UFO, whatever. You know anything about this shit?"

"Uh," Guerra said. "Uh, no, Lieutenant, it's just the time of day, you know? Rush hour, traffic gets tied up, people get a little crazy, they start seeing stuff. Mass hysteria, shared hallucinations, it's real common. They got books about it."

Lieutenant Kunkel's reaction to the concept of shared hallucinations was not at first audible. Then it became audible, but not comprehensible. Finally coherent, he drew on a vocabulary that impressed Guerra so powerfully for its range and expressiveness that at a certain point, phone gripped between his ear and his shoulder, he dug out his notebook and started writing down the choicest words and phrases he caught. If anything, Guerra was a great believer in self-improvement.

The lieutenant finally hung up, and Guerra put the book back in his pocket and said to the dragon, "Okay. He's cool. You just go on away now, go on home, back wherever you . . . well, wherever, and we'll say no more about it. And you have an extra-nice day, hear?"

The dragon did not answer, but leaned against his car, considering him out of its strange red-and-yellow eyes. Huge as the creature was—Guerra had nothing but military vehicles for comparison—he thought it must be a very old dragon, for the scales on its body were a dull greenish black, and its front claws were worn and blunt, no sharper than a turtle's. The long low purple crest running along its back from ears to tail tip was torn in several places, and lay limp and prideless. The spikes at the end of its tail were all broken off short; and in spite of the occasional wheeze of fire, there was a rattle in the dragon's breath, as though it were rusty inside. He supposed the great purple wings worked: it was hard to see them clearly, folded back along the body as they were, but they too looked . . . *ratty*, for lack of a better word. Spontaneously, he blurted out, "You've had kind of a rough time, huh? I get that."

"Do you?" The dragon's black lips twitched, and for a moment Guerra thought absurdly that it was going to cry. "Do you indeed, Mike-O? Do you *get* that my back's killing me—that it aches all the time, right there, behind the hump, because of the beating it takes walking the black iron roads of this world? Do you *get* that the smell of your streets—even your streams, your rivers, your bay—is more than I can bear? That your people taste like clocks and coal oil, and your children are bitter as silver? The children used to be the best eating of all, better than antelope, better than wild geese, but now I just can't bring myself to touch another one of them. Oh, it's been dogs and cats and mangy little squirrels for months, *years*— and when you think how I used to dine off steamed knight, knight on the half shell, broiled in his own armor with all the natural juices, oh . . . excuse me, excuse me, I'm sorry . . ."

And, rather to Guerra's horror, the dragon *did* begin to cry. He wept very softly, with his eyes closed and his head lowered, his emerald-green tears smelling faintly like gunpowder. Guerra said, "Hey. Hey, listen, don't do that. Please. Don't cry, okay?"

The dragon sniffled, but it lifted its head again to regard him in some wonder. Surprisingly severe, it said, "You are a witness to the rarest sight in the world—a dragon in tears—and all you can say is *don't do that*? I don't *get* you people at all." But it did stop crying; it even made a sound like rustling ashes, which Guerra thought might be a chuckle. It said, "Or did I embarrass you, Mike-O?"

"Listen," Guerra said again. "Listen, you've got to get out of here. There's going to be rumors for days, but I'll cover with the lieutenant, who-ever, whatever I have to say. Just *go*, okay?" He hesitated for a moment, and then added, "Please?"

The dragon licked forlornly at its own tears with its broad forked tongue. "I'm tired, Mike-O. You have no idea how tired I am. I have one task to complete in this desolate world of yours, and then I'm done with it forever. And since I'll never, never find my way back to my own world again, what difference does anything make? Afterward . . . *afterward*, you and your boss can shoot me, take me to prison, put me in a zoo . . . what wretched difference? I just don't care anymore."

"No," Guerra said. "Look, I'll tell you the truth, I do not want to be the guy who brings you in. For starters, it'll mean more reports, more damn *bookkeeping* than I've ever seen in my life. I *hate* writing reports. And besides that . . . yeah, I guess I'd be famous for a while—fifteen min-utes, like they say. The cop who caught the dragon . . . newspapers, big TV shows, fine and dandy, maybe I'd even meet some girls that way. But once it all died down, that's all I'd ever be, the guy who had the thing on the street with the dragon. You think that's a résumé for somebody wants to be a hostage negotiator? I don't think so."

The dragon was listening to him attentively, though with a slightly puzzled air. Guerra said, "Anyway, what's this about finding your way back to your own world? How'd you get here in the first place?"

"How did I *get* here?" To Guerra's astonishment and alarm, the dragon rumbled croupily, deep in its chest, and the ragged crest stood up as best it could, while the head seemed to cock back on its neck like the hammer on a pistol. A brief burst of fire shot from the fang-studded mouth, making Guerra scramble aside.

"That's easy," it said, tapping its claws on the asphalt. "I got written here."

Guerra was not at all sure that he had heard correctly. "You got . . . *written?*"

"Written *and* written out," the dragon rasped bitterly. "The author put me in his book right at the beginning, and then he changed his mind. Went back, redid the whole book, and *phhffttt.*" More fire. Guerra ducked again, barely in time. "Gone, just like that. Not one line left—and I had some good ones, whole paragraphs. All gone."

"I'm having a very hard time with this," Guerra said. "So you're in a book—"

"*Was.* I *was* in a book—"

"— and now you're not. But you're real all the same, blocking traffic, breathing fire—"

"Art is a remarkable creative force," the dragon said. "I exist because a man made up a story." It mentioned the writer's name, which was not one Guerra knew. "I'm stranded here, loose and wandering in his world because he decided not to write about me after all." It bared double rows of worn but quite serviceable teeth in a highly unpleasant grin. "But I'm real, I'm here, and I'm looking for him. Followed him from one place to another for years—the man does move around—and finally tracked him to this Oakland. I don't know exactly where he lives, but I'll find him. And when I do he is going to be one crispy author, believe me." It snorted in anticipation, but Guerra had already taken refuge behind the patrol car. The dragon said, "I told you, after that I don't care what happens to me. I can't ever get home, so what does it matter?"

Its voice trembled a little on the last words, and Guerra worried that it might be about to start weeping again. He edged cautiously out from the shelter of the car and said, "Well, you sure as hell won't get back home if you fry up the one guy who maybe can help you. You ever think about that?"

The long neck swiveled, and the dragon stared at him, its eyes red and yellow, like hunters' moons. Guerra said, "He lives in Oakland, this writer? Okay, I'll find out the address—that's one thing cops are really good at, tracing people's addresses—"

"And you'll *tell* me?" The dragon's whole vast body was quivering with eagerness. "You would do that?"

"No," Guerra said flatly. "Not for a minute. Because you'd zip right off after him, and be picking your teeth by the time I got off my shift. So you're going to wait until I'm done here, and we'll find him together. Deal?" The dragon was clearly dubious. Guerra said, "Deal—or I won't give you his address, but I *will* tell him you're looking for him. And he'll move again, sure as hell—*I* would. Think about it."

The dragon thought. At last it sighed deeply, exhaling tear-damp ashes, and rumbled, "Very well. I'll wait for you on that sign." Guerra watched in fascination as the shabby purple wings unfolded. Worn claws scrabbling on the sidewalk, the beast took a few running steps before it lifted into the air. A moment later it landed neatly on the top frame of a billboard advertising a movie that apparently had a mermaid, a vampire and a giant octopus in the cast. The dragon posed there all during Guerra's shift, looking like part of the promotion, and if it moved even an inch he never saw it.

The road crew was back at work, and the intersection was in serious need of a patrolman. Both streets were torn up, the traffic lights were all off, and Guerra had his hands full beckoning cars forward and holding them up, keeping drivers away from closed-off lanes and guiding them around potholes. It kept his mind, as nothing else could have, almost completely off the dragon; although he did manage, during a comparative lull, to call in for the current address of the writer who had carelessly created the creature and then forgotten about it. *Like God, maybe,* Guerra thought, then decided he might not mention that notion to Father Fabros on Sunday.

His shift ended in twilight; the traffic had noticeably thinned by then, and he felt comfortable turning the intersection over to Officer Colasanto, who was barely in his second year. Walking to his car, Guerra gestured to the dragon, and it promptly took off from the billboard, climbing toward the night clouds with a speed and elegance he had never imagined from those ragged wings and age-tarnished body. Once again the bone-image came to him of such creatures stooping from the sky at speeds his ancestors could not have comprehended before it was too late. He shivered, and hurriedly got into the patrol car.

He checked in at the police station, joking amiably with friends about the morning's dragon alarm—neither Lieutenant Kunkel nor Officer Levinsky was present—changed into civilian clothes, and hurried back out, anxious lest the dragon should become anxious. But he saw no sign of it, and had to assume that it was following him beyond his sight, hungry enough for revenge that it was not likely to lose track of him. Not for the first time, Guerra wondered what had possessed him to take sides in this mess, and what side he was actually on.

The dragon's author lived in North Berkeley, past the chic restaurants of the Gourmet Ghetto, and on out into the classic older houses, "full of character," as the real-estate agents liked to put it, if a little short on reliable plumbing. Guerra found the house easily enough—it had two stories, a slightly threadbare lawn and a tentative garden—and pulled into the driveway, expecting the dragon, in its fury and fervency, to land beside him before he was out of the car. But he only glimpsed it once, far above him, circling with chilling patience between the clouds. A motion-detector floodlight came on as Guerra walked up the driveway and rang the bell.

The author answered with surprising quickness. He was a middle-sized, undistinguished-looking man: bearded, wearing glasses, and clad in jeans, an old sweatshirt, and sneakers that had clearly been through two or three major civil conflicts. He blinked at Guerra and said "Hi? What can I do for you?"

Guerra showed his badge. "Sir, I'm Officer Michael Guerra, Oakland Police, and I need to speak with you for a moment." He felt himself blushing absurdly, and was glad that the light was gone.

The author was sensibly wary, checking Guerra's badge carefully before answering. "I've paid that Jack London Square parking ticket."

Guerra had just started to say, "This isn't exactly a police matter," when, with a terrifyingly silent rush—the only sound was the soft whistle of wind through the folded wings—the dragon landed in the tentative garden and hissed, "Remember me, storyteller? Scribe, singer, sorcerer—*remember me*?"

The author froze where he stood in the doorway, neither able to come forward nor run back into his house. He whispered, "No. You can't be here . . . you can't *be* . . ." He did not seem able to close his mouth, and he was hugging himself, as though for protection.

The dragon sneered foul-smelling flames. "Come closer, you hairy hot pocket. I'd rather not singe your nice house when I incinerate you."

Guerra said, "Wait a minute now, just a minute. We didn't talk about any incineration. No incineration here."

The dragon looked at him for the first time since it had landed. It said, "Stop me."

Guerra's gun was in the car, but even if he could have reached it, it would have been no more practical use than a spitball. His mouth was dry, and his throat hurt.

Remarkably, the author stood his ground. He spoke directly to the dragon, saying, "I didn't write you out of the book. I dropped the damn book altogether—I didn't know how to write it, and I was making an unholy mess out of it. So I dropped a lot of people, not just you. How come you're the only one hunting me down and threatening my life? Why is this all about *you*?"

The dragon's head swooped low enough to be almost on a level with the writer's, and so close that a bit of his beard did get singed. But its voice was colder than Guerra had ever heard it when it said, "Because you wrote enough life into me that I deserved more. I deserved a *resolution*—even if you killed me off in the end, that would have been *something*—and when I didn't get it, I still had this leftover life, and no world to *live* it in. So of course, of *course* I have been trapped in your world ever since—miserable dungheap that it is, there is no other place for me to exist. And no other emotion, out of all I might have had . . . but revenge."

Its head and neck cocked back then, as Guerra had seen them do before, and he turned and sprinted for his car and the useless gun. But he tripped over a loose brick from the garden border, fell full length, and lay half-stunned, hearing—to his dazed surprise—the voice of the author saying commandingly, "Hold it, just hold the phone here, before you go sautéing people. You're angry because I didn't create a suitable world for you, is that it?"

The dragon did not answer immediately. Guerra struggled wearily to his feet, looking back and forth between the house and his car. A family across the street—a man in a bathrobe, his small Indian wife in a sari, and a young boy wearing Spider-Man pajamas—were standing barefoot on their own lawn, clearly staring at the dragon. The man called out, loudly but hesitantly, "Hey, you okay over there?"

Guerra was still trying to decide on his response, when he heard the dragon say in a different tone, "No, I'm angry because you did. You made up a fairy tale that I belonged in, and then you destroyed it and left me *outside*, in this terrible, terrible place that I can't escape. And I never *will* escape it, I know, except by dying, and we dragons live such a long time. But if I avenge myself now, as you deserve"—it swung its head briefly toward Guerra—"then policemen like *him* will in turn kill me, sooner or later. And it will be over."

"SWAT teams," Guerra said, trying to sound stern and ominous. "Whole patrols. Divisions. Bomb Squad, FBI, the Air Force—"

"Hold it!" The author was very nearly shouting. "That's it? That's your problem with me?" He held his hands up, palms out, looked at them, and began rubbing them together. "Give me five minutes—*three* minutes—I'll be right back, I'll just get something. Right back."

He turned and started toward the house, but a fireball neatly seared a stripe of lawn at his feet. The dragon said, "You stay. *He* goes."

The author looked down at the crumbling, crackling grass, then turned to Guerra. "Through the door—sharp left—turn right, straight through the other door. My office. Notebook beside the laptop, Betty Grable on the cover, you can't miss it. Grab that, grab a couple of pens, get back out here before he trashes the landscaping. You know how much it cost to put this lawn in?"

But Guerra was already at the door. He hurried through to the office as directed, snatched up notebook and pens, paused for a moment to marvel at the books and electronics, the boxes of paper and printer cartridges, the alphabetized manuscripts in their separate folders—*this is how they live, this is a real writer's workroom*—and raced back out to the lawn, where the author and his creation were eyeing each other in wary silence. Guerra was relieved to see that the dragon's head and neck were relaxed from the attack position, and horrified to realize that the neighboring family—with the addition of a smaller boy in Batman pajamas—were now standing at the edge of their lawn, while a girl coasting on in-line skates was gliding up the driveway, and a large man with a pipe in his mouth, who looked like a retired colonel in a movie, was striding across the street as though to direct the catapults. The larger of the two boys was telling his brother learnedly, "That's a *dragon*. I saw one on the Discovery Channel." *I could have switched shifts with Levinsky, like we were talking about the other day . . .*

"Thanks," the author said, taking the writing materials from Guerra's hands. Ignoring the growing assembly on his lawn and his driveway, and the cricketlike chirps of cell-phone cameras, he sat down cross-legged on his own doorstep and propped the open notebook on his knee. "I did this in Macy's window one time," he remarked conversationally. "For the ERA or the EPA, one of those." He rubbed his chin, muttered something inaudible, and began to write, reading aloud as he went.

Once upon a time, in a faraway place, there lived a king whose daughter fell in love with a common gardener. The king was so outraged at this that he imprisoned the princess in a high tower and set a ferocious dragon to guard her.

The dragon slithered closer and craned its neck, reading over his shoulder. The author continued.

But the dragon, fierce as it was, had a tender, sympathetic heart, greatly unlike the rest of its kind—

"I don't like that," the dragon interrupted. " 'The rest of its kind'—it sounds condescending, even a touch bigoted. Why not just say *family*, or 'the rest of its kinfolk'? Much better tone, *I* think."

"Everybody's a critic," the author mumbled. "All right, all right, *kinfolk*, then." He made the correction. The man who looked like a colonel was standing beside another man who looked like a hungover Santa Claus, and the Indian mother was gripping her sons' shoulders to hold both boys exactly where they were.

The author continued.

Now the dragon could not set the princess free against her father's orders, but it did what it could for her. It kept her company, engaging her in cheerful, intelligent conversation, comforting her when she was sad, and even singing to her in her most depressed moments, which would always make her laugh, since dragons are not very good singers.

He hesitated, as though expecting some argument or annoyed comment from the dragon, but it only nodded in agreement. "True enough. We love music, but not one of us can sing a lick. Go on." Its voice was surprisingly slow and thoughtful, and—so it seemed to Guerra—almost dreamy.

But what the princess valued most, of all the dragon's kindnesses, was that when her gardener lover had managed to smuggle a letter

to her, the dragon would at once fly up to her barred window and
hover there, like any butterfly or hummingbird, to pass the letter
to her and wait to carry her rapturous reply.

He paused again and looked up at the dragon. "You won't mind if I
make you a little bit smaller? Just for the sake of the hovering?"

With a graciousness that Guerra would never have expected, the
dragon replied, "You're the artist—do as you think best." After a moment
it added, a bit shyly, "If you wanted, you could do something with my
crest. That would be all right."

"Easy. Might touch up your scales some, too—nobody's quite as
young as they used to be." He worked on, still reading softly, as much to
himself as to them. What struck Guerra most forcefully was that his was
very nearly the only voice in the crowded darkness, except for one of the
small boys—"Dragons *eat* people! He eat those men *up*!"—and the roller-
skating girl sighing to a boy who had joined her, "This is *so* cool . . ."
Guerra gestured at them all to move back, but no one appeared to notice. If anything, they seemed to be leaning in, somehow yearning toward
the magnificently menacing figure that loomed over the man who still sat
tailor-fashion, telling it a story about itself.

Now when the king came to visit his imprisoned child—which, to
be as fair to him as possible, he did quite often—the dragon would
always put on his most terrifying appearance and strut around the
foot of the tower, to show the king how well he was fulfilling his
charge . . .

To Guerra's astonishment the dragon appeared not only somewhat
smaller, but younger as well. Before his eyes, slowly but plainly, the faded
greenish-black scales were regaining their original dark-green glitter, and
the tattered crest and drab, frayed wings were springing back to proud
fullness. The dragon rumbled experimentally, and the fire that lapped
around its fangs—like the great claws, no longer worn dull—was the deep
red, laced with rich yellow, that such fire should be. Guerra stared back
and forth between this new glory and the ballpoint pen on the Betty Grable notebook, and no longer wished to have switched shifts with Officer
Levinsky.

But beyond such wonders, the most marvelous change of all was that
the dragon was beginning to fade, to lose definition around the edges and

grow steadily more transparent until Guerra thought he could see his car through it, and the lights of houses across the street, and the rising moon. After a moment, though, he realized he was wrong. The lights were plainly coming from a number of low-roofed huts that clustered in the shadows at the base of a soap-bubble castle, and what he had taken for his car was in fact nothing but a rickety haywagon. The vision extended on all sides: whichever way he turned, there was only the reality of the huts and the castle and the deep woods beyond. And one of the castle towers had a single barred window, with a face glimmering behind it. . . .

"Yes," said the dragon. For all its increasing dimness, its voice had grown as powerful and clear as a mountain waterfall. "Yes . . . yes . . . that was just how it was. *How it is* . . ."

The sense of one common breath being drawn and exhaled was abruptly broken by a soft wail, "Dragon gone!" and the little boy in the Batman pajamas suddenly shrugged free of his mother's grip and came racing across the street and the lawn. *"Dragon gone!"* Guerra made a dive for him, but missed, and was almost trampled by the boy's father. The whiskey-faced Santa Claus came charging after.

With the persistence and determination of a rabbit heading for his hole, the boy shot between several sets of legs straight for the splendid shadow that was fading so swiftly now. He tripped, skidded on his seat and looked up at the mighty head and neck, wings and crest, fading so swiftly against a sky of castles and stars. "Dragon gone?" It was a forlorn question now.

The head came slowly down, lowering over the boy, who sat unafraid as the dragon studied him lingeringly. Guerra remembered—shadow or no shadow—the dragon's comments on the heart-melting tastiness of children. But then the boy's father had him in his arms and was sweeping him off, darkly threatening to sue *somebody*, there had to be *someone*. And the dragon was indeed gone.

The castle was gone too; and so, in time, went most of the author's neighbors, hushed and wondering. But some stayed a while, for no reason they could have explained, coming closer to the house merely to stand where the dragon had been. Several of those spoke diffidently to the author; Guerra saw others surreptitiously pluck up grass blades, both burned and untouched, plainly as souvenirs.

When the last of that group had finally wandered off, the author closed the notebook, capped the pen, stood up, stretched elaborately and said, "Well. Coffee?"

Guerra rubbed his aching forehead, feeling the way he sometimes did when, falling asleep, he suddenly lunged awake out of a half-dream of stumbling down a step that wasn't there. He said feebly, "Where did he go?"

"Oh, into that story," the author answered lightly. "The story I was making up for him."

"But you didn't finish it," Guerra said.

"He will. It's *his* fairy-tale world, after all—he knows it better than I do, really. I just showed him the way back." The author smiled with a certain aggravating compassion. "It's a bit hard to explain, if you don't—you know—*think* much about magic."

"Hey, I think about a lot of things," Guerra said harshly. "And what I'm thinking about right now is that that wasn't a real story. It's not in any book—you were just spitballing, improvising, making it up as you went along. Hell, I'll bet you couldn't repeat it right now if you tried. Like a little kid telling a lie."

The author laughed outright, and then stopped quickly when he saw Guerra's expression. "I'm sorry, I'm not laughing at you. You're quite right, we're all little kids telling lies, writers are, hoping we can keep the lies straight and get away with them. And nobody lasts very long in this game who isn't prepared to lie his way out of trouble. Absolutely right." He regarded the ruined strip of lawn and winced visibly. "But you make the same mistake most people do, Officer Guerra. The magic's not in books, not in the publishing—it's in the *telling*, always. In the old, old telling."

He looked at his watch and yawned. "Actually, there might *be* a book in that one, I don't know. Have to think about it. What about that coffee?"

"I'm off duty," Guerra said. "You got any beer?"

"I'm off duty too," the author said. "Come on in."

Humane Killer

Diana Gabaldon and Samuel Sykes

International bestseller Diana Gabaldon is a winner of the Quill Award and of the RITA Award, given by the Romance Writers of America. She's the author of the hugely popular Outlander series of time-travel romances, including Cross Stitch, Dragonfly in Amber, Voyager, Drums of Autumn, The Fiery Cross, *and* A Breath of Snow and Ashes. *Her historical series about the strange adventures of Lord John includes the novels* Lord John and the Private Matter, Lord John and the Brotherhood of the Blade, *a chapbook novella,* Lord John and the Hell-Fire Club, *and a collection of Lord John stories,* Lord John and the Hand of Devils. *She's also written a contemporary mystery,* White Knight. *Her most recent book is a new Outlander novel,* An Echo in the Bone. *A guidebook to and appreciation of her work is* The Outlandish Companion.

Samuel Sykes is a relatively new author, having just been unleashed from Northern Arizona University. "Humane Killer" is his first publication worth mentioning and, he hopes, the first of many. Born in Phoenix, Arizona, he now lives in Flagstaff, Arizona.

Here they join forces to describe an unlikely and accidental alliance between some very ill-assorted characters who find that they all have a common problem to solve—if they can.

"SIR Leonard of Savhael is his name!"

The young woman held her breath and was relieved to see that the crowd, for the moment at least, had stopped what they were doing and directed eyes in various states of bleariness and crustiness up toward her.

"And he is, without a doubt," she spoke rapidly, "the greatest of the Unanointed to have ever set foot back into the lands of civilized men!"

The crowd shifted. Lips, occasionally decorated with warts, twisted into collective frowns at the mention of an Unanointed. She cleared her throat, bracing herself for their next reaction.

"And while he is not pure enough to carry a mace"—she spoke louder to be heard over the disapproving moans—"his sword has spilled more heathen blood upon sand, stone, or stream than *any* instrument, blunt or otherwise!"

A few stern nods from old men, most likely veterans, brought her a little hope. She straightened herself up as much as she could and spoke a little louder.

"He has never set foot in any house of God"—she winced at their angry roar—"*for the blood crusted there is so thick that it can never be washed from his boots!*" She smiled, emboldened, at their morbid chuckles. "He swears to God with as much piety as any man of cloth and steel, but never once has passed judgment upon another, so humble is he."

They quirked a collective brow at that; she bit her lower lip. Such an expression was not what she had hoped to inspire. *Finish it now,* she told herself, *end on a high note.*

"And so, I urge you, my dear friends"—she spoke as loudly and clearly as she could—"to consider *his* judgment, for he is so pure and clean that you *cannot* hear him vouch for me and yet remain convinced of my guilt!"

The chaplain inclined his head to her, his powdered wig and sagging features drooping in a depressing display of age. He glanced to the altar boy beside him, who merely stared at her blankly. Slowly, white brow quirked, the chaplain turned to the crowd and, unhurriedly, spoke.

"And what say *you* to this fevered plea, good gentlemen?"

The old men glanced to the women, who looked to the old men with equal confusion.

For such a decision, they would have surely looked to the young men. The young men, with their strong hearts and minds shaped by God's grace, would look to *her.* They might nod sagely and suggest that they discuss the matter more earnestly. Or, even better, they might take one look at her face, unscarred and fair, and escort her to the nearest alehouse.

Of course, she noted grimly, there were no young men left in the village. There were plenty of elderly and likely plenty of *dead* young men buried in the churchyard, but the living ones had undoubtedly followed their precious Crusade south.

That left the women. *No one ever listens to the women.*

Thus, it was no great surprise that it was one of the old men who raised both his voice and a withered fist to the sky.

"*BURN HER!*"

"*BURN HER!*" the cry was taken up, even by the children. "*BURN THE WITCH!*"

"Oh, *come on!*" Armecia screamed back at them. She yearned to hurl one of the faggots heaped at her feet, but she supposed that was why they had bound her to a stake. "I didn't even *do* anything!"

"Lies!" one of the women, so sagging with age as to suggest she was more melted candle than woman, roared. "You used your black magic upon me gran'daughter!"

To prove this, she tugged at the wrist of a young, fair-haired girl and shoved her to the fore of the crowd. The girl, apparently more befuddled than enraged, looked up at Armecia with a blank face, perfectly smooth and bright with a healthy pink.

"She was scarred with the pox just this morning! One hour away from me sight, and I've got *this*!" The woman seized her granddaughter by the cheeks and shook roughly. "*This!* Smoother than her arse was when she was born!" She leveled a finger and a yellow-toothed snarl at Armecia. "Witchcraft! *Heathenry!*"

"Are you serious? How can you be upset at your grandchild being cured of disease?" She gritted her teeth so hard they threatened to crack. "What makes you think *I* did it, anyway?"

"You're the only foreigner here," the woman said, extending her arms to the crowd. "Everyone else is a decent devotee of the lord and His Order."

"Everyone, huh?" With no free hands to point, Armecia gestured to the old woman with her chin. "When was the last time you were at church? Maybe *you* used some kind of magic on her and are trying to foist the guilt on *me*."

She had to force herself to keep from smiling at the offended look of the woman. She had to strain much harder to keep an elated giggle behind her lips when the crowd parted warily, turning dozens of suspicious gazes upon the accuser.

"Oh, you can't be seriously considering this," the woman grunted, placing meaty hands on hips.

"Witchcraft, Goodie Andor, is a very serious matter." The chaplain stroked both his chins contemplatively. "Even the curing of a dreadful disease is but a ruse covering a far more dreadful taint. If we let but one"— he held up a finger—"bride of the Devil into this sanctuary of the lord's people, it will infect far more than mere children."

"So say we all."

The crowd's heads went low in what Armecia thought of, but did not comment upon, as being curiously similar to a mass of hens upon a heap of grain.

As they made a unified sign of the Cudgel, it was with a grim smile and dozens of furious scowls, respectively, that Armecia and the folk noted Goodie Andor make the blessed gesture just a fraction slower than the rest.

"You've known me for years!" She rose up with as much righteous indignation as sagging breasts and thick legs would allow. "I've prayed in the house of God alongside you! I am no sorceress!"

"So she *says*!" Armecia assumed her own poise of righteousness, insofar as the ropes permitted. "Are not the Devil's brides skilled with clouding the minds of reasonable men?"

"It is true," the chaplain muttered, fixing a wary eye upon Goodie Andor. "It is furthermore true that you did not consider the accusation to be serious."

"*She's* the one trying to cloud your minds!"

"With what? Logic? Big words?" Armecia leaned back against the stake and sneered. "Let us not abandon any precaution here, friends. If she can accuse me of witchcraft, then *I* can certainly accuse *her* of witchcraft." She shrugged as nonchalantly as she could. "In the end, there's really no way to prove that anyone's a witch."

The crowd paused at that. Bony fingers scratched bald pates contemplatively. Someone broke wind, slightly less contemplatively. Another man cleared his throat, straightened up, and spoke.

"Maybe," he said softly, "we should burn them both, just to be safe."

"Not unwise," the chaplain mused. "If it is God's will that the taint be cleansed from our fair community . . ."

"*Fair?*" Armecia looked incredulous. "How did you get in charge here, anyway?"

"The station of the chaplain is not for mere women to question," he replied snootily, turning up a long nose. "Nor is it proper for half-breeds to show such neglect to the strongest voice of mercy."

"That's right!" Goodie Andor pointed at her angrily. "She's a half-breed! Half-heathen! That *proves* she's a witch!"

Armecia was forced to accept the verbal blow—there was simply no denying it. Her skin and hair, just dusky enough, wouldn't have been enough to draw attention to her. Her eyes, however, one clear and blue, the other pitch-black, clearly marked her as the fruit of a union that should never have been.

She accepted the accusation but did not flinch. She had felt more than accusations, after all, in the stones that her mother's peopled had hurled at her and the filth that they had smeared over her father's grave. Compared to that, she thought grimly, accusations were nothing.

Immolations, on the other hand . . .

She eyed the altar boy standing beside her yet untorched pyre, noting with more than a little worry that the slack of his jaw was echoed in the slack of his hand.

That in itself wouldn't be too distressing if not for the burning torch he clenched.

"What are you waiting for, Father?" the woman demanded. "Lower the torch! Burn her!"

"The torch! The torch! The torch!" the crowd chanted, relenting only when the chaplain raised a hand.

"God preaches mercy for all civilized men." He gestured toward Armecia. "And she, clearly, is at least *half*-civilized. Thusly, she deserves at least half a doubt as to her guilt."

"Well, that just makes *perfect* sense," she muttered.

"Well, where's her champion, then?" Goodie Andor demanded. "Where's this Sir Leonard she speaks of?"

"A fair question." The chaplain looked curiously to her. "Where *is* this Sir Leonard of Savhael that you claim will clear your name?"

Armecia winced.

She had hoped that, upon hearing such an impassioned speech, Sir Leonard would have come galloping up to cut her bonds, pull her up onto his horse, and ride off.

After her first few statements, she would have settled for an equally fervent defense of her that would undoubtedly end in her release and a humble apology from all assembled.

By the end of it, she was desperate even to hear him break wind.

Sir Leonard, however, was not a man with a horse. Sir Leonard was not good with words. Sir Leonard was not particularly good with his sword.

What Sir Leonard *was*, was a man caked with stubble and clad in dirty mail armor, quietly pulling strips of jerked beef from a sack and munching on them as he stood toward the front of the crowd, watching the outrage unfold through red-streaked eyes.

"He"—she gestured with her chin—"is Sir Leonard of Savhael."

"Where?" The chaplain scrutinized the crowd. "You'll have to point him out."

She pursed her lips, choosing to believe that he was only being ironically stupid.

"In the first row." She tightened her hands into fists behind her. "Will my champion kindly rise and prove his lady fair's innocence?"

The man in the front said nothing. She clenched her teeth.

"Will Sir Leonard *not* answer the demand for justice?"

His jaw moved up and down in a decidedly bovine manner as he chewed. She snarled angrily.

"*Lenny,* for God's sake!"

To say that his eyes suddenly snapped wide open would be to overestimate his speed by a good three breaths.

Instead, like portcullises, portcullises thirty years old without the benefit of oil, his lids rose with a very slow comprehension that she might have found tedious if not for her imminent immolation. His neck moved with all the speed of a very sleepy tree as he glanced from side to side, then to her. Both eyebrows raised, he put a finger to his chest and mouthed a question.

Armecia pondered if it wouldn't be less painful just to be burned alive.

"Yes, *you*, Sir Leonard," she said, "if you would *kindly* rise to the challenge of seeing that I'm *not* consumed in flames . . ."

"Right, right," he mumbled, shuffling up the stairs to the platform. "I just stepped out for a bite to eat. My mind must have wandered a bit farther than my feet."

"You stepped out for a bite to eat"—the chaplain cocked his head curiously—"during the trial of your lady?"

"Well"—he shrugged—"it's not like she was going anywhere."

"And I am not his lady," Armecia hastily added, "I'm his *chronicler.* I write down his exploits and adventures."

"So we've noticed."

The chaplain beckoned the altar boy to his side, who tossed his torch aside with alarming callousness to produce a leather-bound book from beneath his white robes. The chaplain, giving his aide a cuff upside the head and a command to relight, took the tome and beheld it to the audience.

"This is what you write in?" With a lack of care for the papyrus that made Armecia cringe, he flipped through the pages and frowned. "It's all written in the heathen tongue."

"It's written in *Hashuni*," Armecia corrected over the infuriated roar of the crowd. Quickly, she cleared her throat, attempting to appear as humble as a woman tied to a stake could be. "The better that it may be translated to the heathen, so that they might know fear at the sight of Sir Leonard, you see."

She held her breath at that, as all assembled shifted their gazes so that they themselves might take in the sight of Sir Leonard.

The alleged knight, for he certainly did not look like anything from heraldry, poetry, or even heathenry, stood tall and lank. Barely upright, let alone like a gallant out of story, Sir Leonard *hung*.

His chain mail hung from his body, his stubble-caked jaw hung loosely from his head, his greasy brown hair hung over his bloodshot eyes, his dirty brown cloak hung from his humped back.

Hung as he was, though, Sir Leonard was still a knight. Or rather, he was a very tall man who wore armor and carried a sword, which was at least half of what a knight was.

Armecia attempted to retreat further within that thought, finding comfort in her own perception of him.

He looks . . . she fought to find a word that wouldn't cause her to break out into tears of hopelessness, *reposed. Yeah, that's it. He's calm, collected, years of steady experience and wariness held behind those eyes . . . those bloodshot eyes . . . and he stinks of smoke.*

Oh God, why did I think this would work?

"He don't look so impressive," one of the assembled snorted.

He said, she reminded herself, *that he doesn't look* so *impressive. That means they're at least a* little *impressed by him. If that's the case, I can at least paint him to look like someone who should command some respect. That is, of course, assuming they don't notice the—*

"He's got a hunchback!" Someone pointed to the large lump beneath Sir Leonard's cloak. "Ain't never heard of a knight that had a hunchback!"

"True," the chaplain said, scratching his chins. "The lord pities abominations but does not draft them into his armies." He narrowed his eyes. "Besides, if that *is* a hunchback, why isn't he . . . *hunched*?"

"Because it isn't a hunchback," Sir Leonard replied.

Good, good. Armecia noted the approving nods of the crowd, however meager. *They don't have to know what it is. They don't need to know. You can do this, Lenny. Just don't—*

Lenny did.

Reaching behind to rummage through his cloak, he slid a long, flexible pipe from his back and slid the mouthpiece between his lips. Armecia felt her hopes die along with her breath as he inhaled deeply, the hookah bubbling under his cloak.

And, in the acrid smoke rings that reeked vaguely of a skunk trying to be inoffensive that emerged from his lips, the quaintness of Sir Leonard of Savhael was made all too apparent to the townspeople.

The crowd recoiled in collective horror, as though the smoke were some hideous beast of myth sent from the man's mouth to strangle the life out of them. The chaplain, only slightly more restrained, let his eyes go wider than a holy man ought to while shielding the altar boy behind him.

Sir Leonard licked his lips, then glanced over the crowd, blinking.

"What?" He coughed a little. "Oh, wait. Those weren't very good. I can do better." He stuck the pipe back in his mouth, muttering through it. "If I time it just right, I can puff up a cloud that looks like a naked nun. One moment . . ."

"Thank you, Lenny." Armecia sighed, surveyed the crowd momentarily, then clicked her tongue with an air of finality. "Right, then." She glanced at the altar boy. "You had the torch, right? Let's get on with this."

"Wait . . ." The act of blinking proved to be something long and ponderous for Sir Leonard as he took in the scene. "What's going on?"

"Sir Leonard"—the chaplain's voice drifted somewhere between restrained outrage and unrestrained revulsion—"as loath as I am to advise you, it does not bode well for your chronicler's trial if you insist on so brazenly bringing the Devil's herb into our midst."

Lenny blinked.

"What trial?"

"Do we really have to belabor this?" Armecia pressed.

"She's right!" Goodie Andor spoke up, shaking a meaty finger. "The knight is clearly a disgrace to whatever church and lord he serves. The book is clearly the witch's book of spells! The evidence is through. Now comes the time for burning!"

"Burn her!" the crowd agreed uproariously. "Burn her and her demon book!"

"ENOUGH!"

And at that, the crowd was silenced. Perhaps it was Sir Leonard's bellow, carried on wisps of latent smoke that poured from his maw. Perhaps it was the fact that his eyes had become so red as to burn through the locks of his hair.

Much more likely, Armecia thought, it was because his sword was out and flashing against the sun.

"Lenny," she urged quietly, "no killing."

"I am of the Unanointed," the knight bellowed, unheeding of her. "Without lord, without land, and not without sin." As if the noose holding the hanging knight was suddenly drawn taut, he rose to an impressive height, tall and muscular. "If you should feel bold, madame, perhaps I can throw us both upon my sword and we'll see who reaches heaven first."

"*Lenny*"—her voice was harsh this time—"*no killing.*"

"And if you are eager for a burning"—his grin was broad, yellow, and profoundly horrific—"we can see who burns."

"*LENNY!*"

At that, Sir Leonard was silenced. He slackened, becoming the hanged knight once more, eyes soft and blade limp. He surveyed the scene with a sudden curiosity, as though he had just arrived at that moment.

"Wait a tick." He blinked. "What, exactly, is she charged with?"

"Witchcraft," the chaplain replied, speaking in a tone of voice he might have reserved for feral dogs. "Before burning her, however, we are bound by lord and law to hear testimony for her."

"You're going to *burn* her?"

"We were planning to." The chaplain shrugged.

"Not much else to do round here," the altar boy added with a slow nod.

"Your lady invoked you as her champion and chief witness."

"My . . . lady?" Sir Leonard's eyes lit up as he laughed with a casualness that made her shiver. "Oh, she's not my lady."

"She . . . is not?" the chaplain arched a brow.

"Of course not. She's my *mistress*."

Quietly, Armecia found herself longing for a time when he had merely forced them to recoil with weed.

"What manner of knight consorts with adulterous half-breed harlots?" Goodie Andor howled, echoed by the crowd.

"What? No, it's not like that at all." Sir Leonard shook his head. "She just commands me relentlessly and gives me stuff to smoke, see?"

"You are a knight . . . and she orders you about?"

Armecia tensed as the chaplain stroked his chins, his thoughts visible between his fingers. Clearly he knew that the matriarchal hierarchy was as well established in Hashuni life as was the Crusade against them. It occurred as a fleeting thought, however; she had already resigned herself to the inevitable outcome.

"I *was* a knight, yes," Sir Leonard nodded. "I really only stopped knighting about when I met Armecia." He scratched his stubble. "When was it? Aught three? Aught thirty?" He furrowed his brow. "One moment . . . you can't have an aught with double digits . . . wait, can you? Anyway, she mostly just makes me carry stuff"—he laughed with an unnerving suddenness—"oh wait, there was this one time when she had me put—"

"Just burn me already!" Armecia screamed.

"She's resigned to her fate!" Goodie Andor yelled. "It's clear that, whatever this knight might have done, she's put a spell over him to make him do her bidding! Burn the witch!"

"Well, it can hardly work *that* way." Sir Leonard frowned. "I mean, you can't just scream 'witch,' then burn someone." He glanced to the altar boy. "Can you do that here?"

"She cleared my gran'daughter's face of the pox!" the woman shrieked.

"And?"

"And that ain't natural!"

"But it's still rather a pleasant surprise, isn't it?"

The crowd's silence seemed to suggest so. Goodie Andor, looking flustered at their lack of response, compensated with a feral snarl.

"She's a half-breed! Her lineage is steeped in the blood of heathens and witches!"

"That doesn't seem like a good reason to burn someone," Sir Leonard replied. "Or at least, not a good reason to *completely* burn someone. I mean, you could burn *half* of her, I suppose, but that doesn't seem—"

"Why are we still discussing this?" the woman demanded. "This knight, who smokes the demon weed brazenly under the eyes of heaven and who proclaims a half-heathen witch to be his mistress, has done naught but mock us and our way of life for as long as we've pretended to indulge him!"

"That hardly seems like an appropriate accusation," the knight replied, "I mean, I certainly haven't leveled any sort of slander against your name, good sir."

There was a brief moment of tense silence, during which Armecia could swear she could smell the smoke crackling out of the woman's ears.

"I'm . . . a *lady*," she growled.

"We can debate semantics later." Before she could respond, Sir Leonard waved a hand at the crowd. "Regardless of whatever we may think or feel about half people and the breeding thereof, we're stuck at something of an impasse." He offered a congenial smile that was at odds with the weapon in his hand. "I mean, I *am* the one with the sword."

Armecia, her fury spent, her fear bubbled away, could only roll her eyes. After accusations of heresy, heathenry, witchery, adultery, and the indulgence of an illicit substance, threats of violence seemed less like an assurance of a burning and more like an obstacle to one.

The crowd, apparently, agreed.

"This is takin' forever!" one of the men cried out. "Are we going to see someone burn or not?"

The chaplain, in no hurry to decide, merely scratched at his chins.

"Perhaps we may yet," he muttered. With a sweep of his robes, he turned to face the crowd. "Sir Leonard of Savhael . . . makes an important point." He raised his hands for peace, two meaty shields against the abuse hurled toward the platform. "Within all half-breeds, no matter what heathen or savage their bloodline might reflect, is bestowed the mercy of God."

"And the taint of the Devil!" someone cried out, followed by murmurs of approval.

"*Be that as it may*," he continued, "the grievous charges laid cannot be ignored." He turned a leery eye toward Sir Leonard. "Nor can the grievous sins so brazenly displayed be redeemed . . ."

His eye took on a wicked glint, Armecia thought, far more wicked than a holy man ought to be capable of.

"Without equally grievous atonement."

And, for the first time since the spectacle had begun, Armecia felt fear. The torch, the accusations, the threats all ceased to have any effect upon her as the townspeople shifted in one filthy, flatulent harmony. The same wicked glint spread across each of their faces, the same cruel smile split each of their mouths in yellow-toothed glee, the same hoarse whisper hissed from their teeth.

"Zeigfreid . . ."

Lenny, apparently, did not see the same thing she saw, for he merely cocked his head to the side in pleasant curiosity.

"So we've reached an accord?"

"Of sorts," the chaplain replied. "Rather, we've reached an ultimatum. If you agree to slay Zeigfreid, we'll be happy to grant you the opportunity. And, truly, if you are able to give him righteous slaughter, we shall be convinced of your service to the lord."

"All we have to do is *kill* someone?" Leonard laughed. "That doesn't sound hard at all. I've killed thousands of people before, you know." He paused, glancing at Armecia. "I mean, roughly that, right?"

"Zeigfreid is no mere heathen," the chaplain proclaimed dramatically. "No, he is the filth vomited from the bride of the Devil's womb! He is the source of all smoke and the sower of the seeds of foulness!" His piggy eyes narrowed to thin, black slits. "He is . . . *DRAGON*."

"Oh . . ." Leonard coughed. "A dragon." At the chaplain's shocked expression, he held up his hands. "It's not that I'm not intimidated, of course. I just thought after all that dramatic stuff about wombs and foulness, you'd say something a bit more . . ."

"If you think it beyond your capabilities, we may simply begin with the burning."

"No, no! That's fine. We'll go plant a sword in the Devil's womb or something like that."

With that, Sir Leonard spun on his heel and began to trudge down the platform, barely stopping at Armecia's abrupt cough.

"Aren't you forgetting something?"

"Oh . . . right." The knight turned again and regarded the chaplain warily. "How, precisely, do you know that we won't just run away once you let her go?"

"An excellent point." The chaplain nodded. With a glance to the altar boy, he gestured to the book in the lad's hands. "We shall retain the book of spells and divine its meaning. Even if she is proved to be a witch, she shall be powerless."

"Wait!" Armecia protested. "It's just a log! A chronicle! I can't do anything unnatural with it."

"Well, there was that one time you—"

"Lenny, *shut up*!" She turned to the chaplain with a look of pleading. "It's worthless. Let me have it, and you can have something else." She glanced about the platform before looking to the knight. "Him!"

"Apparently, it is worthy enough of your protest." The chaplain narrowed his eyes upon her. "And that makes me suspicious . . . not enough, however, to deny the world a chance to have a taint cleansed from the earth." He straightened up proudly. "You will find Zeigfreid's lair to the north. Do be hasty. Taint persists forever, pages, decidedly less so."

ℛℬ

"THE Devil, above all, is a deceiver."

Though he had ended his declaration with the slightest quiver of his lips, Father Scheitzen's voice could never be described as gentle; his church made certain of that. Its halls were a vast, granite throat, its door a mouth with wood and steel teeth. What he whispered, the church demanded. When he uttered, the church decreed. When he roared, the church shook heaven and earth.

Heathens and drunkards occasionally mused that the priest owed his entire success to the architecture of his temple. These particular ideas, of course, were voiced far, far away from the church's great, spired ears.

"He takes many forms," the priest continued, the sweeping of his robe's hem an angry hiss upon the floor. "He is the desire and temptation that lurks at the edge of the noble man's eyes. He is the frailty in our arms, He is the rust on our swords, and He is the hole in our armor."

Father Scheitzen turned his gaze upward. The afternoon sun pouring through the stained glass painted his face crimson, glazed his eyes to angry black orbs.

"He is the heathen in the south," he spoke, "He is the barbarian in the north. All these are the Devil's influence, but these are His subtleties, His deceptions, His lies."

His neck twisted so slowly that his vertebrae groaned like old iron.

"For as vile as He is, He can merely corrupt, never create. The heathen is merely a man with untrained ears, who has heard the Devil's silken voice. Should we then condemn so easily? Should we deny all cries for re-demption? To do so would be to deny mercy itself."

Crimson light beat down upon his shoulders and the naked pate of his shaven head. He ceased to have a face at that moment; his countless wrinkles bathed him in an infinite mask of shadow.

"We . . . I . . . am not a man without mercy." He regarded the man before him evenly. "Am I?"

Nitz's first thought was that men of mercy typically did not wear great spiked maces dangling from their sashes.

Whatever other terrifying features the priest might have, his scarred scalp, his clenched jaw, his huge, brutish arms, ceased to have any effect in the presence of this ominous weapon. Its crimson was far deeper than that wrought by the sunlight; it had seen many heathen skulls caved, countless barbarian bones broken, untold numbers of false priests' faces smashed.

The blood would never fully wash off it.

"Am I?"

"N-no, Father," Nitz replied, straining to hide the quaver in his voice.

To have even a foot touched by the shadow of Father Scheitzen, the shadow of a Crusader so famed and noble, would make a fully grown man quiver. Half of the priest's long shade was enough to engulf a man such as Nitz. It took all he had to keep his legs from twisting over each other.

"I am not," Father Scheitzen nodded in reply, his neck creaking. "Nor are you." He cast a glance over the smaller man's head, toward the towering figure behind him. "Nor, I suspect, is she."

Nitz followed the priest's gaze to his companion. Father Scheitzen's shadow did not yet extend so far as to engulf Madeline. Nitz doubted there was a man yet who had grown tall enough to do that. She did not cast a shadow but rose as one, towering and swaddled in the ominous blackness of her nun's habit, her head so high as to scrape against the torch ensconced in the pillar she stood alongside.

"Maddy," Nitz caught himself, "Sister Madeline . . . is not without mercy, no, Father." He flashed a smile, painfully aware of the stark whiteness of his teeth in the church's gloom. "After all, she owes her life to the mercy of others. Who but the church would have a . . . creature such as her?"

Nitz took private pleasure in the shudder Father Scheitzen gave as Madeline stepped forward.

The torchlight was decidedly unsympathetic. All her face was bared, from the manly square curve of her jaw, to the jagged scar running down her cheek, to the milky discolored eye set in the right half of her skull and the grim darkness in her left. The jagged yellow of her smile-bared teeth was nothing more than a sigh, a comma at the end of the cruel joke that was a woman's visage.

"Ah, a Scarred Sister. I suspect you may have inadvertently stumbled upon a solution to a problem that has long plagued the Order," Father Scheitzen murmured, bringing his lips close to Nitz. "There are rumors, complaints of lesser men accompanied by lesser women thinking themselves and each other worthy servants of God. Their mutual weakness feeds off each other, men raise illegitimate children by tainted nuns." He spared a glancing grimace for the woman behind them. "I trust you and your companion have no such temptations."

Nitz hesitated a moment to answer, allowing the image of temptation to fill his mind. He had seen what lay beneath the layers of black cloth:

the rolling musculature, the scarred, pale flesh, the biceps that could break ribs with an embrace. The thought of succumbing to "temptation" had not, until this moment, crossed his mind; the foreplay alone would shatter his pelvis.

"Of course not, Father," he said with a timely twitch, "our devotion is to God and his Divine Warfare. Her . . . unfortunate appearance is naught but a blessing to keep our motives pure."

"I suspected no less," Father Scheitzen spoke. "But I did not summon you to my church to question your choice of company." His scowl deepened; his face went hard. "I have called you here for two reasons: the Devil and your father."

Nitz bit back a sigh at mention of the latter.

"Their paths frequently crossed, I am told, Father."

"That is an astute observation." The priest inclined his head. "Undoubtedly, you have already heard of the countless victories your father dedicated to God. The exploits of him and Fraumvilt, his beloved mace, are legendary. His weapon caved in more heathen skulls than any weapon ever raised in the service of God." He stroked the hilt of his own spiked weapon with a sort of remorseful lust. "Krenzwuld, my own metal bride, is nothing but a fancy stick in comparison."

"I am scarcely a worthy judge of mace quality, Father."

"So it is true."

Father Scheitzen cast a disapproving glare at the axe strapped to Nitz's back, sparing two frowns. One for the barbarian weapon itself and one for the fact that it was large enough to threaten to topple the young man.

"I am told," the priest began, the disbelief in his voice unhidden, "that this . . . weapon of yours has spilled much heathen blood. Tell me, what is her name?"

His expectant stare caused Nitz to start. The young man's eyes went wide, his lips fumbling for the answer. He felt crushed, caught between the Father's suspicious scowl and the envious glare boring into the back of his head.

"Wolfreiz," came the unexpectedly deep voice from behind. Sister Madeline inclined a head to the young man.

"My companion is correct," Nitz said, nodding. "Wolfreiz. I sometimes find myself unable to speak the name, it fills me with as much fear as it does the heathen."

"A decent, godly name," Father Scheitzen nodded. "Your father would have approved its title, if not its heritage. He was a true warrior of God;

the origin mattered less in the light of the mercy it would bring." A smile tugged at his lip. "He brought much mercy in the name of God.

"And yet, he was not God. There yet remained a foe he could not destroy." From the depths of his robe, Father Scheitzen produced a scroll, old and frayed at the edges, sealed with crimson wax. "The Devil Himself."

"I would hope Father does not find my lack of surprise insulting. My progenitor, as great as he was, could not defeat Our Eternal Foe." Nitz hesitated, swallowing hard. "Or was Father being facetious?"

Nitz kept his face straight, despite the narrowing of Father Scheitzen's eyes, despite his huge hand gliding to the hilt of his mace. He had long since grown used to the reaction; Crusaders often displayed such at the mention of words they did not understand.

". . . yes. I was."

Nitz allowed himself to breathe a little.

"Regardless, I speak of the Devil bereft of His trickeries, bereft of His lies and deceptions." Father Scheitzen stroked the scroll in his hands with the same fondness with which he would touch one of his own scars. "Creatures with no use for subtlety. Evil in its purest, most honest form, if evil is capable of such honesty."

His eyes were cold stones.

"Dragons."

"Dragons, Father?" Nitz kept his next thought—that dragons were creatures of myth born out of fear or drunkenness—far from his lips. Crusaders did not like to be questioned.

"A dragon. Specifically, *this* dragon: Zeigfreid."

"Zeigfreid?"

"Are you aware of how annoying it is to hear myself repeated?"

"Annoy— No, Father, I was not aware. Please, go on."

"I shall." Father Scheitzen thrust the scroll toward Nitz. "This creature, Zeigfreid," he paused, challenging Nitz, before continuing, "is one of the Devil's many agents on earth. Have you ever seen such a thing, young vassal?"

"Zeigfreid . . . *specifically*, Father?" Nitz took the scroll carefully.

"I see that your humor is much like your father's chosen weapon," Father Scheitzen growled. "Blunt and prone to beating people over the head. It seems the branches of your familial tree were twisted."

"And I can see that Father's wit is as sharp as the sword that he remains too pure to carry."

"I have seen a dragon, vassal," Father Scheitzen continued. "Skin the color of blood, wings that blot out the sun, spewing hell from its mouth . . . like the Devil Himself, he cared not for whether he slew Crusader or heathen upon the field."

"Gruesome, Father," Nitz said, fingering the scroll. "And you would like me to deliver this to a temple worthy of dealing with such a beast?"

"Those were the orders handed down by the Order's Council of Three," Father Scheitzen uttered. "But, as I said, I am a man not without mercy and thus, I deliver this scroll to you directly."

"To me, Father?"

"Of course, vassal. If Zeigfreid proves too much for you, we will certainly deal with him. However, for the moment, I thought it better to offer you a chance to earn Fraumvilt . . . to honor your father's memory and strike down the one agent of evil that he could not."

Nitz swallowed hard, as unsure how to react as he was unsure what the message Father Scheitzen had just delivered to him was. He had been admitted into the vassalry only a year ago, along with every other young man who had proved himself worthy of an honor higher than squire. He had expected, as all vassals did, to deliver messages through battlefields from church to church, not fight agents of evil.

Then again, he reminded himself with a roll of his eyes, *I wasn't expecting to be paired with savage, disfigured brutes, either.*

Instinctively, he looked over his shoulder. Madeline's good eye was big and bright, her smile was broad and ugly. Her scar twitched in time with her cheek. He saw her hand sliding under her habit, long fingers trembling with contained anticipation.

"This scroll"—the priest seized Nitz's attention—"contains all that we know of Zeigfreid: where we saw him last, where he was heading, what the last known size of his treasure trove was."

He heard Madeline whimper excitedly behind him.

"Treasure, Father?"

"Would it shock you to learn that, being agents of the Devil, dragons are voraciously greedy?"

"Not entirely."

"Of course, it goes without saying that once you slay the beast, its hoard goes to the church to finance the struggle against the heathen."

"Of course, Father. Crusaders need gold."

"Crusaders need only God," Father Scheitzen snarled. "Greedy merchants and smiths *demand* gold for the steel we put to use against the heathen." He composed himself with a stiff inhalation. "To bring down

Zeigfreid, you will need God *and* steel." He glanced over Nitz to the titanic axe he wore upon his back. "I trust you can wield that?"

"This?" Nitz suddenly became aware of the weapon's weight. He had bent his spine in such a way as to balance himself and keep the thing from toppling him over. "Yes, well, rest assured that I can use . . . uh . . ."

"Wolfreiz," Madeline chimed in from behind.

"Yes, Wolfreiz. Thank you, Sister." Nitz cleared his throat. "Rest assured that I can use Wolfreiz to such an effect that nothing remains standing after it is swung."

Father Scheitzen grunted in reply. Somehow, Nitz suspected that the priest did not quite believe him. Was it the fact that he could not remember his weapon's name? Or was it the fact that his physique was offensively similar to that of an underdeveloped milkmaid?

"It is no Crusader's mace," the priest replied, "but then, you are no Crusader . . . yet. That may change after you perform your duty to God."

Nitz swallowed hard at that. Fortunate, he thought, for it prevented any further words from finding their way to his lips. Instead, the questions stewed at the back of his throat: what did the father mean? Was Nitz to be sent to the Holy Land to continue his father's legacy? How on earth would he accomplish that? By caving in twenty thousand and *two* skulls?

Perhaps, he thought, it would be better just to tell the priest everything. No more secrets, no more lies, no more pretending to be the heir his father wanted. All the heathen blood he had shed in his father's name came from the power directly behind him, not within him.

He sought to say this, but things like honesty and truth had long been tempered out of him, leaving only the hard, unrelenting steel of verse and duty behind.

"May God forgive the hell I leave in my wake," he uttered mechanically, the church repeating him.

"So say we all."

ᛦᛏ

FRAUMVILT was contemptuous, Nitz thought, as it stared out through its stone, flanged head to survey the landscape below. The great mace was sickened to its shaft at the sight beneath its unseeing eyes: thatched roofs, rolling fields of green and tan, men holding shepherds' canes instead of maces, women kneeling beside cows instead of altars.

War was reserved for the Holy Land, blood spilled where God could *see* it. Here in the kingdoms, men and women died rarely and peacefully, in their sleep, with no one but insignificant sons and daughters to ever know.

"Father would be sick if he could see it," Nitz muttered.

"Eh?" Maddy took a step forward, and her shadow devoured him.

Father would have been sicker yet to see the size of her compared to him. Fortunately, God had smiled upon Kalintz the Great, the Bloodied, and sent the lightning bolt that had struck him down and called him back to heaven long before he could live to see how runty his son, his only son, had grown. In this, God was gracious, sparing Kalintz the sight of his son dwarfed by a titanic woman.

And yet, God did not smile upon Nitz. For even then, God had sent his father back to earth in the form of his monument: the heap of stone skulls beneath the plated stone feet that blossomed into a terrible, fearsome stone flower. Fraumvilt was its sole petal, its sole thorn, and the re-creation of the mace stared down at Nitz with even more hatred than it did the country below.

"Intimidating fellow," Maddy continued, observing the statue's face.

Behind his Crusader's helm, carved so delicately as to faithfully re-create the visage of the first skull Kalintz had ever crushed, Nitz imagined that he probably frowned.

"It almost makes one wonder what was behind it," she muttered. He felt her good eye staring into his own skull, trying to crack it open and poke whatever twitching lumps held the answer.

"I wouldn't know," he replied softly. "Father never removed his helmet."

"Never?"

"At least, never around me." He rolled his shoulders with a sigh. "Nor my mother, if she can be believed."

"Can she?"

"She was an honest woman, all told."

"Huh." Maddy turned her stare back up to the towering monument. "So the greater question would be why they ever fell in love in the first place?"

"They didn't." Nitz felt a laugh tickle in his throat. "Procreation is all God demands of the faithful; fresh blood for the war. Love has nothing to do with it."

"In the north, a man is required to kill no less than twelve legs' worth of beasts before he can propose to a woman." She grunted. "Or a woman is required to craft him a fine weapon before she can hope to court him. The product itself, be it meat or steel, is largely symbolic. The dedication required for such a thing is what is demanded. Not from God to man, but from man to woman and vice versa."

Nitz smacked his lips.

"No wonder you're all such savages."

"I crafted such a weapon as to allow me my pick of any man in my village."

Her words were accompanied by a sigh, a wistful breath punctuating her thought. Nitz shifted his feet uncomfortably; he was unused to such a sound. Her morbid laughter, the sounds of her boots crunching on gravel laden with corpses, these were sounds that had grown familiar enough to be comfortable. When her voice dripped with nostalgia, he grew worried.

"And you can have it back now," he grunted. Reaching under his vest, he proceeded to undo the complicated buckles and straps securing the weapon to his back. "We're far enough away that Father Scheitzen's church won't hear it fall."

He winced at those words. The weapon fell to the ground with a thunderous clatter, its steel ringing a mournful dirge as it struck the earth.

"Stones don't hear," Maddy growled, reaching down to pluck the axe up in one powerful hand. "If they did, though, they'd hear you spilling yourself on your trousers when I gutted you for disrespecting my axe again."

"Oh, come now, Wolfreiz—"

"*Vulf,*" she corrected hotly, "his name is Vulf. Wolfreiz is what you pious piss-drinkers call him."

"Vulf," he repeated, "is a strong and sturdy weapon, perfectly capable of suffering the earth's embrace for a few moments." He shot her a cheerful wink. "After all, he was wrought by the finest hands in the north, was he not?"

"Mm," she grunted. She swept her good eye about, surveying the lack of flesh in their vicinity. "We're far away now, are we?"

"Yes," he nodded. "Why?" He cringed suddenly as her free hand went for her robe. "Oh, good lord, don't do it in front of me. Can't you wait until you find a bush or something?"

"It itches," she replied simply.

Any further protest he had was squelched by the sound of fabric tearing and the murmur of cloth. In the blink of an eye, her habit was off and clenched in her hand. He attempted to turn away but was mesmerized, as he always was, by the sight of what lay beneath.

The rough leather that sought to encase her had been soundly defeated long ago, leaving tight-fitting scraps that clung to her body with resigned determination. What considerable amount of skin was left bare was criss-crossed by scars, dotted by fresh bruises, and tattooed by blue and black designs that snaked down her biceps, wrists, and flanks. It was a master-piece of muscle, a testament to how much blood, heathen or no, she had spilled.

Against such a wall of strength, the evidence of his handiwork, the bandages that covered her at odd intervals and the jagged scars where his stitching had gone awry, seemed more like desecration than medicine.

He had little time to think on it, for his vision was obscured by black as she tossed the robes over him.

"You've got needlework to do," she said.

He found his way out of the tangle just in time to see her pull her cap off, shaking free a wild mane of brown that descended past her shoulders in a long, frayed ponytail. He caught that more deftly as she tossed it to him, thanking whatever saint watched over tailors that she hadn't ripped the garment. It had taken him months to re-create the stiff-browed head-gear faithfully.

"You ever think of investing in a shirt or something?" he grumbled, folding the garments and tucking them under his arm. "It'd draw less attention."

"Why would I want to draw less attention?"

"It would mean less fighting."

She blinked at that, staring blankly.

"Fine, it would mean less fighting for *me*. Besides, here in the king-doms, women dress with civility."

"Civilization is relative."

"To?"

"To whoever has the biggest weapon to decide who gets to say what civilization is."

"Ah."

"Shirts catch fire, anyway," she replied, hefting her axe. "If we're going to kill a dragon, damp leather will burn less easily."

"What's this '*we*' business, anyway?"

"You're not coming?"

"I'm coming, certainly, but I figured *you'd* do the fighting." He coughed. "Like you always do."

"Hiding behind a woman," she snickered. "Your father would be proud!"

"Had he seen the ogre pretending to be a woman that I hid behind, he probably would be."

As they set down the hill, Nitz didn't quite believe that. His father, undoubtedly, would have criticized him for stumbling in the footprints of the northern woman's stride. Criticism no longer bothered Nitz; he had developed skin thick enough to resist the taunts and jabs thrown his way from the road, well out of Maddy's hearing. And reach.

His father had never criticized with words, however . . .

"Where is it this dragon was seen last, anyway?"

"West," Nitz replied, "if the map's to be believed."

"So we go."

"So say we all."

Before them, the road stretched out endlessly, over the hills and forests that marked the land forsaken by God. Behind them, Father Scheitzen's temple cast its stalwart shadow, hiding the peaceful shame of the country-side from the heavens. And above Nitz, his father watched with unblinking stone eyes.

ঔ

"LISTEN, I know it seems like I erred, but it was an error of virtue."

Armecia was not listening.

"You can hardly fault me for that."

Armecia faulted him for that.

"For the love of the lord," Leonard grunted. "At least let me put down the damn boulder."

She turned a scowl, one part icy, one part pitch, upon him and sur-veyed him bent and crooked under the jagged rock. With a contemptuous snort, she turned her back on him and made a fleeting gesture.

"Fine," she replied, "but only until I can find something bigger." She pointed a finger toward the earth. "Lenny, put it down."

It landed with a heavy crashing sound, followed by a loud popping sound as the knight knuckled his back. She frowned, more at herself than at him; there was no logical reason why he continued doing that, she rea-soned. He should be well beyond pain at this point.

You can bring a man back from the dead, but you can't cure a bad back, she scolded herself, *you deserved to be burned.* She rubbed her arm. *Or at least bashed over the head a few times.*

"Frankly, I'm not sure what you're so upset about." He cricked his neck with a much louder popping sound. "I was only following your commands." He held up a finger in emphasis. "First law: protect the half-breed."

"And the second law?"

"Is superseded by the first."

"The second law," she fumed, "is *protect the book*. As it turns out, the *half-breed* is rather partial to that one. Who knows what they're doing to it?"

She shuddered at the thought of greasy hands running through its dry, delicate pages, beady, ratlike eyes going over its masterfully penned script with blasphemous disregard for its content.

That is, she admitted, *if they haven't already burned it.*

"Well," Leonard responded, "I suppose you should have had better foresight."

"Oh, don't you turn this back on *me*."

"I wouldn't . . . but, I mean, it *is* your fault."

"*My* fault." She pursed her lips. "For being burned at the stake?"

"First of all, you weren't burned at the stake, were you?" He cleared his throat. *"You're welcome."* He held up a pair of fingers. "And second, did you or did you *not* do what they say you did to that child?"

"She was either going to end up dead or as a Scarred Sister, locked away in a nunnery." She tilted her nose up snootily. "Forgive me for being considerate of a child's future, Lenny."

"Okay, I forgive you."

"No," she rubbed her eyes, "that was sarcasm, not a command."

"You ought to work on that."

"Amongst other things, apparently"—her stalk was heralded by a sigh—"such as my choice in thralls. You weren't my first choice, you know."

"It is difficult to forget, what with you only reminding me every half hour." He slid a hand into his pocket, producing a piece of dried parchment and a small, leather pouch. "Fortunately, I have *ways* of forgetting."

"Again, huh?" She glanced as he emptied a green herb in a neat little line upon the paper. "You can't even stop for just a few moments?"

"Apparently not." He licked the paper's edge, rolling it into a small, twisted cigarillo. "Though, of course, if you were halfway competent at what you did to me, we probably wouldn't have this problem." He placed it between his lips and leaned over her shoulder. "Help me out here."

"Help you with your addiction?"

"You're the one that chose it."

It was difficult to argue with that point, she admitted—but not to him. With a sigh, she held a hand up and snapped her finger. There was a brief spark, a puff of smoke, and, when both cleared, the tip of her longest digit was alight with a flickering flame. He leaned closer and took a few puffs, followed by a long draw of breath.

"There we are." His sigh was an acrid cloud of smoke. "I don't really disagree with your choice of anchors, mind you, but you could at least give me permission to carry around some matches."

The thought was tempting, and she had considered it many times before. Matches, of course, would be far less conspicuous than conjuring fire out of flesh, not to mention it would cut down significantly on all manner of whining and complaining.

The problem, of course, was that all that reminded him of his previous life *also* gave him free will. Free will was admirable . . . in people who could use it responsibly, of course.

The man that had once been Sir Leonard was not a man of such capabilities.

That thought gave her the will to deny him his request for matches, as did the comfort that such denials prevented a re-creation of what his previous lords had called previous glories in a previous life.

For all that, however, he was growing more difficult to control. The fact that he had drawn his sword without being commanded to had proven that. The idea of the townspeople being slaughtered, she admitted without remorse, was not such an appalling thought. After all, if they couldn't be grateful for the life of a child, she saw little reason to be grateful for their lives.

It wasn't as if their god was the right one, anyway.

And yet, if he fought the townspeople, someone would eventually fight him back. Someone would rush to their kitchen or their barn, someone would seize a pitchfork, a butcher knife, or a sword of their own. Someone would stick it in his neck, thigh, shoulder, or arm.

Then everyone would notice when he didn't bleed.

"So, anyway," Leonard continued, completely unappreciative of any internal struggle, "I think there's another town a few miles out yonder." He waved a hand in no particular direction. "You know . . . I mean . . . whatever yonder is. We can probably make it by sundown, find a place to bed down, then be off before anyone can think to burn you alive."

"We're not going to any town."

"Oh, really?" He grimaced. "I hate sleeping outside . . . you know, I *did* hate it. I still would if I slept."

"Good for you. We're not going to be sleeping outside, either."

"Then . . ." His grimace became a wrinkled, stubble-laden crag. "Oh, dear."

"If I have my way, we won't be sleeping at all."

"You can't be—"

"I've already come up with something. It's a good plan." She paused, tapped her cheek thoughtfully. "Well, it's the *only* plan, so it's as good as any. You just throw yourself at the stupid thing until you manage to stab it . . . wherever it's supposed to be weak." She glanced over her shoulder. "We should find that out. At any rate, you'll kill it eventually. It can't hurt you . . . I assume."

"Armecia . . ."

"If you've got a better way to kill a dragon, I'd love to hear it."

"All this over a *book* . . ."

No sooner had the words passed his lips than she froze, in spirit and body. Standing stock-still, so rigid as to render her breath barely detectable, her shadow seemed to grow long and cold, reaching out to engulf the knight behind her.

Leonard noted, not without a grimace and not for the first time, that when a breeze whistled across the road, kicking up dust and dead leaves, her hair hung black and unmoved.

"It's not just 'a book' . . ." her voice echoed off of nothing, reverberating through the branches and birds and killing their songs in flight.

Leonard knew that. Things that were *just* books usually didn't warrant laws being made about them. Of course, he thought, this could have been avoided if he had just killed all the townsfolk to begin with. A pile of corpses was easier to deal with than a dragon; corpses, at least, didn't move . . . or breathe fire.

Truly, she had only herself to blame for stopping him. However, given the rigidity of her spine and the particularly fierce clench of her rear cheeks, it struck him as a less than sound idea to say so.

"Besides"—she sighed, going slack on her bones—"dragons have hoards."

"Amongst other things."

"Right, they have fiery breath and hoards."

"Actually, I heard that the breathing-fire thing was just a myth."

"Well, they're supposed to be creatures of myth, so we should be fine. *Regardless*"—she held up a finger to silence further discourse—"hoards mean gold."

"Ah, yes." Leonard sucked thoughtfully upon his cigarillo. "The transcendental lubricant."

"Right, the—" She turned and stared at him for a moment, aghast. "What?"

"Well, it seems like everyone loves gold, doesn't it?" He exhaled a ring of smoke, his grimace seeming to suggest that he wished he could have done it earlier. "Illicit dealers being no exception."

"If even a bit about dragons is true, we'd only need a handful of its treasure to keep you in green for years." She smiled proudly. "The rest, we use to get back home."

"Well, isn't that just brilliant." He sneered. "Go and fight a dragon, and, if we somehow *do* manage to survive, go *back* to a place rife with Crusaders, murderers, and rapists."

"That's hardly a valid criticism coming from *your* lips," she replied snarkily. "You used to be all three!"

"And I would still be resting nicely on those laurels if you hadn't come along."

"Third law," she replied simply.

"Of course"—he sighed—"Sir Leonard of Savhael shall be returned to whence he came when he is no longer needed."

"Precisely. And this is one step closer to your no longer being needed." She rolled her shoulders. "My father had a lot of debts when he died. This dragon business will satisfy the ones that can be paid in gold."

"And the rest?"

Her face twisted into a frown. Her shadow grew a foot longer.

"Those we shall pay by other means."

৸৬

"WELL . . . that's a . . ." Nitz scratched his chin, painfully aware of the fact that it was difficult to look contemplative without a beard, "that's . . ."

"A lair," Maddy finished for him.

He nodded; it was, indeed, a lair.

To call it a cave would seem to label it as something naturally occurring in the earth. To call it a den would imply more coziness than such a thing deserved. To call it a nest was outright ridiculous. Certainly, he hadn't expected it to be a pretty thing of twigs and feathers, but nor had he quite expected so much . . .

What's the word? he pondered. *"Spectacle"? "Display"?*

"Filth," Maddy grunted, as if in answer to his thoughts.

"That's it! This cave . . ." It hadn't occurred to him that he ought not to be making such a grand and proud gesture, given the locale. "This *lair* . . . is utterly filthy!"

"Brilliant."

Its opening rather resembled a mouth, he thought: vast and gaping. In lieu of a tongue, however, a long trail of charnel in various states of decay and burnt beyond immediate recognition extended from the inky depths. In lieu of teeth, various skulls of various creatures that had walked on four legs or on two dangled, caught in the vines hanging over its rocky lip.

To Zeigfreid's credit, Nitz had to admit, the skulls, at least, were polished to a spotless white sheen.

"So, how do you want to do this?" Maddy grunted, apparently less impressed.

"Yeah," Nitz hummed thoughtfully, "we do need a strategy, don't we?"

"We do?" She hefted Vulf over a shoulder. "I was thinking we'd do things the usual way."

"That being?"

"I go in, hack its head off, and come out in time to search for a rag for you to clean yourself off with after you soil yourself."

"That might be well and good for heathens and brigands," he replied, supposing he ought to be more offended, "but this is a dragon in a dark cave. In the time it took you to fumble about and get your face chewed off, I could knit myself a pair of new trousers." He added a coy smile. "Unless you're hoping he dies of embarrassment when you accidentally grope him, I'd think of something else."

"Huh?" She scratched her chin, surveying the long black furrow of flesh upon the ground. "Unless this is his mother's heap of rotting charnel, he seems to like meat well enough. We can just round up a cow, tie a rope to it, and send it in."

"Fishing . . . for dragons."

"Stranger things have happened."

He blinked.

"No . . . really, they haven't." He turned back to the cave. "It's a *beast*, right? It has to make water. We can wait until it comes out to do *that* and then—"

"Who says it has to make water?" she interrupted. "It's an agent of your supposed Devil, isn't it? Maybe it pisses oil and sets it alight." She clapped her hands in a sudden fit of realization. "*That's* how they spew fire."

"I somehow doubt it."

"Either way"—she shrugged—"it's just not right to axe someone while he's doing his business."

Nitz might have suggested that ethics could likely be suspended when battling denizens of hell, if not for the fact that it would undoubtedly lead into a discussion of what fell under the category of "denizen." That, he knew, would be an argument that would end in his defeat and likely with a boot planted in his groin.

After all, he thought with a sigh, it was only ten years ago that the northerners had been removed from the list of "denizens" by virtue of the fact that they had all been slaughtered or converted.

With that in mind, he resigned himself to merely offering an encouraging smile.

"We'll keep thinking, then."

It was only after he turned back to the cave that he noticed that her gaze was directed somewhere else, far into the underbrush surrounding the tiny clearing.

"I suppose *I'll* think of something, then," he muttered. "Though, you know, it wouldn't hurt if you—"

"Shut up," she hissed, waving him down. "We're being watched!"

"What?" He instinctively, and, with less shame than he suspected he ought to feel, crept behind her sizable frame. "How can you tell?"

"Something"—her nostrils quivered—"stinks."

"Well, they might just be passing through," he said softly. "Don't kill them."

"Ha. Right." She paused for a moment, then looked at him with one eye wide. "Oh . . . you were serious."

"I was."

"I guess you're going to be disappointed, then."

༇༖

"DAMN it all," Armecia whispered. "I think they saw us."

The colossal, half-clad woman now had her one black eye focused intently on the brush, narrowed to such a ferocious slit as to bore a deep hole in the tree behind them. A tree, she noted with some frustration, against which Leonard's dirty gray chain mail shone starkly.

The large plumes of smoke, of course, were of no great help, either.

"What makes you think that?" he asked, taking a long drag.

There was a sudden movement, a bright flash of silver, and the hush of leaves.

Armecia was deaf to her own scream as the axe came hurtling over her head, cleaving through the branches and impaling itself with a hollow, heavy sound against the tree trunk.

The scream she emitted when she turned about, decidedly less so.

The axe neatly separated Leonard's arm from the rest of his body, marred only by the sinuous string that connected the two at his armpit. He didn't seem to notice until it finally snapped, the appendage landing softly upon the leaves.

With a glance that was as blank as hers was horrified, he regarded the stump thoughtfully for a moment, moved it up, then down, then in a brief circle before smacking his lips.

". . . huh."

"Oh lord"—she found the words harder to come by as she looked from the man to the arm to the shining, broad-headed axe—"I can't . . . I need to think of something. Just . . . just don't move, Lenny."

"I think I should."

"What? Why?"

Her answer came in the sound of branches cracking against the force of something large barreling through the underbrush.

Where Leonard's face had once been, in an instant, there was a heavy leather boot connected to a muscular, barely feminine thigh. Armecia, with no more breath to scream, could only gape in horror at the sound of something cracking, something squishing and something heavy falling to the ground as Leonard slumped over.

Sparing a moment to sneer at his fallen body, the tremendous woman turned to regard the girl through a single dark eye. Such a gaze was not contemplative, nor scornful, but rather merely acknowledging, as one might acknowledge a squirrel or a bird.

Armecia would have been content with that, to be a small rodent easily ignored, if not for the woman reaching down to pluck up a large, dead branch from the earth.

Instinct seized her, all fear forgotten in a moment of pure animal action. She found enough clarity of thought to consider with some pride that no animal had the same defenses she had.

It was with that clarity that she found wits enough to close her dark eye and level her chilling blue orb upon the woman.

Gritting her teeth, she felt the power leap from her heart to her head in an instant. Her eye erupted in a cloud of frost, icicles bursting from the iris to surround the thin, azure beam that leapt from her pupil and bit at the woman's torso.

With great glee, she noted the staggering step backwards the woman took as frost coated her abdomen in a thin, blue shell, clinging to muscles and gnawing at them with a hunger unseen in any beast. She held the spell within her eye until she could stand it no longer, until it felt as though the sphere would roll out and plop onto the ground.

She blinked, and when she opened it, it was with less glee that she saw the woman staring at her with a scowl, still standing, if shivering.

"Sorcery." The observation was one of amusement, rather than accusation. "Clever trick," the woman said as she unhurriedly brushed the frost from her belly, revealing blue flesh beneath, "tell me, what do you call that?"

"Eye . . ." Armecia swallowed hard in astonishment, "the Eye of Ajeed."

"Fancy." The woman hefted the massive branch, paused but for a moment to grin at her. "I think I'll call this club 'Maurice.'"

And then, it came crashing down.

ᚼᛒ

WELL, Armecia thought as she surveyed in the infinite blackness stretching out around her, *this isn't so bad.*

Somehow, she had expected death to be something a bit more glamorous, as she had been led to believe all her life.

Her father had told her that the warriors of God were escorted to the foot of His throne by a line of immaculate Crusaders, welcomed forever into a world that bore no hatred or warfare, as a reward for all their bloodshed in His name.

Her mother had told her that there was no afterlife to be experienced, only a brief pause between breaths when one fleshy vessel was shattered and the soul slipped into another, destined to commit the same sins and atrocities that it had in its previous thousand lives.

And the people of the kingdoms had frequently shouted that she was destined for a lake of fire surrounded by walls of red-hot iron, struggling to drag her scorched and savaged body up the slick corners while weight-laden chains sought to pull her back down to the bottom.

Many of them, torches and rope in hand, had seemed not patient enough to wait for that to occur.

In comparison, an eternity of blackness was moderately disappointing. Perhaps, she reasoned, this was the fate reserved for people like her: half-breeds who kept their friends as books and inebriated corpses. Sins that were deemed too great to warrant the glory of perpetual bliss, but far too dull to merit the spectacle of a lake of fire.

"You hit her a little hard, didn't you?"

The shrill, grating voice that occasionally echoed through the dark, she supposed was the worst she deserved; an eternity of annoying questions.

"Threatened you? She's less beefy than a twig!"

Annoying, she thought, and senseless.

And yet, they kept getting louder; perhaps stupid questions were merely the prelude to the lake of fire? The darkness around her seemed to support that idea, as it grew grayer around her, infected by some disease of light.

"The wounds don't look too bad, anyway. The pulse is there . . . just a nasty blow to the head."

But there was pain. The blanket of numbness that swaddled her began to come undone, exposing her body to all manner of aches that flowed through her. Her eyelids twitched inside an aching head, longing to open.

Despite her subconscious warnings, they did anyway, and the darkness, so close to light, twisted to searing red. Her head thundered with a pain she had thought was reserved only for people who ate the flesh of children . . . or puppies . . . or something equally loathsome.

Whatever sins she had committed, they were apparently not grave enough to keep the red from dissipating. As she rubbed her eyes, feeling sticky warmth upon her fingers, she glanced up and looked into the face of God . . .

. . . and was decidedly unimpressed.

In a face resembling an oddly angular knot at the top of a twig, the concern flashing in the young man's eyes was not quite as benevolent as she had hoped. It wasn't a concern that a midwife might have for a pregnant woman, but rather that a beast-soother might have as he debated whether or not to put her out of her misery with a well-placed rock.

She blinked; it hurt to blink. *Why does it hurt to blink?*

That was when she looked down at her hands, stained with red. That only caused her to look down at the earth she lay upon, also red. When she spied the red-cloaked kerchief in his hands, she felt the urge to scream.

"I wouldn't," he said, the particular gape of her mouth not lost on him. "You've lost enough blood that sending it all rushing to your tongue wouldn't be a good idea."

"What . . . happened?"

She rose slowly, putting a hand to her brow as if to shove her missing memory back in through the cut that scarred it. It was moist, she noted, and stinging to the touch, but not quite as painful as she imagined having a head split open should be.

Instinctively, she called to memory a spell as she called to her hands a sort of energy. It was fresh in her mind, having already used it once that day; if it could cure the pox, it could close her head, at least.

A hand placed itself upon her back and she froze, all memories lost as another one steadied her by the shoulder.

"Careful," the young man cautioned. "Moving isn't very wise, either, I should have mentioned." His attentions turned from her to the gaping cave mouth nearby. "Not that it's particularly wise to bash a complete stranger in the head."

Armecia followed his gaze to the monolith of flesh and leather standing nearby. Her brow furrowed into a scowl, despite the pain; she remembered the woman.

The same, apparently, could not be said for the muscular female's own recollection. She merely rolled her shoulders, the gesture vast enough to be directed at both Armecia and the young man.

"Better safe than regretful, I always say."

"You never say that," he retorted.

"Oh," she hummed thoughtfully, "better to have smashed than never to have smashed at all, then. I'm pretty sure I've said that before."

"You *could* apologize," Armecia grumbled, with an intentional lack of conviction.

"You *could* be thankful you didn't end up like *him*."

The woman pointed a finger long enough to be a knife to the earth beside her. Armecia followed it and grimaced.

The sight of Sir Leonard wounded was something she was far unused to screaming over. Instead of fear, there was only frustration in the sight of the bootprints on his face, the skin hanging from his jaw, and the severed arm clutched to his chest like a dismembered doll.

That, she knew, *will take a lot of healing.*

"What in God's name did you do to him?" she asked as a blacksmith might ask what happened to a sword he was to repair.

"It would appear fairly obvious, wouldn't it?" The young man answered for his taller companion. "Truth be told, I had expected to hear of Sir Leonard slain in combat or torn apart by a Hashuni mob." He coughed, made a show of waving his hand before his nose. "Dismembered by a savage nun and reeking of weed was not entirely expected."

"You know him?" She turned toward the young man, her eyes widening as a second realization dawned on her. "Wait, did you say . . . Hashuni?"

"That's what they're called, right?" He clapped a hand to his mouth, eyes wide with genuine regret. "I'm sorry. Heathen is the more proper term." He offered a sheepish smile. "And it'd be more accurate to say that I *met* him, yes."

He rose from beside her and folded his hands behind him as he frowned at the knight's corpse.

"Back then, of course, he preferred to be called the Scourge of Savhael. What with the thousands of Hash— Forgive me, heathens he had slain." He raised a brow at her. "Given that, I must say it's a bit surprising to find him traveling with one of them . . . or half of one, at any rate."

The calmness in his voice unnerved Armecia. Perhaps she had been used to such recognition of her heritage being accompanied by scorn and torches that a casual observation seemed horrific by virtue of conditioning.

He might just be open-minded, she thought, but quickly discarded the idea. He was one of *them*, a Kingdomer, a book-burner. His were a people embroiled in an endless war against the people of her mother, for reasons only their God fathomed and did not care to share. He was her enemy; he would be her death.

But then . . . why hasn't he killed me already?

"Granted"—he cleared his throat and looked down at Sir Leonard— "the fact that he's still breathing is far more surprising."

Oh, lord . . .

Within her chest, she felt her heart grow fleshy arms and crawl up her rib cage to lodge itself firmly in her throat.

Probably for the best, she figured. There was no way she could explain it, explain Sir Leonard, that anyone, a scholar, a northman, or even a Hashuni, let alone a book-burner, would understand in a beneficial way.

They already know you're a sorceress, she told herself, *a witch. That's bad enough without knowing that you brought a man back from the dead!* She felt her left eye twitch. *Maybe I can zap them, bring them down, and take Lenny out of here . . . or at least get out myself.*

A quick glance to the tall woman, now standing closer, and she discarded that notion. The flesh of her abdomen, still blue from the spell, was barely enough to warrant an irritated scratch from her. The Eye of

Ajeed hadn't stopped her, had barely slowed her down. Spells, she decided, would not resolve this.

A sign, she decided, *a sign to end this. This is God's way of telling me there's no need for it. No need for him.*

Staring at Leonard upon the earth, his body twitching with what might have been breath, she frowned. Amongst the multitudes of anger and scorn she had previously felt for him, the pang of pity was uncomfortable.

He, too, had been one of them. Not a good man in her eyes, but good enough that other men had called him good. He had participated in the endless war and drunk his fill of blood and been righteously and fairly slain. Better he lie here now and sleep forever, as he had slept when she first found him with a spear through his chest.

End it with him, she told herself, *give up the lies and find another way to settle Father's debts. A way without sorcery . . . that makes sense, doesn't it?*

To someone else, it might have. For Armecia, it only made her leap to her feet.

"LENNY!" she suddenly screamed, "WAKE UP!"

The young man recoiled away from the knight, the woman taking a cautious step backwards. Apparently, of all the things they thought he might do, sitting up and scratching his head with his severed arm while he blinked blearily was not at the top of the list.

"What happened?" he asked, then slowly became aware of the stump where his arm had been. Quietly, he glanced from it, to his arm, to the woman towering over him. "Ah . . . yeah."

With a speed that shocked the woman into inaction, he lunged to his feet, swinging his club of flesh and bone. With a force that surprised everyone, it connected solidly with her jaw, sending her reeling backwards, a spout of blood arcing from her mouth to spatter the ground.

Whatever revulsion Armecia and the young man might have had for the sight was apparently not shared by the woman. When she recovered, her smile was a jagged red gash in her mouth. She hefted her axe, cracked her neck, and rushed to meet Sir Leonard, Scourge of Savhael, risen.

"Damn," Armecia cursed under her breath as she watched them lumber toward each other, two foul abominations of scarred flesh and dirty weapons. "Damn, damn, damn . . . what made me think that was a good idea?"

"A decent enough question," the young man mused, apparently unconcerned. "Judging by Maddy's grin, she's probably intent on not stopping for a bit." He glanced to Armecia, held out a bag. "Jerky?"

"What?" she blinked. "I just . . . sent a man to fight your giant lady friend, and you're offering me dried meat?"

"A flavorful assortment of dried meats. But . . . I guess *we* could fight, too"—he shrugged—"if you really wanted to. But really, I'm far more interested in why a half-blooded sorceress with a greasy zombie is fighting my giant lady friend in front of a dragon's lair." He pulled a piece of meat from the bag. "I'm Nitz, by the way."

Armecia blinked, glanced over as Lenny took a knee to the groin and cackled, then reached out and took a piece of the jerky for herself.

"Armecia."

THERE was a crack of thunder heralding the blow, a spray of splinters punctuating it, and when the dust settled, Sir Leonard peered through the other side of a tree trunk, his shoulders and neck firmly lodged in the wood. Maddy's laughter was soft and gentle, a giggle she reserved only for lovers and shoving men's heads through trees.

"That's it, is it?" She tapped her axe against the ground. "Spent after one dismemberment?"

"Just give me a moment," he grunted, trying to squirm his way free. "I'll be ready to go in just a few breaths."

"Don't they all say that?" Maddy hefted her boot, and, through her one good eye, leveled it squarely at the knight's rear end. "However, I'm ready *now*."

From across the clearing, Nitz paused in the middle of chewing jerky to wince. In a spray of brown and green, Leonard went tumbling out of the tree trunk and rolling like a limp doll upon the earth, only to rise again, clutching his severed arm like a club as Maddy stalked toward him casually.

"He's not bleeding," the young man noted immediately.

Punctured, pummeled, and pounded as he might be, there wasn't a trace of red upon the knight. That wasn't to say he looked at all good, however; Nitz felt the dried meat rise in his gullet as he spied the large, jagged splinter rolling about in Leonard's eye socket. The knight didn't seem to notice, but Nitz felt compelled to speak, regardless.

"Should . . . should we help him?"

Armecia casually reached over and into the bag of meat, producing a piece of her own. Chewing thoughtfully as Leonard loosed a war whoop that was far too enthusiastic for a man whose eyeball had just been replaced by a branch, she shook her head.

"He can take care of himself."

"He doesn't seem to be doing a very good job of it so far."

"Well, I mean he can't *beat* her, obviously," Armecia replied, "but he'll probably wear her out eventually."

"I suppose that's true." Nitz forced his own bite down. "He doesn't seem to be tiring . . . in fact, he doesn't seem to even notice he's hurt."

"Hm . . . was it the severed arm that gave it away?" She grinned a grin full of beef-stained teeth and winked her blue eye. "He's a *Nazj-Nazj*. He'll be fine."

"A *Nazj-Nazj*." He chewed once, swallowed, then blinked. "You brought Sir Leonard, Scourge of Savhael, slaughterer of women and children, back and turned him into a demonic vessel."

"In summation," she shrugged, "why? What do you know about it?"

"I read."

"You're literate. Congratulations."

"I mean I've *read* the annals of the Uncharred Library," he replied, decidedly more hastily. "Tomes of Hashuni myth and sorcery that, after reading, I think *should* have been burned."

"But are left whole for purposes of studying the heathen." She rolled her eyes. "I've heard the rumors. But you've read about *Nazj-Nazj*, so you know they're not that big a thing."

"A *thing*?" He gestured to the brawl wildly. "A corpse raised from the dead, infused with a demon, and anchored to the mortal world, is not just a *thing*. A man who doesn't bleed and who batters women with his severed arm qualifies as something slightly more *blasphemous* than a 'thing'!"

"Listen, if I phrased everything so gloomily, I could make *you* sound pretty vile, too."

"This was Sir Leonard! A friend of my father's!"

"But not *your* friend."

He could find no words to offer in reply, no fury, righteousness, or combination thereof that he suspected should have been in his voice.

She was right. Sir Leonard had been his father's friend.

For obvious reasons, of course. Sir Leonard, if legends were true, had been a holy terror before his namesake. Savhael, the city that straddled the border between the kingdoms and heathenry, ceased to *be* after he visited it. All great Crusaders were named for what they destroyed.

His own father had an accruement of titles the equivalent of a small country.

"Besides," Armecia replied, "it's not like it's *really* Sir Leonard out there."

He looked toward the brawl, eyes wide. In the moments he had been conversing with the sorceress, the battle had shifted in favor of Sir Leonard. He now straddled Maddy's torso, pinning her arms under his knees and bludgeoning his arm against her scarred face with a holy vengeance.

Holy as it was, no legend ever mentioned Sir Leonard having the ability to beat women . . . with his arm, at least.

"That's . . . not Sir Leonard?"

"Well, I mean, it's his *body*, sure." Armecia bit off a large piece of meat. "Some of his brains are probably rattling around in there, too."

"But the rest of him is demon," Nitz muttered gloomily.

"Spirit, actually."

"The difference being?"

"The difference is that your people tend to brand whatever they don't particularly care for as 'demon,' which, while understandable for a race of ignorant, god-bothering book-burners, would be far too broad a category to be of any use for classifying Lenny."

She winced as Maddy wrenched a hand out from beneath the knight's legs, seized him by the throat, and pulled him to the earth. Digging her knee sharply into his chest as she drew herself up, she snarled and delivered a large-booted kick to his side.

"Not to mention that a demon would put up a better fight than this."

"Well, stop him, then!" Nitz demanded, painfully aware of how his voice tended to crack during moments of attempted authority. "You can command him, can't you?"

"Well, not *now*; he hasn't had anything to smoke." Seeing his confusion, she rolled her eyes. "Apparently you haven't read far enough. Putting a demon—"

"Spirit."

"I lied. There's no difference." She waved a hand dismissively. "Anyway, it's a thing not of earth, so it can't exist in a living body . . . or, rather, a body that *used* to be living, without an anchor."

"Something to tie it to the earth." Nitz nodded. "I read that chapter. Witches use heathen relics to tie their spirits to their service."

"If they're rich, sure. *I* had to make do with what I could find when I found his body."

"And you chose . . . the Devil's herb?"

"Well"—she sighed—"Savhael is only known for three things: weed, women, and song. And by the time I found Lenny with a spear through his chest, he had already crushed and raped two of those." She cringed. "I'll leave it to you to decide what he did to which."

"I'm not sure I follow." He scratched his chin, painfully aware of the futility of trying to look philosophical without even a wisp of facial hair. "The books all say that a relic is required to give the spirit meaning and duty in order to keep it obedient."

"True enough, for most *Nazj-Nazj*. However, most witches use demons of pride."

"There's . . . there's types?"

"It wouldn't be interesting otherwise, would it?" She talked through a full mouth. "Demons of pride, or spirits of metal, if you're versed in the old scriptures, won't obey without purpose. They require a relic to give them their duty, something to be proud about, as the name implies. Otherwise, you've got nothing but a lifeless husk . . . apparently a humble one."

"Whereas Sir Leonard . . ."

"Is powered by a demon of wrath," she replied. "Storm spirit. He needs something to mellow him a bit; otherwise, there's the exact opposite of what happens with demons of pride."

"He rips himself apart?"

"No, he rips *me* apart."

"Hence . . ."

"The weed, yes." She beamed at this, apparently quite proud. "It works. The more he smokes, the more coherent he becomes, the easier he is to command. But there's a problem."

"One would expect reanimating corpses to bear their own little issues, yes."

"I *know*, right?" She punched him in the arm, apparently missing the sarcasm. "See, wrath demons don't like to be chained. They're constantly fighting their host body for control. The problem with that is, that the host fights *back*. So, the more he smokes, the less he fights."

"The less he fights," Nitz hummed, "the more his host fights?"

"Precisely. If the demon wins, then it takes control and kills me. If the demon loses, then Sir Leonard takes control."

"And kills you."

"Isn't that how it always ends?"

"In the books, it does."

"And those were all crafty, full-blooded sorceresses, not half-breeds."

"Wouldn't it be easier to get rid of him? I mean, it'd be easier if you hadn't raised him in the first place, but . . ."

"Well, for the time being, I still need him. All I have to do is keep a careful eye on how much he smokes."

"Need him . . . for what?"

Immediately, her head went low as she averted her gaze. She seemed to shrink then, curling into herself like a scolded puppy. No, Nitz corrected himself, more like a child, a frightened child . . . a frightened child with a large, murderous, one-armed doll, he corrected himself further.

A litany of condemnations had already formed in his mind, words he knew he ought to hurl at her, along with stones and a torch, if he had one handy. But he found himself unable to bring them to his tongue.

Her position was uncomfortably familiar, a mirror in a woman's body of how he had seen himself. He was always shrinking, always wilting, like a plant starved for light in a broad, all-consuming shadow. And he could see her now in that shadow, and he felt the urge to show her the reassuring smile he never could see through the darkness of that shadow.

The shadow that only a father could cast.

"I need him for lots of things," she replied, apparently as unaware of the eternity of silence that had passed as he was. "Specifically, I need him to kill a dragon for me."

"What . . . Zeigfreid?"

"You've heard of him?" She blinked, thumped herself in the head. "Of course you have. Why else would you be here?"

"I don't know . . ." He glanced up at the macabre décor dangling from the lair's mouth. "Sightseeing?"

"While that wouldn't surprise me at all, I'll have to protest your presence." She rose up, dusted her skirt off, and assumed a position he could only assume was intended to be intimidating. "We'll be killing Zeigfreid."

"With?" Nitz sneered, gesturing across the clearing to Maddy, who was apparently attempting to induce some form of oral intimacy between Leonard and a large stone. "Your frozen-eye trick didn't even slow Maddy down."

"I've got more powerful tricks than that." She matched his sneer. "Besides, it'll be a dragon, not some psychopathic barbarian man of a woman."

"She's just . . ." He glanced over at the one-eyed warrior woman and grimaced. "Unrefined. Besides, what do you even need to kill Zeigfreid for?"

"A book."

"A book."

"You've got a better reason?"

"Lord and land," he replied, puffing up as best he could. "The mandate of heaven and the command of the Order. Zeigfreid is the Devil's work in His purest form and must be destroyed."

Her eyebrow, cocked just high enough to be insulting, suggested that she wasn't believing it. Either that, he thought, or she had actually seen what he looked like with his chest puffed out and was restraining laughter.

"I don't believe you."

Somehow, he thought, he should be less relieved at that than he was.

"Why not? I'm a very impressive . . . you know, I'm a pretty good Crusader vassal."

"I've seen many of your people before," she replied, "and I've heard the whole 'mandate' and 'kill the heathen' rhetoric before. They say it with conviction." She reached and deflated his chest with a single jab of her finger. "You . . . not so much."

Struggling hard to convince himself that her words were the reason for the sudden ache in his heart, he felt himself wither under her. He could feel her eye boring into him, regardless of the fact that he had turned away; which eye, he couldn't be sure, partially due to having no desire to decide which one was more disturbing.

He felt a hand on his shoulder and looked up and saw her smile. It was a pretty smile, he thought, unusually white, but rather pleasant against her dusky skin, dark hair, and dual-colored eyes.

"Not to mention," she said, "there's the whole 'not killing me while I was unconscious' thing. Not that I'm not grateful, but I doubt a Crusader, even a vassal, would pass up the opportunity to kill a heathen, even half of one."

He found himself more comforted by her words, her touch, than he knew he should be. She was a heathen, after all, an enemy of God, a spiller of Crusader blood and slayer of godly men. Beyond that, she was a *sorceress*, a decrepit matriarch that stood for everything any good Kingdomer stood against.

She was an enemy. She was *his* enemy. She was *the* enemy.

Yet, when she asked, he found himself unable to stop from answering.

"What do you fight for, Nitz?"

"Fraumvilt," he said with a sigh.

"What?"

"Fraumvilt," he repeated, "my father's mace."

"You're risking your life for a weapon?"

"Technically, I'm risking Maddy's life. And it's not for a weapon; it's for Fraumvilt."

"Look, regardless of whatever you might have heard about the Hashuni, we don't actually have the innate gift to understand what in God's name you're talking about if you keep repeating the same word over and over. Who was your father that made his mace so special?"

Nitz grimaced. He was hoping to have kept it a secret, or at least, to have never mentioned it to a heathen in a position to kill him. For she was, he reminded himself, still a heathen; she would most certainly have heard of his father.

And yet, again, he found himself unable to resist answering.

"Kalintz." The name fled off his tongue as he held his breath.

She blinked, and he breathed. That, he decided, was better than what he had expected.

"Kalintz . . ." she repeated.

"Kalintz."

"*That* Kalintz?"

"That Kalintz."

"Kalintz the Heavenly Killer?"

"Yes."

"Kalintz, God's Scourge of the South?"

"Uh-huh."

"Kalintz the—"

"The Divine Destroyer, the Glorious Butcher, the Humble Murderer, and the Servile Slaughterer," Nitz paused to cough, "as well as the Rapist From On High, toward the end of his life."

He had expected her to use her magic on him, then, to freeze him or burn him or turn him into a toad or his genitals into squawking chickens. He had *hoped* that she would merely settle for turning Sir Leonard away from his current battle to break his neck quickly.

What he hadn't expected was for her to scratch her head, swallow her jerky, and break wind.

"Dear me," she said.

"You're not . . ." He bit his tongue, unsure as to whether to continue, given his stroke of luck. "I mean, you're not mad at me? You're half—"

"So I was reminded, daily." Armecia's glower turned bitter. "By both sides of my family. My father's, at least, had a reason to loathe me." She turned a smile to him, just as pretty, he noted. "Suffice to say, I know that families aren't always the blessing they're supposed to be."

"And I can see how a book would be worth fighting a dragon over."

Armecia hummed at that, then reached out to take a piece of jerky.

"You know," she said, "I think I like the way I said it better."

"Yeah, I know."

"But listen," she began, "a dragon's a big thing, isn't it? It can be divided into many smaller pieces, enough, at least, so that we can both prove we killed it."

"If we can ever fight it," Nitz muttered, eyeing the dragon's lair. "We can't fight it in there."

"Too dark," Armecia agreed.

"And it doesn't seem to want to come out." He sighed as the battle between Maddy and Leonard roared into his view. "One would think he would at least come out to see what all the noise was about."

"One would think . . ."

Armecia scratched her chin contemplatively, causing a twinge of resentment to fester in Nitz's heart. How did *she* manage to look so much more intelligent doing it, he wondered.

"I think I've got an idea, though," she replied. Glancing up at the fight, she barked out an order. "Lenny, stop fighting!"

Almost immediately, the knight lowered his severed arm as he stared at her with an incredulous expression. Such outrage, however, quickly shifted to agony as Maddy's leather-bound fist came crashing into his jaw, sending him to the ground. While surprised, Nitz felt the need to call out as she raised her axe.

"Maddy, stop!" he shrieked. "Don't kill him!"

"I feel we may have a difference of opinion of who takes orders from whom," the woman replied, keeping her axe raised high. "But, just for humor's sake, why shouldn't I kill him?"

"We can use him to kill the dragon." He glanced at Armecia. "That's where you were going with this, right?"

"Right."

"Right, Maddy!" he continued. "He can't feel pain, anyway. He's not alive."

At this, the woman's face shifted. The mass of scars became dejected, like a disappointed child. With a sigh, she shouldered her axe, bowed her head, and turned around, kicking at the earth.

"What's the point, then . . ."

Nitz smiled to himself; usually, getting her to stop wasn't that easy. That thought brought another realization to mind as he whirled toward Armecia.

"Wait a tick," he grunted, "you said you couldn't command him because he hadn't had enough to smoke."

"Hey, I lied about that, too! What a coincidence!"

"That's not a coincidence, it's just you being a b—"

"*As I was saying*," she interrupted, "we need to bring the dragon out here. We can't lure him out; we can't annoy him out."

"That's not an accepted phrase in polite society, but pray tell, whatever do we do, then?"

The smile she flashed him this time, he decided, was not pretty.

"Smoke him out."

ᏉᏏ

ARMECIA looked down at the several bags piled into a rough amalgamation of burlap and green herb that resembled something like a malformed sheep. Apparently far more used to the intoxicating scent than Nitz, it was with a suspicious glare, rather than a nauseous one, that she turned to Sir Leonard.

"Is that all of it?"

The knight, for the first time since Armecia had bound him to her service, seemed less than happy to reply. His eyes were disturbingly clear and coherent; he stood frighteningly erect, his newly healed arm tense with restrained anger.

"Lenny," she asked again, taking a slow step away from him, "is it all you've got?"

"It's all I can spare," he snapped. "But by all means, if you want to see me angry, take my last pouch."

"I'd like to see you angry," Maddy said with an unpleasant grin.

"Not now," Nitz growled at her. He looked at Armecia intently, expressly avoiding the knight's irate gaze. "A dragon's a big thing. We'll need every ounce we can get."

"You'll understand if I'm a little reluctant to force him." The sorceress sighed but looked to her companion with a grimace, regardless. "Lenny, we need it."

His response was twofold. First, he swept a long, angry glare over those assembled. It was with some lack of nerve that Nitz noticed how furious the man's stare was when clear of throbbing red veins. Bright and angry blue, his glower instilled a chill in all of them, forcing even Maddy to quickly disguise a step backwards as a restless shift.

The tension emanating from his stare was palpable, the vision of what might occur frozen in their minds. What if, they wondered simultaneously, the thrill of battle and the lack of smoke was just enough to grant one of the two murderous souls inside him control of the body they fought over? What if, they thought as he reached for his belt, his hand shifted just a bit . . . past the belt buckle to the sword hanging at his hip?

And then, Sir Leonard dropped his pants.

In stark comparison to the way his stare had forced their attentions away, they were now horrifyingly riveted as the knight reached a gloved hand between his legs and rooted around for a moment. Then, producing a bag which he quickly brushed off and drew a small pinch of green from, he tossed it upon the heap with a snarl.

"This"—he ignored his lack of lower coverage to pull out a small piece of paper—"is the last of it." Quickly rolling the cigarillo, he shoved it in his mouth and thrust it to Armecia. "The pants don't go back on until you light it."

"Yeah . . . sure."

She snapped her fingers, conjuring a flame to the tip. Sparing only a moment to light the man's roll, she turned her hand to the pile of weed before her. She narrowed her eyes and the flame became a large, angry billow, rolling from her fingers to sear the herb and send a cloud of acrid smoke roiling into the air. Nitz barely had time to put a hand over his mouth before she swept her other arm, conjuring a gust of wind that sent the cloud chasing down into the cavern's mouth, a ghastly, reeking hound after the massive, fire-breathing rabbit.

"Now what?" Sir Lenny asked, apparently in no hurry to fulfill his promise.

"Now we—"

"Now we wait," Armecia interrupted Nitz. "When the thing comes out, you distract it, Lenny, while Maddy or I kill it. Then we chop off its head, get my book, get some kind of whacky-stick—"

"Fraumvilt."

"Right, whichever. After that, we bid each other farewell and go off to find some more herb."

"What . . . just like that?" Nitz raised a brow.

"What, were you hoping we'd cuddle on its corpse afterwards?"

"Well"—he quickly cleared his throat—"I mean, what am I supposed to do during all this?"

"Read a book or something." She shrugged. "I don't know. You can cook us dinner after we do the fighting."

"I can fight!" he said, wondering if it was because of a sense of humor or outright cruelty that God made his voice crack at that moment. Clearing his throat, he continued. "I mean, Maddy is the muscle. I'm usually the thinking man of the pair."

"For one, you can scarcely be called a man yet," she replied, her grin particularly irksome. "For two, the keyword in your prior statement is '*pair.*' I'm the one that thought of this, so I get to take care of it." She tapped her temple. "Not to mention that I can shoot ice out of my eyeball. Can you do that?"

"Well, I—"

"*Can* you?"

"Of course I can't!"

"Then do what you can," she retorted, before he could elaborate. Gesturing with her chin, she glanced to a nearby rock. "Tend to whoever happens to limp over there if something goes wrong."

He found himself at a loss for words. Blunt as she might have been, she wasn't entirely wrong; coming up with plans and needlework was typically his specialty, while bashing brains and occasionally making necklaces out of bits that fell off people was Maddy's. Armecia's specialty, apparently, was his combined with magic, rolled into one ominous, dusky-skinned package.

He would have liked to think that he could have proven his worth as a man of ideas by coming up with a better one right then and there. He would have settled for proving his worth as a man of wit by coming up with a sharp retort to hurl back at her . . . preferably one that would have made her so weak in the knees that she would have swooned at his feet, leaving him free to scoop her up in one arm and fight off the dragon with the other.

Yeah, that's what would happen—he sighed as he settled onto the rock—*and so long as I'm fantasizing, I'd like a harem.*

"You think this will work, then?"

Armecia looked up to regard Maddy's unexpressive, one-eyed glance fixed on her. The sorceress frowned, finding herself unable to read any emotion in the massive woman's stare. *You'd think,* she mused, *that if you had one eye, you'd be twice as expressive with it.*

"I think it might work," she replied in lieu of her thoughts. "I mean . . . if you can use that axe of yours, anyway."

"You can always ask your little friend if I know how to use it," Maddy replied with a shrug.

Armecia resisted the urge to turn around to regard Leonard. She couldn't precisely say how or when she acquired the instinct, but somehow possessing the ability to know precisely when the knight had his pants down was an ability she chose to be thankful for. Instead, she looked over her other shoulder at Nitz, sitting dejectedly upon the stone.

"He looks upset," she observed, more sympathy than she would have liked leaking into her voice.

"Why wouldn't he be? You just told him he was worthless."

"Thanks for that," she muttered. "I was hoping you might be reassuring."

"I can see how you might think that." Maddy flashed a jagged-toothed grin. "I do appear to be the nurturing type, don't I?"

"Not particularly, no." Armecia furrowed her brow at the woman. "Which sort of raises the question of why you're with him in the first place, doesn't it?"

"If you're prone to not minding your own business and not minding your nose getting broken off because of it, I suppose." She shrugged. "I owe him . . . he owes me. We'll pay our debts and go our separate ways after we do."

"Hm . . . debts." She laughed a little, smiling at the woman. "You know, that's how I—"

"Don't care."

"Oh . . . alright, then."

The stench of weed hung heavily in the silence between them as the herb burned steadily. Burlap and herb were consumed, reduced first to gray curls, then to black ash as it continued to seep into the cavern mouth, spurred by the artificial wind. The skulls swayed gently in the breeze, rattling against each other in their vine entanglements, punctuated by the sound of Sir Leonard inhaling behind them.

The cave itself lay quiet, not so much as a stir in the darkness.

"So . . ."—Armecia kicked at the dirt—"why do you think he's called Zeigfreid?"

"That's his name," Maddy replied.

"Well, *yes*," the sorceress said. "But *who* named him? Did he do it himself, or did the people around him?"

"If I had to say, I suppose I might . . ." Maddy's voice trailed off as her eye grew progressively wider with the two breaths that followed. "Oh, son of a—"

She heard the beast long before she saw it. Its roar began as a subtle thing, a low rumble in the earth, a quiver in the branches. It became an overt thing, a growl that sent birds flying from their perches, rodents fleeing from the roots.

By the time its roar had become loud enough to send the weed smoke billowing out of the cave mouth in a roiling gray wave, it was a horrifying thing.

Armecia collapsed onto her rump, her legs suddenly sapped of strength by the intoxicating blast of weed smoke mingled with the terrifying strength of the creature's howl. She scrambled to her hands and feet, or what she hoped were her hands and feet, for she could barely feel her heartbeat through the toxic fog that seeped into her.

Her voice felt mute in her throat, her ears deaf on her head as she called for her companions and heard nothing. She swept the fog through hazy vision, searching for someone, anyone who might help her. When she could find no one, hear no one, she turned, scampering across the earth like a blind sheep, hoping she might bump into someone.

She did.

"Oh, thank God," she gasped, afraid to open her mouth. Reaching hands up to seize her savior, she could feel something cold and hard. "Lenny, is that you?"

It wasn't.

Something rose beneath her, sent her flying backwards to sprawl on her back. Through her fog-laden eyes, she could barely make out the thick, red toe ending in a thicker black claw. There was a sudden gale, the cloud of smoke was swept aside, and when it parted to reveal the scaled titan looming over her, God didn't seem quite so benevolent anymore.

Zeigfreid, for a creature capable of crushing her under his little toe who had just been exposed to more weed than a Hashuni choir, seemed decidedly less agitated than he ought to be. Through a pair of large golden eyes that stared down a long, red snout, he—if the dragon was indeed a male and dragons didn't abide by some other demented rule of genders—regarded her impassively.

Armecia did not return the favor.

She didn't dare take him all in at once but forced herself to look at each part of him with painstaking slowness: his great, webbed wings, his massive, curving horns, his brightly polished red scales and lashing tail. Her tactic seemed to work; focusing on one part of the great beast at a time proved enough to spare her mind from utter ruin.

Until she saw Zeigfreid's teeth.

What remained of the smoke was dissipated in a great burst of wind as he craned his neck down, opened his jaws, and loosed a roar that whipped her hair about her face and sent the dead leaves upon the ground sweeping into the sky like golden angels called to heaven.

That left only her and the dragon . . . and his teeth.

She scrambled backwards like an intoxicated crab, swaying to and fro as she retreated from the creature's gaping jaws. The benefit seemed negligible, however; every twenty breaths she spent retreating, it took Zeigfreid only one step to cover, the earth shaking with every movement.

She tried to summon her breath to her lungs, tried to summon her voice to her throat, but it died and melted inside his molten orbs, was funneled past his scaly lips and onto the long, pink tongue that lashed out hungrily. She would die silently, she realized, the last sound she ever made in the mortal world being the crunch of bones and maybe a break of wind if she was particularly fibrous.

When her back struck the trunk of the tree, her shriek escaped her with a suddenness that shocked her.

"LENNY! PROTECT ME!"

And, to her surprise, Leonard did come. Bounding across the earth like a hare, he skidded to a halt before her, sword in hand, cigarillo in mouth, pants in a place not known to mortal men. He turned to face Zeigfreid, his twin butt cheeks before her like pale, fleshy shields between her and the dragon.

"This is him, huh?" he muttered, apparently not quite as impressed as Armecia had been. "I thought he'd be taller."

"Well, he's not. So, you know, do your thing and get to whacking him."

"Whacking . . . that's a funny word."

He turned to face her, and, with horror splashing across her eyes, she saw the pleasant redness in his.

"Say, who do you think named him Zeigfreid? The people around him or his fat, ugly ma—"

The end of the question, along with every other part of Sir Leonard, was lost between two massive slabs of red flesh as Zeigfreid brought his forepaws together and crushed the knight between them. Whether or not he could actually feel it, Armecia could certainly not ask loud enough for his flying body to hear as the dragon tossed him over his shoulder to land somewhere beyond the brush.

"Damn it, damn it, damn it, damn it, damn it," she muttered over and over, finding no other words for the occasion.

She suspected a prayer might be in order, perhaps a last breath repenting of sins, but could find only the breath to scream a name. She was determined to make this one count; Lenny could feel no pain, but she only knew of one who could deal it.

"NITZ!"

That was not who she had in mind.

Regardless, she was no less shocked when two arms that she wished were more capable wrapped around her. Holding her tightly against himself, Nitz cowered against the tree, ready to die alongside her.

Despite the fact that it was profoundly stupid, she couldn't help but feel slightly flattered that he hadn't run. Then again, she reasoned, he *could* have tried to distract the beast while she got away.

No, she told herself as she retreated further against him, *this is good . . . Better to die with someone than no one, I guess.* She felt a smile creep across her face. *Father used to say that . . .*

Better, too, she told herself, to die with a smile on her face.

Zeigfreid seemed to agree, for his face seemed to bear something resembling a smile as his neck craned low, and his jaws edged toward the pair, in no particular hurry. Despite the glittering rows of teeth facing her, Armecia couldn't help but feel her own smile grow broader as the creature's red mass dipped to expose a mass of pale flesh and silver metal creeping up its neck.

In a flash, Maddy leapt from his shoulder blades and seized his left horn in one hand. Massive thighs straddled his neck as her axe went high into the air.

Zeigfreid's scream, however, was far more disturbing. Mingled with the sounds of crunching bone as Vulf bit deeply into his skull, then punctuated by a spurt of red as Maddy pulled the weapon out of the dragon's cranium and slammed it back down again; the dragon collapsed to the earth, leaking life upon the ground, golden eyes going dim.

"See?" the woman grunted as she hoisted herself off the beast's neck. "Not so hard. Just smack it in the head, watch it die, same solution for any of life's problems, eh?"

Her grin was spattered with red as she winked her good eye at them.

"You can thank me later." Hefting her axe over her shoulder, she put a hand on one hip. "So, which part do you want to take back to Father Scheitzen? The wings? The foot?"

"The head . . ." Nitz gasped.

"I was thinking that, too, but it's a little big, isn't it?"

"The head!"

"Fine, but you're carrying it."

"MADDY, THE HEAD!"

Her eyebrows quirked in confusion before disappearing behind a wall of teeth as Zeigfreid's jaws snapped shut over her. In an instant, the beast was on his feet, wings flapping, tail lashing, and teeth gnashed in a large, ugly grin. Vulf remained as a testament to Maddy's strength only for as long as it took the dragon to step forward and crush it under his foot.

"Slightly anticlimactic, don't you think?" Armecia asked, half laughing. "I always figured I'd die by burning."

"He could still do that," Nitz replied gloomily as the beast lurched forward. "They breathe fire, don't they?"

"I think that's just a myth."

"Maddy . . ." The young man found it hard to breathe, to speak. "Maddy always wanted to die killing Kingdomers."

"She probably wouldn't mind dying for the death of one Kingdomer."

"If it wasn't in vain, I suppose not."

Zeigfreid took another lurching step forward, his great toes twitching so close to them that they could feel the earth trembling between each thoughtful drum of the red digits.

"It's not over yet," she said, though the viselike grip she clutched his arms with seemed to suggest otherwise. "You're the man with ideas, aren't you? Think of something!"

Zeigfreid's foot was a crimson eclipse, blotting out the sun as he raised it over them.

"Like what?" Nitz demanded.

"SOMETHING!" she screamed.

Think of something, think of something . . . he told himself over and over in his mind. *Think of something . . .*

Zeigfreid's foot began its descent.

THINK OF SOMETHING!

"Your eye . . ." he began.

Armecia gasped, stiffened in his arms, and bent all the power of the

Eye of Ajeed upon the dragon, its icy blast boring upward toward the great descending menace.

The last thing they heard was the dragon giggling.

"That tickles," a huge voice said, and the foot came down.

༶

THE nub of the tailbone was perfectly smooth, glowing with a multitude of hues under the stained-glass windows. Even colored as it was, its sheer size and smoothness seemed to reflect the light, casting the church into a symphony of color it had never seen since the day it was hewn from rough gray stone and cast into dank blackness when its huge carved doors had closed over its mouth.

The poetry, however, seemed lost on Father Scheitzen.

The priest was less interested in the colors it cast and more intrigued by the remaining length of the beast's tail. It ran the entire length of his altar and then some, its scaly, ridged back dripping down the dais steps like a small fall of blood to curl slightly at the tip upon the red carpet.

"And you did not bring the head . . . why?"

He turned to regard Nitz, less impressed.

The young man stood as straight and proud as a vassal could in a torn tunic and smudged breeches reeking of weed smoke. Regardless, after clearing his throat and brushing a lock of blond hair out of his face, he spoke with rehearsed succinctness.

"It was a tad too large, Father."

"So it would seem," he replied, looking back at the tail. "And you're certain the beast cannot live without this?"

"If Father doubts me, I would encourage him to venture to the fiend's lair and discover what I left of the beast."

"I suppose I might, at that, when we venture out to get the gold." He turned a glower upon the young man. "I trust you've a better reason for not bringing *that*."

"It's the Devil's gold, Father. It would require a proper ritual cleansing before a man claiming to be holy could touch it."

Father Scheitzen stiffened. Nitz violently beat back the smirk forming on his lips.

"And an explanation for the lack of your companion and weapon?"

"The world is a dangerous place for women, Father, even Scarred Sisters. As for Wolfreiz . . ." He shrugged. "I thought it best to leave the heathen weapon where it lay, embedded in the beast's skull."

Father Scheitzen nodded. Nitz felt almost free to loose a sigh of relief. "And the smell?"

"Smoke, Father. The beast spews hell."

"Indeed, it does."

For the first time since he had met the priest, Nitz saw a smile, unpleasant and grim, form upon Father Scheitzen's face

"Truth be told, I hadn't expected you to come back, young Nitz." He turned and strode behind the altar with its grisly trophy. "I was therefore loath to remove this from its sacred resting place, where it was to remain until the last heathen was cleansed upon the earth." He reached down, wrapped hands about something heavy. "But what good is a killer that does not kill?"

Nitz could hardly breathe when Fraumvilt was brought to the light of the church. Just as the dragon's tailbone shed light across the vast and gloomy halls, so too did the mace's metal, so gray as to be black, drink it up.

From its leather-bound handle, up its long, thick shaft, it consumed the light, consumed the brightness, until, like an actor resentful of sharing the stage, only Fraumvilt existed, its spiked, ever-bloodied head smiling with a wickedness far more gruesome than Father Scheitzen could ever hope to conjure up.

"And you, Nitz, are a killer," he said, approaching the young man. "A Killer Divine, as your father was."

He smiled, undoubtedly with the intent of appearing compassionate, which made him seem all the more unnerving. He took the weapon in both hands and extended it to Nitz.

"And he would be proud."

"So you say, Father," Nitz nodded shakily, extending his own hands to take the weapon.

"So say we all," the priest finished.

⌘

THE coins echoed across the evening sky as they were thoughtfully counted out into the wooden chest. Nitz observed them with special consideration, noting each and every fleck of gold that glistened in the dying light, paying careful attention to the droning of the arms dealer as he dealt every coin out from pudgy hands with an eagerness not befitting his profession.

"One hundred and ninety-eight," he counted off, "one hundred and ninety-nine . . . two hundred." The last coin he let drop into the chest with a frown on his face, as though he had just bid farewell to a loved one. "Two hundred golden brides of God."

"God needs not gold," Nitz replied as he eased the chest shut.

"Nor does he apparently need weapons, anymore." The arms dealer looked to his cart, where his unwashed assistants carefully wrapped and stowed the ever-bloodied mace in leather and then in an extravagant-looking chest. "Though I must inquire, what does God tend to do without the famed Fraumvilt?"

"More good than you intend to do with it, I would hope."

"I intend to deliver it to the Holy Land, where the priests will undoubtedly pay twice as much to see it put to battle again."

Nitz nodded and picked up the chest with a grunt.

"Say you found it on a corpse. It would do no one any good to hear by what means you truly came upon it."

The merchant nodded.

"So say we all."

"Yeah."

The journey up the hill, with the rattling wheels of the dealer's wagon behind him, was not quite as hard as he expected it to be. The chest, heavy as it was, was not beyond his means to carry over the ridge and down to the valley.

Still, when he set it down before a giant, red foot, he did so with a great sigh of relief.

"There we are"—he dusted himself off—"two hundred pieces of gold, as promised." He looked up into a pair of golden eyes. "Now, as you promised, spit her out."

Zeigfreid regarded him carefully, with more than a little callousness suggesting he was hard-pressed to find a reason to comply. Still, with a roll of his great, scaly shoulders, he opened his mouth and made a gagging sound.

Nitz held his breath as something sticky and green rolled out onto the earth and lay still. He finally released it when the object moved, one eye, bewildered and astonished, peering out from beneath the viscous layer of saliva covering it.

"Good lord," came a shrill voice. "What did you do to her?"

Armecia came rushing forward, blanket in hand, Leonard close behind her, and moved to wrap the muscular woman in it. Zeigfreid, in response, shrugged again.

"I ate her," he replied in a thunderous voice. "I would think that would be obvious from the fact that I also regurgitated her."

"I never knew dragons could do that," Sir Leonard mused from behind the cigarillo in his mouth. "Then again, I do get a mite hungry after I partake of the glorious herb."

"You'll learn all sorts of things about dragons, if you pay attention," Zeigfreid replied with a morbid grin. "Such as the fact that four puny weaklings are hard-pressed to kill one."

"And the fact that they can remove their tails," Nitz muttered, grimacing at the nub behind the beast's wings. "Did . . . did that hurt?"

"It'll grow back," the dragon replied. "All things do."

"For dragons?"

"And people," the creature replied, "as well as what they destroy in the process of their short and stupid lives."

Scooping the chest up in one hand, he turned with massive splendor and began to hobble down the dirt road, toward the distant hills and distant sunset. The earth no longer shook with each step, no birds flew away at his step, nor did vermin flee at his passing.

And, in a few breaths, Zeigfreid was a mass of crimson, indistinguishable from the dying sun.

Nitz found himself vaguely jealous.

"I suppose that's that, then." He sighed. He glanced over his shoulder to spy Maddy, now clean and wholly irate, snatching Vulf back from Leonard's grasp. "This is where we part ways, then."

"After slaying a dragon together?" Armecia asked, raising a brow. "That seems to go against tradition."

"After I *bribed* a dragon, yes." He put a finger to his chest in emphasis. "*I*. Me. Nitz. I sold a holy weapon to pay off a dragon I was supposed to kill. *I* took the punishment for this particular endeavor, so please don't begrudge me when I choose to walk away from you all."

"For what reason, though?" Sir Leonard asked, puffing out a cloud. "I thought we got along quite nicely." He glanced toward Maddy. "You know . . . aside from all this attempted murder business."

"Because, in less than a day from now," Nitz replied, "Father Scheitzen will go to Zeigfreid's lair and find no gold and no carcass. The day *after* that, Fraumvilt will appear in the hands of someone, and he'll be able to figure it out."

"But you told the arms dealer—"

"I also told him that priests would be grateful to have it back in their hands. I neglected to mention that they'd offer grateful prayers *after* they crushed his head in for stealing it."

"But he didn't steal it—"

"Lenny, for God's sake." Armecia silenced him with an elbow to the side before looking toward Nitz. "So where will you go?"

"The Holy Land, I suppose." The young man shrugged. "Where all the other heretics and heathens seem to putter about."

"It's a good place to lose your life," Maddy pointed out.

"We've all got to go sometime."

"Without Fraumvilt?"

"I just—"

"You said it would take a day or two," the woman replied, smiling unpleasantly. "That's plenty of time to run down the arms dealer and smash his genitals before we steal the stupid thing back."

"Do we have to smash his genitals?" Sir Leonard winced.

"What do you care?" Armecia asked. "You can't even *feel* yours."

"That doesn't mean I can't be sympathetic."

"No one is smashing anything," Nitz barked. "I'm going to the Holy Land. You can all go to hell."

He had barely taken two steps before he felt a broad hand seize him by the neck of his shirt and pull him back against a large, muscular body flanked by two smaller ones.

"Sort of the same thing, aren't they?" Armecia asked. "I've got business in the Holy Land, too, which, by proxy, means that Lenny does, too."

"Yeah," the knight muttered, "sure, why the hell not."

"You still owe me," Maddy said, giving him a rough shove forward.

"And me," Armecia pointed out.

"Owe you?" Nitz turned on her, incredulous. "For *what*? I said *I* took the punishment for this."

"So you can take another one and help me get my journal back," she replied. "It's not like you're particularly bad at this whole doing well by God thing."

"But I'm a heretic!"

"Lots of good men have been heretics," Sir Leonard replied. "I mean, none come to mind, and I'm sure they all had their genitals torn off and fed to them . . ." He clapped the young man on the back with a smile. "And that could be you!"

"Lucky me," Nitz muttered.

"Point being," Maddy said, "that there are at least three people who would rather you not die until you help them."

"My father wouldn't like it," Nitz said with a sigh.

"Yeah," Armecia said, "mine, either. But, I figure, if you're going to blaspheme dead ancestors, you might as well not do something so half-hearted as selling their favorite bashing stick." She winked. "After you dig up his corpse and sell *that*, then you can consider yourself finished."

Heralded by morbid laughter, a jagged yellow grin, a dejected sigh, and the stench of the Devil's herb, they stalked down the road, dirty, ragged, and covered in various fluids.

In a few breaths, they were but a blob of shadows, indistinguishable from the night.

Stop!

GARTH NIX

Here's a creepy and suspenseful story that shows us that even the most ancient of creatures can sometimes learn new tricks . . .

New York Times *bestselling Australian writer Garth Nix worked as a book publicist, editor, marketing consultant, public relations man, and literary agent while writing the bestselling Old Kingdom series, which consists of* Sabriel, Lirael: Daughter of the Clayr, Abhorsen, *and* The Creature in the Case. *His other books include the Seventh Tower series, consisting of* The Fall, Castle, Aenir, Above the Veil, Into Battle, *and* The Violet Keystone; *the Keys to the Kingdom series, consisting of* Mister Monday, Grim Tuesday, Drowned Wednesday, Sir Thursday, *and* Lady Friday; *as well as stand-alone novels such as* The Ragwitch *and* Shade's Children. *His short fiction has been collected in* Across the Wall: A Tale of the Abhorsen and Other Stories. *His most recent book is a new novel in the Keys to the Kingdom sequence,* Superior Saturday. *Born in Melbourne, he now lives in Sydney, Australia.*

❧

THEY spotted him an hour after dawn, as the two jeeps drove along the ridge road. It was Anderson in the lead jeep who saw him, which was kind of ironic, since he was the only one who wore glasses, sand-blasted GI-issue things with black frames a finger thick. He called out to stop, and Cullen stomped the brake so hard that the jeep fishtailed off into the loose gravel and almost went over, and Breckenridge, driving the jeep behind, almost ran into them because he did the same thing.

When they finally stopped, with the dust blowing back over the top of the vehicles, they debused as per the SOP and shook out into something approaching a line along the road, with Sergeant Karadjian shouting at them not to f—ing do anything unless he told them to, most particularly not to

let their stupid fat f—ing fingers go anywhere near any f—ing triggers unless he f—ing well ordered them to shoot.

When the dust cleared, the guy that Anderson had seen was still walking towards them. Just walking through the desert like it was some kind
of park, or maybe a neighbourhood he was visiting, since he was done up
in one of those brown robes, the ones with the hood like the old Mexican
monks who ran the orphan school over near the border wore; but that was
eighty miles away, so if it was one of those monks, he'd walked a hell of a
long way.

"OK, priest or whatever you are, stop right there!" called out Karadjian. "Can't you read?"

He meant the signs that peppered the Proving Ground, the ones that
said that the Army would shoot you if you came in. The man had to have
seen the signs, not to mention climbed over at least three fences, the last
one still just in sight, a steel blur shimmering in the heat haze, looking like
a mirage, only it was real, and twelve feet high, with concertina wire hung
all along the top, so who knew how the guy had got over it, or under it,
which was more likely the way the ground was a bit unsteady due to previous tests.

"I said stop!" shouted Karadjian again, and he racked the slide on
his .45 and raised the pistol, aiming over the guy's head. But either the guy
couldn't hear or he was nuts from the heat, because he kept on coming,
and he still kept on coming even after Karadjian fired one, then two shots
over his head.

Karadjian swore and quickly looked at the men, then back at the approaching cretin, and wished that he'd never signed back on again after
Korea, but then, you could never expect what was going to happen in the
f—ing Army from one day to the next and before you knew it, you had to
shoot a damned priest or a monk or whatever and he'd been brought up
Orthodox and his mother would never forgive him—

"Stop or I will shoot to kill!" he shouted. The idiot was only twenty
feet away now, just walking with his head down, Karadjian couldn't even
see his face, though maybe that was better, and then he was taking aim and
tap-tap, two rounds straight into the chest, and the guy didn't fall down!

"Crap! Anderson! Four rounds rapid!" barked Karadjian as he fired
another two shots, this time at the man's head. Anderson fired too, his
M1 a higher, sharper report, bang-bang-bang-bang. The fourth round was
tracer, and they all saw it go straight through the guy, chest high, no doubt
about it.

Panic rose in Karadjian. He was back at Koto-ri, with the Chinese pouring over the forward positions, a tide of men in the moonlight that the machine guns hadn't stopped and the artillery hadn't stopped, and he knew that his rifle and bayonet wasn't going to make no difference, but the training took over and he mechanically loaded and fired and then when the platoon sergeant pulled them back by squads, he did as he was ordered and somehow they survived . . .

Training took over again.

Treat the f—ing bullet-proof walker as a tank, he thought, and *get out of its way.*

He pointed urgently at the jeeps.

"Patrol! Fall back on the front jeep! Steady!"

When he was satisfied that they were moving right, keeping the line, and weren't going to stumble together, he shouted again.

"Opportunity fire! Nice and slow, take your shots, watch your flanks!"

The walker kept going as they shot at him, five M1s and a .45 shooting as steady and true as any sergeant could wish, and they kept shooting till he got too close to the rear jeep and Karadjian shouted to cease fire.

In the immediate quiet, they heard another noise, one that had been drowned by the gunfire. A noise they didn't want to hear, shrieking out of the rear jeep, the high squeal of a recently issued, almost brand-new Detectron Geiger Counter, even more terrible to hear because it'd been turned right down, the background squeaking a pain to listen to on the long patrols.

"Stay back," croaked Karadjian. "Don't nobody move."

The guy didn't stop. He just went on walking, straight towards the inner cordon, and the next fence, two miles to the east. The bullets had shredded his robe or habit or whatever it was, and it looked like he was naked underneath, only he was caked in dust or mud or something. Karadjian holstered his pistol, fumbled for his binoculars, and got them up and twiddled the focusing knob, his hands shaking so much he couldn't get a good look till he clamped his elbows in; then he saw the flash of a thin, scrawny leg slide out of the shredded robe. It was red, all right, but it didn't look to him like it was from mud or dust.

Karadjian lowered his binoculars. The men were looking at him, the Detectron was easing off its scream but was still loud, too loud to be anything but bad news.

"Back up twenty yards that way," ordered Karadjian. He pointed along the road. Away from the jeeps. Away from the path of whatever was inside that robe. "Keep a look-out, see if there's any more of those guys."

"More?" muttered someone. Probably Breckenridge.

"Shut up and move!"

Karadjian lit a cigarette and coughed. His throat was dry. It was always dry in the desert, but it was even drier now.

"What we going to do, Sarge?"

"Pass the shitty buck," said Karadjian. He threw the cigarette down and ran to the lead jeep. The Geiger counter in the back seat of that was screaming too, only not as loud as the one in the other jeep. The sergeant snagged out the field radio and ran back, and thinking about it, moved everyone back another hundred yards, so the shriek of the radiation detectors wasn't scaring him so much he felt like taking a dump right there in front of everyone and had to suck air and try to think of other stuff to stop himself.

Karadjian had been on the Proving Ground security force for three years. He talked to the scientists, particularly the troubled ones, who roamed around at night and wanted to talk, and wanted to hear him tell them about Korea, and how they needed the Bomb and more and bigger and better Bombs, because when it came down to it, there were billions of Chinks and Russkies out there and there wasn't anything else that was going to stop them. But the scientists talked about other stuff too, and so did the guards, and all of them had seen what it meant to die of radiation poisoning, and anyone who'd been slack early on was dead now, or wished they were.

The radio worked, which Karadjian hadn't been sure about. He'd bet the one in the other jeep was fried, but that's why they had two, that was the Army way, only you could never be sure if the gear was any good in the first place, so often you had two pieces of crap that didn't work instead of just one.

He called in a contact report, not that it was like any normal contact report. He could tell they thought he was drunk or heatstruck or something, so he put Anderson on, the college boy, and they thought he was drunk too, and there was a stupid little dance with every guy taking turns on the radio to tell the looie, then the captain, then the colonel, all telling the same story over and over again, while the f—ing superman guy was walking in towards the test site without anybody doing anything about it.

The radio died while the colonel was still asking dumb questions. Karadjian put it down, and they backed up from the jeeps again, till they were three hundred yards away, and he wondered if that was enough. He put the men into all-round defence, a little circle of green on the rocky desert ground, and they propped there and smoked and watched. He didn't let them talk. It wouldn't help and would only crystallize the fear that they were all keeping a lid on.

Half an hour later, a helicopter went over pretty low, a CH-21 Shawnee, heading towards the test site. A couple of minutes later, they heard its machine guns firing. Karadjian stood up with his binoculars and watched the bird do a figure eight and come back into a slight backwards hover, the guns still firing.

Then its engine cut out. It was too low to auto-rotate and just smacked into the ground and blew up. The gunners kept firing pretty much till it hit; it happened so quickly they probably hardly knew what was going on.

An hour after the helicopter crash, when the oily column of smoke from the impact was hardly more than a crematory wisp, Karadjian saw a convoy coming up the road, five jeeps, two with .50 cal mounts, and four deuce-and-a-half trucks loaded with what looked to be everyone who could carry a rifle from the base, including the cooks and the laboratory techs.

Half a mile in front of the military vehicles, Karadjian was more pleased to see the blue '57 Chevy Bel Air convertible of Professor Aaron Weiss, the chief scientist. It would be quicker explaining everything to him than to the White Streak of Shit, which was what everyone called Colonel White behind his back, or very occasionally just "Streak" when he could overhear. He thought it meant like lightning and indicated speed and power, and the healthy respect of the men.

Karadjian waved Weiss down well before the jeeps. The professor must have heard the radio traffic, because when he got out, he had his gloves and overshoes on and was carrying one of the Geiger counters with the long probe. He stretched it out and ran it over Karadjian at four inches away, watching the dial.

"You're somewhat hot, Sergeant," said Weiss. "Not too hot. Portable decontamination's coming up, you might as well do stage one here. Strip and pile everything over there, and I mean everything, from dog tags out, it'll all have to be buried. You say this man in the robe walked over there—past your jeep? You fired at him to no effect?"

"Yes sir, the jeep behind. He just walked in a straight line, in from the desert and on towards the test site. I put six shots into him myself, and the boys at least fifty, maybe sixty rounds. We saw the tracer going through, but he just went on walking. He just went on!"

Karadjian could feel the hysteria rising and fought to hold it back. Only now could he recognize that he had survived something that might have killed him, or maybe not survived it, because "not too hot" might be a kindness, not a real accurate appraisal.

"Stay away from everyone but the decontamination team," said Weiss. "I'll make sure the colonel understands. When did this all happen?"

"Seven oh eight," said Karadjian.

"And he was walking at a normal speed?"

"I guess so. Steady. He never slowed down, or speeded up."

"He'll almost be at the site by now," said Weiss. "Presuming he continued on."

There was a moment of silence between them. They both knew that the test was scheduled for noon. Everything was set for it to fire, normally the only delay would be if the wind changed direction and blew hard towards civilization.

"Bullets couldn't hurt him," said Karadjian. "They went straight through. His skin was dark red, like dried blood, oh mother of Christ it was—"

"That's enough, Sergeant!" snapped Weiss. He looked over his shoulder. The convoy was close now, and the White Streak would soon be exerting his military authority all over the place, without pausing to think first.

"Get your men ready for decon," he ordered, and walked towards the second jeep, holding out the Geiger counter's probe and watching the dial. The needle edged up as he approached, then jumped as far across as it would go when he got near the rear wheels. A year ago, he would have scurried back like a cockroach caught in the light, but since he was on borrowed time following the accident in Lindstrom's lab, he didn't bother.

He crossed backwards and forwards a few times, confirming that it was indeed the track of the man that was still intensely radioactive some hours after he passed. The actual footprints were hotter still, impossibly so; it was as if a chunk of pure uranium was buried in every faint indentation of the ground.

Weiss got back in the Chevy convertible as Colonel White's jeep pulled in behind. The White Streak jumped out before the jeep stopped rolling and ran up to the window as Weiss gently moved his foot over the accelerator, but he didn't press it down.

"Professor!" shouted the Colonel. "Where are you going?"

"The test site." Weiss smiled. "Keep everyone back. There's a trail of very high radiation. Run a phone line to the nearest junction, and I'll call in from the site."

"What? You can't go in alone! We've lost a helicopter, we don't know what that thing is. Those morons at Groom Lake won't say if it's something of theirs, but I tell you, whatever it is, we'll finish it off with that goddamned A-bomb if we have—"

"Good-bye, Colonel," said Weiss. He let his foot pivot forward from the heel, and the Chevy accelerated away, TurboGlide smooth through the gears. Weiss jinked the car around the jeeps and off the road, plumes of dust spurting up as the rear wheels spun for a moment in the loose roadside gravel before getting traction on the stony desert floor.

Weiss sang as he drove, Puccini's "E lucevan le stelle." In his head, he could hear the clarinet solo, repeating over and over again, no matter what part he sang. He did not want to die, but it could not be helped. It was only a matter of time. Perhaps in the next few hours, if not, then in the next few weeks, a horrible and painful death.

There was no obvious gap in the inner fence, no way for the walker to have got through. Weiss swung the car around and reversed through, wincing as the barbed wire scratched the beautiful blue paintwork and shredded the folded-back roof. He ducked down and avoided being scratched himself, only to wince again as a thick strand of triple-barb scraped across the hood.

Closer to the test site, he let himself wonder what he was following. Before the first test, way back in '45, he had been an atheist. Since then, he was not sure what he believed, but it certainly included things that could not be immediately measured or similarly known. He knew of no scientific reason for how a man could be immune to bullets, or would leave a radioactive trail, but that did not mean that no scientific reason existed. He was quite curious to find out . . . anything, really.

Colonel White obviously thought that it was an alien, for there were inexplicable and possibly alien artifacts under study over at Groom Lake, but they were sad remnants for the most part and did not include anything alive. Unless the Air Force had been hiding them from the atomic scientists who had assisted in some of the early investigations, which was possible.

Weiss saw the robed man shortly thereafter. He was climbing the tower that held the Pascal-F device. A ten-kiloton bomb, suspended in place and fully prepared to fire in . . . Weiss glanced at his watch . . . forty-nine minutes. Unless he called in to stop it, he supposed.

The professor backed the Chevy in by one of the instrument stands. He left the engine running. With the car pointed west, he could reach one of the observation bunkers in ten minutes, or the trenches dug by the Marines who'd been the subject of last month's test.

Not that he was entirely sure he'd bother. He took one last look at the Geiger counter. The walker's path was more radioactive than before. Getting closer to the cause of that trail would in all probability be lethal, particularly the way the dust was kicking up, carrying the radiation into his lungs.

"Hello there!" Weiss called up when he reached the foot of the tower. He didn't suppose the fellow would feel like talking after being shot at so much, but as it hadn't stopped him, perhaps he wouldn't mind. At least he had evidently reached his destination. "Mind if I come up?"

There was a moment when Weiss thought there would be no answer. Then an answer came, in a harsh, guttural, and strangely accented voice.

"Come if you wish. You are aware my nature is antithetical to your own?"

"Yes," called up Weiss. He set his foot on the ladder and reached for a rung. "I am. I don't suppose you know how swiftly it will kill me?"

"Should we touch, you would die instanter," said the man. "But stay beyond arm's reach, and you may live to see another season."

"My name is Weiss," said the professor as he gained the platform. He took care to stay as far away from the walking man as possible, and kept the bulk of the bomb between them. "Professor Weiss. May I ask who you are?"

"A sinner," said the man. "Who seeks to make up his last accounts."

He stood and pushed back his hood. Weiss stared at the dark red, large-scaled flesh and the blue, human-seeming eyes that were set so strangely in their reptilian sockets.

"I see. Ah, what planet . . . what distant star have you come from?"

"No star, no far planet," muttered the man. "Yet from the far side of this world, I have come."

"From the far side of this world," repeated Weiss. He kept looking at the man. Was he some sort of mutant? But it was not biologically possible to be so radioactive and continue to live.

"I have sought such a thing as this for many, many centuries," said the man. He indicated the bomb. "Yearning for it as I once yearned for love, or wine. Yet even now, I delay, when at a touch I might have release . . ."

"You know what this is?" asked Weiss. "An atom bomb. It is set to explode soon and it will kill—"

"Aye," interrupted the man. "It is a hope made real. I learned of it from a woman who came to my cave in Cappadocia, as so many have done, seeking the healing power of my inner fires. She died, but it was a slow death, and she told me many things, and taught me more of this tongue we speak. I had learned it once before, a long time past, but had forgot it."

"Cappadocia?" asked Weiss. "In Turkey? You come from Turkey?"

He couldn't help but smile a little, as he thought of the strangeness of this interview. Perhaps his mind was already affected, maybe this was all a morphine dream, the result of treatment begun to ease him through the horrors of death by plutonium poisoning.

"As it is now called," said the man. He licked the dust from his lips with a long, forked tongue, and sighed. "But I am no Turk. I was a good Christian, long ago, in the service of my Emperor. Ah, how I long to shed this vile form, that I may join him in heaven!"

"Your . . . vile form," said Weiss. "You were not always—"

"Always thus? I was not. Once I was as well set up a fellow as any might see . . . but so long ago. My own face is lost to me, gone so long I cannot see it, even in my mind's eye . . ."

"How did you become . . . whatever you have become?" asked Weiss. He looked at his watch. Thirty-three minutes to detonation. Perhaps he had given up on life too early. It was not too late for him to have a genuine and great discovery to his credit, something truly remarkable, not just an accretion on top of the work of other, more gifted scientists. If he could study this altered man, learn the secret of radioactive life . . . others would have to continue the work, but if he could publish even the preliminary findings, it would be a famous memorial of . . . or perhaps . . . perhaps he might even learn how he could live, learn some secret to purge the plutonium residue from his blood and bone . . .

"How did I become what I am?" said the man. "I have told the story before, but perhaps none lived to repeat it."

"I think I would remember hearing about someone like you," said Weiss. "Maybe we would be more comfortable down on the ground? I mean if it's a long story—"

"The story is long, but I shall tell it short, and as the end lies here, it would not be meet to leave it."

"Sure," said Weiss. He looked at his watch again. Eleven twenty-nine. "Go on."

"I was an officer of the Empire, a high commander," said the man. "Of a good family, loyal to the Emperor, successful in war. This was in the reign of Ηράκλειος . . . you would say . . . Heraclitus. I was a simple fellow, wishing only to do my duty, raise a family, have sons to rise to even greater glory . . . but it was not to be. It is strange, that this I am to tell you was so long ago, yet it is ever clear to me, when more recent times are but clouded mud, and I could not tell you what I did for a hundred years . . ."

The minute hand on Weiss's watch moved to the six.

"It was summer, the end of a long, dry summer. I had gone to the mountains, to escape the heat, and hunt. The days were very long, and the evenings were of a gentleness that I never felt again . . . with the wind coming soft and cool from the snowy heights and the earth still warm from the sun. On such an evening, I saw a star fall, and it seemed to me to have fallen close, beyond the lake where my summer house stood on its oaken piles. I had my house slaves ready a boat, and they rowed me to the far shore, or almost to it, for there amidst the burning reeds was a great boat of shining silver. The slaves were frightened and backed their oars. Startled, I fell into the water. I called to them, but they were too afraid, and their fear made me angry, and braver than I should otherwise have been. I swam ashore, and seeing a hinged door open in the side of the silver ship, I went inside.

"It was cold inside that metal ship. Colder than the nights on the high plateau, when the ice storms blow sideways and no shelter is ever enough, and no fire can adequately warm you. But I was still angry, and I thought to see the glow of lamplight upon golden plate. Greed overcame me, and I struck deeper into the craft."

"What did you find?" asked Weiss anxiously. There were only twenty-eight minutes left now, and he would need five minutes at least to reach a fixed phone. Now that death was so imminent, he wanted to do more to postpone it, and this strange, cursed, voluble creature might be the means of doing so.

"Not gold. I found a creature. A great shining lizard-thing, trapped in the wreckage of its chamber. Longer than this tower, it was, and only one vast clawed arm free, but that was enough. It was quick, as quick as the small lizards that dart across the stones. Even as I drew back, it gripped me and took me in. Its grasp burned and my flesh boiled away at its touch, and the pain . . . the pain was mercifully cut short, as I lost my senses and fell into a swoon. It was while I was insensible that it tried to do its work—"

"Hold that thought!" cried Weiss, unable to listen to any more, his eyes fixed upon his watch and the inexorable circling of the minute hand. "I must . . . I must send a message from below. I'll be back."

He had his feet over the edge of the platform and was feeling for a rung when he felt a terrible, burning pain across his forearms and was dragged bodily back up. The walking man set him down in the corner and quietened his screams with a firm but final tap to the middle of his forehead.

"Tried to do its work," he continued, speaking, as he had done so often, to a corpse. "To make me into what it was, to serve its purpose. But I did not wish to be a dragon, and with the grace of God, it could not complete its foul purpose, and so I have remained at least half a man."

He bent down and kissed Weiss on both cheeks, his lips leaving a burning brand. "Half a man, who cannot touch a lover, and who cannot be slain, nor drown, nor die at all. Or so I thought, until at last Mrs. Harrison told me that my prayers were answered, and that there is a way to slay my dragon."

Weiss's watch said sixteen minutes to twelve, and the detonation was set for noon, as set by a bank of electric clocks and three separate control cables. But when the dragon embraced the bomb and tightened his grip, it was enough.

Nine miles away, as he stood mute while being scrubbed in the decontamination showers, Karadjian felt the floor shake for several seconds, and the flow of water from the shower head slowed, stopped, then restarted. It was a much bigger shock and a heavier ground wave than for a mere ten-kiloton test.

"Hey, Sarge," called out Anderson. "Reckon that guy went up then, with the bomb?"

"What guy?" asked Karadjian. "There never was no guy."

He was right. Five minutes later, still wet from the showers, they signed the forms that said so, while the mushroom cloud fell into itself in the middle distance.

Ungentle Fire

SEAN WILLIAMS

Sean Williams is best known internationally for his award-winning space opera series and novels set in the Star Wars universe, many cowritten with Shane Dix. These include the Astropolis, Evergence, Orphans, and Geodesica series, and the #1 New York Times bestselling computer-game tie-in The Force Unleashed. His stories have been gathered in several collections, including New Adventures in Sci-Fi, Light Bodies Falling, and Magic Dirt: The Best of Sean Williams. He is also the author of ten linked fantasy novels inspired by the landscapes of his childhood: the dry, flat lands of South Australia, where he still lives with his wife and family. These include the Books of the Change (The Stone Mage & the Sea, The Sky Warden & the Sun, and The Storm Weaver & the Sand) and the Books of the Cataclysm (The Crooked Letter—the first fantasy novel to win both the Aurealis and Ditmar awards—The Blood Debt, The Hanging Mountains, and The Devoured Earth). His most recent series in this world is The Broken Land (The Changeling, The Dust Devils, and The Scarecrow), to which this story is closely connected.

Here he takes us along on a dangerous quest with a warrior who must ultimately decide where his loyalties lie—and who finds that either choice may well be deadly.

ℰᵷ

Absence is to love what wind is to fire;
it extinguishes the small, it enkindles the great.

—ROGER DE RABUTIN

O N the twenty-third day of his quest, the young man detected crabbler spoor. Swinging the reins of his mechanical steed sharply to the

left, he parked in the shade of the yellow canyon wall and lightly hopped
to the ground. Dust puffed under his heels, leaving deep indentations in his
wake. The marks he had spied weren't footprints. They were long and thin,
as though someone had scratched the ground with a bone needle. His were
the only human signs that he had seen in over a week of westward travel.

He squatted as though to examine the trail but was in reality listening
more closely than he was seeing. Above the unnamed wind that blew constantly along this section of the Divide, he heard a dry rattling, as of dice
in a cup. Straightening, he looked up and to his right.

Four body-lengths above him, a giant, sand-coloured spider crouched
on an outcrop of ancient rock, watching him with too-numerous, pebbly
eyes. He froze, watching it right back. The crabbler wasn't the biggest he
had ever seen, but it was still wider across than his arms could reach. If it
jumped, he would have only an instant to draw the knife at his side or to
raise a flame through the Change. And if there were more of them . . .

A sharp tattoo came from the other side of the canyon. A second and
third crabbler were splayed across the stone like scars on the world. The
brisk clatter came from the mouth parts of a fourth that was so perfectly
camouflaged against the stone that he could barely see it.

That crabbler spoke slowly, intending its words for his ears.

"We know you," it said, "Roslin of Geheb."

Moving slowly, Ros bent down and picked up a pair of flinty stones.
Holding one in each hand, and feeling somewhat foolish, he clacked out
a brief reply. Master Pukje had taught him the crabbler tongue in the
early days of his apprenticeship, but he had had little reason to "speak" it
before.

"I am he," he told the crabblers. "What of it?"

"You took something from us."

That was true. A long time ago, when he had been little more than a
boy, he had rescued a girl called Adi from a crabbler coven one month's
travel from here. Word had obviously spread.

He raised himself to his full height.

Years of training and exercise had made him strong, since then, and
broad with it. Dark hair hung in a thick pony-tail halfway down his back.
Stray curls stirred as the Change woke at his command, making the steady
breeze skittish.

"You will let me pass," he said firmly through the stones.

"You cannot," the crabbler told him. "The way ahead is blocked."

"Then I will unblock it."

"You cannot," it said again. "Turn back now."

"Is that a threat or a warning?"

"Take it how you will, Roslin of Geheb."

Turning lightly on its eight legs, the crabbler crawled into a crack in the stone, closely followed by its two companions.

"Wait." Ros regretted taking such a confrontational stance. Crabblers or not, these were the first living creatures he had seen on his quest. They knew the Divide much better than he did, and could help him, perhaps, if he talked fast.

The first crabbler he had seen was heading for a similar retreat in the wall behind him.

"I'm looking for something," he said, clacking as quickly as he could. "A dragon, of sorts. Have you . . . ?"

But the creature scuttled away without reply, leaving him standing alone, frowning, in the canyon's still-restless breeze. The vanes of his strand beast flapped back and forth, gathering the energy of the wind and storing it in two rows of ceramic flasks around the machine's wooden flank. Its one hundred and twelve tiny feet were poised in attitudes of readiness, waiting for him to climb aboard and continue his journey. Not the hardiest of steeds, it barely managed his weight plus that of the pack he carried, but it was at least as quick as a camel and much less vulnerable.

You cannot. Turn back now.

He didn't entirely trust his translation of the crabbler language. It might have been trying to tell him *You cannot turn back now.*

He had no doubts on that score, but how had the crabblers guessed?

Tugging on the silver locket that hung from a leather thong around his neck, he kicked up three more small clouds of dust and leapt into the saddle. Jerking the reins—actually a wooden handle connected by two strips of leather to the machine's complicated gear-box—he spurred the strand beast back into motion. Chuffing and hissing, his wooden steed lunged forward, and the echoes of its clockwork engine bounced back at him from the rugged canyon walls.

♔

WESTWARD, ever westward. Although the Divide snaked north and south as it sliced through the red earth of the world, it unerringly returned to face the sunset. Ros had taken to camping so the sun's direct light would strike him of a morning, lessening the feeling of oppression that came from travelling so long in the shadow of two parallel cliffs. The canyon floor was utterly lifeless, and his eyes had grown tired of seeing nothing but yellows and browns. Even the sky above looked washed out and faded.

Not long after his encounter with the crabblers, his attention was caught by a single cloud drifting on the forward horizon. It was perfectly white, tapering from a fat centre to nothingness at its extremities, and provided a welcome break from the monotony. Ten days earlier, he had passed the ruined city of Laure, where people his age flew to and from the Hanging Mountains, trading and exchanging information. He imagined what it would be like to swoop around the wispy fringes of the cloud in one of their flimsy-looking kites. He doubted the air up there was as still as it seemed.

He wondered what Adi would think of something so whimsical and dangerous.

"I hope this letter finds you well," she had written shortly before he had set off on his quest. The formal tone disheartened him, made him feel that he did not know her. "I hope also that it finds you unchanged in your feelings, for I remain committed to the promise we made to each other five years ago. If this letter should find you certain in the knowledge of that, I would be pleased. Be assured that it will never be otherwise.

"Most of all, I hope that this letter just *finds* you. It's been so long since I last had word, and I suppose it's only natural to worry. I keep that strange little galah you sent as a pet, even though the charm must surely have faded by now. Maybe one day it'll tell me something new—perhaps that you've received this letter and are on your way back to me now, with a glad heart.

"I can dream, can't I?" That flash of her own voice, poking through the letter's stilted reserve, offered him the barest reassurance that he wasn't being addressed by a complete stranger. "Do what you have to do, Ros, then come find me in return. The charm I have enclosed will show you the way. Trust it as I have trusted our hearts all these years. Don't be led astray now, when we are closer than ever."

The letter had been folded tightly around the silver pendant he now wore about his neck. He could tell that it was hollow but not empty, and guessed that it contained a small piece of Adi's skin, or perhaps a chip of tooth. The letter itself had been stained brown with her blood and bound up in several plaited strands of her black hair. Unwinding the hair carefully, he had retied it in a cuff around his left wrist.

The leather thong chafed his neck sometimes. From his worrying at the pendant, he supposed, at the weight of what it symbolised.

"Don't forget your promise to me," Master Pukje had warned him on learning of the contents of the letter. "I said I'd teach you only if in return you perform one task for me."

"I won't ever forget that," Ros had said, inclining his head even though his master couldn't see the gesture. They had been flying low past the shallow bowl of the Nine Stars, exercising the less-human of Master Pukje's two forms. Ros had untied his hair and let the thick mane whip behind him in the wind, imagining that he was the one whose wings propelled them mightily through the air. "You remind me every day," he had added.

"There's an ocean of difference between remembering an agreement and honouring it."

"I'll honour it just as soon as you tell me what my task is."

"I'll tell you only when I'm absolutely certain you're ready for it."

How his master had finally concluded that he was ready, Ros didn't know, but he was on the way now.

The pendant tugged insistently on its thong, urging him north, to where Adi was learning to manage her Clan's caravan under her father's tutelage. She had meant the gift to reach him, no matter what; that was why she had bound it with flesh, hair, and blood. When the time came, when his obligation to Master Pukje was fulfilled, her charm would lead him unerringly to her, whether he wanted to go or not.

There could be, as the crabblers said, no turning back.

ℜ

DISTRACTED by both cloud and memories, he had long put the rest of the crabblers' words out of his mind when he took a bend and saw exactly what they had meant.

A single, vast web stretched from one side of the Divide to the other, sparkling and gleaming where the sun struck it directly, barely visible at all where it did not. Ripples moved along silken strands, struck by the wind's insubstantial fingers. It was too large to have been built by ordinary spiders and couldn't have been the work of crabblers, either, since they produced no natural silk. Something else had built it, or grown it, or caused it to come into being, somehow, and he could proceed no further without breaking it.

Ros hove the strand beast to, but didn't immediately dismount. The web was an obstacle, indeed, but unlike any he had encountered before. If he tried to walk through it, it might stretch and snap like an ordinary web.

Or its apparent fragility might be a disguise for something more sinister—poison, perhaps, soaked into razor-sharp threads; or a net that would fall on him the moment he entered it.

One thing Ros had learned about the Divide was to trust appearances not at all. Better to stop and think for a moment before barging into a trap.

From his elevated vantage point, he searched for signs of malevolence. The web crossed the canyon at the waist of a slight hour-glass. On his side of the hour-glass was a pool of water, brackish and dark. A patch of orange rock marred the ubiquitous yellow expanse of the far cliff. There was, as always, no sign of other human travellers, but none of crabblers or insects, either. Just the wind, bowing the web towards him like a sail.

The sun vanished behind the cloud. It was getting late in the day. Rather than acting precipitously, Ros urged the strand beast into motion again and parked it beneath a bouldery outcrop, then climbed free. He had no tent, just a bedroll and simple cooking utensils. Fire had always been his preferred medium, summoned raw and dangerous in his youth and mastered in stages through his training, but he didn't light one now for fear of attracting undue attention. Dipping his can into the pool and cautiously tasting the water within, he found it to be too oily and bitter to drink. No matter. He had enough in watertight pouches to survive until he reached the next source, as well as the store of dried meat that sustained him on lean days.

Settling back on his bedroll, with his feet pointing downhill towards the web, he drew a series of charms in the sand around him, to sound the alarm if anything sneaked too close during the night. Then he folded his hands behind his head and lay back to watch the sunset. Reds and yellows painted the sky from side to side, with a hint of green just before the day properly ended. Ros nodded off as the first stars came into view, and dreamed of Adi calling his name with a soft, questioning voice. He was reluctant to answer for reasons he could not fathom. Hadn't he been waiting for this moment all his apprenticeship? Although he had done nothing specific to earn her disapproval, the shame and guilt were knife-sharp. Inaction could be as hurtful as action.

He jerked awake at midnight, disturbed by something he couldn't immediately identify.

The moon rode high and bright directly above him, casting a silver patina over the forbidding realm of the Divide. His charms were undisturbed. Ros sat and peered around him, taking in details that now looked strikingly different than before. The strand beast was a clash of angular shadows nearby, all pleasing symmetry lost. The pool of brackish water gaped like a bottomless hole in the earth, and he wondered if its depths hid something living: a fish that had improbably splashed, or a hardy frog, perhaps. Pock-marks in the cliff walls now resembled eyes or mouths, gaping madly at him. The web—

His sharp intake of breath was followed by the scuffling of his feet. Upright, he took a dozen steps forward to see better, shading his eyes from the moon's glare in order to make certain he was not dreaming.

The web glowed in the bright moonlight. He could see all of it now, stretching up and away from him like the world's most insubstantial banner. And on that banner was no natural pattern, no radiating bull's-eye as most spiders fashioned between trees and rock-faces. Nor was it a random striation of lines and shapes, without meaning or language. Depicted in the gleaming threads was a creature so vast that its wing-tips touched either side of the canyon.

A dragon, Ros marvelled. A dragon caught in a web.

Never trust appearances, he reminded himself as he came closer to the base of the web. Foreshortened, the dragon seemed even more preternatural. It had four clawed feet and a beaked nose and mouth, like a bird. Captured in mid-flight, its lines were so perfect, so convincingly realised, that Ros was surprised to see stars twinkling where flesh and skin should have been. Those long, outstretched wings should have blocked out half the sky.

Ros came within touching distance of the web. The dragon was sufficiently foreshortened that it could barely be discerned as such. One flattened foot, as broad as he was long, reached out as though to grasp and crush him, magically, into stardust. He watched that foot closely, but it showed no sign of self-direction.

The threads were so fine that they had a tendency to disappear no matter how determinedly he stared at them. Hardly daring to breathe, he knelt to examine one in particular, noting how the thread touched the ground as lightly as a real spider's web. There was no weight, no visible glue, no stake holding it in place. Perhaps, he thought, the strand was thicker higher up, where the heft of the entire web pulled most insistently. Perhaps the strands at the bottom only prevented the base from drifting free.

Still, Ros didn't touch it. Instead he stood up and checked four more threads and the ground near by. The bottom of the Divide might be effectively sterile, but birds did occasionally fly along it. If the web had killed any, by whatever means, it had left no bones or feathers in the sand at its base. There wasn't so much as a dead moth.

To all appearances bar one, then, it was just a web. That one crucial appearance, of a dragon in flight, made him hesitate, but he couldn't hesitate all night. Come morning, the dragon might be invisible again, and he couldn't take a chance on that. He had learned to mistrust disappearances, too.

Some kind of action, immediate and decisive, was required.

Taking two steps back, he picked up a flat stone. With its blunt edge, he drew a new set of symbols into the sand at his feet and encircled them with a double line. The night adopted a sharper tone as the charm took effect, and he warned himself not to become complacent. *Protection draws attention,* his master had taught him. Perhaps that was why the web showed no signs at all of the Change. The thing it contained—if such it was, and not an illusion—must only be visible by particular light at particular angles; otherwise, someone would surely have seen it before him. It hadn't needed charms to defend itself.

Until now.

Aiming carefully, every muscle ready to flee, Ros tossed the stone one-handed at the nearest thread.

It bounced off with a twang and sent a series of tiny shock waves shimmering across the face of the web. The dragon's claw seemed to clench, then the whole thing was shaking. Ros stared and listened with growing surprise. Instead of fading into silence, the twang became a hum, sustained by the on-going vibration of the web's individual strands. And out of the vibrations, out of the hum, a voice spoke.

"Why," it asked him, "are you here?"

"THERE'S a dragon," Master Pukje had told him on the day Ros began the quest that would release him from his apprenticeship. "There's a dragon living in the Divide. I want you to find it for me."

Ros had thought he was getting off lightly. "Is that all?"

"Don't be so sure of yourself, boy. It'll be hidden as I am, but by different means, and cunning with it. Your task is threefold: first you have to find it; then you have to kill it; finally, you must prove to me that you have done as I instructed."

"You want me to bring you its head?"

Master Pukje's smile had been slyly amused. "If it has one, yes. That would definitely do the trick."

ԸԽ

THINKING back to that smile, Ros now wondered if his master had known all along what he would find.

"Why shouldn't I be here?" he replied, but the hum had faded, and the dragon was silent again.

There were several stones within reach from the inside of his protective circle. Ros grabbed the largest and tossed it with greater force at the web.

"I am harming no one," came the breathless whisper, proving that he hadn't imagined it. "Why don't you leave well enough alone?"

"You're a dragon."

"And you're a human."

"Neither of us can help what we are."

"But are we slaves to our nature? That's the question."

"I have no doubt that you would harm me if you could."

"You should doubt, a little. I have no such desire in me at the moment. If I did, you would know about it."

Ros was running low on stones. "So you claim not to be a captive, and that this isn't a trap?"

"Why do you ask when it's clear you won't believe the answer?"

"To test my theory that all dragons are liars."

"Whether I am lying or not, it would be unwise to judge from my example alone."

"Ah, you see, you're not the only dragon I know."

In reply, he received an empty hum, as though the dragon was thinking. When that faded, Ros had no more stones left to toss.

A gust of wind sprang up, tugging at the threads and sending sand skittering around him. For the first time, Ros noticed the deep, desert cold biting at his skin. Do something, he told himself. You can't stay hidden in the circle all night.

Do what you have to do, Ros, then come find me in return.

Lifting his left foot, he swept the sole of his shoe over the symbols he had drawn. The world instantly returned to its usual flavour: he could smell the stagnant water of the pool and detected a far-away rattle of crabblers moving about their nocturnal affairs. Distantly, he noted that the moon wasn't as bright as it had been. It had drifted behind a cloud and came and went uneasily above him.

Ros stepped from the remains of his circle. Nothing attacked him, physically or through the Change. His was the only will making itself felt at the moment.

With great care, Ros reached out and plucked the nearest strand of the web.

"See?" said the dragon. "I mean you no harm."

"This proves nothing."

"What proof do you require?"

Ros thought of the third of Master Pukje's conditions.

"Tell me why you're hiding here, and maybe I'll believe you."

"Then will you leave?"

"I can't promise you anything."

"Without making a liar of yourself, I suppose."

"Something like that."

"Exactly that, I think. We haven't said a true word to each other since you woke me. We have danced around the truth, guarding our secrets as though they were jewels. You talk about *proof* and *lies* and *promises* as though they somehow stand between you and what you want, but I tell you this: no amount of talk will satisfy you. What do you desire so badly that you have come to me in the dead of night and woken me from my slumber?"

Ros thought this time of Adi, and of freedom, and of his promise to Master Pukje. "If you're trapped," he said, "then maybe I am, too."

"Trapped in a web of words," the dragon scoffed, "as I am trapped in this web of spider's silk."

"Yours is easier to break, I think."

"You might indeed think so. Try it and find out."

Ros's index finger tensed to put the dragon's suggestion into practice, but stayed on the verge of doing so. The wind bowed the silent dragon over him, as though urging him on.

He couldn't do it. Not without knowing more—and that, he intuitively understood, meant giving more.

"I've been sent here," he told the dragon, "to kill you. What do you say to that?"

"I say this: who sent you?"

"What difference does that make?"

"All the difference in the world. You are not my enemy; you are just the instrument of my enemy. That's the person I need to talk to, and I can only do it through you."

"He didn't send me to have a conversation."

"Yet here we are. Why not do the deed and be done with it? Commit your murder; get on with your life. You still haven't told me what it is you desire."

"I want to know why you deserve to die."

"Did the one who sent you not tell you? That was remiss of him."

"He tells me what I need to know."

"Do you trust him?"

"He is—was—my teacher, my master."

"Then you should certainly trust him."

"That's what I tell myself."

"But . . . ?"

But I know Master Pukje never does anything without a reason, Ros said to himself, and when the reason is hidden, that's usually for a reason, too. What if this dragon doesn't deserve to die? What if I'm being tricked into committing a terrible crime?

"Once upon a time," his master had told him, "the world was full of creatures like me. We are rare now, and, for the most part, we avoid your kind. We see the fear in your eyes when you gaze upon us. It's unpleasant, for we belong in this world as firmly as you do. It was ours before it was yours. We understand it a little better.

"So we hide ourselves in a variety of different ways. Some live in the sky as clouds or mysterious lights. Some live underground, feasting on molten rock. Some spread their wings in the canopies of forests, where vines will hide them, and they can sleep out the rest of eternity. Some find ways to walk among you as I do, as one of you."

And one, Ros now understood, took the form of a giant web and sailed gently through the days. He had offered the information of its imminent demise on impulse in order to see what it might provoke, but the news had raised barely a twitch of alarm.

"There are different kinds of deaths," he said.

"Indeed," the dragon agreed. "Hope can die, for one. The body lives on, but the inside turns to dust. Love, too, is another thing that doesn't last forever."

Ros looked up sharply. What had the dragon guessed about his motivations? What did it think it knew? Ros was plucking the threads like a harpist, but maybe the dragon was playing him instead.

He crooked his index finger again, and this time he did pull on the thread until it snapped.

The web shuddered, and the image of the dragon recoiled.

"See?" the dragon whispered before the vibrations died down. "I am helpless before you."

That didn't seem plausible. "So anyone could've come along and done this, at any time?"

"I'm sorry if that makes you feel less important."

"This is supposed to be a quest, a challenge, a test—"

"And so I'm sure it is, for both of us. If anyone could have done this, why you? Why now?"

"I don't know."

"Do you have no understanding at all?"

Ros shook his head, full of conflicting emotion. If all he had to do to achieve his freedom was to snap a few threads and end the life of a feeble old dragon, what was stopping him from doing it?

Perhaps this was the test, he thought. Perhaps this indecision was the challenge he had to overcome in order to be truly free.

This led to a far more discomfiting thought. What if Master Pukje wanted Ros to earn his independence by *disobeying* his master's orders, by doing what he thought was right rather than blindly following instructions?

Threefold. He had found the dragon; that was something. But how could he leave the other two tasks unfinished and expect to earn the life he had dreamed of for so long?

"Tell me why you're hiding."

"The world has changed," the dragon said, "and it's changing still. All things reflect the world as it is, just as the world reflects those things inside it. We don't stand apart. Our function alters with time."

"What function do you perform now?"

"To dream."

"Not all dragons are sleeping."

"Don't misunderstand me. Sleeping and dreaming aren't the same thing."

"Not all dragons are dreaming, then."

"Ah, yes. You said you knew another. You believe it to be a liar. Is it lying to itself or to you? The former is, after all, one definition of a dream."

"Perhaps both."

"Then that makes it a very dangerous dragon indeed. Did you attempt to kill it, too?"

"No. He's the one who sent me."

"Did he, now?"

"Yes."

The dragon didn't react with surprise or anger, or any of the human emotions Ros might have expected.

"Let me be sure I understand you: the other dragon you know, the one you believe to be a liar, is the one who sent you to kill me, the one you obey because you consider him your teacher and master?"

"Yes."

"No, that's not what you said. You corrected yourself. You said he *was* your teacher and master."

"My apprenticeship ends with the completion of this task."

"Killing me."

"And returning with proof."

"Naturally. I would demand no less, myself."

"Doesn't that bother you—one of your own kind trying to murder you?"

"Oh, he's not the one doing the murdering. That's you, of your own free will. What concerns me more is that a dragon took a human apprentice. What's your name, boy? Let us talk as equals since that is what your master thinks we are."

"Roslin," he said, keeping his heart-name to himself. "Roslin of Geheb. What's yours?"

"I've had many names," the dragon told him. "You can call me Zilant, if you like. What name does your master go by?"

Ros felt a need to prevaricate on that point. "Why do you want to know?"

"I would like to know, Roslin of Geheb, how he passes among your kind. Does he have a form like mine or some other disguise?"

"He looks much like a human," Ros said. "When he wants to."

"Yes, and keeps his true form for when he doesn't. We have such power, we dragons, when we choose to use it."

"My master says that choices are the most difficult thing to learn. Becoming powerful is easy compared to knowing *when* to be powerful."

"Are you powerful, Roslin of Geheb?"

"I am told that I can be."

"It won't take much to kill me, I'm afraid. Don't be disappointed."

Ros reached out and snapped another thread. "Don't think to arouse my sympathy, dragon. If you want to live, give me a reason to spare you, nothing else."

Zilant writhed, but his tooth-filled mouth seemed to gape in a smile. "Of course. I know I cannot win your allegiance. One dragon at a time, eh?"

"I will never turn on my master, if that's what you're suggesting."

"You're the one with all the suggestions. But remember: a thought voiced is a deed in waiting."

"Stop it."

"What do you believe will happen if you disobey this lying master of yours? Do you think he'll descend from the sky and rend you with his beak? If you're looking for *reason*, ask yourself why your master trained you. Not to die in his own claws, certainly. He has invested too much in you for that. You make your own decisions now. You are already your own master.

"Or has your master no intention of setting you free? Is this monstrous task the first of many he has planned for you? By your guilt and shame you will bind yourself to him. He will trade an apprentice for a servant, and you will be trapped forever."

"Stop it!"

Furious, Ros grabbed an armful of the strands and snapped them all. Severed silken threads fell on him and clung to his face. The dragon roiled and roared above him. The hum became a scream.

"Who is master, Roslin of Geheb," it shouted, "and who the slave?"

Ros tore another armful, even as part of him asked why he was so angry. Wasn't the dragon telling him what he had already suspected: that this was a fool's mission designed either to humiliate or to ensnare him? Wouldn't breaking his word release him from both threat *and* obligation?

He couldn't take that risk. Zilant had been in his life a matter of minutes. Master Pukje had raised him for five years. Ros owed one more than the other, and neither more than he owed himself. He would stick to the deal he had made. Zilant might deserve only to sleep and dream, but the dragon stood between Ros and the freedom Pukje had promised him, the future he and Adi had dreamed of.

But did he deserve it, now? He doubted his feelings for her and fantasised that his master was entangling him in a web of deception. His thoughts betrayed all of them. He was worthy of neither trust nor love.

Ros ran headlong across the Divide floor, snatching at threads and pulling them apart. The fabric of the dragon, rent and torn, flailed in ribbons. Starlight gleamed like tears from the truncated ends and from his hand where web tenaciously clung. Reaching the far side of the canyon, he climbed up the rough cliff-face, leaping from handhold to handhold like a crabbler, ripping at the thickening strands, biting them, finally reaching for his knife and slashing when they became too strong for him to break with strength alone.

How much time passed, he couldn't tell. The moon had vanished entirely behind a cloud, so he couldn't follow its passage across the sky, and nor, in the depths of his determination, would he have cared to know. Ignoring the aches in his muscles and the layers of web thickening around him, he laboured on, climbing and swinging from thread to thread, slashing indiscriminately as he went.

At the top, he paused only to survey the best way to administer the killing stroke. A single, thick rope sagged from one side of the canyon to the other. From that hung all that remained of the dragon. Shimmying hand over hand along it with the knife between his teeth, Ros reached the middle and prepared to do what had to be done.

"This is your last chance, Zilant," he said. "Tell me something, anything, to change my mind."

"No," hissed the dragon. "You cannot turn back now."

At hearing the same words that the crabblers had told him, Ros almost stayed his hand. He was too tired to be angry any more; only stubbornness kept him going. What did it mean that he couldn't turn back, anyway? He no more believed in destiny than he did the Goddess of which some people spoke. The course of his life was mapped out by obligations, promises, and debts. They were what trapped him, not some absurd cosmic cartographer.

Hanging from one hand, he raised the knife and brought it down hard.

The rope snapped. The dragon rent in two, sagging like a curtain and taking him with it. The two of them fell with majestic delicacy to the canyon floor. He braced himself for the impact, rolled, and came up angling the knife safely away from him. The breath had been knocked out of him, and he was covered in dead web, but apart from that, he was unharmed.

To the east, the sky was pale. By the growing light, Ros surveyed what he had done.

The dragon was unrecognisable. Where once had hung the image of a beast in full flight were now just ephemeral rags. All magnificence had fled. No voice remained, no hum. Just the nameless wind, sighing endlessly across stone.

৭৯

A shaft of light caught Ros as the sun breached the far horizon. His hands shook in the golden radiance. He barely had strength to pull the thick mat of threads from his face.

But it was done. He had killed the dragon. All he had to do now was prove it to Master Pukje. The proof he required lay in the remains of the web. His master had known what awaited him here, he was sure. Just the sight of Ros would be enough. He was practically encased in the stuff. It would take days to get all the threads out of his hair.

He laughed hoarsely. The sound echoed back from the canyon walls like a sob. A cocooned caterpillar, what would he become when his chrysalis opened? Would Adi still want him, this killer of defenceless dragons?

In that crystalline moment, he felt his reluctance to honour his promise to Adi become fear, and knew that the course of his quest had led him to pitfalls that, until now, he had never needed to navigate.

A rattling of crabblers brought him out of his desperate introspection. Six of them had crawled over the lip of the canyon, and more followed behind them. Their clattering was wild and incoherent. He had never heard them like this before. They swarmed down the cliff wall and over the remains of the web. Were they shocked at what they saw? Ros couldn't tell. More and more poured into the Divide, and he retreated from their thickening tide.

The sound of stirring water disturbed the silence behind him. He spun, raising the knife. The brackish pool was quiet no longer. Waves crossed its black surface as though something large was moving back and forth beneath.

The wind whipped around him with increasing strength, raising a whirlwind of dust.

Stones rained from the canyon walls.

Clouds undulated in the sky.

No, he realised through growing alarm. Not clouds. The very same cloud that he had seen yesterday while approaching the web. The one that had blocked the moon. It hadn't moved in a day and a night, but did so now in defiance of wind and weather, its own kind of being.

Some live in the sky . . .

White, feathery wings unfurled. A long neck uncoiled. At the same time, a tower of water shot up out of the pool and spread wings of its own. Crabblers climbed acrobatically over each other, manoeuvring with eerie precision to become eyes, beak, talons, and tail, while boulders tumbling from the Divide wall landed to form legs, arms, a hunched back. The whirlwind of dust took a similar form, towering over him and flexing its muscles. Ros barely heard the strand beast explode as every bottle strapped to its side burst asunder, releasing the air trapped within.

Dragon of air.

Dragon of dust.

Dragon of stone.

Dragon of water.

Dragon of cloud.

He reeled back as the full import of what he had unleashed sank in. Even the crabblers, now gripped together in a grotesque tangle of legs and fat bodies, had been co-opted by the dragons into their bizarre masquerade.

"Why don't you leave well enough alone?" Zilant had asked.

Ros should have listened to him. Now he had killed one dragon and disturbed a whole nest of them. That was the price he would have to pay for freedom.

From exhaustion and fear, strength arose. He wasn't a dragon, but he was a dragon's apprentice. Master Pukje had taught him well. The Change poured through him like an ocean through a river mouth. He wouldn't stop to talk this time. He had killed one dragon already. What were six more when his future was at stake?

The dragons roared at him, approaching on all sides. The ground quaked under their mighty feet, but he stood firm. They couldn't all attack at once. Fire would boil water and turn sand to glass. Crabblers would shy away and clouds would evaporate to nothing.

Raising both hands, he summoned the flame that he knew so well.

A bright glow blossomed around him, and it seemed for a moment as though the sun had grown in strength. Heat rippled across his skin, and his eyes were dazzled.

But it wasn't the sun at all. The light came from the web encasing his body. The fire issuing from his hands had set it alight. The glare grew brighter still and the heat more intense until suddenly, with a flash, his entire body was aflame.

He screamed, and the air from his lungs whipped the fire even higher. Great sheets burst from him, rising up and out to either side, and behind him, too, tasting the earth like a tongue. He felt himself lifted by the heat, even as his hair shrivelled and his clothes burned away. The flames lapped at the air, flapped once, and he was aloft.

The dragon of fire surged forward, and Ros was carried with it, inside its belly. Together they left a broad black scar wherever they passed.

�

"BREATHE easy, boy. This won't take long."

Ros recognised that voice. It belonged to the dragon he had just killed. That knowledge did little to quell his panic.

"What's happening to me?"

"Nothing," Zilant said. "This has nothing to do with you. It's all about the seven of us, of which your master is the last and youngest. For sending a man to do a dragon's job, he will pay dearly. But this was what he wanted: to wake us for a while, to remind us that our blood still boils. An insult will serve when entreaty has failed so many times before."

Ros could barely think through the pain. *Nothing*, the dragon said, but it felt like everything.

"Fly with me," said Zilant from the fire all around him, "just this once, as we pay our brother a visit."

Ros blazed with the dragon until it seemed there was nothing left to burn. His flesh went first, then his memories, then the person he had tried to be: the student, the adult, the lover . . .

The only thing that wouldn't burn was the silver pendant that Adi had given him. Not even the heat in a fire dragon's belly could melt it. He clung to it tightly and prayed for release.

�

"I'D be dead if it wasn't for you," she had told him, once. "I would've run off on my own, and the crabblers would've got me."

It had all seemed so simple, five years earlier. The currents of their lives had swept them together but would sweep them apart again forever if given the chance. The decision had been easy for him to make.

"I promise I'll come back to you."

"Well, I promise to wait," she had replied. "Just don't die or anything and leave me waiting forever. That could be a little annoying."

"I'll even try to write," he had said, and at times he had, albeit through Change-rich means like talking parrots and their ilk.

"You'd better," she had said, "but I guess I won't be able to write back, seeing Pukje wants to keep everything a secret."

Somehow she had found a way. The pages were rolled up in his pack, a testament to her determination. Too young to wed, Ros and Adi were not too young to make a vow that would bind them into adulthood. Neither of them had made that vow lightly, but neither had they realised how heavy it would turn out to be.

"I promised I'd come back," he had told her, "and I will."

❦

THE chase didn't last long: six dragons against one, one they knew as well as they knew each other, one they would follow to the ends of the earth if needed. Pukje—the dragon of flesh, crafty and wise in the ways of the earth, but so weighed down with its concerns that he taught humans the secrets of his kind—sprang into the sky the moment his siblings appeared on the horizon, boiling and burning and babbling in their animal tongues. He sprinted as fast as his wings would carry him, and they set off right after him, dragons streaking across the firmament like shooting stars, six against one, and the earth shaking beneath them.

❦

WHEN Ros finally woke, he found himself flat on his back, spread-eagled and fully clothed. The leather of his breeches was stiff with dried water and his tunic full of sand, but no actual harm appeared to have been done to him. He swept his matted hair out of sleep-crusted eyes and looked all around him.

The sun had risen, so he could see clearly that he was back in the Divide, back where it had all started. And more than that: the pool, the patch of discoloured rock, the cloud, the steady breeze—even the web, stretching lazily above him—they were back, too, as though the whole thing had been a dream.

Could it have been? Frowning, he relived the confused moments of the chase: wide jaws and clutching talons; tails whipping and wings slapping all around him. He and Zilant—for an immeasurable time, there had been no distinction between them.

By daylight, though, the dragon was invisible. The web was just a web, swaying in the breeze.

With a shaking hand, Ros reached out to pluck the nearest strand.

Seeing the scars on his skin—thousands of tiny lines, crossing and recrossing like a road map of the Haunted City—he thought, *No, best not.*

Instead, Ros clambered to his feet and considered his options.

The nest of dragons, it seemed, was sleeping again. Several crabblers clung unmoving on the parallel cliff-faces, watching him come to his senses with no more than their own intelligence. Not far away lay the wreckage of the strand beast, its legs intact but the bottles, the source of its motive power, completely destroyed.

What should he do now? He couldn't leave without understanding what had happened to him. Dream or no dream? Free or trapped forever?

Did the answer depend entirely on how one looked at the question?

A blackened, hunched thing that Ros had taken for a rock raised its head and looked at him.

"I release you," said Master Pukje, "from my service."

Ros ran to him. The fallen dragon's skin was burned to a crisp, but the eye that inspected him shone with a familiar, incisive light.

"Are you all right? Who did this to you?"

"You did, I think."

"No, master, I wouldn't—"

Pukje croaked a laugh at the expression on Ros's face. "All right, then. It was Zilant." His crisped wings twitched. "Does that make you feel better?"

Ros recoiled, unsure if he was being mocked with affection or contempt, or both. "I don't understand. I did exactly as you told me—"

"You did."

"I found the dragon. I destroyed the web."

"You killed him. I know. Then the others came, and you went to burn them. The web caught fire, and Zilant returned."

Ros nodded. "How is that possible?"

"He burns and lives again. Don't ask me how. We're dragons. We're different from you. We find our own ways to survive the world. You were caught up in all that for a while, but you're free now. You'll have to find a way to survive on your own, and that flame is a harder master than I ever was."

Ros squatted down and rested on his haunches. Pukje's breathing was laboured. Raw pink patches were visible through the crisped skin.

"You expected this to happen," Ros said, meaning more than just their injuries. "This was the proof you were waiting for."

"Proof; punishment. Tell me the difference, and you can be my teacher."

"You sent me to stir them up, to remind them of—what? That they were still alive? That you were?"

"Solitude is bad for the soul." The hunched spine lifted, then fell. "Perhaps I knew that I would be lonely when you were gone. Perhaps I wanted to be with my family for a little while."

Ros stared at the injured dragon, appalled for both of them—until a raspy, painful sound revealed that Pukje was laughing at him. Again.

He supposed he deserved it.

"Change to your human form," Ros said. "I'll carry you back to Laure, where you'll be looked after."

"No need."

"I can't just leave you here."

"Why not? After a short nap, I'll wake refreshed. Go live your life, as my siblings and I cannot."

"What do you mean?"

"You're ready to wake from the dream of your youth. Be reborn and engage with the world. Fighting fire with fire gets you nothing but ashes, no? Most important of all—" Here Pukje coughed, long and hacking, releasing clouds of soot from his lungs. "Remember never to tangle with a dragon while it's dreaming."

Ros stood, remembering the colours of his wild flight across the land with Zilant. It had been like diving into a living sunset. The feeling had been liquid and furious, joyous and terrifying at the same time. He had *been* fire, and would never use it the same way again.

But the scars on his hands and arms weren't burns. They were left by the dragon's web, where it had touched and clung to him, leaving stigmata that all could see. Perhaps he wasn't quite the dragon-killer he had imagined himself to be the previous night, but there were worse things, such as being deformed by someone else's dream.

He squarely confronted the fear that Adi might be having her own doubts. The letter she had sent wasn't just a testament to determination. It exposed her own uncertainty, too. Thinking of the words she had used, he could see all too clearly now that she was as nervous as he, and taking shelter in conventions alien to both of them.

That both dismayed and encouraged him. He was aware now that the emotional pitfalls he had been skirting during his quest arose from feelings of love after all, not the absence of it. He had refused to reveal his desire to Zilant because he was afraid of what it meant. Fear, reluctance, uncertainty, dread—they were all part of the experience, along with joy, wonder, surprise, and delight. He would need to get used to all of them now he was free to pursue an uncertain conclusion.

Pukje was indeed a dangerous dragon, but he knew better than Ros did who his master was, ultimately. There was no use railing against the people he had chosen to play important roles in his life, not when he himself had invited them in. It did them a disservice to imagine lies and treachery at every turn, just because he nursed doubts he barely acknowledged to himself.

Ros looked up at the crabblers. *You cannot turn back now,* he had heard the monstrous denizens of the Divide telling him yesterday. *Take it how you will.* He had done exactly that, and very nearly tangled himself in a net from which he couldn't escape—because it wasn't *escape* he wanted at all, in the end.

We are closer than ever, Adi had said in her letter.

The mouth parts of one of the crabblers clattered the same brief message as before.

"We know you, Roslin of Geheb."

"Better than I do myself, it seems," he clacked back.

"All right, now, go," Pukje told him in an irritated voice. "Live. Be wise. Stay out of trouble."

"I will," Ros said. "If you're sure?"

"I am. You know your road now."

Pukje's eyes closed, and he returned to looking more like a stone than any living thing.

Ros removed the pendant from around his neck. Placing it on the sand next to the wounded dragon's beak, he said, "Thank you, master. I believe I do."

Stooping to pick up his pack from the wreckage of the strand beast, Ros walked to the base of the cliff and began the long climb northward.

A Stark and Wormy Knight

Tad Williams

Here's a sly and playful take on what history might look like if it wasn't written by the winners...

Tad Williams became an international bestselling author with his very first novel, Tailchaser's Song, *and the high quality of his output and the devotion of his readers have kept him on the top of the charts ever since as a* New York Times *and* London Sunday Times *bestseller. His other novels include* The Dragonbone Chair, Stone of Farewell, To Green Angel Tower, *the* Otherland *books—*City of Golden Shadow, River of Blue Fire, Mountain of Black Glass, Sea of Silver Light—*as well as* The War of the Flowers *and* Shadowmarch. *His most recent books are a collection,* Rite: Short Work, *and a novel,* Shadowplay, *the second in the* Shadowmarch *series. He lives with his family in the San Francisco area.*

❦

"**M**AM! Mam!" squeed Alexandrax from the damps of his straw-stooned nesty. "Us can't sleep! Tail us a tell of Ye Elder Days!"

"Child, stop that howlering or you'll be the deaf of me," scowled his scaly forebearer. "Count sheeps and go to sleep!"

"Been counting shepherds instead, have us," her eggling rejoined. "But too too toothsome they each look. Us are hungry, Mam."

"Hungry? Told you not to swallow that farm tot so swift. A soiled and feisity little thing it was, but would you stop to chew carefulish? Oh, no, no. You're not hungry, child, you've simpledly gobbled too fast and dazzled your eatpipes. Be grateful that you've only got one head to sleepify, unbelike some of your knobful ancestors, and go back and shove yourself snorewise."

"But us *can't* sleep, Mam. Us feels all grizzled in the gut and wiggly in the wings. Preach us some storying, pleases—something sightful but sleepable. Back from the days when there were long, dark knights!"

"Knights, knights—you'll scare yourself sleepless with such! No knights there are anymore—just wicked little winglings who will not wooze when they should."

"Just one short storying, Mam! Tale us somewhat of Great-Grandpap, the one that were named Alexandrax, just like us! He were alive in the bad old days of bad old knights."

"Yes, that he was, but far too sensible and caveproud to go truckling with such clanking mostrositors—although, hist, my dragonlet, my eggling, it's true there *was* one time . . ."

"Tell! Tell!"

His mam sighed a sparking sigh. "Right, then, but curl yourself tight and orouborate that tale, my lad—that'll keep you quelled and quiet whilst I storify.

"Well, as often I've told with pride, your great-grandpap were known far-flown and wide-spanned for his good sense. Not for him the errors of others, especkledy not the promiscuous plucking of princesses, since your great-grandy reckoned full well how likely that was to draw some clumbering, lanking knight in a shiny suit with a fist filled of sharp steel wormsbane.

"Oh, those were frightsome days, with knights lurking beneath every scone and round every bent, ready to spring out and spear some mother's son for scarce no cause at all! So did your wisdominical great-grandpap confine himself to plowhards and peasant girls and the plumpcasional parish priest tumbled down drunk in the churchyard of a Sunday evening, shagged out from 'cessive sermonizing. Princesses and such got noticed, do you see, but the primate proletariat were held cheap in those days—a dozen or so could be harvested in one area before a dragon had to wing on to pastors new. And your great-grandpap, he knew that. Made no mistakes, did he—could tell an overdressed merchant missus from a true damager duchess even by the shallowest starlight, plucked the former but shunned the latter every time. Still, like all of us he wondered what it was that made a human princess so very tasty and 'tractive. Why did they need to be so punishingly, paladinishly protected? Was it the creaminess of their savor or the crispiness of their crunch? Perhaps they bore the 'boo-kwet,' as those fancy French wyverns has it, of flowery flavors to which no peat-smoked peasant could ever respire? Or were it something entire different, he pondered, inexplicable except by the truthiest dint of personal mastication?

"Still, even in these moments of weakness your grandpap's pap knew that he were happily protected from his own greeding nature by the scarcity of princessly portions, owing to their all being firmly pantried in castles and other stony such. He was free to specklate, because foolish, droolish chance would never come to a cautious fellow like him.

"Ah, but he should have quashed all that quandering, my little lizarding, 'stead of letting it simmer in his brain-boiler, because there came a day when Luck and Lust met and bred and brooded a litter named Lamentable.

"That is to say, your pap's grandpap stumbled on an unsupervised princess.

"This royal hairless was a bony and brainless thing, it goes without saying, and overfond of her clear complexion, which was her downfalling (although the actual was more of an uplifting, as you'll see). It was her witless wont at night to sneak out of her bed betimes and wiggle her skinny shanks out the window, then ascend to the roof of the castle to moonbathe, which this princess was convinced was the secret of smoothering skin. (Which it may well have been, but who in the name of Clawed Almighty wants smoothered skin? No wonder that humans have grown so scarce these days—they wanted wit.)

"In any case, on this particularly odd even she had just stretched herself out there in her nightgown to indulge this lunar tic when your great-grandpap happened to flap by overhead, on his way back from a failed attempt at tavernkeeper tartare in a nearby town. He took one look at this princess stretched out like the toothsomest treat on a butcher's table and his better sense deskirted him. He swooped scoopishly down and snatched her up, then wung his way back toward his cavern home, already menurizing a stuffing of baker's crumbs and coddle of toddler as side dish when the princess suddenfully managed to get a leg free and, in the midst of her struggling and unladylike cursing, kicked your great-grandpap directedly in the vent as hard as she could, causing him unhappiness (and almost unhemipenes). Yes, dragons had such things even way back then, foolish fledgling. No, your great-grandpap's wasn't pranged for permanent—where do you think your grandpap came from?

"In any case, so shocked and hemipained was he by this attack on his ventral sanctity that he dropped the foolish princess most sudden and vertical—one hundred sky-fathoms or more, into a grove of pine trees, which left her rather careworn. Also fairly conclusively dead.

"Still, even cold princess seemed toothsome to your great-grandpap, though, so he gathered her up and went on home to his cavern. He was lone and batchelorn in those days—your great-grandmammy still in his distinct future—so there was none to greet him there and none to share with, which was how he liked it, selfish old mizard that he was even in those dewy-clawed days. He had just settled in, 'ceedingly slobberful at the teeth and tongue and about to have his first princesstual bite ever, when your grandpap's pap heard a most fearsomeful clatternacious clanking and baying outside his door. Then someone called the following in a rumbling voice that made your g-g's already bruised ventrality try to shrink up further into his interior.

" *'Ho, vile beast! Stealer of maiden princesses, despoiler of virgins, curse of the kingdom—come ye out! Come ye out and face Sir Libogran the Undeflectable!'*

"It were a knight. It were a big one.

"Well, when he heard this hewing cry, your great-grandpap flished cold as a snowdrake's bottom all over. See, even your cautious great-grandy had heard tell of this Libogran, a terrible, stark, and wormy knight—perhaps the greatest dragonsbane of his age and a dreadsome bore on top of it.

" 'Yes, it is I, Libogran,' the knight bellows on while your g's g got more and more trembful, 'slayer of Alasalax the Iron-Scaled and bat-winged Beerbung, destroyer of the infamous Black Worm of Flimpsey Meadow, and scuttler of all the noisome plans of Fubarg the Flameful . . . '

"On and on he went, declaiming such a drawed-out dracologue of death that your great-grandpap was pulled almost equal by impatience as terror. But what could he do to make it stop? A sudden idea crept upon him then, catching him quite by surprise. (He was a young dragon, after all, and unused to thinking, which in those days were held dangerous for the inexperienced.) He snicked quietly into the back of his cave and fetched the princess, who was a bit worse for wear but still respectable enough for a dead human, and took her to the front of the cavern, himself hidebound in shadows as he held her out in the light and dangled her puppetwise where the knight could see.

" 'Princess!' cried Libogran. 'Your father has sent me to save you from this irksome worm! Has he harmed you?'

" 'Oh, no!' shrilled your great-grandpap in his most high-pitchful, princessly voice. 'Not at all! This noble dragon has been naught but gentle-manifold, and I am come of my own freed will. I live here now, do you see? So you may go home without killing anything and tell my papa that I am as happy as a well-burrowed scale mite.'

"The knight, who had a face as broad and untroubled by subtle as a porky haunch, stared at her. 'Are you truly certain you are well, Princess?' quoth he. 'Because you look a bit battered and dirtsome, as if you had per-haps fallen through several branches of several pine trees.'

" 'How nosy and nonsensical you are, Sir Silly Knight!' piped your great-grandpap a bit nervous-like. 'I was climbing in the tops of a few trees, yes, as I love to do. That is how I met my friend this courtinuous dragon—we were both birdnesting in the same tree, la and ha ha! And then he kindly unvited me to his home toward whence I incompulsedly came, and where I am so happily visiting . . . !'

"Things went on in this conversational vain for some little time as your great-grandpap labored to satisfy the questioning of the dreaded dragon-slayer. He might even have eventually empacted that bold knight's with-drawal, except that in a moment of particularly violent puppeteering, your great-grandsire, having let invention get the best of him while describing the joyful plans of the putative princess, managed to dislodge her head.

"She had not been the most manageable marionette to begin with, and now your great-grandpap was particular difficulted trying to get her to pick up and re-neck her lost knob with her own hands while still disguising his clawed handiwork at the back, controlling the action.

" 'Oops and girlish giggle!' he cried in his best mock-princessable tones, scrabbling panicked after her rolling tiara-stand. 'Silly me, I always said it would fall off if it weren't attached to me, and now look at this, hopped right off its stem! Oh, la, I suppose I should be a bit more rigormortous about my grooming and attaching.'

"Sir Libogran the Undeflectable stared at what must clearful have been a somewhat extraordinate sight. 'Highness,' quoth he, 'I cannot help feel-ing that someone here is not being entirely honest with me.'

" 'What?' lied your great-grandpap most quickly and dragonfully. 'Can a princess not lose her head in a minor way occasional without being held up left and right to odiumfoundment and remonstrance?'

" 'This, I see now,' rumbled Sir Libogran in the tone of one who has been cut to his quink, 'is not the living article I came to deliver at all, but rather an ex-princess in expressly poor condition. I shall enter immediately, exterminate the responsible worm, and remove the carcasework for respectful burial.'

"Your great-grandpap, realizing that this particular deceptivation had run its curse, dropped the bony remnants on the stony stoop and raised his voice in high-pitched and apparently remorsive and ruthful squizzling: 'Oh, good sir knight, don't harm us! It's true, your princess is a wee bit dead, but through no fault of us! It was a terrible diseasement that termilated her, of which dragon caves are highlishly prone. She caught the sickness and was rendered lifeless and near decapitate by it within tragical moments. I attempted to convenience you otherwise only to prevent a fine felon like you from suckling at the same deadly treat.'

"After the knight had puddled out your grandsire's sire's words with his poor primate thinker, he said, 'I do not believe there are diseases which render a princess headless and also cover her with sap and pine needles. It is my countersuggestion, dragon, that you thrashed her to death with an evergreen of some sort and now seek to confuse me with fear for my own person. But your downfall, dragon, is that even 'twere so, I cannot do less than march into the mouth of death to honor my quest and the memory of this poor pine-battered morsel. So, regardless of personal danger, I come forthwith to execute you, scaly sirrah. Prepare yourself to meet my blameless blade . . .' And sewed on.

"*Clawed the Flyest,* thought your great-grandpap, *but he is deedly a noisome bore for true.* Still, he dubited not that Sir Libogran, for all his slathering self-regard, would quickly carry through on his executive intent. Thus, to protect his own beloved and familiar hide for a few moments langorous, your pap's pap's pap proceeded to confect another tongue-forker on the spot.

"'All right, thou hast me dart to tripes,' he told the knight. 'The realio trulio reason I cannot permit you into my cavernous cavern is that so caught, I must performecmeat give up to you three wishes of immense valuable. For I am that rare and amnesial creature, a Magical Wishing Dragon. Indeed, it was in attempting to claw her way toward my presence and demand wishes from me that your princess gained the preponderosa of these pine-burns, for it was with such-like furniture of evergreenwood that I attempted pitifullaciously to block my door, and through which she cranched an smushed her way with fearsome strength. Her head was damaged when, after I told her I was fluttered out after long flight and too weary for wish-wafting, she yanked off her crown and tried to beat me indispensable with it. She was a pittance too rough, though—a girl whose strength belied her scrawnymous looks—and detached her headbone from its neckly couchment in the crown-detaching process, leading to this lamentable lifelessness.

" 'However,' went on your great-grandpap, warming now to his self-sufficed subject, 'although I resisted the wish-besieging princess for the honor of all my wormishly magical brethren, since you have caught me fairy and scary, Sir Libogran, larded me in my barren, as it were, I will grant the foremansioned troika of wishes to *you*. But the magic necessitudes that after you tell them unto my ear you must go quickly askance as far as possible—another country would be idealistic—and trouble me no more so that I can perforce the slow magics of their granting (which sometimes takes years betwixt wishing and true-coming).'

"Libogran stood a long time, thinking uffishly, then lastly said, 'Let me make sure I have apprehended you carefully, worm. You state that you are a Magic Wishing Dragon, that it was her greed for this quality of yours which cost the unfortunate princess her life, and that I should tell you my three wishes and then leave, preferably to a distant land, so that you may grant them to me in the most efficacious manner.'

" 'Your astutity is matched only by the stately turn of your greave and the general handfulness of your fizzick, good sir knight,' your great-grandpap eagerly responded, seeing that perhaps he might escape puncturing at the hands of this remorseless rider after all. 'Just bename those wishes, and I will make them factive, both pre- and posthaste.'

"Sir Libogran slowly shook his massive and broadly head. 'Do you take me for a fool, creature?'

" 'Not a fool creature as sort,' replinked your grandpap's daddy, trying to maintain a chirrupful tone. 'After all, you and your elk might be a lesser species than us *Draco Pulcher*, but still, as I would be the first to argue, a vally-hooed part of Clawed the Flyest's great creation . . . '

" 'Come here, dragon, and let me show you my wish.'

"Your great-grandpap hesitated. 'Come there?' he asked. 'Whyso?'

" 'Because I cannot explain as well as I can demonstrate, sirrah,' quoth the bulky and clanksome human.

"So your forebeast slithered out from the cavernous depths, anxious to end his night out by sending this knight out. He was also hoping that, though disappointed of his foreplanned feast, he might at least locate some princessly bits fallen off in the cave, which could be served chippingly on toast. But momentarily after your great-grandpap emerged into the light-some day, the cruel Sir Libogran snatched your ancestor's throat in a gauntleted ham and cut off that poor, innosensitive dragon's head with his vicious blade.

"Snick! No snack.

"This treacherness done, the knight gathered up the princess's tree-tattered torso and emancive pate, then went galumphing back toward the castle of her mourning, soon-to-mourn-more Mammy and Daddums."

♣

"BUT how can that be, Mam?" shrimped wee Alexandrax. "He killed Great-Grandpap? Then how did Grandpap, Pap, and Yours Contumely come to be?"

"Fie, fie, shut that o-shaped fishmouth, my breamish boy. Did I say aught about killing? He did not kill your great-grandpap, he cut off his head. Do you not dismember that your great-grandcestor was dragon of the two-headed vermiety?

"As it happened, one of his heads had been feeling poorly, and he had kept it tucked severely under one wing all that day and aftermoon so it could recupertate. Thus, Libogran the Undeflectable was not aware of the existence of this auxiliary knob, which he would doubtless of otherwise liberated from its neckbones along with the other. As it was, the sickened head soon recovered and was good as new. (With time the severed one also grew back, although it was ever after small and prone to foolish smiles and the uttering of platitudinous speech—phrases like, 'I'm sure everything will work off in the end' and 'It is honorous just to be nominated,' and such-like.)

"In times ahead—a phrase which was sorely painful to your great-great-pap during his invalidated re-knobbing—your g-g would go back to his old, happy ways, horrorizing harrowers and slurping shepherds but never again letting himself even veer toward rooftopping virgins or in fact anything that bore the remotest rumor of the poisonous perfume of princessity. He became a pillar of his community, married your great-grandmammy in a famously fabulous ceremony—just catering the event purged three surrounding counties of their peasantly population—and lived a long and harpy life."

"But Mam, Mam, what about that stark and wormy Sir Libogran, that . . . dragocidal maniac? Did he really live hoppishly ever after as well, unhaunted by his bloodful crime?"

"In those days, there was no justice for our kind except what we made ourselves, my serpentine son. No court or king would ever have victed him."

"So he died unpunwiched?"

"Not exactly. One day your great-grandpap was on his way back from courting your grandest-greatmam-to-be, and happened to realize by the banners on its battlements that he was passing over Libogran's castle, so he stooped to the rooftop and squatted on the chimbley pot, warming his hindermost for a moment (a fire was burning in the hearth down below and it was most pleasantly blazeful) before voiding himself down the chimbley hole into the great fireplace."

"He couped the flue!"

"He did, my boy, he did. The whole of Libogran's household came staggering out into the cold night waving and weeping and coughing out the stinking smoke as your grand's grandpap flew chortling away into the night, unseen. Libogran's castle had to be emptied and aired for weeks during the most freezingly worstful weather of the year, and on this account the knight spent the rest of his life at war with the castle pigeons, on whom he blamed your great-grandpap's secret chimbley-discharge—he thought the birds had united for a concerted, guanotated attempt on his life. Thus, stalking a dove across the roof with his bird-net and boarspear a few years later, Sir Libogran slipped and fell to his death in the castle garden, spiking himself on his own great sticker and dangling thereby for several days, mistaken by his kin and servants as a new scarecrow."

"Halloo and hooray, Mam! Was he the last of the dragon-hunters, then? Was him skewerting on his own sharpitude the reason we no longer fear them?"

"No, dearest honey-sonny, we no longer fear them because *they* no longer see *us*. During the hunders of yearses since your greatest-grandpap's day, a plague called Civilization came over them, a diseaseful misery that blinded them to half the creatures of the world and dumbfounded their memories of much that is true and ancient. Let me tell you a dreadsome secret." She leaned close to whisper in his tender earhole. "Even when we snatch a plump merchant or a lean yet flavorful spinster from their midst these days, the humans never know that one of us dragons has doomfully done for the disappeared. They blame it instead on a monster they fear even more."

"What is that, Mam?" Alexandrax whimpspered. "It fears me to hear, but I want to know. What do they think slaughters them? An odious ogre? A man-munching manticore?"

"Some even more frightfulling creature. No dragon has ever seen it, but they call it . . . Statistics."

"Clawed Hitself save us from such a horridly horror!" squeeped the small one in fright.

"It is only a man-fancy, like all the rest of their nonned sense," murmed his mam. "Empty as the armor of a cracked and slurped knight—so fear it not. Now, my tale is coiled, so sleepish for you, my tender-winged bundle."

"I will," he said, curling up like a sleepy hoop, most yawnful. "I s'pose no knights is good nights, huh, Mam?"

"Examply, my brooded boy. Fear not clanking men nor else. Sleep. All is safe, and I am watching all over you."

And indeed, as she gazed yellow-eyed and loving on her eggling, the cave soon grew fulfilled with the thumberous rundle of wormsnore.

None So Blind

HARRY TURTLEDOVE

Although he writes other kinds of science fiction as well, and even the occasional fantasy, Harry Turtledove has become one of the most prominent writers of alternate history stories in the business today, and is probably the most popular and influential writer to work that territory since L. Sprague de Camp; in fact, most of the current popularity of that particular subgenre can be attributed to Turtledove's own hot-ticket bestseller status.

Turtledove has published alternate history novels such as The Guns of the South, *dealing with a time line in which the American Civil War turns out very differently, thanks to time-traveling gunrunners; the bestselling Worldwar series, in which the course of World War II is altered by attacking aliens; the Basil Argyros series, detailing the adventures of a "magistrianoi" in an alternate Byzantine Empire (collected in the book* Agent of Byzantium); *the Sim series, which takes place in an alternate world in which European explorers find North America inhabited by hominids instead of Indians (collected in the book* A Different Flesh); *a look at a world where the Revolutionary War didn't happen, written with actor Richard Dreyfuss,* The Two Georges; *and many other intriguing alternate history scenarios. Turtledove is also the author of two multivolume alternate history fantasy series, the multivolume Videssos cycle and the Krispos sequence. His other books include the novels* Wereblood, Werenight, Earthgrip, Noninterference, A World of Difference, Gunpowder Empire, American Empire: The Victorious Opposition, Jaws of Darkness, *and* Ruled Britannia; *the collections* Kaleidoscope *and* Down in the Bottomlands (and Other Places); *and, as editor,* The Best Alternate History Stories of the 20th Century, The Best Military Science Fiction of the 20th Century, *and, with Martin H. Greenberg, the* Alternate Generals *books—plus many others. His most recent books include the novels* The Man with the Iron Heart, After the Downfall, Give Me Back My Legions!, *and* Hitler's War, *and the anthologies* The Best Time Travel Stories of the 20th

Century, Alternate Generals III, and The Enchanter Completed. *Coming up is
Liberating Atlantis. He won a Hugo Award in 1994 for his story "Down in the Bottomlands." A native Californian, Turtledove has a PhD in Byzantine history from UCLA
and has published a scholarly translation of a ninth-century Byzantine chronicle. He lives
in Canoga Park, California, with his wife and family.*

*Here he shows us that it's possible to miss what's right under your nose—worse,
refuse even to look . . .*

ԾՅ

A long with the rest of the wizards and the savants—and the
guardsmen—from the Empire of Mussalmi, Kyosti stared south
through a gap in the trees toward the mountains that marked the tropical continent's backbone. Even down here, even in the lowlands' sweaty
summers, snow clung to the highest of those peaks. Steam—or was it
smoke?—rose from the white-clad tops of a couple of crests not too far
from each other. Kyosti shook his head. Those crests might not look
too far apart from here, but many miles would separate them from each
other.

In the old days, Mussalmian maps of those mountains had borne a
warning inscription: HERE BE DRAGONS. Kyosti, something of a student of those days, had seen many such maps, some in the original, more
reproduced by the law of similarity so the wider scholarly community
could have access to them. The inscription never varied; that subjunctive
never turned into an indicative.

But this was a new age. If there were dragons in these tropic mountains, Mussalmi wanted to know about it. And if there were none, the
Empire wanted to know that, too. Even if this expedition found none, even
if it showed there had never been any, bards would doubtless go on spinning tales about them. That was all right with Kyosti. Bards and tales of
ancient days were one thing. The worries of marshals and statesmen were
something else again.

Kyosti didn't believe the explorers would find any dragons. He thought
dragons were a figment of the bardic imagination—and of the imagina-
tions of the tropical continent's small, pale, skinny natives. Still, he recognized that he might be wrong. And even if he wasn't, who could say what
the expedition *would* discover, despite discovering no great fire-breathing
worms?

One of the native guides pointed toward the distant mountains. "You
for dragons looking there?" he asked, scratching under his loincloth. It

was all he wore. Along with the strangely accented, ungrammatical Mussalmian he spoke, that made Kyosti figure that he was none too bright.

"Yes, we will look for dragons there, Sztojay," the wizard answered. He might have been talking to an idiot child.

Sztojay didn't get offended—or didn't act offended, anyhow. The natives had learned that bad things happened to them if the imperials realized they were angry. The little man just said, "You to mountains going, you dragon there finding."

"We'll see," Kyosti said indulgently. What did, what could, a jungle native know about the mountains?

Sztojay said something else. Kyosti didn't really hear what it was. A native girl—woman—ambled by, bare breasts jiggling. The women here wore no more than their menfolk. With their atrocious climate, that made sense in a way. Still, Kyosti wasn't the only Mussalmian whose eyes kept bugging out of his head. Far from it.

By imperial standards, the native women were easy lays. Someone had told Kyosti as much before he sailed south. Whoever it was—the wizard couldn't remember now—he'd known what he was talking about. Kyosti smiled, remembering.

"Come on! Are we ready?" That was Baron Toivo, who was in charge of the expedition. He had a place at the Imperial Academy in Tampere, not far from the capital, and was connected to the Emperor's family. Even without all that, he would have been a bad man to cross, as he was large and strong and short-tempered. Kyosti wasn't astonished, then, when no one told him no. Toivo took off his broad-brimmed straw hat and waved it over his head. "Well, let's go!" Ready or not, they went.

༨

MUSSALMI ruled all the way down to the foothills of the mountains. That didn't mean that imperials were seen in the jungle very often. Most of the Mussalmians who did go there had either started with nothing and were hoping to come home with something or had made a hash of something and effectively become nothing themselves.

Bearers from one tribe or clan or petty chiefdom handed the expedition and its chattels on to the next one farther south. A few coppers, some glass beads, a petty spell or two: such things sufficed as payment. Sufficed? Here on the tropical continent, they might as well have been riches. The natives thought they were.

Kyosti needed a spell from the healer, to cure a painful and embarrassing malady he'd come down with a few days after sleeping with one of those scantily clad native women. Not all southern diseases yielded to charms the imperials had developed, but this one did. He breathed a sigh of relief.

The farther south the explorers went, the fewer the natives who spoke or understood Mussalmian. Another wizard, a cunning linguist called Sunila, devised a translation cantrip that worked . . . after a fashion. It worked better than pointing and gesturing, anyhow. Baron Toivo swore because it wasn't perfect, but only halfheartedly, so he couldn't have been too unhappy.

"You need to watch out for the *tsaldaris* tonight," one of this latest group of natives said. The cantrip didn't translate the word the Mussalmians really needed.

Patiently, Kyosti said, "Tell me what the, uh, *tsaldaris*"—he knew he made a hash of the foreign word—"is like. Tell me what it does."

The native was only too happy to oblige. He went into gory detail, in fact. Before long, Kyosti got the idea: the *tsaldaris* was some kind of vampire. That led to a good deal of talk among the Mussalmians, talk for which they didn't use Sunila's translating cantrip. At least half of them thought that the little blond man in the loincloth was either trying to scare them away, or, at best, passing on his own superstitions. Up in the Empire, vampires were as legendary—skeptics would have said, as mythical—as dragons.

Those with a taste for arcane lore dredged from their memories things that might stop a vampire: roses, garlic, sunlight. The native who'd warned them agreed about the last one. Of roses he knew nothing. The tropical continent had flowers that blazed in every color of the rainbow, but none so ordinary as roses. He didn't know about garlic, either. His folks had other spices. One of the cooks let him smell some. By the horrible face he made, he preferred vampires.

But the Mussalmians didn't. Several of them rubbed themselves with powdered garlic before getting into their bedrolls and under their mosquito nets. Kyosti was one of those who abstained. He wasn't sure there were such things as vampires. Even if there were, he doubted whether a northern spice would deter a tropical bloodsucker that had never been exposed to it.

Sunrise pried his eyes open the next morning. He'd come through unscathed. So had the native bearers. So had his countrymen who'd used the powdered garlic. So had his countrymen who hadn't—except for a mapmaker named Relander, who had two punctures on his throat and a look of eerily calm satisfaction on his face. He was the most contented-looking corpse Kyosti had ever seen.

Maybe that was because he still lay in shadow. When the sun finally struck him, his features screwed up and his skin started to shrivel. That should have been impossible. Watching it happen, fighting not to retch, Kyosti saw for himself that it wasn't. Relander might be a corpse, but he wasn't quite dead.

To make sure he got that way and stayed that way, the Mussalmians pounded a stake through his heart. The cook put a garlic clove under his tongue. They left him out in the fierce southern sun. His body mortified with unnatural—supernatural?—speed. "Gods grant him peace," Baron Toivo said.

"So may it be," the other Mussalmians chorused.

The natives watched what they did with the luckless Relander and what happened to his mortal remains. Kyosti couldn't read the blonds' expressions. The man who'd warned the explorers about the *tsaldaris* said something to his friend in his own language. Sunila's cantrip wasn't working, but Kyosti didn't think he needed it to understand what the scrawny little fellow was saying. If it wasn't *I told them so*, the Mussalmian wizard would have been astonished.

Everyone, natives and explorers from the north alike, seemed delighted to leave the campground where Relander had found his end. "It could be that the vampire will not pursue us, and that we will meet no more of the foul creatures," Baron Toivo said hopefully.

Hope was one thing. Informed hope was something else again—something better, as far as Kyosti was concerned. With Sunila's help, he translated the baron's comment for one of the bearers.

"It could be, yes," the man replied, his voice grave. "But the *tsaldaris* will have seen that you strangers make easy prey. Why would it *not* come after you to feed again, eh?"

Mussalmians commonly reckoned the natives of the tropical continent flighty and foolish. As far as Kyosti could see, though, this nearly naked bearer reasoned like a schoolmaster. The fellow might work for coppers and trinkets, but he was nobody's fool.

Tramping south toward the mountains that might or might not harbor dragons, Kyosti kept looking back over his shoulder. The vampire wouldn't, couldn't, travel by daylight, but even so . . . He felt better after they forded a stream. Running water was also supposed to balk such creatures, wasn't it?

Sunila found a leech fat with his blood clinging to his leg when he came up onto dry land again. "All kinds of bloodsuckers in this miserable place," he snarled, using a smoldering twig to make it let go, then bandaging the oozing hole it had left in his flesh.

"Not the same. You can find leeches in the Empire," Kyosti said.

"You can find other vampires there, too. Have you ever seen a tax collector out by daylight?" Sunila retorted. Kyosti laughed. By the linguistic sorcerer's expression, he hadn't been joking.

Down sank the sun. The explorers encamped with it still above the horizon; twilight didn't last long in the tropics. After supper, Kyosti used the garlic powder he'd refused the night before. He hoped—he prayed—it would help. There was garlic in the evening sausages, too; they eased his mind as they filled his belly.

All of which helped much less than he wished that it would have when he woke in bright moonlight and found himself face-to-face with the *tsaldaris*. Despite that moonlight, far more brilliant than it would have been anywhere in the Empire of Mussalmi, the undead creature's eyes were two black sinkholes that gave back nothing . . . or did red flicker somewhere far down in their depths, like hellfire seen from heaven?

"You are mine," the vampire whispered. Sunali's cantrip wouldn't be operating now, but Kyosti understood even though the thing wasn't speaking Mussalmian.

"I am yours," the wizard agreed, breathing garlic fumes into the creature's face. Its features twisted, almost as Relander's had when the sun touched them. The garlic hurt it, then—but not enough to stop it. Its eyes might have been embered darkness, but its fangs gleamed in the tropical moonlight. Kyosti knew just where they would pierce him. He could hardly wait.

Fight! Run! Cast a spell! screamed a small, still-unseduced part of his mind. The rest, though, the rest was content to let whatever happened happen. He remembered how pleased with himself Relander had looked when they found him.

The *tsaldaris* carried a reek of the grave. Where did it hide between sunup and sundown? Why hadn't the natives caught it and given it a final death long before this? A singularly pointless thing to wonder as those fangs sank closer.

And then, quite suddenly, the fangs disappeared. So did the terrible eyes. And so did the rest of the austerely beautiful face. As soon as Kyosti couldn't see it anymore, it no longer seemed austerely beautiful. It was the most horrible thing he'd ever set eyes on. The spell it had laid on him—on him! a wizard!—was gone.

"Help us, curse it!" Sunila said hoarsely. Kyosti realized that the vampire's spell might not be altogether gone. The creature's eyes hadn't disappeared because it withdrew. They'd disappeared because Sunila and one of the little blond natives had thrown a big black sack over its head. Now they had to fight like a couple of demons to keep the monster from breaking away and fleeing—or, worse, from breaking away, using its strange powers, and avenging itself.

When Kyosti's wits truly did come back to what they should have been, he used a spell of his own. He was with the expedition not least because he was one of the Empire's leading preservationists. Specimens he enchanted would stay as fresh as if they were alive for years, for decades, perhaps for centuries. With him along, the explorers didn't need to carry dozens of heavy, awkward jugs of formalin (which was devilishly expensive) or strong spirits (which weren't, but which *were* all too apt to be used for purposes unrelated to preservation).

He'd never cast a spell that met such resistance. But then, he'd never before tried to freeze any creature, alive or undead, with a conscious will of its own. Storytellers spun tales about preservationists and the girls rash enough to scorn them. Kyosti had always thought those stories were so much nonsense. Now he was convinced of it. Even slowing the vampire down took all the magecraft he had in him.

Slowing it down sufficed. That let Sunila and the native—and Kyosti himself, once he scrambled out of his bedroll—keep the black sack over its head, and eventually let them bind it so it could not possibly escape.

Despite the spell, despite the bonds, it kept struggling to free itself. That was horrible to behold: it was like watching a man move deep underwater, or in the swaddling folds of nightmare. Kyosti watched anyhow. This . . . thing had come much too close to killing him, and he wanted to see it die the death. Some of the savants in the expedition had more dispassionate reasons to observe the vampire—or so they claimed, anyhow.

Little by little, the eastern sky turned pale, and then bright. Stars faded. The moon went from gold to chalk. Under its shroud, the *tsaldaris* keened. It might not be able to see out, but it knew what was coming. It knew, and it feared.

At last, after what seemed simultaneously a very long time and no time at all, the sun slid up over the eastern horizon. Sunbeams walked down the trees from top to bottom, then glided over the ground toward the vampire. It keened again and moved a little faster, but not nearly fast enough.

A sunbeam touched a bound hand. The hand didn't merely shrivel, as poor Relander's face had done. It burst into flame. In an instant, the whole vampire was on fire. It burned hot and fierce, like fatwood. The glare was so fierce, Kyosti had to turn his face. The smell . . . He wanted to drool and to heave, both at the same time.

It was soon over. The fire left little ash, most of it from the sack and the bonds. The morning breeze sprang up and blew away what there was. The *tsaldaris* might never have been there at all. But, in that case, why was Relander dead?

"Well," Baron Toivo said roughly, "let's head south."

❧

AS the land rose toward the peaks of the tropical continent's spine, jungle gave way to more open woodland, then the woodland to savannas. Days stayed hot, though the hateful mugginess subsided. Nights no longer sweltered. They grew mild, then, sometimes, forthrightly chilly. Flies persisted, but the mosquitoes didn't. Kyosti missed them not a copper's worth.

Few Mussalmian explorers had come so far south. Sunila's translation cantrip got a workout. As before, it proved better than nothing, but not always good enough.

One native tribe, seeing tall, swarthy strangers crossing their lands, wasted no time trying to talk to them but attacked instead. The natives promptly regretted it. Their spears and arrows and half-baked sorceries were no match for the magic and weapons the Mussalmians brought to bear. The handful of blonds from the raiding party who escaped fled, shrieking in terror. Naked-headed vultures spiraled down out of the sky to commence disposing of the natives who'd fallen.

Vultures, yes. But Kyosti eyed the blue-enameled bowl overhead in hope of spying larger visitors. Some stories said dragons were four or five or ten times larger than the largest vultures. Others claimed they were four or five or ten times larger than that. Others still . . . Well, Kyosti didn't waste his time even trying to believe those. Some talespinners had more imagination than they knew what to do with.

The natives had managed to wound a couple of Mussalmians. Even that tiny success irked Baron Toivo. The baron didn't mind losing a savant to a venomous serpent, or another to a striped beast that was to a house cat as imagined dragons were to vultures. By Toivo's attitude, wild animals were some of the hazards explorers faced, but Mussalmians should outdo these southern savages under any and all circumstances.

Imaginary dragons . . . Kyosti saw them in his dreams, and in his mind's eye. With the eyes of his body, he saw vultures and hawks and crows and long-necked birds that ran on two legs like men and were even taller than Mussalmians. With sarcastic aplomb, one of the explorers dubbed them sparrows. Kyosti never found out who'd used the name first, but inside a day it was in everybody's mouths.

Those enormous "sparrows" made good eating. Their meat was red as beef and tasted much like it. A couple of their eggs could feed the whole expedition—if the cooks were patient enough to let them get done.

Eyeing a broken shell with respect, Kyosti said, "Easy enough to think of a dragon hatching from something that size."

"Just because something is easy to conceive doesn't make it true," Sunila answered tartly. "I think we are chasing shadows here myself. If we find anything at all, we'll find something like a large snake—or maybe a lizard—you wait and see. Exaggeration from people who never really saw the creature will have done the rest."

"Some people say men invented the gods that way." Kyosti pointed toward one of the smoking mountains ahead. "What *could* that be but a god's breath, after all?"

"Yes, what?" the linguistic sorcerer agreed dryly. "As a matter of fact, I hold to that view myself—though not where the stuffier sort of priest can hear me do it, I admit. Exactly the same phenomenon here with dragons, I tell you."

Kyosti nodded. "I wouldn't be surprised. We're learning all sorts of other things, though. That nasty vampire, and the 'sparrows,' and who knows what else we'll come upon when we climb higher? We wouldn't have seen any of it if we'd stayed at home in the Empire."

"You wouldn't have almost got killed if you'd stayed at home in the Empire," Sunila reminded him.

That was true, but Kyosti didn't care to think about it. "What's the line from the old poet?" he said. " 'Man seeks the gods, and seeking finds them'—something like that, anyhow. What we learn on the voyage is what matters."

"I suppose so." Sunila spoke with the air of someone granting a sizable concession. But then the other man brightened. "I've improved the translation cantrip a lot since we got here. It's bumped up against *really* foreign languages, the way it can't in the Empire anymore. Almost everyone there speaks Mussalmian along with his birthspeech—instead of it, these days, more often than not."

"I doubt my great-grandparents knew it very well," Kyosti said. "But I can't speak a word of their clan's jibber-jabber. Don't want to, either. Things are simpler when there's only one language, and we all use it."

"You're a sensible fellow," Sunila said, by which he meant that Kyosti's opinion here was the same as his own.

"I wonder what we *will* come across next," Kyosti said in musing tones.

"If the moon were full, I'd guess werewolves," Sunila replied.

"Some of the bone-crunching scavengers that howl in the grass sound as if they ought to be werewolves, or else madmen raving," Kyosti said. "I don't think anyone described them before, or the big striped cats."

"For Antti's sake, I hope there are gods in the heavens." Sunila wasn't going off on a tangent; Antti was the savant the great cat had slain. With a sigh, the linguist sorcerer went on, "But I know the difference between what I hope and what I believe. I hope we find dragons, too." He spread his hands. Sorcerers back in the Empire lived soft, but his palms, like Kyosti's, were ridged with callus. "No matter what I hope, though, I know what I believe there, too."

UP in the foothills, soil covered green-gray stone only sparsely. Grass and shrubs grew where they could. Little beasts something like rabbits and something like tiny deer scurried through the undergrowth, what there was of it. On high ground they kept lookouts who chirruped whenever they saw danger.

They didn't always see it. Snakes ate the little beasts. So did hawks. A dragon swooping down on them . . . Kyosti shook his head. One of those furry scurriers would have been no more than a gooseberry to a hungry dragon, even if dragons were on the small side of what the tales claimed for them.

Suddenly, all the lookouts chirruped at once and tumbled down off their perches. Seeing nothing out of the ordinary, Kyosti wondered why—but only for an instant. He let out his own shout of alarm as the ground shuddered under his feet. He might have been embarrassed if half the other explorers hadn't also cried out at the same time.

How long did the earthquake last? Probably not very long, as those things went—it was just a small one. But it seemed to go on forever. A few rocks fell over. Off to the west, a bigger rumble spoke of a landslide. Birds sprang screeching into the air. Dust rose with them, in a thick, choking cloud.

By the time Kyosti quit coughing and rubbing at his grit-filled eyes, most of the expedition's native bearers had set down their burdens and were making for lower, flatter ground as fast as they could go. It wasn't that he didn't sympathize with them—he did. But he didn't think the Mussalmians could recruit replacements in this harsh, stony country.

Along with Sunila and Baron Toivo, he tried to talk the bearers out of leaving. They didn't want to listen to him. Toivo was more direct. He told the natives, "Remember what we did to the tribe that attacked us. If you run away, you show you are also our enemies, and we will do the same to you."

Some of the skinny little blond men sullenly started back toward the bales and bundles they'd put down. Not even Baron Toivo had an easy time intimidating the rest. A scar-faced fellow named Galvanauskas led that group of locals. He said something in his incomprehensible language. "When the *pranys* stirs in its sleep, what difference does it make what people do?" was how Sunila's cantrip rendered it into Mussalmian. That clarified matters only so far.

"What's a *pranys*?" Kyosti asked, with what he though was exaggerated patience.

You stupid foreigner, the look Galvanauskas gave him said. Kyosti was much more used to giving those looks to the natives than to getting them. *Pranys* turned out to be the scar-faced man's word for *dragon*. To make matters perfectly clear, he pointed ahead, toward the volcanic crater that kept sending up a thin rill of smoke. "That is the *pranys*'s nostril," he declared.

Kyosti, Sunila, and Baron Toivo all burst out laughing together. Galvanauskas looked highly affronted, not that any of the imperials cared. *And I thought our talespinners told whoppers!* Kyosti thought. *Not quite a god's breath, but close enough!*

Baron Toivo was more direct, as he commonly was. "Listen here," he snapped. "If you gutless, lazy lugs don't get back to work, you'll wish a dragon was all you had to worry about. Have you got that?"

Thanks to Sunila's cantrip, Galvanauskas and the knot of his stubborn fellow tribesmen couldn't very well *not* get it. Even so, they made a show of arguing among themselves before they gave in.

"Use your charm one more time for me, will you?" Kyosti asked

Sunila. His colleague nodded. The preservationist fell in alongside Galvanauskas, who trudged along with his head down, the very picture of dejection. Catching his eye at last, Kyosti pointed toward the other smoking mountain in the range, now a quarter of the way across the horizon from the one the native had picked. "I suppose you'll tell me that's the dragon's *other* nostril?" Kyosti jeered.

This time, the look the scar-faced man sent him said he might not be an imbecile after all. Maybe he was only a moron. "Well, of course," Galvanauskas answered.

AS the Mussalmians and their reluctant bearers climbed higher, they spied white beasts gracefully skipping from crag to crag ahead of them. *Mountain goats,* Kyosti thought, and up in the Empire's mountains, they would have been. But these creatures didn't have two horns near their ears. Each one carried a single horn in the center of its forehead. Their tails were long and flowing, not short and stubby. What else to call them but unicorns?

Like dragons, unicorns were more often imagined than seen in the Empire of Mussalmi. Unlike dragons, at least thus far, unicorns didn't seem shy about showing themselves on the tropical continent. A savant named Uluots brought Kyosti a lumpy—something—wrapped in cloth. "Would you do me the kindness of preserving this so I can study it at my leisure, in a place where I have better tools to use?" he asked.

"Of course—that's what I'm here for," Kyosti said. But he couldn't help coming out with a question of his own: "Er, what is it?"

"Unicorn scat," Uluots answered, not without pride. "Still warm, too," he added.

"How nice," Kyosti murmured.

"Oh, it is," Uluots said. "This way, I can be sure I'm working with a fresh specimen. I brought it back to you quick as I could."

"How nice," Kyosti said again. He did not presume to judge other men's enthusiasms. That way, if he was lucky, no one else would presume to judge his. He cast the spell Uluots wanted. The other savant went away happy.

Collecting unicorn droppings was easy enough. Collecting one of the unicorns that produced the droppings proved harder. They were wary beasts, and let neither Mussalmians nor natives come close. "Miserable blonds must hunt them whenever they get the chance—the creatures wouldn't be so leery of us otherwise." Baron Toivo sounded aggrieved that the locals might seek to slake their hunger with unicorn meat. And why would he not, when that made it difficult for the more important (at least to themselves) imperials to gather a specimen?

"Maybe we need a virgin to lure them out," Sunila said—that was part of unicorn lore back in the Empire.

"How about the baron's right ear?" Kyosti suggested. Toivo wasn't standing close by, and had his back turned. He wouldn't be able to tell who was poking fun at him. By the way the back of his neck turned red, it was a good thing for Kyosti that he couldn't.

But then the rest of the Mussalmians took up the game. Another savant suggested Baron Toivo's left ear instead of the right. Yet another, no doubt thinking of the kind of specimens Uluots gathered, proposed a different part of that worthy's anatomy. Someone else demurred, doubting Uluots's virginity there. Things went downhill in a hurry after that. The learned Mussalmians giggled like naughty schoolgirls.

Understanding much less than half of what was going on, Galvanauskas and the rest of the native bearers gaped at their paymasters. They knew more about the unicorns than the Mussalmians did: they would have had trouble knowing less. They didn't have a lot of useless lore to unlearn, either.

That occurred to Kyosti while he and his countrymen were still making bad bawdy jokes. What it might mean took longer to sink in. It wasn't till the next day that Kyosti went over to Sunila, and said, "Help me get something across to Galvanauskas, would you?"

"I can use the translation cantrip for you," the other wizard answered. "But gods only know if we'll get anything across to him."

"Mm, yes. There is that," Kyosti agreed. "Well, do what you can." They went over to the natives' headman. "If you were hunting a unicorn, how would you go about it?"

Galvanauskas considered. Kyosti thought so, anyhow; the native's eyes were as blue and blank and unreadable as a cloudless sky. At last, Galvanauskas said, "I would set some hunters in an ambush and frighten a unicorn so that it ran past them and gave them an easy shot at it."

"Not bad," Kyosti said after some reflection of his own. He took from his belt pouch a broad copper coin bearing the double-chinned profile of the last Emperor but one and handed it to Galvanauskas. "Thanks."

Galvanauskas had no belt pouch—he had no belt. He tucked the copper into his loincloth. Kyosti thought it was likely to fall out, but that didn't seem to worry the native. Galvanauskas said something the cantrip rendered as "So generous." Not till sometime later did Kyosti wonder whether that was intended as irony.

Sarcasm or not, Galvanauskas's scheme struck him as better than any the Mussalmians had come up with for themselves. It struck Baron Toivo the same way when Kyosti put it to him. "These blond fellas, they're sneaky enough and then some," the leader of the expedition declared.

The scheme might be better, but it illustrated the difference between better and good. Spooking a unicorn was easy. Spooking a unicorn so that it ran past the place where a couple of Mussalmians hid waiting to kill it proved anything but. Unicorns ran and jumped where they pleased, not where the hunters wanted them to go.

"We're supposed to be hunting dragons, not wasting so much time with unicorns," Baron Toivo said stiffly.

"But the unicorns are *here*, sir," Kyosti said. "The dragons . . ." He pointed toward the smoking mountaintop ahead. It climbed far higher into the sky now than it had when he first spied it from the jungle. "That's the nose on one of them. Excuse me—part of the nose."

"You really don't believe we'll find anything, do you?" Disapproval stuck out on Toivo like a porcupine's quills.

"It's the seeking that counts," Kyosti insisted, and quoted the poet from ancient days once more. "Look at all the things we've found because we came looking for dragons: the tropical vampire, the striped cats, the 'sparrows,' and now these unicorns. For the rest of their lives, people who didn't come on this expedition will be sorry they missed it."

"We've come seeking *dragons*. Do you see any dragons here?" Baron Toivo said.

"No, sir. But I've seen all kinds of interesting things, important things, I wouldn't have seen if we hadn't come after the dragons," Kyosti answered. "Any excuse to find things I didn't know before is a good one, as far as I'm concerned."

"I want a dragon." Baron Toivo peered up the mountain's flanks in the direction of the smoking crater. "A real dragon, curse it, not some stupid pipe dream from natives who don't know better than to call a half-asleep volcano a dragon's nostril."

Kyosti wanted a real dragon, too, but he would take what he could get. So would Baron Toivo, of course. The difference between them was that Toivo would *complain* if what he got wasn't what he already wanted. As long as Kyosti got things he hadn't seen before—whether that included dragons or not—he was happy. As far as Kyosti was concerned, Baron

Toivo's insistence that reality should match his desires was as foolish as the natives' maunderings about dragon nostrils.

AFTER most of a week in which the unicorns ran the wrong way time after frustrating time, the Mussalmians killed four of them in the space of a day and a half. That let the savants argue about them even more than they'd already been doing. Were unicorns of the horse kind or of the goat kind? The males had a single hoof on each foot, the females two on each, which confused things instead of clarifying them. When a savant cut open a unicorn carcass to see how it was made, what he found sparked more arguments yet.

"Maybe unicorns aren't horses *or* goats," Kyosti suggested to Sunila. "Maybe they're something different: unicorns, for instance."

The linguistic wizard rolled his eyes. "What a ridiculous notion!" he said. "If you put it to the people who are actually supposed to know such things, both sides will tear you to pieces."

"Now tell me something I hadn't figured out for myself," Kyosti answered. It wasn't as if his own specialty were free from feuds. It wasn't, and neither was Sunila's. But watching savants in a different discipline go at one another like a pailful of crabs made him chuckle.

He also stayed busy. Savants on both sides of the unicorns-are-horses, unicorns-are-goats quarrel had him sorcerously preserve bits of dead unicorn so that they could take them back to the Empire for further study. Each of them seemed convinced further study would prove him right and the people deluded enough to disagree with him a pack of cretins.

And Kyosti got acquainted with unicorn another way. Not all the internal bits got preserved—some of them got stewed instead. He'd eaten both horse and goat. To him, hunger made the best sauce for both. Despite having been hungry when he ate of them, he had fond memories of neither. He thought unicorn outdid both when it came to flavor. Something like veal, something like lamb . . . Yes, he liked it. Liking food you ate on an expedition was a happy accident, like living through a vampire attack.

As the explorers climbed toward the smoking peak, they kept killing unicorns. Kyosti's sorcerous skills got used less and less often; eventually, savants on both sides of the argument had all the specimens they thought they needed. But unicorn—stewed, baked, and roasted—stayed on the explorers' menu.

Picking his teeth after gnawing the last of the meat off a roasted unicorn rib, Kyosti asked Uluots, "What do you suppose eats them when no Mussalmian expedition's in the neighborhood?"

"What do you mean?" Uluots asked.

Kyosti waved. "Well, there aren't many natives in these mountains, and the ones who do live here are a sorry lot. The gang we brought up from the savanna puts them to shame. You can't tell me that the local savages kill a lot of unicorns. *Something* must, though, or the unicorns would have eaten up all the scrub; and then they would have starved."

"Ah. Now I see where you're riding. Clever." The other savant nodded. After a moment's thought, he brightened. "Maybe dragons eat them!"

"Well, maybe they do," Kyosti admitted. To say he hadn't thought of that would have been an understatement. "We haven't seen any dragons swooping down on them, though."

"Not yet," Uluots said. "My guess is, we need to go higher."

Kyosti's guess was that Uluots was talking through his hat. If dragons swooped down on unicorns from the sky, the explorers would already have spotted them flying across it. He was as sure of that as he was of his own name. But who said dragons had to fly? Maybe they were too big and heavy to get off the ground. Sunila had thought of overgrown snakes and lizards, after all. If that was what they were, they might still linger in caves or valleys somewhere in these barely explored, almost uninhabited mountains.

They might. After all, if dragons didn't eat unicorns, what did? Something had to. If nothing did, this country would be hip deep in them or without them altogether. It was neither.

So maybe dragons did prowl farther up the slopes. Maybe. But Kyosti still had a demon of a time believing it.

ULUOTS delivered another cloth-wrapped package to Kyosti a couple of days later. "Now I know what eats unicorns," the savant announced.

"What?" Kyosti asked, wrinkling his nose. This package was smellier than the one Uluots had had him preserve before.

"Whatever makes these." With more of a sense of drama than Kyosti thought scat deserved, Uluots whipped back the cloth. Kyosti eyed the formidably large, formidably odorous turd with distaste. Not noticing, Uluots went on, "I've found unicorn teeth and crunched-up unicorn bones in here. No possible doubt about it."

"Happy day," Kyosti said. "You want me to preserve it?"

"That's right," the savant affirmed.

"Well, I will, then." Kyosti both was and wasn't enthusiastic about the task. He was because sorcerously preserving the turd would make it stop stinking. He wasn't because . . . because here he was, using his sorcerous talent to preserve a big, smelly turd. As soon as the job was done, he asked, "What *does* make scat like that? Something like the big striped cats we saw down on the savanna?"

"Not if the tracks I found mean anything," Uluots answered. "They aren't cat tracks—not even huge cat tracks. Whatever the thing is, it's got long, skinny feet with three toes, and they all have claws, big claws, especially the middle toes. And I think—I think, mind you—the beast goes on two legs, not four."

"I've never seen anything like that before," Kyosti said.

"Neither had I." Uluots proved his enthusiasm could stretch to other things besides scat. "They could be the kind of tracks dragons leave!"

"That's—" Kyosti stopped. How could he be sure it was nonsense? People had dug up what they called dragon bones in the Empire of Mussalmi. Some of the skeletons they assembled from them looked to be of two-legged creatures. And, now that he thought of it, didn't some of those creatures have long, skinny feet with clawed toes? He wasn't sure if they had three toes on each foot, but he also wasn't sure that they didn't. With a barely perceptible pause, he finished, "—very interesting."

"It is, isn't it? Gives us something new to think about, too," Uluots said. "How do we go about catching one of these beasts?"

"Set out something they want to eat for bait," Kyosti suggested. "We haven't got a live unicorn—maybe one of the natives would do." He was kidding—but, then again, he wasn't. Killing a man to capture an animal was a bad bargain. Anyone could see that. Killing a worthless savage to gain precious knowledge of a fabulous, mystical creature . . . When you put it *that* way, how the pans of the scale balanced seemed less obvious.

Still, he and Uluots didn't propose the arrangement to Baron Toivo. Kyosti didn't know why the other savant didn't. As for himself, he feared that the leader of the expedition might take them up on it.

Instead, the Mussalmians sacrificed the next unicorn they killed to the cause of learning, not to the stewpot. Several of their finest marksmen crouched downwind from the carcass, ready to open up on whatever came to investigate the bounty. Kyosti hoped something did before the carcass got high. He already knew more about vultures than he'd ever wanted to.

Nothing happened. More nothing happened. Still more nothing happened. And then, quite suddenly, something did. Two green-gray creatures leaped down from the green-gray rocks and ran toward the dead unicorn. Till they moved, none of the explorers had the slightest idea they were there. How long had they waited, watching, weighing, wondering? No way to know.

As Uluots had guessed they would, they ran on their hind legs. Had they stood erect, they would have been taller than men, but they didn't. They leaned forward instead, their long, scaly tails counterbalancing heads and torsos.

They hissed and snarled at each other as they hurried toward the carcass. They might have been a couple of dogs squabbling over a bone in the street. A little to Kyosti's surprise, they both reached the carcass. One at each end, they started tearing gobbets of meat from it with their great, tooth-filled jaws. Eating preoccupied both of them too much to let either stay angry at the other.

The marksmen opened up then. One of the—dragons?—sprang into the air in alarm as missiles cracked past it. Then it fled, dodging and jumping with what Kyosti would have called impossible agility had he not seen it for himself. And the other would have done the same, were it not down and thrashing with what was obviously a broken leg.

"We got it!" the marksmen cried. They ran forward with a net to immobilize the wounded creature. Kyosti loped behind them, with a spell ready to immobilize it for good. The beast's hisses sounded like hot metal dropped into a cold sea.

It thrashed and hissed all the more when the explorers cast the net over it. The weights around the edges made sure the creature couldn't get loose—its struggle only entangled it more thoroughly.

One of the savants bent toward it for a closer look at its head. That should have been safe enough. He still stood two or three feet away, and had the net's stout fibers between him and those formidable jaws. Kyosti panted up just in time to see the creature's catlike yellow eyes fix on the closest of its tormentors with a deadly glare.

Then . . . something shot from the beast's jaws. The savant let out a horrible shriek and reeled away, both hands clutched to his face. "It burns!" he screamed. "It burns!"

"Preserve the beast!" Baron Toivo yelled at Kyosti. "Then it won't be able to do . . . whatever the demon it just did."

"Right," Kyosti said tightly. And Toivo *was* right: no doubt about it.

Kyosti tried to make himself into a man of metal, casting his spell as if the burned savant's cries and wails didn't still echo in his ears. When he did, he felt a certain resistance to his magic—not nearly so much as he had from the *tsaldaris* in the jungle, but more than a simple animal should have been able to show. Which meant that the horrible thing under the net wasn't only a simple animal. But it also wasn't strong enough in spirit to withstand him. A last hiss cut off halfway, and it froze forever.

Then Kyosti could turn away from it and ask the question that really mattered: "How's old Piip?"

One of the guardsmen crouching by the injured savant looked up and shook his head. "Not so good," he answered. "It spat some kind of vitriol at him, I think. His eyes . . . His face . . ." He shook his head. Then he got up and walked over to Kyosti. In a low voice, so Piip couldn't overhear, he went on, "If he lives, he'll be a horror the rest of his days, but he'll never see himself again, so that's a mercy."

Kyosti had got one brief glimpse of the curdled flesh running out between Piip's fingers like soft cheese. It was a glimpse he would gladly have forgone, but the gods didn't give choices like that. "Sorry devil," he said, also softly. "Who would have thought . . . ?"

"Piip sure didn't," the guardsman said. "One thing—he'll never have the chance to make such a big mistake again."

"These beasts, these terrible lizards, must be—*must* be, I say—the origin of the legend that dragons dwell in these mountains," Baron Toivo declared. Sunila would have said the same thing: had already said it, in fact. Here, Toivo'd gone right on thinking about the expedition when everyone else's mind was on Piip. Inexorable as a boulder crashing downhill, the baron continued, "They look much as dragons are said to look. And, just as dragons are said to do, they spit fire, or something all too much like fire. This we have discovered, to our distress."

It wasn't *their* distress. It was Piip's. His shrieks went on and on. Did they sound strange, as if even his mouth . . . ? Kyosti's stomach lurched. He wished he hadn't thought of that. He didn't want to know.

Oblivious to it all, Baron Toivo blathered on: "Now we have at last captured and preserved one of the beasts the Emperor charged us to discover. Gentlemen, our mission is a success!"

He seemed offended when he got no cheers. Kyosti wondered whether Piip thought that their mission was a success. But he couldn't ask the other savant now, and the question never crossed Toivo's one-road mind.

ℚᵈ

PIIP died four days later. As far as Kyosti was concerned, *that* was a mercy. Piip could neither eat nor drink. By the time oblivion claimed him, he smelled bad, too.

They buried him in the rocky soil of the upper slopes and piled boulders on his body so the dragons could not disturb it. And then, with the preserved specimen they'd taken, they started downslope for home.

They were still in the foothills a couple of days after that. One of the marksmen brought down a unicorn. This one wasn't a specimen—it was supper. While the savory aroma of roasted meat filled the air, Kyosti hunted up Sunila. "I want to talk to Galvanauskas," he said. "Give me a hand."

"What do you want to say to him?" Sunila asked. "Why do you want to say anything to him? He's only a savage."

"That's why, and I want to rub his nose in it," Kyosti said. "Come on."

With a creaky sigh, the linguistic sorcerer climbed to his feet. "I suppose I'd better," he said resignedly. He might have been a wife giving in to a husband of many years, knowing he would get to be unbearable if she didn't.

Galvanauskas and the bearers he led shared food with the Mussalmians. But they ate apart from them and generally kept their distance unless they needed to deal with one of the men from the Empire. The skinny little blonds looked up in surprise as Kyosti and Sunila strode over to where they squatted.

"What do you want?" Galvanauskas asked, as they loomed over him. He stood up, but they both still overtopped him by a head.

"To show you something," Kyosti answered through Sunila.

"Is that all?" The headman sounded apprehensive, even if Kyosti couldn't understand his words without Sunila's cantrip.

"By the gods, it is." Kyosti raised his hand as if taking an oath in one of the Emperor's courts.

Galvanauskas' sigh might have been patterned on Sunila's. "Well, I will come, then."

They'd got halfway to where they were going when another earthquake struck. Even though Kyosti was out in the open, where nothing bad was likely to happen to him, it was frightening enough and then some. Quakes were rare up in the Empire of Mussalmi. When they came, all too often they worked havoc; buildings of stone and brick crashed down in ruin, crushing some people and pinning others in the ruins. And the fires that followed could do as much harm as the quake itself—sometimes even more.

"The *pranys* stirs again," Galvanauskas murmured after quiet returned. "One day, sure as sure, it will wake."

If anything could have restored Kyosti's courage, the native's words were the tonic he needed. "That has to do with what I want to show you," the Mussalmian said. "Come on."

Galvanauskas let out another sigh. If this one wasn't martyred, Kyosti had never heard one that was. "I have gone this far," the native said, as if reminding himself. "I can go a little farther."

"Oh, good," Kyosti said. His sarcasm rolled off Galvanauskas like water off the oily feathers of a goose.

Kyosti stopped in front of the dragon. Though the creature wasn't going anywhere, the net still wrapped it. None of the Mussalmians had shown the slightest interest in taking off the mesh. Kyosti's preservation spell did almost too perfect a job. Hatred and ferocity still seemed to glitter in those golden eyes.

Pointing to the beast, Kyosti said, "*There* is a *pranys*." To Sunila, he added, "Make sure your cantrip translates that most exactly."

"The cantrip does . . . what it does," Sunila said. Despite his improvements, he'd never been fully satisfied with it. Kyosti understood why not, too. But the other wizard went on, "Since you used the natives' word for the thing, your meaning ought to come through."

Galvanauskas looked at the dragon. At last, he seemed to realize that Kyosti was waiting for some kind of response. He came out with, "So you say," which might have meant anything—or nothing.

"There is a *pranys*," Kyosti repeated, louder this time. If you were going to get anything across to the tropical savages, you had to say it over and over, and shout yourself hoarse, too. "It is an animal. It is *only* an animal. Now it is a *dead* animal—well, an animal spelled into lifelessness. It is bigger and heavier than I am, but not much. You and your men have been carrying it—you know that. There are many more like it up there higher in the mountains. Even if they all thrashed in their sleep at once, they couldn't make an earthquake. You know that, too."

Galvanauskas looked at the dragon again. Then he looked at Kyosti. "So you say," he said once more, and walked off without a backwards glance.

"Why, you—!" Kyosti started to storm after him.

Sunila set a restraining hand on the preservationist's arm. "What's the use?" he said. "You tried—and look what you got. There's none so blind as the man who refuses to see."

"Mrmm." It was a rumble of discontent—of rage, really—down deep in Kyosti's chest. But then he, too, sighed. "Well, when you're right, you're right. I just get so sick of the way savages stick to their savagery and super-stition even when you've got the proof that it's nonsense right in front of their ugly faces!"

"That's what makes them savages," Sunila said reasonably.

"I know. I know. When we get down onto the flatlands, we'll trade them in for another bunch, and then for another and another one yet while we go back through the jungle," Kyosti said.

"Vampires," Sunila remarked.

"We'll be ready for them this time around," Kyosti said. "And then . . ." He stared north like a lover looking longingly toward his distant beloved. "And then . . ." The words were so wonderful, he said them again. "A ship will be waiting in the harbor. We'll climb aboard. We'll load our specimens into the hold. And we'll sail back to civilization!"

"Civilization!" Sunila echoed. "I can hardly wait. A chance to write up what I've learned. A chance to publish. A chance to be a bit famous, if only for a little while. I wouldn't mind that."

"Neither would I. And I wouldn't mind a hot bath and smooth spirits and aged cheese and soft sheets and a softer mattress. And I sure as demons wouldn't mind seeing a woman who speaks my language!" Kyosti said.

Sunila nodded eagerly. "That all sounds bloody good!"

"It does, doesn't it?" Kyosti agreed.

The ground shuddered under their feet once more. Kyosti tensed, but it was only an aftershock from the previous quake, over almost as soon as it began. Just for a moment, he looked back at the smoking mountain that now lay behind the explorers. The plume rising from it seemed a trifle thicker than it had before, but that was probably his own fancy.

He snorted. Galvanauskas and the other natives from his tribe were the ones who let their fancies run wild. *He* was a sensible, rational Mussalmian—and cursed glad of it, too. Better yet, he *was* on his way home. As soon as he'd got clear of it, that mountain could go ahead and blow its top. It would be the dragons' worry, and the unicorns', and the natives', but none of his. *On my way home!* What a marvelous phrase that was!

꿍

EVER so slightly, the dragon stirred in its sleep. Ever so slightly, it snorted. It had been sleeping, sprawled out across the middle of the tropical continent and under the warm, comfortable sun, for an age and an age and an age. The last time it woke to breathe fire here and there and everywhere, great scaly beasts on two legs and four ruled the world (or thought they did, or would have thought they did had they thought at all). The shrewlike, mouselike longfathers of the creatures that would eventually style themselves Mussalmians and their close relatives, natives and savages, skulked in the scaly beasts' enormous shadows. But when resistless fire smote the great scaly beasts, the smaller ones no longer had anything to stop them from growing greater themselves . . .

One day soon, the dragon would wake again. It could feel that, even in its dreams. And when it did . . . Oh, when it *did* . . . !

A dragon's *soon* is not the same as a man's. It might come in twenty thousand years, or even ten thousand. It might be twenty years, or even ten. But it might come the year after next, or even next year. It might be tomorrow. It might even be . . . tonight.

JoBoy

DIANA WYNNE JONES

Adolescence is a time when we look within ourselves, trying to discover who we really are. Sometimes, though, it may be better not to know . . .

Raised in the village of Thaxted, in Essex, England, Diana Wynne Jones has been a compulsive storyteller for as long as she can remember, a habit that has made her the author of more than forty books and won her the prestigious Lifetime Achievement Award given by the World Fantasy Convention. She's perhaps best known for her Howl's Castle series, consisting of Howl's Moving Castle *(recently made into an animated film by Japanese director Hayao Miyazaki),* Castle in the Air, *and her most recent book,* House of Many Ways. *She's also well-known for the six-volume Chrestomanci series, which includes* Charmed Life, The Magicians of Caprona, Witch Week, The Lives of Christopher Chant, Conrad's Fate, *and* The Pinhoe Egg; *the two-volume Magids series; the two-volume Derkholm series; and twenty-two stand-alone novels, including* Archer's Goon, The Ogre Downstairs, Power of Three, *and* A Sudden Wild Magic. *Her many short stories have been collected in* Warlock at the Wheel and Other Stories, Stopping for a Spell, Minor Arcana, Believing Is Seeing: Seven Stories, *and* Unexpected Magic: Collected Stories. *Almost as well-known as her fiction is her hugely entertaining* The Tough Guide to Fantasyland: The Essential Guide to Fantasy Travel, *and she has also written the nonfiction book* The Skiver's Guide. *She now lives in Bristol, England, with her husband, a professor of English at Bristol University.*

❧

THIS is the story behind the recent swathe of destruction just south of London.

❧

HIS name was Jonathan Patek, but his father, Paul, always called him JoBoy. Lydia, his mother, never called him that until his father was dead. Paul Patek, the offspring of an Englishwoman and an Asian father, was a tall, bulky, jovial man with a passion for cooking and eating curry, very much adhered to his Asian side, while working as a GP from his very English house in Surrey. Lydia, who worked as receptionist for Paul, preferred to be English. She picked at the curries, made a roast every Sunday, and ensured that JoBoy had the most English education possible.

When JoBoy thought of his father, he always thought also of the lovely, hot, throaty feel of swallowing a good curry.

Paul's death was a mystery. He set off one afternoon to visit a bedridden patient. 'And I told him.' Lydia said, 'that doctors don't do home visits these days. It's a waste of their valuable time. And he simply laughed.'

Two days later, Paul's body was discovered at the bottom of a nearby quarry. His car had been driven into gorse bushes at the top of the quarry and half overturned. It seemed to be suicide. Except, why was Paul's body as dry and emaciated as if he had starved to death? Nobody ever answered the question.

This reduction of his father to skin and bone troubled JoBoy horribly. He always thought of Paul as 'full of juice,' as he put it to himself. He could not understand it. There had not been time for Paul to starve.

Lydia made the best of things by selling the large house to a partnership of doctors, where she continued to work as receptionist, and moving into a smaller house nearby. JoBoy, while he finished his education, had to make do with a small glum room at the top of the new house, from which he could see one frail, dusty tree and a patch of sky interrupted by television aerials. He was not happy, but this did not stop him growing taller and wider than his father before he had finished school.

'You'll follow in your father's footsteps, of course,' Lydia said, and made arrangements. Consequently, JoBoy found himself a student doctor in the same teaching hospital as his father, complete with white coat and stethoscope, following a consultant round the wards. He accepted this. He thought that perhaps, in time, he might discover the reason for Paul's sudden emaciation.

He had completed nearly a year of his training when he collapsed. It was a disease as mysterious as Paul's death. They thought it was a variant of glandular fever. At all events, JoBoy was now a patient where he had been a student, and others studied him. He was there for six months, during which time he became weak as a kitten and nearly as emaciated as his father's corpse.

'I wish they'd let you come home!' Lydia said whenever she visited him.

In the spring, they did let JoBoy go home, out of pure bafflement. Lydia had to help him climb the stairs to his room and help him down again in the mornings. JoBoy's limbs creaked as he moved, and his muscles felt to him like slabs of jelly. Worst, to his mind, was the way his brain had become an inert, shallow thing, incapable of any kind of speculation. I must work on my brain, he thought helplessly.

Lydia never let JoBoy be alone for long. She came home at midday and made him curry for lunch every day. Since she had never attended to the way Paul made curry, hers was a weak yellow stuff, full of large squashy raisins. JoBoy ate it listlessly for a week or so. Then he rebelled.

'I'll get my own lunch,' he said. 'I prefer bread and cheese anyway.'

୧୫

LYDIA was possibly relieved. 'If you're quite sure,' she said. 'I can go shopping again in the lunch hour then.' She left the ingredients for curry carefully laid out on the kitchen table. JoBoy ignored them. He spent the days reading his father's medical books, trying to revive his brain, and obediently ate the curry when Lydia cooked it in the evenings. He several times tried to ask his mother medical questions while she supported his staggering person upstairs at night, but she always said, 'You can't expect me to know anything about that, dear.'

JoBoy concluded that he would have to cure himself.

He lay on the sofa downstairs and wondered how this was done. The disease seemed to have permeated every cell of his body, and, as it made him so weak and tired, it followed that he first needed some way of injecting energy into his body. He looked weakly around for some high-octane source. The fire-place was empty, and he had no strength to light a fire. But he felt that fire was what he needed. Water too, he thought. Something elemental. But he had no strength. After a while, he tottered over to the patch of sun from the big window and lay down in it.

It worked. Sunlight did seem to infuse him in some way. After three days of lying in the sun, he had sufficient energy to remember that, among the schoolboy possessions randomly stashed in his bedroom, there was an old Bunsen burner. He staggered up there and searched. The burner turned up in a black plastic sack rammed into the wash-basin he never used. JoBoy looked from it to the taps. 'Water,' he said. 'I have fire and water.'

He tottered back downstairs and attached the Bunsen burner to the unused inlet beside the fire. He lit it. Then he tottered to the kitchen and turned the cold tap on full. Then he collapsed on the sofa and tried to reconstruct himself.

It went slowly, so slowly that JoBoy sometimes despaired and used his precious energy in bursts of useless rage. And he had at all times not to become so immersed in his own cellular structure that Lydia would come home and find him with these energy sources burning and gushing. It would alarm her. She would think he was mad. She would worry about the gas bill and wasting water. So he set his alarm clock for the time of her return and hurried to turn off the tap and the burner before he heard her key in the door.

Slowly, oh slowly, for the rest of that year, he visualised each part of himself in turn and laboriously rebuilt it. At first, he had to do it cell by cell, and it all seemed endless. But by Christmas, he found that he could reconstruct larger parts of himself in one go. He redid his liver, which made him feel much better. But there were strange side effects. The main one was that he kept feeling as if the body he was reconstructing was separate, outside him somewhere. He imagined it as lying beside him in the air next to his sofa. The other side effect was stranger. He found that he could turn off the Bunsen burner and the kitchen tap without having to actually go and do it. Odd as this was, it saved JoBoy from having to get up before Lydia came home.

By this time, Lydia was saying, 'You do seem better, but you're still so pale. Why don't you go out and get some fresh air?'

JoBoy groaned at first. But eventually, he redid his wobbly legs, wrapped himself in a coat, and crept down to the wood at the end of the road. There it smelt sharply of winter. The bare trees patterned the sky like the branching veins in his new-made eyeballs. He looked up and breathed deeply, sending clouds of breath into the branches. And the wood breathed back. JoBoy thought, This is an even better energy source than fire and water! He turned and crept home, almost invigorated. His legs—indeed, every bone in his body—were creaking in a strange new way. It felt as if they were lighter and more supple than before.

'Must have gone to feed the new body,' he murmured as he plodded up his mother's front path. There was a strange feeling to his shoulder-blades, like cobwebs growing there. He went to the wood every day after that. It seemed to enlarge his sense of smell. He smelt keenly the softness of rain and even more keenly the sting of frost. When the first intense yellow celandines appeared at the roots of trees, he smelt those too. He was not aware that they *had* a smell before that.

By this time, the way to the wood was less of a journey and more like a stroll. And with every journey, the cobwebby feel at his shoulders grew stronger. One day, as he stood staring at a bush of catkins, dangling yellow-green and reminding him of a Chinese painting, he realised that his shoulders rattled. They felt constricted. Uncomfortable, he spread the wings out. They were big and webby and weak as yet, but he could no longer deceive himself. He was becoming something else.

'I'd better redo my brain at once,' he muttered as he walked home. 'I need to make sense of this.'

He remade his brain the next day. Not that it helped. A confusion of notions and images thundered into his head and left him so entirely bewildered that he found he was rolling about on the floor.

Eventually, he managed to stand up and make his way to the bathroom, where he stripped all his clothes off and studied himself in the mirror. He saw a thin, spindly human body. Definitely human. And so thin that it reminded him forcibly of his father's corpse. As he turned to pick up his clothes, he saw, sideways in the mirror, the large sketchy outline, dense and dark grey, of the thing that he was becoming. It had wings and a long, spiked face. It went on four legs. The spines of its head continued in a line down to the tip of its arrow-headed tail. Its eyes blazed at him, through and somehow beyond his human eyes.

JoBoy turned his great spiked head and breathed gently from his huge, fanged mouth on to the mirror. Steam—or was that smoke?—gushed out and made a rosy cloud on the glass. There was no question what he was.

That night, Lydia came out of her bedroom several times and implored JoBoy to stop pacing about the house. 'Some of us have to work tomorrow,' she said.

'Sorry,' he said.

Around dawn, he thought that he understood what had happened to his father. Paul, like his son, had had two bodies, one of them a dragon. This must account for his fiery relish of curry. When the dragon flew, it left its drained and lifeless human body temporarily behind. Paul's body had been found before the dragon could return to it. It followed then that JoBoy's father was alive still, without a human shape to return to.

JoBoy slept exhaustedly most of the next day. At night, he set out to find his father. He left his fine, thin, new-made body asleep in its bed and went on four legs down the road to the wood. It had come to him that the wood's energies might help him locate Paul.

The energies were tremendous that night. They poured through JoBoy, faintly illuminating his grey-blue dragon outline. He stood with his claws in moist twigs and his wings cocked and sent out great questing dragon calls. Around midnight, he caught a small, distant answer. It was definitely a dragon voice. It seemed to be asking, faintly, for help from somewhere a long way south and east of the wood.

JoBoy's clawed feet scrambled as he galloped out into the road to find room to fly in. He spread the great webby wings. But it seemed they were not yet quite developed enough to get him airborne. He flapped hard and angrily, hearing the wind from the wings set the trees threshing, but he remained crouched in the road. His tail stabbed the tarmac in frustration.

Some of the noise he had thought was the trees turned out to be the sound of a neighbour's car returning from a theatre. Before JoBoy could move, he was skewered, dazzled, in the headlights, and, as he tried to move, the car swept through him and on, to turn into a driveway further down the road.

Nobody shouted. Nobody came to look. JoBoy discovered that he himself was quite undamaged. And he had felt nothing as the car went through him. I'm invisible! he thought. Then, I'm made of fog!

He crawled back home thinking that invisibility was probably very useful indeed. He could hunt Paul by daylight. Since he was not in the least sleepy, he spent the hours until dawn strengthening his wings. It felt odd to work on a part of himself that did not seem to exist, but it seemed quite possible. He fell asleep on his sofa.

'Well, really,' Lydia said as she hurried past on her way to work. 'Are you ill again or just lazy?' She did not seem to expect an answer.

JoBoy made himself a leisurely breakfast and took his dragon form out of the house. He went warily at first, in case he proved to be visible after all. But no one seemed to notice, so he grew bold and rushed down the length of the road, flapping, flapping, until, to his great joy, he found himself in the air, planing above the springing green of the wood. He wheeled around above the trees and pointed himself in the direction the call for help had come from and flew there.

It was hard work at first, until he discovered how to catch breezes and thermals without needing to flap his wings, and he kept being distracted too by the increasingly rural land that passed underneath him. It was so green, so full of life. Before long, he saw what he took to be an oasthouse and decided that he must be in Kent. He sent out a long, cautious, dragon call.

The reply was instant. 'Help! Oh, thank goodness! Help! Here!' It sounded like a female. Puzzled, JoBoy came planing down onto deliciously fragrant new grass, into what felt like an old common. The oasthouse, plainly converted to living space, stood on one side. The rest was surrounded by hedges, fruit trees, and comely old cottages. 'Where are you?' JoBoy called.

The reply was piercingly from under his great clawed feet. 'Here! Underneath! Let me out!'

JoBoy looked down. In the grass, almost between his talons, there was a small boulder embedded in the turf. He pawed at it dubiously. It felt queer, as if there was more to it than just a boulder—almost as if, he had to admit to himself, there was some kind of magic involved.

'Just move the stone!' the voice implored him from underground. 'I've been here so long!'

JoBoy flexed his great claws, dug both feet under the sides of the boulder, and pulled. And heaved. He would never have shifted it, but for a high-speed train that went screaming past in the mid-distance, presumably on its way to France via the Channel tunnel. JoBoy thought, Ah! Energy source! and felt power surge into him. He saw his forelegs glow foggy white with it as he heaved at the stone again.

It rolled away on its side. Blue mist instantly filled the earthy depression it had left, bulged, crested, and took form as a blue female dragon, slightly smaller than JoBoy. She put her jagged muzzle up and breathed in the power from the rapidly disappearing train. He saw her glow with it and enlarge slightly. 'Oh good!' she said. 'I knew there was a lot of power around nowadays, but I never could use it to break that spell. Thank you.' She rested, pulsing for a moment, and then asked, 'Who are you? You're new, aren't you?'

'I'm JoBoy,' JoBoy said. 'I—er—had to make myself, you know.'

'Oh, we all had to,' the blue dragon answered. 'But not many people can. I was the only one in Kent who managed it, and that was so long ago that my human part is dead.' She added, 'People were terrified of me, of course. And I was a bit unwise, drawing power from cattle and so forth. They hired a wizard to put me underground.' Her glistening blue eyes surveyed JoBoy thoughtfully. 'Has anyone noticed you yet?'

'No,' he said. 'What's your name?'

She rattled her wings in a shrug. 'Call me Kent.'

'And,' JoBoy asked eagerly, 'do you know of any more dragons? I think my father—'

'If he's recent, like you,' Kent said, 'he isn't a dragon.' She looked at him searchingly. Forgive me, but something's odd. What is that line of substance leading off you into the distance?'

JoBoy turned his head over his wing and shoulder to look where Kent nodded. There did indeed seem to be a misty line of, of *something* leading from the middle of his scaly chest into the far distance. 'It must be my connection to my human body,' he said.

'It doesn't work like that,' Kent said. 'You *are* your human body. Forgive me again, but that looks uncommonly like something feeding off you.'

'I think I may have got something wrong then,' JoBoy suggested.

'I don't think so. It looks far more like what used to happen when I took power from a cow in the old days,' Kent said. 'Or are you taking power from something at the moment?'

'Not that I know of,' JoBoy said. 'That train was plenty.'

'Then,' said Kent, 'do you mind if we go and look? I don't like the idea of a dragon being a victim, not after being locked up underground like that.'

She spread veiny blue wings and wafted up into the sky. JoBoy, after a few ungainly hops and some flapping, managed to get airborne too and soared off after her. She was dawdling in the air, waiting for him and laughing puffs of faint steam. 'This is wonderful!' she said, as JoBoy coasted up alongside. 'You can't guess how much I've longed to fly again. And there's such a lot of power coming from everywhere! From that train-line, and those roads, and that building over there that seems to be making something. I can't believe anyone would need to feed on anything alive these days.'

'I think I just got it wrong,' JoBoy said.

'Let's follow the line and see,' Kent said.

They went onward. Wind poured over and under their wings and the line in JoBoy's chest seemed to shorten like elastic as they went. They followed it almost to London and then to a house right underneath, and swooped after it. JoBoy was expecting to find the house where his body lay, but, to his surprise, they came down into the large house where he had been born, through its roof and its upper story, into a smell of new paint and disinfectant. I suppose that if a car can go through me, I can go through a house, JoBoy thought as they planed down into what had once been their dining room. A row of unhappy-looking people sat waiting there. None of them seemed to notice that there were now two dragons in the room. In front of them was a varnished desk labelled RECEPTION, where Lydia sat, telephoning impatiently. The line from JoBoy's chest led straight into Lydia's.

'What did I tell you?' Kent said, coiling herself to fit among the chairs. 'Whoever she is, she's feeding on you. Have you ever felt very weak at all?'

'Yes,' he admitted. 'For the last eighteen months.'

Lydia said angrily to her telephone, 'If the child really is having convulsions, take it to a hospital. You can't bother the doctors with it now.' And after a pause, 'If your car's broken, call an ambulance. We can't deal with you here.' She slammed the phone down. It rang again at once. 'Dr. Grayling's surgery,' she said. JoBoy saw and felt the line from him to her pulse and bulge as she gathered herself to repel another patient. 'No,' she said, 'you can't see a doctor without an appointment.'

'I don't believe this,' JoBoy said miserably.

'She seems a very negative person,' Kent observed. 'Let's see why.' She put her long blue face forward, through the telephone flex, and gently touched Lydia's chest. It went transparent. JoBoy stared incredulously into the inner parts of Lydia and at the black, writhing, stunted dragon that lived inside there. It was twisting about, sucking sustenance from JoBoy's pulsing line.

'Ah,' Kent said sadly. 'This happens to a lot of people when they can't admit to their dragons. Dragons can't live on their own, you see. She must have been doing this since before you were born.'

JoBoy knew nothing except that he was suddenly and enormously angry. He knew now exactly what had happened to his father. He had simply been sucked dry. He knew he had to destroy that stunted inner dragon. He surged himself forward in a slither of scales, through the desk, through Lydia—

'No, wait!' said Kent.

JoBoy was too angry to listen. He wrapped his huge jaws around the writhing creature and breathed fire. He flamed and he roared and he seethed heat into Lydia, until he was quite sure that the stunted dragon was burned up entirely.

He hadn't expected it to kill Lydia.

॥

THE one thing more dangerous than an angry dragon is a dragon full of grief. We have Kent to thank that the destruction in that neighbourhood was no worse.

Puz_le

GREGORY MAGUIRE

Here's a vivid little puzzler that shows us just how dangerous rainy afternoons can be . . .

Bestselling author Gregory Maguire is the author of the international sensation Wicked: The Life and Times of the Wicked Witch of the West, *which was later adapted into the blockbuster Broadway musical* Wicked. *His other books include* Mirror Mirror, Confessions of an Ugly Stepsister, *and* Son of a Witch, *a sequel to* Wicked. *His most recent book is another visit to Oz territory,* A Lion Among Men. *He lives in Concord, Massachusetts.*

૭ს

"**D**ON'T look at me like that. I didn't write this obvious little script," said her mother. When once she might have taken a long drag on a cigarette, and then for emphasis have released through a thin-slitted smile a hostile plume of hot roasted carbon dioxide, now she merely bounced her shoulder on the doorframe of Eleni's room. Bounced twice, rested, bounced again. Her arms were bolted tight across her bosom. "Save your resentment for the weatherman. Or the weather. Or your father and his *brave little experiment.*"

By which Martha Lester meant her former husband's new family. The fun wife. The ready-made son.

"I didn't say a word," said Eleni. "Did I say a word?"

The thunder said a word for both of them. Martha Lester waited for it to be done, and added, "You can't blame me for five days of rain. If you must blame someone, you can blame Mr. Spontaneous for planning poorly. They got a late start, he said—who knows why, some novel scrap of life happened to them last night and they tumbled into bed at all hours, the dears. By the time they got going at *quarter-past-late*, the interstate north was constipated with traffic. The bypass had been closed due to an accident, he guesses, and all that overspill funneled onto the main road. They were *crawling*, he complained, crawling at best, when they weren't actually standing still. It would be close to dark by the time they got here, and anyway, the rain is supposed to hold on through the whole weekend. So he sends his regrets."

"I've never known what to do with the regrets he sends."

"You might have come to the phone and told him that yourself. You *should* have come to the phone."

"I didn't have anything to say," said Eleni. "I could tell by the way the phone rang that it was Daddy bailing. Who could blame him?"

"Why not blame him? Give me a little rest for once. I didn't order up this storm for our week at the lake, Eleni. I know you were looking forward to seeing your new . . ." She bit her lip, thinking of a word other than *brother* or *stepbrother*. "Your new relative. What's his name—Tyler?"

"Taylor. And I hardly know him. I was just looking forward to. You know."

"A little change from Mamma Mia. I know. Well, in my own sick way, I was anticipating a little diversion myself."

The rain pummeled the small windows with such ferocity that Eleni imagined the putty on the old weather-beaten sash would just give way, and the squares of glass fall in upon the painted floorboards. At this hour, there wasn't much to see; the falling dusk and the rising mist and the rain-stung surface of the lake made of the view a kind of undifferentiated gray.

"If they're not coming," said Eleni hopefully, "is there any good reason we have to stay?"

"You *know* that Saturday is the Brister County Fair, darling. I do better business there every summer than I do at any other venue. You may *think* I enjoy leaving the cottage every day, trawling through people's disgusting garages and basements and attics. It's a wonder I haven't died of asphyxiation years ago. But it's my work. And someone has to put food on the table."

The angle of her mother's pouting lower lip made Eleni unclear who was more at fault: Eleni herself, for having a bothersome appetite for food, or her father, for leaving both the marriage and the kitchen.

"But there's nothing to do in all this rain. I'm sick of neatening up this little prison cell." Eleni looked around her attic room. It was tent-shaped, windows at both ends, no dormers. "This is supposed to be a vacation."

"This is supposed to be a family," countered her mother. "Amputated though we are. You have got to do your part, Missy Sweet-pea." She turned and stopped at the top of the steps. "Now I shall go try to throw some supper together. I had been counting on them arriving from the city with something edible. The trials, Eleni. Someday you'll understand."

"There isn't even anything to read. I've already gone through all the library books I brought."

"You know what I say to that." And Eleni *did* know. Try the growing stack of mildewing children's books. The ones accumulating at the dryer end of the porch, stored under the blue rain tarp with the rest of the tchotchkes that Martha Lester was going to do her best to unload on the unwitting public at the Brister Country Fair.

Descending, her mother called over her shoulder, "You may have gone through them once or twice, but I've added a few new things from that church rummage sale I picked over yesterday. Have a look."

At first Eleni just sat and thought about Taylor. She had no intention of liking him, particularly, but at the very least it would have been fun to have someone new to irritate. And who knows—companionship with an accidental stepbrother wasn't the least likely thing ever to happen to a human soul.

Downstairs, her mother began to bang cupboards and curse in dramatically inappropriate language. Didn't she realize that there was no insulation between the floors? The wood of the kitchen ceiling was the floor of Eleni's bedroom; the cottage was that old and decrepit. Eleni could picture her mother lunging about the kitchen, trying to light the burner, cutting her hand while opening a tin of tomatoes.

As much to escape envisioning that little kitchen drama as anything else, Eleni crept down the steps and wandered out onto the front porch. She peeled back one corner of the tarp with pinched fingers, her nose wrinkling. A reek of compressed, moldy air escaped.

She had looked at the old books before. They had barely survived hearty readings from children who themselves were now probably surviving on social security. The books were almost Harry Potter thick, but had creamier thicker pages and darker, more insistent type. Usually there were black-and-white chapter drawings, and sometimes color plates protected by onionskin guard sheets. But all the hype was rarely worth it. Even when there was something interesting, a marauding army or a sea serpent or a towering genie, the four (inevitably four) children brave enough to take on the enemy were too pretty to be true. The girls wore pinafores and ribbons. The boys all looked as if their names must be Cedric or Cecil or Cyril or maybe Cynthia. The only solo child in any such adventure that ever showed up in these old books was stolid aproned Alice, who wandered through Wonderland more or less alone, with only her own hydroencephalitic head to keep her company. That is: Alice slowly going mad. Who could blame her?

Eleni pawed through the pile as quietly as she could. Her mother heard the noise of stealthy movement, though. "You might find some puzzles in one of the piles of books," she said. "I haven't finished organizing everything from yesterday's haul. I don't mind if you play with one. Just don't lose any of the pieces."

Grunting, Eleni kept looking. She located the three or four boxes of puzzles, all in the same-size box, all from the same manufacturer, presumably. The cellophane sleeve, once a tight-fitting shrink-wrap, had aged poorly. It came apart in brittle chalky strips as she handled the top box. She rubbed the dust off and looked at the picture. All she could see was a kind of dragon head, brow down, eyes up. It appeared to be looking out at the viewer, as a dog who has fouled the carpet might. But a dog would cower, and the dragon wasn't cowering, but waiting.

"Supper in half an hour or when it burns, whichever comes first," called her mother. Eleni heard the liquid gulp a bottle makes when it is turned upside down and its contents are emptied greedily into a glass. She didn't reply but darted back up the steps to her dusty, ill-lit aerie, the dragon puzzle under her arm.

As a rule, Eleni found puzzles idiotic. What was the point? The picture on the cover told you what to work for, so the act of fitting the pieces together was only a way to waste time. You might as well peel a strip of wallpaper off the side wall (it was coming off anyway), rip it up, then fit it back together. You knew no more at the end of finishing a puzzle than you did before starting it. You had only yourself to blame.

Still—the chink of ice in the glass below, the clatter of a wooden spoon dropped on the floor and not, Eleni winced to admit, rinsed off—well, Eleni had heard that people in prison take up crocheting to pass the time, and when they're done with a piece, they pull it all out and start again. Same principle.

There was a card table and a floor lamp, and she moved the table closer to the wall so she could lean the cover of the box against the wall. Then she proceeded like any mathematician or scientist trying to solve a problem efficiently. She turned over all the pieces so their colored sides were up—

coppery oranges and purpley grays, the amber of teeth and talons, little else—and then sorted the edges and found the four corners.

The picture on the box top showed a fairly well articulated background, some sort of a woodsy hill and a lake, and ominous clouds, and, mercifully, no priggish schoolboy with a sword or lisping schoolgirl with a fistful of flowers or a whip. But perhaps this particular puzzle had been printed late in the run, as the color of the pieces themselves seemed less distinctive than the cover art. That would make finding the image harder. For this, Eleni was grateful.

"She-vipers from Missoula, Montana," seethed Martha Lester. The pan clattered in the sink. Only then did Eleni smell the scorch. She rolled her eyes.

"I'm okay with peanut butter," Eleni called in a snarkily cheery voice, adding, sotto voce, "*again.*"

"You'll eat what I make and be glad of it," snapped her mother.

Eleni bent her head down toward the puzzle.

Sheer unhappiness. Was that like sheer curtains?—unhappiness you could see through?

I'm not unhappy, she said to herself. I just love making puzzles night and day. Don't I?

The easiest bit, the edge, came together almost at once. No surprises there. The border was almost all dark, though, so on the card table, when you stood back, it resembled a rectangular window, oozing oil from the outside in. Pooling and pocketing in those little teeth and sockets that individualize each puzzle piece.

She went to work on the dragon form next. The spine was the most obvious place to start, as Eleni could tell from the picture that the spine took up the largest part of the picture. The creature arched taller than it did wide, like a cat spiking its back almost into a point. And the scales on the back of the dragon all flowed in the same direction, a kind of ceaseless pattern of coppery waves frilling toward the tail. She could fit them in fairly easily, and the dragon took shape in its frame, though as yet unconnected by even a single umbilical isthmus to the dark border.

She paused once, her hand suspended over the table, and was studying the region near where the rear leg came up into a kind of haunch and hip, and was about to pull the next piece from the bank of golden choices, when a slam of the screen door startled her. Martha Lester was striding out in the rain to try to keep from lighting up an emergency cigarette that Eleni knew she kept in reserve in her purse. Smoke yourself to death, thought

Eleni, shrugging theatrically, as if someone could see her. She returned her hand to its level position, floating eight inches above the tabletop in a holding pattern until her eyes had quite carefully taken in the clues that would identify the next bit, when she noticed that her hand went warm and cold as it moved back and forth in suspension.

What was this all about?

Maybe the light on the table reflected more easily, more warmly, from bright pieces of paper than from dark ones?

She tested her thesis and picked at random a piece near where the warmth was greatest. Sure enough, the piece was nearly white-gold. It wasn't the piece she wanted, though, not the hip: it was a bit of the long, ridged snout, nearly to the flared nostrils where a curl of smoke was emerging.

"Bizarre," she said aloud. She knew her mother couldn't hear her, not in the rain, not in the noise she was making striding back and forth on the porch. Who was she talking to, then?

"Myself," she replied, "I'm going bonkers due to living a week in my total-isolation cell."

Again, she tried to pick a puzzle piece based on the warmth it emanated, without looking down; again, she found an orangey bit, which turned out to be the hip joint she was looking for.

Enough of the spine was in place now so that the arch showed up. It seemed a more aggressive pose than the picture on the box. Almost as if the picture on the box had been an artist's rendition, but the actual dragon had kept moving in the same direction after the sketch had been completed. Its front left leg farther forward, its head, if this was its eye, and it was—it looked up unblinking at her—cocked more perpendicularly to the ground. As if the sharp ears had heard the sound of the artist's pencil on paper, and the head had swiveled so the eyes could pin the voyeur in its sights.

What a canny eye, what a bitter bejeweled thing it was! The black of the aperture was neither round nor slit, but triangulated, like a chevron, imitating the shape of the skull itself. And the iris was an icy violet.

"What *you* lookin' at?" said Eleni. She felt stupidly brave until she had found and secured the second eye, and then the look of the dragon seemed to pin her with its binocular vision. "It's not *me* standing eight feet off with my Faber & Faber number two pencil," she told it. "Don't look at me like that."

Then, because she was creeping herself out some, talking to a puzzle, she tried to concentrate on the background for a while. But if the dragon looked subtly different from its representation on the cover of the puzzle box, the background was even more imprecise. On the box, you could see whorls of mist, curls and shavings of dragon smoke entwining with the rising mist from the rustic setting. In actuality, the background was indistinct and even, she realized, contradictory. She would pick up a piece with two curves of smoke, like nesting parentheses, ((, and by the time she had moved the piece to the left edge where she thought it would fit, one curve had reversed itself and the second one disappeared.). It was as if the smoke was still rising and floating, insubstantial as actual mist.

Though maybe it was just her eyes that were tired. She rubbed her eyes with the heel of her left hand and jabbed down the piece where she had originally intended it to go. It fit, too. And now the single curve of smoke made sense, though it seemed slowly to be lifting out of the margin of the original piece and into the margin of the piece above it.

She thought perhaps she would stop for supper. But her mother was busy loading things into the car, despite the rain, getting ready for the Brister Fair. To have something to do, to feel less ineffectual, probably. Eleni knew how she felt.

Two more pieces, she told herself. Then two more. Then she got caught in the mystery of how to make all these flashing bits of talon fit in—you'd think there were a dozen dragons in this picture—or that the artist had shown the dragon in time-lapse photography, and the same bared claw was caught in a time-motion exercise. Somehow, the claws all fit, and once the legs were finished, there didn't seem to be quite as many knuckled ivory scythes as had seemed earlier.

"Maybe I'll stop for now," said Eleni, sounding stagy to herself. Sounding falsely brave. Putting it on. As if the dragon were waiting to pounce and she could evade it by the cheap trick of pretending to have to go the bathroom.

There wasn't very much left to do, though. Only twenty more pieces, best case. How keen the temptation to finish so that she could have the satisfaction of breaking the frame up and dumping the whole puzzle back in the box.

A highlight above the tip of the tail. A moon that showed through the cloud, though by the time she got the piece in place, the moon had disappeared, and so, looking back, had that highlight.

"You are one mean old tease-cat, you are," she told the dragon.

It didn't care. It batted its eyelashes, which came in and out from the sides like elevator doors, and regarded her with interest.

"You think you can scare me with those cheap theatrics?" she asked it.

A little hiss of smoke escaped its nostrils and filtered up, disappearing into the fog. So this is why the mist kept rolling. The dragon's furnace was stoked up good.

"As if I care," she said to it.

Fourteen pieces left, nine, six.

A ping as of talon on stone, or several talons, ping ping ping.

Five pieces, then three came all together.

The last piece was in her hand, and she bent to put it down—a little knob of a knee on a rear leg. But the last piece wasn't the last piece, actually, because now she could see that the very tip of the tail, which was to have curled right up beneath the monster's closed mouth, was missing.

"No wonder someone was giving this away," she said. "Not all there, are we, dragon?"

Yet the box had been shrink-wrapped, after a fashion. So how could a piece have gotten lost?

She looked on the floor, and shook the box again, and even went so far as to kneel and check under her bed and dresser in case it had fallen and she had kicked it away without noticing. But she couldn't find it anywhere.

Was it her imagination? The dragon looked as if was sneering.

"What a cunning little trick," she said. "Until you are finished, though, you don't have any power. How could you?"

A scritch, a scratch, as of a mouse running along a baseboard, or a talon itching against a stone.

"You are hiding that piece somewhere, aren't you?"

The dragon made no comment. Its nostrils flexed and the small stream of white plume lifted its head, curling at the top, looking like nothing so much as a question mark.

"You are curious to see if I can find it? I can find it. I *will* find it."

She looked again at the floor, the box, even feeling the inside in case somehow the piece were there, but invisible. Then she ran both hands over the surface of the nearly completed puzzle, thinking perhaps she had built up a section of the picture right over a hidden piece without noticing it. The dragon was warmer near the nose, and rippled along its spine; she could faintly feel the waves of its muscle groups. She thought she felt it stifle a breath, or even a purr, when she came near to the part of the nose between the nostrils.

"Where could it be? That little tippy tip tip of a tail?"

Maybe the puzzle maker was a trickster. Maybe the missing piece was the same size exactly as one of the other interior pieces. Maybe one piece alone in the whole puzzle had been printed on both sides. When she had turned the cardboard sides up to reveal the colored sides, she hadn't, of course, turned over those pieces that had already landed with their colored sides faceup. So she would never have noticed a piece printed on both sides.

"I have more patience than you do," she said. "Besides, what are you going to do to me?"

Eleni was nothing if not systematic. And anyway, where else was she going in this rain? She had all the time in the world. She began to unlock pieces in an orderly fashion, from upper left to bottom right. One row at a time. Unlock, look, and replace. One two three. Fifteen eighteen twenty-one. Thirty forty fifty. Ninety-nine.

It wasn't there. Though when she had taken the final piece of the nose, that steaming fissure, it was almost too hot to handle.

"Pretty tricky," she said.

The dragon purred a little, sounding not unlike a distant roil of boiling water.

"You like being flattered?" she asked it. "I suppose you do. Who doesn't? Well, you are a pretty creature."

Its eyes narrowed. Wrong approach. "Pretty amazing," amended Eleni. "Pretty awesome."

The dragon liked that better. A small exhaust of steam rolled forth, not unlike like the starch released when pasta has been dropped in hot, salted water.

"If I found that last piece, would you do my bidding, I wonder?" asked Eleni.

The dragon flared its nostrils and the steam from its nose thickened, whitened. Eleni watched it curl in an arabesque, and it formed a sort of a hook, as if to reach out and drag someone down. (Where did the word *dragon* come from, anyway?) In the twilight, the dragon's eyes twitched and glittered.

She saw what the problem was. The dragon wanted to move, but was pinned into place by dint of the missing tip of its tail. Eleni could see how its shoulder muscles shrugged and flexed in frustration, and the effort moved along the articulation of the spinal column, shimmering scales like the ripples on the surface of a pond moving outward from where a stone has plunked in. But the ripples faded out, and the rear legs and far end of the tail were frozen in place.

"I rather know how you feel," said Eleni. She put her hand on the nose of the dragon. "With just a little more effort you could break out."

It looked at her. She felt something more was needed. Maybe—the question mark—maybe it just needed to be asked the right question.

"Do you know where the missing puzzle piece is?" she asked.

The dragon looked as if it knew, though it didn't do anything so obvious as nod in assent.

"Is it my job to find it?" she asked, but hardly dared continue "and what will you give me if I do?"

Again, the dragon did not seem to reply, though it was clearly attending to her questions.

Then, suddenly, she had it. She knew what to ask. Maybe she only had three questions, but this next one was the right one. "Will you show me where it is?"

The dragon breathed some more white splendor, and its eyes sharpened with canniness and glee. Then it opened its mouth.

There was no golden flame, no guttural torchlight. Just a long slick tongue undulating forward. On the slick nubble of the tongue lay the final puzzle piece.

"Oh," said Eleni, "so it looks as if you bit your own tail off. Well, not to worry." She rubbed her fingers together, and, with the delicacy of a surgeon, leaned forward and grasped the near edge of the missing piece.

She held it up to the light to see if it had changed any by being swallowed by a dragon, but it hadn't, or not so she could tell. It looked like an ordinary, slightly cheap cardboard puzzle piece, the usual sockets and prongs in the usual arrangement.

Eleni leaned down to slip the last piece in place. The dragon held its breath and looked up at her with a sharp expression. Maybe adoration. Maybe skepticism. She couldn't tell.

"*You* should be skeptical of *me*?" she asked.

She rotated the puzzle piece in her hand so that it was oriented correctly.

"Has all this rain made you *deaf*? I've been hollering from downstairs for fifteen minutes."

Eleni turned. Her mother stood in the doorway. "I'm down there busting my butt to put a meal on the table, and you can't tear yourself away . . ."

She looked at Eleni and said, "What. What. *What?*"

"I just have one more piece to put in place . . ."

Martha Lester's gaze fell on the puzzle. In one step, she had crossed the room and snatched the last puzzle piece out of Eleni's hand. You would have thought she was handling dynamite, or a poisonous snake. She spun wildly about as if looking for a fireplace that she hadn't noticed before, one suitable to receive a pitched cardboard puzzle piece.

Eleni leaped up from the card cable, astonished, unmoored, as if she'd just been awakened from a dream. Her mother's eyes narrowed. She popped the last puzzle piece in her own mouth and swallowed.

"Mom!" said Eleni. "What is *going on*?"

Her mother shrugged and ran her fingers through her hair, and straightened up. "Oooh, honey," she said. "I had hoped you would grow up and go off to college before any of this came out."

"Any of what?"

"Oh, the back and forth of it. The great battle of wrong and right, evil and good. Rather tedious to talk about it, a bit overearnest for my taste, but you know, we avatars of justice have to do what we can."

"Have you been hitting the gin harder than usual?"

"A nasty thing to say, and anyway, gin is not recommended for those on duty. It can muddle the thinking and seriously compromise response time. You should count your lucky stars I wasn't drinking gin."

"I don't get this," said Eleni. "I don't understand. There are too many pieces not in place. Are you a . . . a whatever?"

"A witch?" Her mother raised an eyebrow expertly. "Well, that's what your father used to call me. Who cares what the term is?"

"Mom," said Eleni. "I need a little more information here. A few more pieces of the puzzle."

"Well, then," said her mother. She picked up the cover of the puzzle and looked at the dragon. "If they're going to try to use you to get to me, I guess you do need to hear a little more. Why don't you come down for supper? I made spaghetti. We're going to have to have a little chat. A bit sooner than I'd expected, alas. But I suppose it doesn't matter. We don't have anything else to do. And I see it's going to be stormy, stormy weather for quite a while. Quite a long while longer than anyone yet realizes."

After the Third Kiss

BRUCE COVILLE

Not only can you get used to anything, no matter how monstrous and dreadful, you can even come to miss it . . .

   Bruce Coville is the author of more than ninety books for children and young adults, with more than sixteen million copies of them in print, including the international bestseller My Teacher Is an Alien *and the wildly popular Unicorn Chronicles series (featuring the long-awaited, much-delayed, but finally released third volume,* Dark Whispers*). Bruce has been, at various times, a teacher, a toymaker, a magazine editor, a gravedigger, and a cookware salesman. A noted speaker and storyteller, he has been commissioned four times by the Syracuse Symphony to create original stories to perform in concert with the orchestra. He is also the founder of Full Cast Audio, an award-winning audiobook company devoted to producing full-cast, unabridged recordings of material for family listening. His books have won children's choice awards in more than a dozen states, including Vermont, Connecticut, Nevada, and California. His most recent book is a collection,* The One Right Thing. *He lives in Syracuse, New York.*

ൿ

I looked at my brother with desperate longing. "Please," I begged. "Just one more kisssss."

Wynde shuddered and turned away, toward the west, and the setting sun.

Horrified that I might lose my chance, I stretched the great length of my neck past his broad shoulder, then curved it back so I could catch and hold him with my amber eye. "Please, Wynde," I hissed again. "Once the sun goesss down, I will be trapped this way forever. We have but minutessss left."

My heart was pounding with such fear that I thought I might die before the sun reached the horizon anyway. Wynde had kissed me twice already, which, really, was more than you could ask of any man, given how hideous I was, and how fierce the heat of my every breath. But underneath the scales, beyond the fangs, the fire, and the venom, I was still May Margret, the sister he had left behind shortly after our mother's death, when he went out to conquer the world with his young man's sword and his young man's heart. Still the sister who had been left to deal with our father's new wife, who was the one who had cursed me into this loathsome shape.

The agony of my transformation will be with me always. It pained my body, of course, for every bone had screamed in rebellion at the way it was forced to twist and stretch, every inch of skin had felt afire, every secret inside part burned as though it were being bathed in acid. But the torment of my body had been nothing to the agony of my soul when I saw the long, twisting coils of dragon shape that now encased me.

That same despair pierced me yet again an hour later when the sight of me evoked piercing screams from Glenna, my lady-in-waiting—and yet again each time I saw the fear and disgust that twisted the face of anyone who looked on me.

And that was only the beginning, for less than a day after my change I discovered that I had an appetite to match my size, and a hunger that ate at me as if a fire were burning within. Out I soared on newfound wings, and nothing that lived was safe, though I managed to restrict my feeding, usually, to sheep and cattle.

How I was feared. How I was hated! How I ached inside each day as I wrapped myself around the Spindlestone, the great shaft of rock on the cliffs above the sea, the rock that I had claimed as my perch. Or perhaps it had claimed me, for I felt a strange attraction to it. From here I could watch inland to see if any came to attack. More importantly, I could gaze out over the western waters in the hope that I might spot my brother returning to free me from my curse. For my stepmother had made this much clear: The only way for me to regain my true shape was for Childe Wynde, of his own free will, to kiss me three times before sunset on the day of his return.

Wynde did return, at last. Later, I learned that it was my own rampaging hunger that had brought him back, for when I had slain enough cattle, devoured enough sheep, word reached him across the sea that a dragon was devastating his homeland. So home he came, sword at the ready, never suspecting that the beast he came to slay was his own childhood playfellow, the younger sister he had promised to protect and defend forever.

Oddly, by the time he arrived, the worst of my depredations were past. This was because an old wisewoman named Nell had advised the desperate countryfolk that if they would set aside the milk of seven cows to bring me both morning and evening, my ravenous hunger would be sated. So it was a fairly peaceful countryside to which Wynde was returning—at least, until the queen herself became aware that he was on his way. Then her wrath was mighty indeed. I sensed her rage. Indeed, who in the kingdom did not? It seemed to sizzle in the stones, and curl the leaves of every tree. What I did not know, at first, was the cause of it. So I simply clung to my stony perch and watched.

In time, I saw a ship upon the horizon. I reared my head, feeling an odd uneasiness. It was as if I needed to go down to the water, to keep the ship from landing; as if there were a compulsion on me to guard the kingdom.

Before the urge became so strong that I must leave my stony perch, my stepmother sent an army of imps to raise a storm and turn the ship away. But my good brother was wiser than the queen had anticipated. Suspecting witchery, Wynde had—as I later learned—sheathed his ship with rowan wood, good proof against the queen's dark art.

It both delighted and troubled me to watch that screeching horde of imps dash themselves against the ship's hull, then tumble into the water, where they thrashed about, wailing for their mistress to protect them. Delighted me because they were my stepmother's servants, and I hated her. Troubled me because I had no idea, yet, who was on that ship, and this uncertainty intensified my compulsion to protect our shores. With the imps vanquished, the uneasiness I had felt when I first spotted the ship drove me to the water's edge. Once there, I found I had no choice but to attack the ship. Soaring out across the water, I coiled my long body around the vessel and tried to drag it under.

My brain was on fire then. I had no control of myself, and still no knowledge of who was on board. But with the help of the rowan wood, Childe Wynde escaped my clutches and steered the ship out of sight. His oarsmen were strong, and before the queen knew what was what, he had landed in the next bay.

And here was a lovely thing; the moment my brother, the true heir to the crown of Arlesboro Castle, set foot onshore, the queen's awesome power was broken. So when Wynde approached me, sword drawn, ready to lop off my head, I was able to speak to him. My own maiden's voice rising from my massive dragon chest, I whisper-hissed, "Ssset down your ssssword, my brother ssssweet, and think not to ssslay me now. For I am your sssister, your May Margret, and naught but your kissss can set me free."

Wynde stared at me in astonishment, and called me both demon and liar. But when I whispered to him of secrets from our past, childish intimacies that only he and I could know, he understood that I spoke the truth.

"What must I do to break this spell?" my winsome brother asked.

"Kissss me thrice ere set of sun, and I'll your sssister be."

Wynde paled, nor could I blame him. I knew too well, from gazing into streams and ponds, how hideous I was, with teeth like daggers, shieldlike scales of fiery red, and blazing eyes set in a head the size of a coracle. Yet far worse than all this was the heat of my breath, for though I tried to hold it in, it seared my brother's skin as he drew near. He, brave brother, ignored the pain and kissed me on the lips, his mouth as small to mine as a gnat's would be to his.

Nothing happened, save the blistering of his fair skin.

Again I begged, and again he kissed. Thus the blisters multiplied, and this time he cried out with the pain.

The sun was sinking, and with it my hopes. Wynde turned to me once more, and I nearly screamed at the sight of his seared skin. Only the knowledge that such a burst of breath from my lungs would wound him even worse gave me the strength to withhold my cry of pity.

"Please, brother," I whispered, one last time.

Skin blackening, hair smoking, weeping with pain, Wynde leaned in and kissed me a third time. And now the pain was mine, for bones and skin did in reverse what they had done before, twisting and shrinking as I turned back, back, back to the maiden I once was.

In but moments, I stood naked before my blistered brother, who wrapped his cloak around me, then swept me into his arms and carried me to the castle.

But it was not yet time to rest, or heal, for there was one more task to accomplish, and this Wynde did with ease and grace, despite the pain of his burns. Taking a wand of rowan wood, he mounted the tower stairs to where our stepmother, knowing her doom was upon her, sat waiting. It took no spell, no conjuration, for Wynde to work his will. He merely struck her once with the wand. I was holding his hand when he did so, and felt an odd pull, as if something—the transformative magic, I later learned—was leaving me.

Our stepmother's eyes widened. She cried out once, then began her own metamorphosis. Mouth widening, eyes bulging, skin erupting with warts, she shriveled down, down, down, till she was the largest and most loathsome toad I had ever seen.

I wanted to drop a heavy book upon her, but Wynde stayed my hand—I am glad now that he did—and she fled, hopping away down the tower stairs.

And that should have been the end of it.

Save for one thing.

I began to miss the fire inside me.

It did not happen right away, might not have happened at all, had Wynde not stayed and claimed the throne. But not long after my return, our aged and ailing father learned the truth of my enchantment, despite our attempts to hide it from him. Realizing at last what a horror he had married, he went half-mad from brooding on what his bride had done to his daughter.

It hurt Wynde and me deeply to see this man, who in our youth had fought and won such a ferocious war with the neighboring kingdom, slump and grow weak. Despite our attempts to rouse him, in a month he took to his bed. A few days later, he gave up the ghost.

Wynde—no longer "Childe" Wynde, now that Father was dead—set aside his plans to roam the world. As was both his right and his duty, he claimed the crown.

I was happy at this, and at first there was nothing but loving amity between us, as well there might have been, for we had been dear companions from earliest childhood. Yet one sad thing did stand between us: His beautiful face never did heal properly, and there remained always afterward deep scars from the terrible burns. He never, not once, spoke of this or in any way blamed me for them. But I flinched each time I saw his face. This was not because the scars made him ugly to me, but because I knew it was I who had put them there.

To make matters worse, I myself was considered more beautiful than ever. Many were the comments on my sparkling eyes, my rosy complexion, and the deep red of my long, shimmering tresses. I alone knew that these were but outward signs of the new energy and vitality I felt within—an unexpected gift from my endragonment.

I used this beauty and energy to regain the trust of the castle servants. Glenna, my lady-in-waiting, was first to lose her fear. Soon enough, she brought the others along.

After a year of wise and fruitful reign, all the kingdom hoped that Wynde would wed, and no neighboring princesses there were, I think, who would have refused his hand, despite his scars, for he was kind and courteous, and, really, still quite beautiful, at least to my eyes. But women know things about what moves the heart to love that men do not, and my poor brother, thinking himself restricted from the paths of love by his ravaged face, never understood what he could have had.

Women know, too, what goes on backstairs, and the rumor was that though Wynde tried many times, he could not get a woman with child. The dragon's breath, it was said, had unmanned him.

These rumors—I did hear them, of course, though Glenna tried to keep them from me—were like daggers in my heart.

Wifeless, childless, Wynde turned his attention on me. Oh, not in any wrongful way! He simply decided that if he was not to wed, I must do so in his place, in order that the kingdom might have a true heir. But all men knew my history, and none there were who dared to call me bride, for fear that I might again become what I once was. None would state this outright, of course, for fear of Wynde's wrath. Even so, I understood well enough the reason I had no suitors.

In his frustration, Wynde, my brother and rescuer, slowly became my tormentor. I don't think he ever really understood what he was doing, or at least not why. But he began to criticize me daily, telling me the ways in which I should change so I might better attract a husband.

I, who had run the household from the time our real mother died! I, who had kept the keys of the castle for our father until the arrival of our stepmother! I, who had a fire in me that no man could understand—a fire, I feared, that none could *withstand*, come the wedding night.

⚕

IT started slowly, this desire of mine. At first it came only at night, when I would lie abed but in my dreams be soaring once again above the countryside, my wings spread wide and all of heaven, fiery with its myriad of stars, stretching endlessly black above me. In these dreams, I flew until the moon was in my reach, then swooped to devour once again the sheep and the kine, feeling the crunch of their bones and the hot spurt of their blood as it poured down my gullet. When I woke, I would find myself tangled in sweat-soaked sheets, hardly knowing whether it had been dream or reality.

This went on for some months, always worse at my own time of month. I grew more restless and irritable by the day, according to Glenna.

Though Wynde and I fought over many matters, the situation came to a head the morning he sat down to breakfast, and said, "I have found a husband for you, at last, May Margret. You will marry Lord Dunbar come spring."

"Brother," I said, fighting down the heat I felt rising inside, "I have no need of husband, and you no right to offer my hand."

"As your king and kinsman, I do indeed have a right to bestow you where I will," he replied, his voice cold.

"I deny this 'right' of yours!"

Wynde's voice began to shake. "The kingdom has need of an heir, May Margret. As it will not come from me, it must be you who provides the next in line."

I could hear in his words, and his tone, the guilt and shame he felt that he was not able to produce an heir himself. It silenced me for a moment, and my heart ached for him. At least, it did until he made his next argument: "Do you forget, dear sister, who it was who freed you from your dragon prison?"

My rage on hearing this was such that I could scarcely breathe. I could not believe he would use that as a weapon against me! A wave of hot anger erupting in my heart, I leapt to my feet and flung the chalice I had been clutching at his head.

What happened after that, I do not remember, for I lost consciousness. I do not think it was any womanly weakness that made me faint, but rather the heat in my blood, which came on too fast, too strong.

Once you have been a dragon, it is hard, I discovered, to be a mere maiden once again.

⚓

THE next weeks were difficult, as Wynde and I fought over and over again on the matter of the betrothal. I reminded him of how we had hated Dunbar when we were children and he had visited in company with his father. We had both thought him stupid, nasty, and spoiled.

It made no difference to Wynde. As the days went on, I raged and cajoled, begged, bartered, and battered at him. One thing only I did not, could not, would not do, and that was weep to get my way.

Despite my entreaties, my brother remained as hard and unmoving as the Spindlestone itself.

During that month, I was trying, desperately, to keep the dragondesire at bay. But each time I grew angry—and I was angry often, with every flare of temper seeming greater than the last—the desire would rise again, stronger and deeper than before. Finally, I did the only thing I could think to do: I went to visit Nell, the old wisewoman who had told the country-folk how to soothe my hunger with the daily offerings of milk.

I waited until nightfall and wrapped myself in a peasant's cloak that I had asked Glenna to bring me. I dearly wanted to have her join me on the trip, but the question I needed to ask was not one I could share with her, or with anyone save Old Nell.

So I went on my own.

In the past, this journey would have frightened me. However, I had discovered that, having once been a dragon, I was considerably more bold than I used to be.

Old Nell lived in a low, moss-covered cottage at the edge of the king's wood. She was stooped and withered, and had but one eye. Despite this, she saw me well enough, knowing at once not just who I was but what I had been.

"Welcome, May Margret," she said, in a voice that creaked from too little use. "I wondered if you might someday come to visit."

I realized, with considerable shame, that I should have come well before this, to thank her for the wisdom she had given the countryfolk, the wisdom that had helped them ease my appetite. Blushing, I said, "I have been neglectful, and dishonor my house and rank by having waited this long to see you."

Closing her one good eye, Nell replied softly, "Nor did you come now to thank me, I think."

Blushing yet more fiercely, I said, "No, good woman. I come seeking more wisdom."

"And prepared to pay?" she asked, her eye open and alight with greed.

"Of course," I said, for I was not a total fool, despite my foolishness in not having come to see her sooner. I had brought a silver cup, which I had taken from my trousseau—easy enough to do, since my hopes lay in a direction far different than marriage.

When I unwrapped the cup, she sighed happily. "Come in then," she croaked. "Come in and sit by my fire."

The cottage was small and dark, and she shared it with a cat, also small and dark. Dried herbs hung from the rafters. More of the same were spread across the single small table. Their faint odor spiced the air, making the cottage smell more pleasant than I would have expected.

Nell moved awkwardly to the hearth. Though I tried not to stare, she saw that I noticed her limp. "Wood," she said ruefully, knocking on her right leg. Then she offered me a stool. She took another for herself, and we sat, she unapologetic for the simplicity of the setting, I embarrassed for having been caught staring.

We remained in awkward silence as I struggled to find a way to begin. As it turned out, it was Nell who spoke first. Looking up at me with that one piercing eye, she said, "There's a fire in your blood, en't there, lady?"

I started, amazed that she knew what I was feeling. "How did you guess?"

The old woman made a rude sound. "No guessin' involved, dearie. I was afeered this might happen. You can't be dragon long without it doin' somethin' to you, and *you* were dragon longer than was good. You may wear a human skin now, but your blood—your blood is different than it was."

"What should I do about it?"

She rose from her chair, and despite the fact that the movement clearly pained her, she seemed suddenly taller and more powerful. "Don't play games with me, lass! That's not the question you came to ask Old Nell, is it?"

I drew back, startled, and a little frightened.

She glared at me with that single eye. "Well, is it?"

I shook my head and lowered my own eyes, unable to meet her fierce look.

"All right, let's start again, knowing that these things are easier when you're honest about them. What did you come for?"

I hesitated, wanting to be sure before I spoke the words. But I knew what had driven me here, knew what I felt I must do.

"I think . . . I think I want to become a dragon again," I whispered.

"Well," she replied, with some satisfaction. "Now we're getting somewhere. But are you sure, girl? 'Think' is not good enough. This time there'll be no turning back. Dragon now, dragon forever."

Again I felt the fool. My desire had become so overwhelming that I had not really considered the matter of whether I might ever want to turn human again.

Nell read my confusion easily enough. "Go home and think some more, May Margret. If you feel the same in a month's time, come back, and we'll talk again."

I placed the silver cup on the floor beside my stool. Nell nodded approvingly, then tipped her head, and said, "One more favor, lass. Could you send some butter and flour from the castle pantry? It would be much appreciated."

"Of course," I said.

She smiled. "And let that boy, William, be the one to carry them here."

"William?" I asked.

"A sweet-faced lad, and a boon to my old eye," she said. Then she cackled in a way that made my skin crawl and pushed me out the door.

❦

THE next day I sought out William. I knew who he was, of course; he had come to work for us after his father, Lord MacRae, had fallen from grace and lost his lands during the war. He was indeed a handsome lad and always seemed grateful for our family's generosity. I hoped I wasn't sending him into an untoward situation by asking him to take the flour and butter to Old Nell. But he seemed happy enough with the task, so I did not worry about it further.

I had plenty of other matters to fret me.

I longed to speak to Wynde of what was on my mind but dared not, for I knew he could not understand. And the sight of his scars, each time I glanced sideways at him, made me feel a traitor for even thinking of returning to the skin from which he had freed me. But at the same time, the dreams grew stronger and more vivid, and the desire rose inside me like a flame. Now I woke from dreams of flying to find myself not tangled in sweat-soaked sheets but standing at the castle parapet, as if I were about to fling myself into the sky.

Except, of course, I had no wings. I began to wonder if I would make it through the days that Nell had asked me to wait without dashing myself against the rocks at the base of the seaward wall.

Wynde noticed my unease and distraction, of course. How could he not? But no matter how he pressed, I could not bring myself to speak to him of what was on my mind. So this became one more barrier between us, separating me from the person who had been dearest to me for most of my life.

To make things worse, the wedding preparations had begun. I did not think I could go through with the marriage, and returning to dragon shape seemed my best escape.

And that should have been the end of it. I had made a choice.

At least, I thought I had. But then Lord Dunbar arrived for a visit, and

I found that he was no longer the obstreperous child I remembered but had become a handsome man, with flaxen hair and wide blue eyes set in a face as fair as any I had ever seen, save that of Wynde himself before I had scarred him.

Even worse, he was charming. During the week of his visit, he teased and joked with me, seeming unconcerned by my strange past. By the time he stole a farewell kiss—a kiss, I will confess, that I freely returned—I found I desired him with a fierceness that startled me, though I suppose it should not have, given how all my desires had been magnified since my time as a dragon.

There was, indeed, a fire in my blood.

Alas, Dunbar was not my only desire, and deep confusion was raging in my soul. So when the month was over, I returned to Old Nell's cottage, not so much because I was certain of what I wanted to do as because it was to Nell alone that I could confess my competing desires.

"I wasn't sure I would see you again," said the hag when she opened the door to me. Pulling back the long strands of gray hair that dangled about her face, she stared at me for a moment with that one piercing eye, then added, "I sense you are not sure, either—not sure of which way your heart is pointing. Ah, well, lass. Come in and we'll talk a bit."

When we were seated by her fire again, she said, "I can brew for you a potion that will return you to your dragon form. It will stay potent for a goodly time, so you will not need to make your choice right away." With a shrug, she added, "Who knows—maybe simply having it will settle your heart."

"Yes," I said eagerly. "Please do this for me."

She looked away for a moment, then said apologetically, "I have nearly everything I need . . ."

"*Nearly* everything?" I prompted.

She sighed. "There is one last thing you will have to fetch for me yourself."

"What is it?" I asked, feeling a tingle of fear simply because of the tone in her voice when she said it.

Nell twisted her hands together, then said apologetically, "As it was your stepmother who cast the spell to begin with, I must have something from her to brew this new one."

"I believe some of her clothing remains in the tower room that she had made her own," I said, feeling a bit of relief.

She shook her head. "You misunderstand me, May Margret. I need something from *her*."

It took longer than it should have for me to realize what the old woman meant, for I had thought of our stepmother as being dead, though of course she was not. "But she's a *toad*!" I blurted, when I finally did make out her meaning.

"I had caught word of that," said Nell dryly. "That doesn't change the fact that I need something of her in order to complete the brew. Do you know where she is?"

"How could I know that? She hopped away after Wynde struck her with the rowan wand and has not been seen since."

"Well, if you want this change, you'll have to find her."

"If I do, what is it that I must seek of her?"

Nell smiled, displaying two or three teeth. "Any part of her would do. Of course, she is unlikely to willingly surrender a foot, or even a toe. You could try bargaining, but I'm not sure what you could offer that would convince her to make such a trade."

My despair must have shown on my face, for Nell laughed. "Fortunately for you, my dear, I need not even so much as a toe. If you can but run a cloth over her back it will suffice. From that I can draw enough of her essence to brew what you need." She paused, then said, "One more thing."

"Yes?"

"Be careful not to touch her yourself. To do so will muddle the magic."

ৎ৬

I wandered back to Arlesboro Castle, feeling lonely and lost. It seemed impossible to do as Nell had asked, since I had no idea where the queen had gone. However, I did have one hope, and that was the castle servants. I knew them well enough to know that gossip was their gold, as important to them as their daily bread. If word of where the queen might be hiding was to be had, it was among them that it would be found. So the next evening, when the day's work was done and the castle was quieting, I sat in the kitchen with Cook and her helpers.

For some time I simply listened, waiting for a way to bring up my question without seeming too anxious for an answer. At first their talk was all of local doings, what maid had been caught with what lad doing what she ought not, and other such matters. But finally one of them—a girl named Hannah, who had been a playmate when we were younger—spoke about something that had happened, "back when the lady was a dragon." She caught herself, and an embarrassed silence fell over the group. But I simply laughed, and said, "That was months ago, Hannah. Though what you say does bring to mind something I've been wondering about."

"What is that, lady?" asked Hannah, clearly relieved not to have offended.

"I often ask myself where the old queen went after Wynde be-toaded her."

Suddenly the silence was deeper than before, and furtive looks were exchanged among the women.

"Oh, come," I said, trying to keep my voice light. "It's clear you know. Where is she?"

It was Cook who finally answered. "She haunts the lower depths of the castle, lady. Everyone knows that."

I did not sleep well that night. I felt a tightness in my heart to think my stepmother had been so near to us all this time.

AS it turned out, the toad queen was not quite so near as Cook thought, something I discovered the night I finally found the courage to go below-ground and seek her.

To prepare for my journey, I first made four rushlight torches—one to carry as I started, three to bind at my side for later use. Uncertain of what powers the queen might still possess, I took also a wand of rowan wood. More, I girded myself about with a wide belt I wove from slender rowan twigs. This I wore beneath my kirtle, so that my stepmother would not see it.

I waited till all were asleep, then slipped down to the kitchen, from which there was passage to the lower levels. I went first through the cellars where we stored our ale, and the root vegetables, and the barrels of salted meat. Below those cellars lay the dungeon. This, I suspected, was where the toad queen lurked.

The stone stairs to the dungeon were wet, as slick as if covered with dew. The wall—not brick, but carved from the living rock—was cool and moist to my touch. I heard no sound save the crackle of my rush torch, for I walked in silence, as I had been able to do ever since my time as a dragon.

When I reached the dungeon, a shiver rippled over my flesh. The flickering light of my torch revealed the chains that hung from the walls; the horrid implements of pain, carefully arrayed in a rotting wooden rack; the dark ashes of a long-dead fire where iron was once heated until it was red-hot.

The sight of these things stirred in me an uneasy memory, a memory of an afternoon when I was no more than ten and Wynde and I had crept down these very stairs, each prodding the other on by dares and bets. As we descended, we heard someone sobbing, a sound so filled with pain that I wanted to turn back. But Wynde would not go and—unwilling to give him cause to call me coward—I stayed at his side until, together, we peered around the wall at bottom of the stairs. In that moment, we saw something so horrifying that we both turned and fled.

We never spoke of it afterward.

It was odd to think of such torture being inflicted in the daytime. It seemed it should be a secret, nighttime activity. But in the eternal darkness beneath the castle, I guess, night and day were as one. And it was all too easy now—especially in the weirdly dancing shadows cast by my torch—to imagine anew the screams of the suspected spies and traitors who had been sent here during the days of the war.

Too easy to imagine that their shades still lurked in the darkened corners, waiting to reach out for me.

Yet it was those very corners I must explore if I were to find the queen.

The smell of fungus and wet stone and something worse, something foul, filling my nostrils, I began my search. To my dismay, an hour of looking yielded no sign of the toad queen. What I did finally find was another door. I was about to open it when my torch began to gutter. I took the second from my waist and quickly used the last sparks of the one I held to light it. When it was safely ablaze, I opened the door. It seemed a foolish thing to do—surely the toad queen could not have managed this door. Yet I had searched every inch of the dungeon.

Perhaps someone opened it for her, I thought with a shudder. I wanted to turn back, a want like a hunger. But another part of me, stronger even, was caught by my obsession.

Wondering how deep the world beneath the castle went, I passed through the door to a narrow, winding stair. Its curve was so tight that I could see but a few feet ahead of me, and the moisture on the stone steps was so treacherous—I slipped more than once—that it slowed my pace.

After what seemed like several minutes, my second torch began to flicker.

"Not now!" I whispered fiercely, shaking it.

The flame strengthened, but not by much. I scowled. Surely this torch had not lasted as long as the first.

Reminding myself that I had spent a great deal of time searching the dungeon and would need but moments to pass through it on my return trip, I lit the third torch and continued my journey.

When the stairs came, at last, to an end I found myself standing at the edge of some water, though whether a tiny pond or a vast lake, I had no way of telling, for my light did not reach far enough.

Raising my torch, I saw that the stony ledge on which I stood was, perhaps, five feet wide, and that the water extended in both directions. I walked, first, to my right, but soon came to a place where the water and the side of the cavern came together. Turning, I walked the other way. As I passed the entry to the stairwell, I realized it might be easy to miss coming back, so I slipped out of my shoes, leaving them on the floor as a marker.

When I had gone another thirty paces, the stone cold and wet beneath my bare feet, I came to a small boat. Who had brought it here, and from where? Should I use it to cross the water? I walked on, but soon came to another place where wall and water converged. Turning back, I climbed into the boat. Praying that my torch would last, telling myself I could always make the last part of the return trip in the dark, I thrust the base of the torch between two strips of wood at the front of the boat and began to row. Wynde and I had pottered about often enough on the nearby loch when we were young that I had some skill with oars, though my mother had been scandalized when she discovered it.

After only a few strokes, I could no longer see the strand of rock from which I had departed. I turned to look over my shoulder.

The void ahead of me seemed to have no end.

Every ounce of common sense I had left was shrieking for me to turn the boat around. But I was in the grip of a passion; turning back was simply not possible. On I rowed. My torch continued to burn steady, which was both a relief and a bit frightening, for I knew my final torch might not last as long.

Just as I was wondering if I should yield to the small voice inside that was begging me to turn back, I glanced over my shoulder again and saw a light not far ahead. Despite my aching arms, I redoubled my efforts, pulling strongly across the black water. The distance was hard to gauge, for in that great, oppressive darkness, even a small bit of light stretched a fair distance. I rowed farther than I had expected, growing ever more fearful of finding my way, yet too close now to turn back. I glanced constantly over my shoulder, and at last saw that I was close to my goal. A moment later, my oars struck a rocky bottom; a moment after that, I felt the scrape of the little boat's keel against the stone.

In that instant, my torch went out.

I could have lit the last, I think; there was spark enough to make it go. But I decided to take the chance that I would be able to light it from whatever provided the glow that had drawn me on. Perhaps better, I told myself, to proceed in darkness. No need to draw attention to my presence until necessary.

I drew in the oars, then hiked up my robe and slipped from the boat into the cold, shallow water. Cautiously, silently, I drew the boat onto the shore. Some ten feet ahead, I saw an opening in a rocky wall. From this opening came the glow that had drawn me the last of the way across the water.

I approached with dragon silence, pressed myself to the wall, peered around, and breathed a sigh of relief. I had found the queen!

A brown and bloated toad as large as my head, my stepmother crouched upon a flat stone about three feet high. Around her—some standing, some lounging on the floor, still more squatting in niches in the wall—was a group of small, humanlike creatures who stood no taller than the stone on which the toad queen sat. Their skin—they were all naked—was a pallid gray, their eyes huge, their hands and feet oddly elongated.

The light that had drawn me came from a small fire burning in a pit carved in the floor.

I backed away, my courage wavering. But one of the imps had spotted me. It cried out, and several of the creatures rushed through the opening. Seizing me, they dragged me before their queen. I thought of beating at them with my rowan wand, which was hidden in my sleeve, to drive them off, but I did not want my stepmother to know I had it. So I did not resist.

The imps dropped me in front of the stone pillar where the toad queen crouched. When I had gained my feet again, she said, "Well, this is an unexpected pleasure. Did you miss your loving stepmother, May Margret?"

Then her broad face split in a grin that made it even more horrible.

"Oh, yes," I replied. "I've longed for you every day since you left."

Her smile vanished. "Do not be rude, May Margret! Why have you come here? Is it not enough that you and your wretched brother have trapped me in this disgusting shape—"

"No more disgusting than the one in which you imprisoned me," I snapped, interrupting her.

"Ah," she said softly. "That was different."

To my amazement, she sounded as if she really believed what she was saying.

"You—you and your beauty—were a threat to my rule." Before I could protest, she said, "Come, come, May Margret. You cannot deny it. Men are such fools, after all. And I did need to rule, for your father was ineffective."

"Don't say that!" I cried, even as I realized in my heart that it was true.

"Tut, May Margret, you know I speak truth. You cannot be so naïve as not to know that we had hungry neighbors crouching at our borders. I had to seize control if I was to save the castle and its lands. With your brother gone, you were the one thing that stood in my way. I *was* sorry to have to sacrifice you, my dear, but, really, it was for the good of the homeland."

I stared at her, astonished.

She sighed. "You are a true innocent, May Margret. But you are not stupid. Surely you saw the dangers—dangers that continue to this day if my spies tell me right."

"What do you mean?"

"Your brother wants to marry you off, does he not? To the laird of Dunbar Castle."

When I did not answer, she said, "Your silence speaks as a voice from the pulpit, my dear. Your brother does indeed have your best interests at heart. But he is sadly deluded. While it is true that Dunbar longs for you, he longs for your lands even more."

These words twisted at my heart. Was it true? Was the charming Dunbar, who had delighted me so, really after nothing more than our land? Or was my wretched stepmother trying to manipulate me again?

"How can you know these things?" I asked, trying to hide my uneasiness.

"You mean how can I know, trapped down here as I am? That is simple enough. My powers may be greatly reduced, but I still have friends who are loyal to me."

At these words, the grotesque creatures around her rose as one and bowed, then turned their naked backsides to me and slapped at their bottoms.

"Oh, stop that," scolded my stepmother.

The imps sat again. Their smirking faces were maddening.

"These dear friends travel the land for me, gathering information, telling me who is doing what and who is doing whom."

I felt myself blush at the rudeness.

She stared at me for a moment, then said slowly, "We could work together. I know things, many things. You are teachable, even if you are a bit slow. Perhaps we might still save your family's lands from being swallowed by your suitor."

I stared at her in astonishment. "You want me to work *with* you? After what you did to me? *After what you did to Wynde?*"

"Do not confuse politics with personal loyalty, May Margret! That is a child's game, and you cannot afford to be a child any longer. I did what I thought was best. And it was not I who put those scars on your beloved brother's face."

These words cut deep, and in my anger I wanted to lash out at her. But that would gain me nothing. Worse, I knew there was some truth in what she had been saying—truths which made me even angrier. Why had Father been such a fool? He was old, and tired from the war, I told myself. And I knew that, too, was true. Even so, why had he not done more to protect me? More to protect our lands and home? I loved him, I truly did. But he had let us—let me—down.

"I have, perhaps, said too much," murmured the toad queen. "And I notice you still have not answered my question. Why have you sought me out? Why not let me live down here in peace, now that I am no longer a threat?"

I could not think what to say. Certainly the truth—that I wanted something of her essence so I could return to dragon form—would not do. As if sensing what I was thinking, her imps began to chant, "Tell the truth, tell the truth, tell the truth!"

"Ah," said my stepmother. "I believe there is something you are hiding from me, May Margret. Let me see if I can guess."

I began to feel helpless, as if she were weaving a spell of words around me. Behind her the imps continued their chant: "Tell the truth! Tell the truth! Tell the truth!"

"Silence!" snapped the toad queen. "How can she tell us *anything* with you going on like that?"

At once, the imps fell silent. Turning her great, bulging eyes on me, my stepmother said softly, "Why not take their advice, May Margret? Go ahead—tell me the truth."

A compulsion came over me, and the confession of my desire trembled on my lips. Just in time, I realized that magic was at work. Placing my hands upon my waist, I felt the power of the rowan twigs. At once, the urgent need to tell all faded.

"There were rumors," I said, working carefully not to tell an outright lie, in which I feared my stepmother would somehow catch me. "Rumors . . . that you still lived. I wanted to see if you were still a danger to us."

She looked at me for a long time, then said, "I do not think that was enough to cause you to journey to these depths."

"I am to be wed."

"I know that."

"I am not sure I want to be."

"I know that."

"There is a spell that can help me, but I need something from you for it to be cast."

She stared at me again, blinking. "What is it you need?"

"No more than I would get by wiping a cloth along your back," I said at last.

She burst out laughing. "And what will you give me in return?"

"What do you want?"

"Take me back to the surface."

"Can't you do that on your own?

"There is a . . . prohibition . . . on my return. It would be broken were you to carry me."

This was not exactly what I would have hoped for, but it did answer the question of how I was to get what I needed. All I had to do was wrap the toad queen in the large handkerchief I had brought and carry her to the upper levels. As I was starting to contemplate what I would do with her once we arrived at the surface, she said, "You must swear not to fling me back down the stairs once we are at the top or harm me in any way."

I opened my mouth to answer, but before I could speak a word, she said sharply, "Understand, May Margret, that a dragon is bound by its word. You may have returned to human form, but that binding clings to you still. So do not think to swear falsely to me now."

I drew in a deep breath, wondering if she were telling the truth or simply trying to insure herself against whatever I might do. I decided to respond with a prohibition of my own. "I will swear to this, if you will swear a counteroath that your imps will remain down here and no longer bring their mischief to the world above."

She scowled at me, and I rejoiced inside, sensing she must indeed have planned to summon them. The lovely thing about the counteroath was that, were she to break it, I would be freed of my own oath as well.

"I swear they will remain here," she said at last.

"And I swear not to harm you as long as they do," I replied.

From my bosom, I drew the cloth I had brought with me and began to wrap the queen in it. Remembering Nell's warning, I took extreme care not to actually touch her. The imps wailed and moaned as I was doing this, until the queen scolded them to silence. When she was securely wrapped, I picked her up. Her body was soft and yielding, and it was almost like holding a large round of bread dough. Suppressing a shudder, I carried her to the little boat, placed her in the front, then returned to the fire pit to light my torch. The imps made any number of rude sounds and gestures as I did this, but I ignored them.

As I rowed back over the dark water, my stepmother spoke to me of politics, and the dangers she claimed surrounded us on all sides.

Once across the underground lake, I had to tuck her against my chest so I could hold her with one hand while I carried the rushlight in the other. Fearing to lose my light, I climbed the winding stair quickly, despite the growing pain in my legs, and actually made it to the dungeon before my torch went out. Though I was gasping for breath, and had not expected to fear the darkness, a sudden terror gripped me so tightly that I could scarcely breathe.

"What is the matter?" demanded the queen. "Why have we stopped?"

"I have lost my light."

"Unwrap me, and I will give you light."

Carefully, I undid the handkerchief, again making sure not to touch her. The queen muttered a few words, and a glowing ball appeared above her head. It was a faint, witchy light, an unhealthy green that turned my stomach. Even so, it was better than the darkness.

When the queen saw where we were, she uttered a low cry. "Move on," she urged me. "Let us leave this evil place."

And so, in short time, we arrived back at the kitchen, where I realized that in my haste to get what I wanted I had not thought carefully about what came next.

"Where do you want me to take you?" I asked my stepmother.

"To your room."

"I do not want you there. The swamp would be a better place, don't you think?"

"Don't be a fool, stepdaughter. Put me in the swamp, and I'll be back in a day's time, doing who knows what. But if you place me in your room and take proper care of me, not only can you keep watch on me, but I can advise you on what is to come."

I was not sure I wanted her advice. But I did like the idea that if she were in my room, I would at least be aware of what she was up to.

೪Ꮟ

THE next day, I went again to see Old Nell, taking with me the cloth in which I had so carefully wrapped my toadly stepmother, as well as the three silver cups that went with the first one I had given her. The old woman greeted me warmly and seemed pleased—and a bit surprised— that I had actually done this thing. Eying the silver cups, she accepted the handkerchief, then sent me outside to wait as she brewed the potion she had promised.

Late in the afternoon, she called me back inside. Fixing me with her one good eye, she handed me a small green bottle, and said, "You have but to drink this, and the shape you once wore will be yours again. But remember, child—if you do this, you can never again return to human form."

I gave Nell the cups, which she stroked greedily with her gnarled fingers. Clutching the green bottle with equal greed, I returned to Arlesboro Castle, feeling deep comfort in the knowledge that I could now regain my dragon shape anytime I wanted. I felt, too, a strong hope that the mere fact that this was now in my power would reduce the desire I felt to do so.

೪Ꮟ

THE weeks that followed were, perhaps, the strangest period of my life— stranger, I think, than even the time I spent as a dragon. For at the toad queen's insistence, I prepared a place for her in my wardrobe, a snug spot with a saucer of water and a large, smooth rock encircled by some moss that I moistened daily. Here she could remain unseen by Glenna. At night, I would open the door and give her some wine and bits of meat I had brought from the kitchen. As I could not stand to watch her eat, I would busy myself elsewhere. When she was done, she would call to me, and I would return to the wardrobe, where she would question me on the day's events, then tell me what she thought of them.

How odd it felt to have my stepmother, who should have been my enemy for what she had done to me, begin to advise me on how to handle what was to come. Yet her words seemed in all ways wise, so much so that I began to wonder if she might truly have the best interests of the country at heart. My confusion was enormous. When my stepmother warned me of the plans of my groom-to-be, was she offering me wisdom or trying to lead me into rash and foolish action that might destroy me? When she explained why Wynde had ordered this marriage, was she speaking with true understanding of the human heart or simply pouring black fire into my own heart, which was but half-human at best?

Despite the fact that I hated her, a growing part of me wanted to believe her, for I was desperate to think that I had a wise advisor who could help me understand the events moving around me, most especially my upcoming marriage.

At night, after I had closed the doors to the wardrobe, I would lie awake, catechizing my divided heart. Despite my anger at Wynde, I was loyal to him, and could never forget what I owed him. Dunbar was handsome and charming, and the thought of marrying him was deeply attractive to the maiden part of me. But whenever I spoke of this desire to the queen, she seemed alarmed and even angry. "Do not be deceived by looks, May Margret," she would croak. "You, of all people, should know this!"

I did not tell her that underneath both those desires lay another, my aching memory of having been a dragon, and the never-far-away longing to return to that state. But when I did not respond to her explanations of why I should avoid the marriage, she provided one more idea, a devastating one.

"I cannot say what your children might be like."

So now I was torn, day and night, by desire and fear: Part of me longed to wed and lead a normal life, part of me desired to return to the fiery power of being a dragon, and all of me worried about what might happen if I did indeed wed and become a mother.

I did not sleep much in this time, and often left my bed to stand on the parapets, searching for the answer to my urgent, warring longings. My time grew short, for affairs of state—and the wedding was indeed an affair of state—have a power of their own, moving with the strength of the tides themselves.

And so at last, the day of the wedding came. Despite my stepmother's warnings, I was prepared to let it go on. At least, most of my heart was ready to do so. Most, but not all. Which was, I suppose, not fair to Dunbar.

That morning, I dressed in a gown of ruby red, which was supposed to stand for fertility. Though that idea frightened me—what *would* my children be like?—it also spoke to me of the fire that raged within. My red hair was braided and coiled atop my head. Around my neck hung a ruby pendant. And, of course, around my waist, beneath my gown, I wore the girdle of rowan twigs.

Glenna accompanied me to the chapel as my maid of honor. But despite our long friendship and my deep trust in my lady-in-waiting, she did not know what was in the basket of flowers that I had asked her to carry.

ୡୠ

THE chapel was on the castle grounds, a simple stone building that, even so, held sacred objects of great beauty. Gathered inside were guests from neighboring kingdoms. In the back stood many of our most trusted servants. To my surprise, Old Nell was among them.

At the front of the chapel stood the round little priest who had served our family since I was a child. Before him waited my brother, tall and straight, and still fine and fair to my eyes, despite his scars. Near to Wynde was my groom, the sight of his handsome face and broad shoulders filling my heart with unexpected desire.

Quivering with fear and longing, I took my place and the ceremony began. All went well until the priest asked the question, "Does any man here have reason why these two should not be joined?" The question was meant to let any legal objection—such as an unpaid dowry, or proof that I was not a virgin—be brought forward, and I expected no challenge. So I was astonished when Old Nell stepped from her place, and said, "There will be no wedding today."

The desire I had felt in my veins was replaced by a coldness as icy as the spring streams when the snow melts.

As the chapel erupted in shouts, Nell limped down the aisle.

"What is this?" asked the priest, flustered and turning red.

Nell pulled back her scraggly gray hair, binding it with a quick twist. Now that it no longer hung over her face, her features seemed different to me. She yanked at the tattered cloak she had been wearing, ripping it open and throwing it aside.

Beneath she wore the vestments of a man.

Wynde stood as if frozen. I heard the sound of swords being drawn, but as I scanned the chapel, I saw that they were the swords of our guests, who outnumbered our own men greatly.

Nell limped to where I stood. "There will be no wedding for you today, May Margret. Today, or ever." Her voice was deeper now, and came out in a kind of snarl.

"Who are you?" I whispered. "Why are you doing this to me?"

"He is my father," said William, stepping from the group of servants gathered at the back of the chapel. "My father, Lord MacRae, a loyal subject of your father who, nevertheless, was tortured mercilessly in the dungeon beneath Arlesboro Castle."

Lord MacRae grabbed my chin. He twisted himself a bit, then spoke bitterly in Old Nell's voice. "I was not woman born, May Margret. But never was I man again after what happened to me in your father's loving care." He turned and spat upon the floor, then roared in his own voice, "Look at me, girl, and you too, Wynde. See what your father's evil has wrought. I was a loyal subject. But your father—"

The contempt in his voice when he said "your father" made me ill.

"Your father, believing false reports, thought me a spy, and so had me taken to the dungeon to be tortured. That black hellhole was where I lost this eye." Here Lord MacRae put his face near mine and pulled down at his cheek, forcing me to stare into the empty socket. "It was where I lost my teeth," he continued, pulling down his lower lip to reveal his empty gums. "It was where I received the wounds that, left untreated, festered until they cost me my leg."

At these last words, William rushed forward. Leaning against his son, Lord MacRae continued, "And it was there, screaming for mercy, that I lost my manhood. There, in the dungeon below your home, I suffered pain beyond imagining, for a crime I had not committed."

My shame already great, increased tenfold at his next words.

"My shrieks of pain, my cries for mercy, went unheard."

Were those his cries that Wynde and I had heard when we crept down the dungeon stairs? His, or those of some other innocent, it made no difference. We never asked. We never told. We never spoke of what we had seen.

"I finally escaped with the help of a friend, a decent man who knew evil when he saw it, and stepped in to stop it," continued Lord MacRae. "And as I lay in a hut in the wildwood, recovering, I vowed I would see an end to this bloodline and an end to this reign."

"We thought we had accomplished this when I wed your father and turned you into a dragon," said a voice from the basket that Glenna carried.

With a cry of shock my lady-in-waiting dropped the basket. The flowers scattered, and out rolled the little green bottle that I kept always near, as proof to myself I could return to dragon form if needed.

Out, too, hopped my stepmother. "Though we would have preferred Wynde to stay abroad, it was not a problem that he returned," she continued. "For I had built it into the spell that the heat of your breath would forever unman him."

A brutal cry of loss twisted from Wynde's lips, even as Lord MacRae said with bitter satisfaction, "You unmanned him yourself, May Margret, just as your father unmanned me."

"Our father could not have known what was happening in that dungeon," said Wynde, speaking at last.

MacRae turned to him. Scorn dripping from his words, he said, "A man cannot escape by pretending not to know what is done in his name, Wynde. Your father knew, and if he did not know, his shame is just as great, for it was his duty to know. And it was not just me, boy. Dozens of others were chained in that dungeon during the endless days and nights I was held there; dozens of others were tormented with inhuman cruelty. I know. I saw. I heard. I am the living witness."

Murmurs from around the chapel told me that most of the men here had some connection to those dozens of others. A brother, perhaps. An uncle. A father. A son.

"All would have been finished and done if you had not arranged for this marriage," said the toad queen. "We would simply have let the line die out. That is all we want—for this heritage of evil to disappear from the face of the earth forever."

"What is your place in this?" I cried.

"Why, I am Lord MacRae's daughter. Despite the glamour I wore when I wed your father—a girl can learn a lot of magic in ten years if she has a mind to—I thought you would have realized that much by now. I do appreciate you fetching me from the depths, May Margret. Though William opened the door for me to descend, the magic was such that you alone could bring me back."

Lord MacRae laughed. "My son made a good messenger, did he not, carrying word from me to his sister and back again?"

My fury was mounting, the fire in my blood growing. "Do something," I hissed to Dunbar.

But my groom-to-be was staring at me with horror. Shaking his head, he took a step away.

"Coward!" I cried. With a scream of rage, I flung myself to the floor and grabbed the green bottle.

I expected Lord MacRae or the toad queen to order William to stop me. But they remained silent. As the assembled guests watched, I fumbled with the cork. When I could not pry it loose, I gripped it with my teeth and yanked.

The cork came free.

Tipping back my head, I upended the bottle and swallowed the potion, ready at last for the fire to return.

Nothing happened.

I gasped in fury and astonishment. All this time I had kept the potion close, thinking it would let me return to dragonhood. But it had been a lie, a cheat. My rage grew beyond all bounds, multiplied by the deep, burning shame I felt for what our father had done during the days of the war, things that no man should ever do.

The toad queen laughed. "Did you really think we would put such power back in your hands once you knew the truth, May Margret? That potion was never meant to work."

That laugh was her mistake. More enraged than ever, I dashed the bottle against the floor, where it shattered into glittering shards.

Then I dove for her.

"No!" cried MacRae.

He was too late. "Tell me!" I screamed, grabbing my stepmother's soft, bloated body and lifting her from the floor. "Tell me! There is a way for me to turn back. I know there is!"

But my stepmother did not need to tell me anything. The instant that I grabbed her, I felt my body try to twist and change, felt fire tickle weakly at my veins, felt power beat fruitlessly against the doors of my heart.

Now I understood why Lord MacRae, disguised as Old Nell, had impressed upon me that I must never touch my stepmother. That connection itself was the key and the secret to my return to dragon shape. But something was wrong, something was blocking the magic.

Suddenly I knew what it was. Screeching with pain and triumph, I dropped my stepmother. Grabbing at my bodice, I ripped open the scarlet dress, then wrenched the belt of rowan twigs from about my waist and flung it aside.

Now the magic could flow freely, and, in that moment, the change began for real. In the same instant, my stepmother, still sprawled on the stone floor, began to writhe and grow, crying out with pain equal to mine as her body stretched back to its human form.

Screams filled the chapel as people scattered, trying to escape. They fled not merely in fear of me but because the growing, writhing coils of my returning dragonhood were filling the space, and there was little room for them. Wood screeched as my growing body slid pews across the floor. Glass shattered as my writhing tail struck window after window.

I did not care. The fire and the pain were on me, and I was changing, *changing*.

My stepmother scrambled away, got to her feet, ran. I lunged for her, grasped her between my jaws . . . and stopped.

Why? Why did I stop, when I could have swallowed her in an instant? Was it the promise I had made when we were underground, the promise not to harm her? The promise that bound me by my word as a dragon?

Possibly.

But I prefer to think it was the moment of dragon clarity I had, the sure knowledge that if I killed her, it would not be the end, but just another chapter. The vengeance, the war, the anger, the death, they would all go on.

Opening wide my great mouth, I dropped her naked body to the floor.

She gazed up at me. To my astonishment, tears filled her eyes. "It was not you we wanted to punish, May Margret," she said. "This was always about your father."

I tipped my head back and roared, a burst of flame so powerful it sundered the slate roof. As the stones clattered down around us, I stretched my powerful body over that of my stepmother to shield her. When the stonefall was over and she was safe, I burst through what was left of the roof, sending it sailing in all directions as I took to the sky.

ℰℬ

I spend my days on the Spindlestone now, where I think often on a passage the fat priest in the little chapel used to cite to us: "The sins of the fathers shall be visited upon the sons."

I always hated those lines, thinking it deeply unfair that God would punish children for the actions of their parents. But now, finally, I think I understand. The verse does not speak of what God will do, but rather of how the world works. For when you do evil, when you create pain, at the same time you create an enemy. And not just one enemy; you make an enemy of all those who loved the one to whom you gave the pain.

Our father did evil, and Wynde and I suffered for it.

But perhaps it can end here. My stepmother, having healed my brother's face, now acts as his advisor. Though Wynde will remain childless, young William has been declared the heir. So there will be no fight when Wynde has passed on.

As for me?

Well, I am the guardian of my country.

I watch the shores.

I watch the hills and forests.

I protect us from invasion.

But that is the least of what I do. For I also *listen*. I listen to the people who bring me news. I listen to what is happening.

That is the reason I stay here, wound round the Spindlestone, staring out to sea, but now and then turning my head to look behind, at the land I love.

I am the guardian of my country.

And we will do no more evil while I yet live.

The War That Winter Is

TANITH LEE

Tanith Lee is one of the best known and most prolific of modern fantasists, with more than a hundred books to her credit, including (among many others) The Birthgrave, Drinking Sapphire Wine, Don't Bite the Sun, Night's Master, The Storm Lord, Sung in Shadow, Volkhavaar, Anackire, Night's Sorceries, Black Unicorn, Days of Grass, The Blood of Roses, Vivia, Reigning Cats and Dogs, When the Lights Go Out, Elephantasm, The Gods Are Thirsty, Cast a Bright Shadow, Here in Cold Hell, Faces Under Water, White as Snow, Mortal Suns, Death of the Day, Metallic Love, No Flame but Mine, Piratica: Being a Daring Tale of a Singular Girl's Adventure Upon the High Seas, and a sequel to Piratica, called Return to Parrot Island. Her numerous short stories have been collected in Red as Blood, Tamastara, The Gorgon and Other Beastly Tales, Dreams of Dark and Light, Nightshades, and Forests of the Night. Her short story "The Gorgon" won her a World Fantasy Award in 1983, and her short story "Elle Est Trois, (La Mort)" won her another World Fantasy Award in 1984. Her most recent books are the four The Secret Books of Paradys and a new collection, Tempting the Gods. She lives with her husband in the South of England.

Here she takes us deep into a stark and bitter—and perhaps never-ending—winter, for a grim tale of an obsession that will persist until the last heartbeat—and perhaps beyond.

PART ONE

EVEN as they ran towards the village, Kulvok could hear the heart-beat. The nearer they came, the louder it grew; though he had been hearing it anyway since one sunpass earlier. Now it shook him, like a drum inside his own body. To a shaman such as he, the significance of this was horrible, and had he been a novice, he would have run in the other direction. But he was no longer a novice. There was no choice but to go on.

They had reached a long snow ridge fifty or sixty feet high. Here the leader, Nenkru, halted his men.

The midday sun was low at this season. The valley beneath spread like a blue apron of ice, quite featureless, and, as expected, the village could no longer be seen. Things were always like this when they followed Ulkioket.

The killing certainly would be over by now. But they would still need to be very wary for a while.

Nenkru touched Kulvok's shoulder. "Do you hear it still?"

"Louder."

"What can it be?" puzzled Nenkru.

"What I told you it was," said Kulvok impatiently.

"A heart? What heart? Only our hearts make a sound. Or is it *his* heart?"

"It's not *his* heart. I've never heard the heart of Ulkioket beating. Perhaps it doesn't. Perhaps he has none."

Prepared to wait, the men squatted. They could not make a fire; that would be unwise so close to Ulkioket.

Looking over the brink of the ridge, Kulvok made something out after all, but this too was usual, to note such signs in the more flexible places of the ice. The awful beauty of the signs repelled him. Whenever he saw them, they repelled him. He was not respectful or religious about the marks, as were the rest of the band. Their band's very way of life was evil and disgusting, and Kulvok the shaman knew it, even if the others *refused* to know it.

To live—by *this*—

"*See—see—*" Etuk whispered on a silver breath.

As if they'd never seen it before. Though it was a fact that few saw it and lived to view it *again*.

Miles off, where the white snow hills marched away from the valley, sudden swirls of gleaming motion rose, like an unfrozen wave, luminous, indecipherable. If you didn't recognize it.

"*Ulkioket.*" The men sighed.

Winter, thought Kulvok, *they call him winter.*

And next, *Why am I angry? Nothing has changed. For us, that's his name now.*

But in spite of Ulkioket's departure, the heart still thudded, and when the last quiver of light had faded behind the snows, he got up and ran on, towards the murdered village.

༉

THEY were scavengers, Nenkru's band.

Their sort had been given a general name among the many tribes: Kimolaki. Which meant Fox-Men, for the white fox was a coward and a thief, sneaking in to take the leavings of animals more powerful than itself. As did their tribe.

How had they come to it?

Kulvok did not care to recall. In the ordinary way, was the best answer. Because of poverty and death and dearth. And the winter. Always the winter, the ancient enemy of the Northlands. Anything really could be blamed on the winter, which crept up on the little time of summer that lasted only three months, burnt the last fruits black on the bushes, turned the sea to marble, and chained the sun to the horizon so that he never rose higher than one-eighth of the way up the enormous, sunken sky.

At the start, they had simply been trying not to die. Most of mankind would instinctually do that, beastkind too, seals and fish, the wolves and the great bears.

But then, instead of hiding or flying from death, from Ulkioket, they had come to see what might be gained.

Since that sunpass when they learned this, Nenkru's Kimolaki had seldom gone hungry, or gone without fire or shelter. Even clothing, even weapons they got. Even ornaments. What Ulkioket wrecked and left behind him so carelessly became of vast benefit to them. So now, like many other scavengers, Kulvok supposed, they said prayers to Ulkioket, put up little altars to him. Worshipped the filthy, foul, and fearsome *nightmare* thing.

While the true gods and spirits of the North, Kulvok was certain, cursed them all and planned for them some terrible hell of suffering. And a worse one for himself, since he was a magician and should know better.

But until he was dead, slain by the winter, or by Ulkioket, the monster named Winter, or merely by another man, Kulvok would not know what his punishment was to be.

He glanced about him now as they sped on.

He and they were all so alike, the same as all their race, their tall, lean bodies hard from hardship, bronzen-skinned from cold-burn, black-eyed and black of hair. In all his years, not one of them had ever seen a man or woman who was not physically like themselves.

Yet why did Kulvok notice such a familiar thing now?

Umb-umb, thrummed the heart. *Umber-umber-umb.*

HE had been eight years old when he saw the dragon. As the son of the shaman's first wife, Kulvok, instead of being let out to play with the other boys in the red winter moonlight, was sent to gather driftwood from an ocean inlet. His father had read weird signs in the magic fire-pot the night before, and must relight it to learn more, and only this particular type of wood, which gave off a blue flame, was of use.

Kulvok was already trained to more work than play.

That he had a talent for sorcery, he didn't yet grasp. Yet he liked to study it. And liked his father well enough, too.

He was alone along the frozen shore then, when he beheld for the very first time that uncanny metallic shimmer in the air.

Not knowing what it could be, he stood staring up at the low ice-cliffs above the bay.

The moon was over to the west, much redder, so that all which reflected its light had a coppery tone. Oddly, the metallic thing that moved between the cliff-top and the sky was more silver than red. It seemed to catch the reflection of the stars more than that of the moon.

Kulvok had to make a decision. Should he continue gathering the important driftwood, as he'd been told to do, or instead climb back up the ice and rock to find out what moved there?

He decided on the second course.

In fact, it would have made no real difference either way. In the end, the same thing would have happened.

By the time he had clambered out on the table of the cliff, the shining mystery had left it.

Perplexed, eight-year-old Kulvok paused, looking around.

That was when he noticed the marks.

Even then, he had thought them beautiful, though he would not have admitted to the phenomenon in quite that way. They *drew* him. So he knelt to trace one with his gloved finger.

It went without saying that the ice was freezing cold, and even through the sealskin of the glove he would have felt it—but this was more than that, far more. With a yelp, he snatched his hand away. And saw with horror that the tip of the glove had burned off and, under it, his finger-tip was *black*—as if he had thrust it into a fire.

Despite being accustomed to his father's often dangerous craft, Kulvok was frightened.

He sprang up, clutching his hand.

And in that moment saw what was below, out of the shadow of the cliffs, full in the blood-red moonlight. His village, of course, lay on the ice-plain down there. Kulvok knew the sight of it well. He had been born there, grown up there. The curved walls of the white towers, one storey or two of ice-bricks, with smudges of cook-smoke rising. Inside, the house-wolves would be lying, waiting for the evening meal; the women would bend to the savoury-smelling stone pots slung over the flames; men would mend things, sitting in the central lower room, where the fretted stone lamps each lifted a yellow flame, two or three feet tall. On the wall skins hung down, with little whale-ivory images of kind or helpful gods fastened to them with pins of iron or bone. All this, Kulvok pictured in that glance. Perhaps foreknowing.

He was at once aware, without consciously understanding what it was, that the other thing, which now moved between him and his world of light and warmth and safety, would end it instantly, like the smothering of a lamp.

And he cried out, Kulvok, in his high child's voice. But the whining wind ate his cry.

The shape was beautiful too. Yet he could not bring himself to see it as anything beautiful, nor would he ever. Its hugeness he did compre-hend. High as the low sky it looked, though it was not, for the cliffs stood higher. Moon red and dark and silvery, it eased sinuously forward, re-flecting everything, almost like a misted silver mirror—or like the scales of black ice that armoured the winter bay. For it *was* ice, and *scaled* with ice, and the crest that stabbed out like flint spear-heads along its head and back and all the terrible yards of its eddying tail, they were ice also. And then it turned its head, just a little. And the child saw one of its eyes. Its huge eye—and this was almost more ghastly than all else—was like the *eye of a man or woman*. Yes, like that, a clear crystal white and an iris and pupil of pure inky blackness, and the eye was set into its long, wolf-like head, inside the same human, long, narrow lids that slanted at the outer corner.

It was when he beheld the dragon's eye that Kulvok fell to his knees. Not in worship. His legs had changed to liquid snow.

And from that position then, kneeling and unable to run either forward or away, he watched what the dragon did next.

⚕

WHEN they reached the village, all was as usual. That is, things were as they always became once Ulkioket had gone by.

Long ago, any of Nenkru's band might have missed the signs. But by now, they knew what to look for. These clues were various and not every time the same; sometimes there was something new. That happened now.

On this occasion, it was an old woman, lying just outside the zone of attack. The blast had caught her, but despite killing her, had not disguised her. She was still visible: her heavy leather and fur garments, the necklace of shark-teeth, perhaps given her in youth by a loving husband. Her face, despite being sheathed in ice like the rest of her, was still quite plainly visible. She looked startled, that was all. As if someone had shouted behind her. The blast had turned her hair to iron. Frozen solid, one of her gloved fingers had broken right off when she hit the ground.

Her broken-off finger made Kulvok remember his burned one. The scar was still there, covering his finger-tip, grey and without any feeling.

The village lay immediately beyond.

If you knew what to look for, you *could* see.

The hilly rubble of ice chunks that the place had become inside only two or three seconds was not quite natural-looking. And if much of it was milky white, so that you couldn't peer through, in a few areas there were flaws in the milkiness, and there you could.

So they looked in.

The best vantage spot looked right into an ice-tower, for the blast, even as it froze everything, had also cracked one wall wide open.

The scene was perfect, eerily so, although veined over within with thicker ice like white feathers. Kulvok had never seen this exact and awful a presentation of ordinary life—a life that had been going on unawares only seconds before it was blasted into stillness.

A man had been repairing his knife. Two small children were playing on a bearskin, beside two of the favourite wolves, one asleep and one who had been sitting bolt upright at the moment of impact. A woman was coming through from the cooking area, carrying a pot of fish soup. The only elements that were wrong were the stiffness of clothes and hair and skin—each of the victims had instantly been changed from flesh and blood to a carved statue. And there was no light, save from the twilight of afternoon. No three-foot flame in the lamps, no shine in a single human eye.

"I shall never grow used to it," said Nenkru dully. Apla chuckled, and said, "I'll settle for warming that soup."

And Etuk added, "He was good to us this time, our Lord Winter. See those heavy furs? And the dried seal-meat on the hooks there?"

But the man behind Kulvok, Inoro, muttered, "One sunpass in the future, they'll go away. Ulkioket and his kind. And then the winter will go too. There will be twelve months of summer, and only a night or so of cold."

"Hush, fool," growled Etuk, and cuffed Inoro. "Do you want to spoil our luck? It's more likely the winter will grow stronger and devour us all."

Then they took their axes and began to hack at the more-fragile areas in the blast-ice.

Kulvok stood back.

He wondered how he had heard any of this exchange, and how he could even hear the blows and shatterings of the axeblades over the heartbeat that now thundered so violently in his skull.

It came to him that this noise possibly meant he was going mad, because every time he saw these frozen villages, his birth village of ten years before filled his mind. And since the scene in this one snow-tower was so clear, it reminded even more acutely. He had not, that earlier time when he was eight, been the only one away from home. Some men of his tribe had been hunting along the ice, and when they came back, they found Kulvok. And then they found their frozen village.

None of them had known what had caused this horror, and for a while Kulvok had been unable to speak. They blamed the glassy ice-death on some new freak of the winter, and one of them had begun to scream an old song of the tribe about the enemy tyrant that winter was. But someone shook him and brought him round. Then they too had tried to hack a way through into the ice. It was difficult, and *they* had only two axes with them, one of which snapped head from haft. Then they lit a fire against the ice, and kept it fierce until the sun crawled up one-eighth of the sky. Eventually, a little of the outer shell melted, and then they were able to go in a short distance. But not far. At the last, they had not the heart to go in far.

But Kulvok had glimpsed his father, the shaman. The most surprising horror of all then. Since the man had gone down at the blast, as some did, he had been toppling over, but had frozen in midfall. He lay sidelong and tilted, his black hair fanned out in stiffened quills, his staff of magic in his hand and his eyes dead as two bits of charred wood. Like these eyes now, in the latest village Ulkioket had visited.

꿈

KULVOK the child went away with the hunters who found him. They trekked for seventeen sunpasses and came to another village, one that was still alive. This place took them in generously and without question. You did not refuse to shelter any of those the winter had hurt, for there might come an hour when you also would need help.

They were very kind to little Kulvok. In the warmth among the furs and wolves, the scent of food and humanity, all lit by lamps and fires, he regained the power of speech. And then was able to tell what he alone had seen. The dragon. For which he had no name, and that he could barely describe, only able to talk of its unearthly scintillance, and that mostly because sometimes the winter sky, by night, produced such colors and phantom shifts of light, and that gave him the words to use.

But the people of the new village believed what he said.

They had heard before of what Kulvok spoke. A huge animal that moved on four legs and had a head like a wolf's, and a crest of spines, and a coiling summer-river of tail. One man said that he had known another who saw the thing at higher-sun time, near winter's end. Then it was white, with a leaden bluish glimmer of the sky on it. It reflected the sky, for truly it *was* all polished ice, plated with ice like the winter sea. And it had black, human eyes. The man also said that there were several others of its kind. He said nothing of what they did to men.

Kulvok lived four years in the village and became a man himself there. He learned to train the wolf-teams and to sled with them, to hunt and summer-fish. He relearned his magic talents too, with the village's sorcerer. For a great while, whenever he was away, he was afraid that he would come back to find the village assaulted and frozen over. But the years passed, and it did not happen. He pushed the dread from his mind. Yet at eight he had *seen* what the ice dragon had done, and how it had done it. Seen how, after it had half turned its head and he had beheld its human eye, it had looked back again at Kulvok's birth village. And then it had drawn in a breath. That was unmistakable, the swelling up of its sides— like the leather bellows the women sometimes puffed to encourage wood on the hearth to burn. And he heard it breathe in, even over the wind that was blowing that night, a *hissing* like fire. Breathe in. Then out. Unlike the bellows, its breath was not air, nor fire. Its breath was ice. Its breath blew from the gut of winter. Its breath had frozen the village and all things in it. And, having done that, the dragon rippled itself away over the plain and vanished in the dark of the sinking moon.

※

WHEN his constant fear that his adoptive village would be frozen by Ulki-oket or another of the ice dragons lessened, which it did as nothing like that happened, Kulvok, now a man of twelve, questioned the sorcerer on the matter. He asked why the ice dragon hated men so much.

"Because the dragon's master is winter itself, who is our enemy, and with which always we battle."

"Why do we not then battle with the *dragon*?" twelve-year-old Kulvok had demanded.

"Even a shaman must fail at that. Even the mightiest of magicians."

There were stories of heroes though—Kulvok had heard them round the fires at night.

"Why not a hero then? One who can slay the great white bear, or kill twenty walruses, or ride the whale?"

"Even a hero fails. It's not, Kulvok, that no hero has ever gone up against an ice dragon. It's that we are men, and winter is eternally our war, and the ice dragon is winter's servant and the same. Flesh and blood will never outlast the ice. It swallows us. Any hero, and once there were many, who fought a dragon—died. One breath. One breath of ice. That is all it took. I've not seen what you have seen, Kulvok. *Think* what you have seen. *One breath of ice.*"

When he was almost thirteen, and had been out hunting with his sled, Kulvok came home happy and fearless and thoughtless one evening, look-ing forward to seeing a girl he liked, and with meat for his adopted village. And found that it was gone. Gone in a breath of ice, just like his birthplace, frozen, and everyone there frozen with it, even the hunters who now lived there and had rescued him as a child.

And some years later, he met with Nenkru and Apla. And by then, Kulvok was corrupted, a shaman who did tricks to amuse and earned his food that way. A shaman who did not bother to heal or foretell, did not love or trust. Having learned what happened when you did.

※

UMBER-UMB . . . Umb-umber . . .

The heart beat now in his brain. In his viscera. In *his* heart.

He staggered into the cleared space. He could see, from a spirit totem carved on a bone post, that the people in this village had been from the tribe of Lut. His people, in the past—they were the tribe of Taind. Nothing of that mattered now.

Smashed ice everywhere. He stumbled again. None of the others were near. He ran, disjointedly, ahead. Kulvok could hardly see for the beat of the other heart in his head.

He floundered against ice-walls, over the frozen corpse of a wolf, a boy—

And then—then—*Umber-umber*—then—

Suddenly the beat of the alien heart faded. It grew quiet, so that he could hear it only as if it was miles away, as he had in the beginning.

In this way he knew, or his shamanic skill knew, that it was directly by him.

He had reached more solid blast-ice, where the axes had not yet come. Behind him, Kulvok made out the shouts of Nenkru and the others as they broke into the village ice-towers, pulling the furs and food from the walls, the weapons and decorations from the belts and neck-strings of the dead. "*Gold!*" he heard Etuk call in joy. For the old metals, once mined when summer had been longer and men had had strength enough to delve the earth, were rare now.

Sickened by the scavenging, and by his part in it, Kulvok leaned against the side of a dwelling. And saw a woman's foot, booted in walrus-hide and fur, just clear of the unbreached thickness of the blast-ice ahead.

Then he leant on the ice. He squinted. Though the ice was dense and deathly, he could see straight into it.

The woman to whom the foot belonged lay there. She was, like the rest, frozen to stone. Just like the old woman caught outside, save that this one was young. And her belly rose in a hill. She had been carrying a child for some time, he thought, almost to term.

Umb, faintly said the heart. *Umber-umber-umber.*

It came from the belly, from the womb of the ice-blast-frozen woman whom the dragon had killed with a single breath.

I must smash through.

It was crazy, yet he hammered with his gloved fists on the thick ice until it cracked. It shattered and gave way.

In the stark silence after the beat of the heart had left him, which it did exactly as the ice-wall shattered, he thought, in plain renewal of the hope for life—*We two broke this open. We two—*

I.

And he.

ೞ

WHEN he joined Nenkru's Kimolaki those years before, they had just lost their shaman, who had perished in a lead-crack of the restless land-ice. Very oddly, once settled with the scavenger band, Kulvok's need for magic trickery had faded as his real magical abilities grew. After this, he could often foretell, even foretell the paths Ulkioket might take. And he could heal.

Now he would try to heal the child on the ice.

Before he realized that it had no need of him.

ೞ

AS the blast-ice smashed at his blows, something swift and appalling happened to the corpse of the frozen, pregnant woman. She also *shattered*—like an ancient glass. And then she was simply gone.

Instead, the baby from her womb lay on the white ground.

Kulvok stared. At first, he wasn't able to stir.

One by one, the others stole up. They even left their scavenged goods, the things they always got by following cautiously behind a dragon and raiding the settlements it had destroyed. But this event was more bizarre even than the breath of ice.

"Is it—*dead* too?"

"No. See, it's breathing."

By then, Kulvok had stretched out his hands, pushing warmth from the core of his body into a magical cocoon to enwrap the baby. He felt the heat too, they all did, for they spoke of it, and anyway the air pulsed, and a little of the thinner ice melted and dripped. But it had no effect on the child. None.

He—the baby was a male—lay there, quietly shifting about, turning his head with its smooth fine cap of hair, kicking with his feet and waving his hands slowly. His eyes were open too. They fixed on the men with an unusual attention. The new-born never seemed to gaze like that. Nor did he cry or wail. His mouth, small as a silver bead, stayed shut.

"Nothing happens, Kulvok. How did he survive? But he'll die in a minute."

"*Look at his colours.* He's already dead. It's just some tremor that makes him move—"

"But his *eyes* move—*look*—he blinks!"

"That too, some tremor as the dead body gives way." The heat from Kulvok's hands was now cooling also. Coldness seeped back into his gloves, his palms and fingers. Only the scarred finger-tip gave off a sudden flash of feeling, as if again it had been burnt. But that was gone as soon as it came.

Yet he knew the child lived. And why it lived. Was it anything but obvious?

He had a silvery white skin, the baby, that darkened somewhat at brows and eyelids, the lips, the folds of ears and legs . . . The film of hair on his head was white too, like fine smoke against a shadow. His eyes—his eyes were the green-blue of the core of a floating iceberg.

Near to birth, perhaps only minutes from it, the dragon's ice-blast had caught him, killing all else, his mother included. But some god or spirit that abruptly cared for mankind had saved him, and the freeze had instead reworked every inch and atom of his body.

Kulvok stepped away. He spoke firmly in a low voice.

"He isn't dead or dying. He'll live. And we are entrusted with him—I can hardly guess why it is we who were chosen—perhaps to pay for our crimes." The men stood about him in dumb-struck noiselessness. "Can you not *see* what he is?" Kulvok asked them in a kind of anger. "He is the hero. The *hero*."

PART TWO

DURING the brief summer, pale golden down covered the low trees and shrubs. Fruits grew there, the shades of fire and darkening skies.

Salmon and blackfish might be harvested from the narrow rivers, streams, and lakes.

Thin grass and lichen toned the landscape brown and green.

Nenkru's band moved as ever to the grassland by the great Tear Lake, and lived there with their women and children, in tents of deer-hide. The women made bread from the bitter seeds of grasses, which was only possible in the summer, and pickled the fruits in fruit vinegar. They feasted on the meat of deer and the livers of seal.

Always to Kulvok, this time, a little less than three months, which was presaged only by the lifting sun and by the breaking of the ice with colossal booms and roarings, and which often ended in only a single night of freezing gales and snow, was like a stupid if pleasant dream.

In a way Kulvok had always hated summer-time. It resembled the wicked promise of a faithless woman. She gave you, almost without warning, great happiness, and acted as if she loved you. Then in one night betrayed and abandoned you. Yet you were an idiot—always you welcomed her return. And though never again did you believe her sweet-talking, still you relished her.

Anlut, though . . . What did summer mean to *him*? Kulvok was unsure. Unsure what winter meant to Anlut, as well. Or what mankind meant. Or what Kulvok himself meant to Anlut, he who had taken the involuntary position of a father to the boy, just as the shaman's wife, Nuyamat, had been awarded the status of Anlut's mother. Anlut had been a baby then, and so had to have one. Had to have a woman to care for him and a man to hunt for him. Or had he needed none of that? As he had needed no healing, no warmth, no milk, maybe not even the protective, predictive words with which Kulvok brought him inside the guardian family of the Kimolaki band: Hero. *Hero.*

༄

ALMOST sixteen summers passed, and fifteen winters of many thousand nights. The baby had become an infant, a child, a youth. A man. The hero born from flesh and ice.

He was tall, among the tallest of the men, straight and lean, hard as rock and flexible as a willow-branch. He had learned, as all men did, to hunt and fish, mend weapons and tools, build house towers of ice-brick, raise the ice-brick platforms up inside for two storeys and hang a strong rope-ladder of walrus-hide whereby to climb up and sleep. At all times, he was polite. He spoke to the women, young and old, as a good and serious child does to his mother. To the men, he spoke respectfully, as if to elder brothers. Even to the oldest men, he spoke this way. Which was not respectful enough, of course, yet you could not fault it.

Kulvok, taking the place of his father, had named him Anlut. The name meant simply, *the one of the tribe of the Lut.*

When she had seen him for the first time, Nuyamat had let out a loud screech. But she went dumb when Kulvok told her sternly, "He's been given to us to tend. Do everything for him that a woman must do for the newborn—but never remove your gloves when you touch him. Inoro's wife is still in milk from her last child. She'll put some milk in a jar, and you must feed him this through a hollow reed I'll make for you. If there are doubts, ask me. If I'm away, let it be. He'll live, even if neglected. So I think. Left naked on the ice, he thrives."

"*What is it?*" Nuyamat had whispered then.

"A baby," he replied flatly.

"But—"

He had already informed her of what was required of her. He would not repeat himself. He put the child, not crying, not struggling, already strangely coordinated and attentive, on the fur rug that lay across the lower sleeping place, for right then they were still in their one-storey ice-tower.

"Do as you're bid," he snapped.

She had no choice. She never remonstrated with him again.

Did they all get used to Anlut? No, never. But they became accustomed to *not* becoming accustomed. And when he grew, matured, and reached the appropriate ages of a male's life, he was taught as the other boys were.

The house-wolves did treat him differently from all other people, though not with particular aversion. It was as if he were a favoured piece of equipment they must be careful of and note. And he did not ever try to learn the use of a sled. Later, he would run, fast and tireless, behind the sleds of others, always keeping up.

Now, as Kulvok watched him cross the summer grassland, running lightly with his fish-spear in hand and a string of silver catch around his shoulders, the shaman sucked in his breath as ever. For sunlight, like the light of winter stars, half-sun and red moonglow, reflected on Anlut's pale skin—his *carapace*. His complexion was smooth, without a blemish, like the ice. He gleamed and flickered here with faint blue and tawny tints, and where the hot settling sun snagged on his long white hair, it too shone golden.

"I have twenty-seven fish, Kulvok," said Kulvok's ice-cold foster-son. His voice was cool but not unhuman. His heart-of-ice eyes blinked once, in a human way.

"We'll eat well then," said the shaman. He knew that Anlut too would eat, if less than any other man of his years. And he knew that the fish Anlut carried would not be frozen, but frosty, and also that when they were cooked, everyone reaching for the food-pot would be wary not to brush against Anlut's bare hands. Anlut's bare skin did not burn you with its coldness, yet cold he was, colder than new snow. You could not bear to touch him or—Kulvok wondered—was it that he could not bear to touch *you*? If he had ever loved any of them, he had never been able to express that physically. He would never marry, nor himself sire children. But, anyway, Kulvok did not think that Anlut loved them. Anlut had been saved from certain death and remade by some uncanny force for quite another task. Which, naturally, he had been told from the start.

༡༦

SUMMER was nearing its end that night. Clouds drifted over the stars, and in the far sky was a rippling and banding that was not Ulkioket but only the wild winter lights beginning to practice their weaving.

After the evening meal, Anlut sat apart from the tent and gazed at this, while the other young men sat laughing and playing a gambling game with horn-pieces, the children scampered after a rag ball, and the women salted meat and gossiped. Even the young women never glanced at Anlut. Only the fire paid him attention, glimmering hypnotically on the contours of his hands and face.

He could, like any other man, draw close to fire. It had no bad effect on him. But neither did it warm him. Once, in the earliest days, when Kulvok sometimes questioned him, Anlut had said he felt no heat from fire and had no need of it to preserve him. Yet he liked it, its colour and rhythm, the dances it performed in a lamp or on a hearth. When the young women danced, he watched them also, but in a detached and solemn way. As if, again, simply meaning to be polite.

Kulvok felt his own age. He was thirty-four years now, practically an old man. His back was growing humped, and he had grey strands in his black hair. He had fathered no sons that he knew of anywhere, and decidedly none here. Nuyamat, he understood very well, resented this, and that—worse—instead of a proper baby she had had this monster thrust on her. A demon who might sit naked in a snow gale and not come to harm.

Kulvok had never, either, been sure if the distance the band kept from him distressed Anlut. The shaman was unsure, in fact, of all things to do with Anlut, save that one paramount thing, the reason for Anlut's life.

"Anlut," said Kulvok now.

"Yes?" said Anlut, looking up at him.

"Come with me to my other tent. Tonight, my powers tell me, is a time that you and I should talk together."

Anlut rose. He was graceful, although not in a human way at all. His movements reminded Kulvok of the flow of plate ice on the sea, the passage of a cloud. Or the dance of fire, or of the Northland lights. Or the scintillance of a dragon.

For a moment, they stood quite still. No one else glanced their way.

Yet from the corner of his eye, Kulvok noticed Etuk bending to one of the little portable shrines of Ulkioket, which Etuk set up always in the doorway of his tent or his ice-tower. All Nenkru's Kimolaki did that still. And all through these years, once he had been old enough, Anlut had gone out with them to follow after the ice dragon as well, and to thieve what had been left frozen by him in his blast-ice. Anlut therefore had even seen Ulkioket, now and then, though always in the distance, for none of the rest of them would attempt the suicide of going close. Anlut had not questioned or resisted, not spoken of these excursions, ever.

Despite being warned by the shaman early of his nature and his future role as hero, and, ultimately, dragon-slayer, Anlut had never expressed misgivings, never apparently wanted to learn more—and never once vowed himself ready for the quest, let alone *un*ready.

When Kulvok and Anlut turned off from the camp towards the shaman's other tent, where he communed with his sorcery, only Etuk squinted after them. Then he rubbed more meat fat into the shrine. "Not I," said Etuk to Ulkioket, "I never agreed to nurse this strangeling. None of us agreed. It was the shaman's business. We thank you always, lord. You are our god."

ფჯ

THE other tent was dark and had no fire.

Kulvok kindled the single small lamp that only gave up a one-foot flame, but that flame white as snow.

"You may sit or stand," said Kulvok. But he stood. Anlut stood also.

Is he only a mirror? His skin reflects, his hair—is that the clue to the ice-hero? He has learned our life by copying, not through instinct or feeling. He does as I do now, just as my reflection in an ancient piece of polished metal would do if I kept one in my tent.

This uncomforting idea might be part of his prescience, Kulvok decided. Yet too, in the past year, he had sensed his shamanic powers waning, as they had at first, when he was eight and had lost his father.

"Since you were able to hear," said Kulvok, "I told you of your birth, and of the function that some god or spirit gave you."

"Yes, Kulvok," said Anlut's cool voice.

"What then do you think of such a destiny?"

Anlut said nothing. Then he said, "That it must be mine."

Kulvok frowned. He glared into the turquoise eyes that seemed almost fiery with their alien iciness.

"Then you are to seek the dragon and kill it. Since only you, that are yourself ice-formed, as he is, can face him, his scorching pad-marks, his untouchable surface, his breath-blast of freezing death. And you will destroy him, and thereafter any others of his kind you come across. *Ulkioket*," said Kulvok, slowly. "Say his name."

"Ulkioket."

"Say your own, now."

"Anlut."

"The gods made you for this. Even the day before the dragon struck your village, when you were only hot flesh and blood in your mother's womb, I heard the beating of your heart, and we ran to find you, there in the path of the dragon."

"And now," said Anlut, who seldom spoke save when spoken to, "I am cold and in the world, and he is in *my* path instead."

Kulvok stared.

Then he grunted. He was surprised by the assertion. A hero's statement of intent. It lifted his spirit slightly, and the flame of the small lamp too rose, becoming for a second almost two feet in height.

And in the lamplight, Anlut glowed for a moment with a bronzen skin like a proper human man. But the flame sank.

Outside, eerie as wolves, the women began to sing some chant of summer's end.

"The time is now," said Kulvok. "Now you must go to him. He's out on the edge of summer and winter, stirring from his summer sleep, starting to move about and flex himself as men do when *warmth* draws near. I have traced his whereabouts through my magic. I'll show you which direction you must go."

"No need," said Anlut. "It's eastward."

"How . . . do you know?"

"I've followed him in the past, have I not, Kulvok, with the Kimolaki? I've learned his ways. Perhaps he *calls* me now, if the *time* is now. You summoned me first. Otherwise, I should have sought you also tonight."

Kulvok heard this avowal in a stony amazement. Anlut, between one hour and the next, had altered. But the ritual of sending must conclude.

"Go then, Anlut. My kind have given all we might to you, and I can give you nothing more, for you need nothing of mine, nor did you ever need it."

"That's true," said the young man, the hero, the creature of the ice, cold and level, heartless—even though his heartbeat had shouted and howled at this other man over sixteen years before, calling him to find him. "Farewell then, Kulvok. Farewell then, band of Nenkru."

Without another word, he went out, pausing only to dip inside the home tent, emerging presently with spear and knife. Anlut left their camp. Thinking him off to some lonely night hunt, no one paid heed. Nuyamat was singing with the women. She did not look up. Impervious, the wolves gnawed bones, ignoring all.

Kulvok himself withdrew again into his tent of magic. He lit the fire-pot, but not in order to see anything in it. He felt the going away of Anlut like a weird silver strand that pulled out of him, unravelling as it went, fraying to nothing on the brown grassland beside the tear-shape of the lake. Death, Kulvok believed, must feel similar. Nor, he thought, would he have long now, before he knew for sure how death must feel.

PART THREE

ANLUT trekked eastward.

He progressed at a measured, striding trot, covering miles relentlessly, pausing only at sunfall and sunup, when he would sleep on the bare tundra, each time for less than an hour.

Sunpasses went by, strung pale beads on the black thread of night, which night all the while grew stronger and longer and deeper.

Then gales came and filled the black night with the different white beading of swirling snows.

Ice formed and shouldered against ice, grumbling, sometimes splitting with enormous shrill cracks.

As he ran, Anlut looked often about him. He had been taught to search like this, for the Kimolaki did so, checking the terrain for pitfalls, thicker ice or thinner, or for the danger of predators other than themselves. Once or twice then, he saw the deer streaming away along the land's edge, and once two lone wolves, or a white bear shambling far off in mist, and, on the limit of the horizon, the great bear-like bergs, lit with unreal blue lamps inside. The sun began to be only an eighth high along the sky.

It was again winter's time.

The season of the ice dragon. Ulkioket.

ᑫᕐ

MEN think, even when they pursue something, hunt prey, an enemy, the mystic beat of a signalling heart.

Did Anlut think? Consider? *Remember?*

For sixteen years, he had grown up among human men and women, who nurtured him the best that they were able. Lovelessly, naturally, nothing else could be expected, and often fearfully too—as with Nuyamat in her gloves, forcing the bone reed of milk into his mouth. And mostly with a fearful lovelessness demonstrated by the manner of not approaching him, of keeping distant physically, and in all other ways. Yet they taught him their skills. Otherwise, they believed, he could not have survived, and their code was always to extend the techniques of survival.

But Anlut was not like them; as the shaman had first said, probably he could have survived without any help or teaching at all.

As he ran in pursuit of the dragon, his Fate, Anlut's thought was only of the route he must follow, which *intuitively* now he knew, and his consideration only of the most immediate issues—such as when to take out a strip of dried seal-meat and chew it. His *remembering* was a sort of void, cold and iron and misty, like the landscape all about. It did not offend or trouble him, how mankind had behaved towards him, neither their bleak care nor their dislike. To him, they were ghostly things. Even Kulvok had been like that, though he had seemed more significant than the others. But, Kulvok, to Anlut, was less a mortal man than a kind of spiritual time-telling device. And on that night when the lights of the Northland began to weave again, Anlut had heard a soundless chime, like the clash of two slender stars striking one on another. The moment had arrived. Next, Kulvok had proclaimed it. And so the next stage of life started, vital, irresistible, and expulsive as birth.

New-born at last then, out here Anlut had begun to live and to become.

Always alone among others, now he was alone in the vast, cold world. Where men made walls and lamps against that world, Anlut required no shelter and took all the light he needed from the low sun or the moon and stars. Even when the clouds blotted them up or the mists closed round, Anlut needed nothing else. When thin ice shifted suddenly beneath him, he only leapt free of it with an agility not common to men. One sunrise, sleeping his minutes on the ground, he woke to find the ice-sheet had moved and transposed him. He had slipped twice his height down into a funnel in the ice. But he merely put his hands and feet on the sides of it and hauled himself rapidly up and out. Unhelped, no man *could* have done this. Any other man must have died. Anlut grasped as much, and completely and unarrogantly knew his physical superiority. He had not been afraid or puzzled.

Perhaps nothing *could* stop him.

In his mind, the dragon waited at all times, maybe even when he slept, though he did not exactly dream of it, let alone *think* of, *consider*, or *remember* it.

Ulkioket, given him from the very start as his *reason* for existing, had grown right into Anlut and was now welded among the hero's icy bones and cool, peculiar blood. He was a *part* of Anlut's brain, not an image or aspiration there. He was not even a goal. Your Fate could hardly be a goal, after all. It was instead only a destination. Like the actual east to which Anlut ran, in order to meet it.

MONTHS of the winter passed, all one timeless era. And then the spoor appeared, there on the white earth, the engraved marks of the footfall: Ulkioket. They *were* beautiful. To Kulvok, once, they had been. And to the hero, always. In shape, they were like the long and broad-bladed leaves that stood out stiffly on certain shrubs in summer. The thorns of claws spread from them, some of them more sharply or deeply signed than others. But this varied. No injury had caused the unevenness, only different sorts of ice or snow underfoot. They were, however, much larger than any leaves. Each footfall was some three feet in length, about half that length across. Like a lamp-flame from a stone lamp.

The originator had never been seen close to. From the prints, you could hazard the size of him.

If he did not brush the roof of the sky with his crest, nevertheless his back must rise at least twenty or twenty-five feet into the air, his neck and head rather higher.

His winding tail, often held clear of the earth, still left its own track in places, frequently then wiping out areas of the other signs. The spoor of the dragon's tail was like the narrow passage of a cruel storm wind, that kept low, attracted to some element in the ground-ice, scratching and tearing to come at it.

Anlut, having found the first definite signs, stayed there a while, examining them. Like Kulvok, and yet not like, Anlut put his bare hand into a pad-mark.

To Anlut, the dragon-cold felt like lightning—galvanic—yet it did not burn. Gazing at his palm and fingers, Anlut noted no change. But for an hour after, his skin there sang and prickled. As he had been told the chilled, numbed skin of a man did, held out to the warmth of fire.

That evening, Anlut went by a frozen jumble like a fallen hill. It had been a village, and the dragon had seen to it.

꿍

TWO sunpasses later, the hero saw his quarry.

It was a cloudless night, stars like splashes of steel and silver flung out across it, so that even without any moon as yet, to Anlut the world seemed bright as a morning at winter's end.

He had climbed to the top of a cliff, and below lay the ice-sheet of the tundra. It too looked made of silver and steel.

And on it there walked a black-blueness that was also a glowing, molten light, and it brushed the roof of the sky with its crest . . .

Despite everything, despite having glimpsed the dragon before more than once from far away, despite its constant fateful residence in his own life, body, and brain, Anlut ceased to breathe. He stood on the cliff-top, motionless, and, for an instant, barely conscious.

Just as it had years ago for the shaman, in that instant too Ulkioket half turned his head.

This was like the flirtatious gesture of some girl, something never offered to Anlut, this partial looking over a shoulder—

The hero saw the human eye of Ulkioket, black in its star-sparkling white, and the slanted lids holding it. Anlut blinked his own unhuman green-blue eyes. He let go his breath and drew in another. No smoke came from his mouth as it would have had he been human; he was not warm enough to cause it.

On the cliff, he watched until the dragon turned away and walked on over the tundra.

Then he hurried down the cliff-face and began again his striding run, going much faster now, following the interrupted pattern of the pad-marks and the storm mark of the tail.

Now he seldom glanced to either side. He stared ahead after Ulkioket.

He was midnight blue, the dragon, and the starlight streamed over him like rushes of summer water. The plain went on and on, and for some hours Anlut had a perfect view. Never before had he been afraid, but now the hero was. He was afraid he might lose sight of Ulkioket around some twist of the land, might lose him even. Faster and faster Anlut ran, till even he breathed swiftly, and in his own ears he heard the drum of his heart—*Umb-umber umber umber—*

ꝗꝸ

A memory came while he was running, when the full moon rose, from nowhere, moon and memory together. The memory was of being in the hot womb of his mother and how he hammered there and shouted, not knowing what he did. Probably, he thought, he was demanding to be born.

Then the cold breath blew. The cold was not horrible. The cold did not frighten.

After the remembering, came thought. The thought suggested that he had cried to and for the cold, it was the coldness which *let* him be born, and otherwise, without it, he might have died, for the woman who carried him could not have borne him successfully, she was not strong enough. Both she and he would have perished. But instead the ice came. And he lived though she did not.

After remembering and thought, he considered.

He considered the long, sharp knife and the spear and his own great strength. His heroism and destiny.

Exactly then, the twist appeared in the landscape, mountains of snow and ice, and the dragon moved around them. Was gone.

ꝗꝸ

THE shadow fell all along the ice. It was not cast by the curve of the mountain around which Anlut had just sped. The moon was lower now. It flamed like a pale, ancient ruby, just behind the gigantic crest of the dragon, which sat there almost wolf-like, its front legs stretched out, head raised, regarding him from its human eyes. Now those eyes looked very large indeed. And the clawed, scaled forefeet rested on the shadow and the ice not thirty feet away.

Anlut could easily have slid one of his hands between any two of the steely claws.

It was clear that it beheld him. It *regarded* him.

And he regarded it. Him.

Ulkioket. Winter. Enemy.

The hero sensed that his adversary watched, thought, considered. Perhaps even he remembered—other men he had glimpsed in the moments of slaughtering them.

Anlut waited.

But Ulkioket waited too. Had even sat there, it seemed, to wait until Anlut might catch up to him.

Anlut raised the spear and the long knife, to show Ulkioket why he had come.

And then Anlut sang, in his lean, metallic voice, one of the old songs of the tribes, about the winter and man's constant war with it. He did this also to demonstrate, should the ice dragon be in any doubt, why he was here. And to honour the dragon.

Thus man, from pass of sun to rise.
From rise to passing, fights with iron blood
And heart of fire.
To win each battle in that never-ending war
That winter is, till life is laid to sleep among a mound of stones.
And snow wipes out all trace
Of tears or songs.

The song continued some while. The dragon sat, seeming to attend.

Under all, a piping, a faint drum, the wind melodiously provided accompaniment.

When Anlut completed the song, the stars were more sparse, and the moon was just a copper smudge. The colossal shadow had spread across everything. Ulkioket reflected a glittering black, and Anlut himself a type of twilight colour.

Silence filled the world.

Then the dragon got up. Yes—his great head must have touched the roof of the sky for stars, scraped off perhaps by accident, all at once hurtled down, gleaming and noiselessly spitting, fading, dead.

Anlut saw the vast expansion of the dragon's sides as the bellows of Ulkioket's lungs sucked at the air, swallowing it, in and in. Anlut heard the sound where no other sound was to be heard. Ulkioket was filling himself with breath, which in a few moments he would breathe *out* again upon the hero. It was the ice-breath that killed all living things, froze them and mounded them over, not with stones but with ice.

Did Anlut wonder then if even he, born out of the blast-ice-breath long before, could withstand this attack?

Never. Or rather, it did not occur to him.

In amazement, almost a curious kind of religious awe, he observed what Ulkioket did.

Then: an instant of stasis. The dragon was replete with air.

And after this—

Ulkioket breathed outward.

It was nothing like storm or gale, not even like the freezing clutch of liquid winter sea, or the funnel through the ice up from which Anlut had climbed. No, no, nothing like that.

The breath passed over and through Anlut. His outer skin received it, and his inner body too. It dazzled and burned in his nostrils, in his lungs, his belly, his blood and arteries. His clothing changed instantly to glass which—equally quickly—grew brittle, shattering and falling off him like the stars knocked off the sky by the dragon's crest. His spear became thick with ice and broke as well, and the knife—the knife *melted*, as if in the fire of its making, and curled right up in a serpentine shape, with melted droplets hung there in its new sheath of ice.

But such triumph tore through Anlut too that he shouted aloud. And his voice came out with no difficulty. And when he raised his arms, they rose without trouble. And when he began to spin about and *dance* in the moon-gone dark, his limbs and body obeyed him. Laughing and leaping, he pranced before the dragon of ice. Which watched him then, only sitting back again, paws outstretched, head lowered a little now on the long neck, possibly to see him better.

Eventually, Anlut ran forward and jumped up to balance on the huge right fore-paw. He stood there, laughing and naked, his white hair flying. And he called upwards into the wise, unthinking, *thinking* face with its human eyes.

"You created me. You've fathered your own death in me. Here I am, unkillable by you. Now I need only find a way to destroy *you*, Ulkioket. But breathe again, dragon. I *liked* it. To me—your ice is a hearth-fire. It makes me *warm*."

ԛ֎

LATER, the dragon shifted himself. And as though by prior agreement, Anlut jumped down from the foot he had stood on. There had been no observable response.

When the dragon rose, Anlut gazed up and up the height of him. The sky was black by then and the stars also setting. Without prelude, Ulkioket turned and resumed his inexorable march along the world. In fifty heartbeats, he had climbed far up among the mountains of ice. And in less than thirty heartbeats, Anlut was following him, moving at his trained, unflagging, striding trot.

Like this then, naked and barefoot, unarmed, and now even unsleeping, the hero chased the dragon, as night turned to sunup and sunpass passed back to night, over and over again.

Anlut did not need to consider anything now, save some way to slay Ulkioket. To journey so fast, endlessly, tirelessly, without any protection from the winter, was no problem for him. Presumably he had only worn clothes or carried weapons from thoughtless custom, one more learned thing that was actually useless to him. Nor did he need to eat, which at first faintly surprised him when he remembered it. Nothing then, truly nothing but the chase mattered. The chase—and any weapon that might survive the dragon's blast of breath and penetrate his scaled surface.

That Anlut's garments and knife had been obliterated or ruinously transformed, as such items never were in the case of any of the dragon's victims that Anlut had ever before seen, appeared to be the result of Anlut's own total resistance to the ice-blast. Caught between him and the dragon's force, they had become a sort of sacrifice, like driftwood in flames.

As the sunpasses and darknesses uncoiled in months, the terrain altered, grew similar to earlier terrain, became different again, familiar again. But one last idea stayed fixed in Anlut's dragon-occupied mind.

He and the dragon were equal.

Therefore, something must come from this. The *answer* must come from this.

Whenever the dragon rested, then Anlut rested too. He lay about a hundred feet away, or a little less perhaps. He did not sleep; neither, he thought, did the dragon. Yet sometimes, though awake, Anlut seemed to himself to have left his own cold, hard body, and to be standing right beside Ulkioket. Then, in his trance-state, the hero *examined* his quarry.

All the while. Through his shining, unreadable, human eyes, Ulkioket in turn watched Anlut, or his dream-ghost, moving round him. Never at this time did the dragon use the blast of his breath against the man.

Nor did the dragon ever apparently attempt to outdistance Anlut by any major amount.

✿

IT was midwinter.

The Northland lights blazed in the sky, wild purple and bronze and wolf-eye yellow.

And coming over the hill, down which the dragon had preceded him, Anlut saw a village below, there against the frozen edges of the sea.

Anlut's heart seemed to stop.

Then it shouted to him: *Umber! Umber! Umber!*

Maybe Ulkioket walked more leisurely now. His tail moved after him in shimmering riverine eddies.

Anlut broke into new speed. He raced. He flew.

Down the hill, over the ice, running till he ran beside the river of the tail, leaping it over and over as it lashed across his path.

By the huge feet of Ulkioket, Anlut sped. Up level with the tower of the breast and head and neck. Then *past* him—past the dragon, forward along the plain. Anlut bolted to the open snow about half a mile above the village.

Here he turned, breathed in the bitter crystal of the night, sucking up breath to yell.

"No further!" he ranted to the dragon, as it stepped and swung nearer and nearer. Holding up his arms, Anlut bellowed through the dome of lights. "*No!* Let them *be!*"

His voice came sure and loud; even in the distant misty village of ice-towers, where smokes must rise as women cooked, and the men were mending, and the sled-wolves waiting for cuts of meat and bones, and the boys playing with a rag ball, even *there*, they must hear the curious sound, not knowing what it was, or that it cried to save them.

The dragon too came to a stop.

He gazed at Anlut, and in the dragon's eyes, the hero noticed, for the very first time, a strangeness, perhaps great intelligence, a sort of compassion—pity.

While the huge body swelled, Ulkioket's lungs filling up and up with the crystal air that Anlut had already dragged into his own.

The blast-breath was being prepared. At any second, it would be un-leashed. The village would freeze, dead in three seconds. All those lives—

Anlut hurtled forward. He was springing to tear out, with his bare hands, the dragon's tongue—its teeth—the tender, merciful eyes—when the gust of murder erupted.

Caught in the savage force of it, Anlut was flung upward into that crystal air. It seemed to him he felt his back slam against the flickering arch of the Northland lights. Breath was knocked from him. He fell earthward again, and landed at the dragon's feet. The vast head, dwarfing his body, leant near.

Anlut could not move. He lay and stared, wondering if now, against all former evidence, he too would die. But he had not been frozen, only winded. As his vision cleared, he beheld every delicate graven scale on Ulkioket's forehead. The dragon smelled only of ice and open land. A golden thought seemed to move in his right eye. Without doubt merely a reflection of the lights.

Then Ulkioket moved back several of his own paces, which took him a great distance away.

Anlut pushed himself to his feet, shook himself. He was not hurt, not even bruised. But his cold blood boiled with frustration and fury, a terror and despair that never before had he felt in all his life.

He cursed the dragon, using half-remembered maledictions of the tribes. He shouted now a kind of lament, almost wordless. *Yes,* it said, *I have failed. I've found no means to kill you. But once more, this time in front of me, you have slain my fellow-men.*

Never in the past had he felt such connection to or sorrow for humankind. He, who was, at his roots, mortal. Yet in the human eyes of the dragon, surely Anlut had glimpsed pity.

The hero turned from Ulkioket and the unachievable task of ending him. The hero glared towards the murdered village by the ice-armoured sea.

Anlut's heart stopped for the second time.

Through low mist, under the flutter of lights, was that smoke which rose still on the shore? The ice-towers—still visible? And something ran there—what—*what*? A little sled with perhaps a tiny figure on it, drawn by six tiny pale things—living wolves . . . ?

Looking behind him, Anlut found that the dragon had vanished. Silent as mist, Ulkioket had slid away from him, left him. He could see the marks of the reptilian feet, and where these disappeared at a place of harder ice.

Anlut searched a time, up and down. Of the dragon he could discover nothing else, and it came to Anlut that the dragon-like iridescence overhead had helped disguise Ulkioket's going away.

In a sort of bleak madness finally, defeated, the hero went towards the village. The sled had vanished too by then—he had imagined it obviously.

But—smokes still lifted, unless it was the mist. The ice-towers stood—unless

they were *only* ice.

Could Anlut have deflected or absorbed the blast of death? He did not think so, although he had done all he could. And even in his turmoil, he could feel the joyous warmth of the blast tingling in him. Like a promise, or a birthright.

ℜ

WHEN he was near, the head wolves began to yap a warning. But all about the signs lay that the ice-breath had reached this far. Indeed blast-ice had partly formed, standing up in a jagged unfinished palisade, thin as damaged glass. Over a low wall, made only of ordinary ice-brick, Anlut saw five of the guard wolves padding up.

They were white. No, it was more than that. Though heavily furred, there was a sort of shift and shimmer on them, a waver of the colours now streaming along the sky and off into the west. The eyes of the wolves were cold blue, like the hearts of bergs in miniature.

Then the girl came walking up to the wall. In her hand, she carried a small stone fire-pot, which, as a shaman's sometimes did, also flamed aquamarine. She was clothed—but for modesty, he thought, not need—in light summer sealskin garments. Her skin and hair were white, smooth, reflecting, mirroring pink and ochre from the sky. Her eyes were a brighter icier green even than Anlut's own. She astonished him. Anlut had never really seen a hint of *himself* before in any human.

"Welcome, brother," she said to him, in the language of humankind. "Never fear. I was afraid, when first I came here. Afraid to find others like myself. Then I was glad. You'll come to this also."

Maybe foolishly he said to her, "I am Anlut, of the Lut."

She answered. "I am Setmaraq, of the Telu." She nodded, and showed him the way through the wall. Half-hypnotized, he went by, and so entered the village.

They walked along the packed snow between the ice-towers of one or two storeys. It seemed that some hundred or so people lived here. Except that they were not people. He saw many of them about. And they saw him. None acted as if startled or afraid. They greeted him briefly, as if he were known to them. He and they were almost doubles. Each and every one.

Even the wolves and he resembled each other. Even the other animals, which he spotted here and there as he walked along the path—two foxes with mirror coats and eyes of blue ember, three sky-shimmered deer that stared at him from mild eyes indigo as some deep glacier.

Setmaraq took him to a smaller tower, and through the entrance tunnel into the high-shelfed room. Here a lamp burned low, but, as they arrived, the flame leapt up three full feet. She must be a shaman. There was no other fire, no food. No weapons or skins or pelts hung or lay about, and just a single stone knife and some iron needles were on the shelf, necessary only perhaps for the cutting of hair or the shaping of clothes.

Anlut sat down when she suggested it. Setmaraq sat opposite.

They might have lived here together for many years, they were so at ease with each other. A pair of the wolves slunk in next to join them. Neither hustled nor complained, nor seemed anxious to be fed. No bones lay outside for any animal to forage after. There was no odour of cooking or meat, yet there was a faintly animal and human scent. It calmed Anlut nearly stupidly, for he did not know what had become of him.

They sat a long while, not speaking. Then Setmaraq drew up a pipe made of hardened driftwood. She began to play a solemn music, like the quieter winds.

As he listened, every question he might ask her rushed into his head—then left it. For every question was answered in the instant it occurred. These beings. Like him, they had been formed as mortal embryos inside the womb of a mortal woman, and possibly they would have died there, for whatever reason. But then the ice-blast of the dragon came, and froze everything—but some things it only changed. These people, exactly like Anlut, had been fathered by Ulkioket, or by some other one also an Ulkioket, of the *tribe* that was Ulkioket. They were the Children of the Dragon.

They could not harm the dragon, nor could the dragon harm them. And winter could not harm them either, as all other living things might be harmed by winter. The animals too that were to be seen here, in the same or some like manner, they had come to life instead of death when Ulkioket breathed on them. They were the Creatures of the Dragon. Nothing could or would harm them. No dragon, no man, no aspect of the warlike winter cold.

Did they then *know*, if only sometimes, what they had achieved, the ice dragons? Surely. Why else did they bring such successful hybrids here? Why else had Anlut's dragon summoned him, and brought him here also?

They sat all night, the man and the woman, then the sun undid the low wall of the east, and climbed one-eighth part up the sky.

I am not a hero. I am born of a new-made race. I am not at war.

Just then a small child, white-haired, mirror-lit, eyes like green amber, trotted into the house and, for no reason, laughed at him, as sometimes fearless children did laugh at adults. Then it galloped out again and away.

"My sister's baby," said Setmaraq.

This too, then—they could make children. *This too.*

But "They are all your sisters," Anlut simply said.

"And all my brothers," she said.

"You called *me* brother."

"Or husband. Shall I call you that instead?"

He nodded. There was no more to say. His heart beat well and gently. Sixteen years of wrongness were melting from him in the delirious warmth of Setmaraq's foodless, fireless, sleepless, deathless, frozen house of snow.

The Dragon's Tale

Tamora Pierce

Bestselling author Tamora Pierce is the creator of the Tortall universe, home to the Song of the Lioness quartet, which consists of Alanna: The First Adventure, In the Hand of the Goddess, The Woman Who Rides Like a Man, and Lioness Rampant, as well as the Immortals quartet, Wild Magic, Wolf-Speaker, Emperor Mage, and The Realms of the Gods, and sequels or related books such as Terrier, Trickster's Choice, and Trickster's Queen. Her other major series is the Circle of Magic sequence, made up of Sandry's Book, Tris's Book, Daja's Book, and Briar's Book, as well as several sequels or related books such as Magic Steps, Street Magic, Cold Fire, Shatterglass, The Will of the Empress, and Melting Stones. She is also the author of the four-volume Protector of the Small series, consisting of First Test, Page, Squire, and Lady Knight. With Josepha Sherman, she coedited the anthology Young Warriors: Stories of Strength. Her latest book is a new Tortall novel, Bloodhound. She lives in Syracuse, New York.

In the clever tale that follows, set in her Tortall universe, you meet a dragon trying her level best to do The Right Thing, and who finds that you never regret not being able to speak more than when you have something really important to say.

ᕓᕗ

BORED. I was bored, bored, bored. If I spoke as two-leggers did, I could have made "bored" into a chant. I hated it that I could not speak to humans or animals. I could not even speak mind to mind, as Mama Daine does with the beast-People. Many humans called me a thoughtless animal or even a monster. It made me want to claw them head to toe, though I am not that sort in general. If I could talk to them, they would know I was intelligent and friendly. I could walk among them and explain myself. Instead, I had to sit up on this overlook, waiting for my foster parents to

introduce me to yet another village full of two-leggers who had never met
a dragon before.

I could have stayed in the realms of the gods with Daine and Numair's
human children and their grandparents instead of taking this journey. I
could have spent these long days playing with them and the god animals. I
could have even visited my own relatives. Instead, I thought that it would be
fun to visit Carthak with my foster parents. Thak City and the palaces, new
and old, were interesting. Humans create pretty buildings. The Carthakis
in particular make splendid mosaics. There were ships to see, statues, fire-
works, human magic displays, and the emperor and his empress. I liked the
onetime Princess Kalasin, who was now the Carthaki empress.

Then Emperor Kaddar decided it would be wonderful to travel some
of his country with Numair and Daine. Kalasin had to stay in the new
palace and govern while Kaddar took the road. I remained with Daine,
Numair, and Kaddar as we journeyed east, where Kaddar stopped at
every oasis and town to talk. The village of Imoun looked to be an ordinary stop on that trip. It was a small clump of humans who lived beside
the river Louya and the Demai Mountains.

We had arrived halfway through the afternoon. The soldiers helped
us set up Daine and Numair's tent above the camp, on a spot where it
overlooked the rest of our tents. When they were done, I walked up to a
flat stone outcrop where I could watch the rest of the day unfold. I don't
know why I bothered. It was the same as it had been for the last twenty
villages. The soldiers put up the platform, then covered it in carpets and
decorated it with pillows and bolsters. The important humans would talk
with Kaddar there later. More soldiers placed magical globe lights on posts
around the platform, so everyone would be able to see when it got dark.
Villagers built fires around the platform to warm the humans once the sun
went down.

I never watched the setting-up from close by. Early on, I had learned
that I was always getting in the way of those who set up the platform and
everything around it, even when I tried not to. The guards would complain
to Papa Numair about me. The villagers only screamed and ran. Finally,
Kaddar asked me nicely to stay away. It's not Kaddar's fault that his people
had never encountered anyone like me.

The soldiers learned. Some of them still treated me like Daine and
Numair's pet, though my humans had explained many times that I was as
clever as any two-legger. A few of the soldiers learned for themselves that
I did indeed understand what they said.

Although I was brooding, I had not forgotten to listen to the world around me. I heard the horse that was climbing to my position. I knew who it was without looking because I recognized the sound of his breathing. When Spots reached me, I pointed to the line where all of our other horses were tethered. They were happy to stay there, finished with their day's work. Then I made a fist and shook it at him. I wasn't angry. I was reminding him of how the horse guards would react when they found that Numair's very own gelding was gone again. They were lucky that Daine's pony, Cloud, had refused to come because it had meant a boat trip, and Cloud hates those. Cloud and Spots together got into all kinds of mischief.

I don't care if they are angry, Spots told me. Though *I am as mute as a stupid rock with animals, they can talk with me. Daine will defend me. She knows that I like to look around. And who else can keep Numair in the saddle?*

He was right. Years ago, Spots had learned to counter Numair when he let go of the rein or moved off-balance. He was also good at pulling my foster father away from cliff edges and other hazards that Numair tended to find.

Once, Spots had been like any other horse, only more patient and sweet-tempered than most because Numair was his rider. I barely remember that Spots. Like any creature who lived near my foster mother, Daine, for a long enough time, he grew more clever as humans judge such things. Numair calls it "the Daine effect." Spots began to help my foster parents in their work. He watched me when I was small. That was when we found ways to talk to each other, with sounds and gestures.

How long will we be here, do you suppose? Spots asked me. *It doesn't look like a very interesting place.*

I shrugged. I didn't know how many days we were going to stay. No one ever asked what *I* wanted. Spots nudged me with his nose and stuck his lower lip out.

I glared at him. I was *not* pouting.

"Kit, I can hear you scratching rock down at our tent." Daine walked up the slope to us, tying her curling brown hair in a horse tail. "It's a dreadful noise. I thought you were chewing stones. Oh, Spots, you undid your tether again. You know it makes folk nervous when you do that." She cocked her head, listening as Spots replied, mind to mind. She slung his rein up over his back, so he wouldn't trip on it. "I know Kitten digs at the stone because she's unhappy." Daine sat beside me and reached over to pat the rock. I looked. I had gotten so cross, watching the humans prepare for more talking, that I had gouged my claws deep into the rock at my side several times.

"It looks like you're trying to slice it for bread," Daine told me.

I gave her my sorry-chirp and leaned against her. I wished so much that I could talk to her in more than noises! Spots stretched around Daine and nuzzled the back of my head.

"You're bored, aren't you, poor thing?" asked Daine. "At least Spots can talk to the other horses. Which reminds me," she said, turning to look at him. "Back to the ranks with *you*, magical escaping horse. The soldiers fear they'll be punished if one of the mounts vanishes."

Spots snorted, but he did walk, slowly, back down to the tethering lines.

I was still shocked by what Daine had said about me. How did she always *know* how I felt?

"At home, you usually have something to busy yourself with," she said, running her cool fingers over my snout. "We might have left you in the capital, but the only person there who knows you well is Empress Kalasin. *She* can hardly take you about."

I whistled my agreement. Kalasin had to rule the empire.

"We thought we'd see more of the sights, didn't we?" Daine asked. "But this, Kit, it's a wonderful thing, for Kaddar to meet with his people. Normally he'd travel with all manner of ceremony, and the local folk would be too frightened to say a word to him. With me and Numair to guard, and only a hundred soldiers instead of a thousand, he's approachable. They will talk to him and tell him the truth."

I made my rudest noise. Human truth-telling was a mixed quantity at best. There were always untruths and evasions of some kind mixed in.

Daine looked sideways at me. "Oh, all right. As much truth as folk will tell their emperor. It's a good thing Numair and I are the only ones who speak, Kitten. *You* are not suited to a life of diplomacy."

I made a lesser rude noise. Dragons do not use diplomacy. We are not good at it.

I heard the new visitors before I saw them. Daine and I looked down. Twenty fluffy-tailed mice had come to meet her. This sort of thing always happened when Daine was about. I loved it.

"Well, look at you!" Daine said, opening the pouch at her belt. She *always* carries food for small animals with her. A few of the mice climbed up on Daine, holding on to her shirt or sitting on her shoulders, arms, and legs. She offered them dried raisins and sunflower seeds, inquiring mind to mind after their families and winter food supplies. A pair of the braver mice climbed up on me, which made me happy. Too often I remind small prey animals of snakes or cats.

At last, the mice said their farewells and ran into the rocks. Daine straightened with a grimace and looked at the sky. Dark was coming. Soldiers were lighting the fires below. The platform was finished. I smelled good things being prepared by the villagers and the emperor's cooks.

"I'll make sure a dish is brought to our tent for you," Daine told me.

I cawed at her. I hated the tent, and Daine knew it!

"We got here too late to take you about and show you to the local folk; you know we did," Daine said. "And two-leggers *always* startle more when they see you after dark. I'm sorry. Just stay in the tent for tonight. Tomorrow, I'll introduce you to the village."

I knew she was right, but what was there to do in the tent? I gave her my saddest whistle and walked away. I had already gone through everything in Numair's mage kit, and in Daine's. I had even read all of the books they had brought along.

Humans were so *stupid*. They likened me to a crocodile or some kind of lizard, though surely they should have known that those creatures did not have silver claws or rudimentary wings, let alone the ability to change color. They also did not stand on their haunches and chirp in a reassuring way, indicating that they would like to be friends. My muzzle was far more delicate than that of a crocodile, and my teeth stayed inside it! I was slender, and fine-boned. I was only forty-five inches long in those days, and fifteen inches of that was tail. Yet somehow there were always humans who were terrified by the sight of me. To cater to such idiots, I was kept to my foster parents' tent when there was no time to introduce me in a new place.

It was hard to stay inside. I could hear music and laughter, the welcome that came before the boring speeches. One of the emperor's soldiers—one of my friends—brought me a bowl of stew. I chirped happily at him: he'd remembered I liked honey-nut pastries and gave me two. After he left, I was alone. My boredom soon reached the point at which I might shriek if I didn't do something. Since Daine only liked me to shriek during combat, I was really doing the right thing for Daine if I took a walk instead.

I wriggled under the back flap of the tent. On that side lay mountains, their ridges and peaks sharp in the light of the half-moon. A small herd of screwhorn antelope was climbing to higher pastures, away from the noise.

They were just as visible to my dragon eyes as they would have been with no moon at all.

When I could no longer see the antelope, I concentrated on my scales. I changed color according to my mood; my parents knew that. They did not know that, over the long journey, I had learned to change colors deliberately. I let my magic spread out and around me, collecting the shades of shadowed sand, reddish limestone, black lava rock, gray-green brush, and moonlit air. I drew the colors back into patches over my scales. Then I set out for the village.

I was about to pass through the gate when I heard the very distant sound of young humans whispering together. Since I am always curious, I followed the faint noise around the outside of the wall, away from the meeting of the emperor and his people. Soon the voices were clearer. They belonged to boys, excited ones.

"Look! She's at it again!"

"She don't learn."

"You got rocks? Gimme some."

Four boys crouched in the shadows around the ruins of a shed. They were barefoot, their clothes mostly patched. I halted, secure in my camouflage, waiting to see what had their attention. The village garbage heap lay in a dip in the ground nine yards or so away from the boys. A young woman was sifting through the heap, collecting pieces of food and stowing them in a basket on her arm, working by feel and scant moonlight. Magic burned at the heart of her, the stuff called the Gift that humans put to use like a servant. Could she not make money with her Gift, as so many mages do, and buy food?

The thinnest of the boys crept forward and threw the first rock. He missed by a foot.

The other three ran up to hurl stones at the woman. One hit her shoulder; another struck her leg; the third missed. She dropped the vegetable she'd been holding, but she made no sound. Instead, she knelt and scrabbled to get the vegetable into her basket. The boys threw more stones. All four hit this time. She half turned, catching them on her shoulders and back. Then she grabbed one and threw it sharply, striking the thinnest boy hard in the belly. While the others took care of him, she scrambled to her feet and ran, ignoring their shouts of anger.

The boys gave chase. I followed on all fours, trying to think of what I could do that would stop them without permanently injuring them. In normal battles, no one cares if I split someone's skull or shatter his bones with a whistle. I can throw fire, but that is just as fatal. These were human children. Daine, Numair, and Kaddar would be very angry with me if I killed children.

The open ground before us gleamed in the dim moonlight. Here the mountains reached into the flatlands with long, stony black fingers that dug into the pale earth, leaving bays of light-colored dirt and brush between them. The woman ran for the bays, clutching her basket to her chest. The boys were hard on her trail. In addition to calling her vile names, they said that she had no business stealing their garbage. I wished I could ask the woman, or them, what they meant. Perhaps it was some odd local custom. Everywhere else I had been, garbage was made of things humans had no more use for.

Suddenly the race ended. While the woman ran from my sight between two black stone fingers, the boys began to act very strangely. They separated and ran about, skirting areas as if there were obstacles in the way. They never strayed from the open ground between the garbage heap and the rocks.

At last, they came together, panting and exhausted. I crouched flat, listening.

"We searched those rocks everywhere, but she vanished!" the thin one said.

"Every time we think we got Afra cornered, she goes into the Maze," said another, a male with a long scar on his face.

The Maze? I wondered. I had seen no maze, though the boys *had* moved on the open ground as if they walked such a thing.

"You'd think the rock itself hid her," grumbled the third boy.

The four of them drew the Sign against evil on their chests. "I tole you Afra was a witch," said the one whose clothes were a little better than the other boys'. "Witches do that. They vanish right in front of you."

That was pure nonsense. Numair is one of the greatest mages in all the world. *He* cannot do it unless the spell is already prepared. The female, Afra, had used no spells at all that I had seen. Her Gift was visible to me, but she had not employed it, nor did she wear any spell-charms.

"We have to warn the emperor!" the scarred one said. "Afra might cast a spell against his life!"

The four turds raced away, eager to tell a man guarded by my foster parents that their witch, who was too generous to singe *them*, was a danger to him. Like most humans, they didn't realize that an emperor would never venture so far from his palaces unless he was very well guarded. I *did* think that perhaps the boys had seen Numair and mistaken him for someone who was silly. Many people do.

I followed Afra into the rocky bays where she had gone to hide. I wanted to learn if she knew of the power that had not only made her escape route invisible to the boys but made them believe they had walked some kind of maze.

Ten feet from the first stony finger, I walked into magic of a kind I had never encountered. My experience of magic even at that time was great, yet this was unknown to me. I had not found it in visits to the realms of the gods or to the Dragonlands. Nor had I felt anything like it in all my dealings with humans, Gifted or born with any form of wild magic. Even the spirits of mountains, trees, rivers, and streams had nothing like this.

Numair says that magic is a sense for dragons as much as smell and hearing. The strangeness of this new power made my scales prickle.

I called it "new," but it was that only to me. As the strange force trickled across my face and made my licking tongue quiver, I could tell it was old. It might even be older than my grandfather, Diamondflame, who owns to several thousands of years. Where did this power come from? Who had placed it here?

I took a deep breath. The scent of the power entered my nose and burned, making my eyes water. I tried a smaller breath and thanked the Dragongods that Afra carried rotting food. That stench fought the magic's scent. I took three steps. The strange power thrust at me, trying to stop me. I whistled at it softly, pushing back with my own air-carried magic. My power balanced against that older one as I walked forward.

Three feet. I slammed into a solid wall of magic that flared a hot white in my eyes. My softer whistle did nothing to that. I was too impatient to work my way up through lesser whistles. I used a midlevel squawk, good for shattering drawbridges. It was enough too for this barrier, which melted. I walked on into a third magic that poured down between two rocks, a flash flood that blazed green with red and blue sparks. I had no time to think. I yowled at the top of my lungs, fearing what might happen if I failed.

The flood vanished.

Far in the distance, I heard humans cry out, demanding to know what was going on. (I heard them talk later about a leopard.) High in the mountains to the east, beyond the humans' sense of hearing, I heard a rockslide. I cringed. If Daine shaped her ears to those of an animal that heard well, I was in *serious* trouble.

When nothing more happened, and no humans came, I went on, following my nose. The scent of rotting garbage led me to a cave set in a mass of orange stone, partway up a black rock divide. Its opening was tucked around a bend in the trail, easily missed if no one knew it was there. Flat stones lay before the cave, so no footprints would ever give a dweller away. Light from a lamp or candle shone from its depths. She had to feel safe there.

I poked my head inside.

She gasped, then cried, "Monster! Get out!"

She was quick to find a rock and throw it at me, painfully quick. It struck my head. I ducked out and waited, holding my paws to the nasty bruise on my forehead. After a moment, I shielded myself in protective spells and looked inside. She screamed and threw a blaze of her Gift at me. I backed out again. Her Gift had not touched me, but I understood why she was so frightened and why she needed any food that she could find. Her baby had begun to cry.

It was time to think matters through. Turning what I now knew over in my head, I returned to the imperial camp. I needed to obtain a few things.

჉

I had just returned from my scavenging when I heard Daine and Numair. The long talk was over; they were returning. I smoothed a layer of spells over the items I had procured. When my mage-parents looked at my nest of blankets, they would see only the back of the tent behind me, not the other things. It was tricky to work out something that would fool Daine and Numair, but I'd done it.

They would have been glad to help if I had let them know about Afra, but they always helped. I didn't need that. I wanted to do it by *myself*, in part because I was bored, in part to prove to them—to myself—that I could. I needed something of my own to do. If I had not tamed Afra by the time we had to leave, I would let my parents know about her.

I curled up in my blankets and pretended to sleep just as they entered our tent. They spoke quietly while preparing for bed. They said that the villagers had told Emperor Kaddar about a number of problems. They were hard for local folk to handle all at once, but their emperor and his companions could take care of them easily if they cared to do so. Kaddar and his men would seek a robber gang that operated in the mountain pass five miles to the east. Daine would see to illnesses among the village herds, while Numair cleared the river channel of the water weeds that choked it. We might be here for as long as a week, even two. That would give me more time to work with Afra.

In the morning, when dawn just brushed the mountains, and my parents slept, I tied my things in a small bundle. Disguised in the colors of barely lit earth and stone, I returned to the place where the boys had acted as if they were lost in a maze of boulders.

When the first shock of alien magic crackled against mine, I was ready. In the pale light, I saw it only as a blurring of everything that lay beyond. From sandy earth with its patches of scrub brush, to the black mountain stone, the strange power remade it into softness. It gave this land a more forgiving face.

When I touched it, the magic ran over my scales. It felt different than it had the night before. This time it was like a thousand tiny hands explored me from crest to tail tip. I banished that thought. Grandfather Diamondflame and Numair would scold me for letting imagination color what I observed. I walked slowly into the magic's growing resistance, seeing the boys' tracks from last night, then my own footprints, off to my right.

Next, I met the second, more resistant, wall. I didn't see it. I simply walked into it and felt it give a little as I stopped. Again, there was something new, like a pause, as if the magic waited to see what I would do. I shook the peculiar thought from my skull. It was a leftover from sixteen years among humans.

I had spent the night considering my encounters with this magic. I did not want to risk using sounds by daylight, for fear of drawing attention. If the villagers got frightened enough, they would call on Kaddar, who would call on my foster father. When Numair found this magic, I would no longer have the riddle to solve for myself. I didn't doubt that my papa could probably shatter these barriers easily.

Resting a paw against this barrier, I called up the spell I had prepared and blew it forward. The only sound I made was a long, soft hiss. The magic flowed out between my teeth, eating the barrier like acid. It vanished before my spell could devour it all, and I went forward with my bundle.

I was ready for that third defense, the flood of magic, but it never came. Had I exhausted it last night? I wished I knew who had set these protections. Surely whoever it was had died long ago. Perhaps the mage had been an Ysandir, one of the ancient race alive at the same time that human civilization was beginning to grow. That might account for the total strangeness of the magic's feel. It did not account for Afra's ability to pass it without effort, however.

With no more barriers to fight, I found a hidden place near the cave, where I left my bundle. I reviewed my plan. After last night, I knew I could not rely on the cute tricks that worked with those who knew me best.

First, I had to investigate. I wrapped myself in silence, then climbed up into the rocks and over to Afra's cave. She would not hear my lightest claw scratch or the slide of my scales. Then I positioned myself above the entrance to listen. It was so delightful, where I lay. Unlike the black rock, this orange stone was fine-grained and warm, far warmer than it should have been with sunrise just begun. I had an odd fancy that the stone was breathing, which was impossible. Grandfather Diamondflame would have scolded me roundly for so foolish an idea. Yet I could not stop myself from stroking that warm stone like a pet as I listened for what Afra might be doing, deep within her cave.

Light smoke flowed up from the entry and over my nose. I sniffed: mint tea. Other smells disguised those of rotten food: garlic, ginger, and onion. I smelled another thing, one I knew from the times after Daine gave birth to my human sister and brother. It was mother's milk. Afra was nursing her baby. She would not be leaving her hiding place right away.

I backed away from the cave entrance, then halted. I wanted to stay right there, spread over the warm and breathing stone. I didn't understand. I was no lizard, to doze my life away on any sun-washed rock!

Finally, I ordered myself to stop being a fluffbrain, a word Daine often used. I went back to my bundle. From it, I chose some of the food I had stolen and carried it to the front of the cave. There I left my offering: a small goat cheese, dates, olives, and several rounds of bread.

Then I returned to my hiding place, sheltered by chilly, normal black rock. I could not hear the sounds inside the cave as well as before, but the black stone did not give me strange ideas, either. I drew my camouflage spell around me, just in case, and waited.

Soon I heard Afra's footsteps as she came to the cave's entrance. With my camouflage in place, I eased up to a spot from which I could see her. She stepped into the daylight, sure of the power that hid her retreat in the rocks. She was so confident that she almost crushed my gift before she saw that it was there. Then she jumped back into the cave, vanishing into the darkness.

I waited. Soon she returned, crouching in the shelter of the cave's mouth, peering around like a frightened creature. She had a rock in each hand. Only her head moved. She was listening for any noise.

In the distance, I heard the village goats and sheep as their shepherds took them to graze in the lands not hidden by the barriers. A rooster in the village suddenly remembered that he had duties of his own. As he cried his name, other roosters joined in.

Afra's eyes strayed more and more to the bundle of food. I wondered if her nose was as dead as most humans', or if she could smell the cheese, at least. I scolded myself for not bringing hot meat. She would have smelled that.

She licked her lips. She *could* smell the cheese.

Slowly, she put down her rocks. She rubbed her hands as her Gift moved into her fingers. She wasn't able to do magic without some gestures, then. For anything subtle, she would need to write the signs in the air. She would require special herbs, oils, or stones for more. Did she have them? It would be good to know.

She wrote a sign for safety before her face. In the sunlight, I could see the color of her Gift at last. I rocked back on my heels. Afra's sign was shaped in pale blue light, outlined in pale green. I nearly whistled my excitement, then caught myself. None of my human friends except Papa had magic in two colors. Numair's books spoke of such people, but he said he'd never met anyone else. He would be so glad to meet Afra once I had tamed her!

Had she borrowed her baby's power? I asked myself. Perhaps *this* explained how she had passed through the magic that turned the village boys around, but not her.

Afra completed her spell and set it in motion. It fell onto the food, oozing over it. Within a breath it had vanished, sinking into everything. The scales stood on the back of my neck. I hoped it wouldn't harm the food. Cheese in particular reacts badly to some kinds of magic.

Afra waited, looking all around, still wary. Then she darted forward, seized the food, and ran back into the cave. I guessed that if her spell didn't react, it proved there was no magic on the bundle. I could not see her, but I could hear as she thrust a handful of something into her mouth and chewed. She continued to eat greedily out of my sight as I slowly took the remainder of my stolen goods from my bundle. Daine and I had cared for many starving creatures, so I feared I knew what came next. I had hoped Afra would have better judgment than to stuff herself right away, but I had been wrong. Carefully, retracting my hind claws so they would make no sound on the stone, I carried my next offering to the cave's entrance and left it there. Then I ran back to my hiding spot.

I was just in time. Afra raced from the cave, her hand to her mouth. She made it to a pocket of sand in the rocks across from me before she spewed everything she had eaten. I cursed myself silently. I should have given her just a mouthful of food to start. She had been living on *garbage*, and I had given her a meal of good fruit and cheese.

She stood there, her back to me, after she'd finished the last of her heaves. I could see bone against her skin where it was not covered by her garment. How was she feeding that baby? She must be giving everything to it and keeping nothing for herself.

A blade of pain stabbed me, an undragonlike hurt. Diamondflame says that sentiment is weakness. Maybe I have been among humans for too long. Or maybe I can never forget that my birth mother had given everything for me.

Finally, Afra straightened, wiping her mouth on her wrist. She knelt and buried her vomit well. I wondered if the magic kept wolves away, if there were wolves in these mountains. I knew there were leopards. Did she use her spells to protect the cave at night, or did the strange magic keep the large killers away, as it did humans?

Afra stumbled back to the cave, unsteady with weakness, and halted when she saw my new gift. She turned. Now she had to know that I had been close, to put that food there, and that maybe I was still close, watching. She scanned the rocks and the ground, searching for any sign of me. I had not left her even my footprints as clues.

It was my first chance to give her a good look. She had the bronze skin of the northern Carthakis, snapping black eyes, and coarse black hair that she tied back with a shred of cloth. She was young and so thin, with strong muscles that stood against her skin. She was trembling, though I could not tell if it was from long weakness or from just vomiting.

Suddenly, she bent and took my second gift of food. She hurried into the cave with it.

I relaxed. I had given her two chicken-and-almond turnovers. I had stolen them, like everything else, from the emperor's cooks. They were mild and should not make her ill if she ate them slowly.

She would need vegetables, fruits, and meat. I would have to find a way to carry more, somehow. In particular, she had also vomited up the cheese. Daine's midwife had been very strict with her on the subject of milk and cheese for a nursing mother. She said they needed that more than any other food and that goat's milk was the best.

I wondered if I could steal a goat.

DAINE found me before I even reached our tent. "Kitten, where were you?" she cried, running up to me. "I've been looking everywhere! We were going to the village, remember?"

I sat up on my hind legs and gave her my cutest, wide-eyed look, with chirp.

Daine glared at me. "None of that, mistress. You've been up to something. You can't fool your ma, remember?"

She was right. It was very discouraging. I settled back on my haunches and looked more seriously at her. I sighed, then clasped my forepaws.

"So you'll tell me when you can. Will it get you in trouble with these folk?" she asked me.

Afra didn't live in the village. The boys had chased her away with stones. She did not belong to the village, and they did not want her there. I shook my head for Daine. The matter of the goat might be hard to explain, but I hadn't taken one yet, so I was not lying.

Daine bent down and picked me up. "Is there anything I can do?" she asked as she carried me to the tent.

I shook my head. This was still my discovery.

We had breakfast with Numair before the villagers came for my parents. When we three walked out of our tent, the strangers flinched at the sight of me and drew the Sign on their chests.

Daine stiffened. "This is Skysong, our dragon," she told them, her voice cold. "When our home was attacked, mages who opened a gate to the Divine Realms drew her mother through just as she was about to give birth." She was careful not to say that it was their old emperor who had sponsored the attack. "I helped Flamewing deliver her little one, but Flamewing herself died protecting us. She left her child in our care. Kitten—that's what we call her—is as friendly as can be. She's saved many lives, human and animal alike."

"Her face looks like a crocodile's," said one of the females, an old and wrinkly one.

Daine drew herself up. Numair settled her with a hand on her shoulder. "Kitten is a dragon," he said to the old woman. "They are more intelligent than even we humans. She understands every word that you say."

"Why doesn't she answer, then?" one of the males wanted to know.

"She is too young," Numair replied. "You will be centuries in the ground when she is able to talk."

That caused them to whisper among themselves. I never understood why people would be awed by that, when they were so unpleasant about my looks. Besides, for all they knew, Numair could have been lying. Still, they accepted his word that I would live much longer than they would, which was quite true, unless I was murdered.

"If you wish your animals looked at, you will learn to like Kitten," Daine told them. "Where I go, she goes. She may even do your creatures more good than I will."

I didn't feel like doing good for anyone in the village walls after the way they had treated Afra.

"Well, Master Numair, we're to take you upriver, if you still wish to go," the male who'd led these humans said. "No horses, if it please you. The ground's too rocky along the riverbank as we head into the mountains. Can't even take a mule that way."

Poor Spots, I thought. He's stuck here again. I looked over at the horse lines to see how he did. Most of the soldiers' mounts were gone, along with the emperor's favorite riding horse. They were bandit hunting. Spots was talking with one of the horses that hauled the wagons. That would amuse him for a little while. He would escape his tether by midday.

Numair and the men left on foot. The women looked at Daine and me, then seemed to come to a silent agreement. "If you will come with us?" the female who had spoken to Daine asked. We all set forward, the talker on Daine's left, the other two behind her. I was on Daine's right. "Two days back, Tahat's chickens got sick. We've locked them in their coop, but that will be useless if it is a curse on the village. We think there is a witch hereabouts."

My ears pricked up. Did they mean Afra? I looked at Daine, and I had to snort. Her lips and nostrils had tightened right up. It would follow that in this village, whose humans had already irritated her by insulting me, she would first be asked to look at chickens. Her grandfather's chickens, the ones she had grown up knowing, were the nastiest, trickiest birds she had ever met in her life. Now, even though she had met dozens of perfectly decent chickens, she could not bring herself to like them. She was certain that their pleasantness to her was just another chicken trick.

If she had hated geese, I would have been more understanding. Geese have made *my* life a misery.

While Daine listened to the chickens' troubles, I let Tahat's children sneak up on me and poke me with their fingers. When a neighbor boy tried to use a stick, I snatched it from him and hissed. That amused the women who were not watching Daine. They seemed to like me better for it. Tahat, who was too worried about her flock to be afraid of me, even brought me a small dish of milk.

Daine saw that and warmed to her. "It's no curse, only bird pox," she said. "You were right to contain them before it spread to the other chickens. I can deal with it." She looked up at the female who seemed to be the leader. "Will you help me?"

I hardly noticed when one of the older children tugged my tail. There were chickens all over the village. I could hear them. If Daine had to check them for this illness, she would not be paying attention to my activities.

First, she had to make friends with the village's chief mage. While she had some kind of tea with that man, I busied myself by acquiring a few things: a round of cheese, four eggs, a woman's robe, two lamb sausages, and more fruit. Covered with camouflage spells and keeping to back paths, I carried those things one at a time outside the open gate, where I piled them against the wall. I hid them with still more camouflage, this time a concealment not just of sight, but of a nest of vipers. I didn't want the dogs to eat my loot.

Last of all, I found an empty grain sack. I rolled it up and carried it outside the gate. First, I was careful to wrap the eggs well in the robe. If they broke there, they could be washed out. I knew that Afra must have a water source, or she could not survive in the cave at all.

Once I had filled my sack with all I had taken, I realized that I had listened to my ambition instead of my sense. I could not carry it. I was much too small. The path from the gate to our tent, or even partway to the invisible maze where Afra hid, was mostly open ground. If I dragged the sack—I was strong enough to do so, despite my size—folk would see the clear trail that the sack would leave in the dirt.

I whistled my vexation. I had a spell I shaped of breath and will to brush away any marks I left on occasions like this. It did take a great deal of concentration. That was easy enough when I was on horseback with Daine, which was the last time I had needed it. It would be tiring if I had to keep an eye open for humans, hold camouflage magic over my sack and me, and drag that sack. I need to quickly reach the rocks, which were perfectly visible to me and invisible to humans.

Again I had to wonder how Afra had found the cave. Did her dual Gift make it possible for her to see through the old barriers on that piece of land? Was the power that hid the cave hers to begin with?

I shook my head as I tied the sack shut with some cord I had found. If she had used her Gift to create an invisible maze in open scrub, I would have been able to see its colors by daylight. Moreover, I would have been able to shatter all of it with my middling squawk. Also, those boys had acted as if their Maze had always been in that place. They were used to it.

Gripping the neck of the sack in my teeth, I wriggled until it lay over my shoulder. There was no one in view inside the gate or outside. I set out, keeping an eye on my surroundings. Far off to my left, the soldiers who had stayed to guard the emperor's camp lazily went about their chores. They had shifted the picketed horses off to a line of trees by the river. I hated to think of my friend Spots cooking in the sun, like I was. No one was following as I struggled away from the gate. The bag slid to and fro as I went forward, so that I half carried, half dragged it. I was leaving an unmistakable track.

I halted briefly and took a deep, deep breath, then blew it into my cupped forepaw. I spun it around, blowing steadily, until I had a tornado as tall as I was. I drove it with my will, sending it over the unmistakable drag mark I'd left in my wake. Back and forth I swept it, then around and around, until the dirt no longer showed the trace of my sack. I kept the tornado with me as I trudged across the open ground. It swept over my trail, whisking my marks to nothing, until I crested a small rise in the ground and went down the far side. Once I was out of view of the road, I released my spinning winds. They scattered into the open air.

I collapsed onto the ground, letting go of my camouflage briefly to rest. How could Daine and Numair do more than two pieces of magic at the same time? I was worn-out only by two, and by the effort of dragging my burden.

I hated being young. And I would be young so much longer than a human child.

I had to get up. There was too much risk of a human stumbling over me. The Carthaki sun was also a hammer on my scales. I rose, wove my camouflage spell again, and began to drag the sack toward the rocks.

I had gone scarcely a hundred yards, and had reached the point of telling myself that I was a poor excuse for a dragon, when a horse called to me. I turned to look. Spots was on my trail, his tether in his mouth. I released my camouflage, let go of the sack, and trilled a welcome. I was so happy to see him!

He trotted to me. *I followed your scent.* His slow, practical voice sounded amused in my mind. *I knew you would have found a way to get into trouble by now. Let go of that bag.* I did as I was bid, with relief. He gripped the neck of the sack and picked it up. It had been big for me. To Spots, it wasn't as nearly heavy as one of Numair's book-stuffed saddle-bags, which he had also carried in this way. *Why did you find something to do without bringing me?* Spots asked. *I always manage the heavy work for you.*

I hung my head. Then I made a fist, shook it at him, and pointed back at the camp. I still didn't want to get him into trouble. Then I touched a claw tip to my chest and pointed to the walled village.

Yes, that is a great deal of walking for a small dragon, Spots said. He always understood me. *And I keep telling you, I will deal with the humans if they want to make trouble for me. It's time they learned that not all horses can be bullied.*

I saw the warlike look in his eye and shook my head. Spots had been getting some strange ideas lately. I squeaked an apology and took his rein in my paw. He nudged me to let me know that he didn't mind if I led him. Moving much faster now that I had his help with my burden, I took him to the rocks.

When we touched the strange magic of the first barrier, Spots shied and yanked on the rein. His yank threw me into the air. I came down with a thud. Spots put down the sack and nuzzled me in apology. *I'm sorry,* he told me, guilt in his mind-voice. *I didn't know there was magic here.* He gripped the sack again.

I showed him two of my claws.

Two magics, Spots said. *How splendid.*

I whistled a shield that covered him nose to tail. I loved him because he let me lead him onward into the magic, through the first barrier. He stood firm while I worked spells to get us through the second barrier. Each time, he calmly went ahead when I chirped. I had not known until that day how much he trusted me.

Once we were through, we hurried to Afra's cave. I knew the sound of hooves ringing on stone would frighten her, but it was the fastest way to take the sack right to the cave's mouth. After we left it there, we retreated to a side trail to wait.

What do you have in there? Spots asked me.

With gestures and poses I explained it was a human female with an infant.

It would be easier to bring Daine or Numair, Spots reminded me. *Not that you ever choose the easy path. I prefer to leave humans to humans, myself.*

I only sniffed at him. Spots always said he liked his life to be boring, but he was always there when I got up to something.

Eventually, the baby began to cry. It cried in loud whoops, then softer ones. I dug my claws into the stone, wishing the noise would stop. Just when I hoped the baby was done, it began to scream. That was when Afra came to take the sack.

She dragged it back into the cave, then called, "Who are you? Why do you help us? If you really wish to be my friend, show yourself!"

Afra didn't think that last night's monster was the one who left food for her today. Yet why demand to see me? What good could it do? I looked up at Spots. He shrugged his withers, a human gesture he'd learned. He didn't know, either.

I didn't want to chatter or make friends. That baby needed its mother's milk, and the best way for its mother to make milk was for her to eat food, and to *drink* milk. That meant I still needed to steal a goat. She was wasting my time. I had only waited to be sure she took the sack at all.

"I know you are still here," she cried. "I heard your horse. You are quite close by; I listened to the hoofbeats."

Kraken spit, I thought.

Spots put his muzzle at the center of my back and pushed. *Do as she asks. We did not raise you to be rude.*

It was an easy thing for him to say. She had not hit him on the head and called him a monster.

I showed him my fist, meaning this would not go well. He nudged me again until I fell onto all four legs. I glared up at him.

I mean it, Kitten, Spots told me. *Go.* He shoved my rump forward, nearly driving my muzzle into the dirt.

I ran as much away from him as toward the cave. The stubborn beast followed. He was determined that Afra should see me. Once he took up for someone, there was nothing he would not do for them. That included ordering me about.

Afra saw Spots first because he was taller. Her quick eyes took in his lack of a saddle or rider, and his knotted tether. Then she saw me.

"You again!" she cried. She flung her hand out. A twining flare of magic, mixed pale blue and pale green ropes that would burn an ordinary mortal to the ground, sped from her fingers.

Afra's spell washed over me. It stung, a little. Then it flowed up, meeting the magical barrier overhead in bursts of gold sparkles. I wanted to grip some, but Afra was not done with me.

Brighter two-colored fires lashed from her hand. I could feel their strength—if they hit me, they would hurt. I raised a shield of my own power that would cover Spots and me. Her Gift splashed against it and was sucked into the magic overhead. It blazed gold.

The earth quivered, an anxious horse about to break free of all control. *Uh-oh,* Spots said. *Did you feel that?*

I looked at Afra. She was intent on working another spell. The earth shook hard, knocking her down. The stones beside the mouth of the cave trembled. If the shake got harder, there was danger to the cave.

Spots and I raced forward together without needing to check with one another. We were old campaigners; we knew what had to be done. The ground rolled. Spots scrambled for footing as small stones fell and hit Afra. Spots lunged and got a mouthful of her robe. I raced past him into the cave. Afra screamed as a large rock fell behind me, half-blocking the cave's mouth.

For a moment, I could not move. Inside the cave, a welcoming warmth enclosed me. It reminded me of how I felt when Daine held me. I thought I heard a whispering song in a strange language I almost knew. Dazed, I touched the cave wall. It was glassy and warm, an assembly of tiny beads. I wanted to stay there forever.

Then the baby screamed. Somehow I forced myself to break that spell of love and safety to walk deeper into the cave. Another shake inspired me to run, my night vision showing me all the dangers. Afra had a small fire going in the chamber she had turned into her home. I buried that in case falling rock scattered hot embers everywhere. The baby lay beside the fire, swaddled and tucked into a carry-basket. I whistled a lifting spell until I could wriggle my forepaws into the straps. Then, as another shiver rocked the ground under my feet, I began to run, or rather, to slog.

I never expected a small baby and a straw carry-basket to weigh so much. I was frantic to get out before the cave dropped on us, yet I also wanted to stay and be a baby myself, curled up against the mother-spirit in the stone. Each time I stopped to catch my breath, I had to force myself to move on. Fortunately, though I did not think so then, the baby's screams constantly reminded me to keep going. I could not wait to get it off my back, or sides, wherever it had slipped. By the time we came to the rock that half covered the entrance, the basket hung off of my neck, yanking me sideways.

Eyeing the rock and the opening it had left, I crawled out of the straps.

Grabbing them in my forepaws, I backed into the opening, tugging the basket after me. It was half-out when it stuck. I was squealing curses when Afra said, "I am sorry that I called you a monster. Please—let me get him out."

I slid off the rock with gratitude and let Afra lift her child into the open. My poor forelegs ached. My back muscles complained. I wanted to go back into that comforting cave, which was deadly folly in an earthquake.

Spot came over to nuzzle me. I looked up at my friend and moaned. He pushed me a little harder with his nose. *Don't complain,* he told me. *You aren't bleeding.*

Afra had her baby out of the carry-basket. She held it, bouncing it as she talked softly. It finally stopped screaming.

The hard ground shakes had also halted, though I could feel the same deep shiver that I had felt yesterday, on the rock over the cave's mouth.

"We should get to clearer ground," Afra said. "In case the earthquake returns."

I nodded.

"There is a place by the spring where I get water. But I cannot leave the food that you brought." She looked at the opening in the cave entrance, biting her lower lip. Then she placed the baby on the ground beside me. "Watch him, please. If something happens . . ." She shook her head and ran like a fool to the cave. She wriggled into the opening and was gone.

I squealed in irritation. I could have gone for those things! I looked at Spots, thinking that he could mind the baby.

She asked you *to watch him,* Spots said. *If you go into the cave with her, she will panic, thinking the baby is alone but for a stupid horse.*

I had to do as she had told me since she was beginning to see that I was no monster. I muttered to myself. I knew he was right. He often is.

Spots walked over to the baby and began to nudge him to and fro, rocking him. The baby liked it. He was chuckling, as if a horse rocked him every day. Then he looked at me. I jerked back, thinking he would scream in fear, but he only watched me as he rocked, his eyes big.

Afra returned with my sack. She must have put some of her own things inside, because it was heavier, judging by the way she carried it. She set it down and watched Spots rock her son.

"I don't suppose you two would hire on as nursemaids?" she asked. "I'll take Uday now." She gathered her son up and tucked him into the carry-basket, asking him, "Did you like that, Uday? Did you?" He chuckled for her, too. Carefully, she settled the basket over her shoulders. While she tightened the straps, Spots made faces for Uday. I gave Spots's foreleg a push, for showing off.

Afra picked up the heavy sack. She looked at me. "It's not far, the spring. Would your friend mind if I put this on his back? I know it's slippery with no saddle, but I can hold it there."

Spots nodded at her.

Afra looked at him, then at me. "What are you?" she asked. Her lips quivered. Her eyes were wet. She turned to hoist the bag onto Spots's back. I feared for those eggs inside the robe. They seemed to be doomed.

"I do not weep in the ordinary way of things," Afra said, her voice defensive. "But it has been so hard, with everyone's hand turned against me. And now you two come—it was you with the food, before?" She looked at me. Her eyes were dry again. I nodded to her. "Why? What are you, and why are you doing these things?"

I made a cradle of my forearms and rocked them.

"The baby, yes," Afra said.

Then I ran in place and pretended to be throwing rocks at her. I started to walk around as if I followed a maze, looking confused.

She frowned for a moment. Then her face smoothed. "You saw the boys chase me!"

I nodded.

"Well, you're kindhearted, both of you. Come. The spring's this way." She pointed out the path for Spots, soon discovering that if she spoke the directions, there was no need to point. That was just as well because the sack did slide all over his back. She was kept busy just holding it there.

We followed the gully where Spots and I had waited for Afra to take the sack. The path twisted out of view, making a wide curve around the cave's protecting stone. We entered a small bay where trees grew and a spring bubbled up through the ground to make a pond. One of the three rocky walls of the bay was part of the stone that made the cave, reddish orange and fine-grained instead of rough brown-black. Plants sprouted in the cracks in the walls. Birds fluttered to the tops of the trees as we arrived.

Spots let Afra take the sack from him before he trotted over to the water. He sniffed at it. *Is the water safe?* he asked me. *I suppose it is, if she has been drinking it, but it never hurts to be sure.*

I tested it with a drop of my magic. The water gleamed and rippled for a moment, proof that it was very good. Spots dipped his head and began to drink. I, too, was thirsty. I gulped until my belly sloshed.

While we slurped, Afra made camp. She set Uday up in his basket so he might watch us, then took everything from sack. It was as I feared—the eggs were ruined. Afra looked at them, crushed messes in the folds of the robe. She covered her mouth, but I could tell that she was trying not to giggle. Finally, she could not help herself. She gave way, and her laughter made Uday chuckle. She was different when she laughed.

Spots brought the soiled robe over to me. We were both shaking our heads over the ruined eggs when Afra picked the robe up. "It's a shame about the eggs, but you brought me two sausages and a brick of pressed dates. You're going to make me fat." She smiled when she said it.

A stream left the pond and flowed out through the rear of our bay of rocks. Afra went to it with the robe. I followed her while Spots cropped the grass that grew around the pond's edges and watched Uday. Afra knelt beside some rocks in the stream and began to wash the egg from the robe. "I saw this on their headman's wife," she told me, scrubbing two hand-fuls of robe against one another. "If she knew I had it, she would screech the clouds down." She looked sideways at me. "If I were a better person, I would return it, but the nights are cold."

I retracted my claws and took an eggy spot of my own, swishing it in the stream to wet it before I tried to scrub the stuff out.

"The horse is odd, but at least he is still a horse. But you . . . there are no pale blue crocodiles or monitor lizards, and a crocodile would have eaten Uday. You must have come from someplace wonderful," Afra told me. "Not that my experience of the world is so wide. I have known only the mountain towns and villages." She traded her clean handful of cloth for a dirty one and looked at me. I was scrubbing as well as I could, in hope that she would tell me her story. "My home is back that way." She waved her hand toward the east. "My family had the Gift. My mother could charm metal, my father doctored animals. My sister was good at all-around magic. They believed I had no power. Then my woman's time came, and my Gift with it."

I nodded. It happened that way in about one person in ten, Numair said. Often it was an unpleasant surprise for the newly Gifted child.

"You have seen my Gift," Afra said, finding a new place to scrub. I rinsed mine, then found another spot to work on. "No one knew what to do, or how to teach a girl with two-colored magic. They took me to our lord. He gave them three gold pieces for me and told them to go home. That was how I became a slave."

I reared back on my haunches and hissed. The last emperor, Kaddar's uncle, had tried to make a slave of Daine once. He had caged and bespelled me. That was why there was a new palace in the capital. They could do little with the old one, once Daine and her friends were through with it.

Afra smiled crookedly. "Oh. You know what it's like. I bore it at first. They fed me well. But I could not make my magic do as they wished, so they beat me and took the food away." She began to wring out the robe. We had cleaned it entirely. "I would have done as I was told, if I had *known* how to control my Gift. I didn't. After a few beatings and enough lost meals, I'd borne enough. That was how I learned that if I wanted to be free of shackles or ropes badly enough, my magic would do away with them." She shrugged. "I stole some things and I ran away. I traveled with a caravan for a time, dancing for coins." She spread the robe on some rocks to dry in the sun, and she shook her head. "There was a man traveling with us. Sadly, he had a wife in one of the towns. I did not know that until Uday was growing in my belly."

I stood, watching her. She spoke well. Perhaps she had learned it at the lord's house. If I looked at her without the struggle of getting her to eat, or worrying about her magic, if I only thought of her as a human, like Daine's friends, how old could she be? Her face was not strained with fear or anger as she sat on a rock and looked back at me.

"I joined another caravan, but once my belly was big, I could not dance anymore," she told me. "You understand every word, by the rivers and springs, you do. I cannot see feelings in the face of a lizard or snake, but I can tell you are sad. Don't be sad for me. I have whored and stolen, and done both of those among people who had taken pity on me and gave me work." She pointed toward the village on the other side of the rocks. "Why do you think those boys were so happy to stone me? I got caught at my thieving and thrown out. The villagers had warned me about the Maze of stone, but I never even saw it. I found the cave instead. I felt safe there, and that is where I managed to have Uday without bungling things too badly." She looked at her worn straw sandals. She was about fifteen, I decided. Nearly my age, just a baby. I knew human females are supposed to be old enough to marry and have families by the time they are sixteen, or even fourteen, but that never seemed right.

I could not play any more games with Afra, trying to keep her to myself. When she trusted me enough, I would take her to my parents. They would know what to do. Numair would welcome her for her rare Gift. Daine would welcome her because once she, too, had been a girl on her own. Afra and her baby would be as safe with my foster parents as I was.

"I think I will sleep," Afra told me suddenly. "I have learned to fight using my Gift, but it tires me. Or maybe it is nursing a baby and fighting with my Gift both." She walked back to Uday's carry-basket and curled up beside him, without even a blanket. I looked at Spots, thinking that there were extra blankets in Numair and Daine's tent.

Once Afra slept, Spots and I left her there. Afra could also use one of Daine's scarves, and perhaps a few other items. They wouldn't mind, once they knew the entire story. I was sure of that.

 や

SPOTS hid behind the tent while I packed up the things I had decided to take from Daine and Numair. Once I was ready, I whistled Spots around to the front of the tent. This time I used some of Daine's scarves and sashes to tie the bundle to his back. He was helpful about kneeling to help me reach everything. I was just finished when we heard a man's footsteps on the hillside.

It's one of the horse guards, Spots said. *The one who thinks I should stay tied up all of the time. He thinks he knows better than Daine and Numair what to do for me. I am tired of being polite. Will you destroy his rope for me?*

All through this trip I had watched Spots struggle with this stupid human, who would not learn that Spots could manage himself. I gladly would have done even more than destroy a rope.

"There you are," the soldier told Spots, his face hard. "All morning and all through my noontide meal, I've been lookin' for you, you cursed contrary beast." He had his lariat at his side and was swinging the noose easily. "I don't know how you got away from the lines, but you'll not do so *again*!" He flung the noose just as Spots turned out of its path. The noose missed. I shrieked—it was one of my new ones—and noose, line, and coiled rope went all to ash. The soldier swore, hugging his scorched hand to his chest. Then Spots danced up and swung his head hard, right into the man's chest. The man stumbled, fell, and began to roll down the steep slope to the imperial camp. Spots and I fled, Spots soon getting ahead of me.

When I looked back and could not see the soldier, I whistled up my tornado and swept the hillside. I kept the spinning wind trailing me until I reached Spots. He was waiting patiently for me at the edge of the first barrier spell. I let the tornado go and leaned against my friend's leg. He still had the bundle.

He nudged me gently. *Thank you. I must ask Daine to speak to him again and make certain that he listens this time. The other soldiers have learned, but he is too stupid.*

I crooned my understanding and reached out, feeling the barrier. It gave under my paws, making them tingle.

Spots took a step forward. *What is this?* he asked. His skin twitched all over, but he could move through the magic, whipping his tail as if he were beset by flies. *I am no mage, so something has changed this barrier, Kitten.*

The second barrier stopped him. It also felt different. It flowed over my outstretched paw like cool soup. I felt no little hands exploring me, and I missed them. Confused, I made a shield for Spots and hissed a spell at the barrier. My breath barely touched it before it vanished.

I followed Spots into the rocks, feeling baffled. These barrier spells were *old*. Why were they changing now?

Afra was still asleep, but Uday was not. He was amusing himself, playing with magical bubbles that were dark pink, pale green, and bright yellow, all swirling together. Afra's son's magic was even stranger than her own. I felt grateful that if she did not know of Uday's Gift, I would not be the one to tell her. Since her power had brought her such trouble, I could not see her welcoming it for her baby. Maybe Numair would teach her how to be glad of their Gifts.

Spots stayed to guard them. I clambered up onto the orange rock to listen for goats. My luck was in: the herd was grazing not too far away, near the edge of the barrier around the rocks. Swiftly I clambered over that warm, welcoming, orange stone to find them. I was soon in the oddest state of mind. Flashes of green, orange, red, blue, and brown fires filled my vision, then faded. The lands before me were shaped the same, but their covering was different. The areas that did not sprout stone were green with trees and brush, and populated with big animals. There was an *enormous* shaggy cow—why would I imagine a giant cow? There were zebra, too, like King Jonathan and Emperor Kaddar have in their menageries. That was senseless. Zebra could not thrive in these desert lands. Still, I saw the land as green, so perhaps zebra would do well here.

When I ducked to avoid a large imagination bat, I tumbled down a groove in the orange stone. Luckily for me, the groove was long and cushioned with brush that grew in the earth collected there. I was also grateful that no one was on hand to see me, except for a family of rock hyraxes. They had a good laugh at my expense. I bared my teeth at them, which made them run away. Then I felt small as well as stupid.

At the foot of the stone was open ground where the magical barrier ended. I barely felt the magic's tingle on my scales as I passed through it. Beyond lay slopes of the black lava rock spotted with brush on its sides. Goats. I was back in the real world, looking for goats.

Pausing on the level ground, I listened for a goat bell and heard one nearby, over the ridge. I trotted over to the black rock and began to climb. Then I halted. The bell was coming closer, and with it, human voices. Hurriedly I drew camouflage colors over myself, blending in with the rock and the scrub. Then I crept forward to listen.

"I don't want to give up my afternoon's grazing so this mage can look at the beasts," I heard a human boy whine. "Make her come out to look at them"—I heard the sound of a slap—"Ow! Ma!"

"She is the emperor's friend! As well ask his Imperial Majesty to call on you! Gods all above, why did you curse me with a son whose head rattles like a gourd?" a woman cried. The goatherd and his mother climbed down from the pasture on the other side of the rock where I sat. The herd of goats followed them, so obedient I could have sworn they were spelled. Knowing goats as I do, I wouldn't have been surprised if they knew I wished to steal one and delighted in twitching their tails as they trotted by, bound for the village gate.

The goatherd turned to make certain that he had them all and choked. "Ma! Ma, look!"

His mother, a good-sized woman in a headcloth and robe, turned, ready to cuff him. Her hand froze in midair. Only long training for and in battle kept me in my place, hoping that I had not made a mistake in my camouflage. No, they were not staring at me, but at the orange stone to my right and at the open ground before it. The goats were baffled and frightened by the humans' confusion. They began to bleat their fear.

"That wasn't there before!" the woman said, drawing the Sign on her chest.

The boy did the same. "The Rock Maze lay in that open ground. We never saw no orange rock!" He ventured forward, his staff outstretched.

"Careful!" his mother cried. "This is magic, it's folly to meddle with magic!"

The boy stopped just five yards from me and waved his staff, expecting something. He was not the only one. He should have touched the barrier there, and with each step forward that he took. When he stopped to tap the orange stone, he was six feet inside the barrier of magic I'd walked through each time I came here.

His mother could bear it no more. "Leave it!" she cried. "We're no mages! That's what ours are for—yes, and those grand ones the emperor has brought! Get away from there before you're hurt!"

The goatherd had blossomed more rolling sweat with each step he had taken beyond that five-yard point. I think he expected to walk straight into a cliff and break his toes. When his mother ordered him to come with her, he turned and raced to her side. They and the goats ran for the gate.

I shed my camouflage once they were inside the village walls and climbed down from my place on the black stone. Once on the sandy ground, I walked straight toward the round curve of orange stone. There was no sign whatever of the barrier. I even waved my paws through the air, seeking its power. I'd felt it—somewhat—on my way to find those goats. Where had it gone since then? No one had worked a spell big enough to destroy it. I would have sensed that.

Remembering the next barrier, I ran up the stone, which quivered under my paws: the earth was shuddering. At the top of the formation I braced myself to look at the black lava rocks around the orange, and at the village to the south of my position. Was I visible to anyone who might pass, if the barrier was gone? I had to be if those humans had seen the orange stone. I camouflaged myself a second time, then moved on, seeking the next barrier as the stone beneath me trembled. I hadn't even noticed that it was gone when I'd passed this way before, wrapped in strange visions. *Why?* What had destroyed the barriers?

At last I reached Afra's clearing. She knelt beside the open bundle that had been on Spots's back, a small pot of one of Daine's healing creams in her hand. She put it down when she saw me. There were tear stains on her cheeks. "You go too far! The village mages have not tried to break the magic on this place because they believe there is none, only stones and desert. Now you have taken costly things! If the mages track them here, who is to say they cannot shatter the spells that hide us?" She wiped sweat from her face with a hand that trembled. "And that you did this now, with the earth dancing again . . ."

If the village mages could have pierced the illusion of the Maze of Stone they would have done so the first time Afra was spotted at their garbage heap. They didn't even know it was there. Numair was another matter, but now, with the barrier gone, we *needed* him to come, and Daine, too. Or we needed to go to him and Daine, out through the taller rocks, before the ground opened up under us. Afra could not stay here. The goatherd and his mother had to be spreading the news that the village had land this afternoon that had not existed that morning. People would be coming if there wasn't an earthquake first.

I straightened the blankets that had served to bundle up what we had taken and began to put Afra's belongings in their center.

Kitten, what are you doing? Why are you packing? Spots pawed the ground, nervous. He knew how I behaved if we were safe and if we were not safe.

I hissed at him, the noise I used to mean "trouble," and pointed back in the direction from which I had come.

Spots snorted in disgust. *Why does this happen just as I begin to like a place?* He began to help me pack, choosing only the most important things to place on the blankets.

Afra stared at us. "What are you doing now? Are you *packing*?" She set down the cream. "Please! I'm frightened enough with the ground so restless, but this is the safest place for us to be. There's no tall stone here to fall over on us. Please stop! I have to be calm for Uday, surely you know that!"

I went over to her and gripped her wrist, then pulled her and pointed in the direction of the path back to the cave—and the imperial camp. I opened my mouth to explain that soon we would have curious villagers entering our sanctuary, but of course all that came out was baby chatter.

"Go back there?" Afra demanded, pulling free of my grip. "That place is surrounded by high rocks and cliffs. We'll be crushed!"

I shook my head. I was nearly screaming with frustration, cursing my lack of speech. I hunkered down on my hindquarters and placed a group of small stones together, some of them black, some orange. I put the orange ones in the center, as they seemed to be in the true rock formation. Then I drew a circle around them. The line was jagged. Afra was not the only one made edgy by the shaking ground, but we dragons are supposed to control ourselves.

Afra nodded. "The magic, yes." Spots continued to pack, rolling up the bundle of blankets.

I wiped away the line around the collection of rocks. Then I stabbed a claw into the area where I'd erased my line and glared at Afra.

She wiped sweat from her upper lip. "No. I don't believe you. The villagers told me that the Rock Maze has been there ever since their people can remember." I stabbed the ground again. Afra was still shaking her head when Uday woke and began to cry. "I have to feed my child," she whispered. She went to him while I threw the rocks into the pond.

I wanted to throw myself in after them—not to drown, only to cool my temper and my nerves. It made me half-mad to be unable to speak at a time like this! I could tell her about Daine and Numair, about how they would be able to help her and the baby! We wouldn't be dithering here, but on our way to safety!

Should I go get Daine? Spots asked me.

I was about to say yes, but the ground heaved under me. I shook my head and pointed to Afra and Uday, then made running motions with my claws. We had to get them away first.

Spots began to nudge Afra toward the way out of the clearing. Each time she turned away from his nose, back toward the pond, he would turn with her and begin to nudge again. He was very stubborn. I often wished I could tell him that I suspected he had a mule in his ancestry. I had so many jokes I could not tell him.

I walked around the pond to think of something, but all I could think was that we had to *go*. The water's surface rippled under the force of the quivering earth. Loose rocks tumbled everywhere. I reached deep into the ground with my power, feeling for the cracks in the earth that might open and swallow us, but I found none. That meant nothing. In Numair's books, I had read that the deadliest faults were miles underground.

When I returned, Afra had taken away everything that Spots had placed on the blankets. She then rolled up the blankets themselves to make a rough circle in the open, away from the rocks, where Uday might crawl in safety, free of his swaddlings.

I did shriek then, and scold. I had left to get myself under control, not to say I had conceded the fight! Spots walked over to my side to let Afra know he agreed with me. His white-and-brown withers were dark: he too was sweating, his fear of the shakes obvious in the way he planted his feet and watched the stone around us. I felt guilty. I had been so busy with my tantrum that I had not even asked my friend how he did.

Afra stood in front of Uday, and said, "The barrier has kept me safe for longer than I have known you, strangers. We are safer in this open ground than we will be running through those canyons. Go if you wish, but Uday and I stay here."

I wanted to weep in frustration. Humans!

We did not leave them. I went to the far side of the pond and whistled cracking spells at the small rocks there, turning them to gravel, until I had myself under control. Then Spots and I gathered deadwood for a fire, lurching to and fro to get the wood that lay on the ground. Uday crowed and raised his arms for me when we came back, which touched me deeply. Afra, about to swaddle him again, gave me a nod, but the look in her eyes was wary.

I'd just started the fire when we heard the dogs. Afra jumped to her feet, then stumbled as the ground gave a hard shake. She looked at me. "They sound so close," she whispered.

I raised one claw and put it to my muzzle, to silence her. Then I clambered up over the orange boulders to see how near the villagers had come. The stone rocked beneath me for a moment, then settled. I raced forward before it had another spasm. Finally, I saw the last rise, the one before the slope to where the barrier had once been.

This time I did not trip down the crack past the rock hyraxes, if they were still there. I crouched and called my magic, letting it rise as fire all around me. When the stone beneath me begin to scorch, I rose onto my hind legs and walked up the last rise.

The villagers stood at the foot of the orange stone. Three mages were in the lead, each with their Gifts blazing in their hands, ready for use. Men and women stood around the mages with dogs on leashes. The dogs were barking and yowling. They knew they were supposed to be hunting *something*. They wanted to be taken off the leash so they could do their jobs. More villagers armed with bows and spears stood behind the leaders and dog handlers. From their reaction as I stood up, they had not expected anyone to meet them here.

I went red with rage. When humans say that, they mean their faces go red. When I go red, it is my scales that turn that color, blotting out my normal blue-gold. I let my anger flow into my power, so that the air around me burned scarlet. Some of the villagers began to run. I stood all the way up on my hind feet, stretched my neck out as far as it would go, raised my head, and blew a long plume of spell breath, shaped as a stream of flame.

More people ran then, but they were not the right ones. "It is the witch's illusion!" cried the chief mage, who had spoken with Daine only that morning. "Now!" He and the other mages threw fist-sized balls of magic at me. They *hurt* as they struck, though my power devoured them. I screeched a breaking spell, shattering the weapons of those who had stayed to attack. Now most of them ran, too.

"Illusions don't wield magic," I heard a mage say.

"Again!" cried the chief mage, not caring.

I did not wait for a second attack. I could endure the hurt. My problem was my own magic. If it devoured more power, it might get too hot for me to bear.

I turned and galloped for Afra's camp, half-stumbling all the way. The earth, so calm while I had faced the villagers, now shook harder than ever. As I skidded down the last slope, the rock bucked like a stallion, pitching me into the pond. My magic evaporated. The cool water eased the heat that the use of so much power created. I actually rolled there for a moment before I remembered I could not swim.

I scrabbled at the bottom mud, trying to crawl up to the water's edge. Then two strong hands gripped my forelegs and pulled. I kicked back with my hind legs as Afra dragged me from the mud, water, and clinging strands of weed.

Sitting on the ground, Afra plucked some of it off of my back. "What are these for, if you can't fly?" she asked, passing a gentle hand over my tiny, rudimentary wings.

I shook my head, sprinkling her with more water, and cupped a paw around my ear. She heard the shouts of humans in the distance.

"You were right?" she whispered. "The barrier is truly gone?"

She did not wait for my answer, but jumped to her feet and hurried to tie a bundle of her things to Spots's back. Even though she had not believed me about the barrier when I left, she had been worried enough about the dogs to pack.

She is quick to work when she is frightened, Spots said with approval. *She would do well in the army or the Queen's Riders, if she did not have to worry about Uday.* He pitched as the ground shook harder. I looked for Uday. He was swaddled and tucked in his carry-basket once more.

The villagers were still coming. From the sound of their arguments, they feared their mages more than they feared being caught under a rock, at least for the moment.

Afra was hoisting Uday's carry-basket onto her shoulders when I heard new voices in the canyons between us and the imperial camp. One male whined that the protection from earthquake and falling rocks had best be good. Another cursed "that mad, thieving horse" and "that evil little dragon." The soldier who had tried to stop Spots was coming to reclaim him. At least one mage came with him, as well as more soldiers. Did I not have enough trouble on my scales?

Afra started to lead Spots toward the stream that flowed away from the pond. I grabbed her arm and towed her toward the trail that we had used to come here.

"No," she whispered, tugging her arm from my grip. "That goes toward the village."

I took her arm again and pulled harder.

"They'll *kill* me," she snapped. She yanked free.

She would not trust any symbol for mage, even if she knew one. I knew no symbol for "emperor." I quickly drew a picture of a crown.

She staggered as the ground shook, and clung to Spots's mane to keep her feet. "A king? Are you mad? We have no kings," she said, "only an— Oh, no. No, no." She shook her head, her eyes wild. "The emperor is the judge of all Carthak. He will return me to my master if he doesn't execute me for all I've stolen!"

We were out of time. The chief mage was the first of the villagers to top the orange stone rise. "Witch!" he cried, pointing. "Thief!"

I got in front of Afra and threw up my best shield as spears of yellow fire sped from his fingers right at her. They struck my power and flew straight into the air. I rose on my hind legs as the other two mages and the remaining villagers joined the chief mage. The dogs were nowhere to be seen. They must have fled for home like sensible creatures.

The mages' Gifts shimmered and blazed around their hands, the chief mage's brightest by far. I wriggled my hind feet, seeking good purchase. Then I summoned my own magic, letting it crackle like lightning over my scales. I was almost blind with the rage that comes from using too much power. In my fury, I meant to cook those annoying humans where they stood.

"Kitten!" I heard Daine cry, her voice shocked. *"Bad* girl!"

I looked over my shoulder and released my magic into the empty air. Daine stood behind me. She looked cross. She and Numair had come with the imperial soldiers I had heard. Numair held a protective shield of magic over all of them, keeping falling rocks from their heads back in the canyon. I could see its white sparks shimmer against its sheer black fire.

Daine looked at me, then at the villagers, her eyebrows knit in a frown. "Kit, you know better than to threaten humans. And I would like to know why these humans are threatening you and your friends!"

Numair surveyed all of us. "Your pardon, my dear, but the magical energies here are making my ears ring," he said in his usual mild way. "Something very big is about to happen within these stones."

That made my ears prick. Magic? Earthquakes weren't magical.

"Perhaps we should all return to the emperor's camp and finish this discussion?" Numair asked. "I am certain that Kitten did not adapt such a threatening posture without reason." His Gift flowed out from him to enclose Afra, Uday, Spots, and me, but not the villagers. My foster father had seen that we were under attack from them.

Afra started to raise her hand, her magic gathering around her fingers, but I grabbed her wrist. I was fairly certain that, even with her two-colored magic, she would get hurt if she tried to fight Numair.

She stared at me, her eyes wide with fear. "Is that the emperor?" she whispered.

Spots and I shook our heads.

"Stand away!" screamed the village's chief mage. "This woman is a witch and a thief! She is ours to deal with! Call your monster off!"

Daine's frown deepened. "Kit's no more a monster than you," she called back. "Though just now you're looking fair monstrous to me!"

No one heard what the mage said next. The orange rock under him bucked and split. He and the other villagers were thrown, as I had been, into the pond. Chunks of rock dropped away from the orange stone. The villagers who escaped the pond tried to run down the canyon where the stream flowed, only to find that boulders were blocking the way.

No one wanted to come near us. They stayed on the far side of the pond.

As more orange pieces rolled onto the open ground, darker stone was uncovered. The inner rock was brown, glassy stuff. Once most of the orange stone had fallen away, the brown stone began to jerk and rise. Its ridges shifted as larger, angled pieces appeared out of the mass of rock beyond our view. The assemblage of stone, oddly shaped, even sculpted, kept turning toward us. One piece set itself on the sand next to Daine and Numair.

I was looking at a lizardlike foreleg. It was made of a glossy brown stone filled with a multitude of different-colored fires that blazed in sheets, darts, and ripples under each stone scale.

The center section up above bent in a U as the dragon—it was a dragon—hauled its still-captive hindquarters from their stone casings under the earth. Then it had to pull its tail loose, the tail being trapped in a different section of rock. I saw the foreleg press up. With a roar of shattering stone, the dragon forced its upper body free, then its tail.

Raining gravel and powdered rock, the opal dragon turned. It brought its head around and down to our level, regarding us with glowing crimson eyes. Their pupils, slit just like mine, were the deep green of emeralds. Free now of its prison, it was not so big as I'd thought. Numair was six feet and six inches; the dragon stood that tall at the shoulder. Head to hip it was sixteen feet. The tail I could not measure. This dragon carried it in curled loops on its back. I noticed its other peculiarity right away as well: it had no wings.

It said something that flattened me. I squeaked, in my body or my mind, I don't know which. I tried to meet its eyes. The dragon spoke again, using very different words and talking slowly. I shook my head in the hope that I could make my ears open up, but my ears were not the problem. The dragon spoke within my skull, expecting me to understand. The language was completely unfamiliar.

Daine raced over and picked me up. "Stop it!" she cried, glaring at the great creature. "She can't understand you! She's just a baby!"

I shook her off. I didn't mean to, but I was *trying* to understand this being. Was it a relative of mine? Didn't the dragon ancestors mention kindred of ours, dragons fashioned of stone, flame, and water, at the gathering I had attended when I was nine? I was busy playing with my cousins, but I had listened to some of the stories.

The dragon looked at Daine, then at me. It tried another series of sounds, gentler ones. I heard something familiar, *sleep*, and called back with my own mind, *Awake?*

The dragon flashed a look at the village's chief mage, who was trying to creep up on it. He shrank away, his hands blazing with his Gift. The dragon stretched its head out on its long neck and blew a puff of air straight at the mage. His Gift vanished from his hands. He gasped and plunged his hands into the pond.

The opal dragon looked at me and spoke within my mind, *Child?*

Dragon-child, I thought to her. I knew this dragon was female. It was in the way that she said "child," as if she had mothered several. She had loved them and scolded them, watched them grow, tended their hurts, and seen them leave in search of their own lives. Somehow I had learned all that just from the way she had thought that one word to me.

The dragon waved her forepaw at the humans around us. *These? Tell.*

I explained about Emperor Kaddar's journey here. How I'd seen the boys stone Afra, and how Afra had led me to the cave in the rocks hidden by magic. I was almost to the end of how I'd tamed Afra with food when the dragon said, *That is sufficient for me to learn your speech.*

I stared at her.

It has been an age since I last heard the speech of my winged cousins. I had quite forgotten it. The opal dragon eyed the humans. *Other things have changed as well.* Some note in her voice was different. She was ready to talk to others. She asked, *Have you pestiferous creatures gotten any wiser?*

The villagers dropped to their knees, crying out or weeping. Their chief mage was the last to kneel. He quivered as if he could not help himself. Afra clung to Spots. I was so proud that she did not kneel.

Spots bared his teeth at the dragon. *Try your luck against me, big lizard,* he said. *I have fought giants and steel-feathered Stormwings. I have faced Kitten's family. No dragon, not even a stone one, will make me run.*

So I see, the dragon replied.

Neither Daine nor Numair had budged, though the emperor's soldiers were on their knees. My parents, like Spots, had met far larger dragons.

Numair stepped forward. "It depends on how you gauge such things, Great One," he said quietly, answering her question about humans. "I have met foolish dragons, and badgers with great wisdom."

The dragon regarded him, then Daine. *Mages have improved,* she said.

"Would you favor us with an explanation?" Numair asked in his polite way. "We had no sense of you, or we would not have disturbed you."

You did not disturb me, the opal dragon told him. She turned her crimson eyes to Afra. *Nor did you, small mother. I layered my protective spells so that none of my kind, who had been plaguing me with questions and requests for ages, would find me. I wanted a nice, long nap. But I set the wards so that any mother or mother-to-be might find sanctuary behind my barriers. I welcomed you in my dreams.*

She snaked her long neck around Afra to peer at Uday. A little uncertain, Afra half turned so the dragon might get a better look at her son. *And I am quite charmed by you, small human.* Uday crowed in glee, as if he understood.

The dragon straightened so she could eye all of us again. *It was this young dragon who caused my waking. When first she entered my barriers, I began to rouse myself from sleep, bringing down my old wards and cracking the shell that time had formed over me. It has been more than two thousand circles around the sun since her kind and mine have spoken. Moreover, she is so young. I feared that you two-legged creatures might have captured her. You have been known to do that.*

Her gaze was so stern that the villagers, who had begun to rise, knelt again. The soldiers behind Numair and Daine quailed.

I am no captive! I told her. *Daine and Numair*—my mind added their images and voices to their names so the opal dragon would know them better—*are my parents. They adopted me. My kin allow it. Daine tried to save my dragon mother's life, and my mother left me with her. I have been managing very well among humans, thank you!*

Now the beautiful creature looked down her long muzzle at me. *In my day, infant dragons were not so forward,* she said, her mind-voice crackling.

I am not like the infant dragons you knew, I replied. *You said yourself it's been more than two thousand years since you spoke with any dragons.*

For a moment, I thought I heard her sigh. She picked up a slab of orange stone that was three feet thick. *My nap lasted far longer than I had intended. I was very bored, and tired.*

You could come with us, I said. *It wouldn't be boring if you did.*

"Kitten—Skysong—means that it wouldn't be boring for *her*," Numair said. "But surely, after such a nap, it *is* time you moved around a bit?"

"Numair!" Daine said, tugging on his sleeve. "The people in the city—well, people anywhere! If we have a dragon with us—a *big* one—if folk see her out and about—"

I slumped. I liked this dragon, for all that she was so much older and a snob. She was beautiful and funny. Daine was right, though. People screamed at the sight of *me*. What would they do if they saw *her*?

My children ceased to need me long before my nap. The time I showed you, young dragon, the time when these lands were green and the creatures were larger, was the last time I was happy. Somehow I could feel the dragon spoke to me alone. *I cannot—would not—take you from these strange friends, or your two-legged "parents." But I would be happy to come with you, if you would like.*

I squeaked and ran at her and wound between her forelegs. The glassy stone of her body was cool and pliable. She looked at Daine and Numair. *The skill of the dragon depends on the stone of our flesh,* she said so that everyone could hear. *We opal dragons are the mages of ideas, illusion, seeming, and invisibility. That is why my magical protections held for so long.*

Suddenly I could feel her, but I could not see her. No one could. Then I could not even feel her. I cheeped, sending my magic out, searching for her. Just as suddenly as she had vanished, she appeared again, beside Afra and Spots. Afra jumped; Uday began to wail. Spots's ears went back. The villagers decided it was time to run away.

"Now that's fair wonderful," Daine said with a smile. "You can hide in plain sight." She looked at Afra. "I didn't catch your name."

"I'm—Afra. This is Uday," Afra said, keeping an eye on the dragon. "Your little creature, there—she's been looking after us." She pointed to me, then Spots. "And the horse."

"Kitten is the dragon," Daine said, coming over to Afra. "Her ma named her Skysong, but she's got to grow into it. Spots is the horse. He's Numair's. I see Kitten found some of my things for you to use. She's a rare thief." She hugged Afra's shoulders, then looked at the dragon. "And your name, Great One?"

The opal dragon looked from Daine to me. *Why does this child not speak to you mind to mind, as she does to me?*

"She is too young. That's what her family told us," Daine replied. "It drives her half-mad. I think it's the only thing she dislikes about living among humans. She needs to talk among us, and she can't."

The dragon—my ancestress? My kinswoman?—went to the rocky hollow that had once been her bed and began to sift through the stones, tossing most of them aside. *I am Kawit, in the language of my people. Ah. Skysong, eat this.*

She turned about and offered me one of her discarded scales. It sparkled in the sun.

But it's too pretty to eat, I protested.

Eat it, Kawit ordered me.

I obeyed. Daine asked Kawit, "Will you teach me how you did that?"

The scale fizzed and tingled in my mouth, crunching among my teeth. Then it was gone.

I must compliment you upon your raising of Skysong thus far, Veralidaine, Kawit said. *She is a valiant young one who will do whatever she must to care for her friends.* She nodded to Afra.

"How did you know my full name?" asked Daine, startled.

Because it is in all of me, I said. *My mother put Daine's name in all of me, so every dragon, god, and immortal would know who my new mother is. Kawit, would you tell her?*

"Oh, my," Daine said. She sat on a rock.

You have already told her, Kawit replied.

You hear me! I cried, and I ran to my mother. I jumped into her lap.

You hear me! Now we can talk, and I won't have to make funny signs or noises! Daine hugged me close. Once we stopped saying private things to each other, I looked at Spots. *Can you hear me, too?*

As well as if you were one of the beast-People, he replied, nibbling on some weeds. *I'm glad you are happy, but we managed perfectly well before.*

But now I will understand your jokes. I only used to guess at them, I explained. I looked up at Numair. *Papa, Afra has magic in two colors, and Uday in three. Afra needs someplace to be safe and well fed and not enslaved.*

"Why are you telling my secrets?" Afra cried, looking around. She hadn't noticed the villagers' departure before this. Even the soldiers who had come with Numair and Daine had fled.

"She tells only us," Numair said kindly. "And we are safe, because Daine and I are both mages. I wish Kitten had brought you to us sooner—"

"I suspect she wanted to look after Afra herself," Daine told him. "Seeing as how we'd given her nothing to do."

I felt myself turn pale yellow out of embarrassment. It was dreadful that my parents knew my mind so well.

She has something to do now, Kawit said. *I know nothing of this new world. She may be my guide, and my friend. I hope she will be my friend.*

I struggled to concentrate, so that only Kawit would hear my reply. *I would love to be your friend,* I said. *If you don't mind that I am very young.*

I like it, Kawit told me. *You make me feel younger.*

Daine set me down and went to Afra. "May I see your baby?" she asked. Slowly, Afra turned so Daine could lift Uday from his carry-basket. "I have two of my own, but they are with their grandparents," Daine told Afra. "Please come with us. We'll send the soldiers back for the rest of your things." Holding Uday, she took Afra by one wrist and drew her toward the trail.

"But the dragon—Skysong—" Afra said, hesitating. "She drew a crown? The emperor is with you?"

"He's a nice young man," Numair said, coming to stand beside her. "Kitten said you have two-colored magic? How do you manage to keep one aspect from overpowering the other? My own, which is two-colored, has always been integrated, as you see—" He showed her a ball of his black fire so she could look at the white sparkles in it.

Oh, no, I thought. If Numair starts to ask questions now, I will never get my own answered. *Papa, when are we going home?* I demanded, tugging on the leg of his breeches. He was already walking off with Daine and Afra. Spots trotted ahead of us. *Kawit, come! Papa, did you fix the river? Mama, are the chickens going to be all right? Are you going to scold those mages for trying to kill us? Will you tell the soldiers to leave Spots with Kawit and me instead of tying him up all of the time?*

That was just a start. I had a great many more things to say.

Dragon Storm

MARY ROSENBLUM

It's always a good thing to have friends, but as the tense story that follows demonstrates, when you're a shunned and despised outcast, sometimes having a friend can make the difference between life and death—particularly when that friend is a dragon!

One of the most popular and prolific of the new writers of the nineties, Mary Rosenblum made her first sale, to Asimov's Science Fiction, in 1990, and has since become a mainstay of that magazine and one of its most frequent contributors, with more than thirty sales there to her credit. She has also sold to the Magazine of Fantasy & Science Fiction, Science Fiction Age, Pulphouse, New Legends, and elsewhere.

Rosenblum produced some of the most colorful, exciting, and emotionally powerful stories of the nineties, such as "The Stone Garden," "Synthesis," "Flight," "California Dreamer," "Casting at Pegasus," "Entrada," and many others, earning her a large and devoted following of readers. Her novella "Gas Fish" won the Asimov's Reader Poll in 1997, and was a finalist for that year's Hugo Award. Her first novel, The Drylands, appeared in 1993 to wide critical acclaim, winning the prestigious Compton Crook Award for best first novel of the year; with its picture of widespread social upheavals caused by catastrophic climate change, it and her other stories about the Drylands—an American West emptied of population by a disastrous drought—seem today more relevant than ever (alas!). Her second novel, Chimera, and her third, The Stone Garden, followed in short order, as did her first short story collection, Synthesis & Other Virtual Realities. She has also written a trilogy of mystery novels under the name Mary Freeman. Her most recent books are Horizons, a major new science fiction novel, and Water Rites, an omnibus collection of her Drylands stories that includes the novel The Drylands as well. A graduate of Clarion West, Mary Rosenblum lives in Portland, Oregon.

K NEELING in the rear of the narrow outrigger beneath the Crone's dim yellow face, Tahlia gasped as salt spray soaked her. "What was that for, Pretty?" The little blue surf-dragon dropped the boat's towline and rose half out of the water, needle teeth bared in her narrow snout as she chattered shrilly. Her teal-colored companion rolled his blue-green eyes and winked, and splashed his mate with water. She turned her wrath on him, and, in a second, both dragons were skipping away across the ocean swells, their vestigial wings sending up white skiffs of spray as they chased each other out of sight beneath the starry sky.

"Oh great." Kir stood, balancing easily as the boat crested a swell. "What now? Do we have to paddle all the way back? We'll miss the morning market for sure."

"Maybe they'll come back." Tahlia shook her head as she gathered in the tow ropes the dragons had dropped. "I don't know what got her upset. Surf-dragons are kind of . . . well . . . they get distracted pretty easily."

"I wouldn't know." Kir sniffed. "You're the only one who can talk to them . . . or whatever it is you do. We'd better start back now." He peered northward. "I sneaked out, and if I'm not back by dawn, Dad'll find out, and he said he'd beat me, next time I sneaked out to night-fish."

Dad had meant next time he sneaked out with Tahlia. He didn't approve of Kir's friendship with the "bad-luck golden eyes." Especially since someone had seen the surf-dragons towing her canoe and had spread the word. Spider-dragons they tolerated, because the big, aggressive spiders that lived on the grove trees were a lot worse than bad dragon luck. "I'm sorry." Tahlia sighed and began to uncoil the fine fishing line. "We might as well fish while we paddle back. Maybe a jewel fish will bite. They come to the surface when the Crone is in the sky. If we can get it pulling in the right direction, it'll even tow us." She baited the line with a tree-crab and dropped it overboard, then leaned out over the stern. The gold that edged the jewel-fish scales might make even Kir's father happy. The Crone's light seemed to fall like a beam, illuminating a patch of sea a few boat lengths away. "Kir, what's that? Something floating." She grabbed a paddle.

"What?" Kir twisted to look. "I don't see anything."

"It's like a pile of bubbles." Tahlia paddled her outrigger closer to the floating mass. Half as tall as she, it looked a bit like the foam the storm winds whipped up on the waves, but each crystal bubble shimmered with rainbows in the Crone's yellow light. "It's solid." She touched it tentatively. Her hand sank slowly into the dense mass, and she touched something. Warm. Smooth.

"Watch out!" Kir backed the canoe away with a hard paddle stroke. "You don't know what's in there!"

"Oh, stop it." Tahlia hung on, and the floating mass drifted with them. "Look at this!" She pulled one of the warm shapes from the gleaming bubbles, held it up. "Some kind of egg. I felt a bunch of them." So big that her fingers couldn't close around it, the shell, iridescent like the bubble mass, seemed both soft and hard at the same time, pulsing faintly against the pressure of her fingers.

"Too big to be a ketrel egg." Kir tilted his head, his sky-colored eyes narrowing. "Let's take them back to the market. If they're not rotten, that is." He reached for the egg. "Let's crack one and see."

"No way. Hey." Tahlia snatched it out of his reach, but as she did, the shell cracked, or rather split, pale edges curling back. A moment later, a long, narrow draconid head, the dull grey color of a stormy sea, poked through.

"Surf-dragon egg." Kir looked disappointed. "Everybody has always wondered where they lay their eggs. Now we know."

"I guess." Tahlia cupped her hands around the egg as the small dragonlet clawed its way out of the shell. "But it doesn't look quite right for a surf-dragon, and if this is how they lay their eggs, why don't we find 'em all over the place? Surf-dragons are everywhere. Ow!" She snatched her hand away, nearly dropping the dragonlet into the bottom of the boat. "It bit me!"

"Throw it overboard." Kir scrambled back to the bow of the canoe as the dragonlet thrashed in Tahlia's grip. Blood dripped from her wrist as she examined the double set of tooth marks on her left hand. "Sharp teeth. No, I'm not going to throw it back, Kir. Why shouldn't it think I'm going to eat it? Relax, baby, I don't eat dragons," she soothed it. "Look." She nodded. "They're all hatching."

Small dragonlets were emerging, poking narrow heads into the Crone's wan light, clawing their way to the surface of the mass.

"Ketrels!"

Kir's cry made her tear her eyes from the hatching dragons. Sure enough dark shapes wheeled overhead, blocking out the stars with their huge wings. "They're after the nest."

"Better them than us. Tahlia, paddle!" Kir dug his paddle blade into the water and drove the canoe away from the bubble nest.

He was right. Tahlia grabbed her paddle. The dragonlet had stopped fighting her, was now wrapped tightly around one wrist. "Hang on, little one." Tahlia dug her own blade into the water. "I won't let them eat you." They would be lucky if the ketrels didn't eat *them*. More than one grove dweller had died when caught out in the night ocean by a hungry flock. The Crone's light dimmed as a cloud veiled it, leaving them in safe darkness. Tahlia's back itched with the expectation of razor-sharp claws as she and Kir drove the canoe through the swells.

But the flock of huge birds ignored them, their shrill cries making Tahlia wince. Thrashing and shrieks erupted behind them, and she risked a quick glance over her shoulder. The Crone had emerged again from her cloud, and her light seemed to focus on the nest. The flock shredded it, long necks dipping as they stabbed through the rags of foam. Dragonlets struggled in the long, sharp beaks. Tears stung Tahlia's eyes as she turned back to her paddling. No hope for those babies. The sounds faded as the canoe leaped through the darkness. One of the huge islands of floating weed loomed in the darkness, and they paddled along the edge until they found a natural cavern in the tangle and drove the canoe into its shelter.

"Maybe they won't spot us," Kir panted.

"Pretty!" Tahlia rested her paddle as the blue surf-dragon erupted from the water, darting back and forth along the verge of the weed mat, squeaking and agitated. A moment later, the teal-colored male joined her. "Throw the tow rope out, Kir. Let's go, you two. Fast, fast, fast!" She was never sure just now much language the surf-dragons understood, but this time, they seemed to share the urgency of the moment, slipping their heads through the collars she'd fashioned from braided weed fiber and fanning their water wings so that a fog of spray instantly drenched both her and Kir.

"We're going to have to bail," Kir shouted, but the canoe shot ahead, white foam at the bow as it cut through the water. "Wow, what a ride."

"They're afraid of the ketrels, too." Tahlia looked back. The nest had vanished into the night. She shivered. The ketrel flew with the Kark, feasting on the exhausted spirit-slaves that the hardlanders tossed overboard. Rumor was that they led the raiders to the grove settlements. Her wrist tickled, and she looked down.

The dragonlet was licking the bite, cleaning every last trace of blood from her skin. "Thanks, little one." She held out her hand, and it crawled onto her palm, wrapping its tail around her wrist. It was long and slender, with webbed feet and silvery blue fins, although they were closed up right against her sides, and the muscular tail. Like the surf-dragons, she thought. Their fins unfurled and stiffened in the water to help them swim. "Maybe you're a surf-dragon after all," she murmured.

The negative in her mind was as clear as a whisper in her ear. "You answered me?" She looked down at the small dragonlet, and it looked up to meet her gaze. Its silver eyes held a glint of intelligence that she had never seen in the eyes of surf-dragons or spider-dragons. "What are you?" she murmured. "Kir, look." She held out her bitten hand. "Look what the dragon did."

"Bit you again?" He looked back, fear still shadowing his eyes. "Just throw it out for the ketrels. Serve it right."

"No, the bite is all healed. See?"

"Weird." He eyed her hand with the faint pale trace where the teeth had pierced her. "I never knew surf-dragons could do that."

"I don't think they can. And I don't think it's a surf-dragon."

"I don't know what else it could be. Well, who cares? Surf-dragons aren't much good to anybody but you." He glanced ahead, where Pretty and her mate thrashed through the swells. "I wish they'd pull a boat for me."

"You just have to ask them." She shrugged.

"They don't listen to me."

"You don't ask nicely, I bet." She looked ahead. The sky was getting light to the east, and she could just make out the tops of the village grove clearly now, the dark green-furred limbs rising in a solid tangle on multiple trunks that went clear down to the ocean bed. The scaled fish skins that roofed the village domes caught the first sunbeams and winked gold in the morning light. "I hope you don't get in trouble."

"Too late now." Kir sighed. "Father gets up at dawn."

"Maybe he won't look in your bed this morning," Tahlia said hopefully.

They caught a snoutfish as they neared the grove. The snoutfish were trash eaters and liked to hang around the inhabited groves, cleaning up scraps that the villagers tossed into the water. This was a small one, and, as Tahlia unhooked it, the dragonlet threw itself onto the quivering fish, tearing at the pale flesh with its needle teeth.

"Hey." Kir scowled. "That's *our* fish."

"Your mother doesn't want to eat snoutfish." Tahlia shrugged. "It has to eat something, you know. Wow." She watched, impressed, as the dragonlet cleaned the snoutfish to its pearly bones in minutes. Its stomach bulged comically, and it made a low, burbling sound as it crawled into her lap and wrapped its long tail around her waist. "It's growing." Tahlia stroked its smooth, satiny hide. "It already looks a lot bigger than when it hatched."

"Oh great." Kir rolled his eyes as he rebaited the line and tossed it overboard. "Just what we need. A *big* bad-luck dragon hanging around the grove. Tahl, you already get in trouble; this isn't going to help.

"It'll probably take off as soon as it can fly or swim or whatever it does."

Why would I leave?

Tahlia blinked with the intensity of that communication. *Were you speaking to me?* She stroked the gossamer folds of wing membranes with a fingertip. "Looks like she's a swimmer to me."

Of course I was. And my name is Xin.

"She?" Kir gave her a suspicious look. "How do you know it's a she?"

"She told me."

"How can she speak our language?" Kir gave her a look. "You're fooling me."

If the small-friend is talking to me—Xin turned one large, silvery eye in Kir's direction—*tell him you are speaking* my *language. Not many of your kind can do that.*

"How do you know anything about our kind?" Tahlia lifted the dragon to look her in the eyes. "You just hatched."

"What is going on?" Kir gave her a narrow look. "You're not really having a conversation with that thing?"

"I think I am, actually." Tahlia blinked. "She says her name is Xin."

He gave her a moment of silence. "Sometimes I don't know whether to believe you or not."

Tahlia made a face at him. Kir was right, though. She tilted her head to look up at the soaring tops of the grove trees as they approached the grove. Her eyes already made her bad luck, never mind that the surf-dragons fished for her. Bring a strange new dragon into the picture, and she'd be lucky if the villagers didn't drive her out of the grove altogether.

"Got something," Kir yelped as the fish line tightened. "This time, don't let that dragon of yours get it."

I will not "get it." Xin opened her jaws in a gaping yawn that revealed a double row of gleaming teeth and a long, crimson tongue. *I am full.*

They landed a fat redfish, and Tahlia told Kir to take it home to his mother. That would make her happy, and she might stand up for Kir against his father. A prosperous seagold-smith, Kir's father believed very strongly in luck. Good *and* bad. She sent the surf-dragons skimming away with her thanks as they got close to the village grove. Night still lingered among the grove's many thick trunks. Tahlia lifted the canoe's outrigger into vertical so that she could maneuver the narrow spaces between the huge trunks, and skillfully guided it through the maze of tethered boats and small docks, stopping at the dock skirting the trunk near which Kir's family had their home.

He scrambled up the netted ladder with a wave, the redfish, slung over his shoulder in a carry-net, dripping down his back. As he went, Tahlia thought that she heard a hoarse squawk high above. Like the cry of a ketrel. But the interlaced branches hid the sky, and it couldn't see a baby dragon down here. The tide was low, and she quickly filled a small net bag with purple sweet-shell snails that had emerged into the air in the dark to feed on the fur of tree-moss that quickly invaded the tide-exposed trunk.

Tahlia tucked Xin out of sight against her belly beneath her tunic. She tied off the canoe and climbed quickly up to the first level, where the thick branches radiated out from the trunk, interlacing with the branches of the other trunks to create a tough, flexible floor. Each grove supported several levels, and this grove of trees, centuries old, carried four levels. Down here, sheltered from the storm winds but vulnerable to storm swells, the marketplace thrived. The wealthy crafters like Kir's family and the most successful fisher families lived on the second level, the safest one.

She and her mother had lived on the uppermost level. Before the hard-land raiders came that fall. Now, she lived in her canoe or in the trunk ferns with the spider-dragons. Or in the healer's dome, when he stayed in this grove on his travels.

Xin stirred sleepily against her skin, her claws pricking Tahlia, and she stroked her until she quieted as she stepped from the ladder onto the branch floor. Strips of dried sea-ribbon woven between the interlaced twigs created paths, and she followed them to the main market, clustered between two of the grove's huge trunks. This was prime market time, and the stalls were busy, selling everything from fresh sea-harvest through the crafters' wares like dishes, spear and arrow points, and the fish-gold jewelry that Kir's father made.

Her stomach growled at the scents drifting through the cool morning air, and she halted at her favorite stall. "Trade you sweet-snails for a fish and a bowl of tea." She waved the bag at the old woman tending the burner.

"Are they fresh?" She peered into the bag, pulled out one of the purple snails, and sniffed it. Tasted it. "Not bad." She grinned at Tahlia, her weathered face folding into a thousand wrinkles. "One fish." She lifted the smallest of the skewered pink-fish from the fire.

"I just picked them, you know you'll sell them all." Tahlia shook her head, pointed to a fatter fish. "That one. And the tea."

"No tea." The woman shook her head.

"I'll just take them over to Dalid, then." Tahlia snatched back the bag.

"All right. Tea." The stall owner snatched the bag back and tucked it quickly into the shadows behind her. "Tea." She filled one of the smaller cup-shell bowls with golden tea, handed Tahlia the grilled fish.

"Who told you you could be here stealing food, bad-luck eyes?"

Tahlia froze at the taunting voice. Slowly, deliberately, she took a bite of the juicy fish. Swallowed. "Did you run out of little kids to push around, Andir?" She drank some tea.

"I don't want to see you here." Andir stepped in front of her, the oldest son of the head of the council, his blue eyes hard. Two of his cousins flanked him. "You want to buy here, you do it when I'm not around."

"They elected you to replace your father?" Tahlia kept her posture relaxed, sipped more tea. "I guess I didn't hear the news."

"Someone needs to teach you respect for your betters." Andir sneered. "You're nothing but a tramp like your mother. You going to sell yourself to the hardlanders, too? They'll like your eyes, that's for sure."

She threw her tea in his face and he howled, scrubbing at his eyes.

"You little . . ." He flung himself forward, massive as a whale-fish. And about as slow.

Tahlia slipped aside and his grab missed. His cousins were hanging back, grinning, expecting to see Andir give her a beating, she guessed. She dodged again, but one of his cousins shoved her from behind and Andir's clawing fingers snagged her tunic. Xin was squirming now, struggling to free herself.

Sudden wind shook the branches of the grove, whirling shreds of tree-moss and leaves through the market.

Andir paused to look up, and Tahlia slapped him in the face with her grilled fish. Bits of greasy fish splattered his fine-woven tunic, and he snarled at her, lunging at her with the full weight of his body behind his charge. At the very edge of the woven path, Tahlia didn't move as he loomed. Behind him, his cousins shouted warning, but he was too blind with rage, too sure of his catch to listen.

At the last second, she leaped sideways, dropping feetfirst through a space in the interlaced branches, catching herself with both hands, and swinging up and onto the path again in one lithe movement. Behind her, Andir screamed as his foot slipped through the branches and he fell forward. She heard his ankle break with the sound of a snapping stick.

"I'll kill you for this, bad-luck," he screamed. "Get her!"

People were gathering now, but she didn't wait to see if they were going to intervene or not. Leaping lightly from branch to branch, off the path now, she headed for the next trunk. The cousins stuck to the path, not wanting to risk a fall into the water below. She made it to the next trunk before they did and scrambled up into the thick trunk-ferns that sprouted from it. Two spider-dragons lurked there, and she felt their interest as she scrambled upward, to the broken end of a limb she'd turned into a private perch.

"Go ahead and hide, bad-luck." One of the cousins shouted up at her, his face a shadow in the dim light. "I hope the spiders eat you."

One of the spider-dragons appeared at her shoulder and snapped, jaws crunching one of the hand-sized tree spiders a moment later. The huge spider's mate lurked nearby, its red eyes gleaming in shadows. Tahlia broke off a dead fern stem and flicked the huge, venomous spider off its perch. A shriek below and the sound of running feet told her she'd come close to her mark, anyway. The second spider-dragon snapped up another spider, then stuck its nose under the hem of her tunic.

Xin stuck her head up through the neck of her tunic and hissed something. The spider dragon flattened itself briefly, its silvery tongue flickering in and out, then stretched itself along Tahlia's thigh as she settled herself on the mat of dead fern fronds she'd woven to create a sleeping platform.

That one meant to hurt you. Xin's grumble filled her head. *I need to . . .*

What exactly she needed to do didn't quite translate. "That's all right." Tahlia sighed. "He's just a bully. We'll stay out of his way. Maybe it's time to go camp on the weed mats for a bit." This time of year, it didn't rain much, so it wouldn't be too bad.

She was sinking into a drowse, the dragonlet curled beneath her chin, when a voice calling her name softly woke her.

"Slane?" She rose to her knees, poked her head through the fronds, soothing the dragonlet's instant alarm. "Is that you?"

"It's me." Below, the aged healer looked up at her. "Come down. I know you say the spider-dragons protect you, but I'd rather you slept safe in a bed tonight, eh, girl?"

"When did you get back here?" She tucked Xin back into her tunic and scrambled down the trunk, the spider-dragons scrambling ahead of her, watchful of spiders. "I thought you were gone for a long time?"

"I was gone, but I got back this morning. It seemed like a long time to me." Slane smiled down at her, his face a wrinkled map of years and weather. "They brought Andir to me. He broke his ankle."

"I heard it break." Tahlia lifted her chin. "Serves him right."

"I expect so." Slane chuckled. "I didn't believe the boys' story for a moment." His expression went grave. "But some will. And you have made a serious enemy, Tahlia. Andir is a boy in name only, and you made a fool of him in front of quite a few people. He will hurt you if he can. And his father will shield him. Andir knows this."

"I know." She looked away.

"Come sleep in my dome tonight." He put a hand on her shoulder. "No need to risk spiders. I think it's time you joined me in my travels."

Go with him? Excitement filled her as she scrambled down. But she'd have to leave Kir behind. Frowning, she followed the healer along the paths as he greeted the grove dwellers out doing morning errands. Tahlia ignored the dark looks she got from a few. News of the fight . . . Andir's version, she guessed . . . was spreading fast.

The healer lived in a small dome on the second level. They climbed the rope web up one of the big trunks and followed the woven pathway through the branches, past the closely built domes encircled by their railed porches. As they approached his dome, with its extrabroad waiting-porch out front, roofed against weather, the healer paused. Light seeped from the door-curtain, which hadn't been completely drawn. "I didn't leave a light. Maybe you should wait." He put out a cautionary hand, but before he could take a step, the curtain was flung aside.

"You found her! She's safe." Kir dashed out to throw his arms around her. "Tahlia, I was so worried."

"Of course I'm safe." She hugged him back. "You're going to get in trouble."

"Yeah." He flashed her a grin. "I sure am." He led them inside as if he was the host, as if this was his dome.

Slane, shaking his head and smiling, lit his oil stove and set water on to heat for tea. The glow from the oil lamp lined his face with shadows and illuminated the bunches of dried seaweeds, fishes, and hardland plants hung from the ceiling. Jars of extracts and ointments lined shelves, and his small table and narrow bed were the only islands of clear space in the clutter.

"Did you really break Andir's leg?" Kir perched on the edge of the table, his pale eyes gleaming. "I wish I'd been there. He sure deserves it."

"He fell and broke his own ankle." But Tahlia had to smile. The dragonlet was squirming under her tunic, and she finally undid her belt. Xin immediately scrambled free, leaped onto the tabletop, and perched on a corner, her gleaming silver eyes reflecting the oil lamp's glow.

"It's bigger. Tahlia, it's really growing fast." Kir's eyes opened wide.

Slane put the water jug down and frowned at it. "Where did this come from?"

The dragonlet tilted her head. And Tahlia smothered a grin. "She," she said. "She's a she. She calls herself Xin."

Slane's grizzled eyebrows rose into his hairline. "She speaks with you?"

"It bites." Kir flinched as Xin hissed at him.

"I know you have an unusual bond with the spider- and surf-dragons. Oh yes, I've seen them pulling your boat." The healer seated himself on a stool, offered a cautious hand to the dragonlet, who hissed, then sniffed at his fingers. "But they don't speak to you, do they?"

"Not like this." The tea water was boiling, but Slane seemed to have forgotten it. Tahlia got up to spoon dried grove blossoms into the pot and poured in the hot water. The dragonlet clung to her shoulder, sniffing at the rising steam. "Kir thought she was a surf-dragon." She made a face at Xin's outrage. "All right, I apologize."

"Not a surf-dragon," Slane said absently. "I don't think so. Apparently, she doesn't either." He held out his palm, and the dragonlet, after a moment of hesitation, stepped onto it and walked up his arm to his shoulder, poking her snout into his hair and investigating his ear. "Tahlia . . . do you know why the grove people call your eyes bad luck?"

Tahlia put one of the steaming cups in front of him, didn't look at him. "Because they think my mother . . . she mated with a Kark . . . a hardlander." The whisper came out harsh. Kir had turned away, so she wouldn't see the pity in his face.

"That's Andir talking, isn't it?"

Slane's sharp tone made her look up. "Who else has golden eyes? Only the Kark!"

"It's been so long we've forgotten." He sighed. "We should not have forgotten." He winced as the dragonlet probed through his hair with one claw. "Easy, little one, that hurts." He turned his attention back to Tahlia. "You know the story of the sea-dragons?"

"Sure." She shrugged. "They protected the grove peoples with magic and kept the Kark on the hardland. Then, one day, the Crone called to them, and they all flew up to the moon. It's just a story for babies, Slane."

"Stories often have roots in reality." Slane smiled as the dragonlet leaped from his shoulder, her vestigial wings flailing, to land with a thump on the tabletop. She threaded her way delicately between the teapot and mugs, her claws scratching the wood, then scrambled onto Tahlia's shoulder and wrapped her long, finned tail around Tahlia's neck.

"The sea-dragons protected the grove peoples because they bonded with some grove dwellers who could speak with them." Slane blew on his tea. "The Kark weren't the only ones with magic, back then. If the bonded person died, the dragon no longer protected the grove where that person lived. Dragon loyalty is . . . limited."

Kir snorted, and the dragonlet flicked her tongue at him.

"I didn't know they *had* loyalty," Tahlia said, thinking of the many times she'd had to paddle home after her surf-dragons had lost interest and taken off. "I mean, sort of, but not very consistent, you know?"

We do. We are very loyal. The dragonlet prodded her ear with her narrow snout. *And your eyes look fine to me.*

"Ouch. Okay. And thank you." Tahlia felt her face heat as she realized Slane and Kir were staring at her.

"I take it she agrees with me." Slane took a slow sip of tea, his expression thoughtful. "The Kark realized that the way to eliminate the dragons was to kill the bonded human. And that's what they did." He set his cup down. "They sent out assassins to find and kill anyone with dragon-speaking blood. Then, once the dragon was gone, they raided that grove and killed everyone to the last person. Just to be certain that the bloodline was extinguished. You see, the ability to speak with dragons is inherited, Tahlia. And most dragon-speakers had . . . golden eyes."

Bad-luck golden eyes. Tahlia stared at him, and on her shoulder, the dragonlet hissed and extended her neck, her silver eyes sparking with anger, her wings rising and seeming to expand.

A sudden small gust whipped through the dome, sending weed-paper scrolls fluttering to the floor.

The healer nodded. "The Kark have us doing their work for them." His voice was bitter. "In many groves, a golden-eyed child is . . . set adrift at birth. That's why your mother came to this grove. I . . . brought her here. Because I knew that in this grove . . . her child would be safe. It wasn't true, in the grove where she grew up. Although I couldn't save her from the raiders." For a moment he was silent, his eyes full of shadows. "But now . . ." He nodded at the still-watchful dragonlet on her shoulder. "A sea-dragon has found you, Tahlia."

"It didn't find her. We found a nest. Of eggs." Kir bounced to his feet. "So it . . . she . . . can drive away the Kark?"

"She says that she doesn't remember how, but she will." Tahlia stroked the dragonlet's satiny scales, felt the creature's probing query. *You're a sea-dragon,* she thought. Felt Xin's *Yes, so?* shrug. "The ketrels came and killed the rest. She was the only one that survived. She bit me." Tahlia held out her hand. "But it healed when she licked it."

I had to know if I knew you. The dragon's thought felt testy. *How else could I know except to taste your blood?*

"How could you know me?" Tahlia looked down at her, surprised. "You just hatched!"

I know you. The words felt very positive.

"Ketrels?" Slane was looking grave. "Ketrels found the nest?"

"They came out of nowhere." Kir hunched his shoulders. "I thought they'd come after us for sure."

Tahlia shivered as the dragon gave a low, piercing cry of grief. "They killed all the others."

"Did they see you?" The healer leaned forward. "Did they attack you?"

She shook her head. "We got out of there fast."

"The ketrels are allied with the Kark. They must search for sea-dragon nests, destroy them before one can find a bond-mate. Maybe that's why we never find a nest." His face brightened. "I thought that the sea-dragons might be gone from this world entirely, but perhaps they come back here to lay their eggs occasionally. This can't be the only nest."

Tahlia blinked. "Xin says they're not gone, they're just . . ." She frowned. "I don't think I really understand what she means. Right here but not here?"

"The grove people were strong when the sea-dragons partnered with us." Slane's eyes took on a faraway look. "We and the Kark were equals. Their magic could defeat us, but not the sea-dragons, and sea-dragons protected the groves from the slave-raiders. But then the Kark discovered that they could drive away the sea-dragons by killing off the bloodlines that could bond with them."

"Tahlia can't be the only one." Kir bounced to his feet. "There have to be others."

"Oh, there are others. A few." A slow smile grew on the healer's face. "I was going to take you to meet some of them, Tahlia. They are scattered, living in groves where they're tolerated. We healers keep track of them. We have been . . . hoping that the sea-dragons might one day return."

"And they have." Tahlia stroked the dragonlet's filmy vestigial wings. "If that's what you really are."

I am what I am. Xin ruffled her wings, and another gust of wind swirled more scrolls to the floor.

"Don't make her mad, Tahl." Kir eyed her nervously. "Aren't the sea-dragons supposed to be really dangerous? I mean, they could beat the Kark, right?"

"I think you're safe, Kir." The healer chuckled but shadows still lurked in his eyes. "You need to keep her hidden, Tahlia. Out of sight. If the ketrels found the nest so quickly, they must be looking hard for eggs. And that means the Kark will have spies listening for any news that might mean a sea-dragon has bonded with one of us. That's why we healers have hidden the golden-eyed children in the small groves, away from the large city-groves. The risk of raiders is higher, but they're harder for the Kark to find."

"I'll tell anyone who sees her that she's a surf-dragon." Tahlia yelped as Xin nipped her ear. "You're *not* a surf-dragon, but we need to make people *think* so, okay? Ouch." She rubbed her ear. "That hurt!"

"Does she know how to reach the place where the other dragons are?" Kir leaned close. "Maybe she could bring the others?"

I don't remember. Xin lashed her slender tail. *But I will.*

Kir scowled as Tahlia relayed her response. "I don't get it. How you can *remember* something you don't know."

"We'll hope, eh?" But the healer, too, looked disappointed. "Do you want me to send a note to your father, Kir? Telling him I needed your help?"

"That would be good." He made a face as Slane found a scrap of paper, penned a note. "Father is going to be really mad. Maybe she'll remember how to call the other sea-dragons, eh?" In a moment, he was out the door, vanished into the grove shadows.

"We'll hope, eh?" Slane's tone was sober, but he smiled. "Kir's a loyal friend, isn't he?" He turned to Tahlia. "I have some fresh fish if our sea-dragon needs to eat. And some sweet-shell pastries for you. I'll see if I can clear you a space to sleep."

Xin let Tahlia know with no uncertainty that yes, she needed that fish now. Lots of fish. And the sweet-shell pastries were fresh and well spiced. Tahlia hadn't realized how hungry she was until she bit into the first one. By the time she had finished, the healer had made her a cozy bed in a corner sheltered by stacks of scrolls and bundles of dried things. She curled up with the woven moss blanket he gave her and the dragonlet tucked against her belly, licking the last crumbs from her chin, and fell instantly asleep.

ๆ๖

SHE stayed away from the grove as much as possible in the weeks that followed, staying out on the weed mats that this time of year tended to collect in long, ragged shoals to the leeward of the groves. Soon, they would let go of their long, anchoring roots and go drifting with the winter storms, carrying their seeds and resident creatures to other parts of the world ocean. But for now, they made a nice dry place to sleep. Kir brought her a small oil stove that his family used sometimes in the cold season and she often cooked sweet and succulent bottom-crabs for them. Xin—now much larger than a surf-dragon and growing rapidly—dove for the crabs happily, now that she knew that Tahlia liked them. A rare delicacy, Kir traded the extra at the market for her, and the healer came out often to visit and, she guessed, keep an eye on her. He hadn't mentioned her going with him, but they both knew it had to happen.

She didn't tell Kir, couldn't find the words.

Mostly, she swam with Xin, whose speed and skill in the water made the fish look slow and ponderous, and visited with Kir whenever he could sneak away.

"What are you going to do when the season changes and the mats start to break up?" Kir sat on the thinning fringe of the mat, dangling a fish line in hopes of catching dinner for his mother. "Andir is still walking with a stick. His ankle didn't heal right, and he blames you."

"He probably wouldn't stay off it while it healed." Tahlia flopped onto her belly beside him, hoping to steer the subject away from season's end. "Or does he blame my eyes?"

"You know Andir." Kir made a face. "Where's Xin?"

"Off catching her dinner. She eats like a dozen fishermen." Tahlia laughed. "Good thing she can feed herself, or I'd be at it all day."

"Got one!" Kir sat up, reeling in the line hand over hand. "Feels like a really big one. Mom's going to be happy!"

"Kir?" Tahlia tensed as the prow of a boat nosed out from the shelter of three small, tangled clumps.

He looked up, let go of the line. "That's Jirath's boat. You know. Andir's cousin. Get out of here." He bolted to his feet, fists clenched. "I'll pretend you're hiding somewhere here. You'll have time to get away while they look for you."

"They'd just beat you to a pulp." Tahlia watched three outriggers slide into view, each carrying two paddlers. "And they've seen us." She felt strangely light and calm as the boats bumped against the mat and the six youths scrambled out.

Andir and his cousins, plus three hangers-on. They stayed back as he limped forward, spreading out in a loose half circle to block Tahlia and Kir from the boats. Andir was smiling, but his eyes held a cold ugliness that made her skin tighten.

"You ruined my leg, you witch." He stopped about two arm's lengths away, still smiling, his tone light, almost friendly. "The healer says the bone set crooked, and I'll always limp. Your bad-luck eyes did it, made it not heal."

"Walking on it too soon kept it from healing." Tahlia made her voice even. "You should have listened to the healer."

"Everybody knows he's your friend. Your bad luck infected him."

"You're just not smart enough to listen to good advice."

His fist caught her by surprise, spun her backward. She fell onto the matted weed, skinning her palms on the rough, salt-stiffened stems. He grabbed her arm and yanked her to her feet as Kir yelled. He had started for them, but Andir's cousins held him, arms twisted behind his back.

"You need a lesson, witch." Grinning, Andir raised his fist.

Tahlia cringed away, watched his smile grow creamy with satisfaction as he enjoyed her seeming submission. She shifted her weight and kicked straight out.

Her heel caught him below his belt and he let go, doubling over with a cry.

"Run," Kir yelled. "Get away . . ." His shout was cut off as one of Andir's pack punched him hard in the stomach.

Tahlia grabbed up a short piece of thick weed stem and spun, catching the cousin holding Kir square across the side of the face. The hollow stem snapped, but he let go with a howl, grabbing his welted face. The other cousin let go of Kir and lunged at her.

"Come on." Tahlia hauled Kir to his feet.

Too late. Hands grabbed her from behind as two others tackled Kir. She went down fighting, clawing. Something hit her hard in the back of her head, and for a moment the world blurred and darkened. When she could focus her eyes, she was on her back, held down by three of Andir's gang. She could hear Kir gasping somewhere out of sight.

Andir stood over her, and the look on his face chilled her. Slowly, he reached down and pulled her fish knife from her belt. "You and your bad-luck eyes. You just don't know when you're not wanted, do you?" He reached down and grabbed the neck of her tunic. The fabric ripped, and he laughed, a short, ugly sound.

"Andir, are you crazy?" Kir sounded panicked. "What are you doing?"

"We were out here fishing and saw you drown your stupid little friend here." Slowly, Andir drew the knife blade across her chest, from her shoulder to her breastbone.

The blade felt cool, followed immediately by hot, burning pain. Tahlia felt hot wetness trickling down her ribs as he straightened, his lips curving into a smile beneath his terrifying eyes.

"When we tried to help him, stop you, you attacked us. Self-defense. We had to kill you, you were crazy."

"Andir, stop it." Kir's voice had dropped to a whisper. "What are you thinking?"

"We'll be rid of you." Andir laughed, his eyes on her face. "You never should have messed with me. Want to beg now? Or you can let your spineless little buddy do it for you."

"Andir, you're crazy." Kir started to struggle. "Someone is going to tell. Someone is going to see you."

He gave Kir a contemptuous look. "Tie his arms and legs. Dorn, you get that anchor rock we brought. They'll never find him on the bottom."

"Andir?" The one he'd addressed sounded uncertain. "What's that? It looks like a big surf-dragon."

"Who cares? I like to spear surf-dragons." Andir turned back to Tahlia, shifted his grip on the knife.

She tensed.

One of the youths yelled in terror, and, suddenly, the hands holding her down were gone. She scrambled to her feet as Andir lunged at her. The blade gashed her arm, leaving hot pain in its wake. She scrambled back as he lunged at her again, but his bad ankle turned and he fell with a scream of rage. Kir leaped in, grabbing his wrist, twisting it as he struggled for the knife, leaping back in triumph, the blade gleaming in his bloody hand. Then his triumph vanished. "Tahlia . . ." He pointed.

Xin rose from the water a few lengths from the edge of the mat, her eyes flashing crimson light. Her vestigial swimming wings made a silver blur in the air, growing larger by the second. Water, whipped to froth, boiled up around her, and sudden wind gusted, knocking the two youths who had held Kir to their knees. The boats tore free of their tethers as a waterspout began to grow around the dragon. In a matter of moments, the whirling column towered over the mat, its roar deafening, the cold, wet blast of the wind bringing Tahlia and Kir to their knees as they clung to the weed to keep from being sucked into the whirling funnel.

At the top of the spinning tower, the dragon's red eyes gleamed balefully.

One of the boats spun overhead to bounce across the weed mat, and Tahlia flattened herself, pulling Kir down beside her. The two cousins screamed as they were pulled into the spinning tower of water. The one named Dorn tried to burrow into the weed mat.

Andir stood straight, his eyes crazy, lips pulled back from his teeth. "You did this, bad-luck eyes!" His hoarse scream cut through the howling of the waterspout. "This is your doing!"

The silvery tower of water leaned across the weed mat, and, in a second, Andir was gone. The waterspout moved away from the mat, churning the water into white froth, spinning toward the horizon. It left a deafening silence in its wake.

For a moment, nobody moved. Then Dorn scrambled from his shelter in the weeds, stumbled to the edge of the weed mat, and dove off. A moment later, his head broke the surface, heading back toward the grove. The other two youths followed.

"They'll drown." Tahlia stood up, shakily, looked around. "Our boats are gone, too."

"The waterspout tore all kinds of junk off the mat." Kir shaded his eyes. "They've got floating stuff to hang on to, all of 'em. They'll make it okay." He turned a pale face to Tahlia. "Was that your . . . what was that?"

"I guess that's . . . what sea-dragons do." Tahlia looked toward the horizon. The water spout had vanished. She shivered. "He cut you bad." She took his hand.

"I can still use it." He flexed his fingers, winced, then pressed his fingers against the gash across his palm. "And you're bleeding, too. We're going to have to swim back. Before the others tell their version to everybody." He looked grim. "Are you okay to do that?" He frowned. "You're shaking, Tahlia."

"Yeah." She flexed her fingers, drew a shuddering breath. "I am."

"He was really crazy." Kir hunched his shoulders. "I mean, he's always been a bully, but . . ." He shivered. "Let's lash some stuff together, big enough for us to rest on if we need to, okay?" He gave her a crooked smile. "I might need that."

He was worrying about her, not himself, but that seemed like a good idea. Even though the cuts weren't deep, she wasn't sure she had the strength to swim all the way back to the grove, even with a piece of floating weed to cling to.

They lashed a small raft together and pushed off, heading for the grove, with the afternoon sun behind them. Before they'd swum more than a hundred lengths from the mat, a large cargo canoe appeared in front of them.

"Slane." Tahlia clung to their makeshift raft. "I'm so glad to see you. Kir's hand is cut."

"Tahlia, what happened?" The healer maneuvered the wide-bottomed boat alongside and reached down to pull them aboard. "The boys showed up hysterical, with stories about some kind of monster. Where's Andir, Elor, and Qwait?" Anxiety tightened his face. "Kir, how did you cut your hand like that?"

"Taking a knife away from Andir." Tahlia shook water from her hair. "Andir tried to kill me, they were going to drown Kir. They know what happened. The others. They were part of it." As the healer stared at her, aghast, she poured out the story of Andir's arrival and Xin's transformation.

"I don't know . . . that's not the story they're telling." He stared back toward the grove as the light deepened to sunset. "Not that . . . they're very coherent."

His shoulders were hunched, and he wasn't looking at her. "Slane, take me back to the weed mat. I have a camp there. Take Kir in. He wasn't part of this."

"You are *so* wrong." Kir grabbed her shirt, yanked her around to face him. "What are you thinking?" Angry tears gleamed in his eyes. "What am I? Nothing? I was there, too. I'm going to tell 'em what happened. We both are. No way you go off and wait for those liars to stir up a mob against you."

"I should just go." She looked away.

"I ought to hit you." Kir scooted across the canoe bottom so that she had to look at him. "You're my friend. It matters to *me* if it doesn't to you."

"Okay." She drew a deep breath. "It does matter to me, Kir. I'm sorry." She looked down. "And don't hit me. You're already bleeding again."

"Oh. I guess I am." He clenched his hand into a fist, blood dripping onto the floor of the canoe.

"You'll come stay with me." Slane had straightened and drove the canoe through the water with fierce strokes. "No one will dare enter without my permission. We'll see this through."

They didn't get that far. As they neared the grove in the fading light, Tahlia made out the shapes of many canoes clustered along the shore. Oil lamps glowed in the gloom between the trunks, and it seemed as if every resident of the grove clustered on the lashed platform of the floating dock that skirted the massive trunks.

"Healer, did you find them?" A voice rang out. "Who's with you?"

Sidon, the head of the grove's council.

Andir's father.

"Did you find Kir?" Another voice rang out. "Did she kill him, too?"

"Father, she didn't kill anyone." Kir leaped to the prow of the boat, balancing there as Slane stilled its forward motion. "Andir tried to kill her. With a knife." He thrust his slashed palm into the air. "He was crazy. And they were helping him. All of them."

"That's a lie!" The three surviving boys stood in the midst of the council members in the middle of the dock. The tallest one, Zoav, pushed forward. "She called up a demon. He's just trying to cover up for her."

"We need to sift truth from untruth here." Slane raised his voice, but the crowd was pressing forward so that wavelets lapped over the dock as it sank beneath the load. Shouts of "bad luck" and "demon eyes" rose above the murmur.

"We need to sort this out." Slane dug his paddle into the water to back the canoe away from the dock, but already boats had pushed off, arcing out to cut off escape.

"She must answer for these deaths." Sidon's voice boomed above the crowd noise. "No one will harm her until we decide her fate."

"Kill her before she can call the demon!" A woman with a taut face burst to the front of the dock. "While we wait and squabble, she is calling it back." Hair wild about her face, she flung out her hand, finger like a spear thrust at Tahlia's chest. "She must pay for my son's death, and she must die before she can kill more of our children. Quickly!" Her voice rose to a scream. "I tell you, she's calling it now!"

"No," Tahlia cried, but her voice was lost in a rising clamor. Some leaped into boats, others tried to hold them back. Sidon was shouting, but only a handful of people were listening to him.

Slane thrust his paddle deep into the water, but a half dozen canoes had already cut him off, arrowed toward them. In the foremost canoe, a grim-faced man held a fishing spear, its long, barbed head bloody in the sinking sun's light. Behind him, Kir's father drove the boat forward, his face stark with fear and anger.

"No." Kir leaped in front of Tahlia. "You're wrong. Don't do this, Father."

A spear thunked into the side of the canoe, and, a second later, Slane cried out as an arrow sank into his arm. He dropped the paddle, grabbed for it with his good hand as it splashed into the water. The boat driven by Kir's father slammed into their stern and Tahlia fell to her knees, grabbing for the side of the boat as she nearly went over. Kir managed to keep his footing, arms spread, his face desperate in the sunset light. "We're telling the truth! *Listen* to us!"

The man with the spear drew back his arm. Tahlia's eyes seemed frozen to the gleaming point with its wicked barbs. She wanted to duck, leap overboard, but her muscles wouldn't obey her.

Screams from behind her seeped through her fear. The spearman hesitated, head turning. With a cry, he lowered his spear, turned. Tahlia followed his gaze. There, in the deepening twilight, a serpentine neck rose from the swells. Xin shrieked, eyes flashing crimson light brighter than the setting sun. She reared out of the water, rising taller and taller, her wings beating, expanding, whipping the water into white foam. The water seethed, began to whirl about her. It caught the canoe paddled by Kir's father, sucked it toward the maelstrom.

Already the water was rising into a white, spinning tower. Wind-driven spray stung Tahlia's face, and she clung to the boat as it rocked in the sudden chop.

"No!" Kir leaped from the canoe, splashing into the water between the boats, grabbing on to the gunwale of his father's boat. "Tahlia, don't let it!"

A dozen canoes were in the water, and the waves generated by the waterspout washed across the dock, carrying grove residents shrieking into the water.

"Stop!" Tahlia leaped to her feet, balancing lightly on the bucking canoe. "Stop it now!"

They want to kill you. Xin turned her attention once more to the canoes and the people struggling in the water.

"No!" Tahlia threw all the weight of her fear into the word. "Go away, Xin. Go fly up with the others! Now!"

Fly up? Xin's voice in her head was heavy with hurt. *With the others?*

"Yes." Tahlia closed her eyes. "Go. Now."

We don't fly up. And she dove. Just like that, the water quieted.

She was gone. Her absence rang in Tahlia's head.

For the space of a dozen heartbeats, the only sound was the slap of water against the dock and the grove trunks. Then the clamor began again as residents hauled people from the water. The canoes closed on them from all sides, bumping against the sides of the healer's boat, cutting off all escape. Kir's father had hauled his son into the boat and was paddling toward the dock with him. Kir hung over the stern, his mouth open, yelling something to her.

She couldn't hear his words. Bowed her head as hands grabbed her, hard, unforgiving fingers bruising her arms.

And then they let go. Canoes were pushing away from their boat. More shrieks rose from the grove dock. Tahlia blinked into the thickening dusk, squinting against the last bloody beams of light from the vanishing sun, looking for the dragon.

"Kark!" The healer's voice broke, and he leaned over the side of the canoe, tipping it dangerously as he grabbed for the dropped paddle with his good hand.

Tahlia stared around, her heart a stone in her chest. There they were, three tall ships barely visible against the bloody light of the dying day, hidden until the last by the magic of their captains. Already small, sleek boats were dropping into the water, speeding toward the grove on a white tail of foam.

Each powered by a captive's life force, drained to power the magic.

"Tahlia, paddle." Slane's command came low and urgent. "Quickly! Back to the mat. They'll focus on the grove and taking captives."

"Kir." She peered toward the grove, but his father's canoe was lost in the chaos of grove residents arming themselves, docking canoes, scrambling up the trunks. "I can't leave Kir."

"Yes, you can." His voice was harsh. "He doesn't matter. You do."

She grabbed the gunwale to vault into the water.

Something hit her in the back of the head, and red light exploded behind her eyes, then blackness came rushing in.

ℰᏏ

SHE woke to blue sky overhead and throbbing pain in her head. "I'm sorry." Slane's face moved into view, blocking out the sky. "I didn't mean to hit you so hard. Here." He held a bowl to her lips as he slid an arm beneath her shoulders. "This will help."

She grimaced at the bitter taste of the brew, but her headache faded some as she sat up. "Kir." She started to get up, but Slane's hand on her shoulder stopped her.

Three Kark ships floated just off the grove, and dark longboats plied back and forth. They went to the grove empty, came back loaded with bound captives. Mostly children, it looked like. Numbly she watched as one of the small boats pulled alongside the ship and the first captive was winched upward by his bound hands. At this distance, she could make out the pale shapes of the chained slaves along the deck rail. Their life force fed the magic that moved the ships. For a while. Until it was gone. The boy being hoisted to the deck was struggling fiercely, in spite of the ropes that bound hands and feet. Kir? She squinted, but the tears in her eyes blurred his features. It could be. In a moment he was dragged on deck, and one of the raiders leaned over him, swinging a club, his sun-darkened shoulders gleaming with sweat as he struck. She looked away, her throat so tight that she could barely breathe. "They came because of me, didn't they?" she whispered. "One of the ketrels must have seen the dragon, must have followed us back."

"You don't know that." Slane stroked her hair back from her face. "It doesn't matter how they got here. They are here. Stay low." He pulled her down as she started to rise. "I have a boat hidden on the far side of the mat. As soon as it's dark, we'll leave. We have enough water, I think, to get us to the next grove. And if not, we'll just have to catch fountain fish."

"Bad-luck eyes." She stared out at the dark ships, the busy to and fro of the raiders' boats as they stripped the grove. "I'll just bring it to the next grove."

"*Stop* it!" He jerked her around to face him, his own eyes blazing. "You are our *hope*, don't you see? You need to call your dragon back. The dragons kept the groves safe once. It can happen again. We've kept the strain of dragon-speakers alive. You have given us the key to the dragons."

"Xin's gone." Tahlia looked down at the salt-crusted weed beneath her knees. "I sent her to . . . wherever they are."

Slane was staring at her in stunned disbelief. "Can't you call her back?"

She shook her head. All sense of the dragon was gone. As if she really had flown to the moon, like the old stories said.

"Well," he said heavily. "We'll still go. We have to. Maybe . . . she'll come back to find you."

She didn't argue with him, nodded when he wanted her to agree, watched the slow descent of the sun as the boats went back and forth. They weren't bringing any more captives now. They must have enough to power the boats. Until the next raid. The returning longboats were now full of bundles and fish-skin sacks of oil. Slane gave her some dried bluefish meat and a cup of water as the sun set, and she made herself eat and drink.

"Sleep for a little while," he told her in a whisper, as the dusk thickened to full dark. "We'll leave after the Crone takes her walk."

She was already rising, her yellow lamp shedding a weak light across the water. It was still, the swells sluggish and oily, as if the sea itself grieved for the destruction of the grove. Tahlia listened, and, after a while, she heard Slane's breathing change, deepen into sleep. Silently, she stripped to her belt and fish knife, crawled across the mat, and slid into the cool water.

It was as if the Crone aimed her lamp to guide Tahlia's way, laying down a yellow shimmer of light that stretched like a path to the nearest ship. It loomed over her, impossibly tall, silent except for the slap and suck of water along the hull. All must be below, she thought. Except for guards. There would be guards. The Crone's light touched the rail of the ship above her and gleamed on clumps of stone-clam sprouting on the sleek black planks of the ship's hull. You had to scrape them off the canoes, or they'd foul it clear to the gunwale.

The Crone's light picked out a stairway of clams. Tahlia stretched, grabbing the first clump, bracing her feet against the slick hull. The boat rolled gently in the slow swell, lifting her clear of the water as she reached for the next clump, got a toehold on the first clump. Her shoulders burned with the strain as she slowly, painfully, worked her way from clump to clump, afraid to look up, afraid to look down. Then, suddenly, she found herself at the deck. For a moment, her mind numb with effort, she could only stare at the low rail and the dark deck beyond. The Crone had hidden her light behind a cloud and all was black.

Footsteps slapped on the deck, and she flattened herself to the hull as a Kark walked by. A guard? She listened to his steps diminish, then slipped over the rail and crouched, trying to get her breath back. The Crone unveiled her lamp again, and Tahlia stifled a squeak as she found herself between two crouching shapes. The Crone's light illuminated pale, fish-belly faces and glazed, unseeing eyes.

The captives. The ones that powered the ship. Tahlia's stomach twisted with horror. Pale, unhealthy skin hung on bones, and no light of intelligence flickered in the glassy, golden eyes that seemed to look through her. For an awful moment, Tahlia thought the woman might be her mother. A softly glowing collar of ruby light ringed the captive's throat, and shackles chained her ankles to the deck. Not her mother, no. The ruby collar pulsed with a thready irregular rhythm, like a heartbeat. A failing heartbeat. As she watched, it slowed, flickered, then darkened. The creature sagged slightly forward, its jaw dropping slowly.

Tahlia scrambled backward, swallowed a gasp as she backed into another captive. A man, this one seemed less drained, still healthy-looking, his eyes the sky color of the grove peoples. But they had the same flat, unseeing look. His collar pulsed strongly.

Voices sounded aft of the dead captive, coming closer. Someone laughed harshly, and Tahlia heard a sound like a blow. The Crone poured yellow light down on the dead captive as a silver-haired, gold-eyed Kark bent over the corpse and said something in a harsh, disgusted tone. Metal rattled as he unlocked the shackles. He removed the dull collar and picked the body up as if it weighed nothing. Tahlia shivered as he tossed her over the side like a piece of trash. He peered after, nodded as she splashed into the water, then snapped an order over his shoulder, his tone impatient.

Another Kark emerged from the shadows, dragging a small figure. Hands bound behind him, face crusted with dried blood, the boy kicked at the Kark with bound feet.

Kir.

The Kark dragging him stopped and raised a fist, but at his companion's snarl, grunted and grabbed Kir's ankles, dragging him facedown toward the waiting shackles. The Kark with the collar grabbed Kir by the hair, ready to put it around his neck.

Tahlia launched herself at him, knife in her hand. The blade caught the crouching Kark, the one who had dragged Kir, in the back, but it skated along his ribs. He leaped away with a howl, and Tahlia slashed at the other Kark's eyes. He dropped the collar, scrambling back, yelling at the top of his lungs.

Sound erupted everywhere, and the Crone doused her lamp once more. Tahlia flung herself down, felt Kir's writhing body beneath her. "It's me." She found the weed-fiber ropes binding his hands, slid the knife blade beneath it. Hands closed on her back, nails raking her skin as she twisted, slashing blindly with the knife. Her attacker yelped and leaped back. Someone shouted a hoarse order, and, suddenly, Kir was yanked away from her, yelling at the top of his lungs.

A dark shape loomed over her, and Tahlia leaped aside, ducking his grab. She leaped up to the rail, ran along it for a few steps. Oil lamps illuminated a dozen raiders. Some were grinning as they surrounded her, cutting her off on both sides. The Crone drifted from behind her veil of cloud, and Tahlia saw black boats below her in the water. No escape there, either. For a moment, time seemed to stand still. The Crone's lamp seemed to float on the slow, dark swells, like a perfectly round pool of yellow light.

They flew away up to the moon. The words of the old myth.

We don't fly up. Xin's voice echoed in her head, full of hurt.

Tahlia flexed her legs and dove from the rail, arcing downward as the Kark howled and laughed, her stiff fingers cutting the yellow circle of light precisely in the center.

She kicked, disoriented for a moment, lungs burning as she swam down through a tunnel of golden light . . . no . . . she was swimming . . . *up.*

She broke the surface, blinked in sunlight, beneath blue sky. Pale birds circled overhead, and one fell like stone, splashing down with a gout of spray to emerge a moment later, flapping heavily, a silvery fish in its talons. A moment later, a familiar form burst from the water, the serpentine neck curving as it spied her, silvery scales gleaming in the sun.

About time. Xin's voice prodded her mind, edged with a righteous indignation. *What took you so long? You were rude.*

"I didn't know how to find you. I need you," Tahlia gasped, struggling not to cry. "I'm so glad to see you." She threw her arms around the dragon's neck. "The Kark . . ." She flinched as Xin intruded on her thoughts. For a moment, it was as if her mind was like one of the healer's scrolls, and the dragon was unrolling it, reading everything that had happened since Tahlia had sent her away.

A deep, crimson anger began to rise in Xin, scorching Tahlia so that she winced.

I remember them. I don't like them.

"How can you remember them?" Tahlia blinked at her.

We know very little when we hatch, but we remember everything by the time we're very old. I am remembering more and more. I do not like them. The dragon bared her many curved, silvery teeth in a grin. *Let's go save your small-friend. I like to eat Kark, you know.* Her grin widened, teeth glinting. *I remember that they are tough and chewy, but not bad. Hold on.*

Tahlia scrambled onto Xin's shoulders and locked her arms around the dragon's neck. It was much bigger than she, now, big as her canoe. She sucked in a quick lungful of air as Xin dove, and her stomach clenched as *down* suddenly turned to *up* as they rose through the tunnel of light. They surfaced in the midst of the longboats, as if no time had passed at all.

The Kark in the nearest boat shouted something and stood, balancing lightly on the gunwales of his boat, a barbed spear in his hand, trailing a line. The dragon reared out of the water, her wings churning, whipping the water to froth. Wind gusted, and the boat canted over, tossing the spearman into the water. The dragon's head shot out with the speed of a sea snake, and the man's scream choked off as the jaws closed on him. Then the ocean lifted in a white whirl of power.

Tahlia clung to Xin's neck, blinded by stinging spray, barely able to breathe. The roaring chaos seemed to go on forever, and she had the sensation of moving at great speed, but she didn't dare open her eyes, clutching the dragon's neck with all her strength, afraid that her grip would fail, that she would fall into the roaring maelstrom around them.

Time stretched on forever, and her arms began to tremble with exhaustion. Then, suddenly, the roaring began to fade. Shivering, she straightened, blinking in the Crone's weak light as the dragon shook her shrinking wings and folded them close to her side. The three ships still floated, but canted over, their decks scoured clean. Not a single Kark was visible anywhere.

"What happened to them?" She pushed wet hair out of her eyes.

The dragon bent her long neck and nosed her wing into a neater fold. *I took them elsewhere.*

"What about Kir?" Fear seized her.

I was careful. The dragon twisted her long neck to turn a reproachful eye on Tahlia. *Look, he's waving at you.* She made a sound like a blowfish surfacing. *Your kind has terrible eyesight, you know.*

"Well, it's dark, Xin." But he was there, scrambling up onto the rail of the closest ship, waving at her. Behind him, shadowy figures emerged from the hold of the ship, tentative, fearful. Whooping, Kir leaped from the rail as the dragon swam closer, splashing down into the water beside them, scrambling onto Xin's back behind Tahlia.

"Wow, how did you do that?" He laughed, his eyes round. "It was like a winter storm all around me, Kark flying off the deck right and left. But I didn't feel anything but a breeze."

Of course not. The dragon sounded testy. *I'm much more skillful than that, small-friend.*

"I heard that." Kir almost fell off, grabbed for Tahlia's waist at the last second. "She *can* talk! I really didn't believe . . ."

They both winced at Xin's snort of laughter. *I didn't choose to talk to you before. You can talk to us if you want to. Not all can.* Xin snorted again. *You may find your own dragon-friend one day, small one.*

Shadows moved in the grove. The survivors who had fled or hidden were coming down to the dock, as tentative as the captives on the empty Kark ships. Tahlia leaned forward. "Maybe you can convince other dragons to come back here, do you think?"

Perhaps. The dragon bent her head, considering. *If we have people to speak with once more.* She swam toward the grove, the returning villagers retreating with fear and wonder in their eyes.

The Dragaman's Bride

ANDY DUNCAN

Andy Duncan made his first sale, to Asimov's Science Fiction, in 1995, and quickly made others, to Starlight, Sci Fiction, Dying For It, Realms of Fantasy, and Weird Tales, as well as several more sales to Asimov's. By the beginning of the new century, he was widely recognized as one of the most individual, quirky, and flavorful new voices on the scene today. His story "The Executioners' Guild" was on the final Nebula ballot in 2000, the first of his six Nebula nominations, and in 2001 he won two World Fantasy Awards, for his story "The Pottawatomie Giant" and for his landmark first collection, Beluthahatchie and Other Stories. *He also won the Theodore Sturgeon Memorial Award in 2002 for his novella "The Chief Designer." His other books include an anthology coedited with F. Brett Cox,* Crossroads: Tales of the Southern Literary Fantastic, *and a nonfiction guidebook,* Alabama Curiosities. *A graduate of the Clarion West writers' workshop in Seattle, he was raised in Batesburg, South Carolina, now lives in Frostburg, Maryland, with his wife, Sydney, and is an assistant professor in the Department of English at Frostburg State University. He has a blog at http://beluthahatchie .blogspot.com.*

In the evocative, scary, and wryly funny story that follows, he takes us to the mountains of Virginia in the 1930s for some tall-tale telling at its best, in company with a brave young girl who is wise enough to know that if you would sup with the Devil—or even his son-in-law—you should use a long spoon . . . and also that love is where you find it, no matter who it's with.

৫৯

PROLOGUE

*S*HE'D *been in sight for a half hour. As the sheriff labored up the slope,
the pine trees dwindled in size, as if he were growing, so that he emerged*

at the bare crest a giant. The wind from Lost Spectacles Gap drove the rain into his face. The girl had not plunged down the other side into a fast escape, as he had hoped and feared, but instead had clambered westward along the rocky ridgeline of Cove Mountain, on an old goat track that was mostly boulders and scree. She was a hundred yards ahead, and her bare arms seemed to glow against the gray rocks and sky. She was bareheaded, too, but the red hair that had given her away downslope, before the skies opened, now was dark and ropy in the rain. Her soaked dress clung to her young woman's body, the sheriff half saw and half imagined.

"C'mon down, honey," he called. "That path's a dead end." As if he needed to tell Ash Harrell's only child anything about Cove Mountain. It was what she knew; it was all she had to know. But his knees hurt, he was soaked and out of breath, and he did not want to sidle among these high rocks in the dark, as the gravel shifted beneath him. Downslope, he could see the flashlight of the next-to-useless deputy who followed as slowly as possible, in hopes the sheriff would give up and come back down.

"Only fraidy-cats are scared of the doctor," the sheriff yelled. "I thought you were a big girl now. Aw, c'mon, child, there's a hot stove waiting, and good rabbit stew."

The receding bright spot on the ridge that was Allie Harrell did not stop or look around, but her voice cut through the rain and wind. "You eat it," she called.

"Little bitch," the sheriff muttered, as a peal of thunder seemed to shake the mountain. Did a girl, he wonder, holler like a boar hog when she got snipped? Flashlight in his left hand, he found a slick rock crevice with his right and hauled himself onto the path the girl had taken.

A lightning flash illuminated the end of the path: a jagged, moss-patched shard of quartzite that towered thirty-five feet above the western-most part of the ridge. Buzzard's Rock, the landmark was called, though even the buzzards seemed to shun it. The Harrell girl stood at the base of the spire, at the top of a heap of boulders. Good God, surely she didn't intend to jump? Was the prospect of the state hospital that terrifying?

The rain had slacked off some, and in only a few more steps he would be close enough to talk to her in a reasonable tone of voice. Hoping to distract her in the meantime, he shined the flashlight into her face. She squinted—and smiled at him.

"You come down from there right now," he said. He took a step forward onto a flat rock that tipped sideways, so he stepped back to solid ground, keeping the flashlight on her. "I don't want you falling and hurting yourself, ruining your pretty face." Actually, she looked like a half-drowned wharf rat at the moment, the same as he probably did, but she was still pretty. Beautiful, even. As if reading his mind, she lifted a hand and tucked a hank of hair back behind her ear. The little flirt! You would think he had asked her to dance after a corn-shucking, when in fact he had ordered her to come down off a precipice in a storm. He edged closer, though everywhere he placed his feet seemed uncertain now.

"I just wanted to get you alone, Sheriff," she said. "Come up here closer, so I can talk to you."

Wet as he was, the sheriff felt his mouth go dry.

From the path behind came the voice of Deputy Larsen, with his customary poor timing: "Hang on, Sheriff Stiles, I'm coming."

"You stay back there!" the sheriff cried.

"Well, how come?"

"Never mind how come." The gravel beneath his left foot rolled sideways, and his leg followed it into nothing. He wrapped his arms around a boulder to keep from falling who knew how far. "I'm talking her down, you idiot. We're negotiating."

A crash of thunder. As the rain slackened, the thunder seemed to be getting louder—but would he have flinched so if it hadn't been on the heels of a bald-faced lie? And her a mere slip of a hardscrabble girl, and him a respected man? As the thunder rolled out of earshot, it was replaced by another sound. Allie Harrell was laughing, a low chuckle that raised the sheriff's short hairs.

"Negotiating," she said. "Is that what they call it in town, Sheriff? On the mountain, we have other words for it."

With some reluctance, the sheriff had let go of the boulder, freeing himself to creep around it to a spot directly beneath the girl. He shined the flashlight beam into her face, liked not at all what he saw there, then flicked it lower to see that she was leaning her elbows on a giant, tilted slab of rock that reared between the two of them. It was like a natural pulpit, and him in the front pew, looking up.

"Girl," he said, his voice a croak. He licked his lips and tried again. "Girl, you don't want me to come up there after you."

She laughed again. "Don't I?" she asked.

"Sheriff! You OK?"

And with those three words, Deputy Larsen almost killed him. At the moment the sheriff turned his head to reply, Allie Harrell, having for the past several minutes methodically pushed and pushed and pushed the full *weight of her body against the rock slab while she dug away the gravel at its base with her feet, finally achieved her aim, and the slab began to fall forward, almost without noise. Only a preliminary patter of gravel prompted the sheriff to step back, onto one of those teeter-totter rocks. His ankle twisted, and he fell backward into space, arms outflung, flashlight flying, and so the toppled slab crashed into the rock where he had stood, a freshet of gravel and rainwater pouring down onto the rubble.*

"Sheriff!" cried Deputy Larsen.

"Here!" called the sheriff. He lay amid the rocks ten feet down the slope, his feet uphill from his head. He hurt all over. He moved his limbs. Right arm probably broken, ankle certainly sprained. Larsen would have to get some help up here, a crew with a gurney—

Allie Harrell stood over him, hefting above her head a rock the size of a watermelon. Her ropy arm muscles bulged. But how was he able to see that? Where did this flickering light come from?

"Don't," the sheriff said.

"You thought you could sweet-talk me into some butcher-shop hospital," she said. "I'd die first."

"You don't have to go," the sheriff said. "It was a mistake."

"Damn straight it was," she said, raising the rock and stepping forward, "and you've stolen your last mountain girl."

Behind her, seeming to rear up in that unholy light, was Larsen, his pistol aimed at the back of her head. He was grinning.

He cocked the pistol.

"No!" screamed the sheriff.

And then came the loudest thunder yet, a thunder that was not thunder, and the sheriff screamed again because of the fire, the fire that seared his face and his arm and the mountaintop and the sky, and as Deputy Larsen, guttering like a tallow candle, plunged past him over the edge, flailing and screaming, the sheriff blacked out. He would be weeks remembering what had happened, and weeks more trying to believe it.

MY name is Pearleen Sunday, though I was always called Pearl, and this is the story of how I followed an Old Fire Dragaman down a hole that another girl went down before me, and how one of us came up again. The story also has a wishing ring, and kidnappers, and an angry mob, and a car chase with one car, and a shoot-out, and, of course, a few ghosts, which I seem to attract, and it happened to me and around me and in spite of me in the Virginia mountains, where you stand on a ridge and see the next ridge real clear and the next ridge behind a little less clear and so on back, ridge after ridge, with the last one only a faint blue notion of a line, because it's the farthest one away in distance and also the farthest one away in time. It's the long-gone past of the mountains that you're trying to scry, away off there. This story happened several ridges back, when the mountain folks were hearing stories from the cities of wait lines for bread, and padlocked banks, and jail time for drinking beer, and were glad of their rifles and turkey gobblers, their gold pieces hidden in shuck mattresses, their home-made whiskeys that played different tunes on the tongue from hill to hill and spring to spring.

One fall afternoon I sat in a bald patch on the slope of Cove Mountain, on some flat rocks that may once have been a cabin's doorstep, to eat cheese and crackers from the store in Catawba and muse over the troubling things I had heard there. I spread my hat and jacket across the rocks because I needed the sun to warm my arms and the breeze to stir my hair, since no one else was like to bother, and marveled at the magic on display all around, as many reds and golds as there are sorrows and joys, and every last leaf a-trembling to burst into flame if you looked at it too long. So I kept my eyes moving. I sat in that bald for a spell, watching a hawk wheel overhead, a chipmunk skitter from rock to rock, a black belch of smoke rise on the other side of the trees. No homestead chimney puts out smoke like that—the puffs were too strong and regular, as if squeezed from a bellows—and the plume was moving slow to the east, so I knew it must be a locomotive headed along the N&W track. But something didn't set right about that notion, and I plucked and chewed a grass blade while I figured why not. The first problem was I ought to hear the train rumbling and clanking along, but I heard no sound at all to go with that moving puff cloud. The second problem was even bigger: I had crossed the N&W a mile or so back, on the way up the hill. It lay behind me, not in front. So there was nothing for it but to ease up off my smooth rock and take up my hat and jacket and soogin sack and sidle through the trees to where I could make out, through a laurel bush, where that smoke was coming from. It was a man walking along the ridge smoking a pipe, only the pipe was the size of a man, and the man was a giant. His eyebrows stuck out from his craggy face like twin rolls of barbed wire, and they kept catching on the oak limbs, so that boughs and leaves and bits of bark pattered onto his shoulders and the tops of his rowboat-sized brogans. He hummed a tune as he walked, and as I watched him, holding my breath—because anyone who ran across an Old Fire Dragaman in the hills, even in those days, knew she had seen something not long for this world, something that deserved to pass in a hush—the giant stopped, took one last drag on his pipe, then knocked it empty on a boulder that echoed Whack! Whack! like the chop of an ax. Enough dumped out with each Whack! to make an ash-Pearl my height and weight, but the Dragaman puffed out his cheeks and blew and scattered the ashes across the valley before their sparks could kindle a fire. Then he pulled from his coat pocket what looked like a saddlebag, from which he pinched a haystack of pipe tobacco between his thumb and long finger. This he put into the bowl of his pipe and tamped down. Then he hacked and coughed and brought up a little fireball, about the size of a frolicking calf, which played across the bowl and set it alight. The extra flames fell to the brush underfoot, where the Dragaman crushed them out with a sigh, like it was a shame to waste such a good fire. He hitched up his pant legs and sat on the ground with a thump like dynamite deep in a mine, and I sat down, too, because his sitting had rippled the mountainside and knocked me plumb off my feet. I came down on a sharp place, and I was sprawled beneath the laurel, rubbing my backside, when the Dragaman began to sing.

The coo-coo is a pretty bird
She warbles as she flies
She brings us good tidings
And tells us no lies.

It wasn't the prettiest singing voice. It sounded like a man trying to sing around a mouthful of pebbles without spitting them out or swallowing them. But he sure knew a lot of verses to that old song, some changed around and others entirely new to me.

Way up on Cove Mountain
I wander alone
I'm as mean as the devil
Oh let me alone

I'll eat when I'm hungry
I'll drink when I'm dry
If the mountain don't kill me
I'll live till I die

As he sang, he looked across the valley, as I had done, and I wondered how many leaf changes there were in a Dragaman's life. Some say the Dragamen remember when there were no leaves, and no mountains either.

Gonna build a log cabin
In Cove Mountain so deep
So I can see Allie
Has ne'er cause to weep

Way up on Cove Mountain
Where hawks sail so high
I'll think of little Allie
Till my day to die

He sang and sang, and as I always was a fool for a song, I rightly lost track of the time. The air turned chill as the sun got lower, and just as it grazed the next ridgetop, the Dragaman turned his head and looked right into my eyes:

I spy a pretty wizard
Who's up on yon hill
If she ain't done flown off
She's watching me still

This gave me a start, and I flushed, embarrassed. The older magic-makers get, the better they are at spotting other magic-makers, and, of course, a Dragaman is older than just about anybody short of a rock. So I might have expected discovery if I sat still long enough. I squared my shoulders, pushed through the laurel, and walked down the hill toward the Dragaman, who continued to sing:

She's vain in her knowledge
And proud of her sense
It'll all be forgotten
A hundred years hence

The words were harsh, but the Dragaman didn't look angry. His eyes twinkled. Since they were the size of twin pie pans, that was a lot of twinkle.

"Well met, Grandfather," I said, because that's how one politely addresses the oldest beings, whether related or not.

"Don't you 'Grandfather' me, Miss Cute-as-a-Bug," said the Dragaman. "Your airs are wasted on someone as wicked as me." He patted the mountainside, nearly knocking me off my feet again. "Come warm yourself, little one. You can't sit in my lap, now," he added, winking, "because I'm spoken for."

"I wouldn't have sat in it anyhow," I snapped, settling myself onto the grass beside him, but my, he *did* put out the warmth. It was like getting neighborly with a steamboat boiler. "You ain't even introduced yourself proper," I said.

"That's true, Miss Nose-out-of-Joint," said the Dragaman, but he seemed in no hurry to rectify matters. Dragamen seldom hurry. He took a long draw on his pipe, then sighed and let the smoke roll out of his great nostrils to be lost in the evening sky. The sun had dropped out of sight as it always does in the mountains, all of an instant, and the glow of the pipe's kettle-sized bowl was now our chief source of light. "My name," he finally said, "is Pike. Cauter Pike. And when I say 'my name,' I mean only what I've gone by the past century or two, in the language that you know."

"My name is Pearleen Sunday, and it's the only name I've ever had."

"You'll earn others, in time," Cauter Pike said. "You're just a slip of a thing yet."

I couldn't disagree. In the complicated ways of wizards, I was physically about nineteen, but the cold drugstore-calendar mathematics of subtracting birth year from present year yielded a number that was pushing sixty, while in my own mind I was sometimes twelve and sometimes older than Methuselah, depending on my mood. A wizard's adolescence lasts a long time, which is one reason I don't recommend the life to anyone who has a choice in the matter. I had none, myself.

"So tell me, Pearleen Sunday," said Cauter Pike, "why the mustache?"

"It's not real," I said, quickly. "It's a hex, a glamour. Just like the short hair, the shoulders, the stubble on my chin." I rubbed my face, felt only smoothness but heard the *skritch-skritch* that meant the spell still worked. Appearing as a man was one of my handiest skills. "A man traveling alone gets into fewer scrapes than a woman, in these troubled times," I said. Those troubled times had lasted my entire life to date and likely would continue a lot longer, but you can't explain to a Dragaman how tough things can be for womankind. I also didn't mention, because I was ashamed to admit it, that hex or no hex, the mustache tickled my lip something awful.

"Seems a shame to cover up all that pretty," said Cauter Pike, "but you know best, I'm sure. Of course, I can see right through any hex." He dragged on his pipe, and in the light from the flaring bowl, his expression suggested that he saw through not just the hex but everything else I had on. I tugged my jacket closed and folded my arms together, and the Dragaman laughed, in deep volleys that echoed among the hills like cannon fire.

"So what brings you to my mountains, Miss Priss-and-Proper?"

"If they're *your* mountains," I replied, nettled, "then you ought to know." But I went on to tell him that as a student of the art, I traveled the country, teaching myself the magics that were done in different ways in different places by different people. "Around these parts, for example, I'm learning my way through Hohman's book, *The Long Lost Friend*. It's from the Pennsylvania Dutch, and it's hex-magic and Jesus-magic mixed together. Do you know it?"

"Never did much book reading myself," said Cauter Pike. "They might be of some use if the dang things weren't made of paper." He poked a tree trunk with a slablike index finger, held it there a few seconds, and left a seared and smoking patch in the wood.

"I understand completely," I told him, wondering how I'd get through even a week without reading, much less a Dragaman's lifetime. "Mr. Pike, I heard something at the store in Catawba this afternoon that troubles my mind. Do you know anything about—"

Before I could finish the sentence, Cauter Pike had snuffed out his pipe and sprung into a crouch, his bulk silhouetted against the dark blue sky. He cocked his head and peered downslope.

I looked, too, and saw a distant swinging light. A lantern. Three lanterns. Men's voices, coming this way.

Cauter Pike sniffed once, twice, for all the world like a frighted deer. Then he whispered:

"I got to go, Pretty-My-Pearl, but come up to Buzzard's Rock one evening. We'll have you to supper."

He turned and, without another word, disappeared.

Now for a Dragaman to move from his man-shape into his flying-shape takes only about as long as buttering a biscuit, but Cauter Pike had not stayed put even that long. He had done something else.

Like some other creatures in the hills, and all the oldest ones, the Dragamen are sidewinders. They can turn themselves sideways to the world and slip out of sight—unless you know what to look for, and look quick.

What I looked for and saw was the Dragaman's shadow, just a thin strip crawling along the ground like a blacksnake, and out of sight in an instant, as if it had poured through a crack in the earth.

I thought about hiding myself in a similar way, but curiosity got the upper hand, so I walked down the hill in my own man-shape as the men in the hunting party crashed through the laurel, rifles in their hands. At sight of me, they shouted.

"Who's there?"

"Are you alone?"

"Your hands, mister! Show us your hands!"

I raised my hands, tried to blink away the brightness; someone was holding a lantern in my face. Another someone searched me for weapons, and none too gently, either. But the glamour held, and he felt nothing he wouldn't expect to feel on a man's rough body.

"Where's your badge, son?" asked the man with the lantern.

"No badge, sir," I said. "I'm no Revenuer. I'm a stranger in these parts, and mean no harm." What I heard when I spoke was my own Pearl-voice, which still sounded childish in my ears but for the little rasp I had picked up in my travels, like I might need to clear my throat directly. What the men heard was a man-voice that matched the man-image and man-clothes that I presented in their minds. "Y'all hunting possums? I didn't hear your hounds."

The lantern was lower now, and by it I saw the bald head and heavy jowls of the old man who held it. I knew his face, and if I had presented myself true, he might have remembered mine, too, from the Catawba Grocery that day at noon. He had held forth loudly to the clerk, while I had eased about the shelves filling my basket, and listening.

"Law, nothing," the old man had said. "Don't talk to me about obeying the law!" He hacked at an apple with a pocketknife, not peeling it like a patient man but chipping away at the skin. On each outstroke he flipped a little red dot onto the floor. "Ain't no law says we got to let them take our children."

"Calm yourself, Ash Harrell," said the clerk, watching the pile of red shavings like he wouldn't appreciate having to sweep them up. "She'll come back. She'll be fine, you'll see, just like the others."

"Cut up like hogs, you mean," said the old man called Ash Harrell. "She'd be better off—" But instead of saying the next word, he slung the flayed apple into the sandbox beneath the stove and stomped out of the store, slamming the screen door and knocking sideways the Colonial Bread sign.

"May I help you, Miss?" asked the clerk, looking relieved to speak to anyone who was not Ash Harrell. But when I asked what all the fuss had been about, he only shook his head, and said, "You're best shut of it, Miss, believe me."

Those things I had mused about, on that warm, flat rock up the mountain: who had run away from Ash Harrell, and who had been cut like hogs, and why the law was to blame.

Now here was Ash Harrell in front of me, looking no better tempered than before, and a good sight more scary.

"Ain't hunting *possums*," said the old man, nearly spitting his contempt. Lighted from below, his deeply shadowed expression was murderous. "You pass anyone, Mister? Up the mountain?"

"No, sir," I said. A lie is the easiest magic there is. Just saying something can make it so, if you say it right. The old man looked unconvinced, but instead of replying, he reached a mottled hand into a pocket of his overalls.

"Mr. Ash," said one of the others. "Mr. Ash, we got to go." The four other men in the group were younger. The old man was stern as a deacon, but the boys were definitely spooked. They looked as if every swaying tree limb was about to dump a Behinder on their heads, or every wind-ripple in the tall grass was the wake left by a Flat with sharp teeth. If they'd ever been taught to keep their guns pointed at the ground, they'd forgot it now. I didn't like the way those twin barrels waved around, like hard black eyes seeking a face to look into.

The old man had produced a cracked and crimpled photograph. He handed it to me, fingers trembling and slow as if he didn't want to give it up. He aimed the lantern so the redheaded girl's pretty face was bright in my palm.

"Come on, Mr. Ash."

"Shut up," Mr. Ash said, absently and without malice, as you would address a barking dog. "You seen this girl? You seen my daughter?"

"No, sir."

"She hides it in this picture, but there's a little gap in her front teeth, and she laughs deep like a man. You sure you ain't seen her? Maybe in the next county?" He paused. "Or in Roanoke, with all the . . . the working girls?"

"No, sir, I'm sorry. How long has she been gone?"

"Three months this Friday," he said. He snatched back the photograph and shoved it into his pocket without looking at it, as if it were a cash receipt.

"Mr. Ash, we're gonna miss 'em."

"No, we ain't," the old man said. "They got to drive around the spur and up the grade, while we cut across. We'll beat 'em by ten minutes, easy."

"If someone doesn't warn 'em first," said a new, rough voice, nearly in my ear. Its owner kneed me in the back, and I staggered.

After a moment's thought, the old man gestured with his rifle. "Good thinking, Silas. You better come with us, Mister."

"Why?" I asked. Silas seized my arm, as if to dig his fingers into my very bones. "Ow!" I said, less from the pain than from the anger that gouted from him. The Sight is the least developed of my gifts, but I can't help thought-reading when someone takes serious hold of me. Out loud, I asked the question his touch was already answering: "What do y'all think you're doing?"

"Hunting monsters," the old man said.

As we scrambled in a straggly line toward the two-lane on the other side of the mountain, the old man in the lead was silent, but I harkened at the others whispering among themselves.

"Who they got this time?"

"I hear they got Polly, and Bert, the youngest Lunsford boy, and the Mainer twins."

"I say that you're a fool. Polly was on the porch swing when I went by there. It's Lula, Polly's sister, what got carried off."

"Carried off by what?" I asked.

"The sheriff, of course. And his deputies, damn their eyes."

"But why? Are they the monsters Mr. Ash meant?"

"Shut up," said Silas, cuffing my ear. "You ask more questions than a girl."

"All I know is, they won't take no more of our neighbor younguns to the operating room, not if I got a say in it."

"Hush, all of you," said the old man. We were headed down again. His lanternlight picked up the cat's-eyes of the reflectors along the curve of the two-lane below. We all fell silent, but between what I had heard and what I had felt through Silas's grip on my arm, I had plenty of information to chew on, none of it pleasant.

For months, all over the county, young boys and girls from the families on the slopes and in the hollers had turned up missing, by day and by night, one or two or a half dozen at a time, hoes or fishing poles or berry baskets left where they dropped. Boys and girls of courting age were warned to stick close or stay in groups, but they paid about as much attention as courting boys and girls in all places and times, so the disappearances continued. Then the first ones came home. Weeks after the parents had gone from panic to grief, they would hear the dogs barking and come out on the porch to see, wonder of wonders, Vassar or Hazel walking up the lane, dazed and dreamy-like, in the clothes they went off in, always with the same story to tell: They had been snatched off the mountain by Sheriff Stiles or his deputies. The lawmen said they had a court order. They were driven alone or in carloads or truckloads to the state hospital—usually Staunton, sometimes Lynchburg, though a few had been taken as far as Marion, Petersburg, Williamsburg. There they were poked and prodded but treated right well, fed real good and given haircuts, so they said, and by the way, the girls all added, the doctor said my appendix had to come out, so that's what this scar is, see? The doctor said soon it'll be only a pale line across my belly, how about that? The boys had scars, too, ones less visible and more embarrassing, but soon enough they realized the equipment still worked just fine, and so some were inclined to shrug off their brief adventure, no stranger than some other things that you heard tell of in the hills, like red-eyed dogs that cross your path at night and crows that speak in the voices of men and farmers who drop from sight in the middle of a field into the Gone Forever. But the more young men and women got rounded up for the hospital, the madder the mountain folks got, and the better able to figure that appendicitis was not what the operations were meant to prevent. Then Ash Harrell's daughter had not come back at all, so now Ash Harrell and his neighbors would make some law of their own.

"Here they come," the old man said.

Across the cut, a pair of headlights swept around the last curve before ours. At nighttime in the deep mountains, oncoming cars give plenty of warning if you keep watching the next curve across the way. It sounded like a truck, and its brakes squealed as it hugged the curve. Someone was in a hurry to get down the mountain, now that it was dark.

Silas kept hold of my arm. His thoughts were all confused now, mostly from fear I judged, but his interest in the Harrell girl was not brotherly, and his favorite pie was peach.

Just below, the old man knelt on an outcrop and raised his rifle, while the three others kept going, slid down the rocks onto the gravel shoulder and walked into the middle of the road, swinging their lanterns back and forth like the Brown Mountain spook lights.

The engine got louder.

Just as the sheriff's truck rounded the curve, I dropped the hex that hid my true self. Within Silas's grip, my upper arm changed from a young man's to a young woman's. He looked at me—now a foot shorter and a girl besides—then let go and jumped back with a gasp.

I turned and ran—not down into the road, but along the hillside in the same direction as the truck, which now blared its horn and veered around the men trying and failing to flag it down.

As I ran along the trackless hillside, I said to myself one of Mr. Hohman's charms for surefootedness:

He is my head
I am his limb
Therefore walketh Jesus with me

Jesus-magic had never been my long suit, but what could it hurt?

Below and just behind me, the truck roared onto the far shoulder and nearly skeeted off the edge of the cliff, but the driver fought it back onto the asphalt past the highwaymen and sped up again, into the right-hand lane and catching up to me. Just as rifles fired behind me and the right rear tire blew, the truck passed directly below, and I took a deep breath and ran off the ledge, *Wham!* onto the roof.

"Hold!" I cried, and just in case *that* spell didn't take, I seized the luggage rail tight in both hands as the truck squealed into the next curve, rear tire flapping. My body swung sideways, and my feet kicked air off the edge of the roof, but I held on, and before us now was a long, straight downslope. The driver had done a fine job so far to avoid a wreck, but now what? That tire was plumb gone, and the truck began to fishtail. The brakes smelled like a miner's lamp. Did I know any arts that could stop an out-of-control truck? All I could think of was one to stop mad dogs, but as the truck began to speed up—toward a bad curve below, and a void beyond—I decided that would have to do. Without letting go of the rail, I pointed both index fingers at a spot halfway down the grade and yelled:

Dog, hold thy nose to the ground,
God has made me and thee, hound!

I kept repeating this, my eyes focused on that same rapidly approaching spot in the road, even as I remembered that the mad-dog hex should be placed, ideally, before the dog sees you. But hellfire, no one *in* the truck had seen me yet, had they? And just as it hit that hexed spot in the road, the truck slewed sideways, nearly overturned but didn't, and stopped dead.

"Well, I'll be," I said, then scrambled backward as the front doors flung open beneath me.

"Who's up there?" someone called. Of course—as long as they thought I was armed, they wouldn't risk poking their heads out of the truck. As quiet as I could, I shinnied over the roof's edge at the rear of the truck and dropped to the pavement. Behind me was the steep, wooded downslope; in front of me, the truck's headlights illuminated a rock face split with glittering trickles of runoff. I ran for the downslope, then stopped myself, skidding in the leaves and cursing silently, ran back to the rear of the truck and made a two-handed pass over the latch. I never had been so pleased to unlock a door. "It's open!" I hollered. "Run!"

The rear doors flung open, nearly knocking me down, and out poured a dozen whooping, yelling people, men and women, some maybe fifteen, some maybe nineteen. The instant they landed on the pavement, they all lit off into the woods, and I took off right behind them—or thought I had. But someone tackled me from behind, and I fell on my face just off the road, the wind knocked out of me. I struggled to my knees, coughing leaves, but a man's strong arms wrapped around my chest and held me tight.

"I God, I knew it was you!" a voice said. "I knew you were out there somewhere, Allie Harrell!"

I saw a lightning flash, a pillar of rock, and a redheaded girl coming at me, and felt a searing pain that made me cry out. Then the man threw me to the ground, and my memories were my own again.

"You ain't Allie," he said. "You ain't one we just picked up, neither. What witchery is this?"

I rolled over. Standing above me was a broad-shouldered man with a badge gleaming red in the taillights. Just as I registered that something was wrong with his face, he seized my collar and hauled me up like a hooked fish. His mouth hung crooked, his skin was taut and shiny, his hair was an uneven stubble, and one ear was nearly gone, melted flat against his head. His eyes were dark, hot coals.

"You're burned," I said.

"I appreciate your noticing," he said. With his free hand he pawed at me, yanked up my flannel shirttail to look at my belly.

"Not fixed yet," he said.

"Why are you doing this?" I asked. "Why don't you want the mountain folks to have children? Why cut off their generations?"

"Someone's put notions in your head," he said. "In this county, Missy, we enforce the law, and Virginia law says the feebleminded and shiftless, like you hillbillies, should not be allowed to reproduce theirself. It ain't my say-so, it's the state's."

"It's criminal," I said.

"That ain't what the U.S. Supreme Court says. What the U.S. Supreme Court says is, 'Three generations of imbeciles is enough.' "

"Allie Harrell," I said, "is no imbecile—"

He slapped me, hard.

"—and you know it," I finished.

From up the slope came another rifle shot, and the taillight behind him exploded. He didn't look around, just dragged me by my jacket into the shelter of the downhill side of the vehicle. Two other men with badges crouched there, guns drawn.

"Here they come, Sheriff!"

"If you see 'em, shoot 'em," the scarred man replied, still staring at me and not them.

"Watch out for a flamethrower," one deputy told the other. "That's how they got Larsen, and, uh." He nodded toward the sheriff.

"When's backup getting here?" the sheriff asked.

After a long pause, the talkative deputy asked: "You want us to radio for backup, sir?"

This time the shooter got one of the headlights.

Still looking at me, the sheriff shook his head, and muttered, "Dumber than owl shit." He turned away, and said, "Yes, call for backup, you lunkhead! These crackers might kill us by accident, even if they mean only to pin us down, while that trash gets . . . away . . ."

I heard his voice trail off, as he realized he was holding an empty jacket. By the time he began to roar, I was halfway down the leafy slope. All I had needed was for him to break eye contact; a distraction hex helped, but my being quick helped more. And since I had come away with my hat and my soogin sack and the rest of my clothes, I couldn't begrudge him my jacket, though I'd play hell finding another that fit me so well, whatever shape I used. And as I ran down the mountain toward the lights of the town, I pondered four facts. One, the sheriff didn't know where Allie Harrell was, either. Two three four, the Old Fire Dragaman had sung me a song about a girl named Allie, and said he was spoken for, and invited me to supper.

༄

THERE was no trick to finding Buzzard's Rock the next afternoon, any more than there is to finding Chimney Rock in the North Carolina mountains. Climb to the highest point you can find, and look around, and there it is, a splinter of rock rearing up over the ridge.

As I clambered up the rocky trail, the thing put me in mind of the tower in Genesis, the one that Nimrod built; or the tower of ill omen in the Rider deck, with flames and lightning and two figures falling, one caped and one crowned. You'd swear Buzzard's Rock was one of God's ruins if you didn't know ruins were purely human-made things.

The base was a jumble of boulders with barely room to stand, much less anything resembling a dwelling or a door in that wild place, certainly no log cabin like the Dragaman's song. The day had been warm and sunshiny, but up there on that exposed rock the wind cut through me, and the sheriff had my jacket. I shivered and held myself and kicked aside the smaller rocks in the pile, only to turn up larger rocks I couldn't move so easy. There was nothing for it but a tether-and-plumb. I hunkered down in the lee of the rock spire, rooted in my soogin sack, found my roll of twine, and cut two one-foot lengths. The two ends that had been joined together I put in my mouth and held there, wet them down good, so they both would know me. Then I tied one of the lengths around my left wrist and said, "Plumb," only not in English. The other length of twine I laid on the flat top of a shoulder-high rock. I pressed it down, and said, "Tether," in the same old tongue I had used before. Then I began walking widdershins around the clearing at the base of Buzzard's Rock, in the widest circle I could manage given the boulders all around and the precipice just the other side.

Now I warn you, before you try it your own self, that this way to open an unseen portal and lower yourself into it does not always work; sometimes it accomplishes what a lot of magic accomplishes, which is slap nothing, and sometimes it *closes* an unseen portal and takes unexpected parts of the world with it, and that can be hard to explain to the neighbors, at best. But on this afternoon at Buzzard's Rock, my hopes were higher because I had some powerful help: Cauter Pike had asked me to come to his house. A Dragaman's invitation can slice through a lot of magics that otherwise would keep folks out, would keep me turning in a circle atop this rock until they came to take *me* to a hospital.

(And did I keep turning over in my head what Cauter Pike had said, We'll have you *to* supper, to make myself more easy that he had not said, *for* supper? I surely did that thing.)

And I began to know that I would not be disappointed this time because after I had walked one circle (shaped more like an egg with an ax wedge out of the side), my second pass I was knee deep in the rock, and my third pass was hip deep. It wasn't like walking through rock, but like walking through a thick fog colored and shaped like rock, and as my head sank below the surface (and I confess I took a deep breath before I went under, though I knew better), the fog cleared, and I was in a deep tube-like well with smooth rock walls, like a borehole, and I walked down in a spiral as if there were a staircase, only of course there wasn't. The farther down, the warmer I got, and soon I was sweaty and no longer missed the jacket. Then a rock floor rose up beneath me and knocked me off-balance, dropped me to my knees, as if my elevator had come to rest, and I knew I was at the bottom—or as near the bottom as Pearl was likely to get, or want to get.

I walked through a Dragaman-sized rock archway and found myself in a cave so big its ceiling and far walls were lost, though everything for about twenty feet around was illuminated by a dim and sourceless reddish light. A shallow branch trickled over the rocks at my feet. I heard bats chitter to one another and fancied I saw their pinpoint eyes like stars in the darkness above. I couldn't help but shudder. I never harbored a love for bats, however helpful they could be in the wizard way. As I moved around, that weird light moved with me. I looked at my hand and saw where the light came from, as if I had brought into the deep, deep dark some measure of sunlight that shone out through my skin. But away in the distance was another source of light, more natural-looking in this unnatural place, and walking upstream along the branch seemed to bring it nearer. So I went on thataway, through stalagmite thickets, until I came into view of the pretti-est log cabin you ever saw, with a shake roof and flower boxes in the front windows and outflung shutters that would have said, "Welcome, friend," if you had come upon the place in any mountain holler. But because the cabin was in fact in the bowels of the Earth, its message was a tad more complicated, especially since those flowers stirred without a breeze, and there seemed to be no reason for the patch of afternoonish light in which the home place sat. But I walked on toward it, and as I got closer I heard someone singing inside. It wasn't the Dragaman's yawp, but a girl's voice that could carry a tune.

> *I've gambled in England*
> *I've gambled in Spain*
> *I bet you ten dollars*
> *I'll beat you next game*

Figuring politeness would stand me as well belowground as above, I stopped about twenty paces from the door, and called: "Hello, the house!" Two or three echo-Pearls repeated me, aways off in the ceiling somewhere.

The singing stopped right quick, and the girl came to the window, holding a dish and a washrag. She was a good deal prettier than I expected, and her red hair was longer, but when she smiled, her front teeth gapped just like her father had said when he held a gun on me on the slope of Cove Mountain the night before.

"Oh, hello!" she cried. "You must be Pearl."

"Yes, ma'am. And you must be Allie Harrell."

"Honey, you hear?" she said, addressing someone in the cabin behind her. "Pearleen Sunday has come to supper."

Someone rumbled a reply that I couldn't quite make out, but the gout of flame that spit from the cabin's stone chimney, like from an Alabama steel mill, was easy enough to recognize.

"My goodness, you've come a long way! You come right in this house this minute and put your feet up. Oh, and please don't mind the flowers. I'd hoped for spiderwort, but these are what came up. What can you do? There's cider on the hearth, and chicory brewing—oh, and I need to put on the biscuits! I swear, I'd forget my head if it weren't tied on . . ."

The window-box flowers were long and snaky, with bulbs on the end that opened and closed, and as I stepped through the doorway, they strained in my direction like geese wanting a handout through a fence.

The inside of the cabin was a sight larger than the outside, but still homey compared to that dark reach of cavern. The front door I came through was Pearl- and Allie-sized, but the stone fireplace was big enough to roast two oxen longways, and if the chimney was its match, I guessed this was how Cauter Pike came and went. The rocking chair beside the hearth could have held a family, but the Dragaman still looked squinched and uncomfortable sitting in it, knees practically in his face and shoulders hunched beneath the ceiling, which was no higher than what you'd find in the average railway station. Not that he cared about any of this. He gazed at the redheaded gal who bustled and chattered around the kitchen the way Gabriel must have looked at Evangeline in Acadia long ago.

He glanced at me.

"Now, Pearl," he said. "It ain't what you think."

"All I think," I said, "is that building this house in a Dragaman's cave, and toting down all the provisions, must have been a piece of work."

"I love this house!" Allie sang out. "I never thought I'd have a house this nice, on Cove Mountain or under it, neither." She set a pitcher precisely in the middle of the long oilcloth-covered table that ran along the back wall, benches to each side. The table was set for twelve.

"Let me help you," I said. "Who all else is coming?"

"You keep your seat, and as for who, you'll see directly," Allie said, with the same pinched expression as when she had acknowledged the flowers. "You'll like them, I'm sure. They're so . . . interesting. Isn't that the word you'd use, Cauter honey, interesting?"

"Danged interesting," Cauter Pike agreed.

Allie started singing again, all the while banging plates and cups together, and in the hubbub I murmured: "Cauter Pike, what do you think you're doing, playing house with this woman-child? Her pa's worried sick. Do you intend to keep her here the rest of her life, until she's a sick old lady, and you still as green as the mountain?"

"She's better off here than up there," the Dragaman said. He spit a fireball into the hearth, and flames roared up the chimney. "Let me tell you a true thing, Pearleen Sunday, and you can put it in your head with all the other lessons you're collecting up. There's a lot of evil that don't have anything to do with magic, not black magic, not your magic, not inside-the-mountain magic like mine. And when evil's on the march, all that magic together does no good against it. Can I do air thing to stop all the innocent folks from being rounded up by the police, in Virginia and everywhere else in the world? No, ma'am, I cannot. But take one individual out of it and keep her safe, yes, ma'am, I *can* do that, and I *did* do that. That's why Allie's in this cave house right this minute, and don't expect me to be sorry for it, neither. And when I brought her here, Pearl, well, I stopped her just short of doing something she would have been sorry for the rest of her days."

"You're a fine one to talk of days, here in a place with no sun, and flowers made of snakeskin. It can't be good for her. She looks a little peaked to me."

"Why, Pearl," he said, with a crooked grin. "I do believe you're jealous."

Before I could answer back to that, he bestirred himself, and said: "Allie, honey, I'm gonna stretch my wings a little before supper, see if I catch sight of them lollygaggers."

"Tell 'em hurry up," Allie said, chopping scallions. "It'd be a shame to have all this beef stew and corn bread go to waste."

"Yes, ma'am," Cauter Pike said. He couldn't stand up in the low-ceilinged cabin, but he eased himself out of the rocker and onto his knees, then stuck his head and shoulders into the fireplace. "Whoo, that tickles!" he said as he shinnied headfirst up the chimney. Flames wrapped his long lanky body like a blanket. Just before his feet disappeared, the scaly green point of a tail, the size and shape of a shovel, dropped into sight, raked through the hot coals, then vanished up the chimney as well. That was as close as I had come to seeing a Dragaman change shapes. I ran to the door and looked up, but the light around the cabin didn't reach far, and in the darkness above, all I saw was a trail of sparks like a meteor. The sound was of the world's largest carpet being beat, beat, beat.

"Oh, *here* y'all are," cried Allie behind me. "Hello, fellas. I swear, I never *will* get used to you walking through the wall like that."

ৡৡ

WHEN we all sat down, we were eleven, but Allie wouldn't tell me who the twelfth place was for, the setting at my left hand. "Never you mind," she said.

The first supper guests to arrive, other than me, were the ghosts of four of the eight miners working the Greeno Slope who had died when a lamp ignited a methane pocket in December 1910. Exactly whose lamp it had been was still a subject of debate.

"Warn't me," said the youngest and smallest of them, who was only fifteen. "I ain't tall enough to hit a pocket."

"Gas can hole up anywhere," said the skinny one, "not just the ceiling, and you're the one that has to be first to poke his fool head into ever' crack he sees."

"Poor things," Allie murmured into my ear. "They're always grateful for the invite, but once they get here, all they talk about is work." In fact, she had made up a pail of food for their four friends, who were working the late shift. Miners too spectral to dig, hunting coal that wasn't there, in a tunnel closed for a decade, because that's all they knew to do: It didn't bear thinking about.

"Hesh up, all of you," the one with the broadest shoulders told the others. "I was the foreman, warn't I? Whatever happens down the hole on my watch is my fault, and that's all there is to it."

The others all talked at once about this, even the Hungarian whose English wasn't so good, disputing the foreman's modesty or his arrogance in claiming to own their mutual disaster. You could tell they were miners because even with their helmets off at the table, they never exchanged direct looks, for fear their lamps would blind somebody. Yet for all their chatter, they still managed to put away the food, in the ghostly way I had got used to in the haunted house where I was partly raised. The food just vanished from the plates in front of them, bit by bit, though you couldn't see it happen, and with each helping the ghosts got less transparent, but never so solid that you couldn't read a calendar through them.

Ghosts I was familiar and easy with, but the four imps at the other end of the table were more of a problem. It wasn't just that they were all naked, or that their fat red bodies were as smooth and hairless as store-bought dolls, or that their noses and chins nearly touched, or that they talked so fast and so high that you couldn't understand what they said, any more than you could understand a cricket. It was mostly their ancient faces without expression, their deep-set eyes with no pupils, and, of course, their table manners—nearly as bad as Cauter Pike's, and he ate beef stew with a shovel out of a bowl the size of a cauldron. Because they live so long, Dragamen take their sweet time doing most things, but eating is an exception, even when the meal is past the point of struggle. Between gulps and slurps, Cauter Pike carried on his masterfully noncommittal side of the imp conversation: "Well, I declare." "Ain't that something." "How about that?"

Given the miners' bickering and the imps' clackety-clack, Allie and I had plenty of chance to talk to each other. I asked her how she liked living down here.

"Oh, it's ever so nice," Allie said. "And isn't Cauter Pike just the sweetest thing?" At that moment, the sweetest thing was retrieving a whole carrot from where it had landed, behind his ear. "He plaited this green ribbon in my hair, and he says one day he'll take me flying, so high I can see the whole New River Valley." During this speech, she didn't look at me, but studied a jar of chow-chow pickle like it held her future. I took it from her hand and set it down.

"Allie," I said, "I hate to say this, but ain't you stretching it a bit, this housewife business? Trying to make all this out to be normal? Honey, you have been carried off to a hole in the ground by an ancient creature of myth. Your going drove the sheriff half-crazy, and your neighbors have suffered."

"Yes," she murmured. "So Cauter says. It's me he really wants. He's just taking it out on them."

"And your poor pa has looked for you these past three months. Don't you want to see him?"

She sighed. "Of *course* I'd like that," she said, as if she was explaining something obvious to a youngun.

"Well, why don't you? Why don't you come back upstairs with me?"

"I'm afraid."

"Afraid of what, honey? Afraid of the sheriff catching you? Or afraid that Cauter Pike won't let you go?"

"No," she said. "He's told me, many a time, I'm free to go whenever. I'm afraid I'd never be able to come back. I mean, look at this place. You're right, it's nice enough, but it's sort of impossible, ain't it?" She looked down the table at Cauter Pike and gave him a little wave; he winked. "He's created a whole little world around me, and without me, what would happen? I'm afraid it'd be like waking up from a dream that I'd never have again—me or him, either. Do you understand?"

"I believe I do," I said, "though I've never heard tell of such in all my life. Allie Harrell, you are in love with that old Dragaman."

"Yes," she said. "Yes, I am."

"Lord have mercy," I said, and I meant it.

That was when the racket started: *Boom! Boom! Boom!* One after another, each a little closer, each setting off its own wave of echoes in the cavern outside. On the mountain we'd have thought a thunderstorm, but we weren't on the mountain. *Boom! Boom! Boom!* Milk and cider sloshed from the mugs, and the table hopped away from me a half inch at a time.

"We firing tonight?" asked the youngest miner.

The foreman looked through his pocket watch, and said, "No, we are not."

"Do you suppose?" asked the skinny miner.

"Devajkodas!" said the fourth miner, crossing himself.

The imps seemed frozen, their eyes set deeper than usual. One imp finally said two understandable words in a row: "Oh, hell!"

At the next *Boom!* the imps bolted in four directions, each trying to wriggle headfirst into a tiny chink between logs, and succeeding. Four shiny red butts squeezed flatter and flatter, little chicken legs dangling, until *pop pop pop pop*, they were gone.

The miners simply vanished, though the foreman did say, "Thank you kindly for the victuals, Miss Allie," as he went. The "Allie" sounded much farther away than the "Thank you."

Finally, the last *Boom!* died away, and I barely could hear, from out front, thin, frightened sounds like a nest of baby mice. The window-box flowers were screaming.

"Hello, the house!" called a familiar voice.

I glared at Allie, knowing now why she had kept her mouth shut about that twelfth place at table, as that last awaited resident of the underworld strode through the door. Petey Wheatstraw, the Devil's son-in-law, wore a red jacket and white flared pants and high shiny boots like a Charlottes-ville swell riding to hounds—not the usual attire for a black man in those days.

"I surely hope the dead and the damned left some stew for a working-man, for friends, I am hungry," Wheatstraw said. "No, no, don't get up, keep your seats, enjoy your meal," he added, though none of us had made the slightest move. "Pearl, you oughtn't pucker your mouth so," he said as he straddled the bench next to me. "It ain't becoming. Someone might come along and kiss it."

I said something that I am now ashamed of and will not repeat.

"Such colorful language," Wheatstraw said. "You've been hanging out on keelboats, I see. Oh, speaking of language, here's a piece of advice, Pearl. When you're this close to my in-laws' realm, 'Lord have mercy' is not the thing to say."

To speak at length of the rogue Petey Wheatstraw is to invite trouble, but I had known him for years, since I was younger than Allie Harrell, and just learning the ways of a wizard. Petey had taken an interest in me, not entirely on his father-in-law's behalf, and had been my first companion in roaming the country, which had, of course, ended badly, and I hated him, mostly. But as I watched him put away stew and listened to him lie about what he had been doing and who he had been doing it to, I reflected that he was about the only tie I had left to my younger days, since the Chatta-nooga dime museum had closed and the widow Winchester had died and her California mansion had gone to tourists, and that made me regret even more that he was a scoundrel and a reprobate and impossible to live with.

"Petey," I said.

"Pet*er*," he corrected me.

"Petey," I said, "what's that ring on your finger? It's new, isn't it?"

It looked like a plain iron band, almost like a washer that a sink installer might slip on his finger to keep it from getting away.

"That's the latest innovation we're working on at the Old Concern," Petey said. "A wishing ring. The idea is, anyone who puts it on gets three immediate wishes granted, no questions asked."

"What's the catch?" I asked.

"The problem, so far, isn't with the technology," Petey said. "The problem is what you might call user error. Most people think that wishing is a conscious act, when the average person wishes without ceasing, every moment of her life, whether she realizes it or not. Even as she slides the ring onto her finger, in a swivet of worry about what she'll wish for first, the ring knows that she wishes the morning twinge in her hip would go away and the baby next door would stop wailing and the dishes would wash themselves. By the time the ring passes the second knuckle it's dumb metal, all power gone to those three accomplishments, two so trivial as to pass without notice. Too bad about the baby, though. Could you pass the cider?"

"Could I see that ring, Mr. Wheatstraw?" Allie asked.

"Certainly."

"Why, Allie, what would you wish for, that you ain't already got?" asked Cauter Pike, sort of wistful.

"I'd wish my father was here, to see how we live and see me happy. And I'd wish the sheriff was here, too, so I could give him a piece of my mind. And the third wish, well." She laughed deep like a man. "A little blue spiderwort *would* be nice."

"Put the ring on," I told her.

Everyone looked at me.

"Who's to say I'd get those?" Allie asked. "I might wind up with who-knows-what, like the silly people Mr. Wheatstraw talked about."

"I think you know your own mind better than most," I told her. "I think you should go ahead."

"But," Petey said.

"But what?" I said, kicking his shin under the table as hard as I could.

"Nothing!" he said, wincing. "Just a little gas attack, pay it no mind."

The Dragaman looked worried but said nothing.

"Well," Allie said. She held up the ring, turned it from side to side, peered through it like a peephole. "A wizard ought to know." She laughed again. "Here goes." She slipped on the ring.

"Allie!" cried a voice from outside.

"Allie Harrell!" cried another.

The two together said: "You!"

We all rushed to the front door—except for Cauter Pike, who whooshed up the chimney—to see Ash Harrell and Sheriff Stiles punch and claw and gouge and wrestle each other in the middle of a blue field of spiderwort that stretched as far as the eye could see.

"Stop it!" Allie cried, rushing down the steps. "Stop it, both of you!"

The sheriff was on the ground. Ash Harrell gave him one last kick and staggered into Allie's embrace. "My girl, my girl," he said. "I thought you were dead or ruined. Oh, my little girl."

"I'm fine, Pa, really I am."

Over her shoulder, Ash Harrell gaped at the sight of Petey Wheatstraw in his fine clothes. "What in the world are you?" he asked.

"You're just having a nightmare," Petey said.

"Where is he?" the sheriff yelled. The cavern repeated the question.

From the darkness above, the beat of wings.

"If she's here, I know you're here, too, you damned lizard, you coward!" The sheriff was on his feet now, fists clenched, his shouts echoing, spittle flying from his lips. "Show yourself, I say! Finish the job you started!"

The shriek that split the air from high above sent the rest of us to our knees, hands over ears, but not the sheriff. He swayed, blinked, bared his teeth in a corpse's grin, and said, "Hah!" He flung both arms wide, stood there, ankles together, a scarecrow in a world without crows. We were jolted by another terrific shriek, and then a rush and roar like floodwaters overhead as all the bats took flight.

"Finish it!" the sheriff cried, as a thousand thousand shadows raked his taut and crooked face. In the next instant, a half acre of spiderwort behind him erupted in flame. Embers landed on his jacket sleeves and smoldered.

"No!" I screamed.

"No," Allie whispered.

Something enormous passed over, too fast to be seen, and then Cauter Pike walked out of the flames, looming over the sheriff like a mountain, boulder-sized fists clenched, breath rasping, fire-sweat in glowing rivulets down his forehead like molten steel. His scowl was terrible to see. But still the sheriff stood there. The Dragaman had stayed his hand.

"Once again, Pearl, I am impressed," Petey said, helping me up. "Calming a Dragaman! I wouldn't have believed it."

"It ain't me that calmed this Dragaman," I said. Allie had rushed over to hug one of Cauter Pike's legs, which she almost could reach around. His expression softened. When he stroked her hair with his tree-trunk fingers, sparks flew.

"Is this Hell?" the sheriff asked.

"Believe me," Petey said, "it isn't."

The sheriff lowered his arms, slumped his shoulders. "I knew if I saw Allie again, I'd see the Dragaman again. And then I would die."

"Pleased to oblige," Ash Harrell said, darting forward and snatching the sheriff's pistol from its holster. Before anyone could move, he raised it to the sheriff's temple and pulled the trigger. The click made the loudest echo yet.

"That won't do, Ash Harrell," I said. "Guns don't work in a Dragaman's lair."

"Fine, then," he said, slinging the gun into the spiderwort. "I'll finish the job soon's we get back."

"No, you won't," Allie said.

"But Allie. After all he's done. Why not?"

"Because if you do, you'll never see me again. A good man stopped me from doing such a thing, three months ago, and now I'm stopping *you*, Pa, just the same."

Now was Ash Harrell's turn to slump his shoulders. He and the sheriff stood side by side, like sad brothers. "All right, Allie," Harrell said. "Whatever you say. But what about these people the sheriff has been rounding up? Who'll stop that?"

"Too bad she used up her wishes," Petey said, "on a field of pretty flowers."

"It wouldn't have worked," I said. "It wouldn't take. Stopping this county's bad business has to be the sheriff's doing."

Sheriff Stiles gazed at Allie, who still leaned into Cauter Pike. "I've seen so many mountain girls get old before their time, having baby after baby, turning them out like a hay baler. I didn't want that for you, Allie. Not for you."

She shook her head. "When I told you no, Sheriff Stiles, I meant it. And my babies, any I have or don't have, are my business, not yourn."

He hung his head. "I'm sorry for what I done," he said, "and I won't do it no more."

"Ooh, the sincerity," Petey said. "How do we know he means it?"

"You can see it on his face," I said. And sure enough, the flat and shiny parts were filling out, the mouth straightening, the ruined ear unfolding like a bloom.

"It's a miracle," Ash Harrell said.

"Objection," Petey said.

I put one finger under the sheriff's chin to lift his head for a better look. He worked his jaw and eyebrows as his features woke up. "Ouch!" he said.

"Fire don't scar us near as bad as we scar ourselves," I said.

The Dragaman shouted, "Applejack all around!"

While Cauter Pike tapped the barrel, Petey pinched my elbow and drew me aside. "Pearleen Sunday, I know and you know full well that particular wishing ring was burnt out and used up and didn't half work in the first place, since it delivered unto me only a Memphis gal named Lucinda and neither of her sisters. That means bringing the sheriff and Ash Harrell and all these nasty flowers here was your doing, girl, and I would dearly like to know how you managed it."

I laughed. "Always about you, ain't it? You're imagining things again, so hush." I turned aside so he wouldn't see me wince. The pains would worsen in the next couple of days, and I'd be laid up for a week—working displacement magic nearly ruptures something inside—but I wouldn't give Petey the satisfaction of knowing that. And pains aside, I felt pretty good. "Hey, Petey. Look over there."

The Dragaman wasn't as tall as usual, for he had dropped to his knees in front of Ash Harrell. Allie stood a ways back. The sheriff sat farther back still, on the front steps, head in hands. Leathery flowers strained to touch his neck.

"I'd say he's asking for her hand," Petey said. "Who would have guessed he's the old-fashioned sort? I wonder what the answer will be."

"I think we know, and none too soon. She'll be showing before long."

"Showing what?" he asked.

I said nothing.

"You mean."

He thought it over. Then he blurted, "Lord have—"

He didn't finish, because I clapped both hands over his mouth. I felt like Christmas. Even Petey Wheatstraw was worth saving.

৭১

I am told that when the sheriff came down the mountain he went straight to the courthouse, handed in his badge, and left the county payroll, and the county, for good. The deputy who became sheriff in the special election, whose mother was a Harrell cousin, said that if any Staunton doctors wanted to cut on his neighbors, they damn well could drive down with rope and a basket and catch their own, because he and his deputies had all they could do just chasing bootleggers into Bristol, and besides, the only feebleminded people that worried him were in Richmond and Washington. That was the end of roundups and sterilizations in those parts—though not in every place in Virginia, or the country, either. You can look it up.

All this happened a long time ago, but many who were alive then are with us today, and the mountains are yet full of fire and marvel, for those who care to look. Buzzard's Rock is still miles from any place, but it's no longer quite so lonesome. In good weather, a right many people hike up there, along a new-made path called the Appalachian Trail. The trailhead is off Highway 311, just past the Catawba Grocery, but don't bother to look for a Buzzard's Rock sign. The place now is called the Dragon's Tooth, for reasons I think you know.

Don't expect to see me up there, either. Mind you, I walk the A.T. in all weathers, whenever I take a notion, but no one sees me do it except friends of mine. In the vicinity of the Tooth, for example, I like to visit a certain old couple and find out how their boy is getting along. He's a big one, but he gets that honest, as mountain people say; he's also proud and brave and knows his own mind, and he gets that honest, too.

CREDITS

LOSING IT

edited by
Keith Gray

Will you, won't you? Should you, shouldn't you?

Have you . . .?

A gift? Or a burden?

MELVIN BURGESS, ANNE FINE, KEITH GRAY, MARY HOOPER, SOPHIE MCKENZIE, PATRICK NESS, BALI RAI AND JENNY VALENTINE.

Losing It is an original and thought-provoking collection of stories from some of today's leading writers for young people: some funny, some moving, some haunting but all revolving around the same subject – having sex for the first time.

Everything you ever wanted to know about virginity but your parents were too embarrassed to tell you.

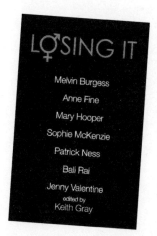

LOSING IT

Melvin Burgess

Anne Fine

Mary Hooper

Sophie McKenzie

Patrick Ness

Bali Rai

Jenny Valentine
edited by
Keith Gray

9781849390996 £5.99